BLOODLINES
THE FIRST BOXED SET

BLOODLINES: the First Boxed Set
ISBN - 978-1-938745-91-1
Copyright © 2021 by Angry Sheep Publishing LLC

This is a work of fiction. All characters, organizations and events in this boxed set are products of the author's imagination and are not to be construed as real. Any resemblance to persons, living or dead, is entirely coincidental.

Blood Magick, ©2011
Zombie Love, ©2011
Zombie Wedding, ©2011

Published by Angry Sheep Publishing LLC
Findlay, Ohio

Cover Design by For the Muse Design
Interior Design by JW Manus

Bloodlines

THE FIRST BOXED SET

SUZAN HARDEN

More Books by Suzan Harden
(Each series is in suggested reading order)

Bloodlines

Blood Magick
Zombie Love
Zombie Confidential
Zombie Wedding
Amish, Vamps & Thieves
Blood Sacrifice
Love, War & a Bulldog
Zombie Goddess
Ravaged
Sacrificed
Reality Bites
Ghouls in the Grocery Store
Resurrected
Bloodlines Shorts Anthology
Bloodlines: The First Boxed Set

Justice

Sword and Sorceress 28
("Justice")
Sword and Sorceress 30
("Diplomacy in the Dark")
Justice: The Beginning
A Question of Balance
A Modicum of Truth
A Matter of Death
A Touch of Mother
A Twist of Love
A Virtue of Child
A Hand of Father
A Measure of Knowledge
A Hint of Thief
A Cup of Conflict

Seasons of Magick

Spring
Summer
Autumn
Winter
The Seasons of Magick Anthology

The Justice Thalia Stories

Snowfall
Murder Most Fowl
The Sweetest Poison
A Granddaughter of Mine
Too Many Fish in the Sea

Tales of the Twelve

The Trickster Priestess and the Demon

Crossover Worlds

Invasion!

888-555-HERO

Hero De Facto
Hero Ad Hoc
Hero De Novo
A Very Hero Christmas
Hero De Jure
Hero In Camera
Hero Amicus Curiae
A Very Hero Wedding
A Very Hero New Year
Hero Ad Litem
Queer Eye for the Super Guy

Solar System Services, Inc.

Alone Is Not Lonely
Halloween Harvest
("A Place at the Table")
A Place at the Table

Millersburg Magick Mysteries

Spells and Sleuths
Fae and Felonies
Magick and Murder
Feline Navidad

Soccer Moms of the Apocalypse

Pestilence in Pumpkin Spice
Famine in French Vanilla
War in White Chocolate
Death in Double Mocha
Demons Run at Halloween

Miscellaneous

Sword and Sorceress 31
("Pig-Headed")
Sword and Sorceress 32
("Unexpected")
Practical Witches
Revenge Served Hot
The Yule Switch
Chocolate for Dinner
Silver Shoes and Pigs' Ears
Snipe Hunt

For updates, news, and giveaways, join Suzan's mailing list at suzanharden.blogspot.com/p/contact-me.html, or visit her website at www.suzanharden.com. You can also check her out on Facebook @SuzanHardenWriter.

Blood Magick

Chapter 1

The bang of the auctioneer's gavel sealed the fate of Grandma Petrov's wardrobe. "Sold! To Bidder 665!"

Another wave of grief overwhelmed Dr. Bebe Zachary, not so much at the loss of the furniture, but from missing Grandma. Why had she let things between them fester for so long? Why hadn't she answered Grandma's last letter? She wouldn't be in this mess if she'd simply swallowed her pride.

No great revelation answered her guilty conscience as the auction house staff scurried to roll the huge wardrobe out of the way for the next piece. Soft coughs and murmurs interrupted the stark silence of the exclusive facility, but the heavy burgundy drapes covering the walls muffled even those slight noises.

Swallowing hard, she glanced at the man two rows down who had outbid her. Striking, with olive skin and dark, wavy hair trimmed in a conservative style, he gave her a mock salute. The glint of an overly sharp canine in his smug grin confirmed her suspicions regarding his aura.

Vampire.

Damn. One more problem she didn't need. How was she supposed to get Grandma's Book of Shadows now?

Apprehension sizzled across her nerves. She ignored him and turned her attention to the next item in the catalog, a milk can once used by Harry Houdini. Grandma's quirky obsession with Normal illusionists never ceased to amaze Bebe. Why bother when a witch had real power at her fingertips? But all the magick in the world hadn't changed Grandma's fate.

If only she'd learned of Grandma's death before the human probate judge had ordered Grandma's estate into receivership, an act for which she could thank her asinine cousins and their petty squabbling. Little did the judge know the real fight was over the coven leadership, not the estate assets. Ironically, the half-elven attorney appointed to oversee the estate knew exactly what he had been dumped into. He'd contacted this auction house, since it specialized in serving supernatural folk.

And supernaturals comprised the majority of bidders. The smattering of humans without abilities, aka "Normals," was most likely Family, scoping the estate for their supernatural relatives.

After another half hour, the auction of Grandma's possessions ended as quietly as it had begun. No other members of the Petrov clan had bothered to show. Probably a good thing since Bebe had the urge to turn every one of them into newts.

Grief mingled with anger and regret in her heart as she dodged the confused milling of the crowd after the auction. A quick glance assured her no one watched her while she sidled next to the wardrobe. She could cast a blurring spell to cover her, but the receiver had boasted that the auction house carried the best spell-detection charms available. Jail time and losing her medical license on a possible fraud charge wasn't worth testing the power of said charms.

She eased the door open, and the silky grain of the wood triggered old memories. Years ago, it had been her favorite place to hide, especially after her parents' deaths. The pain had been too much for a child to bear. Now, Grandma was gone, and old wounds she thought long buried ached with fresh agony.

Anger flared again at both Grandma's stubbornness and her two cousins' greed and lust for power. She had been close to both of her cousins once. Damn their idiocy that had forced her to return to San Francisco. She didn't want to be here. She didn't care about the family fortune or about power within the coven. She wanted to be back in Africa. At least Doctors Without Borders didn't consider her a pawn in some stupid game.

She ran a hand along one of the doors smoothed from generations of use and tugged it open. Someone had to retrieve the ancient tome secreted inside the wardrobe. If Grandma's Book fell into the wrong hands, the results would be disastrous—for everyone, not just her family. She stooped to disable the spell that secured the secret compartment at the bottom of the antique.

"What are you doing to my furniture?"

Bebe lost her balance at the unexpected tenor behind her and fell on her butt. Following the gray pinstripe-encased legs upwards, she met the eyes of her bidding foe. Pressure caressed her shields and receded. The weasel had been trying to read her mind the entire auction.

She climbed to her feet, her movements awkward in the straight navy skirt. "If there's something you want to know, then ask me," she snapped.

One of his raven eyebrows rose in amusement. "I believe I did."

She took a deep, nerve-calming breath. "I was examining the piece."

"And why would a White Rose witch be so interested in the interior of her high priestess's wardrobe?"

Oh shit, he knows! I should just go back to the hotel and wash the day away with a bottle of Jack Daniels.

Instead, she shot back, "Why would a West Coast vampire care about a witch's furniture?"

He shrugged, the motion displaying powerful shoulders. His thumb stroked the onyx ankh set in the heavy gold on his left ring finger. "I liked the piece."

"So did I." Tears threatened. Thanks to her family, she had nothing left to remember Grandma except for the photos in her scrapbook.

He sobered and studied her. Again the pressure of his mind against her shields. A tiny thread of triumph ran through her. It would take a master vampire to shatter her protections. Her secret was safe.

He nodded at the wood behind her. "I'll let you buy the wardrobe."

Shock and mistrust ran along her frayed nerves, seasoned with a healthy dose of fear. Bargaining with a vampire was a dangerous proposition. Since her cousins and the coven elders admitted they didn't have Grandma's Book of Shadows, it must still be in the secret compartment. Bebe didn't dare let anyone get his hands on it, including this guy. Of course, his offer to negotiate could be a ruse.

She suppressed a shiver. "And your price?"

"Dinner with me."

She shook her head. Dangerous proposition was an understatement. She could be dinner for him for all she knew, though he didn't come across as a rogue. If he'd been anything but a vampire, she'd be tempted to take him up on his offer. She couldn't remember the last time she'd been on a real date. "How about my last bid and a couple of cover spells for your coffin?" she countered.

He chuckled at her forced attitude, the timbre sending a shiver of awareness down her spine. The bastard couldn't seduce her if he couldn't get past her shields, and she wasn't about to do something so monumentally stupid as drop her mental barriers.

He pulled a gold case from his coat pocket, withdrew a business card and held it out to her. She matched his unblinking gaze, her arms firmly at her sides. No power on earth could make her take that damn bit of cardboard.

One heartbeat passed. Then another.

Why wouldn't he leave so she could retrieve the Book? All she needed was a few seconds.

With a faint quirk of his full lips, he slid the card into the vee formed by the buttons of her tailored blouse, brushing the crest of her breast with his fingertips. His brazenness shocked any comeback right out of her head.

"If you change your mind, call me." He nodded and sauntered off into the crowd.

She turned back to the wardrobe, only to see the auction house staff cart it into the back in preparation for shipping. There was no way to access the compartment now, not without a lot of questions. Frustration at her lost opportunity welled up inside her.

She pulled the vampire's card out of her shirt with the intention of ripping it to shreds. Horror engulfed her at the name engraved in raised black ink. Caesar Augustine. Not any vampire, but the freakin' master of the western half of the U.S.

She squeezed her eyes shut. Both she and the rest of the witches were royally screwed.

Chapter 2

Caesar Augustine stood back while the movers unwrapped the antique cedar. He inhaled the spicy odor of the wood. Unmistakably Lebanese. Pieces like this weren't crafted anymore. Hades, trees like this weren't even grown anymore. He dismissed the workers with a wave. The men snatched their straps and quilts and scurried out of the room.

He shook his head at their anxious haste. *Normals.*

The polished surfaces gleamed under the recessed lighting in his office. Anticipation racing in his blood, he opened the doors. The little witch at the auction house had been interested in something inside, but the interior of the wardrobe was bare. Not even the faint scent of Natasha Petrov's favorite lavender perfume graced the wood.

He quelled the brief swell of grief at Natasha's death. She had been one of the few people he had called friend. He ignored the tiny voice that reminded him she was one of his few friends in the two thousand plus years of his existence. Not for one moment did he believe her overdose of heart medication was accidental. And if what he suspected were true, the killer would be after the named heir to Natasha's position within White Rose, her granddaughter Bebe.

He released the breath he had been holding as he ran his fingers over the interior wood. There wasn't a whole lot left in this gods-forsaken world he cared about, but he owed Natasha. For her efforts in finding a cure for his blasted disease, if nothing else. A disturbing thought wormed its way through his consciousness. Had the witch at the auction been searching for Natasha's missing notes as well?

No, he couldn't dwell on such selfishness. Honor demanded that he pursue Natasha's murderer. And the minimum he could do for his friend was protect her granddaughter from the assassin, even though he hadn't seen the child since the day of her parents' funerals.

At least, the child had been able to go to her parents' funerals. At least, her parents had the grace of dying by someone else's hand instead of their own. At least, little Bebe had someone who gave a fuck about her instead of being handed over to a sadistic bitch—

He shut down that line of thinking with practiced effort. His parents and half-brothers had been dead for over two millennia. Dwelling on it wouldn't help him locate Natasha's granddaughter or discover what the witch at the auction was trying to do.

He sucked in a breath when he found an indentation in the wood. No, the dip was a worn spot from decades of use.

Air whistled between his teeth in exasperation over his current dilemma. Tracking Natasha's estranged granddaughter down was proving problematic with the current unrest in Central Africa. He'd ordered his sister, Selene, to send her hired eclectic, Lucien, in the hopes the girl would be more receptive to another witch, even if he were covenless. But so far, Lucien hadn't found the girl.

Maybe he should have shown his hand and asked the little witch at the auction.

The woman had been the only White Rose member to bother showing up at the sale of Natasha's estate, the silver flower-shaped stud in her right ear the only sign of her affiliation. He couldn't tell if she was one of the conspirators that Natasha had suspected, but she was definitely one of Natasha's students. He hadn't been able to penetrate her mental shields even with direct eye contact.

He smiled at the scene she had made when he caught her, firm heart-shaped behind in the air as she poked around the bottom of the wardrobe. She wasn't a classic beauty, but her bosom had complemented her behind. And she had blushed when his fingertips had grazed her breast when he placed his business card inside her shirt.

The fact she was flustered by his touch coupled with her un-enhanced breasts amazed him. Few women were that innocent and real in this day and age. The desire for more than the brief touch of her soft skin caught him off guard.

Pushing thoughts of the little witch out of his head, he knelt and ran his hand along the bottom. Nothing unusual presented itself to his touch, only cedar smoothed from years of use. He frowned. She had definitely been looking for something. He knocked on the bottom panel, but no echo indicated that a hollow space lay beneath.

Sitting back on his heels, he stared at the piece. The dark interior of the wardrobe sucked all light out of the room. Even his virus-enhanced vision had difficulty distinguishing individual boards. Good thing he had anticipated such problems.

Grabbing the flashlight and toolbox from his desk, he crouched before the wardrobe again and aimed the light inside. With a careful touch, he probed the wood. No catches, but who knew what booby-traps Natasha may have set. The woman had grown cannier with each passing decade. Pushing his head and chest further into the interior, he ran the beam over each seam and peg.

"That's an undignified position for a prince."

Caesar jerked at Ptolemy's voice behind him and banged his elbow against the right door. Unfortunately with vampire speed and strength, the heavy cedar whip-lashed into his right temple as he tried to extricate himself. Rubbing his head, he sat back and glared at his snickering brother.

"Glad I'm entertaining you." Annoyed, Caesar rose and brushed packing dust off his polo and khakis.

Ptolemy's snicker turned into outright laughter. "Better than any gladiator. Did you find anything?"

Caesar shook his head. "Not yet. This was the only piece the White Rose witch at the auction was interested in." He cocked an eye at Ptolemy. "Please tell me you've identified her from the photo I e-mailed you." Hellfire, what he would've given for a smart phone camera centuries ago when he was in Rome.

Ptolemy's expression grew serious. "You aren't going to like this."

"We've got a potential coven war brewing. I already don't like it," he snapped.

"She's Bebe Zachary."

Caesar clenched his fists. "When did she get back in the country?" The last time he had seen her, she had been a child of eleven. Still, he cursed himself for not recognizing the fiery woman at the auction house.

Ptolemy shrugged. "Don't know. She didn't fly in, or she would have shown up on the Homeland Security airline database. She had to have crossed the Mexican or Canadian border by car. With the paperwork backlog at the crossings, she may have been in the country for up to three weeks."

Caesar groaned. Not only had he made a pass at Natasha's granddaughter, now he couldn't even protect her as he had promised because he had no clue where she was. "Have Anne start working the streets. Send anyone we can spare with her. And have Stan come see me before he leaves for the night."

Ptolemy pivoted on his heel and left to execute his orders.

Caesar closed his eyes and whispered a prayer that his people found Bebe before Natasha's assassin did.

Chapter 3

Bebe eased the dingy hotel curtain aside and peeked out. Night fell early this close to Yule. Red and green lights twinkled in counterpoint with blue and silver tinsel in the shops across the street from her hotel room, the color a half-hearted attempt to drive away the desperation that seeped into the very air of this downtrodden section of San Francisco. Tiny, who had followed her all evening, crouched in the alley between two of the storefronts with her shabby coat pulled tight against the winter chill. The vampire girl couldn't have been much more than sixteen when she was Turned, and Goddess only knew how long ago that had been. Only the faint red haze overlying Tiny's natural green aura gave any indication that she was a vampire and not one of the homeless kids roaming the area.

Bebe let the yellowed fabric drop back into place. The tail didn't make sense. If Augustine had Grandma's Book of Shadows, why bother with her?

A small quiver of relief rippled through her. He hadn't found it yet. Or else hadn't figured out how to open the compartment without destroying the contents.

The furniture in her one-star hotel didn't leave much room, but she paced the four steps. Walking helped her think, and she definitely needed to plan her next step with care. Between the little vamp today and the brown sedan that shadowed her yesterday, she felt wanted in her hometown.

Not.

She rubbed her temples at the growing tension headache as she tried to work out her plans, cursing the nightmare of Grandma trapped somewhere, screaming for help, that had awoken her before dawn. What she needed was to focus on her real problem, not some stupid dream resulting from her own guilt and remorse. If Augustine's people knew she was here, she needed to find a new hotel before she tried to retrieve Grandma's book. She sighed in exasperation at yet another delay.

Bebe glanced at the real estate records and building plans on the utilitarian wooden desk. Breaking into a vampire's estate was not the brightest of ideas. She would have to do it in the morning while the vampire household slept. The trick would be getting past the daytime guards. And she hadn't been able to discover what the guards were yet, though fae magic lay thick around the estate. It didn't make sense given the Cold War situation between the fae queens and the Vampire Nation.

Too bad it wasn't Girl Scout cookie season. If she had an excuse for ringing the front doorbell, checking the aura of whoever answered would solve the question.

Reaching over her shoulder, she dug her fingers into the knots at the base of her neck. If she didn't get a grip on her fear, all of the vamps and weres in San Francisco would be pacing outside her window. Goddess, she wished she could contact a friendly face for help, sympathy, anything. But everyone she knew was either too scared or making their own bid for power.

When applied pressure didn't relieve her headache, she rooted through her shoulder bag. Yes, peppermint oil.

A sharp rap at the door sent already fried nerves haywire, and the small vial flew through the air. Before she could search for the oil, a rich, heady essence slammed into her shields, one that seemed very familiar.

Standing on tiptoes to peer through the peephole, her heart stopped. Caesar Augustine raised his fist to knock again.

Frantic, she searched for a weapon. Any weapon. The fiberboard chair wouldn't hurt him. Everything else was bolted to the floor or walls.

Another knock, more insistent than the last. "Dr. Zachary? It's Caesar Augustine. I know you're in there."

A polite vampire. The world really was about to end.

Damn, surrounded and no way out. Even if her acrophobia allowed her to try the fire escape, Tiny would grab her before she climbed down one floor.

His firm knocks grew louder. "Dr. Zachary, would you please open the door? I only wish to speak with you."

With a deep gulp of air, she concentrated until a decent-sized fireball glowed in her hand. She flung the door open. "Make it quick or I'm having barbeque for dinner."

As impeccably dressed as yesterday, he eyed her with obvious amusement in his expression. "So if I don't make it quick, you're accepting my invitation?"

She glared at him.

"The hotel sprinklers will be set off in another minute if you don't put that out."

She hated to admit he was right. Displaying her abilities in public was never smart. Grandma had drilled that into her head for the entire twenty-eight years of her life. She clenched her hand to extinguish the witchfire.

He brushed past her into the room, acting like royalty. Very good-looking royalty, with a vampire's signature sandalwood scent drifting in his wake. Not for the first time, she wished all the myths about vampires needing an invitation were true. Vampires were jerky, conceited, and dangerous, but not true supernaturals. A freaking virus from 10,000 years ago had created them, not magick, but lack of the occult arts didn't make them any less deadly a foe. He paused at the token desk.

Oh, shit!

The bottom dropped out of her stomach.

He shuffled through the diagrams of his estate lying on the desk then glanced up with a smirk. "If you want to see something, just ask me."

Her eyes closed in resignation. Her marvelous plan for B&E had crashed and burned because she was too damn tired and panicked to think clearly enough to shove some blueprints under the bed.

He didn't wait for her reply. "You really should stick with practicing medicine, Dr. Zachary. I don't believe you're cut out for espionage."

Her eyes snapped open. "Thank you, Mr. Augustine. I'll take your career advice under consideration." She waved toward the door she still held open. "Now that you've done your civic duty, why don't you find someone else to annoy?"

Ignoring her, he flipped through what passed for the room service menu before tossing it back on the desk. "I'd prefer a private venue for our discussion, but I will not subject a lady to swill." He picked up her coat lying on the bed and held it open. "There's an excellent restaurant a few blocks from here."

"I am not going anywhere with you," she said and tried to look as stern as possible. Normally, she could hold her own with anyone. She wouldn't have survived medical school otherwise, but this man's audacity rivaled her worst professor's.

And she wasn't about to go anywhere alone with a vampire. Especially not a conceited, rather attractive . . .

She squashed that disturbing thought.

Her nerves were so wired she jumped when his jacket pocket emitted soft beeps. He frowned, jerked out an older model cell phone and barked, "What? When?" before snapping it shut. He thrust the old gray trench coat at her. "Get your coat on now, Doctor."

"No." She shook her head. "You can't order me around like I'm one of your minions."

Pressure smacked her shields. He wasn't even pretending to be subtle. "Get. Your. Coat. On. Now."

"And I said no." Her arms crossed over her chest of their own accord. Between her family and the Council of Elders, she'd had more than enough of people trying to bully her.

Big mistake. Augustine stalked towards her. There was no time to conjure a fireball, but she could deliver a mean kick if she had to. She shrank against the open door, but he poked his head through the doorway instead. He muttered something under his breath she was pretty sure translated to "manure" in Latin. Wrenching the door from her death grip, he slammed it shut and pushed her towards the window.

"Out the fire escape." When she hesitated, he roared, "Now!"

Blood hummed in her ears, and she scrambled around the bed. When she bent to push up the sash, the pane exploded in a storm of shards. Caesar shoved her down in the middle of broken glass and filthy carpet and threw himself on top. She opened her mouth to yell at him. Then she realized the muffled thuds and grunts were bullets hitting him.

Terror ripped through her as easily as the glass slicing into her palms and knees. Her attempted objection to his rough handling morphed into a scream. One of this stupid vampire's enemies had to have followed him, and now she'd be the innocent victim of some screwed up vamp vendetta.

The firecracker sounds paused. In one fluid motion, Augustine was on his feet and lifting her through the ruined window. She peered back. Holes winked at her from what was left of the hotel room door.

She didn't have time to think about who was shooting from the hallway. Augustine threw her over his shoulder. Vertigo roiled her empty stomach, not aided by the fact she was hanging upside down. Damn, where was her peppermint oil when she really needed it? He climbed down the escape so fast, all she could do was squeeze her eyes shut, hang on to his coat and belt for dear life, and pray she wouldn't puke on his custom tailored suit. She sure couldn't afford to replace the darn thing.

A solid jolt popped her eyes open. They were on the pavement, but Augustine didn't stop. He raced down the street. Each step rammed his shoulder into her already protesting stomach, but the shouts from above froze her blood.

I'm going to get shot in the back while hanging upside down from an arrogant asshole's shoulder.

As if reading her mind, one more bullet pinged off the pavement. She glanced up to see Tiny running behind them. Except the female vampire didn't have a gun.

Bebe's chin smacked Augustine's back at his abrupt halt, making her bite her tongue. He tossed her across the seat of some large vehicle before throwing himself on top of her once again. Tires squealed as whoever drove sped away from the hotel.

The adrenaline surge eased off, but her attempt at a deep, calming breath was impeded by the hunky vampire splayed over her chest. "You can get off of me now." She shoved at Augustine's chest, but she could have been pushing a granite boulder for all the good it did.

"I don't know. I rather like this position." He rose slightly to look at her. His eyes gleamed fluorescent yellow in the darkness.

Her heartbeat tripped double-time at the sudden awareness of his body against hers. Nipples tightened from the press of his chest. Liquid warmth pooled where his thigh lodged between hers. Breath caught in her throat, refusing to fill her lungs for fear he'd realize his affect. His lips were so close. All he had to do was . . .

"Hey, if you two are going to mack in the back, can you wait until Anne and I are out of the Hummer? I *don't* need the PDA tonight."

She reached out mentally. The harsh coppery texture of his shields and the rich scent of sandalwood confirmed the man guiding the Hummer through the streets was another vampire. Underneath the copper was a burnt toast taste, the vamp's personal signature, but she couldn't get past his shields to pick up specific thoughts.

Augustine chuckled and pulled her up with him, somehow managing to sit her so she didn't give the driver a Sharon Stone in the rearview mirror. Why the hell hadn't she put on jeans when she returned to her hotel room earlier?

"How many times were you hit, Caesar?" The tiny vampire, who must be Anne, peered over the front seat.

"I lost count," he said with a dry tone.

"Oh, damn," Bebe muttered. Under the passing streetlights, she realized his cashmere turtleneck was no longer the pristine cream it had been in her hotel room. She ran fingertips over his chest, ignoring the blood, and searched for exit wounds.

She gasped when Augustine grasped her hands tight against hard muscle. "Sweetheart, as much I love what you're doing, trust me. Most of the bullets are still in me." A wicked smirk lit his face. "And with my blood covering you, you make too much of a tempting snack as it is."

She looked down. The blood staining her navy sweater was invisible in the darkness, but the sticky wetness against her skin gave her no doubt that her bra was ruined as well.

Her gaze returned to the glowing eyes that regarded her. "We've got to get them out." She wasn't a weapons expert, but she had done her stint in an ER during med school. If Augustine's enemies had shot him with some kind of explosive bullet, even the vampire virus wouldn't be able to heal him fast enough. The metal obviously wasn't silver or he'd already have gone into anaphylactic shock.

"Do you have a safe house?" she asked.

Anne answered. "We have an adequate medical facility at the mansion." When Bebe twisted to face her, the female's eyes were glowing gold as well and her fangs were fully extended. A quick flick of her gaze to the rearview mirror revealed the driver in similar straits. Augustine's wounds were triggering the bloodlust of every vamp in the vehicle. And she was the only tasty treat inside.

Self-preservation overrode her desire to render medical aid. She silently berated herself for forgetting who she was with as she inched towards the door.

Augustine's hand shot out and grabbed her wrist before she could lunge for the handle. "We've gone to a great deal of trouble protecting your cute little behind. I would *not* appreciate you killing yourself by jumping from my SUV."

She hissed in pain, not so much from his strength but from his thumb grinding into a cut on her palm. He yanked her palm closer to examine it, and the pressure of his thumb eased from the sliced skin.

"Shit," he muttered. Faster than she could follow, he seized her other hand as well. "You're going to need stitches yourself, Doctor."

Shit was an understatement. She had been touching his chest. His chest with his contaminated blood . . .

Anne leaned over the seat to study her hands and wrists as well. "It doesn't look like you severed any tendons or ligaments." The smile Anne gave her would have been sweet if not for the fangs. "We'll make sure there's no shards still in the cuts and get those cleaned up in a jiffy."

Her words jolted Bebe out of the threatening bout of panic. Jiffy? What kind of vampire says jiffy?

Nothing was making sense anymore. The vampires she rode with hadn't attacked her despite the blood oozing from both her and Augustine. He still held her hands, and his gentle strokes sent strange tremors through her body. Her stomach clenched with nausea that had nothing to do with her vertigo. She may have contracted the vampire virus in the last few minutes. Then there were the gunmen at the hotel. If they were after Augustine, why did he bother taking her with him?

His earlier words about saving her hit her addled neurons like a Mack truck. "Those men were after you," she said. Passing streetlights revealed no change in Augustine's stoic expression. Two more blocks passed before she gathered the courage to add, "Weren't they?" She loathed the quiver in her voice, but it was more desirable than tears.

"No, Doctor, they were after you."

"But why?" she squeaked. "And why do you care?"

He exhaled, a long drawn-out affair, and shifted to stare at the traffic. Her father had made the same sound when he prayed for patience after she'd done something particularly annoying. The sharp pain at the memory of her parents jabbed through her soul as it always did. Ironic that she sat in a vehicle with creatures just like the ones that had killed them.

When he faced her again, his eyes had dulled to a faint amber. "You already know why those men were trying to assassinate you, Doctor, so please don't play coy with me. As for why I care—"

He drew a sharp breath as if pain racked him.

"It's because Natasha asked me."

Chapter 4

Bebe wouldn't have been more shocked if Augustine claimed he was the pope. Her grandmother's given name from a vampire's lips? And he spoke as if he and Grandma were more than acquaintances. "I–I don't know what you're talking about."

"I said don't play games—" Another shudder racked Augustine. "I said—" The whispered words barely made it out of his mouth when the convulsions took him.

"Caesar?"

Bebe glanced at the rearview mirror. Raw fright shone from the driver's eyes, matching the gruff tone of his voice. "How close are we?" she asked.

"Another couple of minutes," Anne said.

Years of training took over. She pulled Augustine over her lap to keep him from further banging his head against the reinforced doorframe. She'd never seen a vampire choke on his own vomit, but she struggled to turn him over anyway. Seeing what Bebe was trying to do, Anne single-handedly flopped Augustine on his side.

"What's wrong with him?" Panic scarred the driver's voice.

Horns blared, and Anne yanked the steering wheel hard to get the Hummer back on the right side of the street. "Dammit, Ptolemy, pay attention!"

"He's going into shock. The bullets may be time-released with some kind of compound." Experience forced Bebe to shove her personal feelings aside. She pressed her fingers against Augustine's neck, seeking a pulse. A faint rhythm existed but it was far too erratic, even for a vampire.

Tires screeched in protest as Ptolemy whipped the vehicle into a long driveway. Bebe winced when the barely open gates caught the sides of the Hummer with a nails-on-chalkboard screech. Augustine's seizure stopped as they cleared the ornate ironwork.

A shiver of fear ran through her. What would the other vamps do to her without their master to keep them in check?

The unconscious vampire's weight was the only thing that kept her in her seat when Ptolemy slammed the brakes once the vehicle was inside the attached garage. He was out the door and pulling Augustine from her lap before the rebound bounced her against the back of the seat. After an instant of hesitation, she scrambled out and followed the vampires into the main house. She couldn't violate her Hippocratic Oath even if the patient was a blood-sucking fiend.

Who happened to save her life.

"What in tarnation!"

Another male vampire jumped up from the table where he'd been sitting when the little group charged through the huge kitchen. Bebe spared him no more than a cursory glance. She followed Ptolemy down a hallway into a brightly lit room. The infirmary was small but well-appointed, the equivalent of the after-hours clinics scattered throughout the city.

He laid Augustine face down on the exam table, his manner gentle despite the fear rolling off him. Anne was already cutting away the ruined sweater. Their practiced ease scared the daylights out of Bebe.

The new vampire pushed his way past her. Tall and blond, the vampire had probably used his looks and Texas accent to lure many women to their doom.

Damn. She should leave now while the three vampires were occupied with Augustine's injuries. She bit her tongue. Augustine had saved her life from the gunmen. She couldn't leave, not until she knew he'd be okay.

The new vamp seized a metal probe off the instrument tray. "Shit, I thought y'all were just taking the witch out to dinner."

"Some hitters had other ideas," Ptolemy said.

The new vampire chuckled. "You've watched *The Whole Nine Yards* one too many times." He surveyed the damage to Augustine and glanced up. "Your brother will be fine, Ptolemy."

That explained Ptolemy's excessive worry. Biological siblings in the vampire community were rare, but they did exist. And they didn't take a family member's death lightly. Another shiver of fear gripped her.

The new vampire eyed her before he grinned. "I'm Alex, by the way." He turned back to his injured master and poked the probe into Augustine's shoulder. "This is going to sting." He eased out the first bullet and frowned at it. "Not silver. Why's he out cold?"

Bebe edged closer to the table. "Probably laced with garlic. He went into convulsions on the way here." At her words, another seizure racked Augustine. This one lasted barely a minute.

"Fuck," Alex said under his breath. A new sense of urgency flared in his voice. "Ptolemy, you're going to have to hold him down, or I won't get these blasted things out in time."

"I can help." She stepped forward and reached for another set of instruments, only to hiss in pain again as Ptolemy grabbed her injured hand.

"Let me see." Alex examined her sliced up palm when Ptolemy yanked her closer to them. Alex looked at her with a strange mix of worry and admiration. "The last thing you need is to mix his blood with yours and accidentally Turn."

She met his gaze and sighed, resigned to her fate. "It's a little late for that." If she were infected, if she survived the transformation, she'd probably wake up a raving lunatic.

"Aw, shit." Alex closed his eyes for a split second. "Anne, get her washed and stitched up." Before Bebe could protest, he added, "And find her some of those latex gloves. I'll need the help." His blue eyes carried a naked mourning as he regarded Bebe. "Might as well make the doc's last hours with the living useful."

Despite his pronouncement of doom, a prickle of pride ran through her. Someone here took her seriously.

With terrifying strength, the tiny vamp tugged Bebe over to the sink. The warm water stung almost as much as the anti-bacterial soap Anne lathered over the main slice in Bebe's right palm and the multitude of tiny nicks on both hands. Anne peered at the cut. "No foreign objects and the blood's still flowing." She smiled at Bebe, a small hopeful smile. "There's a good chance you haven't been infected. We can test you in the morning."

Bebe snorted. "Assuming I don't go into a coma tonight."

The vamp shrugged and turned off the faucet. "There's that possibility."

Bebe ran through the initial symptoms of the vampire virus: dizziness, irritability, nausea, and abnormal pain and tenderness around the entry site of the infection. That pretty much ran the gamut of what she was feeling now. Goddess, she didn't want to think about what she could turn into. The vampires may not have a choice about killing her.

She blinked in surprise and looked down at her hand. Anne was already tying off the final knot. With precision, the vamp clipped the suture and handed a pair of surgical gloves and goggles to Bebe.

Anne rummaged in the cabinet before pulling out a bottle of Midol. "I'm afraid this all we have in terms of over-the-counter pain relievers."

Bebe cocked a puzzled eyebrow at the vamp, who shrugged again and smiled, this time in true humor. "They're not mine. Tiffany left it here when she came up during summer vacation." When Bebe's other eyebrow rose to join the first, Anne said, "Tiffany's Family."

Family with a capital "F." Bebe considered Anne's words as she snagged the pair of pills from the vamp's hand and swallowed them dry. So a member of Augustine's coven was young enough to have living Family running around. What surprised her was that the girl was allowed to associate with vampires. Someone needed to have a long talk with her parents. She pulled the goggles over her eyes.

"Are you two finished? We need some help here!"

Another seizure gripped Augustine, so strong that the two male vamps were having trouble keeping him on the exam table. Anne rushed over and flung herself on the unconscious Augustine's legs.

Bebe snapped the gloves on and snatched the bloody probe that Alex had dropped on the tray. A quick count showed he had extracted ten bullets. "How many more?"

"Four." Alex grunted, doing his damnedest to keep Augustine's right shoulder down. "Watch it. I found two explosive rounds."

Her night was getting *so* much better. No, she should count herself lucky. The damn things could have blown up already. And she'd been in close proximity to Augustine the whole time.

One entry wound was uncomfortably close to the lower spine. If he was a normal human and this was a real hospital, she'd send him up to surgery. A little anesthesia would do wonders. But no, she couldn't get that lucky.

The holes where Alex had already removed the bullets were trying to close, but the healing was slow compared to the usual vamp's ability. Sucking in a deep breath, she dealt with the most difficult one first. The metal instrument struck something hard, and she pulled it out.

Damn, a bone fragment.

She dropped it in the tray with a clatter. Augustine's thrashing did not help her concentration. Chewing on her lower lip to distract her from the aches in her hands, she reached back into Augustine's mangled body with the probe. This time there was a definite metal-on-metal clink.

Careful, careful.

She eased the bullet out, and she nearly choked on her own spit. The explosive round was unmistakable. Gently, she set it in the tray.

"Come on, Doc. You've got three more to go," Alex muttered.

"She's taking too long."

She looked up to see Ptolemy glaring at her, eyes still glowing and fangs halfway extended. His partial vamp-out didn't help her nerves at all.

"Do you think your virus will repair all the damage if one of those things goes off inside him?" Bebe snapped.

"With all due respect, Your Highness, shut up and let her work." Anne's tone was polite even if her words to Ptolemy weren't.

Ignoring the vamps, Bebe felt inside the next bullet wound. Bingo.

Working methodically, she removed the last two. Augustine's body gave one last shudder and stilled. She laid two fingers on Augustine's neck. He had a slow, weak pulse, but he had one.

She met Alex's worried gaze. "Do you have any epinephrine?"

"For the anaphylactic shock?" He shook his head. "Nope. Stuff doesn't do jack for us. All we can do is remove the problem and hope for the best."

"And you'd better pray to your gods that my brother survives, witch." The expression on Ptolemy's face promised her hell on earth if anything happened to Augustine.

Swallowing her own fear, Bebe met his threatening stare. "I didn't invite him for a social visit, Your Highness."

Her sarcastic edge on his title wasn't lost on Ptolemy. His eyes, so much like Augustine's rich brown ones, narrowed, but he remained silent. That scared her more that any verbal threat he could deliver. No one outside of these vampires knew where she was. She could be drained before she could blink, and nobody would ever find her body.

"Now, Ptolemy, play nice and use your company manners for once," Alex said. He turned and winked at Bebe before he headed to the sink to wash Augustine's blood off his hands.

Ignoring Ptolemy's menacing stance, she turned to Anne. "Do you have a pressure cuff?"

The girl nodded and pulled one from another cupboard.

Girl. Bebe winced at her assumption of the vampire's age based on her appearance. Anne was hardly the homeless waif she appeared and could be thousands of years old for all Bebe knew. The last thing she needed was to underestimate these people.

Bebe gingerly pulled off her gloves before she took the cuff from Anne's outstretched hand and wrapped it around Augustine's well-formed bicep. She shoved away the memory of that arm wrapped around her, protecting her from the hail of bullets. She sighed in satisfaction when his blood pressure registered normal. Well, normal for a vamp. She reached for his neck again. This time his pulse was a strong, steady forty.

Without the garlic-laced bullets to impede the virus, the holes sealed themselves in four minutes. By five, not even a scar showed on his skin. She shook her head in amazement.

Alex eyed Augustine's back as he wiped his hands with a towel, then grinned at her. "Good work, Doc." He held out a platter-sized palm.

She gave him an apologetic smile and displayed her stitches. "If you don't mind, can we pass on the high-fives for a couple of days?"

"Sorry." He bent closer to examine her stitched cuts. "Anne does a mighty fine job with a sewing needle, doesn't she?" He waved Anne closer. "Let's roll him over, or our boy's going to wake up with a mighty stiff neck."

"You'll take him to his room," Ptolemy said.

Bebe had forgotten he was in the room though she wasn't sure how. "No." Maybe medical ethics overrode her common sense, but Bebe didn't back down from the haughty glare Ptolemy gave her. He was no longer the scared kid from the Hummer, but someone who expected his orders to be obeyed.

"Lady's right, Ptolemy. Why don't you two get some rest? We'll keep an eye on him and holler if there's a problem."

Ptolemy stiffened. "I don't take orders from you, Stanton."

Bebe shifted her gaze between the two men. Now, she had a last name to go with Alex. And by his relaxed stance, he didn't seem all that intimidated by the other vampire's posturing.

"No one's ordering you, Your Highness." Anne's soft voice sounded as if she had to smooth ruffled feathers on a regular basis. "Dr. Zachary has the medical expertise, and Alex can advise her on any peculiarities regarding our physiology."

"Very well. Keep me apprised." Ptolemy shot Bebe another nasty glare. "You would best hope that Stanton's faith in you is not misplaced." He turned and stalked out of the room. No if-then threats from this guy. He probably got that lesson from his brother.

Anne gave her an apologetic look and mouthed, "Thank you," before following him out of the room.

Bebe sighed in relief. Maybe she'd survive the night after all. She turned to the remaining vampire. "By the way, Alex Stanton, I'm Bebe Zachary. Nice to meet you." Not that he didn't already know who she was, but a few manners never hurt.

Alex grinned in response and gave a mock tipping of an invisible hat. "Pleasure, ma'am."

After waiting a few heartbeats to make sure vampiric hearing outside of the room wouldn't catch her next words, she whispered, "Does Ptolemy always have a broomstick shoved up his ass?"

Alex laughed, displaying very sharp and very white canines. "'Fraid so. Hope he didn't offend you too much. He tends to act like a real pisser when it comes to his brother." He placed his fingers against Augustine's neck. With a satisfied nod, he crossed to the mini-fridge and pulled out a plastic pint bag of blood. With a practiced manner, he set up the IV and inserted the needle into his master's arm.

Remembering his earlier skill, curiosity burned in her. "Where'd you go to medical school?"

He glanced up, surprise on his face before he resumed taping down the IV tube. "I did a year at Johns Hopkins, but medicine wasn't where my heart was." He chuckled and waved at the IV. "Of course, medical school was nowhere near as complicated back in 1876."

"You're young for a vampire," she commented.

Alex shrugged. "All depends on your perspective. Anne says I'm ancient because I remember the Civil War." He grinned at the unconscious Augustine. "Caesar here thinks I'm a snot-nosed brat because I haven't had a personal conversation with Jesus Christ."

Bebe returned his smile. "And he has?"

Alex shrugged again and checked the IV line. "Claims he has. I wasn't there."

She looked down at the unconscious vampire. Augustine's aquiline features could be Roman. He definitely had a Mediterranean cast in his coloring. He wasn't drop-dead gorgeous by today's blow-dried and gelled standards, but he was . . . well, compelling would be the best way to put it. In sleep, he had a certain serenity. "Shouldn't he be awake by now?"

She glanced up when Alex snorted, anger surfacing on his face.

"Between the blood loss and the tissue damage, I'd expect him to be out for a couple of hours. With the garlic, it'll take a hell of a lot longer. All we can do is give him a couple of pints and see what happens," he said, concern softening his tone.

"Don't you have a, um, vampire physician to consult with?"

"Darlin', I'm pretty much it." Alex laughed. "Besides, unless our heads come off or we get staked through the heart, there ain't too much we don't recover from."

"What about explosive bullets or dirty nukes?" She smiled sweetly.

"Well, there is that," he conceded with another chuckle. "Why don't I show you a room, and you try to get some sleep?"

Bebe shook her head. "I'll stay here. Not that I don't trust you—" They both smiled at her obvious lie. "But I'm the closest thing you've got to help right now."

He nodded in acquiescence. "I'll go find us a couple of decent chairs."

Waiting for his return, she paced next to the unconscious Augustine. She should leave now. The smart thing would be to slip out of the mansion, head back to her hotel and try to retrieve her purse. Augustine's place was in a decent neighborhood. She could probably get a cab despite the late hour.

She wrapped her arms around her. No, she couldn't leave. At least, not yet. This would be her only chance to search for Grandma's wardrobe and retrieve her Book. Now that the vampires knew who she was and where she was, she wouldn't get another opportunity.

She glanced at the man on the table and tried to quell an even more disturbing thought. He had saved her life tonight. She had a duty to make sure he survived— beyond her Hippocratic Oath, beyond his brother's unspoken threat. Pretending that her motive was purely selfish did no good when strains of the Stones' "Sympathy for the Devil" ran through her head, mocking her.

—•—

Caesar awoke with a start. The dim bedside light could have been a million-watt halogen thanks to the obscene headache that pounded his skull. He checked the luminous display on the clock next to his bed. After sundown, but sundown on what day?

He peered through squinted eyes around the room. He was in his own bed in the San Francisco mansion. Better than dead and the flesh melting from his bones. Instinct warned of another presence. Then he noticed the glossy dark hair that flowed across his comforter.

He frowned and reached for the locks. The muscles in his arm burned like they had in the old days after one of his older brother's taxing sword lessons. Brushing the silky curls aside, the face of Bebe Zachary appeared, her cheek resting on her crossed arms. The rest of her remained in the chair pulled close to his bed.

In sleep, she looked innocent and peaceful, not the frightened, angry and very stubborn young witch who seemed hell bent on making his life difficult. He smiled and continued to stroke her hair. She was so much like Natasha, but there was an emotional vulnerability in her that her grandmother had never possessed. On the other hand, she couldn't have moved him from the Hummer to his bedroom by herself, so presumably she hadn't fried the rest of his household.

Big, brown eyes blinked open, and Bebe jerked herself upright. She wouldn't meet his gaze while she smoothed her wild mane out of her face. "How are you feeling?" Not even waiting for his reply, she busied herself with the blood pressure cuff.

He missed the texture of her soft hair against his fingertips, so he settled for drinking in the sight of her. Instead of the blood soaked clothes she had on earlier, she wore gray sweats and a white t-shirt obviously borrowed from Ptolemy. Her figure was too full to fit into any of Anne's clothes. Not that he objected. Interesting how her nipples perked under his gaze. It was all he could do not to reach for her assets dangling right in front of his face.

Ignoring her question, he asked one of his own. "I take it you don't normally sleep in men's beds?" His teasing was worth the slow blush that crept up her neck and flooded her cheeks. If it wasn't for his enhanced physique, she would have cut his arm off when she yanked the cuff tight. He grunted but managed to keep the smile plastered to his face.

"I'm surprised my people let you stay in here alone."

Still no answer from Bebe, who stared pointedly at her watch as she squeezed the bulb for the cuff.

"I am sorry our dinner plans were interrupted." He gave an exaggerated sigh. "If I'd but known it would be this easy to get you into my bed—"

"You think this is funny?" She ripped the cuff off and impaled him with a ferocious glare. "You think your vampire charm will save you the next time some jerk-off shoots a full clip of garlic-laced explosive bullets into your ass."

"Bet you had fun digging them out." He teased her even though her revelation had his mind churning. The assassins weren't taking any chances. Why else use garlic bullets? Or did they know about his promise to Natasha? Was the culprit one of Natasha's suspected conspirators, or worse, a leak in his own coven?

He needed to keep Bebe out of sight until he knew for sure from whom or what the danger came. And by the way she clenched her fists, keeping the doctor hidden was going to be a problem.

Something was up in that head of hers because she forced herself to calm down and her hands relaxed at her sides. Hades, what he wouldn't give to penetrate her shields. Despite his aching body, his cock stirred at the image of penetration of another type. He blew out a frustrated breath and banished the thought. Fun and games with any non-vampire was definitely out of the question. Bebe might as well have been locked in a chastity belt with the key at the bottom of the Pacific.

"Look, Augustine," she said, totally oblivious to the direction of his mind. She glanced south for an instant before continuing to berate him. He couldn't help the wicked smile that spread across his face. Maybe she wasn't so oblivious after all.

"I appreciate your help last night, even if it's some misguided debt to my grandmother." She crossed her arms over her chest. "If you knew my grandmother, why didn't you introduce yourself at the auction?"

"I wasn't sure who you were. It's not like I could read your mind." And he didn't dare force an attempt now, not if he wanted her trust. She wouldn't accept his protection if she didn't trust him, making an already difficult task a total nightmare. He levered himself slowly into a sitting position, as much to keep from startling her as from the lingering pain from the garlic working itself out of his system. "Once I found out you were Natasha's heir, I tracked you down."

She smirked. "You mean you had Anne track me down."

He nodded. "She's very proficient at finding people who wish to disappear."

Her expression changed to something sad and something else unreadable. What he wouldn't give to know what she was thinking, but he didn't dare touch her body, much less her mind. Not that he feared retaliation at the intrusion, but it would destroy the tenuous link developing between them. The best he could do for the moment was be honest with her.

"If you were that close to Grandma, then you know I refused to be named her heir," she finally said, not meeting his eyes.

Hades, the girl's ignorance of politics was exasperating. He swallowed his irritation. He dared not lose his temper with her. She'd try to run if he did, and the last thing he wanted was to keep her here against her will.

"Did you think it was that simple?" he said, striving to keep his tone even. "Did you really think that denying your heritage would negate your responsibility?" He barely kept himself from cringing when he realized he echoed the same words his twin sister had thrown in his face two millennia ago.

Ire flashed in Bebe's eyes when she met his gaze. "It's not my fault my mother died." She jabbed a finger in his direction. "At the hands of your people I might add. It's not my fault Grandma refused to accept my decision." She dropped the accusing finger and stepped closer to him. "And it's not my fault she didn't name another heir before she died."

An avalanche of resignation crushed Caesar. As much as he hated destroying Bebe's innocent view of the world, some truths needed to be told. "And which one of your cousins was she supposed to trust, Dr. Zachary? The one who poisoned her or the one who tried to shoot you last night?"

Chapter 5

Bebe stepped away from the bed, rage seething through her. No. The bastard was lying. Vampires lie. That was as much a law of nature as the sun rising in the east.

She wasn't about to let him manipulate her. "Is this how you get your jollies, Augustine? Spreading vicious rumors to see what trouble you can cause?" Anger shook her voice despite her efforts. Besides, he was crediting William with lifting a lazy finger to do something. An obvious falsehood.

"I'm not lying about this," he replied with a quiet conviction.

"Both of my cousins know I'm not accepting the leadership of White Rose coven. I've already tendered my formal withdrawal to the Elders. There's no reason to kill me." She couldn't stop the venom in her voice. She shoved her hands into the soft fleece pockets of her borrowed sweatpants to squelch the urge to fry Augustine in his cream silk sheets.

"A withdrawal the Elders refused to accept."

Her face heated at his blatant statement of fact. How the hell had he known about her encounter with the Council of Elders? Had he slipped into her thoughts when she'd fallen asleep? She checked her shields then breathed a silent prayer of relief that they were intact. So how had Augustine discovered what happened between her and the Elders?

More anger flared at the memory of their bullying tactics, and she lifted her chin. "They can't force me to accept responsibility for our coven, so there's no motive for either William or Alice to want me dead. Care to revise your story, Mr. Augustine?"

Dark circles swam under his hazel eyes, and he released a weary breath. "What about your grandmother's suspicions? Natasha contacted me when you refused to answered her letters. She had reason to believe that someone was trying to kill both her and you in an attempt to seize power within your coven."

Sure, Bebe had some close calls over the past few years. The epileptic driver that nearly mowed her down at UCLA. The snapped cable in the elevator in New York, which hadn't helped her fear of heights one bit. Heck, even the Frisbee that gave her the concussion at Golden Gate Park had all been accidents.

Except there had been more accidents lately. The kid who mugged her at the Nairobi airport. The bus from Mexico losing its airbrakes pulling into San Diego.

Oh, Goddess, now she was beginning to be as paranoid as Grandma Petrov!

Deliberately forcing down her anger, she considered her options. Maybe sheer logic would shake Augustine. "My position with Doctors Without Borders is risky in itself. Grandma blew stuff out of proportion every time she read about a terrorist attack or another civil war breaking out. Has it occurred to you that Mom and Dad's deaths messed with her head? She saw assassins under every bush. Their deaths were the result of sloppy governing." She yanked a hand out of its pocket and jabbed a finger in his direction again. "Which, I might add once more, was your fault for not keeping control over your people!"

"I am sorry rogues killed your parents."

Her accusing finger dropped and clenched into a fist with the rest of her digits. How could he sit there so calm and not even apologize for screwing up his job? She held her breath, but he said nothing else.

"Is that it? Is that all you can say? You're the fucking coven master! It's your responsibility to police any rogues!"

He blinked, but otherwise his face remained as impassive as ever. "I'm not disagreeing with your assessment. I dealt with the problem as soon as I learned of the incidents."

Her fingernails dug into her palms. Goddess, she never wanted to hit someone so bad in her life. "Incident? Is that what you call my mom being gutted, my father ripped limb from limb? In front of my face!" Her chest heaved, desperate for oxygen. The memories of that night swam in her vision.

"You may not remember but I visited your grandmother the night after your parents died." He gave her that same pitying look that everyone who knew the truth had given her for the last seventeen years. The look that infuriated her. "You hid in Natasha's wardrobe and refused to come out. I offered to erase your memory—"

Bebe gasped at his audacity. There had been someone at the mansion. Someone she'd referred to over the years as the Dark Man because his face had been hidden by shadows. Someone who had promised to take the pain away. Someone Grandma said didn't exist. Grandma had to have mentioned the story to Augustine, but before she could bitch him out for trying to use a childhood fantasy against her, he continued.

"Natasha would not allow me."

"Damn straight, she wouldn't! Assuming you're telling the truth, how could you even think of doing that to a child?"

"And it was better to leave you in that much pain? Pain you're still feeling? Pain you can't let go?" Something twisted in Caesar's expression. Not the fake sympathy everyone else gave her, but almost a shared experience.

For once, she cursed her lack of knowledge of the local vampire hierarchy. Dealing politely with the bastards was one of many reasons she loathed stepping into Grandma's position. "And you think Grandma let go of her pain? What the hell do you think killed her?"

"I think that she was far too young to die of heart failure."

Somehow, Augustine's calm demeanor unnerved her more than his flirtatious innuendos or even his previous attempts to slip past her mental shields. "Grandma was 102."

He gave her a small, sad smile. "And the current life expectancy for your people is 160. Natasha was hardly ancient."

Bebe bit her lip. Damn, he had her there. Defiant, she lashed out. "Grandma's health was never the best as long as I can remember. She always tired easily. It wouldn't take much for her to forget she'd already taken her nitroglycerin."

"Natasha was hardly that incompetent." For the first time, an edge appeared in his tone. "Do you really believe she would have forgotten that she took fifty pills instead of one?"

"What are you trying to insinuate, Augustine? Grandma was many things, but suicidal wasn't one of them."

"For once, we agree, Doctor," he said, dry irony filling his voice.

"Oh goody, that made my day." Bitterness flooded her. "Assuming you're correct and the overdose wasn't accidental, it doesn't mean the guilty culprit was one of my cousins. Grandma had enemies out the wazoo, not to mention so many secrets she couldn't keep track of them all." *Grandma wasn't the only one*, her personal nag reminded her. Ignoring the voice, she continued her rant at Augustine. "She wouldn't have dared to show weakness. Knowing her, she could have hidden how bad her cardio-pulmonary problems really were from everyone for years until they finally caught up to her."

He looked away as if praying for strength. When he turned back to her, his gaze contained an odd combination of steel and sympathy. "Bebe, we both know the real cause of her health problems was her incarceration at Auschwitz. And you're right about one thing. Her work against the Nazis earned her a lot of enemies, but the only ones to profit here and now by both her death and yours would be your cousins."

Her breath whooshed out of her lungs, his words a sucker punch to her psyche. Her memory tumbled back to the awful day of her parents' funeral. She reached for the chair where she'd kept her daylight vigil over Augustine, collapsing into it as her knees turned to rubber.

"I—suspected she'd been in a concentration camp," she said, unable to meet the vampire's eyes. The morning of the funeral, as Grandma brushed and braided her hair, Bebe had seen the blue-tinted letters and numbers tattooed on the soft flesh of her grandmother's inner arm. When she asked Grandma what it meant, the blood drained from Grandma's face. Despite all the disagreements they had in the successive years, it had been the only time in her life that her grandmother had ever truly raised her voice to Bebe.

Bebe never saw the tattoo on Grandma's arm again. She almost sure she had imagined it until she saw another, similar one on Grandpa Petrov's arm after her grandparents had divorced. By then, a classmate's grandfather had spoken at her middle school about his experiences in the Nazi concentration camps, so she knew what the tattoo meant. Grandpa had admitted being imprisoned in Auschwitz, but he steadfastly refused to discuss the matter. Afterwards, she subtly examined Grandma's arm and detected the small cosmetic glamour.

Was that the reason for the arranged marriage Grandma had tried to force down her throat? A tortured woman's attempt to keep her family line alive?

She raised her eyes to meet Augustine's, twisting her entwined fingers until her knuckles cracked. "It would seem you know more about her life than I do." The confession tore at her.

"I'm sorry, Bebe. I assumed that she would have discussed such matters with you." His expression belied his words though. He schooled his emotions until only the harsh face of a vampire coven leader remained.

How dare he? The problems between her and Grandma should have remained in the family. Now he claimed an intimacy with her based on his knowledge of Grandma. Him. A vampire. Resentment grew until her head ached.

"So now we're on a first-name basis, Mr. Augustine?" Irritation crawled along her nerves, the itch so bad that she didn't wait for his reply. Sucking in a deep breath, she shoved her emotions aside. She needed to deal with one problem at a time. "What proof do you have that my grandmother was killed? And why do you think those men blasting my hotel room were after me? They could have just as well been your enemies, not mine. I don't need a garlic-coated explosive bullet to kill me."

"No, the regular variety would do the job just fine." That annoying smirk of his twisted his lips. "Obviously, someone close to one or *both* of your grandmothers knew they had asked me to become your guardian in the event something happened to either of them. Your assailants came prepared last night."

No!

Her hand flew to her mouth. Augustine *had* to be lying. Fury burned past the numbness in her veins, and her hand dropped.

"A vampire? My guardian? Neither of my grandmothers would have done such a thing to me," she snapped. "Not after my parents—" The surge of anxious energy spurred her feet into action. She jumped up to pace back and forth at the foot of his bed. Granny E. wasn't as anal as Grandma Petrov, but for all her easygoing nature, there was a reason she was the Los Angeles coven's high priestess.

No, not even Granny E. would have sold out to a vampire.

"They didn't inform you of that little decision either." His words were a statement, not a question. He let out a deep, heartfelt sigh and turned to arrange the pillows behind him before leaning back against the ornately carved headboard. "I'm sorry this comes as a shock, Bebe."

"It's Dr. Zachary to you!" But her words came from very far away. She couldn't catch her breath. Something sucked all the oxygen out of the bedroom. Spots swam in front of her eyes. "They wouldn't do that to me," she whispered. Images from that awful night flashed through her brain. Mom shoving her into the entertainment center as Dad's blood splashed across them . . .

She felt rather than saw Augustine climb from his bed. When he tried to wrap his arms around her, she struck at the blurry vision of him. Despite his weakened state, he easily pulled her into his lap as he dropped to the edge of the bed. He rocked her, his hand stroking her wild curls as Grandma Petrov would have done after one of her frequent nightmares. She loathed admitting, even to herself, that his actions were soothing.

Too soothing. A warm tickle of another kind started in her belly and worked its way through her veins. With an awkward reluctance, she leaned away from his hard chest and eyed him. "Why would either one of my grandmothers trust you? Especially after what had happened to their children?" The skin around her eyes tightened as she eyed him. "Let me see the Blood Seal." The magickal oath mark on his skin would confirm his story.

He shook his head. "I don't have one."

"Really? How convenient. Do you expect me to believe that either of my grandmothers wouldn't take steps to guarantee your performance on this alleged promise to protect me?"

"I expect—"

The bedroom door popped open, Alex poked his head around the edge. His good-natured grin faded when he saw them together on the bed. "Good to see you awake, boss. Uh, everything okay in here?"

Bebe slid off Augustine's lap and took two safe steps away before she turned and crossed her arms. "Everything's just fine." She imagined how the picture of her sitting on Augustine's lap appeared to the younger vampire. Heat seeped into her cheeks.

"Uh-huh." Alex flicked his gaze to Augustine and cocked an eyebrow.

"We're both fine," Augustine said.

For once, the bastard didn't make any cracks at her expense. She breathed a silent prayer of thanks when Alex merely nodded and left, shutting the door behind him. She pivoted back to face Augustine.

He remained silent, his expression again an odd mix of concern and wariness.

"Look, you want me to trust you, then you've got to come clean," she said. "Why would my grandmothers come to you without making you take the oath?"

He sighed and ran a hand across the stubble of his beard before giving her a wry smile. "The enemy of my enemy is my friend."

She rolled her eyes. "In English, please."

He sobered. "We had mutual objectives. Your parents weren't the only ones murdered that night. Others were killed by the rogues as well, including some of my people."

"Your people?" Her eyes narrowed. "You mean other vampires?"

He nodded. "And weres and Normal relatives as well."

"Why?"

Augustine shrugged. "Either an attempt to start a race war or an attempt to seize power. We're not sure. None of the culprits were taken alive."

She crossed her arms. "Once again, how convenient."

"Feel free to confirm my story independently."

His story made sense, but why the hell hadn't Grandma Petrov ever told her any of this? The urge to do something, anything, grew overwhelming. "I need to go to L.A." Granny E. would tell her the truth. Give her a direction in this mess.

"I would like to discuss the incident at the hotel with your paternal grandmother as well."

"Where's your phone?"

He gestured toward the modern set sitting on nightstand.

She ignored his smile at her blatant faux pas. The lack of sleep definitely affected her reasoning capabilities. She reached for the handset and started punching in Granny E.'s number.

"You do know she won't be back from Europe until Friday, don't you?"

Irritation washed over Bebe at Augustine's words. "And how would you know this?"

"I called Los Angeles yesterday once I had located you. The housekeeper informed me she would return on Friday."

She couldn't summon the energy to feed the annoyance she should feel towards him. Exhaustion tugged the edges of her mind.

He grinned when she could no longer resist the huge yawn that threatened to crack her face wide open. "However, I think you could do with some more sleep before we fly down. Why don't you lie down in my bed?"

Yeah, right, the spider said to the fly. The man had sported a woody simply from having his blood pressure taken.

"I managed not to contract the V-virus last night. How, I'll never know. Let's not put my luck to the test." Too much was happening, and not just Caesar's continuous flirting. She shook her head at the thought of the last twenty-four hours. If she didn't get a break soon, she might go bonkers.

He rose from the bed, his Road Runner pajama bottoms still freaking her out as much as they had when Alex put them on the unconscious Augustine last night. "Sorry, Dr. Zachary," he said stressing her title. "I wasn't planning on joining you." He gave her a top-down perusal that would have been promising if he weren't a vampire. Then he flashed a wicked grin. "Next time perhaps?" He snagged the rich velvet bathrobe off the trunk at the end of his bed and shrugged it on. "I'll be in my office making flight arrangements for Los Angeles if you need anything."

The bedroom seemed oddly empty after Augustine strode out the door. Bebe glanced between the closed door and the bed. A bed still rumpled from its owner. She squelched the thought that sent tingles through her nerves. He was a vampire, damn it!

A check of the clock showed she had slept maybe twenty minutes before the touch of his hand had woken her. Her scratchy eyeballs reminded her how crappy pulling a thirty-six hour shift felt. Cursing what was probably another stupid move on her part, she crossed to the door and locked it. The heavy click of the deadbolt was only slightly reassuring.

Climbing between his silk sheets, Bebe snuggled in and inhaled the spicy scent of Caesar, sandalwood and something indefinably masculine. It was almost as good as having his arms wrapped around her.

—•—

Once in his office, Caesar paced in front of Natasha's wardrobe, cursing the old witch, cursing the Fates, and most of all cursing himself. After five minutes, his body reminded him it was still recovering from last night's experience at Bebe's hotel, and he sank into the soft leather of his desk chair. Two seconds later, there was a quiet knock at his door.

He wanted to ignore Alex in favor of wallowing in his own self-loathing. Despite Caesar's silence, the Texan strode in balancing a tray with two mugs of warm blood. Mugs that bore the logo of Little Caesars Pizza.

The boy did not know when his perverse sense of humor crossed the line. Waking in the cartoon pajamas Tiffany had given him as a Winter Solstice present last year had been bad enough. He had to assume Ptolemy had already left for the evening and had not seen the mugs. Otherwise, Alex would be nothing more than a puddle of goo with a wooden stake lying in the middle.

Alex finally acknowledged the death glare Caesar aimed at him. After placing one steaming mug on the desk and setting the tray on the credenza, he crossed his arms and said, "If you wanted privacy, you should have locked the door."

"Like that ever stopped you." The familiar surge of thirst made Caesar reach for the mug, but he hesitated at the odd odor. He took another careful whiff before raising an eyebrow. "What the fuck did you put in my cup?"

Feigned innocence spread across the Texan's face. "It's prime Angus. Your favorite."

Not in the mood for the younger vampire's games, he bared his canines.

Alex spread his hands in a defensive motion. "I added a little barbecue sauce."

Caesar narrowed his eyes, and Alex's eyes glowed electric blue in response to his threat.

"It's the only thing that covers the bitterness of liquid ibuprofen. I figured you might be a little sore this evening. No one else knows." Alex held his hand over his heart. "I swear," he finished.

Caesar relaxed a fraction. While he trusted his immediate household, the sheer nature of both ancient Roman and modern vampire politics made him reluctant to show any weakness. Not that passing out in his own Hummer and being dragged into the house wasn't a dead give-away. He gulped half the mug in two swallows, then grimaced and set the giant-sized cup down. "Next time use chocolate or vanilla instead. Your homemade sauce sucks."

"Har-de-har-har," Alex said. "By the way, you want to tell me why Dr. Z is sound asleep in your bed?"

"Yes, brother dear," a soft voice purred from the doorway. Caesar twisted to see Selene leaning against the frame. "Why *is* a witch sharing your bed?"

Alex pursed his lips before giving Caesar an apologetic shrug. "Also, your sister's here to see you."

Chapter 6

The vampire virus eliminated nearly every form of ailment that plagued Norms, but stress migraines were not unknown. And a doozy began pulsing behind Caesar's left eyeball.

"Why, Selene, to what do I owe this unannounced pleasure?" He didn't bother rising, and his twin sister didn't bother crossing the room to kneel before him. Gods forbid she might get lint on her black designer slacks.

"Passing my respects to my coven master, of course."

Her sly smile didn't fool him for an instant. He gave Alex a measured stare. "That will be all."

Alex frowned, but then he nodded and backed out of the office, closing the door behind him.

Selene crossed the room and nestled in the brown suede couch. "So tell me more about your new pet. And why is *my* eclectic still stuck in Africa?"

He wiped a hand down his face. "Why Dr. Zachary's here is none of your concern, Selene. And I told you a couple of days ago to recall Lucian." He reached for his mug, wishing that the ibuprofen were opium. Sometimes progress wasn't all it was cracked up to be.

"Do you have any idea how hard it is to get a last minute flight out of Chad? If I'm lucky, he might be back in the U.S. before the end of the week." She crossed her arms and glared at him. "Don't tell me you're getting us in the middle of the White Rose succession."

He smiled, deliberately displaying his canines. "As you wish."

She leaned forward, elbows on her knees. "What in Isis's name are you thinking? Finding the girl for Petrov is one thing. Involving us in a witch war is totally different. This is why you got your ass shot up, isn't it?"

He took a sip before answering her. "And you came here hoping I had brought Duncan to San Francisco with me, not out of any concern for my well-being."

The faint pink that flooded her cheeks was the only indication Caesar had nailed her real purpose for the visit. Selene's obsession with his Chief Enforcer knew no bounds. She had Turned the man without his consent, then couldn't understand his rejection of her. Five centuries after the fact, she still pursued him. Gods above! For an intelligent woman, Selene did some damn stupid things.

She cleared her throat. "Of course, I'm concerned, both as your sister and as your second-in command. Ptolemy called me last night. Very upset about you getting shot, I might add."

He had to give his twin credit. She could dissemble better than anyone he'd ever known. "He didn't need to call you. As you can see, I'm perfectly fine."

One of Selene's slim black eyebrows flicked upward. "Really? Then why was he rambling about garlic-laced explosive bullets?"

Caesar took another sip of the doctored blood and decided to ignore the issue with Duncan for now. "Ptolemy blew things out of proportion. I wasn't shot in the ass, and I'm fine. Thank you for asking."

"Ri-i-ight." Selene pursed her lips and nodded. "I'm sure that's why Stanton is serving you Advil-laced blood."

He sniffed the cup again. "You can smell it over his nasty barbecue sauce?"

She gave him a 'duh' look. He shrugged and downed the last of the cup before trading it for the second one.

Frowning, Selene sat back and crossed her arms over her ample chest again, which pulled her black turtleneck even tighter. Her move was so instinctual when she dealt with men. She probably didn't realize the effect was wasted on her brothers.

"Let's go back to our original topic," she said. "Want to tell me why you're dragging our coven into the middle of the White Rose succession?"

He needed to have a word with Ptolemy about the kid's big mouth. He matched her frown. "I'm not dragging the coven anywhere. This is a personal issue. Natasha Petrov was my friend."

Selene snorted in disgust. "It becomes a coven issue when you start imitating Swiss cheese. It becomes a coven issue when your second-in-command gets frantic phone calls in the middle of the night that you're in a coma. It becomes a coven issue when you've got the new White Rose High Priestess sleeping in your bed." Her lips curled in a nasty snarl that would have scared the crap out of anybody with common sense.

"Bebe hasn't been confirmed by the coven Elders yet." He started to take another drink and looked down in surprise. He'd already drained the second cup during Selene's rant.

"So what in Hades is she doing here?" A suspicious glint flared in her deep brown eyes. Her arms dropped and she slid to the edge of the couch. "You're not trying to Turn her, are you?"

"Turning the unwilling is your department."

Her eyes glowed neon yellow. "That's a really shitty thing to say, even for you."

Ancient guilt sprang up. When Octavian's army camped outside of Alexandria's city gates, their mother had made Caesar promise to protect Selene and Ptolemy. And here he was, throwing insults without any care. He sucked in breath to calm himself.

"I'm sorry. And no, I'm not trying to Turn anyone. Assassins were after Bebe, and I—" He gave her a wry smile. "—got in the way."

She relaxed slightly but remained perched on the end of the cushion. "It sounds like they were gunning for more than witch."

He shrugged. "Maybe they were simply taking precautions. We would do the same in a similar operation."

She cocked an eyebrow. "So what *is* she doing here? Why not hand her over to the White Rose Elders?"

Caesar propped his elbows on the desk, his fingers steepled. As much as he loathed asking Selene for more help, he needed it if he was going to keep Bebe alive. "Natasha asked me to protect her granddaughter. She believed there was a conspiracy within her coven to assassinate both her and Bebe."

Selene jumped to her feet and threw her arms in the air. "Isis, help me! Since when do we get involved in internal witch politics? In case you haven't noticed, we're vampires!"

"And that's your excuse for letting an innocent woman die?"

"You said Petrov's heir hasn't been confirmed by the White Rose Elders yet." She started pacing, the sharp stilettos on her sandals poking holes in the plush of the beige carpet. "Then it's not *our* concern. Are you even considering the ramifications of your actions? The witches will have a field day if *you*, a vampire master, champion one candidate over another in a succession contest. Not to mention the sanctions the International Council will impose on us." She whirled and pinned him with an irritated glare. "Have you even discussed this with the other North American Masters?"

"No, I have not. As I said, this is a personal matter." Caesar leaned back into his chair. Selene's anger spiked her normal sandalwood into burnt ash. The acrid odor caused the pounding behind his left eye to escalate.

"Good, good," she murmured and resumed her pacing. "If no one outside your immediate circle knows about this, we have a chance at damage control. We'll return your little houseguest to her Elders and no one will be the wiser. Damn, how can we spin this?" She raked her hands through her hair, mussing her stylish black tresses.

She was so intent on her plan she didn't notice Ptolemy slip through the door. He shot a grin at Caesar while she continued her mumbling. "She was mugged, you rescued her, we alter her memory—"

"Are we giving that butt-ugly wardrobe back to the witches, too?" Ptolemy asked.

Her head jerked up at his words and the furrows in her brow smoothed. She walked over and gave him a quick hug. "Thanks for calling me last night."

"Glad you're here." Ptolemy shot a thumb in Caesar's direction. "I just hope you're talking some sense into him."

She snorted and smiled as she looked up at Ptolemy. "Like anything I say has any effect on him."

"So are you going to send that atrocity back with the girl?" He pointed at the corner between the couch and the built-in bookshelves where Caesar had placed the wardrobe.

She tilted her head to examine the piece and grimaced. "Where did that come from?"

"He bought it at the old witch's estate auction."

She crinkled her nose. "Why, in Isis's name, would he do that?"

"You know, I am in the room." Caesar tried to give them his most menacing scowl, but the effort was wasted when all three of them cracked up. Damn, it had been too long since they had been in the same room. And even rarer still since they had shared any laughter. Gods, he missed the old days.

Once the last chuckle died, Selene turned serious again. She strode to the front of his desk and crossed her arms. "We have to send her back to her people."

Ptolemy stepped forward, shoulder to shoulder with Selene. "She's right. I know you're concerned about the witch, but it's not our problem—"

Caesar slapped the desktop, hard. His siblings jumped but didn't back down. "No, it's my problem. This about a promise I made."

Selene leaned forward and slammed her own palms on the hard cherry wood. "To a dead woman who probably wasn't in her right mind when she extracted that promise."

Caesar rose and dipped down until his nose was millimeters from his twin's. "We are *not* turning her over to anyone, Selene."

"Damn it, Alexander Helios Antonius!" Her eyes flashed gold. "For once in your misbegotten life, listen to me!"

"Uh-oh," Ptolemy muttered and backed away from them.

Caesar's pulse pounded a rhythm to match his rage, and the tips of his canines pressed into his lips as they elongated. "Don't you *ever* call me by that name again." The cold calm in his voice contradicted the red that swam in his vision. "That man died the day Octavia sent her immortal pets to assassinate us. Or don't you remember, dear sister?"

Selene deliberately lowered her hard stare and took a hesitant step away from the desk. "I meant no disrespect, Master."

Fire roared in his ears. "You both need to leave." He clenched his fists in an effort to get his blood rage under control. The last thing he needed right now was to lose it and attack his sister. He felt rather than saw Ptolemy take a tentative step forward.

"Do you need more blood—"

"Now!" he roared.

His siblings scrambled out the door. His chest ached as he forced slow, steady breaths. In. Out. Gods, he couldn't let Bebe see him in this way. Her emotional state was questionable as it was, and any connection he had with her tenuous.

In. Out.

He dropped into his chair and concentrated on the cool leather against his overheated skin. Why in Hades did Selene have to bring up the past tonight? Selene's husband, Juba, had done his best to protect him and Ptolemy, but it hadn't been enough to stop Octavia's bitterness. He forced the memory of that terrible night aside.

In. Out.

Caesar wasn't sure how long he sat slumped in the chair before the red haze cleared from his vision. He rose and stretched. The aches in his body intensified, no longer the dull throb now that his temper-fueled metabolism had burned off the painkiller.

Selene wouldn't assist him in protecting Bebe. She'd made that perfectly clear. Not that she was likely to be in a gracious mood after his temper tantrum if she weren't already dead set against getting involved in White Rose's problems.

He shambled up the hand-carved staircase towards his bedroom with the intent of getting some more ibuprofen and then sleep. The earlier talk with the witch flared to life in his brain. Crap, Bebe was still in his bed.

As much as crawling in next to her held its fascination, getting fire-balled in his own bed didn't have the same appeal. And Bebe needed the sleep as much as he did. He had the impression she had stayed up all night and the following day to keep an eye on him.

He'd just grab some more painkillers from his bathroom rather than suffer the torture of making his way back downstairs to the infirmary. Then he'd fall onto a mattress in one of the guest bedrooms. Yes, that'd work. Especially if he didn't look at the bed or touch its occupant. He eased the door open.

Just one problem with that plan.

His bed was empty.

Chapter 7

Guilt and worry stuck to Bebe's consciousness, preventing sleep despite the fatigue plaguing her limbs and eyelids. Rolling over on her back, she stared at the blue glow from the alarm clock reflected against the ceiling. She couldn't wait for morning to search for the wardrobe and retrieve the Book of Shadows. Augustine probably had a private jet, which meant he could come upstairs anytime to collect her for the flight to L.A.

The doorknob rattled. Her breath hitched in her throat, and she mentally reached out. A vampire was on the other side. Alex, from the fruity cereal taste of his surface thoughts. The deadbolt slid back, and she closed her eyes and deepened her breathing to feign sleep. No shuffling foot steps on the carpet. Her willpower hammered to keep her breaths slow and even.

Seconds later, the door clicked shut, and the deadbolt gave a soft *snick* as it locked again.

Bebe opened her eyes and stared at the door, but no other sound came from the other side. Now what the hell was that all about? She swung her feet over the edge of the mattress and eased over to the door to listen. The fruity cereal taste receded down the hallway towards the main staircase when she reached out with a psychic probe.

Goddess, she truly was becoming as paranoid as Grandma Petrov. Alex had probably come up to check on Augustine again. If the Texan were one of Augustine's enforcers, he'd have a key to every door in the mansion. Most likely, when he realized his coven master was up and about, he went looking for him.

Concentrating, Bebe leaned her forehead against the door and reached past the hallway. No one upstairs.

Stretching, she pressed her thoughts further through the house. The rich, beefy taste of Caesar fired through her nerves. He must be weaker than he let on because she didn't get a reaction from her slight intrusion.

She breathed a sigh of relief. No taste of spinach and dandelions, which meant the two half-elven day guards had left for the evening. And no burnt toast or cotton candy meant Ptolemy and Anne were gone as well.

Confirming that Caesar and Alex were still downstairs, she cast a blurring spell around her before she twisted the lock and crept through the door. Not true invisibility, a blurring spell merely kept the casual observer from noticing someone or something was out of place. Once the vampires realized she wasn't in Caesar's bedroom and started a thorough search, she was screwed. She prayed that she'd been in enough rooms during the day that any previous scent would cover her most recent passage. Keeping her own shields tight, she began a room-by-room search through the second floor. The ambient light from the security lamps outdoors guided her way.

Emerging from the fourth bedroom she checked, Bebe cursed softly to herself. The wardrobe had to be downstairs in one of the rooms she hadn't visited. Even with vampire strength, she couldn't imagine the practicality of hauling it up to the attic or down to the basement. And from the functionality and simplicity of every piece of furniture and art, if Caesar Augustine was anything, it was practical.

She jumped at the soft chime of the front doorbell, her elbow knocking into the urn of daisies at the head of the stairs. She snatched the crystal, which she sensed was Anne's touch, before it could crash to the floor. Tension scraped her nerves as she settled the flowers upright and crouched down.

Soft voices drifted up from the foyer, but the hint of anger in Alex's was unmistakable, even if she couldn't make out the words. Dropping to her belly, she crawled to the edge of the landing to peer down through the banisters. The voice of the woman Alex spoke with carried an air of amused arrogance at his irritation. After another exchange, he gestured for her to wait by the entrance before he stalked off toward the kitchen.

Instinct warned Bebe this woman was not someone to screw with. She didn't dare reach out with a mental probe.

The dark-haired woman paced back and forth in the foyer, impatience in every click of her designer shoes. Her skin-tight turtleneck was not something Bebe would have dared wear, much less with the heavy gold jewelry that drenched the woman. The slacks, that had to have been spray-painted on her ass, screamed sex with every twist of her hips.

The woman's head jerked up, and for an instant Bebe would have sworn they locked eyes. How the heck did the bitch see through her blurring spell? Was she a vampire? Bebe couldn't tell by scent when sandalwood odor from the other vampires filled the house. If she weren't a vampire though, who else would be visiting Caesar?

Bebe's heart banged an obscenely loud rhythm the woman probably heard despite the magickal shield. From the hard look on the woman's face, this was not someone who would cut anyone slack for sneaking around the mansion. Bebe bit her lip, clenched her fist and started to summon a fireball. Energy tickled in her fingertips.

The woman's sharp gaze shifted across the banister and flicked across the high windows of the foyer. Bebe stopped her incantation and tracked her line of sight. What was she looking at?

The visitor's eyes settled on the security camera lodged in the corner of the entrance's cathedral ceiling. Her sharp canines gleamed under the chandelier when she smiled at the camera and blew it a kiss. Okay, that came under the heading of weird behavior, even for a vampire. Then the female vamp pivoted and sauntered down the main hallway until she disappeared under the landing.

Bebe held her breath until the clicking of the vamp's heels disappeared. The air in her lungs escaped with a *whoosh*. She glanced again at the security camera. While the blurring spell worked against electronic eyes the same as organic ones, she needed to be more careful not to set off any other conventional alarms.

Last night, when she had questioned Stan Gryffudd, one of the half-elven day guards, about magickal security measures, he had snickered and told her it was none of her Morrigan-damned business. In her experience, that statement meant Stan and his partner, Harry, knew the most powerful spells a half-elf could wield. If their techniques were anything like White Rose security, their spells focused on keeping intruders out, not preventing someone from snooping inside.

In a way, it was a relief Caesar was doubly careful with conventional and magickal measures. Maybe the hotel gunmen would think twice before mounting any kind of assault on the vampire's home.

Rising to her feet, she hugged the wall as she crept down the stairs. She froze when one tread squeaked under her bare foot. After a few seconds, when no one appeared, she preceded the rest of way down the remaining steps.

So far, so good.

No sooner did the thought materialize when the front door lock rattled. Panic started to overwhelm her.

No, dammit! This is no different than freaking triage! What's the priority?

Hiding, except there were no hiding places in the foyer or front sitting room. The blurring spell wouldn't do any good if she was standing in the middle of a room and someone ran into her. If she went into the kitchen, she could say she couldn't get back to sleep and was looking for tea. But then one of the vamps would shadow her for the rest of the evening as they had last night.

The massive front door started to open.

She dived into the tiny half bath tucked under the staircase and closed the door until a sliver allowed her to watch the hall and kitchen door. Anne stopped short when Alex's shaggy blond head poked out of the kitchen door.

"You're home early. Not enough rogues and gang bangers to beat up?"

An odd expression crossed Anne's face, and her wide, innocent eyes narrowed. Her vamp-out happened so fast, Bebe shoved a fist against her mouth to stop the shriek that bulged in the back of her throat. It was too much like the ugly sons of a bitch who broke into her parents' home. The night her father's head was ripped off.

Anne bared fangs at Alex. "What I do on my personal time is my business." A sneer twisted her grotesque mouth when she added a sarcastic, "Father."

Father? Was Alex Anne's sire? What the hell possessed him to Turn her at such a young age? Bebe struggled to keep her breath shallow and even. If the vamps caught her watching their little soap opera . . .

Alex folded his arms over his chest, his calm look and the dishtowel over his shoulder incongruous with the angry little vampire he faced. "If you're finished with your snit fit, I have the address for that plate number Ptolemy got off the gunmen's van. It took me a while to trace it through several different holding companies, but the final one's Bay Area Consolidated. I need you to shadow the principal shareholder, Lionel Hart."

No.

Bile rose in Bebe's throat. Would Uncle Lionel kill her to insure that her cousin Alice was named high priestess by the Elders? Spots swam in her vision. She leaned her head against the cool ceramic of the toilet. Uncle Lionel had always doted on Alice, and as one of the richest men in the country, he had the means to give Alice everything she desired. Everything except Grandma Petrov's approval.

The split between the cousins had started the day of the funeral for Bebe's parents. Grandma had caught Alice making out with a neighbor boy.

In the family crypt.

Alice had accused Bebe of narcing. The rawness of the whole deal was that Bebe hadn't tattled. But if she had ratted out the real tattletale, their cousin William, she'd be exactly what Alice called her.

From there, Alice had decided since Grandma had called her a whore, she'd act the part. Only Patti Hearst and Paris Hilton had received more press than Alice in the spoiled heiress department. And the weekly pictures of Alice in the tabloids hadn't endeared her to their ultra-conservative grandmother.

The last straw had been Bebe's decision to enter medical school. To Alice, she'd done it only to suck up to Grandma.

Maybe it wasn't Uncle Lionel. But if it wasn't, that left only Alice. Bebe swallowed hard. An innocent man almost died because of this stupid family squabble.

No. Augustine was hardly innocent.

She blinked back the tears that threatened to spill. Goddess, no wonder her old friends avoided her like the plague. How many had Alice threatened?

"Call Stan before dawn so he can cover daytime surveillance of Hart." Alex's voice drew Bebe back to her present predicament. Alice, William and the Elders had been careless enough to lose Grandma's Book of Shadows. Bebe needed to find it while she had the chance and get the heck out of this vampire haven before Augustine dragged her down to L.A.

Anne had calmed down and only a dim golden glow showed in her eyes. "Isn't Hart—"

"Yeah, he's the doc's uncle by marriage. She's going to shit a brick when she hears this." Alex raked a hand through his unruly locks.

"We don't tell her."

Both of the vampires and Bebe jerked at the sound of Ptolemy's voice. How the heck did he manage to sneak into the house?

She cursed herself. She'd been so busy eavesdropping on Alex and Anne that she hadn't been scanning her surroundings. If she wasn't more careful, she was going to get herself caught and maybe even killed. As much as she loathed admitting Augustine was right, she definitely wasn't cut out for espionage.

"What? Why not?" Alex said.

She shared Alex's confusion. After her verbal sparring with him, she assumed Ptolemy would have gotten a kick out of skewering her with her family's homicidal bent.

"Contrary to your opinion of me, Stanton, I've no wish to upset Dr. Zachary. Despite her obvious distrust of our race, she saved my brother's life."

Wow. Who would've thought the brat prince had a soft side?

Then he stepped into view next to Anne, his nostrils flaring. He twisted his head left then right, sniffing like a bloodhound on coke.

"Where is she?" His eyes narrowed, but his gaze continued to flick around, obviously searching for her.

Bebe wrapped her arms tight around her knees. Like once before, a long time ago, whimpers gathered at the back of her throat. *Please don't let them find me. Oh Goddess, please don't let them.*

Alex huffed, exasperation evident in the sound. "She's upstairs asleep. I just checked on her."

Ptolemy stared at Alex for what seemed an eternity before he nodded curtly. "Is Caesar still—"

"No." With his sharp answer, Alex shook his head. "He's awake and in his office with your sister."

Sister? Holy crap! How many vampire siblings did Augustine have running around? Remembering the woman's sharp profile, Bebe wanted to kick herself for not recognizing the new vampire's resemblance to Augustine and Ptolemy.

Ptolemy passed in front of the bathroom door, heading towards the back of the house.

"Why's *she* here?" Anne's voice carried a nasty edge.

Alex shrugged. "Fake sisterly concern and the faint hope that she could fuck Duncan."

Bebe swallowed hard. Who's Duncan? Did she need to worry about another vampire?

A nasty smile crossed Anne's face. "Over or with."

Alex turned his head in the direction Ptolemy had disappeared. "Both probably."

"Too bad someone doesn't accidentally stake the bitch." The venom on Anne's voice made the hairs stand up on the back of Bebe's neck. So much for the vampire's sweet act.

Alex laid a hand on Anne's shoulder and guided her into the kitchen. "Down, girl. Meanwhile, you've got a job to do . . ."

Wetness trickled down Bebe's face, and she swiped a hand across her cheek to eliminate the tears. The family feuds and her old friends shunning her were one thing. Facing the fact that someone really did want her dead was another. Alice's normal weapon of choice had been a well-aimed rumor or a nasty practical joke spell guaranteed to embarrass the hell out of the target, not a physical assault.

No. The vampires had to have known Bebe was eavesdropping. The story could have been concocted for her benefit, to fracture any remaining tie she had to her family.

So why didn't they kick open the bathroom door and kill her? Why all the games? Terror wrapped its ugly hand around her heart and squeezed. No one outside of the vampires knew where she was. They could be playing with her. Was Augustine's claim of flying to Los Angeles just another game?

She shook her head. She couldn't afford the distraction of her wild imagination. She needed to find the wardrobe, retrieve the Book of Shadows and hotfoot it south to the relative safety of Granny E.'s place.

Bebe held her breath and counted to twenty. She couldn't take the chance of reaching out with a mental probe. One of them might feel her.

When none of the vampires reappeared, she toed the bathroom door open. Still nothing. She climbed to her feet and eased next to the door. Faint voices came from the kitchen, but the sounds weren't coming any closer. She eased out of the bathroom. The burning in her lungs reminded her that she was still holding her breath. She released the used air out as silently as she could.

Tiptoeing down the hallway, she passed the clinic and paused outside the next door, which was closed. Laughter trickled out, Caesar's tenor unmistakable. What she wouldn't give to join in the good-humor that laced the air. To share a smile and a chuckle with him, the emotional connection that a good laugh—

Cut the romantic bullshit!

The sharp admonition forced her feet to move to the next room, but a flip of the light switch showed the windowless bare room contained only exercise pads on the floor and an open wooden rack full of hand weapons.

The next room held a grand piano, a bench and a small bookcase full of sheet music. Again, no wardrobe and no place to hide a humungous piece of furniture.

Worry chewed at her. Could the vampires have taken the wardrobe someplace else after it had been delivered here? Even worse, could they have destroyed it, not knowing what was inside?

Bebe hurried around the corner of the hall to the last door and gasped when she opened it. Riotous life overwhelmed her senses, both physical and psychic. What had been a cloak room leading to a massive back porch on the architectural diagrams had been combined and transformed into a gigantic greenhouse. Everything inside glowed with life and beauty. Had she bought into the stereotype of vampires so much she underestimated them?

But stubborn loyalty to the coven overrode the desire to bask in the greenery. Augustine wouldn't store an antique in this humidity.

Bebe jumped at the howl of anger that ripped through the thick atmosphere. It was followed by the distinct crash of the massive front door slamming shut. What the hell was going on? Had the vamps discovered that she was no longer in Augustine's bed? She crossed to the greenhouse door and paused to listen. No other noise presented itself, then the faint shuffling of feet away from her.

She double-checked the integrity of her blurring spell then slid through the door, easing it closed behind her. Her breath rattled in her throat, a harsh noise she was sure the vampires could detect. She peeked around the corner, but no one guarded the hall, waiting to nab her.

Holding her breath, she extended a tentative psychic probe. Only one mind met her mental touch. The rich, beefy essence of Caesar receded upstairs, the pace in time with the faint creak of the wood on the stairs. She released the held air when he didn't react to her probe. That was twice now, and the physician part of her worried at his lack of sensitivity.

Light no longer shone from beneath the door of the room where Augustine and his company had been. The only place she hadn't been since arriving at the mansion. She tiptoed over, listening for any other activity in the house, and turned the knob. A sigh of relief escaped her when she discovered it was unlocked. After closing the door, she thumbed the switch on the wall, and light flooded what was obviously an office.

Bebe's knees trembled, and she hung onto the antique glass knob to remain upright. In a corner between the floor-to-ceiling bookshelves and a leather couch, the dark hulk of Grandma's wardrobe loomed over the rest of the furnishings.

She shook her head at the incongruity. Grandma's wardrobe would have fit in any other room in Caesar's mansion. But no, he sticks it in the one room that had been redecorated in a thoroughly twenty-first century style. Crossing to the desk, she hit the switch on the smaller lamp before turning off the recessed lights from the wall switch. She muttered a silent prayer that no one would interrupt her for the few seconds she needed.

Caution was called for though since Augustine employed half-elves. With all her senses, she examined the wardrobe from across the room. Only the same residual elf magic that permeated the mansion shone in her Sight. No active spells displayed themselves.

Bebe crossed the room and whipped open the old cedar doors. She knelt and reached for the bottom panel of the wardrobe. Probing with care, her fingertips tingled when she found the entrance to the pocket of nymph space within the wood. To most other races, and even most witches, the bottom section would appear to be solid, but the living space of the nymph who had inhabited the tree used to build the wardrobe still existed. With the wards set inside the hole itself, the magick would be invisible to almost anyone.

And it didn't appear than anyone had breached the wards. Relief swept through her. Now, she needed to get the Book out of the mansion before one of the vampires discovered it. Despite her anger at her cousins' and the Elders' behavior, she had no wish for the information in the Book used against them.

Sucking in a breath, her nose filled with the odor of sandalwood, along with Caesar's own distinctive scent. The result sent her heart tripping for reasons that had nothing to do with fear.

She squelched the thrill that ran along her nerves. Caesar may have been friends with Grandma, but could she take the chance he would use the information in the Book against White Rose and their allied covens? No, she had to get the Book out of the mansion.

Except she had no money and no clothes.

Wood moaned overhead as Caesar walked down the hallway toward his room.

Retrieve the damn Book and call Beatrice Flannigan.

The Air Elder was sympathetic to her. Even if Beatrice resorted to guilt tactics to get her to accept the high priestess position, at least Bebe would be away from the vampire's mansion.

She was out of time and out of options. Any moment Caesar would discover she was no longer in his bed.

She whispered the incantation to dissolve Grandma's wards and reached into the compartment. Her fingers found nothing but wood.

No leather.

No paper.

Nothing.

The Book of Shadows was gone.

Chapter 8

Bebe yanked her hand out of the nymph hole. Air couldn't get in her lungs because her heart had shot up and lodged in her throat. She reached back into the wardrobe's secret compartment.

So much for wishful thinking. The Book of Shadows had not materialized in the few seconds since she'd opened the space. Her eyes and throat burned. Both William and Alice had accused her of taking the Book when she returned to San Francisco. Neither possessed the talent to hide their auras so she was pretty damn sure they weren't lying when they said they didn't have it.

Auras. Goddess, she was so stupid. She had the perfect opportunity to check Caesar's aura when she questioned him earlier, but she'd been so angry, all she had wanted was to shove a fireball up his ass. And last night, she'd been so scared all logical thought escaped her.

It didn't matter now. Her real problem was much bigger. Where was the Book? And how the hell was she supposed to find it?

"You really cannot keep your hands off my property, can you?"

Her head whipped around, and she found Caesar leaning against the door-frame, his arms crossed. Her game of hide-and-seek was up. She swallowed hard. It no longer mattered. The Book was gone.

The annoying smirk smeared across his face twisted into concern. He strode across the room, knelt and wrapped his arms around her before she could stand. Cradling her head against his shoulder, his simple gesture loosed the floodgates of her tears.

"Can you tell me what's wrong?" His warm breath brushed against her ear.

How could she trust him? He was a vampire. And yet he gave her more simple acts of compassion in the two days she knew him than she received from her blood kin in the seventeen years since her parents died.

Raising her head, she regarded him. "Why did you outbid me for the wardrobe?"

"Truth?"

She nodded and shifted her visual focus. Scarlet, the color of a warrior, surrounded him, edged by the brick red signature of the virus. She waited for the pulse of ugly gray across his aura that signified a deception.

"On my honor, I did not know who you were. All I knew was that you were from the White Rose coven." He lifted a finger and stroked her right ear, avoiding the sterling silver stud, one of the rose-shaped earrings she received at her Initiation. His light touch sent a tremor through her body. If he noticed her reaction, he gave no indication.

"Since I did not recognize you, I feared you were one of the conspirators. You were the only one from your coven to attend the auction. I suspected there was something valuable regarding the wardrobe by the way you pursued it." He shot her a wry grin. "I was actually trying to preserve it for Bebe since I didn't know you were her."

No change in his aura. She sat a little straighter, reluctant to pull away from his hard, comforting chest, but she needed to distance herself in order to think clearly. "I beg your pardon?"

His left hand still clasped her shoulder. "As I told you, I vowed an oath to Natasha to protect you if her death was untimely. This—" He waved his free hand at the wardrobe and chuckled. "—was of value to you, so I knew Natasha would want you to have it. I planned to give it to you anyway."

His aura held steady. His consideration overwhelmed her, but not enough for her to drop her guard.

"You still haven't told me what's your real connection to my grandmother."

The brilliant scarlet outlining his body darkened and her heart fell. He was considering a lie to tell her. Typical for a man. Just when her opinion of him improves, he goes and does something stupid.

Then his aura flared back. He dropped his hand from her shoulder and shook his head. "There are things I shouldn't tell you." He blew out a deep breath.

The faint prickle of his mental touch sent tingles along her skin but it lasted only an instant. He wasn't trying to read her. Caesar's focus wavered, and she realized he was checking for who remained in the mansion.

A shiver of apprehension rippled down her spine. Didn't he trust his own people?

Amusement quickly followed the heels of that thought. She couldn't talk about trust issues considering the situation with her family.

His golden eyes cleared and his gaze bore into hers. "Since your grandmother's actions have dragged you into danger, I believe you have a right to know. But what I say cannot leave this room. Do you understand?"

She nodded, more than a little concerned. What the hell had Grandma gotten herself involved in?

"Bebe, you must understand that Natasha had your best interests at heart, and she never meant for harm to come to you or your parents."

His sincerity ripped at her. She nodded but silently prayed she could bear whatever secret he was about to reveal.

"I met your grandmother in Paris shortly after she was released from Auschwitz II. She confirmed what Ike and I had suspected during the war—the supernatural breeds had been betrayed by their own kind to the Axis powers."

Horror surged through Bebe. What Caesar said went against every rule and custom in the supernatural handbook—if such a thing existed. Okay, maybe the I.C. code counted. "Wait a minute. Are you saying some of us took part in a Normal war? You took part?"

He nodded. "Once stories reached us here in the U.S. about what was happening in the Old World, we didn't have a choice."

She inched back from him and hugged her arms around her knees. "There's always a choice," she snapped.

His cold expression could have frozen Lake Tahoe all the way to the bottom. "So in your opinion, I should have let the regiment of vampire soldiers Hitler had created decimate Europe?"

"No! That's not what I'm saying! But why would any of us—" She waved her hand to include both of them. "—get involved with someone like Hitler?"

He shook his head sadly. "I honestly don't know. And it wasn't just Hitler. There were pockets associated with the Japanese and Italian military as well. A small team of us, including your grandmother and I, tracked down the known collaborators, but we never discovered their ringleader."

She watched him carefully while he related his story. His aura remained a clear, steady scarlet. She shook her head in disbelief. "And President Roosevelt and General Eisenhower, not to mention the International Council, let you waltz in and play Mossad?"

He chuckled. "Not exactly. Ike is, was, Family. Anyone else within the Allied countries was on a need-to-know unless they were also Family."

She understood his slight emphasis. Family with a capital "F" meant General Dwight D. "Ike" Eisenhower was related to a supernatural by marriage or blood and could be trusted with the secret of their existence. It also meant he was smart enough to leave such matters to the International Council, the supernatural equivalent to the Normals' United Nations.

Except the I.C. had a lot more bite, literally and figuratively.

Her eyes widened as a terrible thought struck her. "Why would the Council sanction hunting down and killing supernaturals without a trial?"

A grim look crossed his face. "All we had to do was read the survivors' minds for sufficient cause."

She had so many questions, but Caesar wiped a hand over his drawn face. The action hit the physician part of her in the gut. How could she forget the doctored bullets ripping into his body last night?

"Damn it, Caesar! When was the last time you drank?"

A wry smile appeared on his face. "You're changing the subject."

She shook her head and climbed to her feet. "I'll let you finish your story after we get some nourishment in you." She didn't miss his wince as he rose from the floor but was smart enough not to mention it. For vampires, strength or the perception of such was paramount in their society.

Nice to know she remembered something from her coven cultures class.

Caesar stopped so abruptly she smacked her nose into his back. He whirled around and caught her as she stumbled, his touch sending warm fuzzy thoughts to places in her body that should know better.

"I'm sorry. I nearly forgot to give you something." He strode over to his desk and picked up a plain, white envelope. Smiling, he returned and handed it to her. "I think this was what you were looking for in the wardrobe's secret compartment."

It wasn't, but she didn't know how much she could trust him yet. She glanced down at the front of the envelope. In Grandma Petrov's neat, tiny handwriting were the words, "For Bebe, in the event of my death."

Chapter 9

Caesar expected Bebe's anger, but from the way her right hand glowed and ozone filled the air, he'd be lucky not to be charbroiled in the next five minutes.

She glared up at him, shook the envelope under his nose and bellowed, "How the hell did you get this?"

Her eyes flashed, red suffused her skin and the ripe peach and ginger smell of her was almost more than his depleted body could handle. Blood rapidly left his brain and departed for parts south. Parts he didn't need to be thinking with when it came to Bebe Zachary. He inhaled in an attempt to clear his head, but the effort only drove the rich scent of ginger, peaches and something that was indefinably Bebe deeper.

"One of my people, Stan Gryffudd, was part of our tracking team. He and your grandmother often left messages for each other in nymph holes during our hunts. When I told him about you searching inside the wardrobe at the auction, he surmised that Natasha may have hidden something in the wardrobe's nymph hole." He glanced at the envelope, which happened to be poking his left nostril. "That's what he found."

She drew back, taking the sharp paper with her. The red glow faded from her right hand as she turned the envelope over and over, examining it from every angle. Ozone sharpened the air again, but so faint that it would not be distinguishable by a Normal nose. He waited for her to finish examining the paper magickally. Patience was the key to winning her trust.

Staring at the envelope, she tapped it against her left palm. With her brows drawn together in concentration, he felt certain the tapping was unconscious on her part.

"It doesn't make sense. Why leave this in the wardrobe and not—" Her mouth closed in an abrupt motion, and her eyes widened.

So, she *was* looking for Natasha's Book of Shadows, but she did not want him to know. It took all of his remaining strength not to laugh outright as her reason for the plans to his estate came into focus. Fine, if she were preoccupied with the Book, she'd have less time to plot an escape from him.

He didn't have to fake the wave of dizziness that rammed his brain with blackness. He grabbed the edge of the desk to stay upright. From the corner of his eye, he watched Bebe's expression shifted from suspicion to concern.

"We were headed for the kitchen, weren't we?" Despite the seven-inch difference in their heights, the petite woman slung his arm over her shoulder and wrapped her own arm around his waist.

Unbidden, images rose of her wrapping other parts around his waist. Her body heat penetrated his robe, despite the thick velvet, to coil in his middle as they shuffled to the kitchen. Despite the pain, her heat and scent wrapped a sensuous cocoon around his brain cells. Thank Horus, the trip to the kitchen was mercifully short.

Once Bebe settled him in a chair, she bustled about the kitchen at his directions, pulling out mugs and warming blood for him and water for her tea. He noticed she didn't show the usual Normal squeamishness at preparing his cup. Nor did she flinch when he sipped.

Instead, she propped her fists on her ample hips, a gesture that nearly had him on the floor, whimpering, and gave him a stern, measured look that contradicted her obsequious tone when she spoke. "I'm not trying to offend you, Caesar, but can vampires take painkillers?"

Her sensitivity, for someone who claimed she hated his kind, startled him. He nodded but didn't say anything. Her exasperated expression was worth the effort of teasing her.

"What can you take and where is it?"

"We can take ibuprofen and aspirin." Barely paying attention to what he was saying, he gripped his mug and tried not to stare at her full breasts jutting against her t-shirt.

"And?" She spoke slowly as if to a child. "Where do you keep it?" Her head tilted and her eyes narrowed. "Again, no offense, but you look like death warmed over."

Humor tugged the corners of his mouth. "To some, we are already dead."

She rolled her eyes and her words come out in a huff. "Oh, please! It's a chronic disease, not a curse. You manage your condition just like a diabetic."

His gaze swept over her, and he inhaled her ginger and peach scent. Her cheeks flushed at his obvious perusal. Regret tinged his purely male interest in her. "Diabetes isn't sexually transmitted, Doctor."

Her face went from pink to bright red in an instant but not from her usual anger. "Why do you have to do that?" she asked, her voice softer than usual.

"Do what?"

"Turn every conversation we have into some sort of sexual innuendo."

He gave a slight shake of his head. "I'm truly sorry if I offended you."

She shrugged. "It's okay."

Relieved that another argument had been avoided, he took a long drink.

She tapped an index finger thoughtfully against her cheek. "But you know there are other methods of satisfaction other than penetration. It involves a lot of latex, but I think we can manage—"

Suddenly, blood was going down the wrong pipe and he couldn't breathe. The image of Bebe on the kitchen table, legs spread like a banquet, beckoning him, didn't help one little bit.

Neither did Bebe banging on the partially healed flesh on his back as he hacked and coughed.

Dragging in a pain-filled lungful of air, he shouted, "Enough!" He reached behind and snagged her waist, pulling her into his lap for a second time. His groin throbbed in response to her well-rounded ass grinding against him.

She stuck her tongue out at him before adding, "Serves you right, jerk-off."

All pain in his muscles and joints faded at the thought of her delicate but strong hands gripping him, sliding up and down his shaft. He grinned at her, the tips of his fangs pricking his bottom lip. "Well, jerking off would satisfy your non-penetration criteria. Were you offering?"

Her eyes widened, but instead of her usual tongue-lashing, her mouth parted in an "O" of surprise. The pink tip of her tongue poked out and slid along her bottom lip, leaving a trail of wetness that he wanted to taste. Her breath quickened, but she made no move to struggle. Like she hoped he would do something. Anything.

Her breath whispered against his skin. He knew he shouldn't be letting the temptation she represented get to him. She may be a witch, but she was mortal. She had a life to live, one that could never include him, not in the way he wanted. She was absolutely, positively, without a doubt, off limits.

And he wanted her like he'd never wanted anyone in his long, misbegotten life.

You can't have her.

But he ignored that silent admonishment by his conscience as he dipped his mouth to meet hers. He explored tentatively at first. With a soft sigh, her lips parted, returning his kiss with a passion that surprised him. Not that he was about to argue when her tongue swirled around his.

He couldn't stop the groan that rumbled through his throat when she shifted against his erection, the sensation sending his system into overload.

This is not a good move.

He had to disagree with his all-too-vocal conscience as he cupped her full breast through the thin t-shirt, his thumb brushing back and forth across her nipple until it tightened. Bebe moaned against his mouth, the sound almost as stimulating as the vibration of her lips. She arched her back, thrusting her breast against his palm, the move totally at odds with his first sight of her in her prim, proper suit. He obliged by dipping his head and tongued her rigid nipple through the fabric.

"Ahem."

He and Bebe jerked apart to find Anne standing in the entrance to the garage, arms crossed and a bemused expression on her face.

"Thank you for waiting until Ptolemy and I were out of the house before you two decided to make out."

Chapter 10

Bebe leapt to her bare feet, a different kind of heat flooding her skin. Except for the coolness of the damp spot on her t-shirt. Sweet Goddess, could she and Caesar be any more obvious? Any more ridiculous? Any more embarrassed?

She glanced down at Caesar. Nope, not one iota of embarrassment on his face. A little irritation in his glowing yellow eyes at Anne's interruption maybe, but definitely not any embarrassment.

Damn vampire.

"I'll go get that ibuprofen," she muttered and walked out of the kitchen with the little dignity she had left. Once in the hallway, she realized she had no clue where it was kept. And she wasn't about to go back in the kitchen to ask.

Alex had said few drugs affected vampires. Therefore, her best choice would be their mini-clinic. She trudged down the hallway and flipped on the lights. She blinked in shock. Her reflection in the mirror over the sink left nothing to the imagination. She watched as her hand lifted of its own accord to touch her kiss-swollen lips. Pink flushed her cheeks, and her wild curls were even more wayward than usual. And taunt nipples poked their own accusation through the borrowed t-shirt.

Goddess! What the hell was I thinking?

She had been so close to doing something so idiotic, so stupid, so—

Forbidden.

Was that why she was so attracted to Caesar Augustine? Because he was taboo? Or because he was the sexiest man she'd ever met?

Bebe was the first to admit that her hourglass figure wasn't the modern standard of female perfection. So what the hell did he intend? To follow through to their lusts' natural conclusion? Recrimination flared in the eyes of her reflection. *That's exactly what you intended,* her image seemed to say.

Just one problem.

Unprotected sex meant infection. She'd been damn lucky not to contract the V-virus last night when she'd touched the blood on his turtleneck with open cuts on her hands. To have sex with Caesar would be asking for disaster.

No matter how wonderful, sensual, exquisite that sex would be.

Her reflection's eyes glittered at the erotic thoughts that rushed through her.

She shook her head sadly at the aroused woman in the mirror.

No sex. No sex for you. Especially not with the hunky vampire in the kitchen. Not unless you want to join him permanently.

Her reflection winced at the mental finger wagging and gave a disappointed shrug of her shoulders. No, vampirism was the best-case scenario. In most cases if a witch survived a Turn, she'd end up nuttier than Grandpa Ben's almond fudge cookies.

Before someone put her down like a rabid dog.

Bebe walked over to the mirror and opened the cabinet behind the silvered glass. Next to the Midol sat a bottle of prescription strength liquid ibuprofen. She grabbed the plastic bottle and closed the cabinet.

Ignoring the pleading look on her reflection's face, she turned for the door, flipping off the lights on her way out.

As soon as she popped through the swinging kitchen door, Caesar and Anne halted their whispered and, from appearances, heated discussion. From the pointed stare Anne shot Caesar, Bebe had no doubt exactly what the discussion entailed. What she didn't understand was why Anne, who'd been overly deferential to the Augustine brothers compared to Alex, would dare give her coven master a tongue-lashing over a witch.

Bebe set the ibuprofen on the table, shoving it over to Caesar with a fingertip. She couldn't meet his eyes.

The tiny female vampire rose from her chair, took Caesar's cup to the counter and retrieved a bottle of blood marked Angus from the refrigerator. Bebe eyed the glassware. Was the marking for her benefit, so she wouldn't think they were drinking human blood?

After pouring the contents into the cup and setting it in the microwave, Anne punched the buttons with a little more force than necessary. The electric hum filled the kitchen, drowning the silence. Then she turned to Bebe, a polite smile on her lips. "Would you like some fresh tea, Doctor?"

Bebe resisted the urge to cringe and nodded instead. Her cup had cooled during the make-out session with Caesar. What seemed like seconds had obviously been long enough for the hot liquid to hit room temperature. And given how warm the vamps liked to keep their mansion . . .

So much for worrying about Caesar penetrating her shields and seducing her. She'd practically thrown herself at him the first chance she had.

Instead of nuking a mug of water, Anne pulled out a teakettle from a bottom cupboard. She filled it from a jug of distilled water from the refrigerator before setting the kettle on the stove.

"You don't have to go to all that trouble," Bebe protested.

Anne flashed Bebe another smile before continuing to spoon tea leaves into one-half of an egg-shaped strainer that screwed together. "No sense wasting the good stuff if Duncan's not here to drink it."

Second time this mysterious Duncan had been mentioned. Like she needed another vampire to worry about. "Who's Duncan? I'd hate to piss off someone by stealing his tea."

"Duncan St. James is my chief enforcer," Caesar said.

Wonderful. The vamp equivalent of a police commissioner.

"You'll meet him when we arrive in Los Angeles." Again, an amused smile spread across Caesar's face.

Bebe resisted the urge to smack him. She was becoming far more acquainted with Caesar's security personnel than she cared. Caesar's humor over her transparent interrogation irritated her, but Anne fiddling with spoons, cream and sugar drove Bebe over the edge.

She had a sneaking suspicion that Anne's fidgeting next to the stove was a stall tactic to keep an eye on them. Like she would let herself lose control again. Her suspicion was confirmed by Anne's next question.

"Are you hungry, Doctor?" Instead of waiting for an answer, the vampire turned to another cupboard and pulled out a bag of English muffins and a toaster.

"You can sit down, Bebe. I won't bite." Caesar's grin was heart-stopping. "Unless you want me to." He waggled his eyebrows.

She didn't know what was worse—Caesar's suggestive look or Anne's reproving glare. Taking the high road, she ignored both and marched to the opposite, and safer, side of the table. Pulling out a chair, she plunked down and crossed her arms. Caesar pointedly stared at the swell of her breasts. His grin widened.

She huffed and dropped her hands to her lap. She sure as hell wasn't going to give him any additional pleasure at her expense. From the sly look he shot Anne,

Bebe was sure the female vampire hadn't missed one little bit of their silent exchange.

Anne set the mug of fresh tea in front of Bebe. The aroma alone indicated this brew was far and above the generic tea bags Bebe had found earlier. She took a sip and nodded her appreciation to the vampire. "This is wonderful."

She nearly choked on her second sip when Anne picked up the envelope from Grandma Petrov off the tabletop and asked, "What's this?"

She reached to snatch the envelope out of Anne's hand, but at the last second, she remembered her manners. "It's mine. May I have it back, please?"

Anne shrugged and handed it to her before returning to the toaster, which had disgorged the browned halves of English muffin. Bebe turned it over in her hands again. Still no sense of a witch spell or any other type of magick.

"You could just open it, Bebe."

Her head jerked up and her eyes locked with Caesar's. They no longer held any hint of amusement. Just concern and something else. Worry?

She sighed and looked back down at the envelope rotating between her fingers. He knew her grandmother far better than she ever had, right down to the secret compartment in the wardrobe. What was the sense of hiding the contents of the letter? For all she knew, he'd already steamed open the envelope and read it. "I suppose you're right." Sliding a nail in the corner, she ripped open the top. The envelope contained a single piece of paper. Sucking in her breath, she opened the folds.

> *Dear Bebe,*
> *Sometimes the best magic is old magic. I trust you to find your way.*
> *Love,*
> *Grandma P.*

What in the Thousand Names of the Goddess was Grandma blathering about? Other than the short, cryptic note in plain old ballpoint pen, the white sheet of average twenty-weight paper was completely blank. There was absolutely nothing special about the note. No, she was missing something. Grandma would have left some kind of clue.

She held it up so the light from the Tiffany lamp suspended over the table could shine through it. Still nothing.

Puzzled, she looked at Caesar. A frown creased his face as he leaned closer to examine the sheet. "What the hell was Grandma thinking?"

He looked at her with a puzzled expression. "I have no idea."

"Well, dammit, you sure seem to know her better than me. Don't you have any idea?"

He shook his head. "I'm sorry. This is strange even for Natasha."

Anne sat the plate of English muffins slathered with butter and honey in front of Bebe. She started to step back but edged closer. "Do you smell something odd?"

"Like lemons?" Caesar said.

Anne nodded, and Bebe drew the paper closer to her nose. Sure enough, the citrusy scent of lemon juice permeated the sheet.

A grin split Bebe's face. Maybe Grandma had made this easy for her after all. Turning the search for the family's Book of Shadows into a treasure hunt would have appealed to the old lady's warped sense of humor.

Or at least the sense of humor Grandma possessed before Bebe's parents were murdered.

She didn't dare use a fireball. It would be too easy to ignite the sheet. Jumping up, she edged Anne aside, stalked over to the stove and flipped the electric burner Anne had used to heat the water back to "On." Carefully holding the paper above the heat, she held her breath. Within a couple of minutes, brown, looping letters appeared on the surface.

Caesar and Anne joined her, each peering over one of her shoulders at the sharp, neat handwriting that continued to develop over the heat of the burner. "I rather had the impression you didn't sense any magick on the paper," he said.

Bebe turned to meet his warm, golden eyes and smiled. "You're right. It's not 'magick' with a 'k', but 'magic' with just a 'c' as in a Normal illusionist trick. The spelling was Grandma's hint." She couldn't resist adding a jibe. "And really, Caesar, I'm shocked that you didn't suspect this old military trick of using lemon juice as invisible ink."

He snorted. "I'd put my faith in a sword over a box of citrus any day."

"I'll remember that the next time I'm digging bullets out of your hide." She really shouldn't have heated the letter in front of the vampires. What she should have done was play stupid until she had some time alone. She suppressed the sigh of disappointment welling in her chest. What was done was done. And if Caesar knew Grandma well enough to guess her hiding spot in the wardrobe, then maybe he was someone Bebe could trust to help her find the Book.

Even if he was a vampire.

Pulling the paper away from the burner before the page scorched, she shuffled back to the table and read the text that circled the edges of the page.

I'm sorry to do this to you, Bebe, darling, since you've made your feelings clear, but you must contact Caesar Augustine at (213) 555-8293. Your life is in danger. Trust no one but Caesar. He can protect you. Take him with you and go to Seven Wonders Antiques in L.A. Ask for the owner. She has something for you. I love you. Blessed Be.

Bebe raised her head to stare at Caesar. That annoying smirk of his twisted his full lips.

"I'm not going to say I told you so," he said.

"Thank you for not saying it," she replied. She normally didn't resort to sarcasm, but he seemed to bring it out of her.

Anne raised her cup in a shaky salute. "Home it is." She finished her blood in two gulps. "I'll get us packed."

Shortly after sunset the following night, Bebe sank into the plush seat next to Caesar's on his private jet. The gracious host when not making suggestive comments, he insisted that she take the window seat before heading up to the cockpit to speak with the pilots. Alex took the seat behind her while Anne sat across from Bebe, the tiny vamp's hands twisting in her lap, her face even paler than normal. Ptolemy had flopped in the chair next to Anne, totally oblivious to his seat companion's obvious fear of flying.

Bebe took the prudent course of also ignoring Anne's nervous fidgeting and surveyed the interior of the plane. While her family had hardly been poor, the luxury of the Lear met a whole different standard than what she had been accustomed to on Grandma's estate. The accents consisted of real wood, not fake plastic veneer. The leather seats gave a new meaning to the term "butter soft." The whole plane simply smelled of money.

She'd insisted on Caesar waiting the extra day out of concern for her patient, but ten solid hours of sleep had done wonders for her disposition as well. And unpacking the shopping bags Anne had brought home the night before had sent her into ecstasy. She could swallow her pride in order not to wear the men's extra clothes. What had amazed Bebe was the fashionable taste that the little vampire showed in her purchases compared the drab clothing Anne constantly wore.

The rest of Caesar's "gifts" weren't as easy to stomach. Opening the Prada handbag, Bebe found a wad of cash, a bank debit card, a black American Express card and a California driver's license with her picture and the name 'Elizabeth Levi.'

In the picture, she wore her white blouse and navy jacket, her lips pursed in an irritated grimace.

She had waved the purse in his face, protesting that she couldn't accept his money and she sure as hell didn't appreciate her picture taken by a cell camera at the estate auction. He took her tirade in his usual maddeningly calm fashion before pointing out that she'd left her purse at the hotel room and that should they become separated then she'd need money and identification.

She had been willing to accede on the money and ID issues, but his last suggestion seared to the core. He opened a Tiffany's jewelry box with a pair of silver ball studs and a pair of large delicate silver hoops.

"You can't wear your White Rose insignia in public, Bebe," he murmured. "No one will question an eclectic in the company of vampires."

She hated to admit he was right. She might as well hang a neon sign around her neck for the assassins that said, "Please kill me." Tears stung her eyes as she removed her rose-shaped studs and the tiny Fabergé-style filigree hoops of her coven. Common sense did nothing to stop the sense of betrayal that washed over her. Differences in opinion within the coven were one thing. Total denial of her heritage was another.

When she had said as much to Caesar, he gave her a sympathetic shake of his head and replied, "Your safety is my sole concern. Someone at the estate auction must have identified you the same way I did, by your coven jewelry." He laid his hands on her shoulders, his touch sending a tremor of excitement through her. "I do understand your need to proclaim your allegiance, but I learned from bitter experience the cost of no prudence in such matters. No one questions my sister's hired witch. No one will look twice when you accompany me, provided you dress the part." She had wanted to argue, but he turned his back and left her bedroom.

In retrospect, he had been right. The vampire pilots had given her no more than a cursory glance when she had boarded the plane with Caesar and his party.

Sighing, she fingered the alien earrings as she watched the last light fade from the San Francisco sky. Forty-eight hours was an awfully short time to have a girl's life turned upside down.

The welcome sense of Caesar's electric aura preceded him moments before he sat next to her and buckled himself in his seat. She gripped the armrest, digging nails into the leather, while the jet taxied toward the runway. The fact that she found his presence desirable was not a good sign. Granted, Grandma trusted him, but that did not mean she had to trust him totally. A nagging sense that he was hiding something continued to plague her.

"We should be at LAX in forty-five minutes." He smiled at her. Not the sad, pitying one or the suggestive leer he deliberately used to annoy her, but a genuine smile. "How about that dinner I promised you?"

In her peripheral vision, she noticed Ptolemy roll his eyes before shoving the earbuds of his iPod into place. His lids closed, and he slouched in his seat, looking for all the world like any other rich, bratty twenty-something.

Anne, on the other hand, frowned but said nothing. At least Caesar's flirtation with Bebe seemed to take the female vampire's mind off her own phobia, but Anne's laser-like attention was unnerving.

"Thank you, but that's not necessary," Bebe murmured.

"Your Grandmother Epstein won't be back in Los Angeles until tomorrow—"

"And if you'd let me talk to her housekeeper, I might have gotten a number where I could reach her," she snapped.

"Do you really want to take the chance of letting the wrong person know where you are?" he fired back.

She crossed her arms and said nothing. Why did this self-conceited jerk always have to be right?

"Since Seven Wonders will be closed when we land, you can call the store when it opens in the morning," he continued in a calmer tone.

"Gee, thanks, Mr. Augustine, for letting me act like a grown-up."

A wicked light gleamed in his golden eyes. "If you don't stop acting like a child, I am going to bend you over my knee."

Retching sounds came from Ptolemy's seat, but the obvious younger sibling act took a second seat to Bebe's shock. Her eyes locked with Caesar's. Heat pooled in her middle at the image of her buttocks bared before this man. Wetness seeped between her legs, and she crossed them in an effort to reign in her reaction. Instead, the pressure added to her agony.

Desperate, she ripped her gaze from his, but not before she recognized the raw need in his eyes. Mercifully, no one said anything else on the short flight.

Chapter 11

The interminably long flight home with Bebe tested Caesar's will in ways that other women never had. The desire in her face when he made the spanking joke had been too much to bear. If not for the three other vampires' presence, he would have lost control and ripped Bebe's clothes from her lush body. The way she kept crossing and uncrossing her legs added to his agony.

Only when his pilot, Kensai Osaka, announced their final approach into LAX did Caesar realize he'd left dents in the steel frame of the armrests despite the thick leather upholstery.

Caesar hung back as the other three vampires and Bebe exited the cabin, each of them shooting a suspicious look at him. None of which stopped him from admiring the good doctor's curves as she climbed down the short stairs of the jet.

"Somehow I doubt you're waiting here just to watch your guest."

Caesar turned to find Kensai with a wry grin on his face. "You'd be right."

Kensai shrugged. "She's not my taste, but I concede where you would find her attractive."

Hades. If his pilot had noticed his interest in Bebe, then he really did have a serious problem. His attention shifted back to Bebe striding across the tarmac to where Duncan waited by an armored SUV, even though his words were addressed to Kensai. "Have Miko and Mai on stand-by." The sisters were Family, Kensai's descendants though Caesar couldn't recall how many generations removed from the ronin.

Jamal, Kensai's life and flying partner, joined them. "You're planning a daytime run back to San Francisco?" The Moor's bared fangs gleamed against his dark skin. "Just what kind of trouble are we in?"

The flashbulb pop behind Caesar's left eye signaled the beginnings of another stress migraine. He rubbed his temple in an attempt to alleviate the pain. Despite some sleep, he still wasn't at one hundred percent. "Ptolemy couldn't keep his mouth shut, could he?"

"He only said that someone took potshots at you, something to do with your solitaire witch." Kensai fixed him with a pointed stare. "He did his job as one of your Enforcers by informing us of potential trouble."

"I know, but sometimes the boy doesn't understand the difference between necessary knowledge and gossip." And Caesar needed to have a long overdue talk with his baby brother concerning that difference. Even after two thousand years, some people refused to grow up.

His irritation must have shown. Kensai shot him a reassuring smile. "The subject will go no further, Master. But I want the girls to wear bulletproof vests for the time-being."

Caesar nodded. "You both should as well. Whoever took shots at us knew I was a vampire. They had explosive rounds and bullets laced with a garlic compound."

Jamal whistled through his front teeth, but Kensai merely nodded and said, "We will take the appropriate precautions."

Reassured, Caesar jogged down the steps and stalked toward the SUV. He couldn't shake the feeling of wrongness about this whole situation. Natasha's extreme measures in protecting her Book and her granddaughter were obviously warranted. But the preparedness of the gunmen bothered him. Did Bebe's assailants know that Natasha Petrov and Ziva Epstein had approached him concerning their granddaughter's protection, or were the assassins merely covering their bases when they tried to kill her? And why murder Bebe when she had no interest in taking over the coven?

Too many questions flew through his aching head with no real answers. If he could figure out the why, then he could discover the who behind this insane scenario. And what the Hades was in that gods-cursed book that Bebe was willing to risk life and limb to get it?

A chill having nothing to do with either his current weakness or the balmy Los Angeles night ran through him. Natasha had been researching the similarities of the V-virus to both AIDS and Ebola. She had truly believed that a cure for him, for all vampires, was possible and had joked that one day she'd take him on noon picnic in Golden Gate Park. Had Natasha found the answer before she died and placed the information in her Book of Shadows?

But that begged the question of who knew about her research besides him. Was Bebe playing him to get her hands on the Book and hold the cure over his head?

He didn't like the ugly suspicion. He wanted to trust Bebe, but it would be unwise to base his trust on a woman he barely knew. She wasn't Natasha, no matter how alike grandmother and granddaughter were. Too many people depended on him to let his guard totally down.

All theories concerning the problems represented by the intriguing Dr. Zachary flew out of his head at the intense argument taking place by the SUV. And for once the good doctor wasn't the one shouting. Instead, she stood to the side, observing his brother's temper tantrum with a bemused smile that exhibited her dimples.

"You are not driving this vehicle! You just got your license!"

The petite Normal teenager Ptolemy shouted at didn't back down one iota. Caesar wasn't surprised. Between her guardians' respective training regimens, Tiffany Stephens could and had killed rogue vampires. She pulled a yellow No. 2 pencil, her weapon of choice, from the pocket of her jean jacket and waved it in Ptolemy's face.

"Back off, Prince of Darkness. I've had my license for a year, and I still drive better than you."

"Tiffany, put the pencil down before someone gets hurt," Duncan ordered his niece.

Ptolemy sniffed in disgust. "She'd barely qualify as a snack."

"He was referring to you getting hurt, Prince Asshole," Tiffany shot back.

The idea of setting Ptolemy and Tiffany on each other tempted Caesar. Such a battle would put the old gladiatorial games to shame. Not to mention he'd reap a fortune on the wagers if he publicized the bout. The two had each done their share of annoying the supernatural community so a profit would be a foregone conclusion.

And maybe it would burn off the mutual attraction Ptolemy and Tiffany felt for each other. Not that his brother would ever touch the girl, much less admit his feelings, but Ptolemy's method of needling Tiffany to circumvent her crush on him drove the rest of the household insane.

Unfortunately, such a plan, no matter how enticing, would add one more straw to the camel-load of issues between Duncan and Selene. Bebe caught his eye. Her smirk indicated she had an inkling of his thoughts without any telepathy between them. He rolled his eyes, and she covered her mouth to smother her giggle.

The simple byplay left him with a warmth that had nothing to do with his cock for once. It had been too long since he'd exchanged such an intimate pleasantry with a woman through a look. But a romantic relationship with a non-vampire was out of the question, and most female vampires looked at him as a means to power.

First things first though. He gathered his mental energy.

Enough!

Everyone except Bebe jumped and whirled to stare at him. Bebe, on the other hand, winced as if in pain. His telepathic shout had probably slammed into her shields like a truck. He'd make it up to her later. First, he needed to play daddy, the part of his position as coven master that grew tiresome.

"If you two are finished, I'd like to leave now." He gave Ptolemy and Tiffany a measured glare. Neither cowered but each had the common sense to lower their eyes and mutter half-hearted apologies.

One of Bebe's eyebrows rose when Ptolemy climbed into the rear seat next to Anne. She gave Caesar a curious look but wisely said nothing. Given the daggers shooting out of little Tiffany's eyes, Caesar did not fault his brother for taking the safer choice. If he rode shotgun, Ptolemy wouldn't resist the urge to comment on Tiffany's driving skills. And Tiffany wouldn't resist the urge to stake him with a pencil in response.

From the dirty look Bebe shot Caesar, she must have noticed his pleased smile when he settled next to her in the middle bench seat. She said nothing and looked out the window next to her. For the first time, he understood Ptolemy's dilemma. It was a bitch to be attracted to someone who was off-limits. Following Bebe's lead, he kept his mouth shut as Tiffany peeled rubber across the tarmac.

Two hours later, Bebe smoothed the skirt of the black dress she wore while Caesar guided his Jaguar through Los Angeles traffic. Once again, she couldn't believe the superb job Anne had done in choosing a wardrobe. The dress hugged her curves in a positive way, and it actually made her short, stumpy legs look long.

She leaned back against the headrest. Everything the vampires had done the last couple of days had destroyed all her preconceived notions. Heck, even Caesar's Brentwood mansion had a modern Mediterranean flair with an incomprehensible number of windows, instead of some dark, gloomy Dracula-like castle.

Despite the chaos of her life had become, she looked forward to some time alone with the enigmatic vampire master. He intrigued her in a way no other man ever had. And it wasn't just because he looked delicious in a suit. If it wasn't for the fact that he was a vampire, she could have enjoyed a date or two with him. Too bad such a relationship would never work out.

Caesar brought his Jag to a smooth stop in front of the famed Anthony's and opened her door before the valet had taken two steps. She complimented his driving when he proffered his arm to escort her into the ritzy restaurant.

He chuckled and said, "Then it doesn't take much to impress you, does it?"

She shuddered. "I was just happy to make it to Brentwood in one piece. Escaping from guerillas in Chad wasn't as hair-raising as Tiffany driving through the remains of L.A. rush hour."

He laughed outright as they followed the maitre d'. Instead of seating them in the main dining room, the prim host led them back to a private room. A cozy, intimate room. One with its own fireplace and a multitude of candles in brass sconces on the walls and in matching tabletop holders. Dark wood paneling and burgundy carpet gave the room a sophisticated and sensual air.

Her first impulse was to protest, but the maitre d' had already whisked out of the room after seating them with a few words in French to Caesar. She settled for giving the vampire the evil eye.

One dark eyebrow raised in a questioning look. "Have I done something to offend you?" he asked.

"Don't you think this—" She waved a hand around the room. "—is just a little too much? Who are you trying to impress here?"

A wry smile filled his features. "Obviously not you." He leaned back in his chair, his fingers steepled as he regarded her. "I thought after the activity of the last couple of days you would appreciate a quieter venue. I, on the other hand, appreciate the solitude with a charming dinner companion."

She grinned back at him. "As opposed to the teen terror?"

His irritated expression left no doubt that he had wanted to ditch his entourage for the peace alone. The vampires had protested, rather loudly, about the lack of security. Tiffany had simply pouted at her lack of inclusion in the dinner plans.

When he didn't appear to want to elucidate, she swallowed hard and gathered what little courage she had left. "Why do you let a Normal girl hang out with your coven?" At his dark look, she reached for her glass and sipped water to soothe her suddenly dry throat.

"Why do you persist in assuming Tiffany is in any danger from us?"

She shrugged and set her glass down. "I'm not. I just can't see any parent, even Family, allowing an underage child to be subjected to a potentially hazardous environment."

He folded his hands and leaned forward until his elbows rested on the table. The similarity to his actions and a lion preparing to pounce unnerved her. Her breath caught, waiting for him to spring.

"I'll have you know, Dr. Zachary, that I haven't been shot at in the last sixty years. At least not until I met you." The glint of humor in his golden eyes belied the dry, clipped tone of his voice. "As for Tiffany's safety, she's fully capable of taking care of herself."

Playing with fire had gotten Bebe into trouble on more than one occasion over the years, but her protective instincts reared up. She waved her hand. "And her parents are okay with their little girl trained to play war?"

Caesar's eyes shuttered and became cold, almost pragmatic. She suppressed a shudder. His look reminded her too much of the rebels who dragged the village children off into the night and turned them into soldiers.

"Not that it's any of your business, Doctor, but Tiffany's parents are dead. They were murdered the same night your parents were. So you see, Doctor, you and Tiffany Stephens have something in common."

Bebe's hand flew to her mouth and gorge rose in her throat. "Oh my Goddess." She'd witnessed the horror the rogues had inflicted on her parents, made worse by her inability to do anything to help them. Had the rogues done the same thing to the Stephens in front of their baby? She struggled to get her memories and emotions under control. She had her grandparents, aunts, uncles, cousins, no matter what pains in the ass they were. For Tiffany to have no one . . .

She dropped her hand and whispered, "Didn't she have anywhere else to go?"

"You mean any Normal family?" He could have sneered, but somehow he understood her manner wasn't condescending. He shook his head. "No. Her only relatives left were vampires or Family not old enough themselves to care for her. As one of her great-uncles, Duncan took her in and raised her as his own."

"How? That had to have been nearly impossible with him, being, you know . . ." For the first time, embarrassment at the way she'd acted toward the vampires consumed her. Heat flooded her cheeks, and she reached for her glass to cover her discomfort.

"You mean, how could a cold, nasty blood-sucker possibly care for a three-month-old infant?" Amusement returned to his voice, and he leaned back once again. "Vampires sharing the night bottles made the job a little easier. It was a joint effort, I assure you. Plus Duncan had help from someone who could bear to go out in sunlight."

Bebe shook her head. "Servants and nannies aren't the same as family." She knew since Grandma often left her in others' care. Goddess, she'd forgotten how much she resented the lack of real attention from her grandmother after her parents' deaths. And poor Tiffany didn't even get the small gift of knowing her parents for the handful of years Bebe had known hers.

Caesar grinned. "Once again, you make assumptions." He reached for her hand, his thumb sliding across her palm in sensual circles. "Duncan had a friend, Phillippa Mann, named as Tiffany's co-guardian. Phillippa took the child to the park, made sure she arrived at school safely—"

"And handled those pesky daytime parent-teacher conferences?" Bebe added.

Caesar laughed, a warm sound from the belly. She had a suspicion it wasn't something he did often.

"That is one assumption that is safe for you to make. There were many. We are all praying that Tiffany manages to graduate from high school this May," he admitted. "Phillippa has a patience with Tiffany that the rest of us often lack."

"This Phillippa must be something special," Bebe muttered under her breath. The wave of jealousy at Caesar's tone socked her in the gut. What claim did she have on him?

None whatsoever, her silent nag chided.

From the glimmer in his eyes, he'd caught her barely disguised cattiness. Instead of his teasing smirk, a wistful expression crossed his features. "Tiffany's the closest any of my household came to having a child we could call our own. Perhaps we all indulge her far too much."

His cool fingers turned her hand over and stroked the sensitive skin at her wrist. How could a touch so slight send a sensual tsunami through her nerves? She clenched her thighs in an effort to concentrate on their conversation.

"So whose smart idea was it to give her an SUV for her sixteenth birthday?"

He laughed again, the sound a viable force that curled through her body. She checked her shields. Nope, still solid. If he couldn't violate her mental barriers, how the hell did he make her react this way?

"The vehicle is Duncan's. Tiffany drives for him when she's not in class. Duncan concluded it was the best solution to keep an eye on the child."

She fingered the crystal stem of her water goblet. "So this Phillippa is Family?"

That sly smile she found so damned irritating appeared on his face. "Why don't you ask her tomorrow morning?"

Figures he would try to distract her. She shook her head. "I can't meet her tomorrow. We're going over to Seven Wonders in the morning. Or are you reneging on your promise?"

"I wouldn't dream of doing so. But that doesn't mean you can't interrogate Phillippa about her relationship with me as well."

The inescapable sensation of being sucked under by quicksand enveloped her. "What are you talking about?"

Caesar took a sip of his own water before answering. "Phillippa Mann is the owner of Seven Wonders Antiques."

Chapter 12

Sweet Goddess, I am such a dumbass.

Bebe blinked, trying to wipe away the shock. He'd lied. Again. Maybe his lies were ones of omission, little facts he refused to reveal, but they were still lies. Her life was nothing more than a game to him. She wanted to fry his butt, teach him not to mess with her. Heat flooded her face, her body, her hands . . .

The wine steward entered, pushing the cart ahead of him with the ice bucket perched on top. She squelched the flames on the edge of her fingertips. Embarrassment at her slip replaced her anger at Caesar.

The steward displayed the bottle and then the cork for Caesar's approval. She settled for glaring at the vampire while the steward poured the white wine. Once Caesar sipped and nodded his acceptance of the vintage, the steward filled her glass, and deposited the bottle in the ice bucket before he scurried out the door. Bebe didn't blame him considering the thick tension in the room.

"I thought vampires only stuck with red liquids." The acid in her voice must have surprised him by the look on his face. Well, what the hell did he expect by not telling her of his connection with the owner of Seven Wonders yesterday? He'd had plenty of opportunities. She toyed with the stem of her glass, but she made no move to taste the wine that she was sure cost more than her plane ticket back from Africa. Instead, she continued to stare at him.

Without flinching, he said, "I like my wine like my women." He smiled before finishing his thought. "A little on the tart side."

Her mouth dropped open at the cheesy pick-up line. It was so incongruous with Mr. Sophisticated Controlling Vampire that she started laughing. Not a polite, social laugh, but a deep belly rumbler that left tears in her eyes.

"Oh, sweet Goddess, where'd you learn to seduce woman? James Bond movies?" She started laughing again, slapping the table until the cut glass goblets sang from the vibrations.

He chuckled as well. "I have to admit a particular fondness for Sean Connery, but nothing beats Ian Fleming's original prose."

Shaking her head between hiccupping gulps of laughter, she said, "No, I gotta disagree. Pierce Brosnan's still the best movie Bond." She swiped her tears away with her fingertips. "You're one sick vampire, you know that?"

Soberness replaced the laughter as she remembered why she was furious with him. And she was letting him distract her. But when was the last time she'd laughed at a man's joke?

No, she couldn't afford to let him off the hook. Too many lives depended on her getting to the Book first, not just hers. "I'm still pissed at you for not coming clean. Why not tell me right off this Phillippa is one of your people? Why all the games?"

He leaned back in his chair, his face still as he probably considered a new set of half-truths to tell her, but his aura remained a clear, brilliant red. "First of all, Phillippa is not one of *my* people as you put it."

"She's not Family?" Damn, what she wouldn't give to read his mind.

He shook his head. "No, Phillippa is not Family."

She leaned forward, elbows propped on the immaculate white tablecloth. "Then what is she? What's her relationship with your coven?"

"Her heritage is her business to share with you if she chooses, not mine." He smiled again, as if he enjoyed their verbal sparring. "As for our relationship, we have done favors for each other over the years. Nothing more."

More dissembling. What else had she expected? But dammit, she was not stooping to his level by asking what kind of favors this Phillippa had performed for him. She sat back with a huff. "In other words, you're not going to tell me a Goddess-damned thing, are you?"

He locked eyes with her, but no feathery touch of his shields against hers came. Instead, he said, "Are you going to tell me what you expected to find in the wardrobe?"

She toyed with the idea of coming clean. Just because he said Grandma trusted him didn't mean that was the truth. And if Grandma trusted him as she said in the letter, why hadn't Grandma ever mentioned that she was friends with Caesar? Maybe Grandma's letter had been a carefully-crafted forgery. There was only Caesar's word that the letter came from the nymph hole. Silence dragged on for a minute, then two, as she and Caesar stared at each other.

The waiter burst into the room, carrying a dish on the tips of his fingers. He ignored the sizzling electricity running rampant and placed the plate before her with a flourish.

She looked up at the waiter. "Wait a minute. I didn't order this."

From the corner of her eye, she caught Caesar's fingertips press his lips when the waiter gave her a haughty sniff.

"I am sorry if Monsieur Augustine did not inform the mademoiselle of the rules for the backroom." The waiter whipped around on his heels and marched for the door, leaving it open a crack as he left.

New horror replaced Bebe's confusion. "What have you gotten me into, Augustine?"

———•——

Caesar struggled not to laugh at Bebe's appalled expression. Bebe's leaps of emotion were entertaining, unlike most women he'd known over the centuries. "Unfortunately, the price for using the backroom is suffering through one of Anthony's experiments." He leaned forward and whispered, "Only Zeus knows what he'll do to *my* meal."

She winced before she looked back down at the brown mass surrounded by artfully arranged parsley and a green sauce. She picked up the first tiny fork and poked at the appetizer before she looked back up at him. "What is it?"

"Well, it's definitely not roasted sparrow in honey sauce," he offered.

"Eeewwww!"

He shrugged and leaned forward to inhale the contents of the plate. An all-too-familiar scent from Tiffany's infancy hit his nostrils, making his struggle to keep a straight face that much harder. In all the chaos surrounding Natasha's death, he'd totally forgotten about his bet with Anthony. Leave it to his nephew to pick the wrong damn time. He met Bebe's suspicious gaze. "I'm not sure, but I believe the green sauce is mint."

Eyes narrowed, Bebe laid down the fork. "I think I'll pass. I learned a long time ago, if you can't identify it, don't eat it."

"Bravo! Bravo!" Clapping, Anthony shoved the door open with a hip and strode in. Even though the restaurant owner was forty-five, his beaming, cherubic face and tight brunette curls made him look twenty years younger. He pointed a finger at Caesar. "You owe me a hundred bucks."

Bebe leaned forward. "You were betting on me?" The outraged look on Bebe's face would have been adorable if Caesar wasn't trying to win her trust.

Anthony winced. "Oooo, did I just blow your date, man?"

"We're not dating," Caesar and Bebe said at the same time.

Anthony raised his hands defensively. "Whoa, my mistake, folks."

Bebe's right eyebrow rose. "So what was this bet about?"

"Um." Anthony flicked his gaze to Caesar.

Caesar said nothing. Anthony should have warned him ahead of time. It would serve the child right to sink on his own. A quick glance at Bebe said the ride home would be very unpleasant.

Anthony ran a hand over his unruly curls. "Well, Caesar said I could serve dog food, and no one would know the difference because they assumed expensive meant good. And I bet him a hundred bucks that anyone with common sense could tell the difference between slop and fine cuisine."

The horrified look returned to Bebe's face. "You served me dog food!"

Anthony's expression matched hers, and he waved his hands frantically. "No, no, no!" He pointed at the brown lump. "That's Gerber's ground lamb."

Disbelief replaced horror. "You served me baby food?"

A sheepish grin covered Anthony's mug. "Well, our bet was on the next non-vampire he brought to my restaurant."

Caesar swallowed a groan. He wouldn't be in this predicament if he'd specified the next werewolf. Anthony would have thought twice before serving baby food to the Los Angeles Packmaster.

Anthony shrugged. "For all I knew, he could have brought a health and safety inspector with him tonight, so I played it safe." He removed the plate from the table. "What would you like tonight, Ms.—"

"Elizabeth Levi. She just joined my employ." Caesar ignored the dirty look Bebe shot him. Her safety was his responsibility. He couldn't take the chance that she would, in all innocence, destroy the identity he'd carefully constructed for her.

"So, Liz, what'll it be? I got some fresh scallops in this morning." Anthony winked at her. "Grilled and served with linguini and cream sauce? It's on the house. Come on, what d'ya say? It's the least I can do to make up for you getting caught in the middle of my bet with my uncle."

"Uncle?" She turned to Caesar, and for once, she looked at him with something other than mistrust and suspicion. Her mouth gaped open in confusion.

"Does that surprise you, Ms. Levi?" He couldn't resist baiting her. Again. Even though, he'd mentioned that he had Family, the knowledge apparently was only now registering in her mind.

"Oops, don't tell me I stuck my foot in my mouth?"

Wishing desperately for Anthony to shut up, Caesar dragged his attention away from Bebe's lovely eyes to glare at his nephew. "You do seem to be slipping in the discretion department. I hope you are quite done insulting my guest." He faced Bebe again, who still looked at him with a shocked expression. "Are the scallops and pasta acceptable? If not, Anthony will prepare whatever you desire."

Her mouth snapped shut, and she shook her head. "No the scallops and linguini will be fine."

His attention shifted to Anthony. "Ms. Levi has a fondness for chocolate. I trust you will serve her an adequate dessert." Bebe's mouth dropped open again.

The sheepish look returned to Anthony's face. "No problem. I know just the thing." With the plate of baby food in hand, he strode out of the room.

"How do you know chocolate's my favorite treat?" The suspicion was back in her eyes.

Caesar leaned back in his chair, despite the urge to brush the curl away from her face that had escaped her topknot. He enjoyed keeping the lovely doctor off balance far more than he should. "I sent Natasha a sample box of chocolates from an investment company I was considering. She called me a few days later, saying the company should be sound after she found you asleep on the floor of her wardrobe with the empty box."

Her face flushed a becoming pink, and she could no longer meet his eyes, choosing to stare at the fire. Was she embarrassed by the childhood incident, or like him, did she hate thinking about the innocence that was ripped away from her at such a young age? He wanted to ask but didn't dare, too much history that neither needed to deal with right now.

After a few seconds, she cleared her throat and turned to meet his gaze, all hint of vulnerability gone. "You didn't have to be that hard on poor Anthony."

His eyebrows rose as he regarded her. "He tried to serve you baby food."

"Because *you* insulted him and then made a stupid bet with him." Her lips twisted in a wry grin. "Serves you right that he embarrassed you."

"I was not embarrassed."

She cocked an eyebrow and reached for her glass of wine. "Then why the dressing down?"

Because he had wanted to impress her. Because he'd wanted a quiet place that was reasonably secure to discover what lay behind the cool front she exhibited. Because he wanted time to explore the attraction between them without his household's knowledge or interference.

Not that he planned to follow through on that attraction.

He ground his teeth, searching for a reasonable explanation to give her. One that wouldn't scare her. Or piss her off even more than she already was. "You're right. I was embarrassed."

Instead of the triumphant expression he expected from her at his admission, she sobered and nodded. "It's okay. I won't tell anyone."

For someone who constantly proclaimed her condemnation for vampires, Bebe knew and respected the subtleties of his people's culture.

She toyed with the appetizer fork while she watched him. "Anthony must be one of your sister's descendants."

Her perceptiveness shook him. No one had mentioned Selene in Bebe's presence as far as he knew. "How did you know I had a sister?"

Her face flamed bright pink again. "I, um, well, that is—"

He folded his arms as he waited for her to finish stuttering. How much of the conversation between Selene, Ptolemy and him in his office had she overheard?

"I overheard Alex telling Ptolemy in the hallway that your sister was at the house last night," she finally said.

"When you were snooping through my house, you mean?"

Her face went from pink to scarlet. "Well, if you hadn't outbid me for the wardrobe, I wouldn't have been looking for it."

He smiled at her flustered expression. "Yes, Anthony is one of Selene's descendants. What makes you think he isn't one of Ptolemy's?"

"You're kidding, right? He hasn't been civil to anybody since I've met him, much less any woman."

He roared with laughter at her observation. Despite their parents' vaunted prowess as lovers, Ptolemy had always lacked in the social graces when it came to the opposite sex.

The rest of the meal passed in pleasant conversation. She was remarkably well-read for someone of her generation, and she lavished compliments on Anthony until the young chef glowed with pride.

Later, as they waited for the valet to bring Caesar's car around, she gave a loud sigh.

He glanced down at her. "What's wrong?"

She smiled up at him. "Nothing. That's just it. Nothing's wrong. For the first time in a long time, I feel . . . normal."

Normal.

Something deep inside him responded to her simple happiness in the moment. He leaned closer, giving her plenty of opportunity to avoid him, to step back, to say no. Instead, her mouth opened ever so slightly. He brushed his lips against hers with a feather-light touch.

She didn't back away but eased closer. Her fingers combed through his hair before winding around his neck as she deepened their kiss. Her full breasts pressed against him, igniting a fire that could destroy them both.

A soft moan from her throat was all that was needed to eliminate his fleeting thought. Their tongues met, danced and parted only to meet again. The rich chocolate of her dessert mixed with her own ginger and peach flavor, a taste he couldn't get enough of, would never be able to get enough.

She sighed into his mouth, a sound of both surrender and demand. And gods above, how he wanted to oblige her. Take her to his bed. Tear the clothes from her lush body and love her—

No.

He couldn't love her. Not the way he wanted. Not without destroying her in the process.

He eased out of their kiss, reluctance slowing his movements. She stared up at him, confusion mixed with lust in her huge brown eyes.

In the split second of searching his brain for the right thing to tell Bebe, he caught the scent. Not the ripe apple scent of the Normal staff, but sandalwood.

Another vampire.

The revelation barely formed when a blurred figure rammed them both into the rock-hard pavement.

Chapter 13

Body still reeling from Caesar's kiss, Bebe looked up at him. But something was very, very wrong. His attention was elsewhere, his nostrils flared, like a predator scenting an interloper on the night wind.

Then something slammed them both to the concrete, hard enough to knock the wind out of her. Screams and shouts echoed above and behind them.

Before she could react, before she could even think of reacting, something had a grip on her topknot and yanked her upright. She reached out mentally, and received a psychic slap for her effort.

A female witch.

Pain burned, both through her psychic senses and through her scalp at the manhandling, and she scrambled to get her feet under her. Once upright, she froze at the flesh jammed against her windpipe and the metal grazing the left side of her neck.

Of all the stupid ways to die. Her throat slit in front of an L.A. restaurant by a plain old knife after her first decent date in years.

And that pissed her off. More than any of the posing, politics and plots that had occurred in the week since she'd returned to the States.

Channeling her fury, Bebe stomped on the bitch's instep as hard as she could, throwing her body back at the same time. Caught off guard by the physical defense, her assailant screamed and flailed wildly before they crashed back down on the concrete portico.

The point of the knife sliced across Bebe's cheek as she rolled away from the other witch. Grateful the cut wasn't to her jugular, she continued the roll until her body smacked a potted palm. She swiped her cheek, and reaching up with her bloody fingers, she grabbed a handful of dirt. Using anger and blood as focal points wasn't smart, but she ignored common sense, forced her will into the tiny handful of dirt mixed with her blood, and flung it at the other witch. The glob of mud struck the bitch squarely between the eyes.

More amoeba than humanoid, her hastily constructed semi-golem oozed its way down the other witch's face and into her mouth. While her opponent gagged and choked on the bloody mud, Bebe searched frantically for Caesar. At the sight of him, her inability to catch her breath had nothing to do with the blow to her diaphragm.

He whirled and dodged in a dangerous dance as he fended off three other vampires, obviously trying to draw them away from her. His eyes glowed golden and his bared fangs flashed as he fought. A half-transformed were lay near the curb, its neck broken from the unnatural angle of its head.

The bastard could be pissed all he wanted, but he was outgunned and needed her help. She climbed to her feet, shaky from her own battle. She didn't dare conjure a fireball for fear of hitting Caesar. And there wasn't a damn thing she could use other than the potted palms and the patrons' keys hanging neatly on the valet's rack. Nothing except . . .

Bebe gulped hard. The other witch's knife glittered under the hanging light bulbs that decorated the restaurant entrance. And the witch herself clawed with desperation, trying to breathe past the mud clogging her windpipe. Bebe reached down and snatched up the knife, then cursed herself for not checking if the other witch had bespelled it first.

The bitch hadn't, thank the Goddess. Plain wood met Bebe's palm. Gorge rose in her throat at the thought of what she was about to do. She'd never actually killed anyone. Not even a vampire, despite her years of fear and hatred. She glanced at the writhing witch on the concrete.

So much for doing no harm.

She checked the progress of the vampire battle. Caesar feinted around one of his opponents. He pulled out a push broom hidden behind the valet rack. With a quick snap, he broke off the brush end. A vicious smile lit his face as he twirled the broomstick in his hand, the jagged point whistling in the night air.

The three vamps backed away from Caesar. The one farthest from Bebe met her eyes, noting that Bebe was still standing and the other witch wasn't. The malicious grin he aimed at her disappeared as fast as his legs out from under him when Caesar swept the broomstick under his knees. Only the martial arts kick from one of his buddies kept Caesar from staking him.

The third vampire, an ugly bruiser with a thick shock of brown hair hanging in his face, followed his downed buddy's attention to her. Fangs flashed and an ugly snarl came from his throat.

Then he leapt.

Bebe could only raise her hands in defense before Bruiser slammed her down on the concrete for the third time. Except instead of ripping out her throat, he had a surprised look on his face. She followed his gaze down to where the knife protruded from his chest, her fist still firmly wrapped around the hilt.

"Shit," he said, and his eyes met hers for a split-second before they fell out of the sockets. Skin slid from the vampire's face as he melted. In seconds, Bebe was covered in the gooey, stinking remains of vampire.

She rolled over and, for the first time since medical school, threw up.

"Bebe!"

At Caesar's shout, she swiped congealed vampire flesh off her face. Breathing through her mouth to keep the rotten meat odor from triggering another round of vomiting, she looked up. Distracted, he paid no attention to the vampire behind him. The one that now had a knife in his upraised hand.

"Caesar, behind—"

Before she could finish her screamed warning, the vampire's head rolled across the sidewalk and bounced into the gutter. The corpse collapsed to its knees, the rapid decomposition already sloughing flesh from bones. Behind the melting body stood Ptolemy, a self-satisfied smirk on his face and a bloody sword in his hand.

The last vampire launched himself at Ptolemy, who took a wild swing at him. Having more of a clue than his friends, he ducked and dived underneath Ptolemy's sword stroke, aiming a nasty kick at Ptolemy's knee as he went. Caesar's brother crashed to the concrete.

A solid whack of the broomstick caught the enemy vamp under the chin as he started to rise. He flipped over backwards and rolled left to avoid a jab. When he rose, he clutched the knife of his beheaded friend. With a flick of his wrist, the vampire aimed the steel straight at Bebe and threw.

Before she could blink, the knife went clattering into the driveway. Caesar barely finished the swing that knocked the knife off its flight path when he impaled the vampire on the business end of his broken broomstick. The vampire liquefied even as he attempted to yank the offending wood out of his chest.

Caesar turned and stalked toward her, the expression on his face one of unmitigated fury. His eyes were no longer gold, but shifting rapidly to crimson. Acting on raw instinct, Bebe scrabbled backward away from him on all fours. Her pulse pounded an obscene rhythm as the memory of the night her parents died rushed over her. Caesar's face held the same blood fury as her parents' murderers.

The glow in his eyes faded a fraction. He knelt and held out his hand. "Are you all right, Bebe?"

She eyed his outstretched palm warily before she met his gaze. The red tint disappeared. Neon yellow melted into warm hazel as concern replaced anger. She nodded and reached for his hand, letting him pull her to her feet. Her knees shook as the initial adrenaline rush died. He wrapped an arm around her to support her weight, and she loathed to admit she needed his help. He examined her body, checking for additional injuries.

"I'm fine." She flashed him a weak smile. "I smell worse then I look." She dabbed at the brand new dress. "I'm sorry you wasted the money."

"I'm not."

She looked back up. The glow in his eyes brightened, and this time it wasn't from blood lust. Her breath caught in her lungs and not from her bruised diaphragm.

"The witch's dead."

Ptolemy's voice drew them both back to the present. He crouched next to the body.

"That can't be!"

But Ptolemy was right. She stepped over, and kneeling on the other side of the woman, she checked her pulse and breathing. Or, in this case, lack thereof. She shifted her sight to examine the other witch. The woman's aura had turned black and would soon disappear as the individual cells of her body died. Thankfully, none of their assailants' souls had hung around after their physical deaths. She didn't have the energy to deal with five vengeful ghosts.

Nausea did another queasy journey through her stomach. She'd never killed anyone before. But how? There hadn't been enough dirt to choke the other witch to death. Maybe give her a bad case of pneumonia if any individual dirt particles made it into her lungs . . .

"It's not your fault." Caesar rested a hand on her shoulder. "I'd have preferred to have someone to question, but our attackers were determined. Do you recognize her?"

Bebe shook her head, but then would she recognize anyone from either the San Francisco or Los Angeles covens? Between med school and now, she'd been gone an awfully long time. She tilted the corpse's head. The double piercings in the other witch's ears were empty of decoration. She definitely didn't want to be recognized.

"I think we have a bigger problem." Ptolemy's voice had a worried tone.

Bebe turned to follow his equally worried look. At least twenty Norms were plastered against the huge glass entry doors of the restaurant. In the center of the group stood Anthony, who looked like he was ready to kill someone himself.

"Now's when I really wish I had one of Will Smith's flashy thingies."

"This isn't funny, Ptolemy," Caesar said.

The vampire's attention shifted to his brother. "Who's joking? Between the two of us, we could probably handle the window group, but by now, the entire restaurant knows and someone's sure to have called 9-1-1."

All of Grandma's damage control training prompted an idea. "I could whip something up in the kitchen," Bebe said. "Anthony would have most of what I need. I can wing the rest."

Caesar gave her a wry look. "You can erase everyone's memory before the police arrive?"

She shook her head. "No, but I can blunt it. The customers will know a fight occurred, but they won't be able to remember details or give accurate descriptions. If you two can—" She coughed and nodded toward the two remaining corpses. The remains of the three vampires were already starting to liquefy and dribble across the portico toward the gutter. A good hosing of the concrete would take care of everything else.

"Ptolemy, bring your truck around," Caesar said.

———•———

Two hours later, in the back room where she and Caesar had dined, Bebe breathed a sigh of relief, collapsed in a chair and closed her eyes. A mere flicker of thought was all it took to drop the glamour that covered the cut on her left cheek and the bruises on her throat. She didn't have the energy for anything else. Once again, she was totally exhausted and wearing someone else's cotton t-shirt and shorts. Luckily, one of the female bartenders had workout clothes stashed in her bag. A faint wisp of mourning crossed Bebe's mind for her ruined outfit. She had really loved that dress.

For all of the twenty-four hours she owned it.

Her half-assed memory-erasing spell had worked though. Anthony and his staff managed to serve the spell carrier concoction to everyone at the restaurant through free drinks before the police arrived. Thank the Goddess, they didn't have more people there that had witnessed the incident due to the hour and the day of the week. With her reserves wiped out, she wouldn't have been able to make a larger batch of potion. Without decent descriptions of the attackers, who had allegedly escaped, and since no one at the restaurant had apparently been injured, the two officers wrote the fight off as an attempted robbery, gave Bebe and Caesar fake smiles, and said if they learned anything they'd contact Caesar's office.

Bebe gently probed the cut on her cheek. It could have been worse. She could have been one of the bodies Caesar and Ptolemy had loaded in the bed of Ptolemy's pick-up. She didn't have the guts to ask Caesar where Ptolemy had disappeared with the corpses of the witch and the were.

The clink of glassware drew her attention. She opened her eyes to find Anthony collapsing in the chair next to her. A bottle of Jack Daniels and three shot glasses sat in the middle of the table.

"You pour. I'm too tired." He followed his declaration with a gigantic yawn.

"Are you a telepath?" she asked, not that she believed he had breached her shields.

He frowned and shook his head.

She smiled and lifted the bottle. "My favorite." She poured two fingers and had to wait until he finished another yawn before she handed the glass to him. "I'd think you'd be used to the long hours."

He swallowed the entire glassful before she had her own drink poured. "Long hours? Yes. Almost losing my restaurant because some supernatural hit team tries to off my uncle at my front door? No."

Not knowing how to answer him, she downed her own drink, relishing the burn in her throat, before she poured another round for them.

Caesar entered the room and crossed to give her a peck on the forehead, his actions more comforting than she cared to admit. All pretenses of Mr. Dark and Mysterious Vampire were gone. Missing suit jacket, messed hair and rumpled shirt marred his normally immaculate appearance. He pulled a chair closer to hers and dropped into it. Without a word, she poured whiskey into the third glass and handed it to him.

He swallowed it in one gulp and held it out to her for a refill. "They know you're here in Los Angeles."

"No shit, Sherlock." She handed the full glass back to him. Her fingertips tingled at the brush of his touch. How could she be aroused at a time like this?

"You're taking this remarkably well." He eyed her over the top of the glass as he downed the second shot.

"Would you prefer I scream like a girl and wait for you to save me the next time?"

Both Caesar and Anthony grinned at her thick sarcasm.

She took a deep breath, glad for the vague numbness that allowed her to deal with tonight's scare. "I'm not stupid, Caesar. The were and vamps were there to keep you out of the way long enough for the witch to slit my throat. No fuss, no muss, and no way to link anything back to anyone."

She rose and retrieved the knife that had been at her jugular earlier from the plastic sack containing her ruined dress. Returning to the table, she laid the slimy knife on the pristine tablecloth in front of him. "Do you know what this is?"

He looked at the plain, black-handled steel, then met her eyes, his eyebrow cocked and his smirk back in place. "A knife?"

Anthony leaned forward and examined the knife, but he didn't touch it. "It's a sushi knife." He met Bebe's eyes and frowned. "Why would a witch use a sushi knife?"

"Exactly," she said and turned back to Caesar. "It's definitely not an athame—"

"What's an athame?" Anthony said.

"A ceremonial knife witches use to direct energy during a ritual or spell," Caesar answered. "They don't use them as weapons though. It's considered sacrilege."

Bebe raised an eyebrow and glared at him.

He held up his hands. "Sorry, didn't mean to intrude. Please continue."

"There's no spell on this thing, and no residual magick, which means she couldn't have had it in her possession more than a few hours at most." She shrugged. "And why else remove her earrings?"

Caesar leaned his elbows on the table, his index fingers steepled as he considered her words. "The real question is why use the witch to kill you?"

She shot him a nasty smile. "Because vampires are so much more efficient at killing?"

His expression remained deadly sober, which sent a shiver of fear down her spine. "Yes, we are. So are the weres."

Anthony reached for the bottle of whiskey. "Because whoever's after Bebe wanted someone they could trust to get the job done. Someone with a personal stake in the matter. They just didn't count on how fast she can think on her feet. And the stakes must be pretty fucking high for supes to risk exposure by staging a hit in a public place frequented by Normals, even if it is a Family-owned business."

Bebe and Caesar both turned to stare at the restaurateur.

"Come on, guys. I'm not stupid either." Anthony snorted. "I'm about as much as an eclectic witch as Bebe is. You're one of the White Rose claimants, aren't you?"

She shot Caesar a nasty look and threw her hands in the air. "So much for your brilliant plan. Even a Norm could figure out who I am."

"I'm not telling anyone, Bebe." Anthony grinned, but it wasn't as sparkling as before the fight. "But the White Rose succession has been a big topic of conversation down here. Word around town is Ziva Epstein's been in Africa looking for one of the heirs."

"You are so fucking dead, Augustine." Exhaustion kept her words from packing any real punch. "Europe, my ass. You knew where she was, didn't you? And you didn't bother to tell me?"

Caesar blew out an exasperated breath. "As I told you, I promised Natasha and Ziva to keep you safe."

"And a fine job you've done so far."

Anthony sprayed his third shot of Jack all over the tablecloth at her snarky comment.

"You're still alive, aren't you?" was Caesar's dry reply.

Sticking her tongue out at Caesar, she reached over and poured Anthony another shot. "No thanks to you tonight, but that's not the point. If it wasn't for your brother, we'd both be sushi right now."

An odd frown appeared on Caesar's face. "Yes, we're both lucky Ptolemy followed us."

"Damn straight. Have you actually spoken with Granny E.?" Her eyelids drooped. In fighting to keep them open, she couldn't spare the energy to figure out what his problem was. What the hell happened to all that lovely rest she had gotten earlier in the day?

"No. But I'm assuming that she received my message that you'd returned to the U.S. since her housekeeper said she was expected back tomorrow." He tilted his wrist to check his watch. "Later today I should say." His gaze flicked back to her face. "I'd say it's past time to return home since you can barely remain awake."

"I'm fine."

"Well, I'm not." Anthony rose. "And I have to close, so no offense, Bebe, but get the hell out of my place."

She jerked as she realized Anthony had been calling her by her own name since the fight and not her pseudonym. "How'd you know my real identity?"

Anthony stood and rolled his eyes. "Uncle Jerk-off yelling it on the street wasn't exactly subtle." He held out a hand, which she shook. "It was still a pleasure to meet you. You're welcome back anytime."

"Assuming I live long enough," she murmured as Anthony left the room. Exhaustion wormed its way through her mind.

"You will." Cool, strong fingers encircled her own, Caesar's touch so comforting she didn't want to ever let go.

Except she couldn't relax into the comfort he offered. Something else about the whole attack bothered her, but she couldn't quite grasp the slippery half-thought as it swam through her tired brain. She eyed Caesar. "Is there any way to autopsy the witch? Find out who she is? And more specifically what killed her?"

He winced. "We're trying to identify her from a photo, but the body . . ."

She sighed. "Ptolemy burned it, didn't he?"

He nodded. "There's a jointly owned crematorium that all of us in Los Angeles use for these types of situations."

"And you don't think anyone's going to ask about five missing supes?"

Again, the wry smirk appeared on his face. "Not without tipping his hand."

"Or her hand."

A muscle twitched along his jaw. Damn, he knew Alice was behind this. Was he trying to protect her? Or was he playing a whole different game with the witch community? It took a lot, a lot of money or a lot of threat, for three different races to act in concert as their assailants did tonight, even if the individuals were rogues.

He frowned and rose before helping her to her feet, never releasing his grip on her fingers. "I'm not sure what would be gained by examining her body."

"I want to find out exactly what killed her," she said, grabbing the knife off the table.

He eyed her with concern. "I understand your guilt over her death, but you were acting in self-defense." His gaze flicked down to the sushi knife in her hand. "And I'm afraid to ask why you're keeping that."

Tugging her hand loose from his, she walked over to the corner, dropped the knife in the sack and slung it over her shoulder. "I'll take it with us to Granny E.'s. It might be close to impossible, but we may be able to backtrack where the knife came from." She sighed at the skeptical look on his face. "I know it's a long shot but unless you have a better idea . . ."

He strode across the room to join her at the door and placed his hand on the small of her back as she preceded him out of the room. Despite his lower body temperature, his touch sent a heat through her that was totally inappropriate. She almost stopped just to luxuriate in the sensation.

Instead, they crossed the restaurant's main dining area, empty except for a handful of staff doing last minute cleaning. The employees looked at them curiously but with no real recognition. She should have known. Her spell may have taken care of the customers, but Caesar would have had to erase the memories of the staff while the police interviewed her.

They exited the main doors, and a tall shadow in the corner of her eye made her jump. She whipped around, hand reaching for the knife in her bag because she was, and she hated to admit it, too damn tired to summon a fireball, much less cast any other spell.

The shadow resolved into Caesar's man, Duncan, and she relaxed a fraction.

"What are you doing here?" Caesar demanded.

"Escorting you home, Your Highness." Despite his clipped British accent and deferential tone, steel lay behind Duncan's words. "I was remiss in allowing you to leave the estate unescorted tonight."

She glanced up at Caesar. By the play of emotions across his face, Caesar wasn't happy about needing a bodyguard, but he nodded.

Before either of them could add anything else, Duncan's SUV screeched to a halt in front of them, Tiffany at the wheel. Behind her came Caesar's Jaguar with Anne in the driver's seat, her eyes barely peeking above the steering wheel.

Duncan held the rear passenger door open, and Bebe climbed in and buckled the seatbelt. The last thing she remembered was Caesar pulling her against him and telling her to get some rest. Despite a vague warning in the back of her mind, she snuggled against his chest and sank into the welcoming cocoon of sleep.

Chapter 14

Dense fog surrounded Bebe. She couldn't see anything around her, not even the ground she walked on. Grandma Petrov's voice screamed through the gray mist, whether in anger or pain, Bebe couldn't tell.

"Grandma! Where are you?" She searched in a panic, stumbling because the damn fog obscured everything. Even her spell to disperse the mist failed. "Grandma!" Raw fear squeezed her heart. Something was wrong, terribly wrong. "Grandma? Answer me!" Smoky tendrils swallowed her shout. Grandma wouldn't leave her. She promised.

But the cries faded, and Bebe was alone. All alone. The ground shifted and dipped, then she fell.

Falling through the misty nothingness.

She jerked when her half-asleep brain realized Caesar sat on the edge of the bed. She glanced frantically around the room, the one she'd been shown to by Anne when they had arrived at Caesar's Brentwood mansion.

Except . . .

She didn't remember crawling into bed. A quick glance down revealed someone else's clothes, but then she remembered the bartender who gave the t-shirt and shorts after last night's insanity. Someone must have carried her into the house after she'd fallen asleep in the SUV. And considering who she'd snuggled against in the back seat, she had a good idea who'd tucked her in bed.

So why did the thought of Caesar taking care of her disturb her carefully ordered sense of self?

He's a vampire for crying out loud.

No, the problem wasn't the vampire. It was the man.

A whiff of eggs and toast sent her stomach rumbling, which made sense since the only thing she'd kept down last night had been the Jack Daniels. Triage. Yeah, triage was a great idea. Deal with the immediate needs first, and worry about the things Caesar Augustine did to her insides later.

Much later.

"I wasn't sure how you liked your eggs, so Tiffany scrambled them." He gestured toward the tray perched on the nightstand, and once again, he had a real smile instead of the usual smirk.

She ran a self-conscious hand over her wayward curls and grimaced. Bits of vampire goo had dried in it, making her hair more impossible than usual. Then she cursed herself. Why should she care about impressing Caesar Augustine? She tried to speak and had to clear her throat before trying again. "What time is it?"

"It's a little after nine in the morning. We can be on the road as soon as you're ready."

"We? You're going out in daylight?"

He chuckled. "Not exactly. Phillippa UV-proofed her place a long time ago."

She nodded, slightly curious about how a vampire traveled during daylight hours.

A half hour, one broken comb, and one loud vampire argument later, Tiffany maneuvered the SUV in a manner Bebe noticed left even Caesar's knuckles whiter than usual. Caesar's entire household had put down their collective foot and said neither Caesar or Bebe were leaving the mansion without an escort. She rather had the impression he wished he'd agreed to one of the other human daytime guards driving them around Los Angeles.

UV film covered all the windows in the SUV so Caesar didn't so much as smoke slightly under the bright California sun, and Bebe realized this was the first time she'd seen him awake during daylight hours. When she asked him about it, he shrugged and said, "It seems pointless to be awake during daylight hours when we can't go outdoors, but occasionally we do venture out." He shot her a heart-stopping grin. "If the cause is worthwhile."

Why did he continue to torture her? She smoothed a hand over the khaki pants Anne had bought for her. It wasn't like anything could ever happen between them. Since she had no idea how to respond to his deliberate flirting, she kept silent and watched the mid-morning traffic.

Soon they were rolling down a quiet street that held a mix of residences and specialty shops. Tiffany swerved down an alley and punched a button on the panel above her head. One of the garage doors framing the alley obediently opened, and she pulled into the deceptively cavernous space.

As the garage door slid closed, a woman opened the side door between the garage and the main building. If Bebe leaned in a different direction, her tongue would be hanging on the floor. The woman was statuesque with sun-kissed brunette hair piled on her head, curves in all the right places, and features that Helen of Troy would have killed for. Except her arms were crossed over her ample chest and a stern frown marred the perfect lines of her face.

"What did you do this time, Tiffany?" she said as soon as the girl popped open the driver's door. "And why aren't you in class?"

"It's holiday break, Phil." The teenage whine came through strong and clear.

"I know, kid. Just giving you shit." The woman pulled Tiffany into a hug. She waved as Caesar came around the vehicle. "What's going on—" Then she caught sight of Bebe and smiled. "Hello, Dr. Zachary. I was wondering when you'd appear on my doorstep."

— • —

Bebe couldn't get over Phillippa Mann's kitchen. Blue and white gingham covered the table with matching curtains framing the window over the sink. Pine cupboards with a natural honey stain gave the place a warm feeling. Of course, the freshly baked strudel she served with coffee helped. And she sat serenely in her cream shirt with black linen pants and sandals, a strand of pearls at her throat. The woman made Martha Stewart look positively normal.

Except everyone knew Martha was part daemon.

And Bebe still couldn't figure out what Phillippa was as they sat, munching on delicious strudel and making small talk. Part human definitely. It was the other part that concerned her because the woman practically glowed with power.

When Bebe tentatively probed Phillippa's surface thoughts, nothing came through. Nothing that is but a feeling of sandy beach surrounded by cliffs that blazed in brilliant sunshine. And Phillippa's thoughts were as ephemeral as the afterimages reflected off the limestone cliffs.

Phillippa paused in her conversation with Caesar and Tiffany concerning the merits of UCLA versus Berkeley, turned and gave Bebe a mysterious smile. "I believe Dr. Zachary is growing impatient with us."

Heat flooded Bebe's cheeks. "I'm sorry for my rudeness."

Phillippa merely nodded an acknowledgement and said, "What you're looking for is down there, Doctor." She gestured toward a waist-high stand. An old-fashioned rotary phone sat on top.

Bebe raised an eyebrow for permission, but Phillippa laid a hand on her forearm. "Bebe, dear, if you accept this from me, there's no going back. Do you understand?"

Bebe paused, reminded of Grandma Petrov's mysterious note. "Don't you want to see some ID before you hand it over to me? For all you know, I could be a shifter."

Phillippa laughed, a soft melodious sound. "Tiffany's endorsement is sufficient for me."

Bebe blinked in surprise. Then the realization smacked her between the eyes. The three of them had been discussing her telepathically the whole time, which said something about Phillippa's power. Curiosity quickly followed. "Why Tiffany's word over Caesar's?"

Again, that mysterious smile tilted Phillippa's mouth. "Caesar isn't exactly objective when it comes to you, my dear."

Oh boy, let's make that all public why don't we? Bebe flicked a glance at Caesar and was gratified that he was as irritated as she. Though a small part of her thrilled at the thought he had feelings for her.

She stood, crossed to the stand, and crouched to open the door to the cupboard under the phone. Part of a black leather cover poked from underneath the piles of Los Angeles metro area phone books. Not a real secure place, but Stan had proven that the wardrobe wasn't necessarily safe. Pulling out the various yellow and white pages and setting them aside, she breathed a sigh of relief when the familiar embossed pentacle appeared. Caesar had been telling the truth about finding the letter. She hugged the Book of Shadows to her chest and whispered a prayer of thanks to the Goddess before she returned the phone books to their storage place.

She went to the table and sat, puzzled that she wasn't more excited by finding the Book. The anti-climax was topped when Tiffany gave Phillippa a confused look and asked, "Why the hell did you store that with your phone books? Do you know people are trying to kill Bebe?"

"That's why I asked if she was sure she wanted it." Phillippa smiled and sipped her coffee.

"I'd like to hire you."

Bebe jerked her head up at Caesar's words, but his eyes were aimed at Phillippa, who shook her head. And the look on her face indicated she was someone that not even a vampire should mess with.

Maybe Caesar was suicidal because he didn't shut up. "But Bebe needs to be kept safe while I try to find out who's behind—"

"No," Bebe and Phillippa said at the same time.

Bebe continued, "I don't need—"

"Yes, you do." For the first time, he showed real anger toward her. "Or did you forgot the last couple—"

"No!" Bebe slapped her hand down on the table for emphasis, her fury rising to match his. "I haven't forgotten, but I'm not dragging another innocent person into this mess."

A trace of what may have been sympathy on Phillippa's face as she regarded him. "And this is a witch matter, Caesar, not a vampire situation. I will not interfere, even at your request."

"But you helped Uncle Duncan with me," Tiffany said.

Phillippa's expression softened when she faced Tiffany. "You were a baby. Bebe's a full-grown woman who needs to learn to fight her own battles." She turned back to Bebe. "I'm sorry, Dr. Zachary. I couldn't if you asked me either."

For some strange reason, Phillippa's refusal to help her was reassuring. Bebe smiled. "No apology necessary, Ms. Mann." She wanted to ask Phillippa about Grandma Petrov, how they knew each other, why did Grandma entrust Phillippa with the Book. But something in Phillippa's manner told her that the unusual woman wouldn't answer her questions.

"When your battle is finished, come back and we will reminisce about Natasha."

Bebe's eyes widened at Phillippa's perception, then she nodded. "Thank you." She indicated the book. "For everything."

Ten minutes later as they prepared to leave, Caesar must have sensed her need for privacy because he climbed into the front passenger seat. He wasn't given a choice of the driver's seat.

Bebe hid her smile at his irritation when Tiffany had refused to relinquish the keys. For a teenager, she took her guard duties seriously. Or maybe it was just the power of a seventeen-year-old behind the wheel of a large, military-based vehicle.

Sucking in a deep breath, Bebe flipped open the cover as Tiffany pulled into traffic. The first pages contained the usual recipes, spells and rituals of any witch's Book. She turned to the damning pages to find they were intact. If Phillippa had looked at them, Bebe had no doubt the strange woman would keep the information silent.

Tears blurred her vision, and she blinked them back. What looked like a simple family tree was a quiet network of alliances through marriage and blood that made the acid in her stomach roil. Most of the marriages were indirect, through siblings or cousins, but they left White Rose in control over most of the Western Hemisphere, either directly or through political influence.

And before she died, Grandma had her sights on Europe.

Bebe's index finger traced the thin ink line between her name and that of Alastair Hyde-Smith. The marriage date was still blank. She'd never met the boy so she had no personal grievance against him. But her last real argument with Grandma Petrov ripped at her memory. Even though Grandma's emotional distance since Mom and Dad's murders had bothered Bebe, Grandma had never tried forcing her to do anything until Alastair.

"I'm not attending fucking Oxford so you can shove your claws into another coven! And I'm sure as hell not agreeing to an arranged marriage!"

She had never sworn at anyone in her life until that moment, but Grandma Petrov had merely looked at her with that same imperturbable expression she had worn since the day of the funerals.

"This is not about your personal wishes, Bebe. This marriage concerns the survival of our people. You need to be in a position of strength to succeed me, and Alastair will provide you that strength and more." Grandma didn't even blink, dropping this bombshell on her as if they were discussing whether to have morning tea in the garden or the solarium.

Bebe suppressed a shudder. As a coven's high priestess, she'd have to deal with the leaders of the other supernatural factions. Like the vampires.

She couldn't do it, not without having a nervous breakdown. "Name someone else as your heir. The Elders will rubberstamp whomever you pick and you know it. *I* don't want the job."

Bebe could have been talking to the maid for all the effect her words had on Grandma.

"I've already made the arrangements with his coven's high priestess. You can continue to pursue your medical studies in England with the minimum of disruption."

"You're not hearing me, are you? I refuse to be named your heir, I'm not going to England, and I'M DEFINITELY NOT MARRYING ALASTAIR!" Her scream echoed through the gigantic, empty house. The maid had run from the room when Grandma made her initial proclamation, probably to warn the rest of the staff to stay outside.

"Then you leave me no choice but to cut off your funding." Grandma's cold voice sliced through the remnants of Bebe's scream.

"You wouldn't." But she knew deep down Grandma would and her continuing silence confirmed it. The old woman had done anything and everything to get her way, one of the reasons Grandpa Petrov had left her years ago.

Well, fine. Two could play that game.

"Then I will petition to have the court dissolve the trust, Grandma. I'm twenty-one now, and there's no real reason for it to exist, is there?"

Grandma said nothing, just the slight rise in her left eyebrow her only answer.

Bebe stepped closer. "The only way you can stop it is to have me declared mentally incompetent. Do you really think the Hyde-Smiths will want a nut case in the family? How is that going to look to the rest of White Rose? And even if you manage to retain control of the trust without having me committed, I'll dance naked in a strip joint to pay for school before I let you force me into any kind of marriage."

Calling Grandma's bluff had meant she graduated from UCSF with honors, but Grandma's audacious plan to move Alastair to the U.S. and install him in the mansion following her internship had sent Bebe fleeing to Africa.

Regrets and grief shrouded her. She shouldn't have left things unsaid for so long between her and Grandma. Grandma had been there for her after her parents' deaths, even if her idea of closeness was sending her out for ice cream with the chauffeur. Now, they'd never have the chance to mend their relationship. Maybe Grandma had meant what she said in her letters, that she wouldn't force a marriage if Bebe would just come home.

She flipped back to the page before and stared at the lines showing her parents' marriage. Had Mom been forced to marry Dad too? How had she reacted? Had she been threatened, told she'd be thrown out if she didn't comply with Grandma's demands? Bebe had always believed her mom and dad were totally in love. Were they? Or was it an act thrust on them for political advantage?

Her parents loved her. Of that, she had no doubt. When those vampires broke into their house and the first one grabbed her . . .

Oh my Goddess!

The air in her lungs refused to budge. The viewpoint of her eleven-year-old self crystallized. The rogue vampires had been after her that night!

Dad had managed to get the bastard to drop her. Mom had scooped her up and crammed her into the nymph hole in Dad's gigantic entertainment center before going to help Dad.

Except it was too late.

And all Bebe could do was beat helplessly on the wards of the nymph hole as she watched first Dad, and then Mom, die a horrible death.

The vampires were still shredding the entertainment center, trying to kill her, when Grandma had arrived and blasted them both into the afterlife with fireballs.

She wiped the silent tears from her cheeks. She had been wondering how her life got this screwed up, but she had been fucked from the beginning. Why the hell would vampires target an eleven-year-old, even if they were rogues?

Same reason the three rogue vamps, a witch and a were teamed up to take her out last night. Someone wanted her dead, had wanted her dead for a very long time, and for what? A position of power she didn't desire and a book that proved her grandmother was a power-hungry harpy. What was she missing?

Caesar had said something about a conspiracy to murder Grandma. Why would Grandma trust a vampire and a—whatever the hell Phillippa was—instead of someone in the coven?

And why did Bebe trust Caesar? Because Grandma told her to wasn't a good enough answer. So what was in this for him? He was spending a lot of time and money on her. And a lot of attention.

A lot of attention that she rather enjoyed.

With effort, she wrenched her mind away from his exquisite kissing technique and focused on the more immediate problem.

Had another witch found out about Grandma's master plans? Someone jealous of the power Grandma was amassing? Or maybe someone who resented being forced into a marriage he or she didn't want? If Bebe had been furious, how would William or Alice have reacted?

Except neither of them could have plotted her murder when they were children.

Well, William *had* pushed her out of the tree house when they were eight, and it *had* been intentional. Like it was her fault he sucked at checkers. Her broken arm had healed, but since then, all the therapy in the world hadn't cured her acrophobia.

At least, Grandma hadn't hidden the Book in one of the ancient oaks on the coven's estate. Bebe would never have been able to recover it if she had to climb a tree.

She flipped the Book pages past the proposed future alliances. Maybe Grandma left some clues as to what she knew or suspected. After a few blank sheets, Bebe found more of Grandma's elegant, loopy script.

She stared at the page, squeezed her eyes shut, then looked at the page again. The words on the page made absolutely no sense. The letters were a mix of English letters and what might have been Greek, but the language wasn't one she recognized. Had Grandma placed a spell on the ink or the page?

Extending her senses, she examined the page more closely. No direct magick, just residual power from years of use.

She jolted when the SUV door opened. Caesar stood there with a quizzical look on his face.

"Welcome back to Earth, Dr. Zachary." He must have noticed something was bothering her because his expression changed to one of concern. "What's wrong?"

Her fingers twitched, the urge to slam the Book shut so strong her hands cramped. He was a vampire. He couldn't be trusted.

But Grandma trusted him. Far more than she trusted anyone else in the coven.

Her eyes closed in her frustration. Goddess, nothing made sense anymore. Shoving the fear and worry aside, she listened. To the Goddess for some sign of what to do. To her instinct. To her gut. Her heart.

Her eyes opened to meet Caesar's. "We have a serious problem." She held up the Book for him to see. "I think this has our answers, but it's in some kind of code."

Caesar's gaze flicked to the pages, and his face stilled, that unnatural vampire stillness that never boded anything good for her. His eyes met hers, and her stomach clenched in fear.

"It's Natasha's research," he said.

"What kind of research?" Her stomach tried to crawl back through her small intestine. Maybe she should follow her organ's lead and find a deep, dark hole to hide in from his expression.

"Genetic research. She was working on a way to make witches impervious to the V-virus."

Chapter 15

"What?"

At Bebe's exclamation, any thoughts Caesar had of her holding the cure over his head disappeared. If he'd learned anything over the past couple of days, it was that the doctor wasn't that good of an actress. And he'd met some good ones over the centuries.

He blew out a harsh breath. "Let's go inside. I'll tell you what little I know."

Tiffany, for once, had the intelligence to keep her mouth shut and trailed them into the house. He stopped her at the door of his office.

"Why don't you go to the kitchen and prepare lunch for Dr. Zachary and yourself? Mai should have delivered the grocery order by now," he said.

"Or I could go tell Uncle Duncan about the top secret witch research." She smiled sweetly.

He bared his fangs, letting his irritation show.

Tiffany paled noticeably under her white Goth make-up. "Uh, how does tuna salad sound, Doc?"

"Tuna sounds delicious, thank you." Bebe smiled, despite her fears and concerns that leaked from behind her psychic shields. Her face grew deadly serious as soon as he closed the office door.

She stood there, hugging Natasha's Book to her chest. From the whiteness of her knuckles, the Jaws of Life would be necessary to get her to let go. And the look on her face . . .

He had expected anger, fury, or at the very least, mild irritation from her. Instead, she looked like a lost child as she stood in the middle of the burgundy carpet of his office.

"Would you like to sit down?" He gestured toward the sable leather couch opposite of the huge mahogany desk. Jamal had designed the effect of the furnishings to be both efficient and intimidating, but the room's influence seemed to reinforce the fear Bebe was desperately trying to hide. She remained frozen in place.

He needed a different tactic if he had any hope of getting her to talk. "I'm sorry I don't have any whiskey. Would you like a glass of wine?" He strode toward the mini-bar discreetly hidden behind a large potted palm.

"Why would someone want children dead?"

Her voice was so soft, that even with his enhanced hearing, he wasn't sure he'd heard her correctly. He spun on his heel so fast that she jumped back in fear. "Children? What children?" he said.

"The night—" She swallowed hard, as if her thoughts were so terrible that she couldn't give voice to them. "The night my parents died, those vampires, they weren't—" Big, round tears formed, then they began a slow roll down her cheeks. "They were after me."

He crossed back to her, slow so as not to scare her more than she was. Pulling her stiff body over to the couch, he pressed her into a sitting position and lowered himself next to her. "Bebe, the rogues killed a lot of people that night. It was a stupid, senseless power play. Nothing more."

She shook her head, the motion so violent that the clips fell from her hair. Her riotous curls fell around her shoulders. He wanted to bury his nose in the mass just to imprint her smell in his brain forever. If her mood weren't so dire, he would have.

Fool, as if you haven't already done so.

He ignored his chiding conscience and tried to focus on her. "Bebe, it's not unusual for children to blame themselves for bad things that happen. I—"

He caught himself before the confession came spilling out. She was distraught enough. She didn't need to hear his pathetic past. And he had actually done something. He sure as Hades wasn't an innocent like she was.

"This isn't self-blame, Augustine." The fire burned in her eyes again, and she spoke through gritted teeth. "Something else was going on that night. Grandma's genetic research—what exactly was she doing?"

All of his old arguments with Natasha came rushing back. He'd told her that her family wouldn't forgive her for manipulating them, even if it were for their own benefit. Bebe had proven his point succinctly when she took off for Africa. But no, Natasha had dangled the one thing he wanted in his face, and he'd caved.

He rose and began pacing in front of Bebe, trying to gauge her mood, but her face had turned as impassive as the monuments at Karnak. "You have to understand Natasha was doing what she thought was in the best interest of her family."

"Of course, she was." Bebe released the tome and crossed her arms over the turquoise camp shirt she wore. Unfortunately, her position only emphasized her breasts. To the point what little blood left in his body pooled in his cock.

Gods above, she wasn't making this easy, was she? He shoved his fists in the pockets of his Dockers and tried to think of bad sanitation during the Middle Ages. He sucked in a deep breath and plunged into the truth. Or at least as much as he dared to tell her.

"During World War II, a young male witch was captured by the Nazis. He was given to Mengele for experimentation. By then, the Nazis knew about supernaturals, and—" This part still made him sick. "They experimented to find out how various races reacted to the V-virus."

The slight clench of her hands betrayed her anxiety. "Didn't anyone tell those idiots what happens when you Turn a witch?"

He couldn't stop his own ironic smile. Hybrids were prohibited for a reason. If the witch survived the transformation, the virus usually left the witch a bloodthirsty psychopath. And a hybrid was a bitch to kill. "Probably not, hoping any hybrid they created would take the bastards out."

He raked a hand through his hair, forcing himself to continue. "They dumped the witch into a pit with a vampire they had starved. The vampire managed to not suck the boy dry, but the Nazis were shocked when he failed to die or Turn."

Her brow twisted in confusion. "That's impossible with that much contact."

"So the Nazis thought as well, but before they could follow up, the Allies overran the facility where the boy was held."

Her eyes narrowed. "What does this have to do with Grandma?"

"Your grandmother left Auschwitz II with Mengele's documentation of his experiments on supernaturals."

Her eyes widen. "She should have destroyed that stuff!" Disgust etched into her features, she looked down at the Book and shoved. It dropped to the floor, landing with a thud.

He bent and picked up the Book. "She didn't have time. Do you believe she should have left it for the Normals to find?"

Her cheeks flushed, and she stared at her toes. "No" came her whispered reply. Then her head lifted. "But she shouldn't have used that boy's torture to further her own political agenda."

"What political agenda?" Was there something more to Bebe and Natasha's rift than the Hyde-Smith boy?

"She discovered what made that boy immune, didn't she?"

He nodded, concern rising.

She took a deep breath, as if coming to a decision. She took the Book from his loose grip and started flicking through the pages. "This is what I mean about her agenda." She patted the cushion next to her. When he joined her, she pointed to what looked like a convoluted family tree. "All these marriages and children." She traced a branch of great-aunts and second cousins, and he recognized the names. The individuals were members of Nikolai's family who married into North and South American covens. "I thought she was just extending her political power, but she used her knowledge as a bargaining chip to form alliances." She looked up at him through dark lashes. "Didn't she?"

Bebe wasn't a stupid woman, and pretending the entire situation didn't exist wouldn't make things between them any easier. He nodded slowly, then reached for her hand and added, "You have to understand something, Bebe. Natasha believed she was doing the right thing in protecting her people."

She raised her head and stared at him. "And you think I don't understand what this could mean to your people?"

Old anger rose to the surface. Anger at ancient politics that decided his fate when he was about the same age as Bebe when she lost her parents. He rose, took two steps away from her and allowed all the ugliness to come out. He turned to face her and took a step forward. Her eyes widened and she gasped. "Do you really think I would wish *this*—" He gestured at his face. "—on anyone!" He'd seen himself in a mirror once when he was in a "full-blown vamp-out mode" as Tiffany called it. It scared the shit out of him, so he understood the effect on everyone else. "If Natasha found a way to protect the witches, and even better, all the Normals, then I'll be the first one cheering her!"

She flinched at his words. "I-I'm sorry, Caesar. I never thought—" She couldn't meet his gaze any longer.

Harsh breaths ripped at his lungs as he got himself back under control. "I'm sorry, too. I didn't want to scare you, but—"

A soft laugh burbled from her throat, and she looked up at him and smiled. "But I needed a kick in the ass?"

The image of her buttocks sticking out of the wardrobe changed into one of them naked and displayed before him. And the idea wasn't helping him get his bloodlust under control one little bit. He smiled as much as he dared with his fangs fully extended. "Yes."

She pushed a wayward curl behind her ear, and he couldn't stop wondering what her more intimate curls would taste like.

"I would guess that someone knows about her research." She waved a hand at the yellowed pages. "Someone besides you. The bad guys probably assumed I had the Book the whole time." She frowned. "In fact, both Alice and William accused me of hiding it when I called them after I arrived in San Francisco. Even the Elders thought I had it."

She didn't wait for his reply. Not that he knew what to tell her. With two attempts on her life since she returned to the States, he'd wager she was right. Instead, she flipped a couple pages over to the strange writing. "Do you have any idea what language this is? I don't recognize it."

He bent and examined the pages. The letters were a mix of English and Theban, but the words were still gibberish to him. He shook his head. "Her notes disappeared from her office. I had hoped they had been hidden with her Book of Shadows." He glanced at Bebe. "Or that you had them."

Her expression became quizzical. "And I would give them to you?"

He nodded and his gaze returned to the strange script before she could ask why. Hope that Bebe would continue Natasha's research was too much to ask her at this point. "It's definitely her handwriting. It's not a language I know though."

She sighed in defeat. "How am I supposed to know what she was up to if I can't read her notes? Does Granny E. know?"

He shook his head. "Not all of it. And I doubt if she knows Natasha's code."

"Do you have any bright ideas?"

"Not one you'll like."

She raised an eyebrow, a suspicious gleam in her eyes.

"We're going to have to ask for help."

Chapter 16

Bebe laid down the book she'd been trying to read all afternoon, her mind distracted with the waiting. Tiffany had disappeared shortly after lunch, muttering something about shopping. Caesar had disappeared into his office to deal with his private businesses. He poked his head out about three to give her a paper copy of an e-mail from Granny E.

Bebe couldn't help smiling as she had read it. The clipped style was definitely Granny E.'s and seeing today's date reassured her.

To: aha40bcalexandria@augustinecoven.net
From: noreply@google.com on behalf of hpze23842191@silverbear.com
Sent: 19-12-2010 19:23 PM
Subject: Delay
C
Flight delayed. Gatwick fogged in. UnNorm? Rumors flying here.
Keep my baby safe!
Be in on Saturday. Will come straight to your place.
Z

Sweet Goddess, could Granny E. be right that the fog in London wasn't natural? Could Caesar have arranged the bad weather to keep her out of the way? The delay nixed any confirmation Granny E. could have given her concerning his story. And the e-mail was from a public terminal.

Bebe had even slipped a telephone handset into the bathroom and tried to call Granny E.'s cell, only to have it roll over to voice-mail. Damn, there was no other way to contact her grandmother directly.

But then, did it matter? Bebe was pretty much at Caesar Augustine's mercy as it was. But he could have drained her and buried her in the back yard at his San Francisco place, so why bother with games?

Pressing her fingertips to her temples, she tried a meditation exercise. The die had been cast when she had shown him the Book. Objective reasoning was what she needed, not her own niggling doubts and childhood terrors.

The fog could be the work of whoever wanted her dead. And despite the fact that Caesar ruled the entire vampire race west of the Mississippi and had money out the ass, his behavior earlier indicated he resented his nature. Did he resent it enough to give up all that power and wealth if the opportunity presented itself? If Grandma had found some kind of antibody to the V-virus, could she have been reverse engineering a cure for those affected?

Giving up on the meditation, Bebe rose from the couch and paced back and forth in front of the fireplace. The huge white brick mantel dominated the formal living room. Her bare feet left faint tracks in the gold Persian rug. Is a cure what he wanted from her? Was that the real purpose behind his innuendo and his wild kisses? String her along until she found a cure for him? She sure couldn't continue Grandma's research if she were dead, so he had every reason to keep her alive.

The deepening gloom in the cherry-paneled room seemed a good place to examine her own motivations for giving in to his attempts at seduction. She could have walked out the front door at any time. Tiffany had woken Anne before she left for her shopping excursion, but neither Caesar or Anne had checked on her all afternoon. Well, other than the e-mail delivery. A thrill had run up her arm and through her body just at the brief touch of his fingers when he handed her the sheet. And the looks he had given her over lunch, like he was stripping off her clothes with his eyes alone . . .

So why was being at Caesar's mercy such an exciting prospect? He wasn't model cute, but then pretty boys had never been her style. His sense of humor, when he wasn't deliberately trying to scare the daylights out of her, was as dry as her own. Over lunch, they had a pleasant conversation concerning the latest books, most of which she hadn't had a chance to read yet. They avoided the unpleasant truths hanging over their heads, and not even his mug of blood bothered her, she realized with a jolt.

Unfortunately, not even Dan Brown's latest best-selling thriller could keep her attention when all she could think about was Caesar's delicious body in those ridiculous cartoon pajamas. She had a sneaking suspicion they were a gift from either Tiffany or Alex, and Caesar, being ever Mr. Etiquette, had politely thanked them before stuffing them in a drawer in his San Francisco house. Even though most of that first night was a blur, she distinctly remembered Alex having to dig for them.

And the pajama bottoms had left nothing to the imagination. Not his finely honed butt. Not his long legs. And definitely not his erection.

"Would you like some hot chocolate? Anne's making some for Tiffany."

Bebe jumped at Ptolemy's voice. Heat flooded her cheeks.

"Anything wrong, Doctor?" he said.

"Um, no." She frantically searched her memory. What had he just asked her?

"I see." He shot her a mischievous grin. "Just lusting after my brother, hmmm?"

Horror engulfed her. Had she leaked her thoughts?

Ptolemy's grin widened, his canines shining dully in the thickening dusk. "I don't have to read your mind, Doctor. Your face tells me everything I need to know."

Something about the way he spoke sent a frisson of uncertainty through her nerves. Caesar may try to scare her to prove a point, but Ptolemy seemed to enjoy head games a little too much for her comfort.

She gave him a wan smile. "I hope my face is telling you that Anne's hot chocolate sounds delicious right now."

He didn't speak, merely gestured for her to go before him and followed her to the kitchen.

Rich cinnamon hit her nose as soon as she pushed the swinging door. Undertones of cocoa drifted in the wake of the spice. Anne pulled a baking dish from the wall oven and set it on a cooling rack. Her long sleeves were rolled to her elbows and specks of flour dotted the front of the baggy slate t-shirt.

Vampires getting domestic?

The more time Bebe spent with them, the more she realized how screwed up her preconceptions were. "That smells delicious. What are you making?"

Anne smiled, a soft, shy look on her face. If Bebe hadn't seen the tiny woman in full vampire mode in San Francisco, she'd never believed Anne was one.

"It's my grandmother's cinnamon bread. She always made it at Christmas." Anne sighed. "I may not be able to eat it anymore, but I still love the smell this time of year. Phillippa, Tiffany and the daytime staff usually enjoy the honors. Would you like some?"

While she spoke, she had pulled off the oven mitts and already had a cup of cocoa, complete with mini-marshmallows, sitting in front of Bebe.

Bebe swallowed. Anne had to have heard her answer to Ptolemy all the way in the living room. Maybe she wouldn't have made it out of the house after all. But her stomach rumbled at the smell of the fresh-baked bread. She perched on the same black, leather-covered stool she had used at lunch and nodded. "That sounds great."

Tiffany burst through the kitchen door, a huge red cloth sack packed full and slung over one thin shoulder and a cell phone glued to her ear with her free hand. "What do you want on your pizza, Doc? It's ringing now."

Pizza? If Bebe's mouth watered from the smell of fresh-baked bread, it practically gushed at the thought of pepperoni and mozzarella. Goddess, she hadn't had pizza since she left for Africa. "Anything, but anchovies." She took a huge gulp of cocoa. The temperature was perfect, and the smooth chocolaty milk slid down her throat.

Ptolemy scowled at the teen. "Tiffany, Mai brought in groceries for you and the doctor."

Tiffany dropped the bag on the breakfast table to flip him the bird while she ordered an "Extra-large Super Deluxe, hold the anchovies and jalapenos." She crossed the room and poked her head in the fridge. "Regular cola okay with you?" she mouthed to Bebe.

Bebe grinned and nodded. Screw the healthy stuff. If she had a target painted on her forehead, she might as well enjoy some decent junk food.

"You'd better not leave that crap to rot in our refrigerator," Ptolemy muttered. Anne smothered a smile as she sat a plate of steaming bread in front of Bebe.

Tiffany clicked her cell shut and dropped it in the front pocket of her jeans. "You're just jealous you were born too early to enjoy real cuisine. And it's not *your* refrigerator."

"Then you'd better not leave that pizza to rot in *my* refrigerator," Caesar said.

Bebe nearly fell off the stool at his sudden appearance. She swiveled around to face him. "Quit sneaking!"

A dark eyebrow rose. "I didn't know it was possible to sneak in my own house," he said. "And you have marshmallow on your nose."

Before she could move, he reached up and swiped the white froth off the tip. Then he pressed his finger against her partly opened lips. Instinctively, she licked the sugary foam from his fingertip. Her entire body flamed at the intimacy of the act. By heat in his eyes, he enjoyed the display a little too much. She could no longer meet his intense gaze and took a sudden interest in the marshmallows. Damn, that didn't help either as her mind replayed what just happened and added its own erotic twist.

Thankfully, he stepped away, putting some distance between his body and her overactive imagination. He paused at the table and tugged the drawstring open to peer inside the bag.

Tiffany raced across the room and slapped his hand away. "They're holiday presents, and you don't get yours until Duncan and Alex come down and Phil arrives."

"I'm here, kid. Now what's the emergency about, Caesar?" Phillippa stood in the doorway leading into the utility room between the main house and Caesar's massive garage.

"I promise I'm not asking you to interfere, but Ziva's stuck in London due to the weather, and Bebe and I needed your opinion on something." Caesar set down the mug Anne had just handed him and disappeared back through the swinging door.

On the door's backswing, Duncan and Alex appeared. And the normally boisterous and smooth Alex Stanton stammered when he saw their guest. "H-h-hello, Phillippa."

"Stanton." A penguin could have skated on her words. But her greeting to Duncan was far warmer, and she positively raved over Anne when the tiny vampire handed her a plate of cinnamon bread.

Interesting. Phillippa's attitude reminded Bebe more of a woman insulted by a suitor than any supernatural rivalry. What could Alex possibly have done to offend Phillippa? A necking session gone awry?

She tilted her head at Alex and Phillippa and raised an inquiring eyebrow as Tiffany handed her the cola. Tiffany grinned and mouthed, "Tell you when the vamps go to bed."

Bebe took a sip from the ice-cold can. This group acted more like a family than her own blood did, and they had welcomed her in their little group with no demands and no questions asked. The realization sent a pang through her heart.

Caesar returned with the Book of Shadows in his hand. "Phillippa, I wanted you to look—"

"No!" Tiffany held up her hand to stop him. "We're opening presents first."

"It's Friday," he said, a hint of amusement in his voice.

"Yeah, and with this group—" Her index finger waved in a circle to indicate everyone in the room. "Murphy is the one, true god, so we're doing presents tonight."

Phillippa grinned. "I kind of thought the same thing." She pivoted to drag in a large shopping bag from the utility room.

Caesar gave Tiffany an indulgent smile as well. "Then I guess we're exchanging gifts before we get down to business." He handed the Book to Bebe.

While the male vampires and Anne disappeared upstairs to retrieve hidden gifts, Tiffany explained the bizarre ritual to Bebe.

"Between the Saturnalia, Yule, Christmas, Hanukah, Kwanzaa, blah, blah, blah," Tiffany said, ticking off each holiday on a finger. "We picked the third Saturday in December for a joint celebration. Anne usually cooks a ham or turkey for me and Phil with all the fixings, but, and no offense, Doc, I just know the shit will hit the fan when your Grandma gets here tomorrow."

Duncan strode into the room, a small pile of boxes in his arms. "Tiffany, watch your language or I will wash your mouth out." He glared at the teen before adding, "Again."

"Sorry."

Bebe placed a hand over her mouth to cover her amusement. Tiffany didn't sound the least bit sorry at all.

Once everyone was back in the kitchen, packages were exchanged, and paper started flying.

Tiffany shocked Bebe by handing her a small navy blue box with an intricate silver ribbon. Her eyes watered at the girl's generosity. "But I don't have anything for you."

Tiffany scowled. "It wasn't right those assholes shot up all your belongings and left you with jack, and as far as I'm concerned, you're part of the family now." Then she shot Bebe a wicked grin. "If you want to do something for me, you could take me to see the new *Saw* movie."

"Tiffany!"

The group cracked up at Duncan's indignant tone as he scowled at his niece.

Bebe ripped off the ribbon and opened the box. Nestled inside was a small silver pentacle on a matching herringbone chain. She met Tiffany's anxious eyes. "You shouldn't have, but thank you," she whispered before wrapping her arms around the girl's frail shoulders and squeezing.

And to Bebe's amazement, everyone else in the room seemed to share Tiffany's sentiment. Except, when the hell could they have done all this? She had just arrived in Los Angeles last night.

Phillippa gave her a small wooden case containing an assortment of herbs and a mortar and pestle. Duncan presented a matching case with small vials of essential oils. Alex's package was the proverbial M.D.'s bag, itself an antique by the wear and tear, but complete with a modern stethoscope, blood pressure cuff, and a digital thermometer. Anne's present was a small suture kit with anti-septic pads that fit neatly into the medical bag.

Even Ptolemy handed her a box. Half-afraid, she pulled the gold ribbon loose and tore off the blood-red paper. Inside the box lay a knife. The ivory handle was inlayed with gold and the bronze edge gleamed under the fluorescent lighting. From the yellowing of the ivory, the piece had to be as ancient as the vampire who gave it to her. Her airways clogged in disbelief. Something like this should be in a freaking museum.

Even Caesar had a shocked look on his face when he saw the contents of the box.

"I can't accept this," she whispered.

Ptolemy's face, however, was gravely serious as he shook his head. "In honor of your first victory over your enemies, Doctor."

She couldn't begin to understand his motivations. One minute he acted as if she were beneath him. The next, he'd protect her.

She nodded, unable to speak. Glancing at the last unopened package, her hands started to shake, and she placed the box with the knife on the counter before her nerveless fingers dropped it.

Various expressions of concern surrounded her, with Anne obviously the most worried. Bebe suppressed a wince. Had the tiny vampire blabbed about catching Caesar and her making out in the kitchen in San Francisco?

"It's very rude not to open your host's gift, Dr. Zachary." Caesar's warm breath teased her ear.

She carefully pulled the ivory ribbon loose and lifted the lid. Cushioned in soft silk lay two exquisite teardrop-shaped pearl earrings. Holding her breath, she picked up one of the gorgeous pieces. The wire loop and setting were obviously handcrafted even to her untrained eye. The jewelry had to be centuries old, if not millennia, just like the knife Ptolemy had given her. Earrings fit for a queen.

Or a princess.

She gulped and looked up at Caesar. His pleased expression faded. The last thing she wanted was to insult or disappoint him, but she couldn't accept these. The money and clothes had been bad enough, even if she intended to repay him, but this . . .

This gift was too extravagant.

Too tender.

Way too intimate.

How long had the pearls been in his possession? Had the earrings belonged to another sister? His mother?

Oh sweet Goddess, was it even worse? Had they belonged to his long-dead wife?

She dropped the earring back in the cushion of silk and slapped the lid back on top. "I can't accept these." She held the box out to him.

He didn't reach for it, just stared at her with that damned impassive look on his handsome face. "As I said, it's rude to refuse your host's gift, Dr. Zachary."

Why did he have to put her on the spot like this? Was it some quirk of vampire culture that escaped her? It was bad enough accepting the clothes and money, but that was sheer necessity. Her lungs burned, reminding her that she'd stopped breathing. She sucked in air, desperately searching for the right words. Anything to get out of this situation.

Why couldn't that damn witch slice her throat properly last night? Then she wouldn't have an insulted vampire in front of her now.

No. With her luck, Caesar would have tried Turning her if her throat had been cut.

Tucking an escaped curl behind her ear, she tried again. "Look, I'm sure in your day this would be a perfectly appropriate holiday gift, but things are different now."

His eyebrow lifted. "Yes, I've noticed how manners are sorely lacking in the latest generations."

Her pulse jumped at his acid tone, and she slid down from her stool and jabbed a finger at his chest. "Maybe the real problem is your arrogant attitude. Maybe you can buy and sell every other woman in California. But you can't buy me," she said through clenched teeth. She slammed the box down on the counter before she stormed through the swinging door. Total silence followed in her wake as she stomped upstairs.

Jerk had to go and ruin a perfectly lovely evening. Damn him anyway.

Not until she threw herself on her bed did she realize she left the Book of Shadows on the kitchen counter as well. The hot chocolate and marshmallows became a lead weight in her stomach.

Grandma's coded notes.

In a room full of vampires.

Chapter 17

Caesar stood still in shock while the entire group stared at him with various levels of disbelief on their faces. What the Hades just happened? Any other wom-an he'd ever met would have been salivating over such jewelry.

"Smooth move, Ex-lax," Tiffany muttered.

"I didn't do anything wrong!"

"You put her in a difficult position, Your Highness." Anne's soft voice re-proached him. "Bebe is a proud woman. It's difficult enough for her to accept your assistance right now, but the extravagance of your gift . . ." She shook her head.

"But Ptolemy—"

"While the knife may be a phallic symbol to some, it doesn't say I'm buying my way into her bed the way multi-million dollar jewelry does, brother dear." Ptolemy smirked.

Caesar dug his clenched fists into his thighs. Otherwise, the urge to punch the shit out of Ptolemy would take over. "I wasn't buying my way into anything."

"Go apologize before she does something stupid," Phillippa said.

A chill stole over his soul. "Like what?"

"Right now?" Phillippa shot him a knowing smile. "She's planning on smash-ing the bedroom window, shimmying down the portico awning and hitching a ride with the pizza delivery boy."

The intercom clicked on at the same time a resounding boom echoed through the house. Mai's voice crackled through the speaker. "Duncan, please remind Tif-fany that security protocol at Master Augustine's precludes pizza deliveries."

Caesar closed his eyes. A familiar pain popped behind his left eyeball. What happened to the old days when it was just him, Selene, and Ptolemy? Things were so much simpler then. Suck on an occasional cow. Stay out of the sunshine. Don't get your head cut off.

Much simpler.

Another boom came from upstairs as Duncan punched the reply button.

"Should one of us go up and tell the doc the windows are made of bulletproof glass before she hurts herself?" Alex said.

"Tiffany's on her way out to the gate, Mai," Duncan replied.

Boom.

"Do you need assistance in the main house?" Mai must have heard Bebe bang-ing on the window, whether through the intercom or from outside didn't matter.

Boom.

"No. Dr. Zachary is exhibiting her displeasure with a Christmas gift. Stay at your post."

Caesar tried to ignore the wry humor in Duncan's voice.

Boom.

"If you want any furniture left, Caesar, you'd better get your ass up there."

He opened his eyes to find Phillippa openly grinning at him. Other than his siblings, she was the only one who dared speak to him in that manner, but he wasn't about to argue with one of the few people who could kick his ass. He pivoted on his heels and marched upstairs to teach the little witch a lesson she wouldn't soon forget.

———•———

Bebe was tired. Tired of being manipulated. Tired of being used. Tired of having no control over her life. No, she wasn't going to lie on a bed in a fucking vampire's mansion and be a victim anymore.

Bebe rolled off the mattress. She hadn't bothered with the room's lamps, relying on the hallway lighting to pick her way across the room. Her fingers itched to hit something. Anything to get rid of the anger crawling across her nerves. She needed out of this house. A car horn honked nearby. She threw her psyche in the direction of the sound. Tiffany's pizza delivery boy. If she could just hitch a ride with him . . .

She had to get out of the house first, and she wouldn't make it out any door with five vampires downstairs. Rage gave her strength, and grabbing the chair at the writing desk, she flung it at the window. With a deep boom, it bounced off and landed on the bed.

Damn you, Grandma!

Picking up the antique chair, Bebe swung it against the window with everything her five-foot-four frame held. It only resulted in another deep booming sound that rattled her arms.

I don't need your stupid Book.

Boom.

I don't want your stupid coven!

She threw the chair at the window, and it bounced off again.

And fuck you and your stupid earrings, Caesar Augustine!

Blinking back tears, Bebe heaved the heavy chair against the glass. Muttering a spell under her breath to transform more of the wood's potential energy as well as her fury into kinetic energy, she was rewarded with a sharp *tink*. A thin crack appeared, spider-webbing its way through the window. Except neither the chair or her arms had any strength left. Breathing heavily, she contemplated what to try next.

"What the Hades do you think you're doing?"

She whirled to find Caesar silhouetted in the doorway of the bedroom, his eyes glowing neon yellow amidst the shadows cast on his face. Damn, she'd been so angry she hadn't been "listening" for anyone coming up the stairs. The chair dropped from her nerveless fingers. When it hit the thick carpet, it disintegrated thanks to her spell, its loss of potential energy crumbling the wood to dust. Her fury drained away until only ice-cold fear remained. The air crackled with his anger.

Well, she wasn't going down without a fight. She summoned a fireball, but the magickal energy did nothing to warm her fingertips. "I'm leaving. The witch covens already think you're holding me prisoner." Assuming she was reading between the lines of Granny E.'s e-mail correctly.

Blasting the window would be her only option. She should have anticipated the vampires used reinforced glass. But whacking the chair against the panes had been satisfying. And with a start, she realized she planned to jump out a window, drop to the awning, and let herself fall to the shrubbery below.

What in the thousand names of the Goddess had she been thinking?

She returned her attention to the pissed off vampire. His eyes closed, and he released the metal doorknob he'd crushed. She wasn't sure he realized what he'd done to the device. He rubbed his temple instead of reaching for her as she half expected. When he opened his eyes, they had faded to a soft gold. "You're not a prisoner, Bebe." Even though he made no move toward her, his voice caressed her. "However, if you insist on leaving, would you please use the front door instead of destroying my home?"

His weary tone surprised her. She had expected threats, pleading, even his damn frigid logic, not total capitulation.

Her eyes narrowed. How the hell did his mind work? First, bribing her with jewelry, now letting her leave? Damn, would she ever figure out this man? "And neither you nor any of your people will stop me?"

"There's no reason for you to break your neck in an ill-conceived escape."

"It wasn't ill-conceived." Irritation snapped to life inside her, mostly because he was right.

He crossed his arms, his eyes eerily cat-like in the dimness. "You're afraid of heights, and yet you're planning to jump out a second-story window."

"I—" She swallowed hard. How could this man read her so well without penetrating her shields? "I'm not afraid of heights."

He snorted. "Really? With the death-grip you had on my coat when we were leaving your hotel room in San Francisco?" he said, the weary amusement clear in his voice. He unfolded his arms and crossed the room until he was inches away.

"I was afraid of getting shot that night." Electricity sizzled through her nerves at his presence. Damn, she wasn't about to back away and let him know how much his nearness disturbed her.

"Of course." He reached for her, his cool fingertips stroking her cheek, feeling so good against the half-scabbed knife wound. "I don't want anything to happen to you."

She glanced down at the fireball in her hand. Did she really want to incinerate the man standing before her? After the effort she'd spent saving his life? After all the times he'd saved hers in the last few days? When all he'd done was try to be nice and give her a holiday present? Okay, maybe an incredibly extravagant present. But did that mean he deserved a fiery death?

Dammit, all she wanted was to get out of these stupid political games.

To practice medicine and help those who really needed her aid.

To get her life back.

She clenched her fist to extinguish the witchfire.

Almost as if he knew it was safe, his head dipped to hers. Heat of a different kind flooded her as his lips kissed and nibbled her mouth. His arms wrapped around her waist, tugging her closer.

She didn't object. If anything, she added another want to her list. Her breasts cried for the pressure of his chest against them. Her fingers threaded through the short strands of his hair, seeking any and all additional contact. Tongues tangled and danced.

And before she was ready, he pulled away. Never before had a simple kiss left her so unsatisfied. She wanted more. Far more than she should even dare.

Hesitantly, he released her. "If you insist on leaving, you might want to eat before you go. Tiffany went to the trouble of ordering you dinner." He pivoted and stalked toward the door.

"Wait."

He paused but didn't look at her.

She couldn't stop her words. She had to know.

"Whose earrings were they?"

He froze, the eerie vampire stillness nearly sending her nerves into overload. When she didn't think he would answer, his quiet voice cut through the tension. "They were my mother's. You remind me of her. The same strength to defy everyone to do what you believe is right. I thought you should have them." There had to be more to his story, but he was out of sight before she could dredge up the guts to ask.

Damn, she really *had* hurt his feelings earlier.

Not that the stubborn jackass would admit it.

Never before had she been so unsure of anything. She pressed her fingers to her mouth, only to feel lips swollen from his kiss. She should leave here. She could march out the front door. She had no doubt now that Caesar would keep his word, but where would she go?

Granny E.'s? Her paternal grandmother had always shunned the extra security most high priestesses employed. Since Grandpa Ben was probably with her in London, one elderly housekeeper couldn't protect Bebe from the folks determined to get her out of the way.

And what about the Book? It was still sitting in the kitchen where she'd left it. She couldn't leave it with total strangers.

Okay, maybe not total strangers, but after her little ungracious temper tantrum, the last thing she wanted was to face everyone in the kitchen.

A low rumble came from her belly. She hadn't touched the heavenly scented bread Anne had served her.

Maybe she should swallow her pride.

No matter how big of a lump it was.

She slunk down the staircase. A soft murmur of voices confirmed her sense that everyone was still in the kitchen. The conversation stopped as soon as she touched the door. Taking a deep breath, she shoved it open.

To find everyone staring at her. Was it that obvious that Caesar had been kissing her? Sweat broke out on her palms. What had she expected?

She met Caesar's eyes from his seat at the kitchen table. They had returned to their natural hazel, and they widened at her appearance in the doorway. Then she noticed the Book of Shadows was still sitting on the island where she'd left it. Sucking in a deep breath, she shifted until she found Tiffany, perched on a stool and digging a pizza slice out of the box sitting on the island.

Bebe cleared her throat before she said, "Is the pizza offer still open?"

"Already filled a plate for you." Tiffany scooted the said plate with two slices across the granite countertop until it rested next to Bebe's half-filled mug of cocoa, the now-cooled plate of cinnamon bread, and her soda can.

She climbed onto the stool, took a bite and nearly had an orgasm then and there. Tangy tomato blended with spicy pepperoni, sausage and an array of vegetables, but best of all was the mellow flavor of mozzarella.

"You two had something you wanted me to look at?" Phillippa said from where she sat next to Tiffany.

"Yes. Actually we could use everyone's input." Caesar rose from his chair and crossed to the island. He raised a questioning eyebrow. Bebe nodded, and he reached for the Book of Shadows. Flipping to the mysterious writing, he said, "Do you recognize this?" He pushed the Book across the granite.

Phillippa turned the Book around and frowned while the other four vampires gathered to look over her shoulder. Well, the three guys looked over her shoulder. Anne peered around her elbow.

"It's Natasha's handwriting, but it looks like some kind of code," Phillippa said. Her gaze flicked up to meet Bebe's. "I take it you don't recognize it."

Bebe hesitated. Not wanting to be rude, she still needed to know who or what she was dealing with when it came to Phillippa. She didn't necessarily agree with Grandma Petrov's choice of trusting those outside of the coven, but all the old rules had been thrown out the window the moment she'd returned to San Francisco. "A truth for a truth?"

Phillippa's brow twisted in confusion before she nodded.

Bebe took a deep breath before asking, "What are you?"

Phillippa sighed before answering. "My mother was a nymph, but the sperm donor was an Olympian. I considered your grandmother my friend." She gave Bebe a stern frown. "And that's all of my personal information you need to know."

Demigoddess. Wow. Not what she was expecting. Bebe took a bite of Anne's cinnamon bread, chewing as she considered Phillippa's bombshell. Demigods were rare these days. And due to the rivalries between the pantheons, the few remaining on earth hadn't bothered to band together and demand a seat on the International Council.

Bebe pointed to the strange script. "That section wasn't in the Book of Shadows before I left for Africa, so Grandma had to have added it in the last few years."

"Do either of you know what this text is supposed to be?" Duncan asked.

Bebe bit her lower lip. With the vamps super-hearing, there was no freaking way she could ask Caesar privately. Taking a leap of faith, she dropped her outer shield and sent a tentative probe to him.

Caesar?

To his credit, he didn't jump at the sudden intrusion, but she could sense the surface of his surprise.

Yes?

How do you think your people will handle learning about Grandma's research?

The link was silent as he mulled her question, but his worry came through loud and clear. He'd obviously been questioning the wisdom of informing other vampires of what Grandma was up to. *I don't believe they will overreact, but I cannot guarantee it. However, full disclosure may be necessary to adequately protect you and the Book.*

Time to take another chance. She took a second deep breath and met Duncan's look squarely. "We believe Grandma was doing some kind of genetic research. She had discovered certain witches are resistant to the V-virus."

Six sets of eyes stared at her in stunned disbelief. Several seconds passed before Duncan's dry voice commented. "In other words, the attempts on your life are about more than the White Rose succession."

"We don't know that for sure," Caesar said.

"Who else knows about this?" Ptolemy's tone was more animalistic snarl than human, and his eyes started glowing. Bebe silently thanked the Goddess for Caesar's comforting presence. Otherwise, she had the definite impression Ptolemy would be smacking the shit out of her.

"We don't know. Bebe wasn't even aware of Natasha's research until I told her," Caesar said.

"So she claims," Ptolemy shot back. "Have you read her to be sure?"

Fear rippled down Bebe's spine. She'd managed to keep Caesar out of her head when he tried to read her at the auction and later in her hotel room, but if all five vampires joined forces, she wouldn't have a mind left when they were done.

"That's unnecessary, Ptolemy," Caesar said.

Phillippa twisted on her stool to eye Ptolemy. "*I* didn't even know until now, so you need to calm down, child." She turned back to examine the Book, flipping through additional pages. "It explains why Natasha asked me to keep the Book for Bebe." She looked up at Bebe again. "And if others know about the witches' resistance to the virus, it would explain the cooperation between your attackers at Anthony's."

Bebe popped another bite of bread in her mouth. Something didn't quite make sense in Grandma's plan. She swallowed before she said, "Why not leave the Book in the wardrobe's secret compartment though? She could have warded the nymph hole so that no one but her Confirmed successor could remove the Book." The memory of sitting under the huge oak in the back yard of Grandma's house and reading one of her favorite novels during summer vacation made her sigh. "If she'd left the Book where William or Alice could find it, my two idiot cousins wouldn't have started the asinine court battle."

Caesar and Ptolemy shared an uncomfortable look that irritated her.

"Would you two stop trying to protect me? I'm not entirely stupid. One of my cousins is behind the assassination attempts, and you suspect it's Alice." Her outburst was worth the surprised look on Caesar's face. She tore into the slice of pizza to keep from smiling.

"How did you find out?" he finally asked.

She eyed him with what she hoped was a disdainful stare. "You know the problem with you vampires is that you're arrogant. Unless someone's another vampire or older than dirt—" She shot an apologetic glance at Phillippa. "No offense."

"None taken," Phillippa said with a smile.

Bebe turned back to Caesar. "You think their knowledge and opinions mean nothing."

Tiffany shot a tiny fist into the air. "Go, Bebe!"

Bebe sighed. She could sympathize with the teen, but with too many questions, she needed to focus. "Rather than carving her own life, Alice would rather stew in her jealousy. It doesn't take a rocket scientist to put two and two together. And—" Caesar deserved the truth no matter how much it pained her. "I overheard Alex saying you had traced the hotel gunmen to Uncle Lionel," she finished in a small voice to the stunned looks from the vampires who'd been in San Francisco.

"You'd better watch out for your job, Duncan," Phillippa said, amusement in her voice.

"So it would seem," he answered, but the twinkle in his eyes indicated he shared the demigoddess's humor.

Caesar crossed his arms, a perturbed look on his face. "So is there a point to this besides attempting to embarrass me in front of my people?

Bebe chewed on her bottom lip. Maybe she should have kept her mouth shut, but she was tired of the head games. "Grandma went to a lot of trouble to get the Book out of San Francisco after adding her coded notes to it. She's not the type to do something without a definite purpose. So what was the purpose in putting her notes in the Book to begin with, and why give the Book to Phillippa for safe keeping?"

"The doctor has a point." Phillippa pushed back her plate and propped her elbows on the countertop, her chin resting on her entwined fingers. Her eyes narrowed. "Natasha was sure Bebe would come down to get the book from me."

"Because she left a letter for me in the secret compartment of the wardrobe, where the Book was normally hidden." Bebe slid her own plate aside, no longer hungry even though she'd only taken a few bites. Instead, her stomach ached as worry began gnawing on the contents.

Phillippa tapped the Book with a manicured index finger. "You said yourself,

Natasha did nothing without a reason. Why not just give me the coded notes? Why put them in her Book of Shadows?" She raised an eyebrow. "What is it about that wardrobe that she knew you'd find a way to access it?"

"I-I don't know," Bebe said. Goddess, she didn't want to go through the marriages and family trees again. That thought started the acid churning in her stomach.

"Yes, you do," Caesar prompted. "You were determined to pay more than it was worth at the auction."

Bebe snorted. "So says the man who *outbid* me for it." She shook her head then shrugged. "The only thing it meant to me was sentimental. I used to hide in it when I was a child whenever I was upset about something."

"That's where I found you," Caesar said.

She didn't realize she was trembling until his hand engulfed hers and gave a comforting squeeze. She turned to him and understanding dawned. The night of the funerals. He had told the truth the other night. He had been there.

She'd put on the brave face Grandma Petrov had insisted, but as soon as the ceremony finished, she had raced for the comfort of the wardrobe. She wasn't sure how long she'd been in there, weeping, when the dark man had come, offering to take away the pain. Grandma had appeared, scolding the dark man.

When she had asked Grandma about it the next morning, Grandma had said she'd dreamed the whole thing. And like everything else from those horrible days, she'd blocked it from her memory. Goddess, what other knowledge had she forgotten that her survival now depended?

With an effort, she dragged her attention back to Phillippa. "I'm sorry. What did you say?"

"I said," came Phillippa's dry voice, "you need some kind of key to decipher Natasha's code." She tapped the incomprehensible pages with a forefinger. "She knew the Book would be preserved and given to Bebe no matter what. My guess is she destroyed any other notes due to her suspected conspiracy. The only reason I can think of to move the Book is to separate it from the key."

Bebe shook her head. "But Caesar's guard Stan and I checked the wardrobe. We didn't find anything else."

"Whoa, people!" Tiffany waved her hands. "We're making a lot of assumptions here." She jabbed a black fingernail at the text. "This crap may be Grandma Natasha's secret recipe for matzo balls for all we know."

Tiffany's attitude restored Bebe's humor. "If Grandma Petrov ever deigned to enter the kitchen except to castigate our cook, I'd agree with you." Remembering the e-mail earlier, her throat closed in fear. She turned to Caesar. "You said Granny E. didn't know all of Grandma Petrov's plans. Did Granny E. know about the resistance to the virus?"

"She knows your step-grandfather, Ben Epstein, is immune. He—" Caesar started.

Then something happened Bebe never thought she'd see. His pale olive face flamed scarlet.

He gave a little cough before continuing. "Ben's helped certain witch couples who could not have children."

Tiffany giggled. "Talk about donating for the cause."

Caesar regained his composure by glaring at the girl. "I cannot vouch for any other information Ziva might know. Other than the evening of your parents' funeral, the three of us were never alone. I'm afraid we were all occupied with more pressing concerns that night, and Natasha would never have mentioned something like this in front of someone she wasn't sure about. Why?"

A terrible suspicion niggled Bebe's brain. Her heart tried to claw its way out of her constricted throat. She choked out the words anyway. "Are you sure this afternoon's e-mail was from Granny E.?"

He gave a slow nod as her concerns were mirrored on his face, but his attempt at a smile didn't quite reach his eyes. "I'm fairly sure. She's one of the few that has that particular address of mine, other than my sister and the people in this room, and no one could have used her e-mail account without her password. Do you want me to contact Eleanor Hyde-Smith?"

His reassuring smile, though sweet, did not reassure her one bit. She shook her head. "It would be better if I did. You're already in enough trouble with my people from the sounds of it, and a high priestess would respect a request from another witch."

Phoning Alastair's mother ranked right up with being staked on top of a fire ant hill.

Naked.

With honey smeared all over her body.

But protocol demanded that Granny E. notify Mrs. Hyde-Smith of her presence in England.

"Before a vampire, you mean." He checked his watch. "It's two in the morning their time. Are you sure you want to wake her at this hour?"

She couldn't stop her exasperated sigh. "For just once, could we please do things my way?"

He chuckled. "Well, since you did say please . . ."

Two minutes later, he had produced Mrs. Hyde-Smith's phone number and a portable receiver. Bebe said a silent, calming prayer. She didn't relish calling Alistair's mother after refusing to marry her son, but she had to make sure Granny E. was okay.

The phone rang several times before someone answered, "Hyde-Smith residence."

"M-m-may I speak with Eleanor Hyde-Smith, please?"

"Who is this?" The woman's nasty tone indicated she didn't appreciate the late night call.

"Bebe Zachary. I apologize for phoning so late, but this is very important. It's about my grandmother, Ziva Epstein."

"Brigid in a basket! This is Eleanor. Is it really you, Bebe?" Now the woman at the other end sounded positively frantic. "Are you safe? Rumors here are flying that you've been captured by vampires."

Bebe flicked her gaze to Caesar, who listened to the whole conversation with his freaking vampire hearing. She suppressed a smile. Tiffany was the only person in the kitchen who *couldn't* hear both sides.

At her telepathic question, he nodded confirmation that she was speaking to Eleanor Hyde-Smith. Since Eleanor was one of the witch representatives on the I.C., Bebe didn't doubt him.

Deciding not to address the vampire issue, she said, "Yes, ma'am, I'm fine. I'm trying to reach my grandmother. Bad weather delayed her flight out of London, and I thought she might be at your estate."

"She's here, child, along with Ben." Eleanor's tone pronounced trouble. "I'm afraid I have bad news. An unseelie attacked the airport shuttle they rode between Heathrow and Gatwick. Thank Brigid, we were able to extract them from the accident scene before the bobbies arrived. Use of magick such as that alerts every fae and witch in Britain. She's alive, but she's in terrible shape. Been unconscious since we found her. Ben's conscious but not too coherent yet. Apparently the bloody bastard hit him with some kind of confusion spell."

Bebe's heart threatened to explode where it lodged in her throat. "When-when did this happen?"

"Early yesterday morning. About seven our time. I would have rung you . . ."

The rest of Eleanor's words faded as Bebe calculated the time difference between London and Los Angeles. From the shocked look on Caesar's face, he realized the problem at the moment she did. Granny E. was attacked around midnight last night. There was no way she could have sent that e-mail.

"...hearing all the problems concerning Natasha's succession. Is there anything I can do to help, dear? Are you somewhere safe?"

Bebe forced her mind to register Mrs. Hyde-Smith's words and answered. "When Granny wakes or Grandpa Ben recovers, please tell them I'm all right. I'll call again later to check on them."

"Wait! Where can we reach—"

Bebe clicked off the phone. "We've got to get out of this house. Now."

Chapter 18

A trap.

Caesar cursed himself as he gave orders to evacuate the mansion. He should have known better. Documents could so easily be forged this day and age. Not to mention all of Natasha's fears of an internal conspiracy within White Rose. Apparently, the problem extended to Ziva's coven as well.

No, that wasn't the only problem. He couldn't lie to himself. He had wanted Ziva to tell him to keep Bebe here with him. He wanted the excuse to spend time with the beautiful doctor, to verbally spar with her, to enjoy the fire that coursed through him every time he touched her.

And now his slip in common sense had put her in danger. Kensai and Jamal's arrival to relieve Mai and Miko would be the time to strike.

Which meant they had less than ten minutes to get Bebe out of the house.

He reached out telepathically. *Kensai?*

Yes, Master Augustine?

Where are you?

The ronin confirmed he and Jamal were only two streets away.

We have unwelcome guests outside of the mansion.

Am I to assume you would like an adequate greeting?

Caesar couldn't resist a telepathic chuckle at the eagerness in Kensai's mental voice. *Not just yet. Ptolemy will provide them a distraction. Stay back and observe how many friends we have and how many take Ptolemy's bait.*

Understood, Master.

Caesar released the telepathic connection only to have Tiffany grin at him as she loaded coolers with blood.

"Told you Murphy would strike," she said, slamming the lids shut.

"Now's not the time, Tiffany." The instant the harsh words swarmed out of his mouth, he regretted them. He'd been the one who'd been thinking with his cock when it came to Bebe. Thankfully, Tiffany kept quiet while she started packing two smaller coolers with regular food. Bless Mai and her efficiency with the groceries.

A minute later, Bebe charged through the kitchen door. "Here we go." She tossed the clothing she'd been wearing into Tiffany's outstretched hands. Clean jeans and one of Duncan's black t-shirts from the dirty clothes hamper now clung to her breasts and swam down her thighs.

He bit his tongue to keep from commenting. It would have been preferably seeing her in one of his shirts, but she needed to resemble his chief enforcer's niece as much as possible.

Despite the mixed company rushing back and forth between the kitchen and the garage, Tiffany skimmed out of her own black t-shirt. Ptolemy opened his mouth to harass the girl about her lack of womanly curves.

Don't. We do not have the time for your usual bullshit.

Ptolemy's mouth snapped shut, and he tossed Caesar the sword and harness he'd retrieved from the master bedroom.

Tiffany slipped on Bebe's bra while the doctor wadded paper towels to stuff the cups.

Caesar tried not to remember the heat of Bebe's all-too-generous breasts filling his palms as he checked the blade and harness for his spatha. A replica of his first sword, the steel slid home with a satisfying snick.

"I don't see why she can't glamour Tiffany. It'd be more convincing," Ptolemy muttered. He snapped a clip into his Glock 34.

Bebe glared at him before stuffing one last crumpled towel in Tiffany's borrowed undergarment. "Because any witch or fae will be able to detect a glamour spell. The witches involved will be checking." She stepped back to survey Tiffany's new cleavage and nodded. The girl pulled Bebe's khakis over her own jeans. The result gave the scrawny teenager the illusion of hips.

"And because they've probably been watching my place all day," Caesar said, his irritation with his own behavior spilling out in his voice. "They'll have a head count by now." He prayed Bebe's scent on the clothes Tiffany had donned would throw off any were or vampire, no matter how temporary the effect. He pocketed the extra magazines Ptolemy slid across the island countertop to him. Normally, he preferred steel to using a gun loaded with modified bullets. But the weres shared the vampires' allergy to silver, so now was not the time to be picky. He tucked one of Ptolemy's spare Glocks in the waistband of his jeans.

"Ready," Tiffany said, stuffing the hem of the camp shirt into the oversized khakis. She pulled on a baseball cap while Bebe attempted to tuck her unruly hair under another cap she borrowed from Tiffany. The effect wasn't as clean as he would have liked, but paired with the UV film on their vehicles' windows, it would have to do.

I would prefer remaining by your side, and Duncan is not pleased putting his niece in this kind of danger.

Caesar grinned at his brother's continued complaints at acting as Tiffany's escort. *But who else do I have who can play me?* He kept silent on his opinion that Tiffany was more than capable of taking care of herself. Such a comment would only distract Ptolemy further.

Within seconds, both his Hummer and Duncan's Escalade had been loaded with fuel, food, weapons and people. Per their plan, Alex and Anne would escort Ptolemy and Tiffany to Caesar's canyon safe house in his vehicle, while Phillippa followed in her Mustang as an extra precaution. Before Caesar could point out that Phillippa was getting involved in a witch matter, the statuesque brunette shot him an arch look as she climbed behind the wheel and said, "I'm protecting my ward. Nothing more."

The only part that truly concerned him was the fact that Bebe would have to drive Duncan's SUV to maintain the illusion that Ptolemy and Tiffany remained with his Chief Enforcer.

As the garage door rose, Kensai touched Caesar's mind again. *Mai and Miko have slipped out undetected and are on their way to the airport in our vehicle.*

Caesar passed the information to Duncan, but he couldn't resist a chuckle that two Normals had evaded the supernaturals sitting at his door. Maybe this would be easier than he originally thought.

Maybe the foes at the gate knew what he planned and everything was for naught.

Sitting in the garage didn't distract that possibility from his mind. The minutes waiting to see if Bebe's enemies took the bait stretched on for an eternity. Her fingers tapped an impatient rhythm on the steering wheel. Somehow, knowing the interim bothered her too helped his own nerves.

"It is time to go. Do not forget to emulate Tiffany's driving style," Duncan reminded Bebe.

Caesar grinned at the dirty look she shot Duncan. He pressed the earbuds of Ptolemy's iPod in place and slouched down in the second seat.

"How is it you're supposed to be protecting me, but I'm the one who has to drive the five and a half hours to San Francisco?"

Despite Bebe's aggrieved tone, he had the impression she was happy to be doing something constructive. She threw the SUV into reverse and peeled out of his garage. Her two-point turn sent him sliding into the door.

"Any questions about my driving, Mr. St. James?" she said, racing down the driveway.

"None whatsoever, Dr. Zachary," came Duncan's arid reply.

Master? We've counted five vehicles. We cannot confirm the actual number of occupants or their status without revealing ourselves, but there appears to be at least three persons in each vehicle. Three vehicles followed your Hummer.

Thank you, Kensai.

Caesar repeated the information to Duncan, who nodded before he added, "Dealing with only one team will even the odds."

"How do you know we'll only have to deal with one car?" Bebe asked. "Your man said there were two more."

"They'll leave one vehicle to watch my place," Caesar said. "Just in case."

"Yeah, but you're assuming only three occupants in a vehicle. I hate to point out that you boys sent your big guns with the other vehicle. What if the bad guys following us have a demigod with them?" Tires screeched as Bebe whipped the Escalade in a sharp right once she cleared the gates and gunned the engine.

"Do you think so little of the ability of Duncan and me to protect you?"

"Forgive me, oh great and powerful Caesar." She obeyed the stop sign at the first intersection and slammed on the brakes.

If not for the seatbelt, he would have flipped past the front seats and smashed into the windshield. "How can you drive like a maniac and speak with a normal voice?" Caesar asked.

She flashed a grin in the rearview mirror. "Experience is the great teacher, and Chad guerillas provided the ultimate opportunity."

"You were a medic for a mercenary squad? I thought you worked for Doctors Without Borders," Duncan said, incredulity in his voice.

She shook her head. "More than once they made grabs for our medical supplies. When you don't carry guns, you learn to run like hell."

The fourth vehicle is pursuing you, Master.

"We've got company, boys," Bebe said at the same moment Kensai reported.

Caesar eased up to peer over the back of the seat. The blue Taurus rental held back a quarter of a mile, making no move to overtake them. "They don't seem that anxious to make our acquaintance."

"They may only be observers. If they are aware Dr. Zachary is with us, whoever is behind this will wait until they have a more secluded opportunity, such as when we reach your private hangar so as not to attract the attention of airport security."

Duncan's analysis sent a chill through Caesar. He wracked his brain for a way to evade the car following them that wouldn't result in the death of Bebe or an innocent bystander.

"Tiffany would still try to lose them." Bebe's hard tone gave Caesar enough warning to brace himself before she swerved to the left. She headed for a busier street.

Her zigzag maneuvers through the heavy Los Angeles traffic sent a thrill straight to his groin. She showed the same fire she had at Anthony's when they had been attacked, and for some strange reason, her attitude excited him. The zipper of his trousers dug into his growing erection. He slumped back down to ease the bite. The sadist who decided placing metal teeth next to a man's penis should be crucified.

I can't touch her. But the reminder did nothing to quench his desire for the brilliant, fiery woman in the driver's seat.

He tried to focus on the other immediate problem. "Our friends still back there?"

Her big, brown eyes reflected the headlights' glare from the vehicles behind them when she flicked her gaze to the mirror. "Yep. They're keeping their distance though."

As much as he'd rather engage the bastards head on, he couldn't take the chance of Bebe getting injured or worse. He also didn't want an encounter at the airport.

Duncan flashed his cell phone. "Perhaps it is time we use Normal paranoia to our benefit. I could give a description of our friends to Homeland Security?"

Caesar chuckled. "A very good suggestion. Please do."

As Duncan punched the number on the cell, Bebe's eye flashed in the rearview mirror. "Are you crazy? You'd be setting up those poor police to be slaughtered!" She swerved around a semi-truck.

"If our friends are supernaturals, do you think they'd really risk exposure?" Caesar said.

"They did at your nephew's restaurant," she shot back.

"Which was Family-owned. They knew we'd have to clean up the mess to avoid questions ourselves. Natasha's conspirators have worked too hard to destroy all their efforts in a major encounter at LAX. My guess is they will depart at the first sign of the local authorities."

"That's a big gamble on a lot of innocent lives," she said.

"I play to win, Dr. Zachary."

Her slight shudder wouldn't have been perceptible to normal eyes, but she kept silent and her attention remained fixed on traffic the rest of the way. At least until her triumphant shout of "Yes!" as the Escalade maneuvered onto the exit ramp for the airport.

He sat up to look behind them. Red and blue lights blazing, a half dozen LAPD cars converged on the Taurus, effectively trapping their pursuers on the ramp.

Duncan directed her through the back roads to the private areas, security a little heavier than usual thanks to his tip to the Normal authorities. Mai and Miko waited for them in the hanger when they pulled into the cavernous space.

"Did anyone follow you?" Caesar said to the girls. He covered his amusement when Bebe ignored his hand to help her down from the SUV. Her refusal was a good thing. His groin tightened when he detected the scent of her arousal over Duncan and Tiffany's clothing.

Miko shook her head. A couple inches taller than her older sister, she didn't have quite the sternness or dedication to rules that plagued Mai, but it didn't make her any less efficient. "No, the fifth vehicle remains near the mansion. Grandfather will inform you if it departs prior to daybreak."

"Good. File a flight plan to Las Vegas and get in the air as soon as you can. I want you two to stay there until you hear from me or your grandfather."

Mai stepped forward, her bun wound nearly as tight as her whip-thin body. "Master Augustine, are you sure you want us to fly to Las Vegas and stay there without you?" She had to be damned upset to even contemplate questioning one of his orders.

In fact, he didn't recall her *ever* questioning him.

He nodded before glancing at Duncan, who had his cell glued to his ear again. Turning back to Mai, he said, "I need you to buy us some time."

"But, Master—"

He held up a hand. "My orders stand." He softened his voice at the stricken expression on her face. "If you're questioned, and you will be questioned by my sister's people, I don't want you to have any knowledge of our whereabouts."

She gave a slow nod. Even Miko's delicate features twisted in concern. He rarely kept anything from Selene.

And he couldn't even answer to himself his reluctance to let Selene know of the immediate problems. He'd always trusted his twin. His first thought had been to ask for her help. Now, he'd pared vampire assistance down to just Duncan.

Understanding of his own motive hit him like a concrete block.

Because Duncan would be the one vampire who'd understand and sympathize with his desire to find a cure for the virus.

Duncan clicked his cell phone shut. "The police commissioner has verified our friends are in custody. He is concerned however about how long he can keep them. Their attorney is Jimmy Hanson, and he is already down at holding."

"Jimmy Hanson?" Bebe incredulous gaze flicked between the two men. "Wasn't he the one who got off that pedophilic pop star and then the basketball player who murdered his ex-wife?"

"Yes." Caesar's hand clenched. Shit. For Hanson to be down at holding to post bail before the ones following them had even been processed . . .

Now, he had confirmation of how deep this conspiracy of Natasha's ran. And he'd lay his entire fortune it had nothing to do with the White Rose succession. For the first time in centuries, the cold fingers of fear stroked his spine. He couldn't fail Bebe. "We need to leave town before they make bail."

Chapter 19

Hours later, a neck muscle gave Bebe a sharp reminder of how long she'd been behind the wheel. She rolled her head trying to ease the tension. Caesar had driven the first leg until they needed to stop for gas. He finally gave in to her insistence that she takeover the steering wheel. It gave her something to do besides sit and worry in the back seat.

"Pull over at the next exit," Caesar said.

Irritated with him ordering her around like she was one of his minions, she glanced in the rearview mirror. "Why? This was your idea. I told you we should have stuck with the Escalade instead of taking your pilot's Vue." While she enjoyed driving the sporty mini-ute, she had no sympathy for the two large men crammed into the seats.

But she couldn't stifle the yawn that threatened to dislocate her jaw.

"Because you need a break."

At three in the morning, she didn't feel like arguing with him. Besides, she wasn't the one who'd turn into flaming shish kabob if they didn't make it to his San Francisco house before dawn.

A few minutes later, she pulled into a twenty-four hour service station. Surreptitiously checking the other vehicles, she climbed out of the seat and stretched her tight, aching muscles.

"Are you trying to entice every male here?"

She jumped at the warm breath tickling her hair. Turning to glare at Caesar, she said, "You really need to stop doing that."

"Doing what?" he said, a mischievous look on his face. Even though the virus had frozen him in the appearance of a man in his mid-twenties, his true age normally shone in his eyes.

Except when he decided to tease her, which was becoming a constant occurrence despite their predicament. And she liked it. A lot.

Not sure if the irritation was at her behavior or his, she shook her head and stomped into the convenience store to find the ladies' room. Holding her breath, she used the facilities as fast as possible. Damn, she'd used ditches in Africa that were cleaner.

Thank the Goddess, the food area wasn't as dirty. The warm aroma of roasted pistachios cleared her head once she left the restroom, but the siren song of chocolate led her away from the nuts. She paid for the dark chocolate Hershey's bar and found Caesar waiting for her at the door, somehow holding three large coffees. She smiled her thanks as she took the top one and shoved the door open.

Then she felt it. Not a psychic probe but the pressure wave of a search spell.

"What's wrong?" he said, his voice soft in her ear.

A tickle of fear rippled through her nerves. "We need to get back in the SUV. They're looking for us." She started for the gas pumps.

Don't run. We'll attract attention.

His words jerked her out of the instinct to flee. Heat rushed to her cheeks. Not that he had to remind her to remain calm, but that she hadn't reestablished her outer mental shields since she had spoken to him privately in the kitchen earlier. And even more surprising, he had not sent a telepathic compulsion. He spoke to her as an equal. A little thrill ran through her that he took her seriously. At least, he hadn't slung her over his shoulder again.

She took a sip of the scorching java and tried to stroll nonchalantly to the waiting vehicle, Caesar close behind her.

Duncan leaned against the passenger door, but his eyes belied his stance. *What is it?*

Company's coming. The buzz of the spell drew closer, the subsonic energy making her teeth rattle.

Can you perform a counter spell? Caesar asked her as he handed the second cup to Duncan.

She nodded, wishing she had the spell memorized, but she'd never had to worry about hiding something or someone from a magickal search before. Damn, how could they act so calm? Their behavior made her want to kick them both, but that wasn't fair. Caesar and Duncan didn't have the fingernails-on-chalkboard sensation of the nearing spell sparking their neurons.

"Keys." Caesar held out his hand.

Balancing the Hershey's on top of the hot cup, she yanked the set from her jeans pocket and dropped them into his waiting palm. Climbing into the back seat, she set the coffee and candy bar on the floor and leaned over to pull the Book from her bag in the cargo area. Nerveless fingers flipping through the pages of the Book, it took her a couple of precious seconds to find the blocking spell. If she survived this whole mess, she was definitely indexing the damn Book for future generations.

Only one item was listed in the ingredients section. "Oh, fuck!"

Caesar slammed on the brakes, tipping over her cup and flooding the back seat floor with coffee. "What?"

"I need a turtle shell. Pull over there." She pointed to a free parking spot to the side of the building.

The Vue hadn't fully stopped before she flung open the door. Racing back into the store, she grabbed a bag of pistachios and dropped a twenty on the counter. Such an extravagance would have sent Grandma Petrov into an apoplectic fit, but now . . .

Now, everything she thought she knew about Grandma had turned into total bullshit anyway.

Launching herself back into the mini-ute, she yelled, "Go!"

And tried not to think about the very big gun sitting in Duncan's lap.

"Bebe, honey," Caesar said, trying to catch her attention in the rearview mirror and keep an eye on the road at the same time. "I hate to be the one to point out that turtles are animals, not nuts."

"It's sympathetic magick, so I can substitute if I have to." She ripped open the bag and carefully pried open a pistachio with a nail. It went to show how crazy the last two weeks of her life had become when her normally short, immaculate fingernails had grown into talons. "Now, shut up, let me concentrate—" *And don't ever call me 'honey' again!*

His silent chuckle echoed in her mind as she dropped half of the pistachio back into the bag. She placed the remaining half shell-side up on the palm of her right hand and closed her eyes. Envisioning the half nut as the Vue, she murmured the old spell to reinforce the shell protecting the tiny pistachio.

With a warm rush, golden energy snapped into place over the vehicle. She opened her eyes to find Caesar merging onto the interstate, the traffic light due to the early morning hour.

And dead ahead, a boiling wave of red energy flowed southward toward them. Her breath hitched in her throat as they rushed to meet the ugly smear. She braced herself.

But the golden haze of the shielding spell sliced through the blistering energy, a slight pressure in her head the only indication that her protective shell deflected the search around them. She twisted in the seat and watched the red wave pass on into the night. A sigh almost escaped her, but she tasted a bitter, iron tang at the back of her tongue. Icy fear gripped her. Someone had powered the search spell with blood. A whole life's worth of blood.

"Bebe? Are you okay?" Caesar said.

She turned to find him glancing at her in the mirror again. Duncan peered around the edge of his seat. Both vampires had concerned expressions on their faces.

"Yeah, I'm fine." She sucked in a deep cleansing breath.

"Did it work?" Caesar asked.

She nodded and curiosity rose. "Didn't you see the spell coming down the freeway toward us?"

"Truth for a truth?" he said, repeating her earlier question to Phillippa.

As old as he was, what could he possibly not know? But she nodded her agreement anyway.

"If we're close enough to the caster or the subject, a vampire can smell the ozone of a spell's energy, but we can't See the energy itself." He grinned, flashing fang in the mirror. "What is it you see? Natasha would never tell me. Said it was beyond my comprehension."

Bebe smiled. She'd heard something similar from her grandmother in the past, particularly when she had problems mastering a technique. "It is kind of difficult to describe to someone who can't detect the patterns."

Caesar snorted. "Now who's being arrogant about their power?"

She couldn't get angry at his teasing tone. "Would you let me finish? Geez!" She whacked his shoulder. "The energy colors reflect the caster's personal aura, and depending on the spell, the caster's intent." She waved her hand to indicate the vehicle. "My shielding spell would appear as a golden sphere to another witch." She jabbed a thumb toward the rear. "That search spell was a nasty-looking dark red."

"Because of the other witch's aura or the intent," Duncan asked.

"Probably both."

"What aren't you telling us, Bebe?" The reflection of Caesar's eyes glowed in the mirror as his gaze bore into her. Not neon yellow, but getting there.

She sighed and leaned back. Was she that transparent to him? The iron aftertaste left her slimy and wishing desperately for a shower. "Whoever cast it used a blood sacrifice for extra power."

Caesar's eyes narrowed as his attention flicked between her and the road. "Natasha told me witches don't use sacrifices in their spells."

Leave it to fuzzy bunny propaganda to make this difficult for her. She shrugged. "Most won't. And if they do, they use their own blood, not another being's. There are … repercussions down the road when using someone or something else's blood without permission. You're taking a part of their life force. And death releases all the energy at once. Someone's pretty desperate to find us to take that kind of risk."

She leaned forward and laid a hand on his shoulder. For some reason, it was important that he understand. "I never have used another person's blood if that's what you're concerned about."

But would you?

I don't know. The question bothered her more than she wanted to admit. She hated to use her own blood in spells, but she'd been desperate last night at the restaurant. Regardless, Caesar deserved nothing less than a straight answer even if it showed her ugly side. *To save someone I loved, I might.* Even if it meant she'd be damned for eternity.

He nodded as if satisfied with her admission. "Thank you for your honesty."

She nestled back into the seat and retrieved the soggy candy bar from the floor. After tearing open the damp wrapper, she bit into the chocolate that was as dark as her thoughts.

What would she do? A few months ago, she would have unequivocally said no blood magick. But then, a few months ago, she'd never pictured Grandma Petrov as a ruthless Nazi hunter or Alice capable of ordering someone killed. Did she have it in her to kill?

The image of the witch, lying on the pavement in front of Anthony's and choking on the blood mud golem, gave her the answer.

Acid crept up her throat. She wrapped up the candy, dropped it in the pistachio bag, and tried not to cry for her lost innocence the rest of the way to San Francisco.

——•——

Two hours later, Bebe was still wide-awake without the coffee when Caesar pulled into his garage. A highly irritated Stan met them at the door to the kitchen.

"Somebody want to tell me what the fuck is going on?" The half-elf's deep voice practically barked out his words. "Your sister's been calling here every hour since midnight wanting to know where you are. When I call down to the Brentwood house, Jamal will only say you're out, and he'll take a message." He propped his fists on his hips. "When I call the safe house, Alex gives me the same Morrigan-damned story. And everyone at the Seattle compound says they haven't seen you either!"

"You'll do the same. It's imperative that no one knows we're here for the time being. Do I make myself clear, Stanley?" Caesar's eyes glowed and his fangs extended, sending a tiny shiver down Bebe's back.

Stan held up his hands, his fingers fanned. "Sure, boss, no problem." He cocked an eyebrow. "But if there's something in particular Harry and I are supposed to be guarding against, we need to know."

"Duncan, would you brief the Gryffudds? Have Harry remain on the perimeter watch. Dr. Zachary and I will be in my office when you're finished," Caesar said. Before she could say anything, he hooked a hand under her elbow and towed her through the kitchen.

Goddess, had it been only four days since Ptolemy carried a comatose Caesar along the same path? Too much had happened since then. Too much on her conscience.

She needed a break. Just a little one. Digging in her heels, she said, "Hey, don't I even get a potty stop?"

Caesar halted at her protest, his face contrite. "I'm sorry. I forget you don't have our stamina."

"Stamina's one thing. A full bladder's another." She shrugged out of his grip and shoved her bag into his arms. "Why don't you start a pot of tea while I use the ladies' room?"

She dove into the half-bath without waiting for his answer. She turned on the faucet and lowered the toilet lid. Then she sat and let the tears she'd held in for the last one hundred and some miles fall. As much as she wanted to chalk her weepiness to exhaustion, she couldn't. She was as screwed up as the rest of her family. The real question was how did she convince the Elders they needed to select a new high priest or priestess. *And it harm none, do what ye will.* Yeah, right. The Petrov line really deserved the title the way they upheld the Rede.

She never wanted the H.P. position. She didn't deserve it. And neither did Alice, if her cousin was truly behind the attacks.

But a tiny sliver of doubt remained. Maybe someone was trying to set Alice up. Or was she clinging to the wish that her cousin and she could reclaim their childhood friendship?

Yanking off a wad of toilet paper, she blew her nose and wiped her eyes. Goddess knew William wasn't qualified. He'd rather party with his toadies than deal with the day-to-day administration of the coven.

And she still needed to call Eleanor Hyde-Smith to check on Granny E. and Grandpa Ben. Maybe the London H.P. would have some information on who was responsible for the attack on them. If Grandpa Ben had been hit with a fae confusion spell, the effects should have worn off by now. She couldn't afford to think about what might have been done to Granny E. Not without totally falling apart.

Damn, her life sucked when the only dependable person in it was a vampire. A shiver ran down her spine at the image of Caesar. She brutally shoved it aside as well. Wanting a relationship with him made as much sense as wanting back her friendship with Alice.

No, she needed to deal with a real problem that she might have a chance at solving. Which meant finding Grandma Petrov's cipher key.

She rose and checked herself in the mirror. At least, she didn't have raccoon eyes from her tears. The make-up she'd applied to meet with Phillippa at the antique shop yesterday morning had long since worn off. Splashing some cool water on her face, Bebe tried to make herself presentable. Another look in the mirror as she dried her skin. The red rims around her eyes were weariness. That's all.

She exited the tiny half-bath and walked down the hallway to Caesar's office. Inside, he had already moved the wardrobe to the center of the room. He stalked around the antique, eyeing the piece like a lion trying to figure out if a strange object was edible.

She leaned against the doorframe and crossed her arms. "So have you made it talk yet?"

He smiled at her tiny joke and shook his head. "With your permission, I would like to consult with Stan about the code." His attention returned to the silent wood. "He may have some ideas."

"Sure." She pulled the door shut before she threw her hands in the air. Not that the wood could really stop Duncan from hearing her yell at Caesar, but it'd probably block Stan and Harry. "Would you like to take out ads in the *Chronicle* while you're at it?"

"It was merely a suggestion."

His conciliatory tone made her feel even guiltier for lashing out at him. "I'm sorry. It's been a long two weeks since I first got the telegram about Grandma Petrov's death, and I haven't had much sleep." She tried to knead her neck muscles.

"Here. Let me." He moved behind her, his hands brushing hers aside. Powerful fingers dug into her tight knots.

She blinked in surprise, but the sensation of her muscles loosening under his ministrations felt too good for her to protest. His massage followed the tension lines up along her scalp. She closed her eyes, letting relaxation wash over her.

Then he swept her hair aside, and lips replaced fingers. Cool, sensual lips nibbled and sucked and did so many other delightful things that her skin clamored for more. She leaned against his hard chest with a sigh.

Her conscience niggled in the back of her mind. Necking with a vampire was a bad idea. It could lead to sex. Sex led to madness. Madness led to death.

She smacked her conscience's Yoda imitation aside when Caesar's fingers skimmed her waist. Too many clothes in the way. Her t-shirt disappeared, and the skin-to-skin contact sent heat straight to her pelvis. His hands moved to cup and mold her breasts, tweaking and rolling the nipples through the satin of her bra. His seduction had nothing to do with power or manipulation, but pure male appreciation for a woman. And she reveled in it.

Turning in his arms, she pressed against his solid chest. And even more solid erection. Twining her arms around his neck, she tugged his head down to meet her lips. Yes, that's what she wanted. His tongue still tasted of the extra-strong coffee he'd drank on the last leg of the trip. It swirled and dipped, caressed and tasted her. Hands gripped her rear, lifting and pressing. Automatically, she wrapped her legs around his waist.

She wasn't a virgin by any means, but something about Caesar made desire a living thing inside her. And she wanted him enough to consider risking her life just to ease the burning in her soul.

A loud knock on the office door jerked reality back into focus.

Caesar leaned his forehead against hers while they both fought to catch their breath. *I seriously need to fire my entire staff.*

Unwrapping her legs, she smiled up at him as she slid down the length of his body. Her action elicited a groan from deep in his throat.

She didn't bother to hide her laughter. *That's what you get for starting this*, she sent.

He waited for her to whip her t-shirt on before he called, "Enter."

Duncan brushed the door open and strode into the room, a tray with a steaming pot of tea and several cups balanced in his hands. Stan trailed him into the room. "You wanted to speak with us?" Duncan prompted. He busied himself with the tea.

Bebe resigned herself to the inevitable. She pulled the Book of Shadows out of her bag and laid it on Caesar's desk. "We wanted you to take a look at this, Stan." Flipping to the pages with the mysterious code, she asked, "Do you recognize this? We thought it may have been a code you and Grandma may have used."

The half-elf leaned over and examined the writing, his white-blond brows twisted in concentration before he shook his head. "It definitely looks like Natasha's writing, but it's not a code I recognize." He stood upright, scratching the top of his buzz cut, his gaze darting between Bebe and Caesar. "Must be pretty serious if you're showing all of us a White Rose BOS."

Caesar gestured at the Book. "We believe the assassination attempts on Bebe have something to do with this."

Stan folded his arms over his chest. "It's not going to do them much good without the key to the code."

"That is assuming whoever is after the Book does not already have the key," Duncan countered.

"It doesn't matter whether *they*—" Bebe made air quotes with her fingers. "—have the key or not. My cousins and the Elders are all looking for the Book." She jabbed a finger at the coded notes. "If I don't know what *this* is, I'm not about to hand it over to anyone just to save my own skin."

"And that's assuming your 'they' don't want you dead for an entirely different reason. So where does that leave us?" Stan said. "There's no way the four of us can defend this place against a full-out assault if White Rose comes knocking in force. And no offense, boss," he said, shooting an apologetic look at Caesar. "No matter how quiet we keep, eventually someone's going to figure out you're here with the doctor. Your sister's already in a tizzy."

Duncan stiffened at the mention of Selene. Poor guy. Bebe didn't know how she'd react to the constant reminder of an unwilling Turn. She wished she hadn't gotten quite so much information out of that eavesdropping session.

Caesar must have noticed Duncan's reaction as well because he said, "I'd better call her before she does something we'll all regret." He headed for the door, but stopped short and turned. "Phillippa suggested that the key to Natasha's code may still be in the wardrobe." He disappeared in the direction of the kitchen.

Bebe murmured her thanks as she accepted the hot cup of tea from Duncan. He then excused himself to assist Harry with security. She couldn't blame him for not wanting to be in Caesar's office. Selene's scent must be all over the place.

Facing the confused Stan, she said, "Did you find anything else in the nymph hole besides the letter?"

He shook his head. "No. Caesar was in here when I opened it too. Is there another hole I couldn't find?"

"No." She paced around the wardrobe, willing it to unlock its secrets, but unfortunately, only the heroine in Disney's *Beauty and the Beast* had furniture that talked. So where was the key to Grandma's incomprehensible writing? She did another slow circuit around the wardrobe, sipping Duncan's English brew.

She reviewed the few facts she knew. Grandma had made a point of ensuring that the Book got into her hands by entrusting it with Phillippa. Then Grandma had left the letter in the nymph hole, a letter meant for her, one that relied on an old illusionist trick Grandma taught her to unlock the secret.

Illusions. Normal magic.

A false panel?

Setting her cup on the desk, she started knocking on the outer panels.

"The boss and I already checked for conventional hidden compartments." Stan crossed his arms over his broad chest. He definitely didn't get his build from the fae side of his family. On the other hand, Caesar's chest was perfect, well-defined but not looking like he'd overdosed on steroids. Perfect to snuggle against, perfect for . . .

She clipped that line of thought before she had to change her undies. "I'm sure he did," she murmured.

"I tell you you're wasting your time, Doctor."

She shot him an arch glare. "Thank you for your opinion, Stan, but I'd like to check for myself."

He stalked out of the room, mumbling under his breath. She distinctly caught the word "stubborn."

Well, she'd been called worse. She completed her circuit of the exterior with no luck. Opening both doors, she knelt and felt around the inside of the nymph hole, praying something had been taped, nailed, hell, even super-glued to the interior. Nope, just the same smooth surface.

Oh Grandma, why didn't you tell me you were in this much trouble?

"Why in Hades didn't you tell me you were in this much trouble?"

Caesar held the receiver away from his ear while Selene continued her rant. The volume of her voice would have been painful even to a Normal. And he hadn't gotten past "Hello" before she started.

"I'm supposed to be your second-in-command! And not only do you *not* tell me, you don't even tell Ptolemy. How is he supposed to back you when he doesn't know where you are? I'm coming to San Francisco."

"No. On the off-chance the people after Bebe still think I'm with you in Vegas, I don't want them following you here."

"Have you heard the rumors? Half the supers in the U.S. think you've kidnapped Zachary. If White Rose comes after you, you'll need help." She paused for a heartbeat. "Whether you want to admit it or not."

"I have help," he said through gritted teeth. The dull pulse behind his left eye grew more insistent. He prayed there was still some ibuprofen left in the infirmary.

A short bark of laughter burst through the receiver. "The halfings?" She sighed. "At least Duncan's with you. The Homeland Security tip about the car tailing you to the airport was his idea, wasn't it?"

"Yes. Unless there's anything else you'd like to lecture me about, I need to go." He regretted the curtness the moment the words were out of his mouth.

"Fine. But don't come crying to me when some witch tries to fry your ass." With an abrupt click, the phone line went dead.

Setting the receiver in its cradle, he leaned his head against the cool stainless steel of the refrigerator. Selene was only trying to help. He repeated the mantra a few more times before he stood straight and opened the fridge to snag a bottle of blood. After pouring the contents in a mug, he popped open the microwave, shoved the mug in and punched the buttons to warm it.

The conversation with his twin bothered him. Something he couldn't quite put his finger on around the pain of another stress migraine. No, it wasn't so much the conversation than the implication. His problem was with one witch in particular, and the problem involved keeping his hands to himself and his pants zipped.

"You know, I'm really beginning to like this view of you."

Bebe didn't jump at Caesar's rich tenor as she had at the estate auction. Instead, pleasant heat flooded her, despite the fact he admired the body part she hated most.

"It's not fair that you can admire my chest, but I can't admire your rear end," he said.

You were eavesdropping.

You meant for me to hear you, he sent back.

She ignored his accusation as well as the fact that they were once again alone in his office. Her motives were seriously in question when it came to Caesar Augustine.

A faint brush of air and a more definite sizzle of sexual electricity indicated he had crouched next to her. "I've already checked both the interior and exterior for conventional hidden compartments," he said.

Pulling her upper body out of the wardrobe, she sat up to face him. "So Stan informed me, but what about wood overlays glued to the original panels?" She raised a questioning eyebrow.

From his faint frown, the possibility hadn't occurred to him. It didn't matter though. She hadn't found any such overlay either. But it felt good to know she'd outthought him on something.

He dropped to the carpet and extended his legs, leaning back on his hands. "Have you checked for any enchantments on the wardrobe?"

She nodded and grinned, slightly pleased she was now two steps ahead of him. "Yeah, the first time I was here, but Stan didn't find anything when you had him check either. I'm thinking Grandma may have used something more conventional. She was utterly paranoid about someone or something in the coven. So far, everything she's done to protect the Book of Shadows has been non-magickal. She may have done the same with the key . . ."

No, it couldn't be that ridiculously simple, could it? She cleared her throat. "Caesar, did Grandma tell you to deliver the wardrobe to me?"

He shook his head. "No, not specifically. You were the only heir who was supposed to receive anything. She went out of her way to disinherit your cousins in her Last Will and Testament."

"How do you know what was in her Will?"

He grinned. "It became public knowledge the minute the Elders offered it for probate." He shrugged before continuing. "She definitely intended for you to receive all her possessions under the terms."

Had Grandma gambled that Caesar would remember what the wardrobe meant to her and would find a way to save it?

All of the sudden it was hard to breathe. "Where's the key to the wardrobe?" she said.

His frown indicated he wasn't following her train of thought, which was probably a good thing. She wasn't too sure about her sanity herself at this point.

"I placed it in my safe before we left for Los Angeles. Why?"

"I need to see it." Her whole body shook, whether from anticipation or fear that she was wrong, she couldn't tell. "Why did you put it in your safe?" Had Grandma put a compulsion on him that he was unaware of?

Caesar's frown deepened. "Duncan suggested it when I phoned him that we were flying back to Los Angeles. It seemed like the sensible thing to do at the time." He rose and crossed to the bookcase behind his desk. Tumblers clicked as he rotated the old-fashioned combination dial, and then a deeper thunk when he opened the door. Returning to her, he held out an antique brass key. The patina had dulled from lack of care, but it was the thick, intricately molded key she remembered.

Her fingers shook as she took it from him. Extending her senses around the brass, she didn't detect any magick. If she were right, Grandma had used sleight of hand to fool the conspirators. Just like Normal illusionists entertained their audiences. She bit her lip as excitement and fear mingled.

Bebe twisted the key. It took some effort before the shaft unscrewed from the ornate bow with a high-pitched squeal. A tiny scroll of white paper protruded from the hollow of the key.

"Hades!" Caesar swore and leaned closer.

Pulling the paper gently from the brass, she unrolled it. Her breath released with a rush, and she blinked away the tears of relief that filled her eyes. In Grandma's neat handwriting lay the key to the encoded notes.

Chapter 20

Leaning back in his chair, Caesar stretched before he rose from the kitchen table to grab another cup of coffee. Even his muscles ached after he, Bebe and Stan had spent the last twelve hours translating Natasha's notes.

It was the first time in centuries he'd been awake from dawn to sunset. Once a vampire, he had learned daylight was a one-way ticket to the Underworld. With the advent of UV-film on windows, he found the view of a sunrise wasn't quite the same, and he hadn't bothered after the initial novelty wore off. It reminded him too much of dawn training sessions millennia ago. He never thought he'd miss those, but he did, and the sight wasn't worth the temptation of stepping out into the now deadly sunshine.

Coffee pot in hand, he returned to the kitchen table littered with notepads and topped off Bebe's mug. Her brow knotted in concentration, she didn't even register the fresh coffee as she automatically gulped the contents. If his muscles were tight, hers must be in agony, but she showed no sign. She continued scribbling on the pad in front of her, chewing on her bottom lip as she went.

Forcing away thoughts of nibbling on her bottom lip himself, he caught Stan's eye and raised the pot. Stan shook his head, sat straighter and stretched his hulking frame.

"I hate to say it, but I don't understand ninety percent of what I've translated," the half-elf said.

"It's genome mapping for a recessive gene that triggers the immune response against a certain family of viruses." Bebe didn't look up at Stan. Instead, she continued writing, her gaze flicking from Natasha's notes to her copy of the key and back to the pad she used.

"Oh, that makes a whole lot more sense to me," Stan grumbled.

Bebe raised her head and blinked in surprise when she looked out the window behind Stan. "When did it get dark?"

"At sunset. The same as it does every night," Caesar teased.

In response, she stuck her tongue out at him, which didn't help the carnal direction of his thoughts. He should be thankful for Stan's presence. It kept him from doing anything idiotic, like telling her where to put that tongue to good use.

Duncan stalked into the kitchen, ignored everyone and made a straight line for the refrigerator. He retrieved a pint bottle, emptied the contents into a giant mug, and set the mug in the microwave, shutting the door with more force than necessary.

Caesar swallowed an exasperated sigh. For once Duncan and Selene agreed on something, not that he'd point that little fact out to Duncan. After Selene had finished chewing him out on the phone this morning, Duncan had argued the need for additional personnel when Caesar had ordered him to get some sleep.

Caesar raked a hand through his hair. Considering the rarity of both Duncan and Mai questioning his orders, maybe he was being foolish.

A rhythmic tapping behind him drew his attention back to Bebe, who stared at him without apparently seeing him. The cheap plastic ink pen in her hand banged in an unconscious motion against the last set of notes she'd translated. She jerked out of her trance when he gave her a questioning look.

"It says here the actual test results are at Augustine Research's San Francisco facility." Her eyes narrowed. "Anything you want to tell me?"

He shrugged, slightly uncomfortable with the looks both Stan and Duncan were giving him. "I loaned her the space and equipment for her research. The actual results mean nothing without knowing the original question."

"Does this have something to do with the blood samples you requested from each of us?" Duncan's eyebrows drew together with a suspicious look since his "us" referred to the vampire contingent of the coven employees.

Time to come clean. Caesar nodded before he gave Stan a sharp look. "This information does not leave this room."

"Understood, boss." Stan's eyes glittered with curiosity.

Caesar met Duncan's gaze. "Since Natasha's research concerned certain witches who were resistant to the V-virus, she believed she might be able to develop a cure by reverse engineering the witches' gene."

Duncan's mouth dropped open. Caesar almost smiled, but managed to hold it back. It wasn't too often he could catch his chief enforcer off guard.

"Shit!"

Caesar's attention snapped to Stan. For the first time he could remember, Stan actually looked scared.

"Who else knows about this besides the witches?" Stan asked.

"As far as I know, only the four of us in this room."

Stan shook his head. "This has something to do with the Mengele stuff Natasha retrieved from Auschwitz, doesn't it?"

Caesar nodded.

Stan sucked in a deep breath. "I hate to point this out, but we never found out who was the lead supernatural collaborating with the Nazis. We've got one other person out there who knows about this crap, even if he doesn't have the original research." He waved a beefy hand at the papers strewn across the table. A sympathetic look crossed his face. "And I'm not trying to be a pisser, but the other problem is not every vampire will be jumping for joy at a cure. Not like you two would."

Caesar exchanged a look with Duncan. Were they that obvious?

"He's right." Bebe's eyes didn't shine with fear the way Stan's did. Instead, obvious worry pinched her brow. "Your Nazi sympathizer, if not a member of White Rose, is probably collaborating with a coven member." She pursed her lips while she thought. "It may not be William or Alice behind the assassination attempts.

Our conspirator may be using the leadership contest as a cover to get their hands on Grandma's research."

"That's a very big 'if', and if so, how do we expose him?" Caesar said.

"There's one way to find out."

At Bebe's soft voice, a shiver of apprehension ran up Caesar's back. "I will not use you as bait!"

She winced at his shout, but she squared her shoulders. "We already know some of the supernaturals are working together. If I call the Elders for a Confirmation ceremony, we'll draw out whoever's behind this within White Rose since he or she obviously wants me out of the way." She shrugged. "From there, we should be able to track down their accomplices."

"No." He crossed his arms over his chest and let his nasty vampire side come out. Fangs slid down, but she didn't so much as flinch this time.

Instead, she rose and glared up at him. So much for the intimidation factor of his extra height with fangs and glowing eyeballs. "I *will* call the confirmation for tomorrow night, and I *will* go." She crossed her arms over her ample breasts, sending a different type of heat through his body. "With or without you," she finished.

"The doctor has a point," Duncan said quietly.

Caesar didn't like the implications of Duncan's unspoken remainder of his statement. His chief enforcer would go with Bebe even against a direct order. He swallowed a groan. Hades, he'd been cornered, and he seriously hated that feeling. "Why tomorrow night?"

The smile on Bebe's face was frightening in its own right. "Tomorrow's Winter Solstice. The coven generally conducts major ceremonies on the sabbats unless there's a pressing need otherwise. If I ask for Confirmation and insist on tomorrow night, the Council will assume I've acceded to Grandma's wishes and bend over backward to set it up."

— • —

A couple of hours later, all arrangements were in place. Like Bebe planned, the White Rose Elders had fallen over themselves when she called Confirmation, if only to "clear any questions" as it was put. One interesting tidbit in her phone conversation with the Air Elder, Beatrice Flannigan, was that the Elders had bought Grandma's house from the estate representative. Beatrice said it would be a shame if Alice and William's fighting led to the loss of the high priestess's residence, especially since the coven held their major ceremonies in the privacy offered by such a large facility, including a Confirmation. Of course, the fact that the Elders planned to deed over the Nob Hill estate to the new high priestess had been an added incentive in Beatrice's eyes for Bebe to accept her fate.

She smiled to herself while she pulled the soft cotton nightgown over her head. Part of her rejoiced a total stranger didn't have the house where she'd spent half her childhood. The other enjoyed imagining how the Coven would react when she walked into the Confirmation escorted by vampires and fae.

Even better was her conversation with Grandpa Ben. He'd fully recovered from the confusion spell. Apparently, the unseelie's magick had affected the driver of the shuttle, which was why he hit a retaining wall and flipped the vehicle. Granny E.'s injuries had been a result of the accident, and she'd regained consciousness shortly after Bebe had called Eleanor Hyde-Smith. Grandpa Ben couldn't say enough good things about the London Coven's healer, though Granny E. had thrown a fit when the healer ordered her to bed early. Grandpa said it was a good sign, and Bebe had to agree.

Eleanor filled in the rest of the details. Her security had arrived before the dark fae was able to get into the vehicle to complete his job. Unfortunately, the culprit escaped while Eleanor's people rescued Grandpa Ben and Granny E. from the wreckage before the Normal authorities got to the accident scene.

Remembering the end of the conversation, Bebe smiled to herself. Eleanor had alternated between assurances of the Epsteins' safety and dire threats of what would happen to the unseelie if she caught him. The edge in the London High Priestess's voice told Bebe the results wouldn't be pleasant.

Reaching for her brush, she sighed as reality set in. Tomorrow would be ugly even discounting the possibility of another assassination attempt. While she'd like to believe in the inviolacy of the White Rose Elder Council, she wasn't that naïve. Nerves could wait until tomorrow though because she definitely needed the sleep. She hadn't been awake this many hours straight since she'd been an intern.

A soft knock at the door jolted her out of her reverie. The rich, beefy essence left her little doubt who waited on the other side. Snatching her robe out of the open overnight bag, she shrugged it on while crossing the room. She yanked open the door. Caesar halted his fist in mid-knock.

She crossed her arms. "I thought you ordered all of us to get some sleep." Her tone let him know exactly what she thought about his orders.

"I—" His jaw twitched, as if he were working up the nerve to say whatever he came to say. The silence dragged on for several seconds before he bit out, "Could you please put on some clothes so I can talk to you?"

"I have clothes on," she said, swallowing her smile with difficulty. What the hell was bothering him? He had seen Tiffany shirtless for crying out loud.

"I'm not attracted to Tiffany, and your nipples are showing."

She glanced down. Her nightgown wasn't that sheer, but sure enough, her breasts were thriving under Caesar's heated stare. Goddess, she hated admitting what he did to her.

Pulling the edges of her terry robe over the betraying white cotton didn't help one iota. It only served to remind her how sensitized her body became around him. "What's so important it couldn't wait until morning?"

Too much of her discomfiture must have shown in her voice. His annoying smirk returned. He leaned against the doorjamb, his stance easy and confident. Ri-i-i-ght. She'd sooner let one of her many potential assassins in her bedroom.

She must have accidentally leaked because his attitude vanished. He reached up and cupped her face, his thumb stroking her cheek. "That's what I wanted to talk to you about."

"Damn it. I don't need you listening to every stray thought that passes through my head." Men. Give them a bite, and they take the whole freaking pizza. Closing her eyes, she started to raise her outer shields.

"Don't," he whispered. "Please don't shut me out."

Her eyes popped open at his impassioned plea.

"I want you to call this Confirmation off." His gaze bore into hers, and a wave of purple-gray emotion hit her, not an attempt to influence her, but raw, honest fear.

Her hand rose of its own accord to cover his. "We've been through this, Caesar. It's the best way to draw out whoever's behind Grandma's murder and the attempts on my life. You're not compromising your honor or your promise—"

"It's *your* life that concerns me."

His statement touched her. The idea that someone cared about her, not her position, not her power, not what she could do for that person, melted a part of her she thought frozen. Her lips turned upward in a warm smile. Drawing his hand from her face, she twined her fingers through his. She had no doubt he'd protect her through whatever was to come.

"Thank you," she said giving his hand a gentle squeeze. "But we need to end this. Now. Before one of your people gets hurt."

"My people can protect themselves." He bit the words out.

He looked so serious she couldn't resist teasing him. "So a big, bad vampire like yourself—"

He jerked from her hold, his eyes flashing gold. "This isn't a joke! You could get hurt, or—"

His fists clenched, and the scent of burnt flesh rushed through her mind. The conflagration of fear, anger and pain swirled through the corridors of her soul until she couldn't see, couldn't breathe, couldn't think. She swam through the violence he exuded to find herself still standing inside the door of her bedroom.

Before she found her balance, he yanked her to his chest and bent his head. This kiss wasn't the passionate exploration of earlier. No, this one was possessive, demanding. The liquid fire of his thoughts turned into a different kind of heat. Insistent. Penetrating. Claiming.

His body pressed hers against the doorjamb, a wool-covered thigh shoved roughly between hers. Fingers stroked and molded her flesh as if it were soft clay. He left her breathless and needy when his head dipped lower. Shoving the terry bathrobe aside, his mouth latched on her nipple, the engorged tip welcoming his attention.

An electric current shot through her as he sucked and nipped through the damp cotton, the sensation more arousing than if he had access to her bare flesh. Soft cries filled the hallway. It took precious seconds for her to recognize her own voice encouraging him to continue his exploration.

Pushing her nightgown to her waist, his hands palmed her bottom, the motion pressing his covered erection against her core. She would have cursed herself for not putting on underwear after her shower, if the wonderful pressure against her clit let her think. But he didn't give her that chance. His hands and mouth were everywhere, soft touches alternating with the slight scrape of fangs. Not enough to break her skin, but enough to give a thrill of danger, a counterpoint to his rhythm.

Then he lifted her. His strength would have frightened her if she didn't welcome the freedom to wrap her legs around his waist. She clung to him, grinding her body against his.

With her more than enthusiastic response, he didn't waste time. A finger, then two, plunged into her weeping flesh, stroking and pressing the sweetest spot on earth. Every touch made her greedy for more, until the slightest pressure of his thumb sent her plummeting off the edge of the cliff. The inferno of her mind and body exploded.

His mouth over hers swallowed her hoarse cry. All she could do was hang onto his neck for dear life as she shook with tremor after tremor. His fingers inside of her refused to stop until every bit of pleasure had been pulled from her.

Instead of lowering her to the floor as she expected, he swept her into his arms.

Striding across the carpet, he deposited her in the turned-down bed. Gently tugging off her bathrobe, he laid it at the foot of the bed before pulling the covers up to her chin. His kiss to her forehead jerked her out of her shock at the reversal in his behavior, but he was halfway across the room before she could find her voice.

"You're just going to leave?"

He paused at her words. For long seconds, she didn't think he would answer even though she could still sense his fiery desire.

When he turned, his eyes glowed with the same intense lust she'd seen the first night in the back of his Hummer. The night he'd been shot saving her life.

"Bebe—" He could have been saying a prayer instead of her name. His eyes closed. Then she noticed his body trembled as well. When he opened his eyes, the golden glow had not diminished.

"If I don't leave now, I'll do something we'll both regret. Goodnight, *amora*." With that, he stalked out of the room, turning off the lights and closing the door behind him.

Bebe took a deep shuddering breath in the darkness. That had been a close call. She burrowed into the blankets, the first tears leaking from her eyes. Caesar was right. She wouldn't have been able to stop herself from saying yes if he hadn't left.

And the fact she wanted him so bad she didn't care if she were Turned or died scared her more than the assassins after her.

Chapter 21

The next morning dawned with a typical rainy San Francisco winter day. The gray, bleary sky matched Bebe's mood. She'd slept little. The times she'd managed to doze, her dreams would start with Caesar doing delightfully wicked things to her body. But just when she was about to climax, she'd hear Grandma Petrov's screams. Then Caesar would turn into one of the rogues who'd murdered her parents. She'd jerk awake when he tore out her throat.

She chalked the nightmares up to her guilt over her parents and for her own unresolved issues with Grandma, but no amount of meditation or prayer helped. The couple of times she'd return to a fitful sleep where once again, the dream Caesar would take her in every imaginable position until Grandma's cries intruded. Finally, she gave up on sleep, but even a session with the guest bathroom's shower massager hadn't taken the edge off her body's neediness.

After putting on jeans and a sweater, she pulled her hair into a loose ponytail and headed downstairs to the kitchen to scrounge some breakfast. Duncan sat at the table, reading the *Chronicle* and sipping from another mug, when he glanced up at her. Him, she could deal with this morning, even with the metallic scent of blood permeating the air. In some ways, he was far easier to figure out than his boss.

And he hadn't given her the most mind-blowing orgasm of her life.

"Good morning, Doctor. Stan left a plate for you in the refrigerator."

"Thanks," she said, crossing the kitchen. "And you can call me Bebe, you know." She found an omelet covered in plastic wrap on the top shelf. Damn, she hadn't been this well taken care of since she moved out of Grandma's. Placing the plate in the microwave and punching the "On" button, she turned, only to have Duncan looking at her with that eerie vampire stillness. Not menacing but unnerving nonetheless.

"Do you mind if I have some of your tea?" Not that she really wanted it, but anything to break the uncomfortable silence. Maybe dealing with him wouldn't be so easy after all.

He nodded, but when he started to rise, she waved him back down. "Would you like some as well?" she asked while measuring out the leaves.

"Please."

A few minutes later, she pulled out the warmed plate and set it on the table before bringing over the cups of tea. Once again quiet fell, punctuated occasionally by the clink of her fork against ceramic. He didn't touch his cup or the nearly empty mug of blood. Those intense green eyes bore into her, but he didn't try to touch her mind.

Finally, she couldn't stand it any longer and laid down her fork. "Are you going to tell me what your problem is or are you just going to continue staring at me?"

He laid aside the paper before folding his arms and leaning his elbows on the table. "Are you going to continue your grandmother's research?"

Okay, that question came out of left field. Pushing her plate away, she leaned her own elbows on the table. "I honestly hadn't thought much past surviving tonight. Why?" And why the one-eighty from his position last night, but she couldn't bring herself to voice that snide question.

"Caesar is gambling our coven's future on his belief that you will continue Natasha's work. I need to know if his faith in you is misplaced." Despite his words, his tone was quiet. Even. Matter-of-fact.

"You were the first on the 'human again' bandwagon last night." She kept her voice as neutral as his. "What changed?"

A small, wry smile quirked his lips. "Too much time on patrol last night to think about my own foolish desires overriding my duty to Caesar."

She nodded. If Caesar prized his honor so much, he'd surround himself with people who thought likewise. "I can't give Caesar the Book of Shadows itself of course, but he has copies of the research notes, both the coded and translated versions. Even if I don't personally do it, he's got everything you need to continue looking for the cure."

Duncan shook his head. "There are not very many people he would trust to carry on the research besides you."

Alex's comment a few days ago about the vampire lack of medical personnel came back to roost. "Surely, someone's willing to get the education in order to finish the project. Goddess, you people live forever!"

Again, he shook his head. "It's already taken Natasha over sixty years to get this far. And after tonight, there is no assurance that anyone from the Augustine Coven will last long enough to start over again. We are about to start a war on your behalf, Doctor. The least you could do is let us die human."

As if Duncan's guilt trip wasn't bad enough, Caesar chose that moment to saunter into the kitchen. He didn't look much better than she felt, between his grayish skin pallor and the dark circles under his eyes. Despite his exhausted appearance, his faux cocky attitude permeated the room.

Good to know his night had been as tortured as hers.

"Good morning." His greeting included both her and Duncan, but his steady gaze held hers. His eyes had a hint of last night's hunger, but a little speculation as well, which meant he'd overheard Duncan's little discussion.

She broke first, reaching for her now cool tea to avoid the looks from both men. The gene-viral research wasn't her project. Dammit, it wasn't even her problem. Grandma's the one who had made the deal with Augustine, not her.

So why do I want to find a reason to stay?

After fixing his own mug, Caesar pulled out the chair next to her and sat down. He took a healthy gulp of his breakfast before he spoke. "Are you planning to return to Africa tomorrow if everything is resolved tonight?" His tone indicted he didn't care one way or the other, and for some reason that cut deeper than his abrupt departure from her room last night.

She lifted her gaze from her cup and met his squarely. "There's no real reason to stay, is there?" Shoving her chair back harder than she intended, she jerked to her feet. "You boys—" She couldn't stop the scathing condemnation in her tone. "—need to give me a personal object, something you'd normally wear that won't arouse suspicion."

"Why?" Caesar's coolness could have frozen the entire bay solid.

"For personal shield charms, unless you want to become a crispy critter the moment someone launches a fireball at your face tonight." A slight shake broke the haughtiness she tried to affect.

Duncan reached beneath the neck of the black sweater he wore and pulled out a locket on a medium gold chain. "Will this do?"

She nodded, and he handed the jewelry to her. Once again, Duncan surprised her. The jewelry was delicate, feminine and very old. A keepsake from his past? But she didn't ask. She didn't want to get in deeper with these people than she already was.

When she turned to Caesar, he stared at her for a long minute before yanking off his gold and onyx ring. When she reached for it, he seized her wrist with a grip that, while not exactly painful, was damn uncomfortable.

"If your spells do not work properly—"

She didn't wait for the rest of his statement. A tiny flare of heat through her hand served as her own warning while she stared deep into his eyes. "I have no intention of anyone dying tonight, Mr. Augustine."

He released her, and a teensy thrill shot through her when he rubbed his overly warm hand against his slacks. Served the bastard right.

"Will you need anything else besides the two cases we brought from Los Angeles?" Duncan said.

She shook her head. "Please don't disturb me for the next hour." Pivoting on her heel, she marched for the kitchen door.

"What about Stan and Harry?"

She turned back to Caesar, an angry smile twisting her lips. "It seems I'm not the only ignorant one in the room." His eyes started to gleam dully in the morning light. Maybe she'd pushed him too far in her horrible mood. Well, he deserved her bitchiness after what he did last night. Especially since he shouldn't have started what he did when he had no intention of following through.

A sigh whistled past her lips. "Elven and witch magicks don't play nice with each other. I'll speak with them, but I'm sure they both will have defensive charms. I doubt if any of the White Roses would be stupid enough to throw a spell at them. If they try anything with Stan or Harry, it would have to be a conventional physical attack."

She waited a couple of heartbeats, but Caesar kept quiet. Damn vampire. It felt good to slam the kitchen door behind her.

Caesar listened to Bebe's footsteps as she climbed the staircase, emotions roiling so bad he wasn't sure what to think or feel.

"I discovered who the eclectic from the restaurant was."

Surprise slammed into him at Duncan's words. "What? How?"

"I . . . borrowed Ptolemy's phone. He had taken pictures of your assailants. The witch was an eclectic named Lily Franklin. Originally from the Cleveland Coven. She had been exiled five years ago for fraud and robbery. She was freelance as far as my contacts know. I am still working on the were's identity."

Caesar blinked in surprise. "When did you do this?"

"I returned Ptolemy's phone before we left Los Angeles." Annoyance tinged Duncan's voice.

"No, I mean when did you have a chance to research her?"

"When you ordered me to bed." The mild reproof hung in the air.

Irritation narrowed Caesar's eyes. "So you're making disobedience a habit?"

"Only because you are being a bloody idiot," Duncan muttered.

"I don't believe I asked for your opinion." Anger rose from the ocean seething through his mind.

"Maybe that is part of the problem." Duncan's voice continued at normal volume. "In the past, you would seek our counsel, weigh the options and take action based on a well-reasoned decision. Those qualities made you an excellent leader, Caesar."

"Made?" The past tense verb kicked him harder in the gut than if Duncan's foot had actually connected.

Duncan raised an eyebrow. "I am your chief enforcer, and I carry Lady Natasha's Blood Seal on your behalf. I do not resent my service to you. However, you are letting your feelings for Bebe cloud your judgment."

"I don't have any feelings for Bebe."

Duncan's other eyebrow joining the first spoke his thoughts on the subject more eloquently than any words he could have said.

Caesar leaned back in his chair, staring at the tabletop. *Hades.* It wasn't very often Duncan nailed him committing self-deception. Actually he couldn't think of a time the English vampire had forced him to face facts. But Duncan was right. He was in love with Bebe Zachary. He raised his eyes to meet Duncan's. He hadn't been this uncomfortable when his brother-in-law had caught him losing his virginity with Selene's maid when he was fifteen. "Is it that obvious?"

Amusement flared in Duncan's eyes even if his lips didn't curl into a smile.

"Other than Anne catching the two of you in here, Bebe's cry of pleasure last night, and Harry's complaints concerning the lack of hot water when he came off duty, no."

Caesar closed his eyes in exasperation. Duncan was right. His behavior when it came to Bebe had been atrocious. And even worse, Ptolemy had been right in abusing him about his choice of Saturnalia gift for her. The sounds of Duncan rinsing his tableware made him open his eyes.

Duncan closed the dishwasher before turning back to Caesar. "What I am about to say, I am saying as a friend."

Caesar nodded for him to continue. The rarity of Duncan's claim of friendship set his curiosity ablaze as to what the other vampire would say.

"Have you considered asking her to join you?"

He couldn't have been more surprised if Duncan had just shoved a garlic-soaked silver stake into his heart. It took a couple of seconds for the shock to die down enough to speak. "You're the last person I'd expect to suggest that she be Turned."

"I am not suggesting you Turn her. I am suggesting you should ask her. First of all, Bebe is much more like Natasha than she is willing to admit. She needs to make her own decisions." A wry smile crossed his face. "Even though we are both old enough to know life does not always allow one's decisions to bear fruit. Secondly, by her answer you will discover how she really feels about you without invading her thoughts."

"No." Caesar shook his head. "I won't even suggest Turning her. The odds of a witch surviving a Turn—"

"Are astronomical at best," Duncan finished. He shrugged. "I know, but she is Nikolai's granddaughter as well as Natasha's. She is stubborn enough to survive the infection if she truly desires it."

Caesar turned to stare at the few brown leaves that clung to the trees in the back yard, dancing under the raindrops. How much of Nikolai did Bebe truly carry in her blood? If she had enough, the question was moot, but she couldn't be with him. At least, not forever.

But maybe she could be Turned. Maybe she could survive. Maybe she'd be one of the rare few that didn't go psychotic. His cock stirred at the thought. Was he willing to risk her life on such a slim chance?

No. Too many maybes. Knowing she was alive somewhere he could deal with, but causing her death would tear his heart apart.

He met Duncan's gaze. "I'm still surprised *you* are suggesting this. Are you sure you're not hoping to give Bebe added incentive to find a cure?"

Again, Duncan shrugged. "I would be lying to say it had not crossed my mind." His attention flicked away for an instant before he cleared his throat and continued. "Love is such a rare thing. I would hate to see you throw it away without finding a way to make things work with Bebe. You both owe yourselves the opportunity to discuss the subject properly before dismissing it." He started out of the kitchen, clapping Caesar on the shoulder as he passed.

"Duncan." His voice made the other vampire stop at the door and look back.

"Thank you for your honesty." His voice wasn't more than a whisper, emotion so thick in his mouth, but Duncan nodded and left the kitchen.

When alone, Caesar buried his face in his hands. Gods above and below, didn't he have enough shit to deal with? He scrubbed the heels of his hands across his grainy eyeballs in an attempt to banish his weariness. Last night was the first time in decades he'd had trouble sleeping. He'd failed miserably in his purpose of speaking with Bebe.

One look at her lush body through the light cotton had destroyed any rational thought. And Bebe's responsiveness to his touch had fired his own lust to the point it took all his strength to walk out of her bedroom. They both needed to be fully dressed before he tried having any discussion of their future with her.

Assuming she wanted a future with him. Such a path would mean no children, no family of their own, and she had never voiced her feelings on having babies, much less if her attraction to him went beyond raw, unadulterated lust. He lifted his head to stare at the barren backyard.

He shook his head at his stream of thought. Had he already given up any hope of a cure? Bebe hadn't really said she wouldn't continue with Natasha's research, but neither did she say she would. And she hadn't specifically said she was returning to Africa either. No, she had said she had no reason to stay. Then he needed to give her a reason.

Two separate problems, for neither of which he had immediate solutions. He sucked in a deep breath and rose to re-warm his mug of blood. After tonight, he'd deal with his emotions where Bebe Zachary was concerned. First, he needed to make sure they both survived the White Rose Confirmation ceremony.

Chapter 22

Anxiety rasped across Bebe's skin as Stan braked the Hummer to an easy stop in front of the Petrov mansion. She tried to remind herself they'd done everything they could to prepare between the protective charms and briefing the men on the coven's major players.

She threw out her senses, but blocking spells rebuffed her efforts. As she had warned Caesar, she had no way to confirm who was inside the building. No doubt, the vampires had already picked up the presence of the hidden security personnel outside of the house. She glanced out the window at the place she'd called home for fifteen years, half-expecting Grandma Petrov to march out the door and scold her for missing curfew. Instead, two black-clad armed guards, a man and a woman, stood sentinel in front of the massive oak doors leading into the house.

Guards who brought their weapons to bear once Duncan cleared the passenger door. He didn't give the White Rose security so much as a glance.

She had to give Caesar's right-hand vampire credit for dismissing the guns so readily. She'd lay odds that the guards' weapons held the same garlic-laced bullets that had nearly killed Caesar a few nights ago.

Duncan opened the Hummer door for Caesar, who in turn, assisted her out of the vehicle, even though she could have easily climbed out in the smart black pantsuit with a matching calf-length jacket Anne had selected for her. As she'd suspected, both guards had been briefed on her appearance, so their mouths fell open when they realized who the vampires were escorting. With all the dignity she could muster, she climbed the steps, her heels tapping smartly on the flag-stones. Caesar fell in step on her right, Duncan on her left. The spinach taste of thoughts reassured her Stan brought up the rear. Just as she reached the portico, the female guard regained her composure, shooting nasty looks at the vampires as she stepped to block Bebe.

"I'm sorry, Ms. Zachary, but you can't leave your vehicle here."

"Doctor," Caesar said, his smooth tenor brushing over Bebe both physically and mentally. She hated to admit his support bolstered her flagging confidence.

"Huh?" The woman jerked as if shocked that a vampire would dare speak to her.

"It's Dr. Zachary," Bebe said, giving the woman a saccharine smile. "Don't you think it would be best to start off on the right foot with your new high priestess?"

If possible, the woman's look became even harder. "I'm sorry, *Doctor*. You're not Confirmed yet, and *no* one's allowed to park here for security reasons. You need to park behind the house." She nodded toward the section of the drive that curved around the side of the mansion.

Bebe looked over her shoulder and gave Harry, still sitting in the driver's seat, a single nod. An energy shield, the color of new leaves, sprang over the Hummer. She turned back to the guards, still wearing her sweetly nasty smile. "If you'd like to remove my bodyguard's wards, you're more than welcome to try, but my ride stays here."

Once more, the female guard's mouth opened in shock as she stared at the Hummer now protected by fae magick. Bebe moved to brush by her, but the bulkier male blocked her way. Caesar stepped forward, eyes gleaming and fangs extended, but Bebe held up a single hand.

"You know we can't let *them* in an official coven function, Doctor." The man's brown eyes gave her a sympathetic look that made her wonder just how much the Council of Elders and their security staff knew about the assassination attempts. Could the Elders be in on the scheme?

Raising her chin, she stared the man in the eyes. Well, as much she could when he towered a foot over her. Playing on that sympathy, she said, "It's a sad day when witch kills witch, and I have to depend on outsiders for my safety, don't you think, Mr.—"

"It's Geoffrey, Lady." He nodded, a serious expression on his square face. His abrupt switch in title boded well. "And yes, ma'am, it is." His decision made, he stepped back and waved her forward.

"No! You can't let *vampires*—" The female guard practically spat the word. "—into a Confirmation." She jumped in front of Bebe, but with no support from her partner and a glare from Bebe, her defiance wilted. She stepped back, muttering imprecations under her breath.

Only with supreme self-control did Bebe manage not to sigh in relief. Maintaining her haughty expression, she swept past the woman, Caesar and his men on her heels. The male guard backpedaled to open one of the massive oak doors for her and her entourage, and for the first time in two years, she stepped into her grandmother's home.

The difference between then and now ripped the breath out of her lungs. The heavy, burgundy drapes were the only things that remained in the foyer. The paintings, the sculptures, even the atrocious Napoleonic side table that held Grandma's favorite vase was gone. For the first time, the fact that *everything* had been sold by the estate receiver struck Bebe in the heart. She'd been so angry and so fearful she hadn't let the enormity of the auction hit her.

Until now.

Tears blurred her vision as her gaze swept up the stairs. Even the delicately rendered still life that had perched at the first landing was gone. And thanks to her stupid-ass cousins, she'd never see it again.

No, it wasn't the missing belongings. It was the sterile atmosphere. No joy. No grief. The place held nothing for her.

Bebe, you must collect yourself.

She nodded at Caesar's empathetic urging, literally pulling strength from the surrounding stones in the walls to keep herself upright. She took a deep calming breath just as Beatrice Flannigan charged through the side parlor door into the foyer. Beatrice's warm greeting faded on her lips as Bebe's escort registered. If her salt-and-pepper hair hadn't become completely silver in the intervening years, it probably would have done so in the instant she realized vampires and a half-elf flanked Bebe on the marble tile of the high priestess's mansion.

Flustered, Beatrice tried to speak three times before she smoothed her intricate braids coiled at the nape of her neck and a much dimmer smile stuck to her face. She held out her hands to Bebe. "I'm so glad you came to your senses, dear. It makes things so much easier for all of us."

Bebe threw out a probe before taking Beatrice's hands, but no spell lurked around the other woman. She returned Beatrice's lukewarm smile and double handshake. Now, if she could only make her crazy-ass plan sprout wings and fly. "There are some things I need to discuss with the Elders before we start the ceremony, Beatrice."

The Air Elder's expression grew serious. "Some of us wished to speak with you as well, but I'm afraid Alice and William discovered our plans. They've challenged your Confirmation." She sighed. "If we met with you privately—"

This time Bebe's smile grew genuine. Caesar's information network had done their job. The bait had been scented. For the hundredth time that day, she gave the Goddess a silent prayer that her cousins didn't have the resources to cause anyone significant harm when the trap was sprung.

She patted Beatrice's hand and said, "Don't worry about it. I'd rather have this out in front of everyone, so there's absolutely no questions later."

Beatrice nodded slowly, acting like she seriously considered Bebe's words. "Yes, their accusations have been disturbing to say the least." She met Bebe's eyes, her smile broadening. "Not that I believe a thing. Lady Natasha was so proud of the work you were doing with the children in Africa. I know you had nothing to do with her death, despite your disagreements." She gave Bebe's hand a squeeze as if that cemented her opinion.

At least, now we know what else your family will throw at you during this little hearing.

Bebe inclined her head, knowing Caesar would pick up her acknowledgement even though her words were directed to Beatrice. "My sole regret is that I left things unresolved between me and Grandma. All I can do is make sure her true wishes are followed." She gestured for Beatrice to precede her into the old ballroom where Grandma usually had held her council meetings.

Beatrice ran her hands down the tailored mustard skirt she wore, the motion to collect herself rather than to smooth the non-existent wrinkles in the fabric. She tugged on her matching short jacket before she nodded and headed down the hallway.

Sweet Goddess, why was Beatrice so nervous? Maybe Caesar was right and this whole thing was just another trap aimed at killing Bebe? She shot a glance at Caesar. A reassuring warmth flooded her, and she gave him a small smile in return. She strode after Beatrice, the click of boots behind her. Tomorrow she'd dwell on how upside down her life had become in the last couple of weeks. Right now, she needed to focus on the next couple of hours.

Gasps rippled through the assembled coven members when Bebe and her party entered the ballroom. Shock and outrage, she expected, but there was a healthy amount of curiosity emanating from those who recognized Caesar.

She didn't dare raise her outer shield to block the slurry of wild emotion that threatened to overwhelm her inner shields. Caesar had been right to keep silent communication open in case trouble erupted. Instead, she focused on the bareness of the room.

Once again, everything movable had been stripped but the heavy draperies, which were closed despite the high walls and landscaping that would prevent anyone from observing their rituals from outside. Candelabras, probably borrowed from other coven members since she didn't recognize them and none of them matched, stood at regular intervals to provide light for the proceedings. Good. She wouldn't have to rely so much on her internal resources if a literal firefight broke out.

With all the furnishings gone, the parquet wood strips forming the giant pentacle that took up nearly the entire floor stuck out. The only other object was a makeshift altar in the center of the room. The too-big white tablecloth covering the waist-high table pooled on the hardwood. Each of the ceremonial objects representing the four elements already lay on top of the altar. The chalice, wand, athame and clay plate were the responsibility of the Elders as were the silver and gold bells that represented the Goddess and the God, and therefore hadn't been lost in the asinine estate sale.

An uncomfortable itching sensation of someone staring at her from across the room made her scan the crowd. Ahead and on her left, Alice huddled next to Pierre Le Croix, the Fire Elder. She glared daggers at Bebe.

Amusement rippled through her. For once, Alice wore a sedate black dress, not one of her slinky, sequined party numbers. She stretched up to whisper something in Pierre's ear, revealing a thigh-high slit. So, the dress wasn't that conservative after all. Somehow, it went well with Pierre's flashy burgundy suit.

No sign of Uncle Lionel, but then, he often missed coven events. So why not show up if he supported Alice's bid for high priestess? His absence didn't help Bebe's nerves given the current situation.

She gave Alice a slight acknowledging nod before her attention swept the rest of the room. William stood directly on her right in a semi-circle with three of the Lesser Elders and two others she didn't know. His bland face revealed nothing as he and his little group regarded her, though his associates' distaste for her presence was rather obvious from their expressions. Standing on opposite sides of the room, Alice and William were hardly the portrait of steadfast allies.

As I pointed out, they each could have engineered a separate assassination attempt.

Thanks for that pleasant reminder. It so helps my nerves.

Caesar's soft mental chuckle tickled her brain. *You knew which Elders have thrown their lots in with your cousins.*

Nerves sent the butterflies in her stomach spinning. *I wish your little network hadn't been correct about how many Elders sided with them.* So much of her plan had hinged on convincing the Elders that Alice or William or maybe even both of them jeopardized the entire coven.

Soft ringing cut through the scattered murmurs. The rustling of the crowd replaced the chiming as Beatrice set down the bells and the coven members moved to their positions around the circle. Each of the Greater Elders took their places at a pentacle tip with their Juniors on their right hand sides. Alice stayed close to Pierre in order to take the spot on his left.

Sucking in a deep breath, Bebe strode across the floor to her place at the northernmost point of the pentacle. The point reserved for the high priestess.

Grandma Petrov's spot.

She'd stopped standing at Grandma's right hand after the second huge fight over marrying Alastair and had left the country a week later. Her feet wanted to carry her one spot over, but reality slammed home. She would never again stand next to Grandma in a coven circle.

She blinked back the tears that threatened and turned to face the assembled coven. Caesar gave her shoulder a quick, reassuring squeeze as he passed her. He,

Duncan and Stan ranged themselves behind her. Not part of the circle, but where they could keep an eye on the proceedings.

No one stood in the space to her right. Similar to Arthur's Siege Perilous, it would remain empty until someone worthy could take that place, or in the coven's case, a confirmed h.p. named an heir.

Bebe swallowed the sigh that threatened. Maybe she should accept the Confirmation. With an h.p.'s autonomy, she could institute the democratic conventions so many other American covens had adopted instead of the European hereditary method White Rose had clung to after immigrating to San Francisco.

"Elder Flannigan, I must protest the presence of—" Pierre obviously decided to skip whatever insult he'd originally planned to lob at Caesar by his slight hesitation. "—these outsiders. Confirmations are closed to all but adult coven members."

"Elder Le Croix." Bebe stepped forward, letting her eyes narrow. "Mr. Augustine and his associates are here by my grandmother's request."

"So now we allow the Silver Bear High Priestess to dictate our laws and traditions." An ugly sneer spread across Pierre's sharp features.

Bebe quelled the anger under a veneer of calm. It figured he would try to muddy the issues. "I'm so sorry for your confusion, Elder. I was referring to Lady Natasha Petrov, not Lady Ziva Epstein. Conspirators within our own coven planned and carried out my grandmother's murder."

That little proclamation elicited a number of gasps and exclamations of alarm. Bebe's eyes scanned the crowd, but everyone looked genuinely shocked. Everyone except the Greater and Lesser Elders as well as Alice and William.

Plunging ahead before Pierre could cut her off again, Bebe said, "Suspecting such problems within our coven, she feared for my safety as her heir, and she asked Master Augustine to provide security for me upon my return to the States should any *misfortune* happen to her."

Tension crawled through the room as the initial surprise gave way to anger and fear.

"How do we know you didn't murder Grandma to control the coven?" Alice's low-pitched fury carried through the room. "Everyone here knows you were pissed at her for suggesting that you marry Alastair Hyde-Smith to cement relations with London. Now her Book of Shadows is missing. As the named heir, you are the only other one who knew where it was, and you said you didn't have it."

Game on.

It took all of Bebe's willpower not to clench her fists and march across the circle to beat Alice into a pulp. No wonder she clung to Pierre. She'd always needed her daddy to bail her out of trouble, so now the bitch planned to use the Fire Elder as a substitute.

Well, not this time.

"You know, cousin," Bebe said, letting the sarcasm drip from her words. "I'd suspect me too, if it weren't for a couple of things. I'm not the one who challenged Grandma's Last Will and Testament in court after she couldn't find the Book's hiding place, which, by the way—" She lowered her voice in a pseudo-whisper. "—was the smelly old wardrobe you hated." She raised her voice to a normal volume. "I also didn't get the wardrobe sold along with every other thing Grandma ever owned at an estate auction. Want to guess who bought the wardrobe for me since someone was taking great pains to make sure I didn't get back to San Francisco in time for the funeral, much less the auction?"

She and Caesar had decided it would be best not to mention Phillippa's involvement in the safekeeping of the Book. Besides, there was a certain delight in rubbing Alice's surgically enhanced nose in the fact that the Book had been right under it the entire time.

"Then there's the matter of someone trying to kill me ever since I received the telegram from the estate receiver, including a group of gunmen who destroyed my hotel room here in San Francisco." She paused a beat before delivering the coup de grace. "We traced their getaway vehicle to a subsidiary of Bay Area Consolidated. By the way, where is your father tonight?"

Alice's eyes narrowed as the entire assemblage turned and stared at her, but what concerned Bebe more was her aura. The bloody orange energy shifted and flared with Alice's rising anger. The coven hadn't raised a circle yet. If her cousin didn't get a grip, her unchecked magick could kill someone.

Then abruptly Alice laughed, a bitter sound that had the woman next to her take a not-so-subtle step back. "Ooooh, that's clever. Steal a van from one of Daddy's companies so you can pin your power trip on me. What amazes me the most is your pet vampires after the years you've spent trashing them."

Bebe smiled back, a wide one that would have bared fangs if she had them. "It's a lot easier to trust Mr. Augustine after a witch tried to slash my throat two nights ago."

"That's a very serious accusation, Bebe." Morton Sinclair, White Rose's Water Elder, spoke for the first time. "Who do you claim attacked you?"

Somehow, relief flooded Bebe when no one called her an outright liar. Yet. "We've identified the woman as Lily Franklin, a freelance eclectic with no known affiliations." Confusion rippled through the circle at her words. She couldn't blame them. The attempted murder by another witch still shocked her.

Alice made a sound of disgust. "Even if you're telling the truth—"

Aha! The expected slam.

"—who's to say she wasn't someone else you set up, Bebe. And that's no reason for *them* to be here. Our ceremonies and traditions are none of *their* business." Alice sneered at the three men behind Bebe.

"Franklin attempted to murder Dr. Zachary while assisted by three rogue vampires and a packless were in front of a restaurant owned by a member of my Family in the presence of Normal witnesses in my capital. That makes White Rose's Confirmation my business." Caesar's steel voice sent a wave of discord through the coven. The rich, beefy texture of his thoughts enveloped her, a cocoon against the hostility raging through the room, and a sharp boot click said he'd stepped forward on her right, not quite in the circle but in the one spot everyone could see him. He continued his speech as if any coven member's objections meant nothing to him. "Furthermore, Lady Natasha did ask for my assistance in protecting Dr. Zachary. As I explained to her, Augustine Coven will not interfere with the White Rose succession, but I will honor my word to Lady Natasha and ensure that Dr. Zachary survives long enough for a Confirmation hearing to be held."

"Well, you've certainly done your duty." Miranda Doucette's voice carried an oily contempt. Her forest green dress appeared black in the candlelight. "But since this *is* the Confirmation, I hardly see where your services are still necessary."

Bebe suppressed a shiver. The Earth Elder had never disguised her personal dislike of Bebe during their tutoring sessions. When she'd tried to broach the subject with Grandma, she'd been told that Miranda held a potential h.p. to higher standards than her other students. Grandma had added that the Earth Elder had been equally hard on Bebe's mother. Now, Miranda's raw antagonism shone on her pinched face.

"With all due respect, Elder Doucette, I believe the Confirmation has been challenged by Ms. Hart and Mr. Petrov. Until a Confirmation ceremony is actually performed, my duty to Dr. Zachary remains."

Bebe didn't have to see Caesar's face to know his familiar condescending smirk filled his features. It was further confirmed by the ugly look Miranda shot both of them.

"And all we have is your word concerning Lady Natasha's wishes," Pierre said.

"Would a Blood Seal suffice?" Caesar said.

Bebe whirled to face him, her heart pounding. What the hell was he playing at? An h.p. Blood Seal couldn't be faked by another witch. She hadn't seen a Seal on his body the night he'd been shot. Not only had she gotten a very intimate look at every muscle-sculpted inch, he admitted Grandma had not requested him to take the oath.

To her surprise, Duncan stepped forward and shoved up the sleeve of his black leather jacket. He raised his right arm. A wine-dark stain formed a filigreed circle on his pale flesh, the same design the coven used for the earrings worn by its members. Under the multitude of candles, occasional flashes of silver light could be seen in the mark. The Blood Seal promised immolation if a bargain went unfulfilled so it was invoked only in the direst of situations.

"That makes no sense!" snapped Pierre. "If you made the promise, Augustine, why don't you bear the Seal?"

Caesar favored Pierre with an arrogant smirk. "Lady Natasha trusted me to fulfill my promise, but she had concerns that my chief enforcer would not be so willing to assist me with my obligation. He graciously acceded to her wish for insurance."

For once, something Caesar said regarding Grandma made sense. She would have wanted a guarantee of good behavior from the coven master's right-hand man. She already had Caesar on the hook with the lure of a possible cure to the V-virus.

"We have no wish to create a dispute with your coven by preventing you from fulfilling your oath, Mr. Augustine." Beatrice's mouth twitched as she tried to suppress a smile. "Unless any of my fellow Greater Elders has an objection, you and your men may remain until the end of the ceremony."

"If I may remind you, Elder Flannigan, there's still the issue of Lady Natasha's death." Pierre's strident voice rang through the room.

Beatrice sighed, a long exasperated sound.

Bebe bit her tongue to stifle her nervous laugh. Had Beatrice and Morton really expected to force the confirmation through without Pierre and Miranda raising every possible fuss they could? Not to mention Alice and William.

Except William hadn't said a word yet. So what was his motive in all this, or was he waiting to see who survived once the dust cleared?

That would totally be his style. His inherent laziness made her question his role in this charade.

Morton spoke first, his voice soothing and reassuring despite his actual words. "Dr. Zachary, since you brought up the charge of Lady Natasha's murder, please present your evidence."

Bebe swallowed hard, her stomach rebelling at the nervous energy swirling around her. She wasn't sure how much was her own anxiety and how much was the imposed emotions of the people surrounding her. A strange sensation surged up her spine, something she couldn't identify. There was no time to question it. She had no choice but to proceed with the miniscule evidence she had.

"The Elders already ordered an autopsy prior to my grandmother's cremation. They are aware she died from a heart attack triggered by an overdose of nitroglycerin. In that regard, I agree with my cousin, Alice Hart, in that her overdose was not accidental." Goddess, she hated this drama. She pulled a plastic bag from the deep pockets of her jacket and displayed the ziplocked baggie that held a knife.

The gore-encrusted sushi knife Franklin had held at Bebe's throat.

She eyed each of the Greater Elders in turn as she spoke. "Since I believe that the attempts on my own life were orchestrated by the same person or persons who engineered Lady Natasha's overdose, I ask the Elders permission to cast a spell on the knife Franklin used in order to trace who hired her. I would then ask the Elders permission to question that person once the circle's been cast."

And Uncle Lionel wasn't here. How convenient. The stunt could blow up in her face, but Caesar seemed so sure there was more than one member of White Rose involved in Grandma's little conspiracy.

"Wait a minute! How do we know you haven't already bespelled the damn knife to point to whoever you plan on casting as the scapegoat?" Pierre broke circle, stepping forward, his face red with fury even in the dim candlelight.

"All four of the Greater Elders will examine it at the same time while it remains in Dr. Zachary's hand." A sardonic smile twisted Beatrice's face, and her eyes fixed on Pierre. "I would hate for the knife to be sabotaged to kill her the moment she casts her discovery spell. Is that satisfactory?"

The affronted look on Pierre's face lasted barely a second before he gave a curt nod of agreement. All four Elders crossed the circle and laid their right hands on the knife Bebe had pulled out of the baggie and placed in her raised right palm. Magick tingled and pulsed across her skin as the Elders examined the knife, but no one tried anything.

Beatrice met the eyes of each Elder, and one by one, they nodded their satisfaction that the knife was taint-free. Simultaneously, they pulled away and returned to their places at the other four points.

Beatrice gave a sharp nod. "Please proceed, Dr. Zachary."

Bebe took a deep, calming breath and concentrated on the nasty piece of steel. While the Elders could have performed the same spell, the knife had been intended to kill Bebe. Her connection to the knife would create far more accurate results. It was a saving grace Pierre hadn't disputed that point. She didn't relish the thought of confessing to the coven that she'd killed Franklin. She hoped she wouldn't have to. But it was another degree of relationship that added fuel to the spell, no matter how it turned her stomach.

As she focused, strands of golden energy flowed and danced around the steel, mixing with faint orange-ish wisps, the miniscule revenants of Franklin's power. She called on the bits of information Duncan had pulled about the woman and shaped as complete a picture as she could of the living, breathing person that once existed. Then she murmured the ancient Latin words that completed the circuit of magick.

The knife leaped from her palm to land with a clatter at William's feet.

Chapter 23

Stunned silence filled the room.

Bebe gasped. Not that William wasn't a conniving little weasel, but for him to gather the gumption to have her killed?

She was still trying to wrap her brain around the revelation when William whirled and charged for the closed door, only to crash into Duncan's broad chest. The vampire had crossed the room before any of the witches could react. Her cousin landed hard, sprawling in an awkward heap across the parquet floor.

Duncan reached down to pull the dazed William up by the collar. "I believe Dr. Zachary has some questions for you."

"Let go, you rat bastard." William struggled in the vampire's grip. Not that it did him any good. "I didn't hire that eclectic bitch. Let go!"

"Why did you hire Franklin to kill me, William?" Bebe said. Goddess, she didn't want to hear the answer.

"I didn't! Tim did." William stopped wriggling and jabbed an accusing finger at Timothy O'Leary. The Lesser Earth Elder.

"No, you just provided the money!"

Bebe blinked in surprise as the Lesser Elder stepped forward, his counteraccusation still echoing through the room. She didn't know the man very well, but he had been in the cluster standing with William before Beatrice called the hearing to order.

Miranda stepped forward as well, her claw-like hand grabbing O'Leary's arm and turning him to face her. "What are you saying?"

Bebe didn't miss the maniacal look that shone in O'Leary's eyes as he faced his senior.

"I'm the one who hired the idiot. We gave that stupid little eclectic bitch everything she needed to slice Zachary's throat, and she still fucked up the job." O'Leary sneered at his Greater. "Come on, Miranda, you're always saying that Zachary didn't have the balls to be high priestess. That we needed new blood. That the Petrovs had no talent. No strength." A smile that could only be described as pure evil leered from his face. "No vision of the future."

"I *never* advocated killing Natasha, much less Bebe." Miranda forced the words through her clenched teeth.

"Hey, what do you mean I have no talent?" came William's pathetic complaint.

O'Leary jerked free of Miranda's grip and sauntered closer to the altar. "You're all idiots." His voice rose as he addressed the coven. "You've merrily followed Natasha Petrov to your own slaughter. Do you have any concept of what our precious high priestess has been doing behind our backs?"

Air caught in Bebe's lungs, electricity racing up and down her nerves. Where did he think he was going?

Miranda stepped back onto her point, met Bebe's eyes squarely, and nodded. That single nod spoke volumes where the Earth Elder's change of mind was concerned. Bebe may not be Confirmed, but she was the acting high priestess.

Each of the Greater Elders followed suit, even Pierre, and for the first time tonight, relief spread through Bebe's soul. Coven members began locking hands with their neighbors, and a slim thread of magick began twirling around the room. Within seconds, only two gaps remained in the circle.

Caesar, step back. A whisper of air told her he'd complied, even though the essence of him didn't leave her psyche. She edged as close to her neighbor on the right as she could without leaving her point of the pentacle. A quick glance showed the woman's outstretched hand, the other witch waiting for her signal.

"She's used her own blood kin to consolidate her personal power, regardless of any benefit to White Rose." O'Leary continued his rant against Grandma, oblivious to the growing tension.

Bebe locked eyes with the vampire across the room. *Duncan, when I tell you, shove William into the circle.*

Like Miranda, Duncan gave Bebe a single nod. The gaze of the two male witches on either side of him flicked from her, to Duncan, and back to her. Their bodies stiffened as they prepared to make the final connection.

She sucked in a deep breath and shouted, "Now!"

In a single fluid motion only a vampire could accomplish, Duncan pushed William forward and leapt back out of the pentacle. The two male witches clasped hands as soon Duncan was clear.

The instant a hot, perspiring palm met Bebe's, a hemisphere of brilliant white energy arced into place over their heads. Except her bodyguards were now on the outside of the shield, and she remained inside with a couple of nutcases.

"You're trapped, O'Leary. Start talking. Who else is in on this plot of yours?" Bebe said. Her anger kept her voice steady.

O'Leary slowly pivoted until he faced her. His leering grin stretched his narrow features into a death rictus. Black danced along his crimson aura. "Would you like to find out, baby?" When she didn't respond to his mockery of her name, he reached toward the altar, his long fingers closing around the athame.

He wouldn't be stupid enough to desecrate the coven's ceremonial knife, would he? She met his eyes. Not stupid.

Insane.

"Put that down, O'Leary," she said, bending a fraction of the circle's magick to lend power to her voice. "You've got no way out. Not with the entire coven, a couple of vampires and a fae between you and the door."

"Who said I was leaving, baby?" he said, and then plunged the athame into his heart.

Chapter 24

For the second time tonight, Bebe found she couldn't make a sound as shock ripped at her.

The psycho had made himself the blood sacrifice.

Black energy bubbled out of O'Leary as his body collapsed. With the circle's shield in place, there was nowhere for his soul to go. The soul energy swirled, collected itself, then arrowed straight toward her, its intent to possess clear.

She couldn't let O'Leary leave the circle. Who knows what innocent person he'd take advantage of in his insanity? No, she only had one choice.

"Don't let go! Don't let the circle collap—"

O'Leary's soul oozed into her, cutting off her words. Sticking a finger in a light socket would have been less painful. She wanted to scream from the agony but couldn't. The blackness filled her nose, her mouth, her throat until she couldn't breathe, much less cry out. It swallowed her vision, sucked away any sound, destroyed any taste, touch or smell.

Her lungs burned, desperate for air. Goddess, was this how Franklin felt when she was dying? Fresh pain seared each brain cell. No, this had to be much worse. Fire scorched every nerve ending as the connection between matter and energy shredded under O'Leary's attack. The bastard was trying to force her out of her own body, ramming his own soul roots into her flesh.

Bebe, fight him! Damn it, woman! Fight!

Caesar was there with her, cocooning her, but he only muffled the pain. Her psychic fingers were losing their grip. Hatred, rage and fear whipped at her, O'Leary's emotions a hurricane wind in her mind, knifing through everything that made her unique.

On the edge of her awareness, chanting sliced through her, but she couldn't spare the power to figure out if the voices were hurting or helping her. It was all she could do to maintain her hold on her body.

C'mon, Busy Be. Don't let that son of a bitch win!

Alice? Her cousin hadn't used that nickname for her in seventeen years. A trickle of energy, like the taste of fresh-picked oranges, flowed through her.

Remember what Grandpa Nick used to say?

Alice's words triggered old emotions, ones Bebe had buried under her grief long ago. *We were his Sunshine Girls, day or night.* He'd compared their auras to sunbeams dancing when they'd played together as children, racing through the gigantic backyard, whether chasing butterflies or lightning bugs. When she found her tears, she'd shed them for the memory of how she and Alice used to be.

No rain, Be, not now. Think sun, think fission, think solar power burning that bastard away.

Fresh rage pummeled Bebe, searing her raw. She couldn't stand any longer against the pain. Hell, she didn't even know if she still had legs.

Bebe, amora. Caesar's sandalwood and steak mixed with Alice's tangy orange. *I love you. Don't you dare leave me.*

Love her? Did he really say he loved her?

Yes, dammit! If you can battle me and a whole cadre of assassins, you can annihilate a measly-assed, cowardly witch!

Caesar was right. She'd faced worse. Her mental hold tightened tenaciously around her body. Hell, she'd done worse. The image of the golem she'd thrown at Franklin sprang into full bloom. But there was nothing to use within the Circle. Nothing except the coven tools.

No, not matter. Energy.

Carefully shaping the memory of the golem she'd created to kill Franklin, Bebe launched the psy-bolt at O'Leary's ghost.

An eerie low-pitched wailing assaulted her suddenly returned hearing. She fell to her knees, pain shooting up her thighs. But Blessed Lady, it was physical hurt, not the psychic agony O'Leary had inflicted. The soul tendrils of the insane Earth Lesser made one last grab at her, but were forced back by the other witches. The tight grips of the witches on each of her hands kept her from totally collapsing to the floor. Kept the circle intact.

The chanting resolved into the voices of the seven remaining Elders, a counterpoint to the keening that rattled her bones and grated her nerves. Bebe blinked, trying to clear her vision of tears that had collected. A white-hot ball of energy surrounded O'Leary's black soul, forcing the miasma into the silver chalice on the altar.

Ashes and despair coated her tongue when the realization of the type of spell hit her. The Elders condemned O'Leary into a Soul Sphere. The ultimate punishment for their people, to be incarcerated for all eternity in a special glass ball. To see and hear everything around you, but to never touch reality again.

Unless someone took pity on you and released you from that horrible prison.

She swallowed the bile that rose at the back of her throat. Someone had placed the Sphere in the ceremonial chalice prior to her arrival, and she hadn't thought to scan the objects on the altar, so unnerved she was by discovering the possible truth about either of her cousins.

The pure white light flared as the dark energy disappeared into the cup with a final scream of desperation and pop of displaced air. The whiteness faded and another type of blackness swallowed the room.

And losing her hold on the two witches, Bebe fell headlong into that other blackness.

Chapter 25

Anger, fear and pain tore a howl from Caesar's throat when the last shred of Bebe's essence slid from his mind. The protective sphere around the circle faded the instant Bebe slipped from the grasp of the witches, landing with a boneless thud. Caesar charged forward and knelt to cradle the unconscious woman in his arms. Blood seeped from both of her nostrils. In the vee of her blouse, the silver pentacle Tiffany had given her had charred to slag though her skin was unmarred.

She couldn't be dead. Dammit, Osiris, it's not her time!

Someone tried to take Bebe from him, but he hissed at the person, bloodrage turning everything around him scarlet. Clutching her to his chest, he bared his fangs. She couldn't be dead, she just couldn't.

"Boss, it's me. Stan."

Caesar blinked hard several times to clear his vision. The pale blur in front of him coalesced into Stan's concerned face.

"The doc's alive, boss, but we need to let the witches check for residual magick from that asshole." Stan's pale blue eyes widened, a pleading look that didn't mesh with his hulking figure crouched on the floor beside Caesar. Stan reached out his arms in supplication, but the half-fae was smart enough not to try touching Bebe. "Please, Caesar."

Swallowing the horrible taste in his throat, Caesar rose, Bebe in his arms. He couldn't leave her on the cold, hard floor. Stan stood as well, and for the first time, Caesar realized the Elders clustered behind the half-elf.

He let his gaze sweep across the candle-lit ballroom. Duncan must have entered the circle as soon as it dissolved too because he had a firm grip on the squirming William. However, Duncan held his eyes and fangs in check, any hunger that might have been triggered by Bebe's or O'Leary's blood well under control. The rest of the White Rose members huddled against the long side walls, as far from each of the vampires as possible, their fear seasoning the very air.

No, from him.

Everyone that was, except Alice Hart. The auburn-haired witch must have been the one he'd snarled at because she wore an expressionless mask on her face, but still stood close to his side. Only a slight tremor of her lower lip showed her unease.

Damn, she was so much like Bebe.

"She needs someplace to rest." Hades, his voice didn't sound human to his own ears.

Beatrice eased forward to stand next to Stan. "There's a donated sofa in the front sitting room." A weak smile lit her face, but she reeked of fear like the rest of her coven.

Fear of him, of what he'd do next.

He gave a slow nod, as much because he barely clung to his own self-control than to reassure the frightened witches.

"Pierre—" Beatrice pointed to O'Leary's body, the tainted athame still sticking out of its ribcage, his dark blood staining the center of the pentacle.

The Fire Elder gave a curt nod of his silvered head. "I'll take care of all three items."

Stalking after Beatrice, Caesar paused and speared Duncan with a glare. "Natasha has a windowless room upstairs. Second floor, third door on the right. Keep the little bastard there until I come up." He let his eyes settle on the cowering witch in Duncan's hands, who noticeably shrank to the floor in a desperate attempt to evade his gaze.

Beatrice started at his instructions to Duncan, whipping around to stare at him. Her eyes widened in alarm. "William is not your responsibility."

He allowed a small smile to cross his face. "I'm not disputing your authority, Elder. However, he hired three rogue vampires to attack me while one of your people tried to slit Bebe's throat. I will be involved in his questioning."

The Air Elder flushed bright red, but instead of arguing, she pivoted on her sensible heels and marched from the ballroom.

Good. He didn't know if he could maintain his control if she'd chosen to pick a fight while he was in this condition. As he followed Beatrice, the soft click of heels indicated Alice trailed behind him.

The front sitting room was a bare as the rest of Natasha's house except for two worn chairs and an equally shabby couch. He carefully laid Bebe on the threadbare cushions, then knelt next to her, keeping her small, delicate hand in his. In his peripheral vision, Beatrice stood near Bebe's feet and clutched her hands together. Anxious worry added more wrinkles to her visage. Alice sidled next to the Air Elder, almost as if the younger woman wanted comfort but was afraid to ask for it. He had no sympathy for the girl after the way she'd treated Bebe.

"Master Augustine."

He cast a baleful glare at Morton Sinclair, who crouched next to him on the right.

The elderly witch gave him a sympathetic look and laid a hand in Caesar's shoulder. "I need you to step aside so I can examine her.

Caesar continued giving Sinclair a nasty look. Trust was something he had in short supply right now when it came to any White Rose member.

Stan leaned over the arm of the couch where Bebe's head rested. "Boss, I can watch him. He makes a move I don't like—"

"You're perfectly within your rights under the Blood Seal to rip my throat out, Master Augustine," Sinclair finished smoothly. His scent carried only the faintest trace of his nervousness, which could easily be attributable to his concern of what he might find lurking within Bebe. Brown eyes gazed serenely out from under bushy white eyebrows.

Caesar gave the slightest of nods before laying Bebe's hand down on her waist and stepping out of the way.

Sinclair rested one palm on Bebe's forehead and the other over her heart before he closed his eyes and mumbled a few words. An electric sensation rippled through the sitting room, and sharp ozone filled the air. Seconds seemed to drag into hours before he opened his eyes.

It took Sinclair another second before his eyes found their focus, and he looked up at Stan. "Do you detect anything I might have missed, Master Fae?"

Apparently, the old witch knew and respected fae culture enough not to say Stan's name. No fae, even a half-breed like Stan, would give a possible foe a weapon to use against him. And in magick, knowing a being's true name was the most powerful weapon of all.

But he'd given the witches his personal name in his efforts to draw Caesar out of his bloodrage. The enforcer's sacrifice rattled Caesar.

Stan shook his head. "Nothing magickal I can See." He met Caesar's gaze. "The doc's clean as far as spells, but she could have some internal bleeding from the sheer power forced through her body. We should get her to a hospital to double-check."

The acrid smell of ammonia assaulted Caesar's nostrils. His hand shot out and nearly broke Sinclair's fragile mortal bones when he grabbed the Elder's wrist. "What are you doing?"

The old witch seemed unperturbed. "Just smelling salts, Master Augustine. I agree with your fae though. I didn't detect any internal damage, but I'd prefer a second opinion. And if we can't wake her up this way, she may need an M.D."

Caesar released Sinclair's wrist. The Elder broke the capsule, but a single pass under Bebe's nose was all that was needed. She jerked up so fast she nearly knocked heads with Sinclair.

"For the love of the God and Goddess, get that shit out of my face."

Her voice was a bare whisper, but the sound of it sent a wave of relief through Caesar. Shoving Sinclair aside, he bent and pulled her into a giant hug, murmuring, "Thank Isis," over and over again.

"Ouch! Hey! My nose! Caesar, let go!"

Wetness trickled down his face in his joy. He eased up on his hold to examine her. Pins had fallen from her hair, strands escaping to curl wildly about her face. Dark smudges remained under her eyes, but her all-too-familiar annoyance blazed out of her gaze.

She reached up to shove at his shoulders. "Let me up, dammit! I need to go kill that no good little shit."

"O'Leary's dead, Bebe," he gently reminded her.

"I don't mean him." Her words came out in a gruff snarl, her throat scraped raw by her earlier screams when the traitor had attacked her. "I mean the son of a bitch I have the misfortune to call family."

Bebe struggled against his hold a second before her face dissolved into tears. "He killed her, Caesar. He killed my grandma." She repeated the words in between hiccupping sobs, clutching Caesar in her grief.

Sinclair disappeared for a moment, but before Caesar could send Stan after the witch, he returned with a glass of water that he pressed into Bebe's hand.

Caesar stared at the Elder, who just gave his benevolent smile and said, "Your fae can assure you it's safe, Master Augustine."

Caesar glanced at Stan, who nodded at the same time Bebe whispered, "It's okay, Caesar." She wiped her eyes with the heel of her free hand then took a huge gulp of water, nearly choking in the process.

Caesar rescued the glass and held her tightly as she recovered her breath. "You all right?"

She nodded but grief still shone in her eyes. He could only imagine what the confirmation of William's involvement in the conspiracy had torn inside of her.

"W-what—"

He and Bebe both turned to find tears streaming down Alice's face. She cleared her throat before trying again.

"How did he do it, Be?" The expression on Alice's pale face contained the same morbid look of someone who'd seen a horrible accident but couldn't stop staring at the carnage.

"He swapped out Grandma's normal dosage of nitroglycerin with capsules at ten times her dosage mixed with Viagra," Bebe said. She gave a wry smile. "Whoever did the autopsy probably didn't bother to check for blue diamonds in a 102-year-old woman." Her smile disappeared and she shuddered. "O'Leary knew about the plan for Grandma, but William did the deed. Someone outside of White Rose was helping them though. William insinuated it was a woman to O'Leary, but never introduced O'Leary to her or mentioned her name."

"You got all this from O'Leary?" Caesar asked.

Bebe nodded, and another shiver took her. "He was too intent on killing me to guard his own mind. Or what was left of it. We need to question William."

"In a minute, *amora*." He gently pushed her back down on the cushions when she tried to rise. "You need to rest, and Duncan will make sure William stays put. We also have other concerns." He cast a nasty look at Alice. Running his tongue deliberately over his canines made the young witch take an involuntary step back.

"I-I-I didn't—" Alice said at the same time Bebe laid a hand on his shoulder and said, "She didn't have anything to do with William and O'Leary."

He swung his head back to face Bebe. "How can you be sure? William could have lied to O'Leary that the woman helping them was an outsider." He gave Alice another glare. Bebe was far too forgiving, and he wasn't about to let the other witch verbally attack her, much less physically. "I noticed Lionel Hart wasn't present."

Alice couldn't meet his eyes, focusing on her toes instead. "Daddy refused to support my challenge and wouldn't come tonight. He said I—" She swallowed hard before continuing. "He said I was a spoiled idiot."

A tug on his arm brought his attention back to Bebe. A gentle smile spread across her face. "Trust me. I'm sure Alice and Lionel aren't involved in William's plan." She looked up at Alice. "Thank you for your help in the circle."

Caesar turned back to the other witch to find a mix of surprise, regret and embarrassment in her expression. A little confused himself, he asked, "Help? What help?"

"Didn't you feel Alice in the link?' came Bebe's bemused voice.

Red crept up Alice's cheeks. "I didn't realize you and Be—" She coughed before continuing. "I mean, I didn't know you and she . . ." She twisted her fingers, looking everywhere around the room but at him and Bebe. "I didn't mean to eavesdrop. I'm sorry."

She'd "heard" his declaration to Bebe during the battle with O'Leary.

He looked back to Bebe, his lips twisting in a wry grin. This was definitely an opportunity he couldn't let pass. "I believe I said something to you to which you have not responded, *amora*."

She blushed and opened her mouth, but whatever answer she had disappeared in Duncan's shout.

Caesar, get up here! Now! Alarm tinged Duncan's mental tone.

Caesar rose, but Stan had already jumped up and raced for the door. Bebe's eyes widened, and she swung her feet to the floor.

"You're staying here," Caesar said.

"Like hell, I will." Her expression promised fury and brimstone. "William's my problem."

"Our problem," he countered.

"Do you two want to stand here arguing?"

He and Bebe both turned to find Alice standing with her arms crossed over her chest, the response similar to Bebe's but not as delightful.

"Or find out what our son of a bitch cousin is trying to pull now?" Alice finished.

Caesar shook his head in resignation and held out a hand to help Bebe up off the couch. He led the way out of the sitting room, Bebe and the other three witches following close on his heels.

Stan already stood next to Duncan inside the door to the windowless room. He looked at Caesar, shock on his face. "Someone's possessed him, boss."

Caesar pushed past his men to see William for himself. The witch sat on the floor, back propped against the far wall, no longer the sniveling, broken man Duncan had hauled upstairs. William's head tilted at an angle, a sly smile on his face.

The expression was all too familiar, and Caesar's gut clenched in confirmation when William began to speak.

"Hello, brother dear. Still slumming with the witches, I see."

Chapter 26

Bebe sidled into the room next to Caesar and stared at William, the change in him too confident and too secure to be the skunk who ran for the door when the magicked knife fingered him. She shifted her sight to find a riot of dark color surrounding him instead of his normal blue-tinged orange aura. Stan was right. Someone else was inside William's body. More than one someone from the psychedelic rainbow that surrounded his body.

"Well, Selene, at least I'm not pretending to be one of them." Caesar's cool voice carried a hint of wariness.

A vampire couldn't possess a person. She would have to be channeled through a witch. It was the how that made her stomach cramp. More blood magick. Her jaw clinched so tight the muscles hurt. She shot a look at Alice, who had edged into the room beside her.

No hint of black marred the sunshine orange aura. A baffled expression appeared on Alice's features. *Who's Selene? Another vamp?*

Yes. Now be quiet. When Alice's aura remained clean, Bebe's last shreds of suspicions regarding her cousin dissolved, but an uglier thought replaced them. Selene had to be William's mystery woman. Bebe's stomach did a nauseous flip that had nothing to do with O'Leary's attack. Did Caesar know all along? Had the conversation concerning Alice's involvement she'd overheard between Alex and Ptolemy been a set-up after all? Cleaving an already strained relationship so no one discovered the truth until it was too late?

"Sorry for the unconventionality, but we need to talk, brother," William/Selene said. "Alone."

"Anything you need to say you can say in present company," Caesar said.

Bebe's head spun, trying to puzzle out what was happening. If Caesar knew of Selene's involvement, he wouldn't want everyone to hear it, would he?

"Fine." William, or Selene that was, gave a dramatic sigh. "You still don't get it, do you? Petrov played you. Kept you all nice and tame while she plotted to destroy our people."

"The only person playing games here is you, Selene. Did you provide William with the doctored nitroglycerin pills?" Caesar's voice carried a harsh undertone.

"Stupid bastard was so eager to do it, but he didn't have the balls to get his hands really dirty. He just couldn't wait to get his mitts on his granny's money." William/Selene giggled. "Got a little too greedy, and he still blew it, didn't he? Should have taken both of the girls out when he had the chance."

Bebe swallowed the bile in the back of her throat. Oh sweet Goddess, everything Alice and she had accused each other of doing, and William had been behind it all along. And from her conversation with Caesar in what seemed like eons ago, Caesar knew, or suspected, William's involvement in the overdose-triggered heart attack.

"That explains William's motives, but it doesn't explain yours," Caesar said.

"Do you know what that bitch was doing?" Selene's shriek using William's male vocal cords set nerves on edge. He/she beat fists on the floor in fury.

"Yes," came Caesar's quiet reply. "I do. She was looking for a cure for the V-virus. Is that why you had her killed?"

A frozen mask of anger fell over William/Selene's face. "Has it occurred to you that her 'cure' was a mutated version of the virus that would slag us before we had a chance? What do you think the newborn witches are carrying in their modified genes? One sip from a blood bag with that crap and that's it. No more vampires."

Bebe sucked in a breath. That's not what Grandma's notes specifically said, but Selene was right. It wouldn't take much alteration for that odd little gene to do exactly what she said.

"I don't know who you get your information from, but you might want to do a breathalyzer test on your snitch." Caesar crossed his arms, his expression one of total disgust.

"Really?" The sly smile returned to William/Selene's face. "Why don't you ask you little pet witch beside you?"

Bebe shivered at the murderous look Caesar cast her. "You were with me, Caesar. You saw her notes in the Book. You know that's not where Grandma was going with her research."

"Ahhhh, so the bitch's notes *were* in her Book of Shadows." William/Selene's cackle would have scared the piss out of the Crone herself. "She led us on such a merry chase." He/she leaned forward. "Tell you what Bebe, darling. You give me the Book of Shadows, and I'll let you have your precious Grandma's soul back."

"What are you talking about?" But deep in her gut, she knew. She'd had the nightmares for nearly three weeks now, but she still didn't want to hear it. She'd seen it done to O'Leary moments ago. But condemn someone to that fate without a trial, without a real reason? No one could be that cruel, that amoral, that evil.

"Don't play stupid, dear. It doesn't become you." William/Selene held out a hand, and the image of a brilliant purple Soul Sphere appeared to float just above the palm. Not the white of a sealed sphere. A purple the same shade as Grandma Petrov's aura. "Miko is waiting for you at San Francisco International." An obnoxious smirk spread across his/her face. "I'll be generous and allow for traffic or any delays by Homeland Security. We all know what a bitch they can be." He/she scowled. "You have three hours to get to the Karnak for the exchange. You don't show or you bring any other witches and Granny dearest goes poof."

An expression appeared on William's face that Selene probably thought looked seductive, but was just downright creepy. "You know, Duncan, since you don't like me as a woman, maybe you'd like to take a spin with me as a man."

The disgusted look Duncan gave him/her was all the vampire needed to make his feelings clear.

"Oh well, maybe some other time then."

The insane rainbow surrounding William faded. He slumped over and proceeded to vomit all over the dusty maple floorboards.

This cannot be happening. Bebe reached behind for a wall as dizziness swept through her overloaded body. Not finding any support, she landed unceremoniously butt first on the floor. The sphere was the only explanation for the bizarre nightmares of Grandma, trapped and screaming for help. The witch who cast it hadn't sealed the thrice-damned thing properly, allowing Grandma to touch her subconscious. And it had to be Selene's eclectic.

Goddess, how could any witch do something like that to an innocent?

"Bebe."

She blinked away the tears of despair to find Caesar crouched next to her, concern lining his normally marless forehead.

"I'm so sorry, *amora*," he whispered. "I'll go with you to Las Vegas and try to talk my sister out of her foolishness."

"Foolishness? Is that what you call what she did to my grandmother?" Fury replaced shock, igniting a fire that needed to strike out at someone, anyone. And Caesar was the closest target. "That bitch engineered my grandmother's murder." She jabbed a finger into his granite chest, her voice rising. "Someone who was your friend, or so you say. And worse, your sister is holding my grandmother's soul for ransom. And all you want to do is *talk* to her?"

Caesar stood, his expression icy. "I'm tired of you blaming me for everything that's wrong in your life just because of what I am. In case it hasn't occurred to you, Doctor, my sister needed one of *your* people to curse Natasha's soul into that sphere when she died."

He spun on his heel and stalked toward the door, his fists tightly clenched at his sides. But he paused at the door and turned back to her, his face devoid of emotion. That lack of anything scared her more than his anger.

"One more thing, Doctor. I saw from the look on your face that my sister was telling the truth about the possibility of converting the gene. If that was your plan—"

"Stop it!" Alice screamed the words at the same moment Duncan shouted them.

"Alice?" Bebe scrambled to her feet. Her cousin may have four inches on her, but that only meant Alice's head came to Caesar's nose instead of his chest. And now, Alice shoved every inch she could in Caesar's face.

"If you were friends with our grandmother, you are not walking out of here with that attitude." Alice shook a fist beneath his eyes, setting her silver bangles jangling. "And you are not treating my Be like shit and think you'll get away with it."

Caesar quickly suppressed a flinch and took a step back, though probably more concerned over the metal touching him, not from the fist waving beneath his left nostril. "You seem to have a rather abrupt change of heart for someone who accused Bebe of murder less than an hour ago," he said, his voice leaden.

"Ms. Hart is right. Both you and Dr. Zachary—" Duncan paused to give Bebe a meaningful look. "—are letting your pride consume you. This is a time to make a rational plan." His right eyebrow rose a fraction of an inch. "In the Hummer on the way to the airport. Selene does not bluff."

"We're coming, too."

Bebe looked over her shoulder. Miranda stood outside the room, a look of murderous fury on her face. A look that for once wasn't aimed at Bebe personally. Pierre, Beatrice and Morton crowded next to her. From the looks on the Elders' faces, they'd heard every word of her exchange with Selene.

She shook her head. "I appreciate the offer, but you heard Selene's terms. If I show up with any of you—"

"Then the bitch shouldn't have left a loophole in her terms," Stan said. "We're coming with you."

Turning, Bebe saw him and Duncan wearing the same terrible grin, grins that promised death and destruction to whoever got in their way. She found herself clutching Caesar's coat sleeve to keep her hand from trembling.

"You and your coven are not the only ones with a stake in this," Duncan said.

Chapter 27

Now, Caesar's world was literally falling apart in front of him. Selene's betrayal was catastrophic, but how dare Stan and Duncan volunteer their services without his authorization!

Duncan faced him, and the other vampire's expression sobered. "Caesar, think about it. This is only partly about Natasha's research. If Selene were behind the attacks seventeen years ago—"

Old habits jumped into place, despite his own heartbreak. "Duncan, I've heard enough of your accusations against her." Caesar bit out the words through gritted teeth. "I understand your personal feelings regarding Selene, but you have no proof—"

"Then why the hits on both you and Lady Petrov, boss?" Stan's quiet voice cut through the tension between Caesar and Duncan. "On the same night at the same time? I saw the doc's family tree. If Selene's that pissed off about the witches' immunity, then the hits on Natasha's people make sense. Eliminate anyone who might be carrying the gene. But why the attacks on us?"

No. Caesar felt his intestines knot. Selene was his twin. They'd shared their mother's womb for gods' sakes!

Stan didn't stop his relentless analysis. "Without you here, Ptolemy would side with her out of blood loyalty. With both you and Duncan gone, the rest of us would have been mincemeat for those loyal to her. None of the other supernatural leaders would have interfered with an internal vampire matter, but if you had asked Natasha for assistance, she'd give it. You know it, boss. Selene had to take you both out at the same time. She just didn't count on both you and Natasha reacting as fast as you did that night and foiling a majority of the attacks."

"She knows you'll insist on accompanying Dr. Zachary to Las Vegas. She will use this opportunity to remove both of you from the picture," Duncan said.

"Permanently," Stan added. "Which is why we're going with you."

Bebe's fingers twined between his, the gesture oddly comforting in his numb insanity. How could he have been so blind? If Duncan and Stan were correct, Selene's involvement went back more than seventeen years.

Gods above! It had. The teasing puzzle of thought snapped into place. Selene knew about the research, just as she had known about Duncan's stunt with Homeland Security, when Caesar had spoke with her on the phone. And he hadn't told her. Stan had pointed out that the only person who knew was the Nazi conspirator. Oh, sweet Isis, what had he done?

All those people. Dead. Because he hadn't wanted to see what evil Selene was truly capable of committing.

"Caesar?"

He looked down. Beside him, Bebe peered up, concern on her features.

"We have to go now. Are you coming?"

How can you still want me?

She smiled, a tremulous one that struggled through the tears welling in her eyes, but it still managed to light her face brighter than the sun he hadn't seen in centuries. "This started with both of our families. We need to end it. Together."

His promise to Natasha must be kept, for Duncan and Bebe's sake if not for himself. At his nod, Bebe gave his hand a squeeze.

As the group strode down the hall after leaving William in Pierre's tender mercies, Bebe named Alice as her heir, even though her Confirmation hadn't been completed. Thankfully, the Elders weren't questioning her decisions or her orders. Being the high priestess was what she'd been trained for since she was eleven.

On the way downstairs, the Elders decided Alice, Miranda and Beatrice would accompany Caesar's group to the airport.

Bebe hid her grin at the female guard's dismay to the camaraderie between the vampires and the Elders. Morton waved Miranda and Beatrice off at the door of the mansion with a thumb up, saying he'd contact all the other High Priests and Priestesses and alert them to the possible danger.

With Harry behind the wheel and Stan hexing the traffic lights to keep them green, the Hummer raced toward the airport. Caesar and Duncan twisted to face the four witches crowded in the third seat.

"What if we buy a book at the airport and spell it to look like the BOS?" Alice said.

Miranda whacked the younger witch in the back of the head, earning a nasty look. "Why the hell do you think that vampire has an eclectic working for her?" She turned to glare at Bebe. "You couldn't name someone brighter to replace you? You damn well better not get yourself killed, girl."

"She wants the White Rose family trees as much as she wants the Book of Shadows," Duncan said. "She needs it to make sure all the lines are wiped out to prevent the genetic engineering she fears."

"She's going to know if I rip out any pages." Bebe shook her head. "I don't see anyway out other than not give it to her."

"You're not seriously considering leaving Grandma in that bitch's hands, are you?" Alice's face held a horrified look under the passing streetlights.

"No!" Appalled that Alice would think her capable of such an act, Bebe struggled to complete a plan. "I need to let her have it long enough to set Grandma free, and then steal it back."

"You have one thing on your side." Caesar let his fangs show in his smile. All the witches, but Bebe, recoiled.

You are so wicked. Bebe's smile took the sting out of her admonishment.

You have no idea, amora.

"Natasha's notes are in code," he said aloud. "The key isn't in the Book. If we can exchange the Book for the Soul Sphere before she realizes she's been duped—"

"I could 'port the Book to Harry before Selene's witch could do anything. The eclectic wouldn't dare to stop my spell for fear of destroying it," Stan volunteered from the front seat.

Harry glance at his partner before returning his attention to the road. "Hey, I'm coming with you guys!"

"No." Caesar leaned forward to give the younger man a reassuring squeeze on the shoulder. "I appreciate your desire, but I need an elf back-up on this end as well as a witch back-up. Stay with Alice Hart at all times unless you hear orders from me otherwise."

"I don't need a fucking babysitter."

Caesar chuckled at Alice's complaint and glanced at Duncan. "I thought we left Tiffany in Los Angeles."

Duncan nodded, his expression serious. "The similarities between Ms. Hart and my niece are disturbing to say the least."

All conversation ceased as they made their interminable way through the security checkpoints to the private hangars. Caesar checked his watch for the thousandth time. He'd lay money that Selene had called in the latest terrorist tip that had the guards in an uproar, retaliation for Duncan's tactic when they left Los Angeles two nights ago.

He clenched his fist in frustration. No, he didn't need money. Natasha's soul was already on the table.

Harry slammed on the brakes the proscribed distance from the Lear. A dark figure stood next to the entry ladder, someone too tall for either Miko or Mai.

Caesar narrowed eyes. It couldn't be. Wasn't anyone around him listening to him anymore? He charged out of the Hummer. "Ptolemy? What the Hades are you doing—"

Ptolemy pulled both hands out of his pockets. The Glocks in each fist froze Caesar's blood.

No, not his baby brother too.

"We've figured you'd come with her." Ptolemy shifted to aim the right gun at Duncan. "Don't try it, St. James."

"Like that piddly piece of shit could do anything," Duncan said, his voice a snarl of rage.

Caesar risked a look at his chief enforcer, whose eyes glowed neon green with his fury. "Don't do it, Duncan. He's loaded with garlic-laced bullets."

"Caesar can tell you how bad they feel, and I don't want to kill you." Ptolemy actually had the balls to look regretful.

"No, just me." Bebe stepped around Caesar before he could stop her.

"No, I don't, Doctor. Just give me the Book and I'll let you walk."

"Not without my grandmother, you snake," she hissed.

Ptolemy nodded, weariness in his eyes. "I figured you say that." He gestured at the plane. "Just you and Caesar."

"You can't—" Stan started.

"This is a family matter, Gryffudd. Stay out of it." Ptolemy met Caesar's gaze, even though his other gun was now pointed at Stan. "We don't have a lot of time. You know she'll destroy the Sphere without blinking."

Caesar sucked in a breath. He'd counted too much on Stan and Duncan's backup when they reached Las Vegas. Without Stan along to keep Selene's eclectic in check, it would be up to Bebe to magick the Book back to Alice. Once she did, and that was a big assumption on his part that a witch could pass objects through Otherwhere like a fae could, he didn't know how he was getting both of them out of the Karnak alive. None of his usual sanctuaries in the city would be safe, and it would be too close to dawn for him to reach any of the mountains surrounding Las Vegas, much less find a deep enough cave or crevasse.

We've got to go, Caesar. Your brother's getting an itchy trigger finger. Bebe started for the ladder.

Deliberately ignoring his brother, Caesar faced Duncan. "Get Alice back to the witches' mansion and stay with her. It's spell-protected. Contact Los Angeles and Seattle and keep them apprised of the situation."

Duncan stiffened but nodded.

Caesar stalked to the jet and climbed in after Bebe. He'd have to trust Duncan to ferret out those vampires who were loyal at the other compounds. Anyone in Las Vegas was suspect. Once he reached the cabin, Miko's quiet sobs from the cockpit were audible over the roar of the engines. He threw his senses forward, but Mai was noticeably absent.

"Put your sword in the closet and lock it."

Caesar gritted his teeth at Ptolemy's words. He might as well walk into the Coliseum and try petting a pride of starving lions without his spatha.

"Do it." Ptolemy shifted until the barrel pointed at Bebe's head. Something flickered in his eyes for a moment.

Regret? But the emotion wasn't enough to risk Bebe's life on. Slowly, Caesar pulled off his jacket, unlatched the harness and shoved the leather and steel into the tiny luggage locker.

"Sit down and buckle up." Ptolemy had pocketed one of the Glocks, but the other gleamed in his right hand.

Caesar ground his teeth in frustration. What had Ptolemy done to Miko, and where was Mai?

Bebe laid a soft hand on his and shook her head. Damn, she was right. Now was not the time, but gods help his siblings if Mai was dead.

Dropping into the seat next to Bebe, a sense of déjà vu stole over him. Three days ago, they had been sitting in these same seats on their way to Los Angeles. Now, his life was as inside out and upside down as Bebe's. The irony forced a chuckle out of him.

Ptolemy shot him a suspicious look as he made his way to the cockpit but didn't say anything.

Care to share what's so funny? When he turned to her, Bebe's delicate black brows were twisted in concern. *Because if you're having a nervous breakdown, a little forewarning would be nice.*

He lifted her hand, basking in her scent as his lips brushed her delicate skin. *Merely reflecting on the Gray Ladies' sense of humor. You were right,* amora. *Three nights ago aboard this very jet, I arrogantly believed I could protect you. Now I find we share a similar position with each of our blood kin.*

She smiled at him, a sweet, loving smile he desperately wished he deserved. *You're right about something too. You bared your heart to me, and I never answered. I—*

"Oh, for the love of Venus, can you two stop making googly-eyes at each other for two seconds?" Ptolemy threw himself into the seat across from them and scowled.

"Jealous?" Strange how their positions had been reversed in more ways than one. Normally, he was the one chiding Selene for baiting Ptolemy. But he needed any information he could get, which meant playing nasty.

Ptolemy snorted. "Hardly."

No one spoke as the Lear rolled toward the designated runway, pausing only for a moment before gravity and momentum shoved Caesar deeper into his seat. Leaping into the air, the jet performed a slow sweeping arc before orienting southeast.

Caesar's stomach rolled along with jet. They were committed to Las Vegas. A silent prayer to Neith rose from his mind. If ever he needed divine inspiration to come up with a strategy, now was the time.

"You know, Ptolemy, I never pictured you as the greedy type. When did you and Selene decide to kill me?" he said.

Ptolemy's eyes widened. "This isn't about taking over the coven." He waved the gun at the bag Bebe had shoved under her seat. "Natasha's notes need to be destroyed before anybody else gets the bright idea of using the information against us."

"So what are you saying? I accidentally got in the way of the gunmen you sent after Bebe? Gunmen using bullets specifically designed to—" He turned to Bebe. "What's the strange gesture your generation makes with their fingers?"

"Air quotes. Also known as bunny ears." She demonstrated.

He smiled. "Thank you, *amora*." He faced his brother again, widening his smile. "Kill vampires?" Using his index and middle digits, he repeated Bebe's gesture. He deliberately left the middle digit in the air when he was finished.

Ptolemy's cheeks flushed only the faintest of pinks. Interesting. Did he not drink enough before leaving Las Vegas or had Mai and Miko put up more of a fight than he anticipated and drained his strength?

"I tried to stall you that night, but you were too intent on reaching Dr. Zachary." Ptolemy grimaced. "And the men William hired were late. You weren't supposed to get to the hotel until after they'd stolen the Book."

Who was lying to whom here? The men at the hotel were definitely there to kill Bebe. Caesar made a soft *tsk*-ing sound. "It's so hard to hire good assassins. I would have thought you would have learned a thing or two from Octavia."

Ptolemy sneered, but his grip tightened slightly on the gun. "I learned plenty. Maybe not as much as you, *Alexander*."

"Alexander?"

Caesar turned to meet Bebe's questioning look. "My birth name. I gave it up centuries ago." He faced Ptolemy again. "My so-called siblings like to throw it in my face."

"I'm not the one who brought up the past," Ptolemy shot back. "Or sick enough to take the name of our parents' murderer."

Ptolemy's verbal strike hit far deeper than he realized. What would happen if he knew the truth? That Caesar had helped their mother die?

Taking a slow, deep breath, Caesar forced his muscles to relax. He needed to hang onto his control and swallow his ancient guilt, or he and Bebe both were doomed. Letting his fingers form a steeple, he peered over the tips at his brother. "You're right, of course. Forgive me. So let me guess? You came to Anthony's Thursday night to make sure the second team succeeded."

To his surprise, Ptolemy shook his head, a morose look on his face. "Selene sent the second team, even though I told her I'd be able to get the Book from Phillippa. So I followed, and when it looked like you were—" He sucked in a harsh breath and couldn't meet Caesar's gaze any longer.

Hades, curse him for a fool! Caesar wasn't sure what made him angrier, his own blindness or the unnecessary guilt his brother had inflicted on Bebe. "You didn't give a shit about me. When you saw Bebe take out two of your assassins, you killed Franklin so neither of us could question her."

Ptolemy's head jerked up, his eyes blazing gold. "And it should have ended there. I told Selene she'd gone too far, but she still sent a squad to the Brentwood mansion to retrieve the Book."

"If the Book is all she wants, why is she trying to kill me?"

Ptolemy jerked at Bebe's soft voice, a look of shock on his face. After a moment, he shook his head violently. "She's not, I swear."

"One of the White Rose witches tried to kill Bebe tonight during their Confirmation ceremony. And then Selene had Bebe's cousin William possessed in order to demonstrate her power," Caesar added.

Again, Ptolemy shook his head, a firm expression of denial planted on his face. "No. That had to have been William's idea, not hers." He faced Bebe. "In case you haven't noticed, Doctor, your cousin is nuts."

"Then why was Selene killing our people seventeen years ago?" Caesar didn't let his voice rise above a soft murmur. His heart ached too much to make the effort. Ptolemy was still defending her, just as Caesar had to Bebe earlier before heading to the airport.

The ragged disbelief on Ptolemy's face gave way to a slightly hysterical laugh. "St. James's using the current trouble to make a case against her, isn't he? When is he going to give up his insane need for retribution? Selene screwed up by fucking him, but she's paid her fine."

"If it was only the situation with Duncan, I'd agree with you. But I have reason to believe she was the supernatural who collaborated with the Nazis as well," Caesar said.

Ptolemy's mouth fell open.

Caesar willed himself to stay still. His brother couldn't dissemble to this level. On one hand, he was relieved Ptolemy wasn't involved deeper than he was. Selene used the same line of bullshit on their baby brother she had tried feeding him through William. And she'd nearly succeeded.

"Where on earth did you get that idea? From her?" Ptolemy pointed the gun at Bebe, waving it uncomfortably in the direction of her all-to-vulnerable mortal heart. "Selene's our sister, and you believe someone you've known a week. Or is this more of St. James's bullshit?"

"Why don't you ask her when we arrive in Las Vegas? Ask her why it was necessary to hold Natasha's soul prisoner. Ask her why Bebe needs to die." Caesar couldn't look at his brother any longer.

His chest hurt, and it wasn't from his gunshot wounds of the other night. He almost wished it were. Something physical would be so much easier to deal with. He closed his eyes against his seething emotions. Despite Mother's best efforts, the three of them had ended up plotting against each other, just like she and her siblings had done. Was the Ptolemaic dynasty doomed to repeat the same pattern until the end of time?

The subtle shift of air pressure indicated Miko had begun their decent. They needed a plan before they reached the Karnak.

Bebe, don't react. We can't let Ptolemy know we're talking.

Okay.

He breathed a soft sigh of relief that no sound of her shifting in her seat came to him. *Can you transport the Book and the sphere to Alice magickally?*

The Book, yes. The sphere, no.

I thought witches could transport objects, but not living things through Other-where.

Her silent laughter fluttered against his mind. *Sounds like Grandma left something out of the translation.* Deadly sobriety came with her next thought. *The key is whether what's being transported has a soul. Technically, I could transport a dead elephant if I have the power to move that much mass. But the sphere with Grandma in it? I might as well slap a strobe on it with a sign saying 'Blue Light Special' for all the nasties in the Otherwhere.*

Damn. He was running out of ideas. The landing gear sliding into place made a soft grinding beneath them.

Caesar, where would your sister be keeping Mai?

He barely suppressed his start of surprise. Slitting his eyes open a fraction, he checked Ptolemy. His brother wiped his free hand along his thigh, as though trying to wipe blood and remorse off on his jeans. *She may be dead. Miko was crying when we first boarded.* And had stopped at some point, though the occasional sniffle came from the cockpit. He didn't dare touch her mind. Ptolemy would be waiting for such a tactic, but the deep connection he'd forged with Bebe in the circle passed under his brother's radar.

If she is, Ptolemy doesn't know it, and I can't see Selene killing Mai until she was sure Miko had delivered me.

How do you know what Ptolemy's thinking? Can you get into his mind without him realizing it because he's sure acting guilty?

Again the soft fluttering like a butterfly's wings. *No, silly, his aura. Yeah, it's gray around the edges, probably subconscious regret at setting me up for Franklin's death and being conned by Selene. But there's no black.*

Which means?

He has no involvement in a murder.

But Franklin—

Wasn't a murder in his eyes. To him, he was saving your life.

Amora, you scare me.

The fluttering sped up until it became a buzz. *Good, maybe you'll stop treating me like a porcelain doll. Is there any place we can get a UV-protected vehicle?*

There's a small, private area located in the main parking garage. The keys will be in the security office. The odds of us reaching Los Angeles—

No, she'll expect that and have the airport and any routes to California blocked. Do you have any other compounds east?

That I trust right now? No.

What about the other vampire masters?

He punctured his tongue with a canine to keep from laughing outright. *No, amora, Virginia and Jean-Pierre will consider this situation my problem to clean up.*

Fine. Her snort of derision was audible. *We'll hole up in a hotel in Utah before dawn—*

"What's your problem?" A harsh note buzzed in Ptolemy's voice.

Caesar opened his eyes to find his brother staring at Bebe suspiciously.

She turned from the window. "I'm continually amazed how you big, bad vampires get your rocks off by beating up defenseless girls."

"I haven't touched you, Doctor." Ptolemy's lips peeled back from his fangs. "Yet."

Unfazed, Bebe stared back, anger twisting her full lips. "I meant Mai and Miko."

Again, Ptolemy flushed the faintest pink. A Normal wouldn't have even noticed.

She must have seen something in his aura because her lips tilted in a nasty smile. "Leaving aside me and Caesar, what do you think Kensai will do when he finds out?"

Whatever retort Ptolemy planned to throw out was swallowed by the sharp series of jolts when Miko touched the jet down on the runway.

"Sloppy," Caesar remarked. He gave the same nasty smile to his brother, releasing some of his pent-up fury. "I'm sure Selene will leave Miko's punishment in your capable hands."

Instead of answering Caesar, Ptolemy clenched his free fist against his thigh and addressed Bebe. "Last chance, Doctor. Give me the Book, and I'll let Miko fly you back to San Francisco."

"My terms have changed. I want Mai, Miko and my grandmother in return for the Book." Her expression would have done any professional poker player proud.

An exasperated sigh blew from Ptolemy as the jet pulled to a stop in front of a hangar. He didn't take his eyes or the gun from them when he yelled over his shoulder. "Miko, shut everything down and get in here!" He unclipped his seatbelt, rose from the chair and pulled the second Glock from his coat pocket.

A moment later, the cockpit door opened. Miko limped into the main cabin with only one eye red from crying. The other sported a shiner that had nearly swollen the orb shut. But both eyes glared naked hatred at Ptolemy.

"Let me guess. Mai wasn't in any shape to fly." Bebe's voice dripped with sarcasm.

Ptolemy stepped back behind Caesar's chair. With some amusement, Caesar noted his brother was out of the reach of Miko's legs as well.

"Open the door, Miko."

"I just hope I'm there when you get your evil heart staked, you bastard," she spat, but she moved to obey him.

Ptolemy nudged Caesar's back with what definitely felt like one of the Glock muzzles. He must have poked Bebe too, because they unclipped their seatbelts and stood as one. Bebe reached beneath her seat and pulled out her shoulder bag that contained the Book of Shadows. Without a word, they followed Miko down the ladder.

Caesar scanned the area. No one waited to meet them. He resisted the urge to smile. Selene had spread her people too thin in the effort to seize the Brentwood mansion, and Ptolemy must not have been able to notify her in time or tip off the Los Angeles assailants without revealing himself to those who were loyal to Caesar.

Ptolemy avoided the ladder altogether and leapt down, landing lightly next to Caesar.

"Show-off," Caesar muttered under his breath.

Ignoring him, Ptolemy waved toward the SUV parked on the tarmac. "Doctor, you'll drive. Everyone else in the back."

Caesar's heart skipped a beat. No, Ptolemy wouldn't shove Bebe out the door while she was driving. It would attract too much attention. Still, being that far away from her left an antsy feeling that Caesar found annoying. His fingers automatically moved to stroke the pommel of his spatha, and he was reminded that it sat locked in the Lear.

Ptolemy waited until Caesar and Miko had climbed into the rear bench seat, then he flicked the child safety locks on the door before shutting it.

Well, on the plus side, he and Miko weren't getting tossed from the moving SUV either.

"You're going to have to give me directions, asshole," Bebe said.

Again, Ptolemy gave an exasperated sigh, but surprisingly made no comment on her insult. "Follow the signs out of the airport, then make a left at the light and then another left at the Strip."

The good doctor deliberately squealed the tires as she accelerated away from the hangar.

Caesar laid a hand on Miko's arm and winced at the way she flinched from him. "Where's Mai?"

"She was still at the Karnak the last time I saw her." Miko's voice trembled, whether from anger, fear or exhaustion he was uncertain. "The bitch deliberately broke her leg. I'm sorry, Master." Her breath hissed in pain. "I shouldn't have—"

"It's all right." He gave the girl's forearm a gentle squeeze. "I'm not thinking very generous thoughts about my sister either."

A single tear rolled down her cheek. "I shouldn't have left her there. Selene had her arm wrapped around Mai's neck and threatened to pull her head off. If she—" She choked back a sob.

"Where else are you injured?" he said at the same time he sent *I have a plan, but are you well enough to help?*

She nodded and for the first time tonight, hope shone in her good eye. The injured one was now completely swollen shut. "A sprained ankle and I think my cheek bone may be broken." A wry smile curved across her lips. "The bitch needed me well enough to pilot the plane."

Bebe braked at the first traffic light, tapping a fast rhythm on the steering wheel as she waited for the left arrow light.

"So Ptolemy, how did you manage to ditch everyone at the safe house?" Caesar pitched his voice to carry over the bass of the truck that had pulled up next to them. When his brother ignored him, he laughed. "Oh, come on. You can tell me. Aren't you the one saying the younger children don't know shit?"

Ptolemy refused to look at him.

He leaned forward to rest his folded arms on the back of the bucket seat in front of him. "Let me guess. You claimed you would try to lead them away in order to let the others make a break for San Francisco. You then left the safe house, but the idiots Selene hired were too stupid to follow you, so you couldn't warn them where I'd taken Bebe and the Book."

Ptolemy whipped his head around to glare, but the vampire glow of his eyes was washed out in the bright streetlights and neon signs. "You should have told me where you were going."

"It seems now I had good reason not to."

The gun came up, pointing at Caesar's head, but it quivered in Ptolemy's grip. "I'm fucking sick and tired of you treating me like I'm stupid."

Keeping his voice even, Caesar said, "What are you talking about?"

"You just think you're all superior, don't you? 'Look at me. I'm the coven master. I know everything.'" The glow faded from Ptolemy's eyes. "Guess what? I'm tired of living this fucking existence, too. But I'm not letting some half-assed witch plot to kill me without even a fight. I am *not* turning into our parents!"

Caesar stared at his younger brother, words clogging in his throat. Today was the first time Ptolemy had spoken of their parents' deaths since they were children. Old guilt rose up, threatening to swallow him whole. What would Ptolemy say if he knew the role Caesar had played in their mother's suicide?

"We're here. Or would you boys like me to find a playground where you can duke it out?" Bebe turned into the Karnak's long curving driveway and headed for valet parking.

Ptolemy jerked before shoving the guns in his pockets, but his hands remained inside, hanging tight to the metal by the tension in his shoulders.

The valet opened the front passenger door. "Welcome to the—" Eyes bulging, he stammered for a few seconds before finding his senses. "Mr. Antonius, why aren't you—"

Shoving past the poor valet, Ptolemy said, "My brother wanted to do a spot inspection, and frankly you are sorely lacking at this point."

If the man's eyes were bulging before, they jumped out of their sockets when he caught sight of Caesar. He gulped loud enough to be heard over the crowd of pedestrians on the Strip and the constant dinging of the slot machines from the casino inside.

"M-M-Mr. Augustine! My apologies. We didn't know you were coming." He scrambled to open the rear passenger door, and Caesar climbed out.

"That's the point of a spot inspection, isn't it?" Ptolemy said, his snarl scaring the valet even more.

If you didn't want the entire staff to know we were here, you should have instructed Bebe to drive around to our private entrance.

Slightly amused at his brother's nasty glare and silence despite the circumstances, Caesar turned and assisted the limping Miko down from the SUV. Bebe already stood next to him, her knuckles white as they clenched her bag.

The valet still shook from Ptolemy's reprimand. "Shall I get a wheelchair for your friend, Mr. Antonius?"

"That won't be necessary." Ptolemy shot Caesar a pointed look. "If you'd lead the way to the private elevator?"

Sucking in his breath, Caesar lifted Miko's left arm around his shoulder and wrapped his right around her waist to support her. Sharing a look with Bebe, they entered the hotel. Straight into an encounter either he or his twin wouldn't be walking away from.

He just had to make sure Bebe and the girls walked out with him.

Chapter 28

Any other time, Bebe would have stared at the sheer opulence of the Karnak, the newest of the Vegas hotel/casino resorts at the south end of the Strip. Despite the late hour, or early morning depending on how one viewed it, noise blared in the casino, crowds of tourists talking, laughing, and gambling. The difference between here and the African villages where she worked would have boggled her mind. All that food and money wasted.

But now . . .

Now, she wondered how the hell they were getting out of the hotel alive, despite Caesar's assurance. She glanced at Miko hobbling along with Caesar's help. The swelling in the girl's lower leg matched the swelling on her face.

Miko needs to get off that ankle and get some ice on it.

Caesar glanced down at Bebe, a half-amused and half-irritated expression on his face. *I won't undermine her confidence by carrying her through the lobby.*

Grimacing back, she sent, *Neither of which will matter if we all die here.*

He neither said nor thought anything, just gave a look that clearly proclaimed, "Thanks for the vote of confidence."

She followed as he led the way to a private alcove where a man stood, dressed in the stylistic black of expensive private security. A quick shift of Sight confirmed the guard was a vampire. Selene wasn't taking any chances.

The guard nodded to Caesar and pressed the "Up" button.

Tightening her grip on her bag, she risked a peek behind her. The minute her eyes met Ptolemy's though, he found a sudden interest in the huge statue beside him, the one that blocked the alcove from most scrutiny.

Interesting. She dredged up the basics she'd learned in her psychology classes years ago. Good to know Ptolemy wasn't entirely comfortable about this whole situation, but would she have a chance to use that knowledge?

The elevator pinged and its doors slid open. Bebe let a soft sigh of relief escape when the muscle-bound vampire didn't step on board with them. Instead, Ptolemy pressed "P1" and the car stated to rise.

Clearing her throat gained Ptolemy's attention, but she'd have to tread carefully. "What has my grandmother done to you?" When he didn't answer, she shrugged, trying to make it seem as nonchalant as possible. "I ran away to Africa because she tried to make me marry Alastair Hyde-Smith." She gave a self-deprecating chuckle. "She threatened to cut off money for school too. So whatever she did, I would probably sympathize."

Bebe, what are you playing at?

Ignoring Caesar's warning, she focused on Ptolemy and allowed her sincerity to shine through. "No matter what happens, I want you to know that I appreciated your Saturnalia present."

An emotion flickered across his features so fast she wasn't sure it happened, much less what it represented until he spoke.

"I meant what I said in Los Angeles."

Had it occurred to the idiot that he may be the next enemy she had to vanquish? Bile rose in her throat. What if he did? What if all this was an elaborate charade to get someone else to kill him? Did he hate himself that much? His tirade in the SUV suddenly made sense. The elevator halted and the doors slid open once again before she could respond.

"Welcome to the Karnak, Dr. Zachary."

The smooth, velvety tones belonged to the female vampire who'd arrived at Caesar's San Francisco house the night after he'd been shot. She stood in front of one wall that was nothing more than floor-to-ceiling windows. Any other time, Bebe would have admired the view of the Las Vegas skyline.

Instead, she focused on the vampire. As before, she dripped in designer clothes and expensive jewelry all the way down to her snakeskin stilettos, but this outfit shouted business. The rose shell top and medium gray pantsuit set off her olive complexion. Her black hair was wrapped into a no-nonsense French twist, not a strand out of place. She exuded control, but unlike Caesar, her attitude carried a nasty, oily taste.

The black sparks in Selene's orange and red aura confirmed Bebe's impression.

"I'd feel a lot more welcome if your brother wasn't holding guns on us."

Selene laughed, a sound she probably meant to sound musical and ladylike, but it sent shivers down Bebe's spine.

"Ptolemy won't hurt you, Doctor. In fact, my baby brother spoke rather highly of your fighting abilities." Her gaze shifted to Caesar. "Why don't you help Miko over to the couch? I'm sure standing cannot be comfortable on that injured ankle of hers. Lucien, would you get some ice for Miko?"

Bebe looked over in surprise. Standing near the wet bar was a witch. For some reason, she'd assumed Selene's eclectic was a woman. Dressed from head to foot in black, he had pulled his greasy brown hair into a queue at the base of his neck. Obviously, Selene kept her witch well in check. This guy reminded Bebe of a pit bull. A very dangerous pit bull that would only respond to his mistress's command.

Another chill ran down Bebe's back. Now she knew who'd been teaching William and his friends how to cast sacrificial blood spells. No hint of the original color of his aura remained, and what existed was so black that it blended into his designer suit.

And his eyes bore into hers.

She had the barest instant to fling up her outer shields, but even then, she staggered under the psychic blow. Only a firm grip on her elbow kept her from falling to the plush carpet.

"Lucien! Behave yourself. Dr. Zachary is my guest." The obscene pressure disappeared at Selene's reprimand.

Bebe didn't believe for one instant that the attack hadn't been sanctioned. Blinking away the tears that had sprung to life at the pain, she found it was Ptolemy keeping her upright, not Caesar. She swallowed hard, pulled herself erect on shaky knees and muttered, "Thanks."

Once again, Ptolemy had the strange look on his face. This time it stayed long enough for her to identify a mixture of regret and pain. When she tried to shrug his hand off, he kept a firm grip on her, but not with the effect of intimidation.

"Why don't you sit down, Doctor?" He steered her over to the armless chair next to the couch where Miko sat with her injured ankle propped on pillows.

Closer to Caesar, Bebe realized with a start. She reached up to finger the pentacle Tiffany had given her, but it was gone. Incinerated in the magickal battle back in San Francisco, and in the frantic drive to the airport, she hadn't had the chance to replace it. She was down to raw strength and the protection charm she'd placed on Caesar's ring. Goddess, she hoped it would be enough.

"Where's Mai?" Caesar's voice held a touch of anger underneath its surface calm. He strode toward his sister from where he'd arranged Miko on the couch.

"Resting in one of the guest bedrooms." Selene sauntered forward and looked up at her twin, but the stilettos put her close to the same height so she didn't have to look far. "Don't worry. Her leg has been set, and she'll recover fully." She gave a mock frown. "Though I'm afraid she isn't as comfortable as I would like. She refuses to take anything for the pain."

"How does she know you aren't trying to poison her, you treacherous cow!" Fury rolled off Miko in waves.

Making a clucking sound with her tongue, Selene shook her head. "You girls brought this on yourselves by disobeying my direct order and then attacking me." The smile she gave Miko would have made the nastiest predator on the planet tremble. "But I keep my word. You and your sister may leave."

Another male security vamp appeared from the hallway, pushing Mai ahead of him in a wheelchair, her broken right leg propped up. A grimace of pain twisted her ashen face. It was all Bebe could do to remain seated and not check on the girl.

A small cry sprang from Miko's throat. The security vamp parked the wheelchair next to the elevator. Caesar made no move to stop Miko when she scrambled off the couch and hobbled to her sister.

Mai's anger-filled eyes sought out Caesar. "I'm sorry, Master. We failed you."

"No, you didn't, Mai." He glared at his sister.

Selene ignored him. "Marcus, please call the motor pool and have one of the Normal drivers take the Osakas back to Los Angeles." The guard nodded, pressed the down button and moved to wheel Mai onto the elevator.

"Marcus."

The guard paused, a glint of fear in his eyes at Caesar's sharp tone.

"I'd make sure that the girls arrive in Los Angeles intact if I were you. Kensai will not take kindly to his granddaughters disappearing or suffering any additional harm en route."

Marcus's Adam's apple bobbed before he nodded at Caesar's veiled warning. A whoosh of air announced the arrival of the elevator. He pushed the wheelchair through the open doors, Mai limping along behind. The doors closed, and a hum indicated the car's steady descent to the lobby.

Bebe's hands dug into the leather of her bag. Damn, if only she and Caesar were leaving with the girls.

Selene turned to her brothers and Bebe, clasped her hands together, and grinned. "Let's get down to business, shall we?"

Chapter 29

Caesar willed his hands to relax at his sides. Any other time he'd play his opponent like a puppet. But this time . . .

This time he was definitely in deep horse manure. If anyone on this planet could read him, it would be his twin. The reek of steel and garlic coming off Ptolemy next to him clogged his sinuses. The harsh *chunk* of the elevator locking in place thirty floors below sent his stomach plummeting.

"We want to see the Sphere before we discuss anything," he said.

"We?" Selene raised an eyebrow, mocking him.

"You've been going out of your way to make enemies, my dear sister." He smiled, giving her a full view of his extended canines. "Smacking around Family members is not the way to win best coven mistress."

Eyes narrowed, she said, "I warned you that taking sides in the witches' dispute was not in your best interest."

"Especially since you'd already taken sides." He laughed outright at the sheer irony. "All of Mother's efforts to build a strong family, and you've ended up just as backstabbing as our aunts and uncles."

"At least I'm not getting dragged around by my dick like Father." She practically purred the words.

"Maybe so, but unlike you, I didn't turn into a power-hungry whore. And that was one of the nicer insults the good citizens of Rome threw at Mother."

In two quick strides, Selene crossed the carpet, but he didn't bother evading the slap. A slap that would have dislocated his jaw if he were Normal.

He didn't give her the satisfaction of rubbing away the sting. "What's the matter? A little too close for comfort?" He seized her wrist millimeters from his face as she tried to slap him again and gave her a vicious smile. "Sorry, sister dearest. You've had enough free shots."

"Stop it! Both of you!"

Ptolemy's shove took Caesar off guard, and he stumbled back against the couch where Miko had been moments ago. Apparently, he wasn't the only one surprised from the stunned look on Selene's face. Unable to catch her balance on the obscene modern shoes she wore, she landed on the cushions with a soft *whoof*.

His brother stood there glaring at both of them. Even though Ptolemy's face was flushed with anger, the color was even paler than during the flight here. "Give Bebe the Soul Sphere." When Selene paused for the barest instant, he snapped, "Now!"

Selene climbed to her feet taking a few healthy steps back from both Caesar and Ptolemy. An analytical expression appeared on her face. Did his baby brother realize he'd just made himself a target of Selene and her lackeys?

A sly smile replaced Selene's strategic look, and she waved at her eclectic. "Lucien."

From behind the wet bar counter, the witch produced the pulsing glass ball, brilliant purple swirling and shifting inside it. He practically slithered over to where Selene stood.

She took it from him and fixed Bebe with a nasty look. "I want to see the Book first."

Caesar glanced down at Bebe. Huge brown eyes stared up at him, filling with tears. What was the worse crime? Condemning Natasha to non-existence or unleashing whatever horror Selene twisted the research into?

It's your play, amora.

Giving him a slow nod, Bebe stood and crossed over to Selene. Reaching into her bag, she pulled out the Book. She paused, looking for all the world like the innocent child who had been orphaned years ago.

Then Bebe swung the Book with everything in her tiny frame at Selene's arm that held the sphere. The glass ball flew into the air.

Catch it, Caesar!

But he was already moving before Bebe's telepathic shout. Leaping over the couch, his fingers extended and wrapped around the surprisingly heated glass.

"Hand it over or so help me, I'll kill her." Selene clutched Bebe by the throat with one hand, holding her high in the air, the other hand held out to him. The Book of Shadows lay underneath Bebe's wildly swinging feet.

"You have what you want, Selene. Let her go."

"Not everything. Give the sphere back before your little girlfriend strangles to death."

"Let Bebe go," Ptolemy said, taking a step toward Selene. "We have the Book and the notes that were in Caesar's possession. There's no reason to kill her."

No. Horror rippled through Caesar. The translated notes he'd left at the San Francisco mansion.

A smirk twisted his sister's lips before she dropped Bebe, who lay gasping and choking on the floor.

If he'd known Ptolemy was in on this little conspiracy, he'd have changed the combination on his safe. He should have had Stan lock them back in the wardrobe's nymph hole. Or given them to Duncan for safekeeping. But it was far too late for any regret now. He stared daggers at his sister.

In that second, all Selene's schemes shone in her eyes.

And sorrow filled his soul. For Ptolemy's naiveté. For not listening to Duncan all these centuries. For finding an excuse for every stunt Selene pulled. For putting his beloved Bebe in danger.

He faced Ptolemy. "If you wanted control of the coven, why didn't you ask for it? You're my brother. I would have given it to you, dammit!"

A stunned look filled Ptolemy's features. "What in Hades are you talking about?"

"The attempted coup seventeen years ago." *Bebe, crawl away from Selene.*

Bebe, her face still blotchy, gave a slight shake of her head, tendrils of escaped hair making the most miniscule of motions. The pins that originally secured her knot gleamed dully from where they clutched the haphazard curls. And he wanted nothing more than smooth those wild strands out of her face and reassure her.

I don't need any reassurance.

The sound in his mind was more growl than words. Her right hand clenched in front of her, a slight red glow surrounding her tiny fist.

"Rogue vampires were responsible for those deaths." Uncertainty filled Ptolemy's voice.

Caesar's attention returned to his siblings. "I have to give credit where credit's due. You almost had me fooled on the jet." His lips curved into a slight smile, and he held up the sphere. "I'd applaud if I didn't have my hands full. Killing two birds with one stone. And if both birds manage to survive, then make sure the birds blame each other for the damage. Ingenious." He propped one hip casually against the back of the couch. "You learned well from Hitler, kids."

"We didn't have anything to do with that bastard!" Ptolemy's eyes glowed golden from his anger.

"Come on. The jig's up. He knows."

Selene's predatory smile sent a wave of rage down Caesar's spine. The bitch had him on the ropes, and yet, she still was trying to make Ptolemy look like one of the bad guys.

Other witch . . . dangerous . . . Bebe out . . .

The faint words whispered through Caesar's brain. Except the familiar voice didn't come from any person standing in the room, but seemed to come from the pulsing amethyst light in his hand. No. Was such a thing possible?

"I'm sorry you found out." Selene pulled the tiny pistol from her pocket, aiming at his heart. "Good-bye, Alexander."

Then she screamed in pain and fury as a fireball exploded in her face.

Chapter 30

The second the witchfire left her fingertips, Bebe clutched the Book of Shadows tight against her chest and launched herself away from Selene. Gaining her feet, she scrambled toward the elevator. She turned to see if Caesar followed her.

The world shattered in a knife-edged wind. Caesar and Ptolemy dived below the deadly hail, but the wind did nothing more to Selene than blow out the flames in her hair. Bebe's vision caught every detail before she thrust the Book in front of her, shouting the Latin spell to raise a shield. It wasn't enough to stop the wind though. Gale forces slammed the energy bubble into the elevator doors. Raw inertia smashed her against the inside of the shield.

But Blessed Goddess, the multitude of fragments that had been penthouse windows couldn't penetrate her shield. Shards slid around her and embedded themselves in the plasterboard or shattered against the steel elevator doors.

With an abrupt shift, the wind disappeared, and the protective bubble dropped to the floor, dragging her and the Book with it. Glass tinkled all around her as she landed hard, her left ankle bending at an unnatural angle until bone snapped. The shield failed with the wave of agony. Tears spilled down her cheeks, but she swallowed the cry of pain. She wasn't about to give the asshole the satisfaction.

A wild roar sounded, but not from the wind. Caesar charged over the couch and tackled Selene. A wrestling match ensued as Ptolemy joined the fray, each of the siblings trying to grab the woman's pistol.

The other witch didn't even lend his mistress a hand. His attention was focused solely on Bebe. With a sharp gesture and muttered words, he summoned a miniature whirlwind.

The dirt devil sucked up shards of glass and aimed straight for Bebe. The idiot had to be totally loony-tunes. If that thing sliced her to shreds, it would set off the vamps' blood lust. They were already pissed off, and he was the only other meal in the penthouse.

She shoved the pain of the broken ankle into a mental compartment and focused. Calling up a wind as well, she used to it slide her and the book along the tile floor. If she could get behind the bar, she'd have a little protection and maybe find something to use as a weapon.

Seeing her tactic, Lucien dropped the tiny tornado and added his magick to hers. Her gentle slide became a headlong rush through the blown-out patio doors. She tried grabbing anything to stop the wild trip, but it was next to impossible with only one free hand, and she didn't dare drop the Book.

She managed to angle her path toward one of the heavy iron tables decorating the ledge. A cry ripped from her throat when she slammed back first into the wrought iron. Fire shot through her broken ankle. Eyes closed against the wind and glass shards, she reached blindly for a table leg and held on.

The wind cut off, and glass tinkled against the tile. She opened her eyes. A new fear rippled through her as she stared at thirty stories of empty space below her. In answer to her phobia, the building groaned as the decorative latticework and concrete of the balcony bent and pulled apart, leaving a person-sized hole next to her. Vertigo wove through her brain, making the tiny dots of light below spin.

"So, the little witch is afraid of heights." A maniacal gleam in his eyes, Lucien stood inside what was left of the patio's sliding glass doors. "Give me the book, and I won't shove you over the side." He held out his hand. The malevolent blackness of his aura stretched from the tips of his fingers toward her.

Every cell in her screamed to take the offer, even though deep down, she knew he'd shove her over the side as soon as the Book was in his tainted hands. He'd use her violent death to fuel his spell to destroy Caesar. With no one to stand against Lucien and Selene, the world would become a nightmare.

"I'm not asking again, child." Lucien flicked his wrist, and the concrete underneath the tile she lay on rumbled and bucked. Cracks appeared and spread around her.

A faint tickle came from the back of her mind. So ephemeral and familiar, and for a weird, wild moment that stretched on forever, Grandma's voice, clear as a bell, said, "He's given you the ammunition, darling. Use it."

And Bebe knew. Earth and air and blood.

Releasing her death grip on the precarious safety of the table leg, she snatched up the nearest piece of dirty glass. The shard sliced into her thumb, the pain and blood searing and coalescing with the energy she drew. Muttering the words, she threw her intent into the surrounding fragments, and as one, they shot through the air carried by a current of wind.

In that split second, only the slight widening of his eyes gave any indication that Lucien realized his fate. Glass shredded his flesh, the largest piece ripping through his throat. The words of his spell died stillborn as his jugular sprayed the white carpet with sticky red droplets.

For the second time, she had harmed someone using blood magick. A mixture of filth and sorrow swept through her.

Lucien's momentum brought him stumbling yet another step toward her before his heavy body collapsed on the broken tiles of the patio. Pitch boiled out of the corpse.

Oh, Goddess, she couldn't do this again!

The miasma twisted. A feeling akin to maggots on her skin rolled across her as it focused on her. Soul energy pooled and spread across the damaged floor, cutting off her escape.

A scream perched on the edge of her bruised throat.

Scarlet hooks poked up through cracked concrete and tile. They latched onto the dark ooze, pulled and stretched until it tore. Too much like her father's flesh under vampire teeth. A bass note rattled the lime chips and hunks of glass beneath her legs. The tone rose and rose until she clamped her hands over her ears.

What in the Thousand Names of the Goddess had Lucien bargained with? She managed to raise another shield, but it couldn't block all of the harmonics in that obscene noise. Her very bones thrummed with the note until she thought they would shatter too.

With a final burst of sound, the hooks dragged the soul fragments apart and disappeared back into the floor of the patio.

Her shield dropped. Blackness edged across her vision from the effort she expended. She needed to get back inside. Goddess only knew how much Lucien had weakened the structure, not to mention those things that had ripped his soul apart. But she couldn't summon the physical energy amidst the throbbing in both her head and her ankle.

"Bebe!"

Strong hands lifted her and carried her away from the traffic sounds and back inside the penthouse. Caesar's clean sandalwood scent engulfed her. Tears of relief coursed down her cheeks now. A hot smooth ball was shoved into her hands. A reassuring heat. A familiar mental warmth accompanied the physical sensation.

Grandma was safe. She slipped the sphere into her left pocket. Relief washed through her.

Until the soft snick of a safety being released made her eyes open.

With her clothes hanging in strips and her hair haloed like the snakes on Medusa's head, Selene glared at Bebe. "Get away from the bitch, Alexander." One of Ptolemy's Glocks shook in her two-handed grip. "Now!"

Somehow, the pistol was less scary than the bugged-out glowing eyes and fangs. Bebe's heart sank. No doubt, the vampiress would rather tear out her throat, and she had nothing in her to hold Selene off. Killing Lucien had drained the last of her energy.

Careful not to jar her ankle, Caesar lowered Bebe until she stood on her good leg. Ptolemy lay sprawled on the floor next to the couch. A black wooden handle stuck out of his chest.

"This is over, Selene." Caesar's voice was barely human. He shifted to cover Bebe's body with his.

Bebe clutched his jacket, more to keep upright than for comfort. It wouldn't matter if he took a bullet for her. Selene would just wait for the garlic to kick in, shove him out of the way and blow out Bebe's brains.

"All I want is her. Stand aside." Selene waved the gun, naked fury turning her patrician features ugly.

"You didn't have a problem with shooting Caesar earlier. What changed?" The fear and anger made Bebe's voice sound alien to her own ears. "Got your rocks off by killing one brother already?" Damn, they needed a plan.

Caesar must have heard her. *The charm you placed on my ring?*

It's our only shot. Keeping the book tucked under her right arm, she linked the fingers of her left hand with his, touching the gold and onyx. It pulsed with the magick she laid on it yesterday.

A wet cough from the floor grabbed everyone's attention.

"I wouldn't worry. Her aim sucks." Ptolemy used the coffee table to pull himself upright. A little gasp of pain escaped when he pulled the knife free from his chest. He tossed the offending steel aside and dragged himself to his feet. "F-Y-I, Selene. The heart's on the left side."

"I wasn't trying to kill you. I just needed to borrow your gun for a moment." Selene smiled, a vicious grin that reminded Bebe too much of the bastards that had killed her parents. "There's one witch I want dead."

A clap of thunder filled the penthouse. Caesar's coat and the Book were ripped from Bebe's grip. She found herself crashing to the floor and smothered underneath a broad chest. Fire burned in her ankle as the broken bones grated against each other. She swallowed the tears spurred by the scorched nerves. It didn't matter. Once Caesar's body dissolved, Selene would finish off Bebe, smash the sphere and still have the Book of Shadows. Bebe wanted to scream in frustration as well as pain. There wasn't a damn thing she could do to stop any of it.

An all-too-familiar scent of rotten meat filled her nostrils.

No. Tears brimmed under her closed lids. *Not like this.*

The weight holding her down disappeared, and she blinked before wiping slime from her face. She wanted the bitch to see her eyes when she died. But it was Ptolemy standing there beside her, a sad look on his face.

Except she could clearly see the light fixture through his head.

Oh, Goddess! The puddle she lay in was what was left of his body.

An animalistic roar of fury burst from Caesar's throat. He charged Selene, tearing the gun out of her hands. She fought back, but she was no match for his rage-fueled strength. Seconds later, he dragged his struggling twin to the crumbling balcony.

Bebe carefully placed the Book on an overstuffed chair. The she pulled herself to her feet, a difficult task between the goo-coated marble and her broken ankle. She carefully picked her way across the debris to the balcony where Caesar stood, dangling his sister over the edge and shouting at her in a language Bebe didn't recognize. Fear made her hesitate at the frame of what had been the sliding glass door. She wasn't sure what was worse, this side of Caesar or the thought of going out on a damaged balcony over three hundred feet above the ground.

A faint glimmer shone out of the corner of her eye. Oh Goddess! Despite the stars shining high above, pale blue spread across the eastern horizon. In the insanity, she'd lost track of time.

"Caesar!"

The man who turned to face her wasn't the man who'd kissed her so tenderly, who'd told her truths that were agonizing but that she needed to hear, who'd told her he loved her. The dark man who'd promised to take away her pain had disappeared. No, this man was just like the monsters from her childhood.

And she couldn't bear letting him take that fall into absolute blackness by killing his sister.

Releasing her death grip on the frame, she inched forward, as much from her own vertigo and pain than to prevent him from dropping Selene. "Caesar," she said, keeping her voice low and gentle. "You need to put her down."

He growled at her, actually growled, but he didn't let go of Selene. Probably a good thing since a thirty-story drop would smash even a vampire into sidewalk jelly.

Bebe sucked in what was left of her courage. *Caesar, please, you don't want to do this.*

"She-she—" He fought for the words, like he could barely remember English.

"I know what she did, but this isn't going bring anyone back." Her voice broke. She struggled to draw a breath. "Not my parents or Tiffany's. Not Grandma." Glancing back at the putrid remains slowly being absorbed by the carpet and the sad-faced phantom still standing next to them was all it took for the tears to cut loose. "And not Ptolemy." She choked back a sob. "Don't become as warped and twisted as she is. This isn't what your parents would have wanted." Holding out a hand, she whispered, "Please."

His panting slowed, and his head shifted back to look at the sister he held by the throat. A deep-throated growl emerged, and with a sudden violent throw, Selene went sailing through the air to slam into the beige concrete above the missing doors before landing with a sick thud on the patio.

Her head rose, blood pouring from her nose and a nasty cut in her scalp. Black hatred boiled from her aura.

Caesar's hands flexed, but he didn't move toward his sister. "I declare you rogue, Cleopatra Selene Antonius. You are a non-entity to the Augustine coven."

At Caesar's pronouncement, Selene's eyes widened. "I didn't mean to hurt Ptolemy. You know I didn't. She's the threat!" A shaking finger pointed at Bebe.

"You will have no comfort, no succor, no shelter from any member of the Vampire Nation," Caesar continued in a monotone, ignoring Selene's pleading tears. "Harm to any sentient will result in the death penalty."

You would choose her over—"

"You made your own choice when you tried to kill me. When you—" Emotion flared in his voice. His fists clenched at his sides. "When you killed our brother." An ugly smile spread across his features. "But you are my twin. We shared a womb, so I'm being far more generous than I should." He glanced at the brightening sky before turning back to Selene. "You have until sunrise to get out of my territory."

The vampiress scrambled to her feet. Naked loathing twisted her sharp features. "You have no idea—"

"Go to New York. Maybe Virginia will be more generous to you than me."

Selene's face blanched at his taunt. Limping awkwardly on a broken stiletto, she backed up until she was inside the penthouse. Keeping her eyes fixed on Caesar, she inched toward the slime that had been Ptolemy.

"And don't even think about reaching for one of those guns in there, sister dear. You won't survive."

She stiffened for the barest second before she dashed for the stairwell door and disappeared.

"Caesar?" Bebe whispered.

His attention returned to her from somewhere else. She wasn't sure she wanted to know where. A small quiver of relief spread through her aching body when his fangs began to recede.

"You need to get inside," she said, but he didn't seem to hear her. "Now, Caesar. Is there a secure room further inside?"

He nodded, a weary motion, and held out his hand. When she took it, a small sigh escaped his lips. He swung her into his arms and entered the trashed penthouse. Skirting the broken furniture, smashed glass and the two sets of remains in the living room, he carried her down a dark hallway and shut them in a bedroom as the first rays of sun peeked over the mountains.

Caesar set her gently on the bed and wrapped his arms around her. She didn't resist his soul-searing kiss. At least, she didn't until he hit a tiny cut on her bottom lip, and she jumped at the new pain.

"I'm sorry, *amora*," he said and pulled back a few inches. "We need to get you a doc—"

Bebe let out a little yelp of surprise. Phantom Ptolemy peered over Caesar's shoulder, rolling his transparent eyes and making a gagging motion with his index finger.

"What?" Caesar's head whipped so fast to look behind him it was wonder he didn't give himself a kink in his neck. "What's wrong?"

"It's okay. I—" She bit down on her lip, and fresh pain reminded her of the cut. How the hell did she broach the subject of his brother with Caesar?

Ptolemy gave her pleading look. He may have unfinished business with Caesar, but after the last several hours, she sure didn't have the strength to deal with a permitted possession. At least, Ptolemy wasn't trying to force his way into her body, and she sighed at that small grace.

The glass in her pocket warmed to a near uncomfortable temperature. Something else she needed to deal with. The heat faded and flared again. Yes, she had the strength to complete this one small act.

She met Caesar's concerned gaze. "There's a couple of things we need to take care of."

His eyes shifted to take in the amethyst sphere she pulled out, and he nodded as he rose. "Of course. I'll give you your privacy."

She laid a hand on his arm, stopping him from retreating from the room. "I need you here. I want—" She swallowed hard. What she was about to ask him would require the most intimate contact. When they were done, he'd know her heart and soul, the inner face she'd never shown anyone. "There's something you need to see."

His eyes narrowed. "What's going on, Bebe?"

"Nothing bad," she said, more to reassure herself than him, and gestured with the sphere. "We need to say our good-byes, and by linking with me, you'll be able to See."

She wouldn't bother casting a circle. It wouldn't be needed in this case. Instead, she patted the bed next to her. Confusion filled his expression, but he climbed carefully next to her on the bed, trying not to jar her ankle.

Reaching out with her senses, she double-checked that Lucien was in fact gone. Phantom Ptolemy must have understood what she was doing because he nodded confirmation that it was just the three of them. The glass gave a little pulse of heat. Okay, four of them.

Reaching for Caesar's hand with her own, she twined her fingers with his until palms met. The touch sent a tremor of heat through her that had nothing to do with the magickal energy she summoned. Then she shifted to her Sight and dropped her shields.

All of them.

The effect amazed and stunned her. It was like looking through two different sets of eyes at the same time. She *was* looking through two perspectives at once. And the loving cocoon she'd felt in the circle at Grandma's mansion enveloped and surrounded her. Hints of Caesar's fury at Selene's betrayal and his grief over Ptolemy swirled through her emotions, but the majority of his feelings held relief that she was safe and alive.

"Ptolemy?" he whispered, and his jolt of surprise rippled through her.

It's all right, Caesar. I wanted . . . I needed to say I'm sorry. So sorry. For everything. I shouldn't have listened to Selene. Ptolemy's voice held an odd dissonance.

Caesar shot her a worried glance, and she gave him a reassuring squeeze. He turned back to his brother. "You've got nothing to apologize for. You saved Bebe. I—"

The words clogged her throat as if they were her own, not Caesar's. Tears trickled down her cheeks at the double portion of pain and regret.

Ptolemy's gaze shifted down. *I know I don't have any right to ask this . . .*

Caesar coughed softly. "Y-you can ask me anything."

Keep an eye on Tiffany. She— Ptolemy raised his head to meet his brother's eyes, a fierce determination in his expression. *She'll try to go after Selene once she knows the truth. I don't want anything to happen to the kid.*

A wry smile curved Caesar's lips. "I'll try. I can't guarantee anything."

Matching amusement twisted the ghost's visage. *That's the reason I didn't make you swear by the Styx.*

Another pulse of heat warmed Bebe's palm, reminding her of her own promise. Raising the Soul Sphere to eye level, she whispered the words to dissolve the glass. The freed energy shifted, misted and finally coalesced into a familiar form. Wrinkles gone and standing straighter than Bebe had ever seen, a much younger version of Grandma gazed down at her and smiled. It was a broad, genuine smile, the kind she hadn't seen her grandmother wear in over seventeen years.

I knew you could do it, my baby. And I'm sorry too. Please understand. I wanted to protect you. I never meant to hurt you.

Bebe nodded, tears clogging her throat again, but this time her own.

A brilliant white light appeared behind the two ghosts, spilling and flooding everyone with a nearly tangible glow. Caesar had to turn his head away, and even Bebe had to raise her left hand to shield her eyes. Grandma glanced over her shoulder, then back at Bebe. The soft flutter of wings filled the bedroom.

We have to go. I love you.

The strange resonance of the words coming from both ghosts at the same time made Bebe shiver. Grandma blew her a kiss and disappeared into the light. Ptolemy turned to follow, but he paused to look back at his brother.

Don't let her go.

Then he too was gone. A flash and almost audible snap closed the doorway between the living and the dead.

Tears trickled down Caesar's face. He pulled her into his lap and kissed her, a gentle loving kiss. "Thank you," he murmured against her hair.

And they sat like that for a very long time.

Chapter 31

Two days later, Bebe hung up the phone and cradled her head in her arms on top of the writing desk. If she weren't so damned exhausted, she'd collect the energy to call room service for some dinner. Her rumbling stomach reminded her that she'd missed lunch hours ago. Adding its own complaint, her ankle throbbed in time to her pulse.

"That bad?"

She lifted her head to find Caesar standing before her, a glass of water and her bottle of painkillers in his outstretched hands. "Any food with that?"

He grinned. "Crabcakes are on their way up. The vegetable of the day was asparagus, but I can call for something else for you."

"That sounds like heaven to me," she said before she took the bottle of pills and popped a couple into her mouth. Then she took the glass from his proffered hand. The simple brush of his skin shot a wave of heat straight to her pelvis. Choosing to ignore it, she sipped the water, swallowed the meds and leaned back in the executive chair he'd appropriated for her temporary "office" in a spare bedroom of the Karnak penthouse.

"To answer your original question, no. Alice and I shoved our compromise solution down the Elders' collective throats. It's pretty sad when we're being the reasonable ones."

He tried to hide his chuckle. The scent of wine mixed with the metallic tang of blood meant he'd had his dinner already. "Beatrice wasn't happy about your abdication," he said.

A sigh escaped her lips. "In her mind, she lost face backing what to her was the losing side." She shook her head in disbelief. "Even though I'm Alice's named heir until her first child is born. Alice is going to try to amend the coven by-laws to switch to American-style elections instead of European succession, but . . ." From the pensive look on Caesar's face, he doubted her cousin's success as much as Bebe did. Alice's political acumen left something to be desired. Especially after she called Miranda Doucette a dried-up hag during one discussion/argument.

Bebe rubbed her temple at the dull pain that had plagued her the last several hours. Somehow, the headache overshadowed the rest of the bruises, breaks and other assorted damage to her body. The hotel's Normal doctor had offered to give her a Vicodin prescription, but she needed her wits a little sharper in order to deal with the White Rose mess. Now, she almost wished she'd taken him up on the offer.

"At least, our tentative truce is holding now that she's realized just how much William manipulated her. In the meantime, I'll pray to the Goddess every day that Alice doesn't get herself killed before she pops out a kid."

A frown creased Caesar's face. "You don't think Pierre and Miranda flushed out all of William's co-conspirators?"

Sitting face level with the zipper on his pants was not helping her concentration one bit. Her thoughts keep turning in a direction they shouldn't be going. One that involved the bed less than a yard away. She could seduce Caesar. That would accomplish her plan. Hell, it'd be the fastest way to heal her broken ankle too.

No, she wouldn't stoop to those tactics. The poor man had been yanked around enough by his own family the last few years. She couldn't do that to him.

The chair squeaked when she shoved away from the desk and stood. "I just don't know." She shook her head as Caesar handed her the crutches. "He was more than willing to spill his guts in return for having his magick bound and making a conventional plea bargain with the D.A." A smirk spread across her lips. "Given his fate if left in the hands of the coven that was the smart road for him to take.

The Elders questioned him under a truth spell before they turned him over to the police, but there's the possibility Lucien altered his memory."

Caesar raked a hand through his dark hair, leaving the short strands standing on end. "Given Selene's alterations to the Karnak's books, I wouldn't be surprised if she had Lucien do so."

"Any idea where the money went?" She took another sip of water, just a small one to calm her nerves. The problems they discussed seemed insignificant compared to what she wanted to propose to him. She didn't want him to think her idea was drug-induced bullshit.

Propose. What a funny way to put it, considering that was what she would be doing. Another nervous gulp of water caught in her throat and resulted in a major choking fit.

Cool fingers plucked the glass from her, and then she was being patted on the back like she was an infant. Goddess, was that what he thought of her? A baby that needed to be cared for? He'd been caring for her enough the last few days.

"Are you all right?"

"Went down the wrong pipe," she muttered before she gave a final racking cough and wiped her eyes. "What were you saying about the money?"

"Duncan tracked it as far as a series of transfers made to a private account in the Caymans." An exasperated huff indicated his annoyance. "After that, it disappears." Caesar's handsome features grew pensive. "If it were just the couple of million, I wouldn't be worried, but . . ."

Except it wasn't just the Karnak Selene had stolen from. His people found altered records going back at least a century. The current estimates of the siphoned funds he'd received from his various businesses were closer to the mid-ten digits. A rogue vampire with a fortune at her disposal could wreak havoc.

And nearly every vampire loyal to Selene had disappeared when she did. The ones who couldn't escape committed suicide before they could be questioned.

Without another thought, Bebe propped the crutches against the desk, wrapped her arms around Caesar's waist and hugged him. "You did the right thing by letting her go. It would have destroyed your soul to have killed her."

Strong arms held her in turn, and he nuzzled her hair. "I don't know what I would have done without you the last couple of days."

The passionate heat emanating from his psyche erased any doubts she had what she wanted most in the world. She knew who she wanted and where she wanted to be. Her only fear was his reaction.

Pulling back a fraction, she gazed up at him and cleared her throat. "I've been thinking about what you asked." The words clogged in her throat, and she drew a deep breath. "About continuing Grandma's research."

A hopeful light flared in his hazel eyes. "And?"

"I'm worried about not completing it before I die." She held up a hand when he opened his mouth. "Please let me finish before you say anything else. The learning curve I'm facing is bad enough, and even if I trained someone else, there're so many other things that could happen. But I've been doing some research myself and—"

Her body trilled in anticipation. This was it.

"I want you to Turn me."

Caesar jerked away from her embrace so fast she had to grab the desk edge to keep her balance. Anger and disbelief mingled on his face. "You want me to what!"

Wincing at the pain in her eardrums, she held out her hands. "Listen to me. Caesar, please. I've been doing some research, and I believe there's a common reason that some of the hybrids survive—"

"No! I won't. Don't even ask me such a thing." He whirled and stalked from the bedroom.

"Wait! Caesar!" Bebe cursed her broken ankle and her emotional ineptitude. Could she have handled this conversation any worse? "I know what I'm getting into." Snatching the crutches, she hobbled after him.

She caught up to him in the living room when he pivoted so fast she crashed into his chest. Grabbing her by the arms, he lifted her in the air. The crutches dropped and her feet dangled. Glowing neon yellow eyes bore into her, his pupils shot with blood red.

"You have no clue of what you are asking of me." His words were low, dangerous, full of his raw masculine power.

And she wasn't afraid. Despite his appearance, despite her past, despite everyone else's schemes and lies. She drew a deep breath, and said, "Yes, I do know what I'm asking. Please put me down."

He set her down as if she were a porcelain doll. Then he backed away from her, staring at her like she'd grown a second head. "You were lucky that night I was shot. If—" He shook his head fiercely. "And you're injured now. No, I can't—"

Bebe took a tentative hop toward him, reaching out mentally as well but his shields were tight. "Caesar, listen to me. I know—"

"No, you don't!" His howl still echoed in the air when vampire speed made him seem to disappear in thin air.

"—I love you," she finished to the slamming stairwell door.

Chapter 32

It was close to midnight before the door to the rooftop garden creaked open. Bebe's scent reached Caesar long before she did. The thump-slap of the crutches and her one slipper made a sobering counterpoint to the shouts and laughter of the holiday revelers on the Strip. He stood at the ledge surrounding the garden and stared at the lights of the city. He couldn't face her, not sure of what stopped him. Pain? Guilt? Love?

Or a combination of all three?

"Watching the skies for Santa Claus?"

That made him turn around. "I beg your pardon?"

Neon lights from thirty-one stories below cast a soft light on her face. "Santa Claus? St. Nicholas? Father Christmas? The fat guy in the red suit with flying reindeer?" A sad, sweet smile spread across her face. "You do realize it's Christmas Eve, don't you?"

Christmas Eve. That meant in a span of minutes it would be the twenty-fifth of December. His and Selene's birthday. And for the first time he could remember, there would be no family celebration. No phone call to Selene if they couldn't get together. Not even wisecracks from Ptolemy about their age.

The loss ached deep inside of him. How could their relationship have shattered so thoroughly?

Because it had been stressed over his failure to protect Ptolemy when they were barely more than children. Because it had been cracked for centuries when he refused to see Selene for the conniving bitch that she was. Because it had been fucked up from the beginning when their mother had seduced two married Roman generals in the desperate hope of retaining Egypt's independence.

And what did he have to show for it? He couldn't love the woman in front of him, not the way she deserved.

"So you're still not going to talk to me?"

He raised a quizzical eyebrow at Bebe's question until her original query rushed back to the forefront of his thoughts. "I'm sorry. I was just surprised you celebrate the holiday." For some reason, it hadn't dawned on him that she would. Good to know Nikolai had some influence on her upbringing before he and Natasha divorced.

She shrugged, a slight gesture, before pulling her jacket tighter against the cold desert air. "My family's just as mixed as yours when it comes to religions." Reaching for her throat, she tugged the silver chain, all that was left of Tiffany's holiday gift to her, and said nothing else as they both turned to stare at the cityscape.

Family. Maybe that's what his strange little household was. He'd never before considered that concept. Alex was nearly as annoying as his nephew, Anthony. Anne had become the daughter he'd never sired. Even Phillippa was closer to him than Selene ever truly was. And Duncan reminded him so much of his older brother, Caesarion. So serious, so intense, so capable.

He didn't force any of them to live in the Brentwood mansion, even though everyone had their own room for those times they spent the day there. They all had their own houses, apartments or condos. Well, except Tiffany, but he had no doubt she'd find her own place as soon as she graduated. And she'd dropped enough hints that she wanted to be an enforcer, despite Duncan's well-intentioned objections.

Some coven masters were far more controlling than he was, but he'd viewed the room arrangement as convenient. The younger vampires didn't drive him crazy and vice versa. In fact, he wasn't that demanding of any of the vampires in his territory. As long as they registered their presence, paid their taxes for group services like the blood banks and didn't kill anyone, he let them do as they wished.

Sure, he employed his household staff and enforcers, but that didn't account for the little traditions like their winter holiday present exchange, celebrating birthdays and the personal joking. Even Tiffany's repeated attempts to egg Ptolemy—

A hard lump rose in his throat at the thought of his brother. Hades, he couldn't even bury Ptolemy's remains properly, no mummification, not even a coin for Charon under the tongue. He'd failed Ptolemy so many times before, but this time sat like ash in his mouth.

Even worse, he'd taken his anger at himself out on Bebe. Thank the gods he hadn't harmed her. A soul as beautiful as hers didn't deserve his crap. What she deserved were children, a real family, a life without constant turmoil. So much more than he could offer her. It had been millennia since he'd felt this powerless.

He had to clear his throat twice before he could speak. "I apologize for handling you so roughly. You didn't deserve such ill treatment."

She hobbled closer to him, quiet and sure. Her tiny, soft hand reached up and cupped his cheek, her thumb stroking as soft as a butterfly. "There's something you need to get through you thick skull, Caesar Augustine. I love you, and you're not getting rid of me so easily." A gentle smile replaced her somber expression. "No matter how far you run, I can still limp after you. Or were you planning to break my other ankle to get away?"

A few days ago, his heart would have leapt at her words, but now? Now, he couldn't be a selfish bastard, no matter how much it broke both of their hearts. He took her petite hand from his face and held it in both of his. "Listen to me, *amora*. I will not condemn you to my fate."

She sucked in a deep breath. "Caesar, I didn't propose this lightly. Every hybrid who has survived and remained sane, did so because they had a vampire mate helping them through the Turn. I'd survive because I want this. I want to be with the man I love. Knowing you would be with me the entire time—"

"And we'd break every law of the International Council."

"If we petition the Vampire National Congress for my Turning, they'd be required to say no. If we do it, then tell them . . ."

Hades, he was tempted to go along with her insane plan, but there were too many other factors, too many things that could go wrong, too many enemies against them. He shook his head. "No, we'd have the witches crawling down our throats as well."

She smiled, a look so wicked and enticing at the same time, he wanted her right there on the roof. Pulling her hand free, she ran her fingers down his chest. His gut clenched in anticipation when those tempting digits paused at his waist.

"The only one who can officially object would be the White Rose High Priestess, and she's already given her *unofficial* approval," she said.

A snort of derision escaped him. He didn't know what was worse—Bebe's naiveté or Alice's blatancy. "Of course, she'd approve. Has it occurred to you it's the most convenient way for her to get rid of you?"

She huffed, grabbed her right crutch and whacked him on the shins. "Has it occurred to you that she was in that link with us back in San Francisco? She Saw how we both felt about each other. You wanted a declaration from me. Well, here it is, buster." Dropping both crutches, she flung herself at him. He caught her before she toppled them both into the raised flowerbed next to them.

Her broad grin shone with its own light. "I love you, and I'm sure as hell not leaving you."

He pulled her closer until her body was snug against his, her heat radiating through him. He returned her embrace, inhaled her sweet scent and wanted the night to never end. Wanted what she offered. Wanted her warmth. Her laughter. Gods above, he wanted her.

Guilt poured through him. No. He'd already caused the deaths of his mother and Ptolemy. If anything went wrong, if Bebe came out of the Turn dead, or worse psychotic, he'd be required to kill her. And he'd never forgive himself.

"No." He tried to let go, needed to walk away, but his limbs refused to obey him.

Her body tilted slightly until her dark eyes met his. "Talk to me. Tell me what it's like, so I know what to expect."

A lot of things blurred together after two thousand plus years of living, but that gods-awful nightmare remained crystal clear. "What happened to us—" Shifting his attention to the neon-lit skyline, he sucked in a lungful of crisp air before he could face her again. "I never want to hurt you, Bebe, but you need to understand something. Ptolemy and I weren't supposed to be Turned. They came for us with the intent to kill, but then that was common practice in Rome. Assassinate your enemies before they get you. How much do you know about the early Roman empire?"

"A little." She shrugged, and again the slight smile appeared. "I've already figured out you weren't on the good side of one of the emperors."

Her wry tone elicited a chuckle. "Actually, that would be my parents. My misfortune was worse. I got on the wrong side of Father's ex-wife, who happened to be the sister of an emperor." Soberness hit him. "My parents were Marcus Antonius and Cleopatra VII of Egypt."

Shock filled her features, and she leaned away from him to examine his face. He could practically see the cogs turning in her head.

"Mark Antony and Cleopatra? *The* Antony and Cleopatra?"

He nodded.

She covered her mouth for an instant to get her obvious humor under control. "Oh, you poor thing."

He rolled his eyes. "See? This is why I don't tell people."

She laughed outright this time. Waving a hand, she said, "No, no. I'm sorry. It's just—" Another spate of laughter shook her. "You're the only one I've met who has more family issues than me."

"Thanks. That makes me feel much better." But no real acrimony filled his words.

Without a word, Bebe took his hands in hers and pointed over to a bench. He swung her into his arms. Already petite, she weighed practically nothing since she barely had a chance to eat over the last couple of weeks. Once at the bench, he settled her gently on his lap, and they huddled on the sun-weathered wood. Soft quiet filled the private garden, blocking out the cheers and shouts from the streets below. The warm cocoon of her spirit filled him as he continued.

"We were taken to Rome after our parents' deaths, and Octavian gave us to his sister to raise as proper Roman citizens. Octavia had been humiliated by Father and—" He suppressed a shudder at the memories. "—took her displeasure out on us. No physical marks on Selene, of course, since she could be used for marital alliances. But that didn't stop Octavia from—" He clenched his hands at the old pain. "She used little things against Ptolemy and me. Barely enough food, no blankets or heat in the winter. Working us like servants hoping we'd get sick and die. She was sorely disappointed when we didn't comply."

Bebe said nothing, merely rested her head on his shoulder. The spicy ginger of her hair filled his nostrils, and the heat of her arms wrapped around his neck warmed his soul. He didn't think he'd be able to get the words out if she looked at him.

"After three years at her tender mercies, Juba of Numidia asked for Selene's hand. One of Octavian's stipulations was that Juba take responsibility for Ptolemy and me, keep us contained. As far as the great Caesar Augustus was concerned, that ended the matter." He snorted at the memory. "You'd think Octavia would be happy not having to look at us, not having everything rubbed in her face. But sending us across the Mediterranean didn't appease her.

"There was a lot of unrest in Numidia. Octavian had raised Juba, so the locals resented the 'Romanization' of their king. When the typical attempts at poisoning us failed, she sent vampires. It was easy for assassins to slip into the palace."

Slim fingers stroked his hair in comfort. He didn't deserve it, but Gods above, it felt good.

"They found Ptolemy first. I'd borrowed his saddle while mine was being repaired. I stumbled on the attack when I went to his room to return it. I threw the saddle at them and shouted for the guards, but before I could draw my knife . . ." He closed his eyes as the past and the present blurred together. "The odd thing was how little blood there was." Blinking away the wetness collecting in his eyes, he drew a deep breath.

"Did you even know what was happening to you?" Bebe raised her head to look him in the eye.

He shook his head. "They had nearly drained Ptolemy. He was already slipping into the Turn coma by the time the guards arrived, not that we knew what was happening. We didn't think he'd live through the night. As far as we knew I just had a couple of odd bites on my forearm."

Old guilt mixed with new and spilled out of him in a bitter torrent. "I failed to protect him that night. Just like I failed three nights ago. Just like I always fail everyone I care about."

"You can't blame yourself for Selene's actions. She's a big girl. Big enough to make her own choices. She's the one who shot Ptolemy, not you."

Hades, how did he make Bebe understand? "I can't do this to you! I can't be responsible for—" The words caught in his throat, ancient pain and new grief choking him.

Understanding dawned in her eyes. "Who was she?"

Bebe needed to know the truth. Maybe then, she'd walk away from him. So what if she'd take his heart with her? Gods knew he deserved having it ripped out.

"My mother," he whispered. Silence weighed down the night. The winds paused, and the stars held their breath, waiting as he did for her reaction. There was a reason the Kindly Ones kept a special place in Tartarus for those who murdered their mothers.

But confusion twisted her brows. "Did you try to Turn her?"

He shook his head.

"But how—"

"I'm the one who smuggled the asp to her."

"Oh."

He found himself holding his breath along with the rest of the universe. She leaned her head against his shoulder, and her arms wrapped around his neck again.

Tears were in her voice when she spoke. "She had no right to ask that of you."

"I would have done anything she wanted." Bittersweet love filled him. "You simply didn't question her orders."

"But you were what? Nine? Ten?" Anger tinged her voice. "You don't ask a child to help you commit suicide."

"She didn't ask me that," he said softly.

Bebe sat up straight, eyes blazing when she met his gaze. "Did you know what she planned?"

"No, but—"

"Then quit blaming yourself because she conned you into helping *her*. It wasn't your fault."

Somehow, Bebe's quiet, furious defense of him sent a wave of comfort through him, but it didn't change things between them.

The butterfly touch of her thoughts lit his mind. *Yes, it does change things.*

Gods help him, she was stubborn. He stared at her. "How?"

"I'm asking you straight out to Turn me. No tricks. No manipulation. I love you, and I want to be with you."

Her face was so earnest he wanted to believe her.

Then read me. Defiance flared in her eyes, daring him to Look.

With a tentative mental probe, he reached for her. And Saw blinding radiance. Love, nearly a tangible thing, spilled out of her. No shields blocked him. Warm yellows and golds caressed him, washed through him. This was Bebe's soul at its purest, and it made him want to weep. He pulled her close and hugged her.

"Now tell me what to expect," she said, her voice muffled by his chest.

He sighed. "You're not going to let this go, are you?"

"Nope." A slight giggle followed the word. "You should know by now I'm just as stubborn as Grandma." She raised her head from his shoulder. "And if you don't do it, I'll find someone else who will."

He didn't have any doubt she'd do exactly that. Another wouldn't have the incentive to make sure she survived the Turn. Staring up at the few stars that pierced the light pollution brought him no alternatives. Finally, he looked at her and said, "All right. We'll do it your way. But if this goes wrong and you haunt me, so help me, I *will* have your ass exorcised."

A wide, triumphant grin spread across her face. "I understand."

He shook his head, wondering what the hell they were both thinking. He kept the explanation clinical. There was no fucking way he'd romanticize it. "You're looking at fever and vomiting within the first thirty-six hours of exposure to the virus, followed by coma. Onset of coma depends on the initial blood loss and the location of the contamination. The length of the coma depends on the age and general health of the person as well as the amount of blood lost. Seventy-two hours is the average."

He paused, making sure he had her attention. "It hurts Bebe. You may be in a coma, but you're going to remember the pain. Selene—" His throat closed at the mention of his sister, but he forced the words past. "Selene compared it to giving birth to all three of her children at the same time."

Bebe gave a small, dry laugh. "Well, I've never been pregnant so I couldn't say."

"You will *never* be able to have children if we do this, *amora.*"

She sobered and seemed to give it some thought before she shrugged. "We could always adopt." Another grin lit up her face. "Or we could ask Tiffany to be a surrogate." The grin flipped to a frown. "Wait. Bad idea. There's a chance the kid would be exactly like her."

That statement ripped a belly laugh from him, only to be replaced by worry and fear for Bebe's life.

"Caesar, I can handle this. Honest. And you'll be here with me every step of the way." But a tiny hint of fear flickered in her eyes.

"We don't have to do this," he repeated.

"It's just . . . I mean, when you were bit—" She licked her lips. "D-did the bites hurt?"

He couldn't help smiling at the trepidation in her voice. "I don't *have* to bite you, you know."

"I know." She swallowed hard before returning his smile. "I was kind of hoping to do it the other way."

He laughed. He couldn't help it. No one had ever made him so angry and so happy all at the same time the way Bebe could. And it drove away the morbid melancholy of the past. "Are you trying to seduce me, Dr. Zachary?"

A scowl darkened her lovely face. "I know I suck at it. You don't have to rub it in." She squirmed in his lap, struggling to escape his hold.

He swallowed a groan at the effect of her warm, round ass on his body, but he wasn't about to let her go hopping across the roof and break her other ankle. Actually, she didn't seem to be fighting him as hard as she could have. She finally gave up though, probably because she realized the effect her movement had on his cock, which very obviously poked her hip. She pursed her lips and huffed a curl out of her eyes before she glared at him.

"This is not fair. If you're not going to succumb to my feminine wiles, at least let me make a dignified exit."

His right eyebrow rose of its own accord. "Explain to me how a slipper and a cast equate to dignity?"

She stuck her tongue out at him in response.

"I can think of a better use for that tongue."

Her winsome smile lit her face. "So can I."

The groan that rolled from his throat was fully audible this time. He buried his nose in her hair. "You have no idea how I want you, *amora*."

Wriggling her hips, she giggled. "I have a pretty good idea."

"Are you absolutely sure? Once we do this, there's no going back," he whispered into her hair.

A deep sigh shuddered through her body. "I'm tired, Caesar. Tired of being alone." Her voice hinted of tears. "And so are you. We have something good here. Why do you want to throw it away on maybes and what-ifs?"

A chuckle rolled through his chest. "Have you been talking to Duncan?"

"No. Why?"

"He suggested that I use the same reasoning on you."

"Really?"

The incredulous note her voice made him look at her. "Why are you so surprised?"

A wry smile twisted her lips. "Guess I never pictured him as a romantic. Smart man though. Maybe you should listen to him."

Amora, you need to think carefully about this. Right now, there is no cure. There's no guarantee you will be able to find one. You will never feel the sun on your face, never taste another morsel of food—

So I have to give Tiffany all my silver jewelry. And I was never a big fan of garlic anyway.

What happens when you accidentally immolate yourself with one of your own fireballs?

She laughed, a joyous sound in the glittering night. *I will trust you to have fire extinguishers in every room.*

He didn't know what else to say to convince her this was a very bad idea. He couldn't convince himself that it was a very bad idea anymore. It wasn't just the thought of making love to her every night for an eternity. She was right. He wanted someone to love, wanted someone to call his own, and wanted that someone to be Bebe and no one else.

A sigh whispered past her parted lips as she stared at him. Not intruding on his thoughts, though the awareness of her hovered on the edge of his mind, but giving him the space to make that commitment.

He couldn't resist any longer. His lips sought hers of their own accord. His tongue swept hers, peaches and ginger invaded every breath he took, and his arms pulled her tighter against his chest. The kiss was exquisite, not full of want, not demanding, but a promise.

Her hands and mouth urged him on, but he broke the contact and simply watched her face. Gold, red and blue neon reflected from her pale skin. A slow smile spread across her dimpled cheeks, and she nodded once. No words, verbal or otherwise, passed between them. Caesar stood, Bebe's petite frame cradled in his arms, and he headed for the staircase.

He paused, looking from the narrow passageway to her. "How'd you get up the stairs with the crutches?"

Brown eyes sparkled as she laughed. "I defied gravity."

Groaning from her bad joke, he treaded down the stairs, careful of the cast on her ankle.

— • —

Bebe had been in Caesar's bedroom twice in the past few days since coming to the Karnak, but this time the golds and browns that decorated the room shimmered and moved as if alive. Depositing her gently on the king-sized bed, he moved with a contained grace while he lit the candles stationed on various surfaces.

Excitement and fear warred along her nerves. He'd given plenty of chances for her to change her mind, to back out of this. No, she wanted him, accepted what the Turn would do to her, even made peace with the pain and problems that would come with their defiance of the International Council's laws. Then her real worry hit her.

It'd been an awfully long time since she'd had sex. And he had over two thousand years of experience.

Goddess, please don't let him be disappointed.

"*Amora.*" He sat next to where she sat propped on the gold and chocolate pillows. "Are you sure—"

"Yes," she snapped. And immediately regretted her tone, though his arrogant smirk mitigated her guilt. "I'm sorry, but you're ruining the mood when you keep asking."

His dark eyebrow cocked upward. "Gods forbid I should ruin a lady's mood."

A heartfelt sigh escaped her lips. She laid two fingers on his soft lips. "No more words."

He complied by wrapping his lips around her fingers, tongue stroking the pads. The effect bypassed her brain and flooded her pelvis. A soft gasp followed as his mouth released the fingers, kissing and stroking its way across her palm.

Ripples of pleasure swept through her at the slight scrape of a fang on her wrist's pulse, the hint of danger adding to the tension in her body. Even with lids hooded, his eyes shone gold when he left her wrist and looked at her. Grasping the clip holding her hair up, he tugged it loose. Curls fell, tickling her cheeks, until he brushed the wayward strands back. He cupped her face, his lips meeting hers for a soul-searing kiss.

Shields gone, their desire mixed and danced. Mental and physical touch melted together until Bebe wasn't sure where she stopped and he began. His lips found her earlobe, nibbling and sucking along her neck. Her back arched of its own accord, and she couldn't get enough sensation.

His cool flesh was the only thing that contained the fire threatening to destroy her. When that touch disappeared, a whimper rose in her throat. In a flurry of motion, her sweater and bra vanished.

Except he didn't touch her. He sat there, looking at her. Not the unnatural predatory stillness of a vampire though. His jaw muscles clenched and shifted under his skin, but he made no move toward her.

"Caesar? What's wrong?"

A slight smile creased his face. *Nothing. You're just so beautiful. I want to remember you like this.* His aura flared brilliant scarlet. He wasn't lying.

A mixture of embarrassment and pleasure burned her skin at his words. No one she'd been with had ever called her beautiful. For the first time in her life, she felt truly desired and desirable.

Not breaking eye contact, his head dipped and lips grasped a hardened nipple. She nearly came from his rough tongue brushing the sensitized skin. Her eyes closed as she luxuriated in the heady feelings.

Cool air hit damp skin, raising gooseflesh, and her eyes popped open. Easing sweatpants and panties over her hips, he tugged the knit and lace down her legs and gently stretched the fabric around her cast before tossing the clothing over his shoulder.

She reached for his face, but he caught her hands and pressed them to the comforter. "No, *amora*, this is my time."

He gently pushed her legs apart. She sucked in a harsh breath, feeling more exposed than she'd ever had. Rough fingers stroked the soft flesh of her inner thigh. Gold cotton and stuffing bunched in her fists as she resisted the urge to touch him. Lying down between her legs, he gave a tentative lick across her hot, wet center. A sob ripped from her throat at the electricity that fried her nerves.

A soft chuckle hummed across her clit before he began kissing and sucking her in earnest. His want wrapped around her in a soft cocoon of love. Desire flew back and forth between them.

Her eyes closed again as she sank into the sensations, mind and body. Her hips matched his rhythm, and the pressure and heat built until it had nowhere else to go. She screamed while her body shuddered and convulsed under his touch.

She blinked away the tears that had collected under her lids. By the time, her vision cleared and her senses returned, he'd shed his clothes. Muscles, defined but not overdone, shifted under the candlelight as he climbed into the bed and lay beside her, pulling her close. He kissed her, a delicate, sensual exploration that left her breathless. She clung to his neck for a moment, trying to collect her scattered thoughts.

Last chance, amora. *I won't be able to hold back this time.*

Laughing softly, she reached down and stroked him in answer. His groan rumbled against her ear. The sound sent a surge of wickedness through her. Kneeling proved awkward with the cast, so she wiggled around until she could prop herself on her elbows. The maneuvering caused them both to howl with laughter, but the amusement gave way to his moan with the first swirl of her tongue.

The heady scent of him penetrated her brain, spurring on her boldness. Salty, sweet taste met her tongue as she ran it up and down his length. A glorious feeling of power enveloped her at giving him pleasure. Nothing else matched in her life, and she didn't want it to end.

He grabbed her upper arms, drawing her up beside him but still careful with her injury. His action tore a whimper of disappointment from her throat.

"Not this time." Brilliant yellow lit his face as he settled her on her back and nudged her knees apart. His tip pressed against her entrance, and she lifted her hips in response, wanting, needing him. She couldn't bite back the squeak of impatience.

"I love you, *amora*." He entered her, slow and steady letting her body adjust to his, filling her until she thought she would burst. There was no going back now.

The friction against her already sensitized flesh sent a frisson of erotic energy bouncing between them. Wet heat enveloped hard strength until she didn't know who she was anymore. She just knew she never wanted it to stop.

The tempo grew, ebbed and crested again until it exploded in a wash of light. Muscles seized as waves of pleasure and heat flooded her. Just as she started drifting back to earth, he went rigid in her arms. His climax sent the waves crashing through her again, and her body echoed his release.

Caesar rested his forehead against hers as they both sought a calm breath. *You can't leave me*, amora. *I couldn't live without you.*

Tears blurred her vision as she reached up and cupped his face. *I won't. I promise.*

He withdrew and shifted them both around until they were huddled under the covers, clinging together.

Neither said anything. Bebe realized there was nothing more to say. It was a long time before Caesar relaxed into sleep, though his hold on her waist was just as secure as before. But despite the boneless satiation and deep weariness, sleep eluded her. Not from regrets, but from concern over the next stages that would change her life forever.

Goddess, please, oh please, grant me the courage to survive the next few days.

No answer, no sign, came though Bebe didn't really expect one. Finally, exhaustion claimed her, and for once, no nightmares of her parents or grandmother intruded on her slumber.

Chapter 33

The horizon above the Muddy Mountains gradually shifted through the spectrum from midnight blue to rose. Bebe bundled the blanket tighter against the chill and took another sip from her mug. Mint chocolate swirled around her tongue while she waited for the first sliver of Sol to peek over the distant range.

No twinge of discomfort nudged her, no urge to run and burrow in the loose desert soil. She would have known by now, from the need for the wool encircling her if nothing else. Vampires had more resistance to environmental changes.

A sliver of scarlet poked over the black mountains. Liquid orange flared to blinding yellow-white. She closed her eyes to the caressing rays. No frying of skin, other than the standard UV messing with her lily-white nose. No screaming in agony. No spontaneous ignition into flames.

Nada.

Nothing.

She sighed, not sure if from disappointment or relief. On the plus side, the energy from all the sex over the last three days had channeled itself into healing her ankle. The new walking cast could probably come off by the end of the week.

She chugged the cold remains of chocolate and limped from the rooftop garden back down the stairs to the penthouse. Shedding blanket, coat and her one boot, she made her way back to Caesar's darkened bedroom where she ditched the rest of her clothing before crawling under the comforter with him. He pulled her tight against him, and she listened to the ultra-slow beat of his heart.

"Still nothing?" He sounded amused.

She shook her head. "What's the point of sacrificing yourself to the dark side if you don't become one of the undead?"

He chuckled in earnest and kissed the top of her head. "I'm not dead." As if proving his point, his cock pulsed against her thigh.

Irritated, she turned and socked his chest as hard as she could. Not that it made any difference. He only laughed harder. She propped herself on one elbow and glared at him.

"I appreciate your attempt, *amora*." Those eyes, the soft stroke of his fingertips on her cheek were almost enough to make her forget her annoyance. No wonder his parents were considered the most famous lovers on the planet.

She sat up and the comforter and sheet dropped from her chest. With anyone else, she would have been scrambling to cover herself, but with him, her nakedness felt—wonderful. "We need to try again."

He blinked in surprise before he answered. "We've been *trying* for over three days now. Not that I'm objecting." To prove his point, he raised his head enough to pull her right nipple into his mouth, sucking almost to the point of pain before releasing to it with a slight pop.

She swallowed hard against the erotic warmth pooling in her center and struggled to remember the thought she'd been trying to verbalize before he distracted her.

"I know. It's just—" She huffed an exasperated breath and brushed fingers over the bites on her left breast and neck. They weren't as unintentional as the one on her inner thigh. And they'd turned her on more than she cared to admit. "We obviously screwed something up, or I'd be a vampire by now."

"No, we didn't screw anything up" he said. He tugged her arm until her head fell to rest on his chest. "You read Natasha's work."

She gave up with a deep exaggerated sigh and snuggled in the crook of his shoulder. He was right. Within four generations, there would be no way in hell he or any other vampire would be able to Turn any witch.

The realization hit her like a two-by-four. She popped upright and socked Caesar in the chest again. This time must been hard enough because he grunted. Rage engulfed her at his betrayal. "You knew!" She punctuated each sentence with a blow. "You knew Grandpa Petrov was the boy the Nazis found! You knew your bite wouldn't affect me. You knew I wouldn't Turn!"

He blocked her next swing and flipped her on her back before she could take a breath to protest. By the time she took that breath, he had pinned her wrists above her head with one hand and straddled her legs. "That will be quite enough Dr. Zachary."

He grinned, fangs and all, while his free hand cupped a breast. A few weeks ago, she would have found the sight terrifying. Now, her anger melted into need. She moaned and closed her eyes to the sweet sensation of the pad of his thumb brushing her nipple ever so lightly.

She bucked and pleaded, but he extended the torture with lips, tongue and fingers, before switching his attention further south. Then he released her wrists and plunged his fingers into her dark, tight curls until she screamed with a different kind of release.

Boneless, she whispered, "Not fair."

"What's not fair?" Raw desire flared in his golden eyes when he rose to position himself between her thighs.

"Changing the subject using sex." She wrapped arms around his neck and legs around his waist, feeling the pent-up tension in his corded muscles. He plunged into her with a hiss. The sensation of him sliding home nearly sent her into orbit again. He whispered something that her overloaded brain couldn't translate, but his magical hands could.

Damn, they don't call Latin the father of the romance languages for nothing.

An age-old rhythm seized them both, and her petty grievances flew from her mind on the waves of the second orgasm. He collapsed on top of her, spent as well. Rolling off, he tugged her snug against him once more.

"Still not fair," she murmured in the drowsy aftermath. He wound and unwound a curl of her hair around his index finger for so long that she believed he wouldn't answer her.

"I—suspected that might be the case."

The situation was so ludicrous she laughed. Not a girly giggle, but that deep belly laugh you hit when you realized how ridiculous the universe is.

When she could finally control herself, she propped up on her elbow again. Caesar scowled, irritation and—was that hurt feelings?—on his aristocratic features.

She kissed the tip of his nose. "There are easier ways of getting my undying declaration of love. But—" She frowned and wagged an index finger to emphasize her point. "If you *ever* use me as a guinea pig again, I'll stake you."

He sat up and nailed her with a glare. "Is that what you think? That I'd risk your life to satisfy a curious whim?"

"Didn't you?" Her heart stopped. She wasn't sure she could handle it if his answer was yes.

He seized her shoulders, yanking her up until their eyes were inches apart. "I had to be sure you wanted to be a vampire. If Natasha had miscalculated, if something went wrong—" He dragged in a deep breath and pulled her into his arms, squeezing her tight against his chest. "I didn't want you to hate me if you did Turn."

"Grandma wouldn't have made that kind of mistake," she whispered into the hard muscle smashed against her face. She pulled back to meet his eyes. He had to understand without any vampire or witch tricks, only the simple honesty of a man and a woman who care for each other. "And I wouldn't have hated you. I chose my own path. I always have."

He cupped her face in his hands. "And I chose you." An expression of raw emotion crossed his face. "If you will have me."

"What are you saying?"

"Marry me, Bebe."

"No."

The stricken look on his face made her realize how harsh her answer was.

"Goddess, I'm fucking this up again." She closed her eyes, praying for strength before she opened them and her mind to him. "I mean, not yet. Let me find the cure first."

His thoughts reached for her, but underneath the assessment was affection and sexual desire. "You weren't sure you could find it in your lifetime."

"I've got incentive now, don't I?" She shrugged. "I figure I've got a hundred, hundred-ten good years unless I have some early onset senility problem."

"So you'll stay in Los Angeles?" Apprehension filled his features, a look so contrary to the arrogant smugness she'd become accustomed to.

She grinned. "Try to get rid of me."

He cocked an eyebrow. "I meant, live with me in Los Angeles."

"And I said, try to get rid of me."

"For how long though?"

"Till death do us part?"

His eyes flared with annoyance. "That's not funny."

"Oh, come on, it is."

His eyes gleamed yellow.

She gulped. "A little."

He began tickling her, but her shrieks of laughter soon turned to something else much more enjoyable.

———•———

Snow fell in a quiet blanket outside Selene's Boulder safehouse. The one her brothers didn't know existed. It had been a better investment than she ever dreamed.

Leaning back in her chair, Selene twirled the crystal goblet of blood, curious of the reaction of the man sitting across the table from her. Tyrone Mallory didn't recoil, not so much as flinch. Good. Maybe this was a Normal she could deal with. She leaned forward and handed the copies of the research notes Ptolemy had taken from Caesar's safe to Mallory.

He glanced through them before looking back up at her. "This was all you could retrieve?"

"Yes." A frown tugged at the corners of her mouth. Once again, no obvious re-action from the man. His heartbeat remained constant. She skimmed the surface of his mind. Just deadness. No spark of hope remained. She couldn't even find a vague sense of despair. He'd already given up on life.

"I don't want my daughter to become a vampire," he said.

"That's why I brought this to you. With your research facilities and our com-bined capital, we could find a way to help your daughter."

"And what do you get out of this, Ms. Antonius?" For the first time, curiosity flared in his eyes.

"What all good little Romans want, Mr. Mallory." She sipped her blood and smiled. "Revenge."

Zombie Love

Chapter 1

My transformation into the undead started with a pregnancy test stick.

A used pregnancy test stick.

Not mine, thank you very much.

I slammed the plastic zippered baggie, used pregnancy test stick enclosed, down on my boss's desk. "Here's your proof. Jessie Alton is knocked up. Her housekeeper confirmed it."

Ralph O'Malley recoiled in disgust. His blue eyes narrowed, and he snarled, "Jesus, Ridgeway, get that thing off my desk!" He poked at it with his pencil, pushing it away from him, until I snatched it up.

I didn't blame him. I wasn't thrilled about dumpster diving for the proof just because a major TV star peed on the damn thing, but I also didn't want my editor destroying valuable evidence. Legal would want the little stick for DNA testing in case Alton sued.

The A/C kicked on, but the weak circulation did nothing more than stir the lingering cigarette smoke in Ralph's tiny windowless office. Despite the ban on indoor smoking in Los Angeles, the publisher of *The National Scoop* ignored Ralph's predilection for cancer sticks.

"Have the copy on my desk in an hour." He eyed my grime-laden clothes. "Make that two. Get a shower first."

I hesitated a moment.

Ralph guessed at my question. He shook his head and said, "When I told you and Bill I'd have my decision on the assistant editor position on Friday, I meant on Friday." He snatched up the cigarette smoldering in the overflowing ashtray and took a puff before he added, "You've got one hour and fifty-nine minutes."

That wasn't the question I was going to ask, but a cheap thrill filtered through my aching muscles. Bill hadn't bested me out of the job.

Yet.

I focused on my pitch. "I want to do a follow up story on the private investigator—" With the baggie still in one hand, my fingers made awkward bunny ears. I suspected the man was a mercenary, not a P.I. "—Brent Poole hired to rescue his girlfriend—"

"No."

My watering eyes blinked under the double assault of his smoke and my clothes. "What?"

"I said no." Ralph's bulging orbs and quivering jowls resembled his bulldog, Emerson. At least, Ralph didn't drool all over my leg when he visited my desk.

My boss could have knocked me over with the test stick. Alton and Poole sold more issues in an hour than any other celebrity could in a week. I glared back. "This guy rescues the highest paid, most popular actress in television history who's knocked up by the highest paid, most popular movie actor—"

"You got garbage in your ears, Ridgeway? I said no." Pink crawled up Ralph's neck and invaded his cheeks. "Now, have you and Agnes discovered what rehab center Sierra Mallory's holed up—"

I ignored his blatant change of topic. "She's kidnapped by some doomsday cult and saved—"

Ralph rose to his feet, teeth chewing on the butt of the cigarette.

I ignored the warning. "—by someone Poole hired, and you don't want a follow-up?"

A growl filled the room. My editor was actually growling at me. I couldn't ignore that fact. I took a careful step away from the desk.

Twin columns of smoke blew from his flared nostrils. "I said no, and I meant no."

The gray haze quivered as we matched glares. Then air seemed to whoosh out of him, and he collapsed back into the ancient leather chair. Glancing at his watch, he muttered, "You've got one hour and fifty-five minutes if you want the fucking cover for this week."

He knew how to push my buttons. Sheer pride kicked in.

"Fine, boss." I pivoted and charged out the door, careful not to slam it on the way. What the hell was going on? Ralph never nixed one of my ideas. Okay, that wasn't true.

He had.

Once.

Two years ago, I'd snapped the Sabretooths' power forward and the lead singer of a certain boy band having a very good time in a hot tub. Even though Ralph ran my initial story, he refused to let me pursue the rumor of a stalker threatening the outed basketball player. His negation now made about as much sense as it did then.

A smile stretched my lips. Good thing I'd already started on the story, or maybe I would've walked away like I had the last time. I may be a slow learner, but I did learn.

I strode through the bullpen, ignoring the gagging and retching sounds in my wake. Everyone backed away from my aroma, except for . . .

Damn. No way could I dodge the lanky woman headed straight for me. Agnes Durley, AKA Agnes of God, because the rest of the staff agreed only the Almighty could love the crazy bitch.

"Samantha, I need to talk to you." Agnes's idea of a whisper carried through the huge room. The snickers started close to us and quickly spread. At least, she wasn't wearing her tin foil hat today.

"I'm kind of in a hurry." I tried to slide past her, only to be nailed by Agnes's claw-like grip and the pungent scent of garlic. I swallowed my impatience and a little nausea as the garlic aroma mixed with the cigarette smoke and garbage wafting from my clothes and hair. She may be missing a few screws, but no one could match the woman's research skills. And she had saved my ass on more than one occasion. Besides, Ralph needed someone to write the Elvis/alien baby stories.

"This is serious, Samantha." Agnes lowered her voice only a couple of decibels. "You need to be careful. The streets are dangerous."

"So's Ridgeway's smell," someone muttered from behind a cubical wall.

Tell me something about Los Angeles I don't know. Too many disappearances and murders had been happening lately, way too many for even Los Angeles, and no one knew what prompted the new round of turf wars. Two of the more notorious gangs had actually called a truce through a network affiliate in order to proclaim their innocence.

I breathed through my mouth since the combination of smells overwhelmed even my junk-food-hardened stomach. "Agnes, please, can't this wait? Ralph wants my story now." I patted the hand digging into my upper arm and tried not to wince. The woman had a grip that rivaled the Governator's. "I promise I'll come talk to you in two hours."

Agnes leaned closer. "People are vanishing. Kidnapped by bad vampires."

Great. Another one of her conspiracy stories. The last one involved the FBI covering up the fact the former vice-president had been possessed by doves. "Agnes," I began while prying her fingers off my bicep. "Vampires don't kidnap people. They eat them."

Agnes shook her head, the greasy, graying strands whipping wildly. It was hard to believe she'd once been a beauty queen contestant. The porcelain skin over gorgeous cheekbones didn't counter the wild-eyed look she gave me.

"The good ones don't eat us." She yanked a strand of garlic bulbs out of her safari jacket pocket and thrust the aromatic veggies at my head. "Wear this. It will protect you."

"Ridgeway doesn't need those. Her reek would drive away any self-respecting vampire." Bill Morton, my office nemesis, hung over his cubicle wall, smirking at us. A noticeable silence fell over the bullpen.

Eyeing the forty-something definition of kiss-ass, I mustered a bored look. If the rest of the guys saw me getting pissed, their jibes wouldn't stop. I didn't have time to deal with their crap. Not with a deadline in less than two hours. "Geez, Morton, just because you didn't get laid last night doesn't mean you have to take it out on the rest of us." Gales of laughter followed my comeback, and Bill slunk back down in his chair, his lips pursed in a sour grimace.

I turned back to Agnes and tried to give her a reassuring I'm-taking-you-seriously smile. Otherwise, Agnes would hound me the rest of the afternoon, and I wasn't about to miss my deadline. Not with the cover bonus. I needed that cover bonus. "If I wear my grandmother's silver cross, I'll be okay, won't I?"

She eyed me suspiciously for a couple of seconds, her gaze boring into my skull. I tried not to flinch. Maybe Agnes really could pick up thought waves without the damn foil hat on and knew I was lying.

Finally, she nodded and said, "Silver should be sufficient." She grabbed my arm again. "Just be careful on the streets at night. They have Normal help." With her bizarre statement, she released me and marched back to the closet that served as her office. It was sadder than her hat. She'd requested the damn closet and had lined the walls with foil too.

Then her words registered. Normal? As opposed to what? Zombies?

I sighed and shook my head. It wasn't worth the effort to figure out what the heck Agnes was blathering about. Not to mention I had to plan a way to convince Ralph to print the follow-up on Poole's hired gun.

I headed for the ladies' room amid another round of chuckles and snickers.

<hr>

Selene Antonius strode down the antiseptic hallway of Mallory Labs toward the section converted into an ICU. The staccato clicks of her heels echoed against bare tile. The vampire guard at the door bowed slightly, but she ignored him in favor of the man standing vigil at the observation window. The set of Tyrone Mallory's shoulders was one she recognized.

One she remembered all too well despite the passing of the last two millennia. A death watch.

"How'd the trials go?" he asked as she halted by his side. He didn't look at her.

She folded her arms and stared into the room at the still figure on the bed. The girl's pale neck blended into the white blanket covering her. It might as well have been a funeral shroud. Despite the airlock, Selene's sensitive hearing could pick up the soft beeps of the EKG unit and the muffled hiss of oxygen. "When did they put her on the ventilator?"

"An hour ago." The despair in his voice nearly drowned the last remnants of his hope.

She could feel Mallory turn his piercing grey eyes away from his only child. "You didn't answer my question."

"The results with the chimpanzees look promising." The last thing she wanted was to lose the gifts the vampire virus had granted her. Unlike her asinine brother, she wasn't throwing her immortality away on a cure. Someday, he'd learn his lesson the hard way when his little witch whore staked him in the back. And if Selene found a way to let Duncan walk in daylight again, maybe he'd forgive her.

"'Promising'?" Mallory stepped closer to her. "My daughter has days, maybe hours, and all you can say is 'promising'? This research is the only chance she has."

She turned to face Mallory. The guard flicked a questioning look. A slight shake of her head deterred him. A Normal could hardly be considered a threat to her. Mallory's lack of fear where she was concerned was one of the appealing things about him.

"Do you want to use Sierra as the human test subject?"

The stubborn set of his jaw gave her his answer. His gaze shifted back to the dying girl. "You could—"

Her sigh whispered through the air. It always came down to that request, didn't it? "Is that what you really want for her?" She waved her hand between her and the guard. "To be one of us?" She shook her head. Pain stabbed through her heart. The girl couldn't even give permission. Another lesson learned the hard way. "There's no guarantee she'd survive the Turn, Tyrone." *There's no guarantee she'd still love either of us if she survived.* But there was no gain in burdening him with that knowledge. She knew from bitter experience he wouldn't listen to reason at this stage. No grieving family member ever did. "It's been two years since we started the V-Prime Project. Give the team a few more days."

"Fine." His attention returned to the girl struggling to hang onto life. "But if Sierra dies before they're ready, I'm feeding the entire science team to the prisoners."

Chapter 2

I whipped my little Civic from its parked position into an illegal U-turn. The bag of stale B-B-Q chips I'd been munching slid across the passenger seat and crashed into the car door, sending a shower of crumbs to join the empty wrappers on the floor. The chips were nothing compared to the midnight Suburban barreling down the street after exiting the private garage. I was not losing Duncan St. James tonight.

My resolution had nothing to do with my growing personal interest in Mr. Tall, Dark and Yummy. This was about a story. Not about the six-two, raven-haired, broad-chested hunk who was the subject of said story. No siree, not at all.

God, I needed to get laid.

His driver nearly sideswiped a Mercedes, resulting in an obscene gesture from the other motorist. A slim, black-nailed hand shot out of the SUV's window and returned the bird.

I slid through a yellow light to keep up with St. James. The facts I'd discovered about my suspected mercenary were sparse. The gaping holes in the man's history ignited my curiosity. To top it off, what kind of alpha male hires a teenage goth to drive him around the city at night?

Agnes's eerie warning echoed through my brain despite the reassuring streetlights. What could possibly happen if I stayed in my car with the doors locked?

The theme of *COPS* chirped from my cell phone. Finally.

I smacked the speaker button before I swerved around a braking city bus. "You'd better have something good for me, Fred."

"You're price just went up, Blondie." Anger crackled in the voice of my source in the LAPD.

"What? No way! We agreed to center court, two home games." In the years I'd known Fred Nguyen, he'd never reneged on one of our bargains.

"I just got my ass suspended!"

Dividing my attention between my irate friend and the SUV, I pressed the accelerator. "Suspended? Why?"

"For leaking sensitive information to the press!"

"Wow." I pondered the implications for a moment. What the hell was going on? Fred had mentioned St. James met with the police commissioner after rescuing Jessie Alton and escorting her to Cedar Sinai. The police hierarchy couldn't possibly know about Fred's extra-curricular hacking. Fred was too careful to be discovered. So what could possibly set the brass off over a meeting with a P.I.?

On the other hand, it was kind of cool Fred's boss treated me as a legitimate reporter. "Do you think you could have your captain call my mom?" She considered my job with the *Scoop* a step above prostitution. Barely.

"This isn't funny, Sam!"

I sighed. Despite a nagging sense of guilt, I couldn't make this too easy for him. "The best I can do is a couple more Sabretooth games." Only because Dad took Mom to Europe, and he let me have the tickets while he was away.

"And beer money." The edge eased from Fred's voice.

"And beer money," I agreed. "Now spill."

"The picture you sent me is of one Tiffany Stephens. Nineteen. Graduated from high school two years ago. 'C' student though her school psych profile indicates she's a genius. No college record I could find. Half a dozen speeding and reckless driving tickets. Nothing criminal."

The genius Goth Girl missed a Mustang by millimeters as she changed lanes again.

"Her parents were murdered when she was a baby, and the court made St. James her legal guardian. Sam—"

The last time I'd heard that same quiver in Fred's voice was the night we'd met. The night a beat cop saved a foolish twelve-year-old girl who thought she'd beat her brother to the Pulitzer by snapping the riots in South Central. The night he shot a kid my age saving my ass.

He'd had desk jobs with the LAPD since that night.

Fred's exhalation whistled through the speaker. "You need to back off this one. St. James has connections."

"No shit if he managed to get you suspended."

"Like Poole couldn't put enough pressure on?"

Thank God, I had both hands on the steering wheel and no vehicles were next to me. Some idiot in a Miata decided against turning in front of the charging Suburban at the last second and swerved into my lane. "Fuck!"

"Sam! You okay?" Panic filtered the speaker.

A bead of sweat trickled down my neck despite the winter air. "I'm fine, but I'm wondering how little Miss Stephens passed her driver's test." I took a deep breath and tried to relax my fingers' death grip on the wheel. "What makes you think Poole had anything to do with your suspension?"

"He's got the resources, and no one in City Hall would ignore someone making those kinds of charity donations."

Fred had a point. Brent and Jessie dumped a huge chunk of change into the city coffers after last year's quake. My gut said Fred was also deliberately sidetracking me.

"You said St. James had connections. What kind of connections?"

Fred's silence drug out for a second or two before he cleared his throat. "The kind of connections that can get you killed. Let's just say he belongs to a certain Family."

Family? "Oh my god, are you saying Poole has mob contacts?" The wheels in my head churned. Frank and the Rat Pack were one thing when it came to organized crime. America's super couple were another. My heart palpitated. Breaking this story was going to make my career.

"Not Mafia." I could hear him take a deep breath. "Sam, there are worse people to mess with than organized crime. You need to drop this. Now. Before someone gets hurt."

"Fred—"

"I've got more than just Internal Affairs breathing down my neck." His voice shook. "This isn't South Central, kid. I won't be able to pull your ass out of trouble on this one. You need to let go of this story."

An annoying ping followed Fred's plea. I glanced at the readout. One bar left on the power.

"Fred, I'm going to have to call you back later. I'm about to lose power."

He got as far as "Damn it, Sam!" before I hit the "Off" button.

I managed to keep an eye on the SUV while plugging in the car adaptor. A reassuring beep sounded as my little lifeline began recharging. Quiet unease filtered through my overloaded brain when I realized where they were headed.

What kind of business did Mr. Yummy and Goth Girl have in the warehouse district? After Fred's hints, good, old self-preservation kicked into gear. I no longer had additional traffic to cover me.

The SUV slid to a stop next to a typical, non-descript storage facility. I had no choice but to drive past them. They didn't even look in my direction as I rolled by.

Which made it a hell of a lot easier to swallow my heart.

I turned at the river to circle back and stifled a nervous giggle. The Los Angeles River was a misnomer. It's more like a gigantic drainage ditch. I found a parking spot on the cross street behind them. Not that it was hard to find one at this time of night.

I climbed out of my car and paused. The night was strangely quiet for the second largest city in the U.S. Agnes's warning flittered through my mind, but I smacked the disconcerting thought away. There was no such thing as vampires.

Slipping my camera into my shoulder bag, I eased down to the corner and peered around the pre-fabbed concrete. Nothing. The SUV was still there, but the pair had disappeared.

Damn. I sauntered down the street as casually as one could this close to midnight when an area's deserted. At the end of the block, there was no sign of anyone down the side streets.

I frowned. Something was definitely wrong. Not even one of the city's ever-present homeless shambled down the street or hid in one of the doorways.

Doubling back, I eyed the dumpster across the street. It was about half a block behind St. James's vehicle. Not the best vantage point, but I didn't want to throw in the towel yet. I spent too much time on St. James to give up that easily.

But I didn't relish spending another night in someone's garbage either. I swallowed hard before forcing a decision. Maybe I'd get lucky and just share the space with cockroaches and flies. Rats were another story ever since a junior high sleepover. Crossing the street, I headed for the only potential hiding place.

A shudder trailed up my spine and nestled in the hairs on my neck. Dark, empty doorways stared at the street like eye sockets on a skull. I couldn't shake the feeling of being watched. I raced for the dumpster.

The last thing I expected was to run into someone's chest. I hugged my bag to protect the camera, so my ass took the brunt of the impact on the sidewalk. It took me a split second to catch a tiny wisp of the air that had been knocked out of me. When I looked up, I found the deepest, greenest eyes staring down at me. They practically glowed in the dark.

Before I could think about screaming, Mr. Yummy pulled me to my feet. Before I could thank him, he spun me around, wrenching my right arm behind my back and pulling me snug against his chest. My bag landed on the pavement with a disheartening crack as his other arm snaked around my throat and choked out any oxygen I'd retrieved.

"Who are you and whom are you working for?" The man gave a whole new meaning to growling. He twisted my arm for emphasis.

I didn't fake the whimpers of pain as fire rippled from wrist to shoulder. "I don't know what you're talking about." The words came more as a gasp than real speech.

He shoved me against the warehouse wall, knocking the last little bit of gas out of my lungs. Sharp bits of concrete ground into my cheek. Struggling against his grip sent excruciating waves of pain through elbow and shoulder. Any fear was forgotten when my lungs burned in protest at their deprivation. I settled for trying to gulp air past the forearm across my throat. Despite my desperate gasps, I couldn't miss the subtle scent of sandalwood.

When I didn't answer, his low voice rumbled in my ear. "Only one more chance, my dear. Who are you?" He twisted. I whimpered. "Whom are you working for?"

I squirmed, trying to find any kind of leverage to get him off me. I only succeeded in having more concrete shoved against my face. Damn, this guy was strong.

Despite my predicament, I realized something else. Threats delivered with a British accent still sound sexy. I've always been a sucker for English guys.

Struggling against him wasn't getting me anywhere. "Sam. Sam Ridgeway," I said, answering his first question.

He must have understood the choking sounds I made. The agonizing pressure on my shoulder eased, and the arm encircling my throat disappeared. Something brushed my waist and hips, then the unmistakable feeling of fingers against my left breast sent shivers through me.

Irritation at his audacity warred with the trickle of warmth in my pelvis. What was wrong with me? The man had just slammed me into a wall for chrissakes. The weird attraction only served to escalate my annoyance. "There are more comfortable positions if you want to cop a feel."

St. James chuckled, and his warm breath tickled my ear. He jerked me away from the concrete wall. "Darling, this is 'copping a feel.'" His hand slid to cup me fully, the feeling surprisingly soft and sensual. Totally at odds with the face full of wall he gave me a second ago.

Maybe it'd been too long since Jake and I broke up. The fact a total stranger toyed with my sex-deprived body on a deserted street didn't faze me. I should have been scared witless. Instead, I leaned into St. James' touch, enjoying the wave of heat through my body.

"When you're finished frisking her, let me know."

He whirled us both around to face Goth Girl, who stood on the sidewalk four yards away, tapping a shiny black boot against the concrete. Her rigid arms crossed her perky, teen chest, and she favored me with an ugly scowl.

I glared at Goth Girl. Talk about a mood killer.

"She's not armed." St. James' smug voice indicated he didn't think I was dangerous either. He kicked something over to Goth Girl. "Take care of this."

It took precious seconds for me to slap hormone-addled thoughts into shape.

By then, Goth Girl had pulled the camera out of the bag, yanked out the memory card, dropped it on the sidewalk and smashed it with her size-two spiked heel.

"You bitch!" I lunged at the girl, but the firm and painful grip on my arm brought me up short.

"Can you believe she cut me out of nearly every shot she took of us?" Goth Girl rolled her eyes. "And, yes, I took care of the other cameras."

My heart plummeted to my stomach. My extra digital and the 35mm had been hidden in the Civic's spare tire well. What had the little bitch done?

"God, Duncan, you would not believe what a pig she is." Goth Girl continued her rant. "Her car's filled with enough junk food bag—"

"That is enough." St. James's voice held a touch of humor.

Irritation flared even higher that he found the destruction of my personal property so amusing. Oh, he was so going to pay for this. I struggled again, with the same lame results.

"Now, Miss Ridgeway, whom do you work for?" he said.

I fumed at the loss of the pictures. No way was I telling this jerk anything.

"Miss Ridgeway . . ." The menacing edge returned in his tone.

If I could see his face, I could determine how serious he was, but he held me tight against his chest. His very solid, very masculine chest. I was calculating the return on a dislocated shoulder when the pressure on said right joint escalated.

Yep, he was serious.

"I work for *The National Scoop*." A tear trickled down my face, more from the humiliation at getting caught than the pain. I hadn't broken this easily when cornered by Mel Gibson's Dobermans.

"What the bloody hell?" Confused annoyance filled his voice.

Goth Girl smirked at me. "Well, well, well. You've picked up a tabloid reporter, Duncan."

The cocky grin on the girl's too-purple lips added to my mounting irritation. "That's investigative journalist to you. And isn't it past your bedtime?"

A nasty look covered Goth Girl's face. "Shouldn't you be wiretapping Nicole Kidman?"

Before I could come up with an appropriate rejoinder, the grip on my wrist disappeared so suddenly I stumbled.

"Go home, Miss Ridgeway." St. James' voice almost sounded weary. His suggestion sounded good, real good, but his story sang its siren's song.

I turned to find St. James stalking towards his SUV, Goth Girl hot on his heels.

Mobsters didn't just walk away from a potential problem. Or maybe I'd watched *The Sopranos* one too many times.

Despite the numbness running down my arm, I couldn't give up that easily. Not to mention they trashed some expensive equipment. I snatched up my bag and camera, awkward with only one functioning arm.

"Wait!" They turned in unison as I ran to them, matching impatient expressions on their faces. "What about my photo cards?"

He crossed his arms over his fabulously broad chest. "What about them?"

"You destroyed my property," I huffed out around my panting. Damn, I really needed to work out more.

"You have been stalking me. Consider us even." He rounded the vehicle and reached for the door handle.

Dammit! This little encounter had been a set-up. Well, I knew how to play rough too.

I followed and laid a hand on his. Electricity shot through my nerves at the sensation of his cool skin beneath my palm. "Give me the story on the kidnapping by the Sunshine Believers, then we'll be even."

His scowl deepened. "What are you talking about?"

"Jessie Alton." I resisted the urge to slap the arrogant look off his face. "You know, the pregnant star of *Buddies* you rescued two weeks ago."

"I do not know what you are talking about." Madonna's publicist couldn't have said that with a straighter face.

"Look, St. James, give me the interview and I'll stop following you."

"Or?"

I gave him my most convincing smile. "I'll keep following you until you do."

He snorted and climbed into the SUV. Goth Girl had the engine running before he slammed the door shut. I banged a fist on his window. The impact had the unmistakable feel of bulletproof glass.

The passenger window slid down to reveal a still scowling St. James. "Go home, Miss Ridgeway," he repeated. "You have had a very long day, and you are very tired."

Again, the desire to burrow under the covers rushed through my system. What the hell was wrong with me? I shook my head to clear the cobwebs clogging the neural pathways and matched his annoyed look. "Answer my question first."

An exasperated look replaced his scowl. "Go home."

"And if I don't?"

A wicked smile spread across his face. "My 'copping a feel' will be the least of your problems."

Why did St. James' threat sound more like a promise? The desire to push him to see if he'd carry through overwhelmed me.

Tires squealed as Goth Girl tore away from the curb. I jumped back to keep my toes intact.

Before their taillights disappeared, I raced back to the Honda. Four smashed spark plugs laid next to the shattered spare photo cards on the pavement. The only saving grace was I'd pulled the 35mm roll out last night to develop it.

I sighed. So much for locking the damn car doors in this freakin' city.

Chapter 3

Dawn threatened to peek into the bedroom window as I shed my clothes and climbed beneath the white eyelet sheets. The brass bed was one of the few indulgences in an otherwise industrial beige and bare apartment. The parents were constantly on my case about getting furniture. Okay, Mom was on my case. She'd lost on the name change issue, so she'd taken up harassing me about the lack of furniture. It's not like Mom and Dad ever came over or I entertained on a regular basis.

Or even a semi-regular basis. Not since Jake and I broke up a year ago.

And spending my money on Lasik surgery was the better bargain in my line of work.

I tossed my cell on the nightstand and collapsed on the pillows, but I was too tired to think and too wired to sleep. What the hell was going on? Old guilt swirled through my volatile emotions.

I didn't care about Poole or Alton. They played the celebrity card, which made them fair game. What I didn't like was the resurrection of feelings I'd thought had died when I walked away from Jake's marriage proposal. And then there was my unintended fallout landing on top of Fred once again.

Trying to clear the ancient hash from my brain, I watched the hypnotic pattern of passing headlights from rush hour worker bees on the bedroom ceiling and focused on the current situation. The bribe to get a tow truck out to the warehouse district in predawn hours swallowed what was left of my stash of mad money. I could expense the tow with the *Scoop*, but the extra cost wasn't what bothered me. Without wheels, it was nearly impossible to tail anyone in this city. Despite Fred's freaky warning, I wasn't about to let this go.

Duncan St. James intrigued me. What kind of man leaves so little trace of his life? What kind of guy doesn't have his driver's license in the 21st century? Better yet, what kind of James Bond alpha male has a teenage car burglar as a sidekick?

I stretched, a slight twinge in my right shoulder the only physical reminder of the evening. That and the scratches on my cheek, but those could be covered with a little make-up. I had to give St. James credit. He knew how to inflict the maximum amount of discomfort with the least amount of damage.

I frowned at the last disturbing thought. Maybe I'd been in this business too long if I was starting to enjoy the pain.

Rolling over, I smiled at the twenty-four by thirty-six photo pinned to the bedroom wall, the other reason my stash was so low in the first place. Dim pre-dawn light illuminated powerful shoulders and raven hair. Goth Girl hadn't destroyed all my pictures of him.

I had taken this one three nights ago through the massive front window of an antique shop. Part of me wished his warm smile aimed at the beautiful brunette behind the counter could be turned my way. I sat up to examine it a little closer as the first rays of the sun flooded the room, and I grinned as something else dawned on me.

Goth Girl was right. I had cut the annoying little bitch out of this picture, too.

— • —

Duncan rocked back on his heels, trying not to let fury override common sense. "I fail to understand why you thought not informing me of these rumors concerning rogue vampires was prudent."

Caesar Augustine, Master of the Western United States Vampire Coven, relaxed in his office chair, fingers steepled, as he returned Duncan's glare with a cool, measured look. "Because I need you looking for our missing people, not settling a vendetta with my sister."

Red filmed Duncan's vision. "How can you even say—"

"I'm not arguing with you about this." Despite the calmness of Caesar's voice, his hazel eyes flared gold in warning.

Duncan sucked in a deep breath, forced down his anger, and resorted to formality. "I am not arguing with you, Master Augustine. I am merely pointing out the rogue—" He'd be damned to the ninth level of Hell before he'd say the bitch's name. "—has used similar distraction tactics in the past. As your Chief Enforcer, I should have been informed. The two situations might be linked."

Pink tinged Caesar's face at the not-so-subtle reminder of the deaths and chaos his twin had caused.

"Duncan." The gentle voice of Dr. Bebe Zachary drew his attention. She rose from the black leather couch, where she'd been sitting next to Tiffany, and crossed the office to face him. "If I had concrete information on Selene, you'd be the second one I'd tell." A small smile curved her lips at her joke. Without a doubt, she'd tell Caesar first, and she had.

Duncan's anger drained away at her words. Caesar and Bebe had suffered as much as his own family had at Selene's hands.

"Right now, all I've got is rumors from patients hoping to curry favor with both Silver Bear and Augustine Covens. These disappearances have all the supernaturals on edge," Bebe said.

"Your grandmother—"

Bebe shook her head, and a few more of her haphazard curls slipped from their pins. "No luck tracking any of the missing. Granny E. has all of Silver Bear on alert." She sighed. "There haven't been anymore coven disappearances since the high school girl snatched in December. That doesn't account for any eclectics who might be passing through Los Angeles."

Duncan's fists clenched at the unspoken worry in her voice, one he shared. Without help from a coven to watch his or her back, any solitary witch would be a prime target. He turned back to Caesar. "Has John heard from the San Antonio Packmaster?"

Caesar gave a solemn nod. "He has concerns their requests to aid the search are a prelude to a takeover. Of course, having a rival Packmaster's pup disappear in John's territory . . ."

Breath hissed between Duncan's teeth at the implied political problems. Los Angeles was one of the few cities in the world where the vampire, witch and were leaders not only cooperated, but actually liked and respected each other. It normally made his job as Caesar's chief enforcer a hell of a lot easier.

And normally, his right hand, Alex Stanton, would be here to assist him. Except Alex had been missing for nearly four months now, along with Logan Polk, the son of the San Antonio alphas. The two friends had gone to a bar one night and never came home. The waitresses remembered the two fellow Texans flirting and dancing with the ladies, but the men had left alone.

Duncan ground his teeth in frustration. This was exactly the sort of game Selene would play. Create suspicion among allies in order to set pack against pack and coven against coven. In any other circumstance, Alex and Logan could take care of themselves, but she wouldn't have allowed a fair fight. He swallowed the accusation. No good would come of rehashing the argument.

"What about Anne? Have we received any word from her?"

Caesar shook his head. "She refused to take a cell phone out of respect for her brother. We'll have to wait for her letter." He rubbed his jaw. "I wish she'd taken the jet."

Duncan paced across the thick carpet. Anne was the only Enforcer who resided in the master's Brentwood mansion full-time. While he would have preferred she remain in Los Angeles during the current crisis, he understood her desire to assist the last living member of her immediate family. It didn't mean he had to like it.

Bebe chuckled. "If I could prescribe an anti-anxiety medication that worked on vampires, I would have to get Anne on the jet."

The byplay snapped Duncan's last reserve of patience. "Instead of worrying about Anne's fear of flying, we need to focus on our immediate problem. What about the International Council?"

Caesar's hand slashed down, the motion as sharp as his tone. "We have no solid evidence of who's responsible."

Duncan took a step forward. Why did his master have such a blind spot for procedure? "We have fifteen known supernaturals missing."

"Before you two totally freak out, let's look at the evidence we've got," Tiffany said.

Duncan looked down at his niece, who sat cross-legged on the couch, boots discarded on the carpet. Thoughtful brown eyes stared up at him.

"Every solid lead we've followed so far points to Tyrone Mallory, a Normal with no known Family connections, not some major league supernatural conspiracy, so we'll need the I.C.'s blessing to go after him. Let's eliminate him as a suspect before we start whittling stakes for Selene. If this is really a good old-fashioned Normal witch hunt—"

"Hey!" Bebe glared at Tiffany.

"Sorry, Doc." As usual, his niece did not look the least bit sorry. "But you guys know what I mean."

Unfortunately, the child was correct. The International Council had been formed to keep cross-species aggression to a minimum, which meant Normals were included, even if the majority of them didn't know it.

Bebe's musical laughter filled the room. "The universe is surely messed up when she's the logical one."

Tiffany scowled at the grin on Bebe's face. "Gee, thanks for the vote of confidence."

Duncan couldn't help smiling at Tiffany as well. Maybe there was hope for the brash girl after all. He raked a hand through his hair and focused on the immediate task. "I need to get inside of Mallory's lab. Surveillance has not produced any results." But then there hadn't been any reports of missing supernaturals in the last three nights either. He eyed Bebe. "Do you have a spell that can breach a wall and still hide the hole if I need to bring anyone out?" He trusted his own skills, but he didn't want to impale a kidnap victim accidentally during the rescue. Steel spikes reinforced the concrete blockade of Mallory's facility, rivaling any defensive works he remembered from his childhood in England.

Bebe nodded. "I can have something to dissolve the wall ready by tonight, but if it's the size you're describing, it'll need forty-eight hours to work or someone will notice it." She tapped her chin and her eyes focused elsewhere as she ran through a mental list. "You're going to need a blurring spell to hide from any electronic surveillance inside the compound, but I can't mix that potion until just before you head out."

His lips tightened in a grim smile. "I can wait. The labs will have the fewest personnel on Sunday evening anyway. Thank you." He turned to leave, only to be stopped by Tiffany's blatant cough.

Caesar's eyebrow rose as his gaze flicked between them. "Was there something else?"

Tiffany leaned forward on the couch and fixed a pointed look at Duncan. "Aren't you going to tell him?"

Confusion filled Duncan, along with the sense of a chasm opening beneath his feet. "Tell him what?"

"Your fan club?"

Irritation returned at Tiffany's comment, but his groin tightened at the thought of the firebrand he'd caught last night. Maybe his self-imposed celibacy was cracking under the stress of the last two years, but she'd felt so warm, so right when he held her.

Quelling the wayward thought, he shot Tiffany a stern look. "That problem has been dealt with." Granted, Miss Ridgeway seemed to resist his telepathic suggestions last night. He'd looked up the woman's information on his laptop as Tiffany drove to Mallory Labs. A personal visit to the pretty, little reporter may be necessary.

"What problem?" Caesar cast a suspicious look at both of them.

Tiffany chuckled. "Duncan has a tabloid reporter stalking him."

"I do not." He'd never struck Tiffany in all the years she'd lived with him, but now he understood why some parents advocated corporal punishment.

A grim expression filled Caesar's face. "Who is it and which magazine?"

"Her name's Ridgeway. She works for the *Scoop*," Tiffany chimed.

"I have already taken care of the situation." Duncan crossed his arms and faced Caesar, his irritation back in full force at the insult to his competency.

Caesar nodded in acknowledgement. "I'm sure you have. However, a call reminding O'Malley to keep a leash on his people will be additional insurance you are no longer bothered. I believe we've had a problem with her in the past."

Even though Duncan would have recommended the same action under any other circumstances, the thought Caesar had to babysit him grated. Granted he had been distracted by the investigation of the recent disappearances, but his preoccupation didn't mean he couldn't handle one little girl.

Except the curves he caressed last night were hardly girlish.

Some of his emotions must have leaked because Caesar added, "This has nothing to do with my opinion of your abilities, Duncan. As Family, O'Malley has responsibilities to our coven. Setting one of his reporters on my chief enforcer hardly fulfills his obligations."

While Duncan was sure Caesar's words were meant to be reassuring, they still left an acid bite in the air. He didn't envy Ralph O'Malley the tongue-lashing Caesar was about to deliver the editor.

Bebe clapped her hands together. "In the meantime, while I whip up the spell, why don't you two go upstairs get some rest? Miko's already laid out fresh bedding."

Tiffany's yawn reminded him his niece was still Normal, despite how hard she pushed herself to keep up with the supernaturals. And common sense told him they both needed to be fresh to deal with the espionage they planned for the next few nights.

He nodded his thanks to Bebe before he and Tiffany left Caesar's office and climbed the stairs to the mansion's second floor.

"What time do you want to head out tonight?" Tiffany's words were garbled by another yawn, but his scan of her surface thoughts caught the question.

"Shortly after sunset, but we need to perform a small errand before we set out for the labs."

Tiffany's thin, black brows drew together in her confusion. "Errand? What errand?"

"A personal visit to Miss Ridgeway's abode. I want to make sure she has no more information concerning me or any member of the supernatural community."

A grin lit Tiffany's face. "Sure you're not really planning a panty raid?"

"No, I am not." The tightening in his groin belied his stern words. Because he'd very much like to see Samantha Ridgeway in her undergarments.

Chapter 4

"I need to ask a favor." I propped the cell phone between my shoulder and ear as I opened the third pack of sugar for my daily dose of java. The aromatic steam caressed my face like a long-lost lover.

"Can't you ever say hello like a normal person?"

"Hello, Max. I need to borrow your car tonight." Catching the phone as it started to slide off my shoulder, I grabbed the steaming cup from the counter. A quick glance around the coffee shop showed I had my pick of seats.

My brother's deep, exasperated huff blasted through the cell receiver. "Jack Nicholson get yours towed again?"

"No." I bit back the usual sarcastic reply. I wasn't the most pleasant person after four hours of sleep, but today I had to try extra hard. I really needed Max's help. "It's in the shop."

"Uh-huh," Max drawled. "Seriously, who had your car towed this time? Brent Poole still pissed at you about the pregnancy test thing?"

"*I* had it towed last night. I had some problems with the spark plugs, and it wouldn't start." Which was part of the truth. I'd never been able to lie to Max. Mr. Pulitzer Prize can sniff a fabrication faster than the Beagle Brigade could detect an unauthorized apple in customs. His lie detection abilities didn't mean I had to tell him the whole truth. I slid into a seat and managed not to spill my desperately needed caffeine.

"Sure you did." His drawl scraped over my sleep-deprived nerves. "George Clooney?"

"Don't you read the papers? He's living in Italy these days. And I really did have car problems!" I winced at the desperation in my voice. It wasn't pretty. I counted to ten, but Max gave in first.

"Sorry, Sam. You can borrow it, but I can't get to your place until six."

I expelled a sigh in relief. I wouldn't need Max's car until dark anyway. With no mad money left and the credit card maxed out for the car repairs, I was up a creek until payday. Goth Girl had sabotaged more than the spark plugs. Someone needs to tell dear, sweet, little Tiffany paybacks are a bitch. The sugar in the gas tank really burned me. Thank God, my mechanic had discovered it before he started the car, or I'd be looking at a whole new engine. With replacing the tank, pump and gas line, I couldn't pick up my car until Tuesday morning at the earliest, and it's damn near impossible to trail someone using public transportation.

I hated to say it, but I didn't have any friends to call. At least none who would trust me with their cars without wanting to horn in on my story.

God, I really needed to find some friends outside of the business.

A soft beep warned the battery was low. New annoyance added to my general irritation. I'd forgotten to plug the phone into the recharger before I'd crawled into bed. Time to end this conversation before it totally died.

"Thanks, big bro. I owe you one." I flipped my phone closed and tapped my fingers on the black laminate table. This morning, the coffee shop was quiet. The rush hour crowd was long gone, which would suit Fred, assuming he arrived soon.

When I had called him earlier about delivering the Sabretooth tickets, he insisted on meeting me here. His voice sounded weird. Not like he was still mad at me for getting him suspended, not like his anxiety-ridden warning last night, but something else. I was too damn tired to figure it out though.

I glared at the few jots in my notebook, wishing more information on St. James would appear. I tapped my pen against the table, earning ugly looks from the elderly chess players two tables down. I smiled in apology, and they returned to their game. Jerry Springer on the overhead T.V. was slightly more interesting than the chess match.

Swallowing the bitter dregs of my triple espresso did nothing to ease my exhaustion. The expected jolt wasn't much more than a love peck. I glanced at my wrist again. An hour late. Something else unusual for my favorite police geek.

I seriously contemplated leaving when a strange character outside the window caught my eye. He had a baseball cap pulled low over Poison-era hair and mirrored shades. The wig and glasses did nothing to enhance the portly man in the trench coat. I just prayed he wasn't planning to rob the place. He'd shoot me for spending my last five dollars on the caffeine. Then his sleeve slid up as he reached for the door, and I caught a glimpse of a red watchband.

Fred's vintage Disney Pooh timepiece was the only recognizable thing about him when he sat down across from me.

"Fred—"

"Don't use my real name. I'm George. George Carver."

Great, just great. My favorite police informant included a racial identity crisis in his nervous breakdown.

"Okay, 'George.' What's going on? Is this about our friend and his family?" If Fred didn't want me using his own name, I wasn't about to send him over the edge saying St. James's.

"Sam, I can't—" He licked his lips, the mirrored shades swinging across the room. I followed his sweep of the place. Other than the kid behind the counter and the two men intent on their game in the corner, we were alone.

"You can't what?" This quivering wreck wasn't the man I knew. The man who had fled Vietnam as a child, shepherding his younger sisters to safety against all odds. The cop who pulled me to cover during the South Central riots. The man who killed to save my life.

"Other people are asking questions."

"What people? What are you blabbering about?"

"Don't ask!" he hissed. A bead of sweat trickled from under his wig and down his cheek. "I don't want to see you get hurt."

"You said that last night." I laid a hand on his wrist. "Fred—"

He shot out of his seat. "I-I-I'm sorry, Sam. For your own sake, don't call me ever again." He scurried out the door, trench coat flying behind him.

And the Sabretooth tickets still sat in my purse.

Shit! Worry won out over anger at Fred's erratic behavior. I snatched my bag and charged out the door. Spotting Fred as he headed for the crosswalk, I jogged to catch up and yelled his name.

Fred was road pizza before I even noticed the van scream through the red light. I froze, unreality penetrating my bones as Fred flew through the air to land with a sickening smack on the pavement. The van never slowed as it spun around the corner and disappeared from sight.

Something clattered at my feet and I looked down. Pooh stared at me through shattered crystal.

—•—

"Sam?"

I pried apart sleep-gummed eyes to find Max leaning over me.

"You've got drool running down your face."

Brothers are so good for the ego.

Leveraging myself upright, I looked down and swiped one jacket sleeve across the wet spot on the hospital's avocado vinyl couch and the other across my cheek. Max nudged me over so he could sit on the drier side.

"You okay?"

"No." I never would be again. Not after the ride in the ambulance with a mangled Fred.

Dragging my thoughts into some form of coherence, I focused on the blue eyes examining me through black frames. The memory snapped into place. I had called Max a couple of hours ago to meet me at the hospital instead of my place. "Thought you wouldn't be here until after work."

I really did need to get more friends. I couldn't rely on my big brother to fish me out of jams. Heaven knew Fred never would again.

He leaned back, raked a hand through what was left of his receding blond hair and grinned. "Business. I'm here to interview a witness to a hit-and-run."

Anger boiled away the threatening tears before I could stop it. "Fuck you!"

He spread his hands. "Hey, I was just teasing."

"Fred Nguyen didn't deserve to be murdered."

His frown looked sincere despite the crappy fluorescent lighting. "Murder? That's not the official word."

I leaned back, the scene playing in slo-mo across my closed lids as I returned to my previous misery. "You weren't there."

"So tell me."

My eyes popped back open. "And let you scoop me? Not!" One of Max's eyebrows rose above his Clark Kent frames. So much for my fake bravado.

None of this made sense. I pursued a guy who rescued pregnant sitcom actresses from apocalyptic cults. Who went out of his way to cover his tracks. Enough to stage an accident to kill an innocent cop?

This story had taken a whole new context. I owed Fred far too much to let his death slide into oblivion. I stood up and held out my hand. Max dug into his jeans and pulled out his Bugs Bunny key ring. He paused just short of my waiting palm.

"Let me buy you dinner first."

Damn. He knew I couldn't pass up free food.

— •—

By mutual, unspoken agreement, Little Sicily was neutral territory in our sibling rivalry. The cheap pine and red vinyl gave the place a tacky appeal, but the food was excellent. Waving to the hostess, we claimed our usual corner booth.

Heading off Max's inevitable interrogation, I started with the small talk. "So, have you heard from Mom and Dad?" I pretended to examine the menu. My parents' nouveau riche status didn't bother me as much as the fact they never called me on their trips. Ever.

"They phoned from their hotel in Venice." Max closed his own menu. "They're staying an extra week."

"Mr. Cuddles is going to love that."

He grimaced at the reminder of his dog-sitting duties for Mom. "You know you could watch him next week in return for borrowing my car. We'll trade when you drop it off."

"Let's not. You know he hates my guts. And you don't want to be responsible when a certain toy poodle takes a suicidal leap from my bedroom window."

No comment from Max. Not even a slight smile at my snarky comment. He stared at the plastic-coated cardboard. I didn't want to bring up his own depressing situation, but I couldn't stop my mouth.

"Heard anything from Anne?" A homeless girl Max kept an eye out for, she had disappeared a couple of weeks ago. Max had dragged me along at first, searching the shelters and local teen hangouts. I wasn't sure why he cared so much. The kid was overly pale, too thin, never smiled and always wore dark, long-sleeved shirts with long, dark skirts in sunny Los Angeles. All the signs of someone trying to hide her heroin tracks.

Then again, maybe she was one of Agnes' imaginary vampires since the couple of times I'd encountered her were at night.

My brother had almost decked me when I pointed out the evidence to him. I hoped for his sake she had moved on to San Francisco. Or Seattle. Or anywhere. I tried not to think about the other possibility.

"No, I haven't heard anything." He yanked the menu out of my hands. "You always order the same thing, so quit stalling."

Over lasagna, I spilled my guts, starting with the possibility of Brent Poole's mob connections and ended with the bizarre incident at the coffee shop, including how Fred went into cardiac arrest and died on the ambulance ride to the hospital. Somehow, I managed to edit the story so Mr. Yummy didn't make an appearance. A girl can only take honesty so far with her big brother when it comes to members of the opposite sex. Or scooping my story on a murderer.

And I had to face the possibility Mr. Yummy may have ordered Fred's "accident."

I handed Max the remains of Fred's watch. "Do you know anyone who could repair this?" I should have given it to Fred's sisters at the hospital, but some bizarro feeling of sentimentality made me want to get it fixed before I gave it back to them.

This caring about others could indicate a serious problem. Maybe I should make an appointment with Mom's shrink.

He looked over the smashed crystal and dented casing, then cocked an eyebrow as he glanced back at me. "You're kidding, right?"

"Never mind," I muttered. "You wouldn't understand." I held out my hand.

Instead of giving it back, he slid the broken timepiece into the breast pocket of his blue oxford shirt. "Let me see what I can do. Consider it your birthday present for this year."

"You didn't give me a present last year so you still owe me."

He ignored my comment and flagged our waiter for coffee. When he turned back, he wore his "serious investigator" face. I should have run but I wanted the coffee too much to move. Maybe there's an AA group for the caffeine-addicted.

"Did Fred have any enemies?"

An image of the blood-splattered man lying on the ambulance gurney rose, threatening to bring my lasagna back up.

I swallowed hard and held up my hand. The waiter misunderstood and started to take away the coffee tray. "Stop right there." The waiter froze. "You," I said, waving him towards the table, "bring that back." I glared at Max as the waiter poured. "Fred didn't have a mean bone in his body."

"He was suspended," Max pointed out.

"For spilling info to me the commissioner tried to squelch."

"This wasn't the first time."

"The other time was normal procedure when investigating a police shooting. And you know damn well that reason." I concentrated on dumping two huge spoonfuls of sugar into my liquid love. It beat meeting Max's eyes.

Max waited until the waiter cleared the rest of our dishes and we were alone before he continued. "Could he have been involved in something dirty?"

"No. Not Fred." I blew on my after-dinner coffee to cool it. "He made Mother Theresa look like Darth Vader." I took a sip and still managed to burn off the top layer of my tongue.

"Sam, I hate to tell you this, but there's been some unusual activity in Fred's bank account."

I didn't like the way he was watching me. "What do you mean 'unusual activity'?"

"Some large sums passed through his checking account. Way too large for an IT guy with the LAPD," Max tapped his fingers to the theme of "The Lone Ranger." Not a good sign. Heaven help whoever he was tracking down.

"Where's it coming from? Are you sure it's not one of his sisters loaning him money or paying him back?" I took another sip, willing myself to stay calm. It was bad enough Max insulted my friend, but Fred couldn't even defend himself anymore.

"What about his sisters? Any idea why they'd be paying him?"

I shook my head and took another painful sip. Tranh, the youngest, had threatened to serve me at her restaurant if I showed up at Fred's funeral. And she didn't mean as an honored guest.

Other than Tranh's penchant for threats when it came to me, the two sisters were good people. I couldn't fault them for blaming me for Fred's death. Hell, I blamed me too. Fred had raised them, educated them—

My head jerked up. "Wait a minute here. Tranh and Mary could be paying him back. He put them both through college," I said. "And he helped Tranh open her restaurant."

He shrugged. "Assuming you're right about the money, what makes you think Fred was murdered?"

I opened my mouth, then clamped it shut. I wasn't about to spill the beans about Duncan St. James and his "Family." It wasn't worth the hassle from Max. And my very dark suspicions were growing faster than the mold in my fridge.

Max gave me a knowing look. "If you're right and the money's clean, you've got nothing but a police nerd under suspension and a van driver who can't use his brakes." He spooned ice from his water glass into his java. "I hate to say it, Sam, but this kind of thing happens all the time."

I eyed Max over the rim of my cup. "You didn't see him. He was scared out of his mind. And why would he warn me not to contact him?"

Max laid down his spoon but didn't take a drink. He leaned on folded elbows, his stare intense, coffee forgotten. "What aren't you telling me?"

I blinked. "What are you talking about?"

"Sam, it's me, and you're involved in something over your head." We both had practiced stare downs with our Siamese cat, DC the First, so it was a long time before he broke and took a sip. "You're lying."

"Am not!"

"Your left eye's twitching."

I rubbed the betraying orb. "Something's in my contact."

"You got Lasik two months ago."

I cursed him under my breath. "Either Alton's or Poole's connections got Fred suspended when I asked him a few questions about Alton's rescue from a cult." Technically, St. James was Poole's connection.

"God, are you still going on about that alleged kidnapping?"

It wasn't alleged, but I wasn't going to argue about it with Max again. "The only other possibility I can come up with is someone with a vendetta in IA."

Max huffed at my lame-ass theory. "Are you sure?"

No, but I wasn't about to admit it aloud. Besides, why would IA kill a police officer for giving me copies of St. James's files? Which brought me back to St. James and his "Family" connections.

Max took my silence as permission to press on. "What about the van?"

I rolled my eyes. "What about it?"

He held up his index finger. "The make and model were so generic the description matches ten thousand vans in the metro area."

I opened my mouth. Max zipped his free hand across his lips.

Another finger joined the first. "By your own admission, the windows were tinted to the point you and the rest of the bystanders couldn't see the driver." A third finger joined the other two. "And the license plate was missing."

Max grunted, lowered his hand and leaned back in the booth.

Damn, he could be exasperating. He wasn't going to let this go, so I went on the offensive. "Why would Malibu Barbie or Malibu Ken go to the trouble of knocking off a police computer analyst, who, by the way, could tell me squat?"

Max stared at me.

I threw my napkin at him.

Instead of tossing it back in my face, he folded the red and white checked cloth. His voice was so soft I could barely catch his next words. "I think you're right about what happened to Fred. There's more to this than a pissed-off Hollywood power couple."

My brother? Believing me?

Hell had just frozen over.

Chapter 5

Duncan stood before the front door and extended his senses into the apartment. Nothing but the dull silence of empty space. He shook his head, and Tiffany went to work on the lock. In less than two seconds, she had the deadbolt picked and the door open.

The idea had been to give the child some practical experience, but now he wondered how much she already knew. During his pause, her expression melted from pleased to a scowl.

"Don't thank me all at once." She stomped past him and into the apartment. Light flared inside.

Swallowing his exasperation, he followed her into Samantha Ridgeway's living room. Stunned, he looked around.

Samantha Ridgeway's totally bare living room.

The only thing between the four beige walls was a sad, broken cobweb fluttering from the ceiling. He closed the door.

"Oka-a-ay." Tiffany pivoted. "Am I the only one getting creeped out by this?"

"Let us check the rest of the rooms."

The kitchen wasn't quite as pathetic as the living room. The counter held a coffee maker, a toaster oven, and an open package of biscuits. He checked the refrigerator. The appliance gave the mold colony in a Chinese take-out box a home, a partially consumed six-pack of diet soda its only company.

He swung the door shut in time to catch Tiffany reaching for an Oreo on the counter. Smacking her hand away, he said, "Do not touch the biscuits. In fact, do not touch anything unless you must."

"They're called cookies, Duncan. You've been living in the U.S. over a century. Learn the language."

A grunt expressed his opinion of how Americans mangled the Queen's English.

She grinned at him. "Here I thought you may have been concerned for my health."

"That too." He surveyed the spartan cooking area. What a sad life Miss Ridgeway must have. Was the emptiness of her home indicative of an emptiness in her life? He gestured for Tiffany to follow him.

And stopped short at the bedroom door.

"Holy shit. Someone's been here before us."

"No." His eyes registered the papers scattered across the floor. A computer desk was tucked in the corner. Empty mugs and CD cases littered the space between a flat screen monitor and the phone on top. Piles of clothing didn't make it into the open closet or the various open dresser drawers. Somewhere in the chaos, a pattern existed, but he couldn't think past the rumpled bed sheets holding her apple-sweet scent. Pushing aside the wave of desire, he surveyed the room with a critical eye. "No, I believe this is the room's natural state."

"Ugh." Tiffany brushed by him and stepped into the room. A foil wrapper crinkled under her boot. "This is worse than her car. Uh, Duncan—"

He spotted the poster-sized photograph pinned to the right wall the same moment as Tiffany. Under other circumstances and with other subjects, he'd have offered to buy the piece. It showed an excellent eye for detail and naturalism of the subjects. The window of Phillippa Mann's antique shop framed the shot, an aesthetic black and white print that captured the humor shared by him and the proprietress.

Stepping closer, he examined the clothing they both wore in the photo. "Bloody hell!"

"Yeah, this was taken Monday night." Tiffany's eyes narrowed. "Bitch cut me out of this shot, too." She shook her head before grinning. "You seriously have a stalker problem here."

Through gritted teeth, he growled his niece's name.

Sobering, Tiffany shifted into enforcer mode. "This confirms she's been tailing us at least four days." Maybe there was hope for the girl. She slid into the desk chair, hit the tower's power button and started rifling through the files in the little two-drawer cabinet while she waited for the computer to boot.

Dumbfounded, he returned his attention back to the photo. How the bloody hell had he not noticed Ridgeway had been following him? If it weren't for Tiffany spotting Ridgeway's vehicle, Duncan would have blindly exposed himself, not to mention the entire coven.

"Because you've been a little preoccupied with Alex and Logan, along with the other missing folks," Tiffany said.

He turned to her, surprise at her perception interrupting the shock of Ridgeway's game. Tiffany shrugged her thin shoulders before she said, "You're leaking."

Hands clenched into fists. Damn! He needed to get himself under control. He hadn't accidentally transmitted his thoughts since his seventy-fifth birthday party.

Tiffany gave him a little reassuring smile. "It's okay. I'm worried about them too. Here." She handed him four files. "Nothing about supernaturals. Looks like she's working on a story about Jessie's kidnapping."

"How the devil did she find out? Davis kept it—"

A sly smile lit Tiffany's face. "Look at Ridgeway's file. Remember, Jess said there was a witness in the alley when those nutcases grabbed her. And Commissioner Davis had to cover up an anonymous 9-1-1 call."

"Ridgeway," he muttered as he started looking at the reporter's notes.

"Ridgeway." Tiffany nodded in confirmation. "According to her notes, she was trying to get a shot of Jess coming out the back door of the maternity shop when our dear cousin was nabbed by those fucking idiots."

"Language, child."

He ignored whatever obscene hand gesture Tiffany not so subtly aimed in his direction. How did a simple search-and-rescue operation get so screwed up? He flipped another page of the file concerning him. Ridgeway thought he was "yummy"? Blood started flowing south. *Spanish Inquisition. Remember the Spanish Inquisition.* "Anything on the computer?"

"More of the same. Doesn't look like we're in trouble." She snickered. "She's aiming to make you the *Scoop*'s 'Hunkiest Man Alive.' I'm downloading Kensai's virus now."

He couldn't help a smile at the little piece of revenge on Ridgeway. The Japanese-born enforcer's program would corrupt anything on her hard drive. Of course, she might recover the information.

If she coughed up a year's salary for a data retrieval expert. From her bank account records, she'd be lucky to produce next month's rent.

They both froze when the phone rang. On the heels of the second ring, the answering device on the set beeped and Ridgeway's recording said, "You know the drill."

"Sam. Ralph." A severe bout of coughing interrupted the man's voice. When he spoke again, the hoarseness almost obscured his words. "I just talked to Max. I'm sorry to hear about Fred. Let me know the funeral arrangements, and I'll have Agnes send flowers." Another bout of coughing echoed through the speaker. "Max's worried about you and this mystery project of yours. He'd better not be talking about the Jessie Alton follow-up. Call me."

Tiffany's breath released with a hiss. She shot Duncan a look. "Be glad she doesn't use the phone company's voice mail."

"O'Malley." His fists clenched. "Caesar was supposed to speak with him."

She nodded, a thoughtful expression on her face. "You know he has. Sounds like Mr. O'Malley had already nixed her story on you."

So what was Ridgeway up to? "Let us finish before she returns." He crossed the room. On top of the dresser lay more digital photo cards and three packages of conventional 35mm photos. Air froze in his chest as he examined them. Every single one featured his image. When he found the negatives in each of the envelopes of prints, he released the pent-up breath in a small prayer of relief and shoved the entire mess into the huge pockets of his coat.

Something caught on a sleeve button as he turned. He lifted the flimsy material to find a pair of black lace panties. His breath didn't catch but turned into a solid lump in his chest.

"Okay, done."

Somehow he managed to shove the lingerie back into the drawer while Tiffany swept the CDs on top of the desk into her messenger bag, shut off the computer and wiped down any surface area she touched. He thanked every saint he could name she hadn't noticed the undergarment.

Careful to turn off lights and lock the door again, they exited Ridgeway's apartment. As they headed for the SUV, he paused.

Tiffany stopped, her hand reaching for her favorite weapon. "What's wrong?"

Something crawled along his spine. He tasted the night air, but no particular scent aroused suspicion. No stray thoughts. Nothing.

He shook his head. "I had the sensation of being watched."

She brandished the standard yellow No. 2 pencil. "Can you be any more vague?"

He shook his head at his discomfiture. No doubt Ridgeway's lucky success at following him on top of his failure to find their missing people played with his mind. The first problem was rectified. The second problem could be solved in the next forty-eight hours.

"It's nothing. Come." Long strides brought him to the vehicle's door and forced Tiffany to run to keep up with him. "We have an appointment at Mallory Labs."

— •● —

The plastic casing of Selene's cell phone creaked under the strain of her tense grip. "Are you sure?"

"I think I can recognize my former boss." Marcus's sardonic reply filtered through the tiny receiver. "His snot-nosed little whelp is with him."

Fury iced the blood in her veins. She rose and began pacing in front of her office window. Two years ago, Marcus would never have dared to speak to her in such a disrespectful tone. "Do you regret following me into exile, my grandson?"

"No, Your Majesty. I am merely following up on the woman seen with Nguyen this morning as my queen requested." The younger vampire's voice held the proper contrition.

Maybe she depended on Marcus's loyalty too much. Most of those who followed her into banishment were opportunists, but she counted on the real family bond between her and Marcus to keep the rest in line.

She couldn't worry about Marcus's discipline now. Her suspicions concerning Nguyen's behavior were justified. "Have they discovered your presence?"

A soft snort, one not audible to Normal hearing, came through the speaker. "Of course not. I'm on a rooftop, downwind and nearly a block away."

She let his sarcasm slide. There was too much to be accomplished in the next few hours to allow any complications. "Search the apartment and question the reporter. I want to know what Nguyen leaked and if she's spoken to any of her superiors."

"Shall I dispose of the reporter as well, my queen?"

"Yes." She pressed the "End Call" button. A manicured fingernail tapped against the cracked plastic as she stared across the Los Angeles skyline and considered her options. Nguyen obviously tried to reach Caesar through a subsidiary company under the Augustine Conglomerate. At first blush, Nguyen's choice of the *Scoop* seemed suicidal until one considered the editor was a supernatural. No doubt, O'Malley would have reported an employee's findings to Caesar by now. She and Mallory would need to move up their timetable if her take-over of the Augustine Coven was going to succeed.

And the only way to accomplish her goal would be to prove the V-Prime project worked.

Crossing back to her desk, she punched the number for security.

"Adams here."

"Mr. Adams, we need a candidate for human testing. Tonight."

Chapter 6

I wiggled my butt deeper into the soft leather seat of Max's car and sighed in pleasure. Definitely worth the crap he gave me at dinner. He had finally backed off when I told him he wasn't coming with me tonight for the umpteenth time. Then he piled on the dire predictions of what he'd do to me if I so much as scratched the clear coat on his car. I smiled sweetly before peeling rubber out of his driveway and speeding into the brightly lit Los Angeles night.

Yummy and Goth Girl already knew what I looked like so I wasn't taking any more chances. I may not be the chick from *Alias*, but I can hold my own in the disguise department, not to mention driving a different vehicle. A quick stop at my apartment before tonight's fun and games would be sufficient.

My fingers drummed a rhythm on the steering wheel as I headed home. What was Fred's connection to the Jessie Alton story? It was definitely something more than me asking him to run a couple of illegal background checks. I rolled it over and over but came up with nothing. Nothing but me, which sent another round of guilt-ridden acid to join the lasagna sitting in my stomach.

I had to be missing something, a major piece of the puzzle. Fred's death less than twelve hours after St. James threatened me made no sense. Guilt gnawed at my conscience. What little conscience I had left any way. Why not come after me?

In my brain fog, I nearly rear-ended the Saab ahead of me when he slammed on his brakes. The two other drivers in front of him had also slammed on their brakes to avoid a black SUV roaring out of the driveway to my apartment building.

A very familiar black SUV.

My heart lodged in my throat, but Goth Girl didn't spare the Camry a glance, much less the other drivers giving her friendly one-fingered waves. The gas-guzzler sped down the street, my suspects intent on their own destination. Had they been waiting for me all day and had finally given up for the night?

Annoyed honking erupted behind me and I tapped the accelerator. A smile tugged my lips. Two could play the follow-and-wait game. And I tried very hard to shove the thought they'd been waiting at my apartment to kill me into a deep, deep hole.

I hung back, not making the overeager mistakes I had last night. Goth Girl also wasn't driving in the same erratic pattern, which made me want to kick myself for falling into her set-up. This time they headed for a different section of the city.

Pre-fab office buildings rose from the overly landscaped terrain of a city park on my right. On the left, the blue and white neon of the Mallory Laboratories, Inc. sign glowed under the halogen streetlights. They passed the biotech campus and pulled into the overflow parking lot between the labs and another set of office buildings.

Damn, no way I could get closer without revealing myself.

Glancing up the street, I headed for the parking garage serving the next huddle of offices. A few cars were still scattered on each level. I breathed a sigh of relief that the top deck was deserted. I parked and climbed out of the car. Snatching my equipment, I crossed to the concrete barrier edging the deck. A nearly full moon and the lack of Los Angeles's usual smog gave me an unobstructed view of both the bio-research complex and St. James's SUV.

I couldn't resist a smirk when I peered through the telephoto lens. Goth Girl's profile edged the driver's window, but no large shadow sat next to her. Where was St. James?

I frowned and pulled out the nightscope I'd picked up on eBay. Maybe St. James thought the damage to my Civic and the photo cards would discourage me. Maybe he believed he had scared me off between his threats and Fred's death. I nibbled my lower lip as I considered the events at the warehouse district. If he wanted me out of the way, why not kill me when he had the chance? No witnesses and a handy dumpster would have been much easier than mowing down Fred in broad daylight.

A lot of this wasn't making sense. Okay, most of it wasn't making any sense whatsoever. Like the one security camera on the Mallory complex's outer wall that seemed to stare at me for a couple of minutes before it continued to scan the grounds.

I was getting paranoid in my old age. And I still had nearly four years until the dreaded three-oh.

A slight movement a hundred yards from the SUV caught my attention as I peered through the night scope. From the ground, St. James would be invisible to the rent-a-cops in their go-carts. Heck, he was nearly invisible to me even with the nightscope. Only his movement crossing the grounds gave him away. He seemed to flow in and out of the shadows faster than humanly possible as he approached the campus wall.

Mallory Labs had spent some serious dollars on the landscape surrounding the main complex. Instead of one gigantic concrete slab, the area was broken up into smaller parking lots with contoured hills, shrubs and trees giving the illusion of the wild. Probably some idiot exec's idea to mimic the forest around his retreat in Colorado. I hated to think about the water bill for this place. But the foolish expenditure definitely gave St. James an advantage.

Timing his moves with the rhythmic sweep of the cameras, St. James froze next to a tree when a pair of guards passed before he proceeded to the next shrub for cover. My appreciation for him leveled up a notch when he shinnied up the brick wall encircling the main buildings. His gloves and boots must have climbing hooks on them, but the similarity to Spider-man was eerie. Except . . .

I blinked a few times before I peered through the lens again. He wasn't wearing gloves.

Deadly looking steel spikes embedded in mortar ringed the top of the wall. They were spaced too closely for even an anorexic like Goth Girl to slide through. Anyone insane enough to try to climb over them would impale himself. And as much as St. James annoyed me, I didn't want him eviscerated. Otherwise, I couldn't watch his sexy ass squirm in jail.

St. James reached the top of the wall and stretched out. Lying on his side despite his bulk and the spikes, he pulled a small object from his clothing and tied it to the spike above his head. Curiosity drove me crazy, but I couldn't make out what he held.

He pulled something else from a pocket and tied the second object to the spike closest to his waist before he crawled back down the wall. St. James retraced his steps and climbed back into the SUV. Goth Girl departed the parking area at a sedate speed. Whatever they were up to, they weren't worried about being caught.

I noted the position of St. James' objects before gathering my equipment. His acrobatics had to have been the weirdest thing I'd seen since I started with the *Scoop*. Running through possibilities, I settled into Max's car, switched on the ignition and headed for the exit. The auto attendant had its wooden arm raised for the night so I didn't have to climb out to dismantle the thing.

I considered heading for Mallory Labs, but I didn't have the equipment or the fingernails to climb the wall like St. James. Daylight would give me a better opportunity to discover what he tied to the wall spikes.

Spy cameras were a feasible prospect. Somehow, I didn't think it was a bomb. Taking out a small section of brick wall didn't make sense if he wanted to damage Mallory's operation. I'd have to check with Agnes to see if she'd found where the billionaire's celebutante daughter was taking her "vacation." Maybe a little bargaining was in order to find out if any new projects of the biotech firm had pissed off someone like PETA.

A giant yawn reminded me how little sleep I was working on. After a full eight, I could come back in the daylight, check out what St. James left behind and still be in position when he and Goth Girl came back tomorrow evening. Whatever they were planning wasn't happening tonight. A shudder reminded me they had been at my apartment earlier. Maybe I could talk Max into letting me stay at his place. Just for tonight.

The tension wringing my neck and shoulders eased as I regarded my game plan. I left the car window down, trying to stave off my sleepiness. The chill breeze helped as I turned onto the little two-lane road cutting through the northwest side of the recreation park parallel to the main thoroughfare and headed for home.

What was up with the Deranged Duo? There wasn't a link between Mallory and St. James that I had found unless St. James had added industrial espionage to his resumé. What would interest him in a squeaky-clean biotech corporation?

I frowned while I considered St. James's path each time I had followed him. The visit to the antique store in one of the older neighborhoods of the city. Talking to a bunch of homeless kids in an abandoned building downtown. A visit to Reno's, a notorious biker bar in an ugly section of Los Angeles. Last night's escapade by the river. Tonight's visit to Mallory Labs. And then losing them near Brentwood the first three nights. What was the connection between the disparate destinations?

A droning sound behind me caught my attention. The flash of moonlight on metal in the side mirror warned me a split-second before the van rammed into the back of Max's car. *What the hell?* The jolt nearly ripped the steering wheel from my death grip.

The idiot didn't have any headlights on. High-pitched whining warned me, and I wrenched the wheel hard to the left, avoiding the van's second try at me. All moisture disappeared from my mouth. The driver gunned his engine to bring the van even with the Camry. A quick glance sent my heart into overdrive. It looked just like the van that mowed down Fred.

Thank god, I had metal and plastic around me. That didn't mean I was safe. I sucked in a harsh breath through dry lips and stomped the gas pedal. The van careened as the attempted sideswipe launched it into the narrow, grassy berm between the road and the duck pond.

I risked a quick look back. The van was an inky spot against the moonlit vegetation. Still no headlights glared from the rearview mirror. The spot grew to a blob as the van sped towards me.

Fear and anger chased each other through my brain. Anger won the race. This bastard was not making me pay for any more damage to Max's car. Bracing myself, I yanked the emergency brake and a hard left on the wheel at the same moment. I would definitely send a thank you gift to Jake, ex-boyfriend and stuntman extraordinaire, for the driving lessons.

If I survived the night.

The bumper screeched a mournful protest as the van caught and ripped it from the backend as I whipped around. With any luck, the jagged plastic would poke a hole in the van's radiator. The one-eighty complete, I punched Max's six-cylinder forward and flipped off the headlights. Two could play this game. Aiming for the picnic area, I prayed I could find a hidey-hole in one of the spots long enough to call the police for help.

No one ever told me how hard it was to drive at night without lights. Moonlight turned everything either into pale imitations or gigantic shadows, potentially hiding the bogeymen chasing me. I slowed to avoid dunking myself in the duck pond. There was no hint of the van's telltale drone between the whistling wind and my own pounding heartbeat. I really wanted to believe it wasn't the same vehicle that mowed down Fred.

Taking the curves among the barbeque pits as fast as possible under the pitch-black grove, I headed for a picnic pavilion with a lean-to. Glimmers of moonlight between the trees guided the way. Pulling up short behind the slanted sunshade, I switched off the ignition. With all the screeching tires and crunching metal on plastic, the park wildlife had fallen silent. As the rasp of my own breathing slowed, the chirps and whispers started again.

The lean-to would cover an infrared signature from the Camry's engine from the main road. The metal shade didn't quite meet the concrete pad so the tires would be obvious if the bad guys had a nightscope. A familiar engine hummed louder as the other driver wound down the main lane through the middle of the park. My breath caught, lungs refusing to work.

Please go past. Please go past.

The sound of the van's engine remained steady as it continued past my hiding place. I waited until it faded completely before I gulped some air and flipped the ignition. Not daring to turn the headlights back on, I eased the car back towards the park's west road while I dug for my cell phone in the bottom of my purse.

Panic dropkicked my heart at the blinking low battery light. I'd forgotten to recharge it at the apartment earlier. I hadn't been home since Fred's death. And my car adaptor was sitting in my Honda.

Please God, all I need is a few seconds of airtime. Just let me get through.

Time dragged on forever. In the corner of my eye, the phone's icon blinked faster.

"9-1-1. Please state your city and state."

Yes! I was definitely going to church on Sunday.

My voice was shaking so bad it took three tries to rattle off my location to the cell company's 911 operator before she could patch me through to the local emergency line.

The second operator clicked on. "9-1-1. Please state the nature of your emergency."

"I'm being chased by a van. It's trying to run me off the road, but—"

A soft click and both the display and the line died along with any possibility of help. I drew in a deep breath and released it, counting to ten in Spanish. *Think, girl!*

Okay, I'm on my own with these guys. I nodded to myself. No problem. I've gotten out of worse scrapes. Except I've never had someone actually try to kill me. Russell Crowe and a hotel phone not withstanding.

Up ahead, the lights of the tennis courts winked a friendly greeting. I was almost to the park's west entrance. The next instant my last little twinge of hope I had died a fast, painful death. A dark van sat waiting in the driveway to the courts' parking lot.

Damn! How could they have swung around me so fast?

My blood froze in my veins as two and two finally made four in my sleep-deprived head. There was more than one van after me.

I eased up on the gas. My pulse beat an erratic rhythm in my ears. If I hit the brakes, the driver would see the taillights. Just a few yards between the van and the park exit. Freedom was close enough to taste.

Fingers clenched around the leather steering wheel cover. No choice then. Coast as close as possible, then hit the gas and pray I'd make it to the street before the van's driver reacted. If this worked, then it would be a race to the closest police substation.

Quarter of a mile. 300 yards. 200.

I jammed the accelerator hard. The Camry's injectors whined in protest. Lights blinded me the instant I was past the park billboard. A sickening crunch sent me and the Camry spinning like a toy top.

For the couple of seconds I could think clearly, I wished vertigo made me see two vans. Then the guy who had been hiding behind the park's announcement billboard revved his engine, aiming to broadside me again. My heart clambered up my throat in its own desperation to get out of the car.

I stomped the accelerator. The Camry roared but went nowhere. Flinging the gearshift into reverse, I pumped the gas again to no avail. All I could do was watch as the huge shadow charged.

The van nailed the driver's side, sending me sliding down the embankment towards the retaining pond. A lurch as something caught the car, a deeper dip on the right side. Then the car started to roll, the ground rushing up to smash the passenger windows.

My last coherent thought was Max would kill me for wrecking his car.

Chapter 7

Consciousness came back with painful reality. My head throbbed in time to the beeps next to me. I eased my right eye open, then pressed it closed as the fluorescent bulb spiked new agony in counterpoint to my headache. Maybe drowning in the retaining pond was a better idea after all.

If I was lying in a hospital, someone must've found me. Maybe a patrol car passed through as the Camry and I were rolling down the embankment.

I started to reach for my head. Nothing moved. I tried again. Okay, right arm not responding. The left hand couldn't lift any further than the right. Neither leg so much as twitched.

Shit! I'm paralyzed!

Panic eased when I realized I could still feel the nubby texture of a blanket underneath my immobile fingers. Despite my brain's best efforts to shut off, I raised my head and opened my eyes. The wave of nausea left me choking, but I registered the straps holding me down. The accident must have been worse than I thought if the hospital staff had to tie me down.

A round of dry heaves left me gasping for breath. Damn! If the idiot hospital staff were going to anchor me to the bed, they should have left someone to watch me. I really needed some water to drown the sandpaper and acid exfoliating my throat. Not to mention the probable concussion beating its way through my gray matter. I didn't see a call button, not that I could reach it if I found one. I would have to wait. And patience was never my strong suit.

I must have drifted off because the sound of the door swooshing open woke me from a dream about Daniel Craig leaving his wife for me. I considered looking at who had entered the room but refused to surrender to another round of heaves.

"No faking, honey. I know you're awake," a saccharine-loaded voice said.

God, I hate cheery nurses.

I peeled one lid open. Except I never saw nurses before who could pass for goodfellas. The two ladies in the center dressed in traditional puke green scrubs. A couple of blinks revealed only one nurse, but she had the broad build of a Rams defensive lineman though she lacked the height. The muscle with her wore the proverbial black t-shirt, black sports jacket, and black slacks. The color did nothing to slim their bodies or hide the guns they both carried under their coats. The double-vision returned with a vengeance, threatening another bout of dry heaves.

Wonderful. So much for my sweetly imagined, last-minute rescue.

I groaned and closed the one eye. "Water." The raspy noise from my throat was not recognizable as my voice, and it burned to make the sounds, but Nurse Ratchett must have comprehended. Fingers slid under my skull and raised my head up so I could sip from the cup held to my lips. She took away the blessed coolness too soon. "More," I croaked, a little more coherently this time.

"Sorry, honey. We need to ask you some questions first."

"Head hurts."

Acid fire shot through my left hand, and I screamed. Both eyes shot open.

"Oh, I know, honey. Unset bones can be so painful."

Through tears, I saw the bitch smile at me as she pointed an index finger at my swollen left hand, something I hadn't noticed earlier with the overwhelming headache. Nerves screamed along with me as she deliberately jarred the broken appendage again. Bones scraped against each other under my skin.

"Now we've taken your mind off your headache, let's talk, shall we? Girl to girl?" Nurse Ratchett pulled a chair close to the bed and plunked her fat ass down.

The combined pain brought the threatened dry heaves close to the surface. I swallowed hard and gripped the nubby blanket with my right hand. The insane part of me rejoiced my writing hand wasn't hurt, which meant I was damn close to shock. And I needed what brains I had left to figure a way out of this.

"Now, dear," she started, laying a motherly hand on my arm, "what's your affiliation with Duncan St. James?"

My "huh" ended with a scream when she jabbed my injured hand.

Anger mixed with pain so I saw red either way. It took a couple of minutes before I could think coherently enough to talk. "What the fuck are you talking about?"

"He was seen leaving your apartment tonight."

My thoughts could have been ice cubes in Dad's martini shaker. I had more people than St. James watching me? "What?"

She poked me again, waiting patiently for my howling to stop.

"You fucking bitch—" I started, but my words dissolved into another hacking round of dry heaves. The aches in my throat and stomach were closing in on the ones in my head and hand.

"Now, now, now. I get after the boys for that kind of language." She wagged her torture instrument at me. "Let's try again, shall we? What's your affiliation with Duncan St. James?"

"I don't know what you're talking about."

She raised the finger.

"I'm serious! I don't work for him or anything!"

She poked anyway.

I must have passed out because the next thing I knew she was spraying icy water in my face. Heckyll and Jeckyll were in the corner of the room, trying not to piss their pants from laughing. Tears dripped down my cheeks to join the freezing mist. Now I understood why cats hated getting spritzed in the face so much. I was ready to claw Nurse Ratchett myself.

I settled for the hissing and spitting part of feline behavior.

"You can torture me all f—" At Ratchett's warning look, I changed my word choice. "—freakin' day. You can have Heckyll and Jeckyll start cutting off fingers." I nodded toward the duo in the corner before returning her look glare for glare. "It doesn't change the fact I can't tell you jack."

I could rat out his business address and his PI license number, but the basics obviously wasn't the information Nurse Ratchett wanted. And what was he doing at my apartment? From the grin on her face, Ratchett enjoyed the torture way too much to stop while I puzzled everything out.

She aimed the finger. I squeezed my eyes shut, gritted my teeth, counted each breath, and waited for the shifting bones to set fire to my nerves.

When I got to fifty, I dared to peek at Ratchett. She was still poised, but her lips pursed as if she actually considered my words. I wasn't sure how long she stared at me, but finally she lowered her hand and stood.

"Keep an eye on her," she ordered her two goons. She favored me with a frown before she marched out the door.

Once the door stopped swinging, my jaw muscles relaxed. Until I noticed that Heckyll eyeballed my lowly little B-cups. A brand-new queasiness developed in my tummy. My concussion and broken hand wasn't going to deter a gangbang if Ratchett gave them the go-ahead. Probably wasn't going to even if she didn't, but I still found myself praying for her quick return.

Someone must have been listening to me because the door whipped open. A tall, thin man in a lab coat strode in, Ratchett on his heels. Peering at his clipboard through coke-bottle glasses, he hummed to himself like my pediatrician used to, but I definitely wasn't getting a lollipop at the end of this visit.

He looked down at me and smiled, his face reminiscent of someone who enjoyed his job. From what I read in history class, so did Mengele.

I was screwed.

His attention flicked from me to the chart then back to me. "She's baseline. If she can't tell us anything about St. James, then we should find a better use for our patient."

"The pit?" asked Ratchett.

He nodded.

"Aw, man!" Heckyll whined. "What a waste!"

What could possibly be worse than rape and a bullet through the head? Not wanting to find out, I made a pathetic attempt at struggling with Heckyll and Jeckyll as they unstrapped me. So pathetic they held me over a waste can while I puked up the miniscule sip of water in my stomach.

Waves of dizziness prevented me from memorizing the layout of the place as they dragged me to "the pit." Anger kept me from passing out. Anger at these bozos for not realizing I wasn't worth the effort of kidnapping. Anger that Max would blame me for his demolished car. Anger my end would be in some crappy pit.

Maybe it was the concussion, but I giggled. *Garbage made my living, garbage would be my ending.* Maybe shock was finally setting in, but I was laughing hysterically by the time my escort dragged me into some room with a metal grate floor.

Ratchett crossed to the middle and bent to pull up a trap door. She motioned to Heckyll and Jeckyll, who hauled me over and lifted me off the floor. Survival instinct butted aside the insane laughter. I flailed, screamed and kicked. Ratchett grabbed my face and squeezed hard.

"If the boys drop you in head first, you won't survive the fall." She pressed a vicious smile against my face. "If you land feet first, you might have a fighting chance."

Once again, blood froze in my veins. Whatever was about to happen wasn't going to be quick. Or painless. Her words startled me long enough for Ratchett's boys to shove me through the opening.

I landed hard, remembering at the last instant to roll right, not left. Even so, the impact flashed searing pain through my broken and cracked parts.

Soft whimpering filled the space, and it took a minute to realize I was making the noise. Boots on metal echoed as the quartet tromped out of the room above. I caught a glimpse of concrete walls and a sawdust-covered floor before they shut the door behind them. A small splash of light fell through the tiny window in the door upstairs, then filtered past the grate to land in the middle of the wood chips. So the sick bastards weren't even going to watch.

I sighed. For all I knew, microscopic web cams lined the wall, and Ratchett and her boys didn't want to chance my blood splashing up through the grate and staining their clothes.

Hugging my broken hand to my chest, I rose to my knees, dizziness tracking every move I made. I carefully tilted my head up and gauged the grate to be ten feet above the floor. I was damn lucky not to break anything else in the fall.

Rising to my feet, I stumbled and waited for the nausea to lessen before examining my cell. The couple of inches of sawdust on the floor wasn't enough to pile, even if the stuff was remotely stable. The walls appeared smooth except for some darker areas at the rear of the room. No way was I going to climb out of here.

I crossed the cell and ran my good hand over the wall. No, just one dark area. Not concrete as I first thought but matte steel. I frowned as foreboding flooded through my tattered nerves. Not wall at all but a door to who knew where. Or what.

The hinges were on the other side—not that I had any tools to pry the pins out. I swallowed hard then cursed my captors. They couldn't come up with anything better than some "B" horror flick ending for me. I checked what the bad guys had left me with.

Not much, I discovered. T-shirt, jeans, bra and panties. Nothing in my pockets and no socks or shoes. Damn. If I had something to cut with, maybe I could make a rope of my clothes. Then I remembered Heckyll's leer and decided I'd rather meet the monster behind the door clothed than Heckyll while I was naked.

I ran my good hand through my hair, desperate to think. How the heck was I getting out of this?

My fingers brushed the goose egg behind my left ear. The tender flesh ached but didn't give to the slight pressure. It seemed my skull was intact under the knot. I sucked in a deep breath and concentrated. Injuries were the least of my problems.

I shuffled through the sawdust, hoping to find a piece of wood bigger than a Frosted Flake. Any weapon was better than no weapon, but all I accomplished was to stir up enough dust to set off a round of sneezing. My head pounded harder than ever.

I sat down in the middle of the pool of light and let loose the tears of despair. Giving up was not in my vocabulary but I figured I might as well add it before I died.

The bad guys didn't let me wallow in self-pity long. I had sniffed twice when the metal door swung upon on silent hinges. I rose to my feet. I had more of a chance than Fred had against the stupid van. Ratchett and her boys were probably stuffing their faces with popcorn while they watched me, hoping for a good show. Then dammit, I'd give them one.

An awful reek flooded through the black opening. I took two steps toward it when something dark, filthy and incredibly thin slunk through the doorway. My first guess of a rabid dog crashed when it seemed to alternate between all fours and its hind legs. I heard a snuffling sound as it slid along the perimeter, like it was testing my smell. No, not a dog. More like a starved baboon with mange.

I tensed every muscle and backed slowly, circling toward the gap in the wall as well to keep as much distance as I could between us. I didn't dare move too fast and provoke the creature, but my effort was for nothing. The door swung shut, dashing any hope I'd get out before the thing attacked. My attention shifted to the thing trapped in the pit with me.

What I assumed was thin fur at first appeared to be a thick layer of dirt embedded in sparse body hair and possibly ragged cloth. I couldn't be sure without a closer look, and its atrocious body odor and my own fear didn't make checking a desirable option. I wasn't sure how the thing could distinguish my smell from its own. I sure as hell couldn't.

I matched its pacing around the room until I was once again on the side farthest from the steel. When the creature reached the door again, it sank to the floor on its rear haunches and stared at me. I bit my tongue to keep from screaming. Large eyes regarded me through matted, dank locks. I'd never seen anything like the neon blue orbs glowing softly in the dim cell. Worst of all were the two-inch fangs protruding from the sunken, almost human face.

Raw fear gripped me. My pain receded to a dim throb in the face of my panic. Why was the thing just looking at me instead of attacking?

"You know they expect me to eat you, don't you?"

I jumped at the hoarse sound coming from the creature. It was right on that count, but a monster with a Texas accent was the last thing I anticipated.

"Well, actually they expect me to drink your blood," it continued. Or was that he? The voice sounded masculine. He gave me a grotesque grin. The skin on his skull resembled a facelift gone horribly wrong.

"What are you?" I tried to project confidence. The quiver in my voice didn't help.

"Don't worry, darlin'. I'm not doing the sons of bitches' dirty work. Hear me!" His voice rose to a bellow though how he got volume out of his emaciated chest I'll never know. "I'm not doing your goddamn dirty work!" He seemed to collapse upon himself after his outburst, like he used the last of his life in his show of defiance.

He looked so pathetic I took a tentative step towards him, but he gave a small shake of his head.

"Don't come any nearer, darlin'. The bastards've been starving me, hoping I'd lose all reason." He favored me with another hideous smile. "I can't guarantee my gentlemanly behavior will continue if you get too close."

I nodded and eased back to the wall opposite from him. Once seated in the sawdust, the throbbing pain returned full force now that my adrenaline charge was shot. We watched each other for a few minutes before he spoke again.

"To answer your question, I'm a vampire."

I couldn't help the laughter burbling from my throat. "I'm sorry," I said, attempting in vain to smother the giggles. Yep, definitely going into shock. Either that, or this guy needed one of Agnes's tin foil hats.

He just watched me, like a predator who finds an unknown animal curious and isn't sure if he wants to take a bite.

Finally controlling the laughter, I cleared my throat and tried again. "I think they've held you here too long. You're delusional. There's no such thing as vampires."

"Used to think the same thing until I met one a little over a century ago." He shrugged. "Doesn't matter if you believe me or not." Another grin. "Wouldn't happen to have a stake on you? Or some silver?"

"What do you mean? What for?"

He sobered, sending a skitter of fear down my spine. "They're planning to leave us in here until you die of thirst or I kill you." He shrugged again. "You killin' me would prevent option number two."

"I'm not killing you any more than you're killing me. Got it?"

He smiled again. Maybe I was getting used to him, but the fanged grin didn't quite scare the beejeezus out of me this time.

"You got spunk, girl. What's your name?"

"Sam." No sense giving whoever might be spying on us any more information than I had to. Oh, who was I kidding? They'd probably retrieved my ID from the wrecked Camry.

"Short for Samantha, I bet." At my nod, the glowing eyes seemed to leave me for another place and time. "I knew a saloon girl by that name once. Pretty thing." His eyes returned to me. "Not as pretty as you though."

His comment didn't have the same vulgar quality as Heckyll's. I laughed and began to relax. Maybe I wasn't going to have to battle for my life after all. Not that I relished dying of dehydration.

"Are you always this charming in challenging situations?"

"Charm enough to make up for my looks and smell."

I laughed again, wondering what he'd look like after a full hot-water heater and a bottle of soap. Not as good as Yummy. Not even Brent Poole cleaned up as good as Yummy.

"I don't clean up half bad, darlin'."

The skitter reversed course back up my spine. Was he reading my mind?

At my pause, he gave me another toothy smile. "I can't stand the smell of myself, so I sure as hell don't know how you can stand me."

I grinned. "I don't usually comment on strangers' hygiene."

He laughed at the easy camaraderie. "So what'd you do to piss off the bastards upstairs?"

I frowned, not sure how much or what to tell this man. Sorry, vampire. The possibility of Ratchett and her boys spying on us remained. "If we're going to exchange life stories, how about you tell me your name?"

"Alex."

I couldn't help another grin. "Short for Alexander? I knew an Alexander once. I beat the daylights out of him in fourth grade after he dropped a rat down my shirt at his sister's sleepover. You're definitely uglier than him."

Alex's laughter turned into a coughing fit that left him prone on the floor, panting.

I started crawling toward him, but he waved me off. "You may not believe my story, but it's not worth risking your life over," he said, his voice gruffer than ever. If he wasn't starving and filthy, he was the type of man every woman in the room would swoon from his personality alone.

"So where in Texas are you from originally, Alex?"

"Born in Baltimore actually. Father moved us west when I was three 'cause of Mama's health. He was mortified I picked up the local accent."

I laughed softly. The story was all too familiar. "It's not hard to disappoint parents, is it?"

"What'd you do to yours?"

Hot blood rush through my cheeks. I don't know why I was embarrassed telling Alex about my job. I sure as hell wasn't last night with St. James. Assuming it was last night when I'd had my run-in with St. James in the warehouse district. I'd lost all track of time since the van clobbered me and the Camry.

Still, my reticence had nothing to do with potential spies. I swallowed hard before I said, "I work for a tabloid."

"Not fond of the yellow press, are they?" He grunted. "So you got too close to Tyrone Mallory and his kidnap and torture club?"

I gulped. "Is that where we are? Mallory Labs?"

He cocked his head. "Where did you think you were?"

"I wasn't sure." I sighed and rubbed my temple, trying to ease the obscene headache. "I was driving through the park on my way home last night—" I frowned and shrugged with one shoulder, not wanting to aggravate the broken bones. "At least, I think it was last night. This van rammed my car and ran me off the road." I gave Alex a wry grin. "Actually, it was—" I couldn't take the chance of mentioning Max. "—a colleague's car. I guess I don't have to worry about him killing me now."

Alex's chuckles dissolved into another coughing and choking fit. I couldn't stand seeing him suffer. The frustrating part was not being able to do a damn thing to help the man. I didn't try to approach him again, but the reporter in me kicked in once he caught his breath.

"What do you mean about Tyrone Mallory's kidnap and torture club?"

He shook his head. "You don't believe in vampires, remember?"

"Indulge me."

"He snatches supernaturals—"

"Supernaturals?"

A chuckle escaped from Alex. "You really are a journalist, aren't ya, darlin'?"

Funny. Alex calling me "darling" didn't send my heart racing the way St. James had. Or maybe it had been the way he'd touched me when he said it.

An odd look came over Alex's face, but his voice retained some humor as he continued. "A supernatural is someone who isn't Normal. Witches, weres, and vampires fall into that category."

His emphasis made "normal" sound like a proper name. Almost the way Agnes said it when she warned me about bad vampires. I rolled it over a couple of times in my head before I asked, "Upstairs, they said I was baseline. That means a normal human, right? Why the hell would they grab me?"

"Good question."

Well, wasn't he just the font of information. My gray cells may have been damaged, but there was an unspoken statement in his story. "So you're saying there are other races?"

He chuckled again. "The fairies are another tale."

Fairies, huh? Maybe the poor guy had lost it down here in the dark. If Alex believed he was a vampire, I wasn't going to correct him about the non-existence of the rest. Then I frowned as I remembered the mad scientist's opinion of me. What the heck was going on here?

Before I could formulate another question for my compadre, the steel door swung open again. Three men in full combat gear marched into the room. Two had giant guns at the ready. Alex had no chance to react before the assholes pulled the triggers. No crack of bullets, but the double electric shock of the tasers left him screaming in pain.

I scrambled to my feet as Thug Number Three strode towards me. I aimed a kick at his shin. Bad move because he only grunted when I connected. Before I could aim higher, he grabbed me in a headlock and dragged me towards the door.

Alex yelled, "Leave her alone!" But the reward for his attempted chivalry was another round of electric shocks. If he wasn't starved to near undeath, I'm sure he would've taken all three bastards.

Maybe my concussion was worse than I thought if I was beginning to believe his insane story.

My eyesight started to go fuzzy, but I wasn't sure if it was the head injury or lack of air. The door slammed behind us, but I could still hear Alex's hoarse cries behind the steel. Tears of rage and pain leaked down my face as I clawed at the arm encircling my throat.

The thug half-dragged, half-carried me through a couple of more doors. When we stopped, the thug tossed me on linoleum tile. Without thinking, I tried to catch my fall with my broken hand. I collapsed at the excruciating pain. Through my moans, I heard him march away and another door slam shut.

Uncurling from the fetal position on the floor, I raised my head. A utility folding table rose in the middle of the stark, white room, flanked by two equally utilitarian metal chairs. Two more goons stood in opposite corners with stun guns ready.

The only color in the room was a scarlet tie. It took a few minutes for enough oxygen to reach my brain to register the tie was connected to a man. A man I recognized from the Mallory Labs website.

Like most CEOs, Tyrone Mallory had the well-preserved look of someone who works out without actually working and the hard eyes of someone who sold his soul decades ago. His immaculate black helmet hair held the right touch of gray at the temples, looking distinguished and powerful instead of ancient and weak. The artful dye job would have made Mom's stylist proud. Manicured fingers strummed next to a stack of papers on the tabletop. He examined me with the same distaste displayed by the head of a soft drink distributor after finding a mouse in a can of his product.

"I expected better of both Maxwell Howell and Duncan St. James."

I frowned, but the best comeback in my pained state was "Huh?" I was really slipping in the smartass department. And what did my brother have to do with this? I'd been careful not to mention him to Alex.

"Don't play coy with me, Ms. Ridgeway. I know you spied on my research facility. My people mistook who you were working for." The smile on Mallory's face would have given Jaws the shivers. "Howell and St. James have joined forces, haven't they?"

"I don't know what you're talking about." The sad part was I really didn't know. Even without the recent brain rattling, I'd have a hard time connecting my nerdy brother with Mr. Yummy. But if I wasn't any use to Mallory, I wouldn't survive long either. I had too many puzzle pieces, even if I had no clue of how they fit.

Mallory frowned and stared at me. "Sitting on the floor is uncivilized, Ms. Ridgeway." When I failed to move, both goons crossed the room, jerked me up and slammed me down in the other chair, hard enough to rattle my teeth. Stars swam in my vision as my brain protested the additional shaking.

Fear flooded my body. What the hell had I gotten myself into? This sounded less like some Hollywood-Mafia deal and more like one of Agnes's conspiracy theories every minute.

"The games aren't necessary, Ms. Ridgeway. I'm aware of Howell's investigation as well as St. James's."

I swallowed the hard lump of nausea collecting at the back of my throat. Time. I needed time. "I don't know what investigation you're referring to. I'm working on a story about Jessie Alton. You know, the TV sitcom *Buddies*?"

Mallory's right eyebrow twitched. He didn't believe me.

My neurons struggled to work past the pain. How was Max involved in this? He didn't mention anything about working on a story at dinner. He'd been more worried about his street snitch, Anne . . .

Oh God! My stomach lurched as four and four jumped to eight. Agnes had mentioned folks disappearing off the streets. Alex said he'd been kidnapped as well. Was the Jessie Alton incident related to the other missing folks? Had Mallory's goons fed homeless teens to their monsters in the basement? Had Max and St. James both followed leads to Mallory Labs?

And Fred? Fred had paid for my stupid curiosity with his life.

The fear contorted my insides. My body curled as dry heaves racked it. I expected to hit the floor, but one of the goons held me in the chair. When the retching stopped, he held a cup of water to my lips. The blessed coolness disappeared after a few greedy sips.

The shark smile returned to Mallory's face. "Isn't that better?" He checked the manicure on one hand. "Now then, Ms. Ridgeway, what do Howell and St. James know and what do they expect to discover?"

I blinked the tears out of my eyes, trying to make the spinning stop. "Max doesn't have anything to do with this. I borrowed his car because mine's in the shop." If Mallory didn't hesitate in killing Fred, kidnapping me or torturing Alex, then he'd do worse to my family. I needed to stall long enough to find a way to warn Max and my parents.

"You haven't illuminated me as to why St. James was at your apartment earlier."

I licked my cracked lips. "I didn't know he came by."

"So you don't deny your association with the Augustine Coven?"

The man was obviously missing more than one screw. "Coven? What coven? Do I look like a witch to you?"

"Just because you're not a coven member doesn't mean you're not Family."

Family again. My vision blurred as I connected the dots. Fred had said there were things worse than the Mafia. I blinked until the two Mallorys melded into one once again. "You might want to get your accusations straight. Am I supposed to be a witch or a mobster?"

Ice gray eyes bore into the core of my soul, and I shivered in response. "We've already recovered Mr. Howell's car. The only question is whether you'll be in it and conscious when I have it destroyed. I suggest you answer me."

I had no doubts about his sincerity, so I launched a little of my own. I returned his gaze, but it took all my willpower not to flinch. "Max doesn't know jack. Nurse Ratchett was closer to the truth than you. I borrowed the car to tail Duncan St. James for a story I'm working on."

Forefinger and thumb framed Mallory's face as he leaned an elbow on the table.

I needed to talk fast. But how the hell to spin it to keep me alive long enough to call for help? Would Alex live long enough for assistance to arrive? He was already in pretty bad shape. First, I needed to give Mallory a reason to keep me alive.

I sucked in a deep breath. "This isn't Max's story. I'm writing a follow-up on St. James's rescue of Jessie Alton from the Sunshine Believers a few weeks ago."

"Waitaminute! You're Sam Ridgeway? From *The National Scoop*? I read your stuff all the time. I thought you were a guy." The goon behind Mallory grinned in pleasure until the death glare from his boss shut him down. Despite the situation, I felt a little thrill. I would have offered him my autograph if the guy wasn't under orders to kill me.

When Mallory turned back to me, his grimace of distaste was reminiscent of my mother's. I couldn't help the smug look I knew was spreading across my face. "Guess your people aren't crack investigators after all?"

"I find it hard to believe a Pulitzer Prize-winning journalist would let a tabloid reporter borrow his car." He drew out the last few words like it pained him to force them from his throat.

In that moment, I knew Mallory had no idea of the real connection between Max and me, so keeping the smart-ass look on my face wasn't hard. I had legally changed my name to Grandma Neel's maiden name as soon as I turned eighteen, more to piss off Mom as much to sever any connection professors and potential employers might make between my brother and me.

Now, I had to make sure Mallory didn't have a reason to dig deeper. Mom and I had our differences, but I didn't want her dead along with Max and Dad.

"Then where did Max work in high school?" At Mallory's suspicious look, I added, "Long before he joined the *Times*?" An annoyed edge came with my words. Not smart in my situation, but no sleep and a concussion will seriously mess with your head.

His attention flicked to the papers in front of him, and an eyebrow rose in surprise. Narrowed eyes returned to me, and I shrugged. It wasn't my fault he didn't bother to read Max's full résumé. "My editor used to be Max's, and Max owed him a favor. Everyone at the *Scoop* already knows you're behind the disappearance of a bunch of people, and we've already connected you to the Sunshine Believers. Anything happens to me, and they'll run the story."

I held my breath, waiting for him to call my bluff.

Dark red suffused Mallory's neck and face. "Have Howell's home and office searched again to be sure," he snapped. "And have someone search the *Scoop*'s offices." Static crackled behind me as Goon Two relayed the order on his mike. "Has anything been recovered off Ridgeway's hard drive?"

"No, sir. The harddrive's been corrupted with a virus. The techs are still working on pulling the residual data."

Crap. They'd already searched my place and found St. James on my wall. No wonder they thought I was an obsessed employee. Had they found my backups stashed in the crawlspace behind my tub too? No, they couldn't have if they were messing with my harddrive. And what virus were they talking about? I was meticulous about my virus protection. Is that why Yummy and Goth Girl had been at my apartment? To search it and fuck with my computer?

Another worry poked my damaged brain. Neither Max or I were big on photos. Okay, photos of each other or family members. My conceited brother only had framed pictures of him with the rich, the powerful, or the popular on his walls. I was fairly certain they wouldn't find anything at his place connecting us other than the birthday card I sent him last month, the one signed "To Snotface, From PITA."

But if Max really was working an angle on Mallory or they decided to search Mom and Dad's . . .

And Mallory's people had already visited Max. Now, I knew the real reason he had talked our parents into staying in Europe for an extra week. Oh God, what if they ignored him and came home? I tried to shut off the ugly train of thought, but it chugged right along through my consciousness, amping up the fear and nausea.

Mallory's holier-than-thou demeanor didn't lessen. "The question becomes what do I do with you, Ms. Ridgeway."

"How about sending me to a hospital so I can get my hand set?"

Instead of answering, he motioned to Goon One. "Please have Dr. Able and Dr. Kane join us." Goon One hesitated for a moment before turning smartly on his heel and marching from the room.

This wasn't good. "No offense, but I think I'd like my own doctor."

"I assure you, Ms. Ridgeway, we have the finest medical facility in the city." The smile he flashed me was not reassuring at all.

"Murdering me isn't going to hide what you're doing here. If you let me go, I can kill the story. We can go our separate ways. No harm, no foul. Right?"

"I don't plan on killing you." My shoulders didn't have the chance to relax before he added, "At least, not yet."

Which meant I was about to become someone's play toy, or worse, food. *Think, girl!* Shoving the looming hysteria aside, I analyzed the situation. I'd never make it to the door. Not with Goon Two's stun gun leveled at me. It would take a distraction of some kind, maybe the next time they moved me.

I managed to keep my mouth shut until Goon One returned with the so-called doctors. Ever the fake gentleman, Mallory introduced them. Dr. Able turned out to be the asshole who ordered me thrown into the pit with Alex. Kane was Hardy to Able's Laurel, a rotund little man with a cheesy Adolph moustache.

"Dr. Able, please explain why you choose to put Ms. Ridgeway into the pit."

Able's sadistic bravado from earlier disappeared, and his Adam's apple bobbed at his audible gulp. "She's baseline, sir. We didn't need her for research." He swallowed again. "Her usefulness seemed limited to breaking Stanton."

Alex's last name? The information would be useful if I managed to escape. Maybe even notify his family. Poor folks were probably worried sick. Focusing on Alex and his family kept thoughts of my own fate at bay.

"I see," Mallory murmured, though his tone clearly indicated he didn't. "And your opinion, Dr. Kane?"

Able's partner visibly shook, but his voice remained steady. "As I told my associate earlier, Ms. Antonius ordered testing of the V-Prime project. We shouldn't waste a viable human candidate." He shot a withering look at his partner who turned white.

V-Prime project? Candidate? Oh God, they weren't using me as a guinea pig?

Mallory watched them both like a cat deciding which mouse to eat first. "If we're ready for testing, I see no reason to wait." He rose from the table but paused next to Able. Without looking at the scientist, he said, "Next time, remember to clear any disposals with me." Then he strode from the room.

As if Mallory's words hadn't told me what was coming next, the goons started towards me. I jumped from the chair, shoved Kane into Able with my good arm, and dodged to keep them between me and the goons. There was a crash behind me as I charged for the door.

The first electric jolt slammed through my body as I wrenched the door open. Unlike Alex, I didn't have the luxury of screaming. White-hot bolts exploded in front of my eyeballs as every nerve short-circuited. I collapsed to the linoleum, writhing uncontrollably. By the time my five senses returned, the goons had carried me to another room.

I bucked and clawed against the straps holding me to the gurney, broken bones grinding in my desperation. The mad scientists busied themselves at the counter and ignored my cries and curses.

Nurse Ratchett appeared above me, syringe and needle ready. "Now, sweetie, I'll take good care of you."

I renewed my futile attempts to escape. Her elbow, sharp for the amount of flesh surrounding it, jammed into my chest and knocked the breath out of me. As I struggled to get air, her fingers tied the rubber tourniquet to my right arm and jabbed the needle into the vein.

The weight disappeared from my chest, followed immediately by a floaty feeling from whatever she injected into me. Ratchett reappeared with a pair scissors and went to work on my clothes.

"Bitch! Those are my favorite jeans!" My words sounded slurred even to my ears. I wanted to fight but couldn't muster the coordination to blink, much less spit at her. My mouth felt like it was full of marbles. Ratchett must have understood me because she chuckled and said, "I don't think you'll need these again."

The disassociated sensation became worse. I couldn't wiggle my bare toes. And the panic-induced tears trickling into my hair and ears didn't even tickle. The waft of air from the A/C raised goose bumps on someone else's naked flesh.

Soft voices murmured around me, but I couldn't understand the words. Then Kane appeared in my blurred vision, gripping a needle that had to have been a foot long.

I started screaming before he touched me and continued long after the fire he injected burned its way through my veins.

Chapter 8

The nightmare jolted me upright. The hospital-issue gown I wore was soaked with sweat. I ran a hand through my damp hair, trying to remember the dream. Something about a group of Frankensteins turning me into their monster.

I took a deep breath and looked around. Soft blue walls reflected the fluorescent tube above the bed. Electronic beeps timed my heart's rhythm. The wire from the EKG machine dived down the sleeve of the gown. Solution dripped through the IV tube taped to my right wrist. I read the bag hanging next to the bed.

I frowned, squinted, blinked, then read the bag again. Damn, I could actually see the microscopic print of the Cleveland manufacturer at the bottom. My ophthalmologist said it could take up to three months for my eyes to settle from the Lasik, but dang! I needed to call and congratulate him for the terrific job.

I relaxed a little at seeing the clear liquid was standard glucose. I plumped the pillow. Or I tried to. I have the firm opinion powdered cement filled hospital pillows.

Focusing on the tiny spider weaving away in a corner of the room, I leaned back against my cement pillow and tried to remember why I was in a hospital. Fuzzy thoughts twirled inside. Closing my eyes, I breathed yoga-style until something materialized.

Fred!

I bolted upright again. Fred had been hit by a van. I had been following him from the coffee shop, and he had been plowed over.

Lying back down against the bed, I battled through the confusing images clogging my neurons. Fred died. No, he'd been hit by a van first and his Pooh watch broke. Max picked me up at the hospital. I had dinner with someone. Was it Fred or Max? I had been tailing St. James until someone named Alex said he was supposed to eat me. More vans chased me or was it the one that hit Fred? A really bad Elvira impersonator licked her fangs. The rest fell apart in the fog.

I rubbed my left hand over my face, trying to clear the cobwebs. If Fred was killed by a hit-and-run, the emotional trauma would explain the nightmares about vans, weird doctors, and secret labs. Had the same van clipped me when it hit Fred?

No, I was in Max's Camry when the van crashed into the side. The car rolled with me in it.

Or had it? I held out my left hand and stared at it. The distinct memory of broken bones and agony haunted me. I flexed the fingers and rotated my wrist. No discomfort and everything bent and stretched like it was supposed to. I never had a dream so . . . vivid before.

I was searching for the nurse call button when the room door swung open.

Nurse Ratchett!

Everything poured back into my brain in an instant. The look on Ratchett's face said it all. I wasn't supposed to be awake.

Raw fury drove me. I leapt from the bed and crossed the room before Ratchett could grab the door handle. The electrodes ripped off layers of skin as I moved, and the EKG screamed a warning. The IV needle tore from my hand, but the adrenaline rush must have overridden any pain I might have felt. Slamming Ratchett against the door, my fingers dug into the wattle of flesh below her chin and squeezed.

Her eyes bulged as her nails clawed at my hand. I heard frantic thumping and looked down to see her feet kicking the door a good six inches off the ground. So, the stories about extreme strength in extreme stress were true. I set her down and eased the pressure from her neck but still kept a firm grip on her.

"Where am I?" My voice sounded alien, a demonic growl.

Naked fear shone in her eyes. She didn't like the tables turned. I tightened my grip and released to encourage some cooperation.

"Where am I?" I repeated.

"You're in Mallory Labs." *Damn, I was still here?*

"Show me where to get some street clothes." The idea of trying to escape from a bunch of mad scientists and their armed thugs with my ass hanging out the back of a hospital gown sucked the big one.

"Down the hall." Ratchett choked the words out.

Survival instinct made everything so clear. Ratchett smelled of fresh apples covered in ash. I could count the beads of sweat on her pasty face. If I wasn't so focused on escape, I'd question my own sanity.

I yanked her away from the door and peered through the tiny, vertical window. No one out there. Good.

I looked at the woman whose neck I had my fingers wrapped around. I had a good four inches on her, but she probably outweighed me by seventy or eighty pounds. From her quivering flesh, she was scared shitless right now. I should have been scared shitless, but I felt good. Better than good. Like I could take on Mallory's entire fucking army.

Eventually this fabulous adrenaline rush would wear off, and she'd try to take me or escape. I frowned at her, deciding to deal with that when it happened. Ratchett shook harder.

Easing the door open, I took a longer look up and down the hallway. Still no one. Considering my luck lately, it wouldn't be empty for long.

I jerked her in front of me. "Which way?" I snarled. Might as well make the most of my advantage.

She pointed right so I marched her in that direction. Four doors down, she pointed right again. "H-h-here. Th-th-this is the employee locker room."

What the hell was wrong with her? She was shaking so bad I could barely keep a grip on her. She acted like I was the sadistic bitch who tortured her.

Then again, helping me escape would probably land her ass in the pit.

With something a lot worse than Alex.

I yanked the door open and shoved her inside. Cream ceramic tile flooring reflected industrial green walls. A small kitchenette flanked the left side of the room while rows of lockers and benches dominated the right. The overwhelming smell of disinfectant and soap indicated a bathroom somewhere close. I pushed Ratchett toward the lockers before I grabbed a chair from the kitchenette and wedged it against the closed door. The flimsy plastic and aluminum wouldn't stop Mallory's goon squad, but it might buy me a few precious seconds.

Ratchett had edged further away from me as I dealt with the door. I turned in time to see her hit a bench with the back of her knees and thud down ass-first.

"W-what are you going to do with me?"

I couldn't believe it. She and her cronies had kidnapped me, tortured me, experimented on me, and she was worried about what I would to *her*?

"I need a size twelve. Both pants and shirt." I swallowed because I really hated admitting the next thing to anyone. "And size ten shoes."

Ratchett blinked. "Locker seven. Shelly's a fourteen. I-I-I don't know about the shoes."

I took a step towards her, and her face went from pasty to blotchy. Good grief, the woman was going to give herself a heart attack before I could escape. "C-C-Charlie wears eight in men's. Locker sixteen!" Her voice had risen to a shriek, and she threw up hands as if to ward me off.

My head shook with disgust. The bitch was super brave as long as I was tied down or she had backup.

I popped open the first locker she pointed to while keeping an eye on her. She quivered in place, all her joints locked by her fear. My own worry and panic disappeared at the sight of the shopping bag from my favorite lingerie store. I poked a finger in and pulled it open. Tags still hung from the aqua bra and panty set. I smiled, flung the hospital gown at Ratchett's face, and wiggled into the smooth satin. I wasn't about to don someone's used undies. Mallory and his people owed me. Big time. My boobs swam in the C cups, but I didn't care.

I pulled on the denim next. Shelly was not a fourteen. The three-sizes-too-big jeans started sliding down my hips. Not good if I needed to run during my escape. Rummaging through the locker, I found a gaudy scarf serviceable as a belt. The rose-colored ruffled shirt wasn't my taste, but it was better than the hospital gown. I grabbed socks and athletic shoes from Charlie's locker and pulled them on. I stood up and wiggled my toes. A little roomy, but I could run in them.

Ratchett hadn't moved from the spot where she landed. I crossed to stand over her. Whites completely surrounded her pupils.

I crouched next to her. If I tried to find Alex, the odds of me getting caught were pretty high. If I were caught, I'd die, no one would warn Max that Mallory was onto him, and Alex would starve to death. Choosing between a stranger I barely knew and my family tore at my gut.

But if I made it out, I could report Alex's whereabouts to the authorities.

Okay, Max could report Alex's whereabouts. My cachet with the LAPD still sucked from the Alton kidnapping.

I glared at Ratchett. "How do I get out of the complex?"

She shook her head. "Y-you can't." She wetted her lips. "T-t-too much security."

I reached for her, and she flinched, sliding away from me along the bench until she hit the floor. I stood and stalked after her, and she crab-crawled until she slammed into the row of lockers against the wall behind her.

"You can tell me how to get out of here, or I can give you the same treatment you gave me." I prayed she wouldn't call my bluff.

"He'll kill me!" she wailed.

"You think I won't?" Not that I would, but she didn't need to know that little tidbit.

The door rattled against the chair. I whipped my head around, searching. There was no place to hide. My only chance would be to take the person at the door by surprise. I raced for the entrance. Part of me wondered if I'd totally lost my mind.

A sharp blow to the door sent the chair skidding across the tile.

"Charlie!"

Before Ratchett's scream died, I reached Charlie, jerked the stun gun away and rammed the butt into his groin. As he collapsed to his knees, I brought the stock down on his head. Hard. Both his helmet and the gun shattered with a sickening crunch.

I stepped back in shock. It was the goon who stood behind me during Mallory's interrogation. Who gave me water. Who wasn't breathing, his chest way too still. I couldn't have hit him that hard.

My own gasps were harsh in the silence. The fragments of metal and plastic fell from my nerveless fingers, and I took a step back. *This is not happening to me.*

Ratchett didn't give me time to contemplate my new career in assault and manslaughter. She landed on my back, screaming and hitting. I staggered under her weight and the force of her leap but managed to stay upright. I backpedaled into a steel locker. She didn't loosen her grip. Nails raked across my lids. I rammed her into the bank of lockers again and again until she sank to the floor.

Gulping for air, I turned. The corner of the first locker had caved in. My view slid down to the floor. Ratchett's eyes stared blankly at the ceiling.

Oh God, this isn't happening! It's just a nightmare. Drugs from the accident.

Blood seeped from the back of Ratchett's head and oozed across the tile. Backing away, I whirled and raced for the bathroom on the other side of the lockers. Bending over a toilet, I hurled. Instead of normal vomit or the expected dry heaves, a dark, curdled liquid flew from my lips. When I was done, I just stared at the reddish stuff in the john. Something was terribly wrong. The normal, post-puking ache in my gut turned into something worse. Vicious cramping drove me to the tile. Every breath stretched my limit for pain. Curling into a ball, my body spasmed in agony. I needed a real doctor, and I didn't know how I would crawl to the bathroom door, much less get out of the complex.

After a few minutes, the agony eased enough for me to drag my shaking body upright. Not looking at the toilet, I flushed and stumbled to the sink. My hands shook so bad it took me three tries to turn on the water. I couldn't bear to look at myself in the sink-to-ceiling mirror. I rinsed and grabbed a towel from the basket sitting on the counter. It came away from my face stained pink. I dropped it and fled the bathroom.

Only to face the bodies of the two people I had killed.

Self-defense, the rational part of me told the horrified part. *They were going to kill you.* It didn't change the fact I had murdered two people. Tears welled, but I brushed them away. *No time for this,* the rational part ordered. I needed a way out, or I'd be joining Ratchett and Charlie.

I stepped over the corpses, trying to avoid the blood pooling underneath

Ratchett's head and spreading across the tile. Easing the door open, I peered up and down the hallway. No one had come to investigate the commotion.

Not sure which way to go, Eenie-Meenie-Mienie-Mo seemed my best option. On Mo, I turned left and jogged back up the hallway, trying not to think of the dead man whose shoes I wore.

Knowledge tickled the back of my gray matter. Somehow, I knew I was underground. I also knew it was after sundown. The certainty I felt of those facts scared me.

At the first intersection, a bank of elevators appeared on my left. I glanced at the single control panel. No option but up, so I punched the button. The chrome doors slid open, and I jumped aboard, afraid another goon would come around the corner of the hallway any second. The buttons were sequential so I had no clue how many underground levels there were. I pressed "7", and the doors coasted shut. I figured worst-case scenario, climbing down stairs was a lot easier than climbing up.

"Please enter your security card."

I jumped a foot at the computer-generated voice. Once my heartbeat returned to normal, I prayed the damn machine would let me back out. As the doors opened, I breathed a small sigh of relief, then swallowed the acidic taste of nausea and guilt and headed back down the hallway to the employee lounge.

Once I grabbed the badge clipped to Charlie's belt, I ran back for the elevators. My imagination worked overtime. I would have sworn I heard screams echoing faintly down the corridor.

Just don't let the damn thing ask for more than the badge. If the elevator required retinal scans or fingerprints, I was screwed. I was not chopping off anyone's hand or head to make the damn thing work. I inserted the badge into the key slot.

"Identification: Charles Adams. Please select destination."

Damn, now "The Addams Family" theme ran through my head. I hit "7" and released the breath I hadn't realized I'd been holding. As the machine rose, my muscles tensed the closer each number blinked to "7", scared the elevator would stop and I'd have company. Finally, the doors parted. I took a tentative step out.

This must be an executive floor. The plush burgundy carpet offset the silver and gray striped walls. Recessed lighting gave the hallway a relaxed atmosphere, totally opposite of the sterile nightmare below. I glanced right. Out the window at the end of the corridor, I spotted the parking garage from which I had watched St. James, not sure if the incident had been last night or several nights ago.

The lawn was a good thirty or forty feet down.

Okay, I went a couple of floors too high.

The elevator doors had already closed, so I punched the button.

Instead of the elevator opening, claxons howled and the subdued golden light turned a flashing red. Damn it! They must have found Ratchett and Charlie's bodies. I jabbed at the button again, but the doors weren't opening this time. I spotted a glowing exit sign and dived for the door to the stairwell.

I whipped it open to come face-to-face with one of Mallory's armed squads. Slamming the door shut, I raced back up the hallway. *Please let there be another set of stairs!*

Bullets ripped through the metal door and shattered drywall as security unloaded their weapons in their blind attempt to nail me. So much for the stun guns. Mallory must have decided I was now a liability.

The bang of metal on plaster and men shouting echoed up the corridor as I rounded the far corner. Just visible through glass and plants, open space appeared ahead. An atrium. The reception area and the front doors would be close by. If I could make it to the street, I could flag down a driver.

Yeah, right, Sam. This is fucking L.A.

I glanced back at my pursuers. They weren't behind me. Yet.

I turned back in time to run nose first into someone's chest. I bounced off, both of us landing in a tangle on the floor.

"You!" St. James' green eyes glared at me from between my legs. A black turtleneck and tight black pants emphasized the planes and angles of his body.

He picked tonight to break into the labs?

Approaching boots stamped a rhythm. Fear-induced adrenaline ripped through me. Survival overrode lust. I scrambled to my feet. "I've got to get out of here!"

St. James yanked my wrist. Hard. Hormones and fear spurred a reaction the opposite of my usual fast-talking solution. A roundhouse left connected with his jaw. My left fist. He flew backwards. His head slammed into the drywall, sending out a spider-web of cracks.

No pain. I must not have broken my hand after all. St. James wouldn't be so gentle if he got a hold of me this time. Mallory would be worse.

Whirling, I circled the landing and raced for the atrium's decorative staircase. If St. James had any sense, he'd follow my lead. Another squad shot out of an intersecting corridor and spotted me. There was nowhere to go. For a long, slow, horrible instant, I watched the leader raise his gun and aim it at me. In the back corridors of my mind, I heard St. James yell a warning.

Something hit me in the chest. I fell into gray and red mist.

An instant later, St. James held me in his arms. There were sounds of firecrackers all around us. Something stung my face, but the pain seemed so far away. I looked up and his eyes were no longer just green but glowed neon like Alex's had. His lips were drawn back in a snarl. Fangs protruded from his mouth.

I wanted to scream but couldn't find the breath. No. Alex was wrong. Vampires didn't exist.

Still carrying me, St. James leapt on top of the planter ringing the landing. I caught a glimpse of the main floor, three stories down. Then he jumped. I gladly landed in the blackness rushing up to meet me.

Chapter 9

Fine cracks rippled across the marble from the impact of Duncan's boots. The girl hung from his arms, literal dead weight. Brilliant crimson streamed out of her flesh and soaked his clothing. No breath, no heartbeat and his mission blown to bloody hell.

He couldn't help her, but he couldn't just drop her either. He didn't wait for the Normals to recover their wits. Another leap covered the lobby. The glass may have been shatterproof, but a kick sheared the metal bolts locking the front doors. Wind rushed across his face as he ran. Behind him, the crackle of radios called for reinforcements. No time to head for the gap in the wall Bebe's potion had created before he was intercepted.

Tiffany, meet me at the front gates.

No coherent answer, just a stream of vomit green disgust flowed through the mental link. The spicy scent of sandalwood interrupted his partially formed rebuke.

Supernatu—

Sharp reports echoed across the campus, swallowing the remainder of his warning. Panic hammered at his heart. *Tiffany!*

Brick-red anger replaced his niece's disgust. *Nailed three of the bastards. Hurry!*

Another crack of gunfire, this time from the building, not the parking areas. Gathering his strength and clutching the dead girl to his chest, he launched his body straight up and over the front gate. Concrete crunched beneath his feet when he landed.

The putrid smell of rotten meat mixed with burning rubber as the SUV slid to a stop in front of him. He wrenched the rear door open and threw himself and his load on the seat. "Go!"

Acceleration slammed the door shut as Tiffany executed a tire-squealing J-turn. "Holy crap! All I can smell is dead vamps. Were you hit?"

"No." He brushed blond hair from the girl's oval face. Skin, translucent from the lack of blood, seemed to glow pale silver. The only thing marring her visage was a small cut above her right eye. His fingers sought a pulse in her neck. Nothing.

"Who is it? Who'd you find?"

He glanced up to find wide brown eyes reflected in the rearview mirror. "Samantha Ridgeway."

"What! You rescued a Normal? What the fuck was she doing there? Did she blow this whole operation?"

He let Tiffany's tirade continue as the SUV zig-zagged through the streets. He twisted to face the rear window, scanning for anyone following them. After a few minutes with no sign of pursuit, he relaxed enough to consider Tiffany's questions. What was Miss Ridgeway doing at Mallory Labs? Guilt stabbed at his heart. Had his mental suggestion to drop interest in him not taken effect? Had she shaken the compulsion by reviewing her files at her apartment?

Or had she really been working for Mallory all along? No, the security team had definitely been chasing her, not him. He glanced down at the still form. Curiosity may not have killed the cat, but it certainly had snuffed the life of the reporter lying in his arms.

Now that the immediate danger had passed, something odd struck him. Miss Ridgeway's scent wasn't right. No longer crisp Granny Smith with citrus overtones, her scent was more like, like . . . steel. He inhaled deeply, letting the odor sit on his tongue. No, the hint of apple and grapefruit was still under the omni-present metal.

"Is she dead?"

Tiffany's soft question drew his attention. "Yes. The guards shot her."

His niece slammed a palm against the steering wheel. "Great. That's just fucking great."

But there should have been a touch of decay in Ridgeway's scent already as the individual cells collapsed and died. The bullet had hit her point-blank. Her mind was the empty slate of the deceased. He peered closer at the obscene hole in her ribcage.

A horrible squelching came from the cavity in the girl's chest.

"What the hell was that?" A note of panic edged Tiffany's voice.

Miss Ridgeway's lips parted. A wet moan filled the passenger compartment.

Another squelching sound, and her chest rose ever so slightly. His fingers rose to her neck. A soft thrum pulsed beneath his touch. Was her body tricking him into believing she was alive? One last firing of neurons?

Again, the veins jumped beneath his fingers. The spongy sucking as her chest rose. Then the ephemeral sensation of *presence*.

"Duncan?" Tiffany's panic no longer edged just her voice. The emotion filled the passenger compartment, clogging everything with ashes.

Miss Ridgeway struggled with another breath, the sound of lungs expanding in the wound no longer as horrifying. The beat in her throat grew stronger, less erratic.

"She is alive."

"You just said she was dead."

As Tiffany spoke, the small cut on Samantha Ridgeway's forehead sealed and faded.

He frowned. "Apparently, I was incorrect." The same steel scent flavored another deep inhalation, not a vampire's distinctive sandalwood. He hadn't spotted her since their encounter Thursday evening, had assumed his suggestion had worked. "Three days" rang through his mind, but she hadn't been Turned.

He should detect musk if she were part were. A witch couldn't heal with this speed, and a fae wouldn't smell like an iron blend. No, something else was going on.

Tiffany made a hard left.

He braced a leg against the frame to keep him and Miss Ridgeway from slamming into the opposing door. "Where are you going?"

"Nearest hospital's Cedars. We're too far from Good Sam."

"No."

Tiffany glared at him from the rearview mirror. "She's a Normal. She needs a Normal hospital. If you're worried about the ER reporting the GSW, we can buzz Commissioner Davis and have him meet us there."

Protectiveness curled through his chest. Whatever was happening in his city, Samantha Ridgeway was in the middle of it. "Our townhouse is closer."

"Are you fucking insane!" Tiffany flicked a harried glance over her shoulder before turning her attention back to the traffic. "We don't have the equipment to take care of her."

"I do not believe supplementary medical assistance will be necessary."

"What do you mean?"

No, additional aid definitely would not be necessary. The obscene squishing sound Miss Ridgeway's chest made grew quieter, approximating normal breathing. He held a palm over the wound. It no longer extended past his spread fingers. She was healing with the speed of a vampire, but why? And what did it have to do with the missing supernaturals?

He looked up to find Tiffany staring at him from the rearview mirror. "I mean you will drive us to our townhouse. Now."

"Fine," Tiffany muttered, zooming through a yellow traffic light. "But I still think this is a really bad idea."

An icy finger of unease poked the back of his skull. Samantha Ridgeway was the key to this whole situation. So why did it seem she was about to do more than turn his world upside down?

Chapter 10

I woke to the sharp smell of alcohol. My brain took a few minutes to focus. An alien picture snapped in place, and I jumped out of the strange bed I was lying in.

Duncan St. James stood in front of me with an open first aid kit and a mass of bloody towels in his hands. His aristocratic eyebrows knitted in a puzzled frown as he stared at my chest. "I really think you should lie back down."

Ri-i-ight. I'm going to do what the nice vampire tells me.

Like hell.

Part of my brain chanted, *Vampires aren't real.* The rest screamed, *Get out now!*

Putting on my best charming smile, I edged along the bed. "Thanks for all your help back at Mallory Labs." I estimated about eight feet between me and the door. "I promise your name won't be mentioned in any story I write."

Six feet. "Or your ward's."

He just stood there watching me. I had a sinking feeling he was playing with me. Just like Mallory had.

"Where do you think you are going?"

"Home."

"You will not make it very far in your current condition."

I reached for my neck, checking both sides for bite marks.

Again, an arrogant smirk covered his face. "Do not worry Miss Ridgeway, I have not bitten you. You are not exactly my taste."

It's always amazed me how polite a British accent makes an insult.

"Then where did all the blood come from?" I pointed to the towels in his hands. I can't say I was courageous by asking an alleged vampire the source of all the blood. I'm pretty sure the drugs the mad scientists at Mallory Labs had given me were damn wicked. Maybe that's why I saw glowing eyes and fangs. But the blood had to come from somewhere, and I couldn't deal with anymore dead bodies today.

He ignored my question and continued to stare at my breasts. Granted, my little B cups were nothing to write home about. Besides, weren't vampires supposed to be neck men? I looked down to see what he found so damn fascinating.

Then I realized St. James wasn't staring at my breasts but at the bloody, fist-sized hole between them.

A nightmare of memories flashed. The armed squad facing me on the balcony. The leader raising his weapon. The thud of something hitting me.

I wanted to scream. The rational part of my brain, the part I wished would shut up, pointed out with a hole of that size, both lungs were probably punctured from breast bone shrapnel and had collapsed. Therefore, I couldn't scream even if I wanted to. The rest of my brain voted to pass out and try waking up again.

St. James dropped the towels and kit, caught me before my ass hit the floor, and carried me back to the bed. After everything that had happened, his arms felt oddly comforting.

Not that I'd tell him.

"She's awake." Goth Girl stood in the doorway, carrying another armful of towels. "You still need these?"

"I do not think so. The bleeding seems to have stopped." Sitting next to me on the edge of the bed, he reached for my chest.

My sanity returned, and I slapped his hand away. "No touching without permission."

"May I?" he said with an ironic twist of his lips.

My stomach roiled at the thought of what had been done to my body. Getting shot was simply the icing on the freaking wedding cake. I tried to breathe deeply and evenly to control the nausea. Nothing's worse than the dry heaves, and I'd had quite enough of those the last couple of days. Then it dawned on me I was still breathing. I looked down at the gaping wound, which didn't appear quite so gaping.

"She's healing almost as fast as you," Tiffany offered.

"I noticed," St. James replied dryly. He raised a questioning eyebrow, and I nodded. I must have been in shock to let him touch me in such an intimate manner. As he probed the rapidly healing wound, I marveled at the gentleness of his fingertips. Too bad this wasn't one of my recent fantasies involving him. It would've been a lot more fun.

He frowned again. "Am I hurting you?"

I shook my head. All three of us watched as my skin sealed itself without even a scar. After a few minutes, the only evidence of my close encounter with a bullet was the bloody hole in the ugly ruffled shirt and the gory towels on the hardwood floor.

"Tiffany, take the towels downstairs. There are new test strips and solution in the bottom drawer next to the dishwasher. There should be enough of Miss Ridgeway's blood in the towels to sample. Then package them for destruction."

Tiffany made a disgusted face at St. James but scooped the gross linens off the floor and stomped out of the room. Then it registered with my overwrought brain she wore rubber gloves.

"Turn around," he ordered.

I didn't want to, but something about his voice made me. Maybe Bram Stoker was right about the hypnotic powers of vampires after all. It would explain the weird desire to go home when he told me to the other night in the warehouse district.

I felt a sharp tugging, and then he tossed a blood-soaked pillow onto the bed in front of me. My teeth worried the inside of my right cheek at the sight. I hadn't even felt the pillow stuck to my back. Bile swam in the back of my throat at the crusty, reddish-brown bits flaking the lime cotton. Back meant exit wound. At least I wouldn't have a bullet taking a joyride around my guts.

Once again, strong but gentle fingertips probed my skin, sliding the borrowed, and now ruined, bra out of the way. I shivered in response, but St. James didn't seem to be paying attention to my current state. How the hell could I be turned on after Mallory's mad scientists had done who knew what to me? After I'd killed two people? After I'd been shot point-blank in the freaking chest?

Warmth pooled in my belly. The familiar and much-missed heat spread through my limbs. A delicious musk filled the air. I wanted to bury my face in the smell. What was wrong with me? I'd nearly been killed tonight. No, not nearly.

She's healing almost as fast as you. Tiffany's words finally sunk through my poor overloaded brain, along with those final moments in the hallway of the lab. Those *were* my final moments.

I flung myself across the king-sized bed, trying to get as far away from St. James as I could. "You changed me, didn't you?" I accused once I had my back against the opposing wall.

A farmer could have planted a garden in the deep furrows on his forehead. "Changed you into what?"

"I saw you. Right after I got shot. Y-y-your eyes were glowing and you had fangs." I sucked in a painful breath. "You changed me into a vampire."

"You are not a vampire. And I did not Turn you even if you were one." He actually sounded offended. It was more of a response than he gave me Thursday night at the warehouse.

"B-b-but . . ."

We both looked at my chest. When I glanced back up, I noticed he seemed to take a little more interest in my boobs this time.

"We do not know what you are. Tiffany is testing your blood to confirm my . . . suspicions." St. James tore his gaze from my partially exposed breasts and rose from the bed to shuffle through his closet. After pulling out an ebony v-neck sweater and a matching pair of drawstring cotton pants, he held them out to me and pointed to another door. God, didn't the man wear any colors?

"You can clean up in there." He smirked again, bringing out the cutest dimple in his cheek. Not that I'd tell him that either.

I scooted as close to him as I could to snatch his clothes. I jumped back into my corner as soon as I had them.

Irritation replaced the smirk on his face. "I believe there are a couple of my towels left on the linen shelf you have not ruined. Join us in the kitchen when you are finished." With his imperious proclamation, he grabbed the blood-soaked pillow and stalked out of his bedroom, slamming the door behind him.

I looked at the remains of his beautiful paisley comforter. Crossing back to the huge bed, I flipped blue and lime fabric down. The matching solid-color sheets underneath it were soaked as well. But then again, maybe blood in bed to a vampire was the equivalent of cracker crumbs for us humans.

I sobered quickly. Except I wasn't human. Not anymore. A normal human couldn't have done the things to Charlie and Nurse Ratchett I had. A normal human couldn't heal from a point-blank gunshot wound within minutes.

What the hell had I become? What had those assholes done to me?

Trying to focus on practical matters, I sucked in a breath and headed for the door Duncan had indicated. Behind it, his bathroom was some dream out of *Architectural Digest*. Marble tiles covered the floor and the steps up to a whirlpool tub that could easily fit the entire Rams cheerleading squad. Golden fixtures accented the white, cream and beige tones.

While I longed to go for a spin in his tub, I opted for a quick shower. I needed answers more than I needed a luxurious bubble bath. But even the shower was extravagant. Double shower heads with a ledge wide enough to shave comfortably. Or do other fun things.

I tossed the ruined clothes into the trashcan under his sink. Thankfully, the can had a plastic garbage bag lining it. Duncan and Tiffany must have been concerned about some kind of contamination, given the precautions they took. I climbed into the shower stall and set the water as hot as I could stand it before I leaned into the flow.

The steaming spray did nothing to halt the instant replay that wound through my brain. Too much death. Fred. Charlie the Goon. Nurse Ratchett. And I caused it all out of my stupid pride. By not letting this stupid story go. And now my stupid family was in danger. I sank down to the ledge and sobbed, my tears mixing with Los Angeles tap water.

I've been chased, hit, bitten and almost run over in my career. In my line of work, you expect the rough and tough stuff. But not having psycho scientists experiment on you. And turning into the living dead was definitely not part of the bargain. There was no way I could be alive. Was this my punishment for getting Fred squashed in the street?

By the time my skin turned pink, a proper heat-related pink not bloody-water pink, the tears had stopped. Numb, I turned off the water and dried with the one remaining fluffy white towel. Poking through the drawers of Duncan's bathroom, I found a wide-toothed comb, a hair dryer, and some extra toothbrushes.

Maybe the stress was getting to me, but I had a fit of giggles at the sight of the toothbrushes. A vampire who had toothbrushes. His bathroom looked so normal.

He looked so normal. At least until the fangs came out. I thought the fangs came out. Oh hell, I wasn't sure of anything at this point.

When I headed for the stairs to join Duncan and Tiffany, I almost felt normal myself. Normal enough to take quick peeks in the rest of the upstairs rooms. Besides the master bed and bath, there were a guest bedroom and a study. The last room, a black-walled cave plastered with Sandman and Dark Hunter posters, had to be Tiffany's. I followed the stairs down to the light at the end.

The kitchen they sat in held the same understated elegance as the rest of the townhouse. Duncan's soft murmur stopped when I appeared in the doorway. Rather than saying anything with her mouth full, Tiffany just shoved the bag of Doritos across the granite bar to me. I sat on the stool opposite of them and popped a chip in my mouth. Bless her for having my favorite junk food.

My stomach gave a gurgle of delight, and suddenly I was ravenous, shoveling chips into my mouth as fast as I could chew. I stopped when I realized Duncan and Tiffany were staring at me.

"Sorry," I mumbled. I scooted the empty bag away from me. A loud rumble filled the kitchen. Hunger clawed at my insides, making itself known rather rudely. It made sense in a warped way. I wasn't sure how many days it'd been since I'd eaten.

Tiffany grinned. "It's okay. Given your speed healing, I figured this might happen." The ringing doorbell interrupted her. "That should be our pizzas."

When she returned with eight extra-large pies with the works and a couple of 2-liter bottles of soda, I wondered who she planned to eat all of it. Turned out, it was me.

Tiffany only ate two slices, not even the whole pieces, since she had a thing against crusts. I scarfed those as well as the rest of the pizzas. Duncan settled for a glass of red wine. That's what it looked like, and I wasn't about to ask. Definitely too much information.

After eating the pizzas, a humongous belch escaped before I could slap a hand over my mouth. Duncan glared at me. Tiffany giggled at my lack of manners while I muttered an apology.

"Ignore him. If he had his way, we'd still be wearing corsets," she said.

I eyed the empty boxes and bottles and shook my head. "I've never eaten so much in my life."

"Really? I would not have guessed considering the amount of debris Tiffany described in your vehicle." Duncan's dry comment should have irritated me, but I was feeling too drowsy to care.

Tiffany leaned across the counter. "Don't let him needle you, Sam. If one of his werewolf buddies is hurt, they can go through ten pizzas in five minutes." Tiffany snapped her fingers to emphasize her point. "He can drink a gallon of blood—"

"We do not need to discuss everyone's eating habits," Duncan said. He turned his gaze back to me. "Though it is good to see you're eating like a human."

"As opposed to?"

"You can relax. You're not a vamp." Tiffany sipped her soda as she watched me.

"So if I'm not a vampire, what did they make me?"

"We don't know." She shrugged. "We just know you don't have the V-virus."

"The V-virus?"

"The virus that causes vampirism." She hopped down from the stool. "You like mint chocolate chip ice cream?"

I frowned at the abrupt change of subject. My gut burbled, but I confirmed the answer to her question anyway. "Love it."

She yanked open the freezer door on the side-by-side. Pulling out a pint carton, she yelled, "Catch!"

She would have made any Major League pitcher proud. I barely snagged the ice cream before it beaned me on the forehead.

She pulled out another carton. "She definitely has vamp reflexes though," she pointed out to Duncan as she grabbed two spoons from a drawer.

Duncan rolled his eyes. "Tiffany, please do not throw any more objects at our guest."

The man who had shoved my face into a wall coming to my defense? I had to admit he did rescue me from the mad scientists.

Tiffany shrugged and bumped the drawer closed with a black leather-clad hip. "Just testing her. I still can't believe you came out with her instead of Alex." She shoveled a huge spoonful of ice cream straight from the carton into her mouth.

He shook his head. "I have no reason to believe he is still alive. There were several were bodies—"

"Alex?" My head jerked up from my carton. "Alex Stanton?" They both stared at me with their mouths hanging open. A dribble of melted ice cream slid down Tiffany's chin.

"He's alive. At least, he was." I frowned as the thought hit me. "What day is it anyway?"

Fury flashed across Duncan's face. He reached across the bar, grabbed my arms and shook me. "Where is he?"

I yanked out of his grip. "In the goddamn labs, you idiot." I couldn't look at them. I jammed the spoon into the carton, trying desperately to ignore the guilt crowding into my soul. I had completely forgotten about the poor guy between my futile efforts to evade the firing squads and waking up here.

I twirled the spoon, making a soupy mess. "At least he was alive between Friday and Saturday, I think. Mallory's men grabbed me late Friday night." I grimaced at the memory. "Then they tried to make Alex eat me."

A very odd look flashed across Duncan's face. Almost like jealousy.

With a clatter, Tiffany's carton and spoon landed in the sink. "We've got to go back!"

"Tiffany . . ." Duncan's warning stopped the girl from diving through the back door she had wrenched open. Lights bounced off the familiar SUV in the garage behind her.

"Duncan!"

"I will go but not without a plan."

She snorted but closed the door. "I'm going with you."

"No, you are not. The stakes in this venture are unknown."

Tiffany jammed a thumb toward her chest. "I'm a full enforcer now, remember?"

"And we do not know how many of Mallory's security forces have been altered as Miss Ridgeway has been. I will not risk your life."

Her anger and defiance melted into whiny teen-ness. "I've been your backup all along in this investigation. You've got to let me come."

"I said no." He left the impression this wasn't the first time they've had this type of conversation and his answer wasn't changing any time soon.

"In case you haven't noticed, Duncan," Tiffany bit out sharply, "I'm nineteen."

"And all of your ancestors thought they knew everything at nineteen as well, which is the reason so many of them died at such an early age."

Real affection lay behind their banter. I wondered if my family would be as accepting of my new status. No. Dad would ignore the situation, Max would turn me into his next Pulitzer, and Mom? Mom would rant about how I'd never find a man and get married now because what live man would want a dead bride. And I wasn't even sure what I was. Undead?

Tiffany crossed the room and laid a hand on Duncan's arm. Pain and determination filled her huge brown eyes. "We have to get him out of there."

I couldn't think about Alex trapped in Mallory's dungeon. Not naked and filthy and starving. "Not that I'm unsympathetic or anything," I interjected, "but you still haven't told me what day it is, much less what I am now."

My smart mouth. My best defense against uncomfortable thoughts instead of vodka. God, I was becoming my mother with an alternate addiction.

"It is Sunday evening. How—" Duncan cleared his throat. "What were they doing to him?" The guilty look on his face mirrored my own feelings.

Damn, he was going to drag me into the abyss anyway. I sucked in a deep breath and twirled the spoon in the ice cream some more. They needed to know what was happening to plan a rescue, but the image of the pathetic creature Alex had become turned all eight pizzas in my stomach into a putrid mess. "They were starving him, trying to break him. That's why they threw me in the pit with him at first. When Mallory's boys dragged me out, they were shocking him with stun guns." My jaw muscles jumped at the memory and my own frustration. "For the fun of it, too."

Duncan's hands clenched into fists on the counter. If he hit the granite, I had no doubt it would crack in two.

I raised my head to meet Duncan's frustrated gaze. "Is there anyway we can contact his family?" My voice squeaked as I tried to avoid the tears threatening to spill.

Tiffany shook her head and waved a hand between herself and Duncan. "We're pretty much it."

I didn't want to know the answer to my next question, but the reporter in me asked anyway. "How long can a vampire last without—" I gulped hard. "—blood?"

"Years. The real danger is insanity after four or five months." Green eyes bore into mine. "And Alex has been missing for four months today. How did he seem?"

"Other than the atrocious b.o. and the starved dog look, he seemed okay. He's very charming."

Again, the weird jealous look appeared on Duncan's face. "Really?"

My eyes dropped to the now melted ice cream. "He wanted me to stake him before he lost control and hurt me," I whispered.

I raised my head at Duncan's sigh.

He gave me a rueful smile. "That would be Alex. Always the hero."

Tiffany's scowl remained in place. "We need to get him out of there before it's too late."

Duncan's face went sober. "We will. However, I used all the charms I set getting Miss Ridgeway out tonight."

I blinked. He didn't just say what I thought he said. "Charms? Like magic charms or Lucky Charms?"

"Magick charms," he said.

Tiffany rolled her eyes at his faraway tone and grinned at me. It was nice to know someone got my really bad joke. "He means 'magick' with a 'k'," she said. "As in the real deal, not Vegas showman crap."

Duncan rubbed a hand across his jaw before he returned his gaze to me. "And first, we need to find out what was done to Miss Ridgeway. The information may give us an edge over Mallory."

"What do you mean?" I really didn't like the gleam in his eyes.

"We know you're not a vampire, a were or a witch," Tiffany proclaimed, ticking each item off on her black-nailed fingers.

My head bobbed back and forth, looking at each of them. "Are you sure? I may not have this V-virus, but the full moon was three nights ago. What if I sprout hair and start licking myself next month?"

Tiffany chuckled. "I tested for both were and witch too. There's a particular blood enzyme each one has, and neither showed up"

"The vampire skills do concern me." Again, Duncan watched me with a thoughtful look on his face. "Especially, your recovery from being shot. You did not have a pulse for nearly five minutes."

"Yeah, but if I died, then . . ." My voice trailed off as the horror engulfed me. "Oh my God, I'm a zombie!"

"Zombies are a myth, Miss Ridgeway." Duncan rose to refill his glass from a green bottle in the fridge. He took this awful revelation way too calmly. "And I certainly have not seen you take any orders."

"Or eating any brains," Tiffany chimed in cheerily.

"Okay, smarty-pants," I shot back. "Then how come vampires are real?"

He sighed wearily, sitting back down. The rich acidic odor of wine mixed with sandalwood. "Samantha, if we fully explain the other races to you, you must promise not to repeat this to anyone."

"I promise nothing until I hear the whole story."

Duncan and Tiffany exchanged looks, obviously coming to some silent understanding between them. He took a deep drink before he started. "Weres and witches are mutated branches of humanoid evolution."

"You mean, like the X-Men?"

He gave me a confused frown.

"No," Tiffany said, waving her hand at me. "Forget all the comic book jazz." Leaning close, she continued. "Their abilities are based in scientific fact, using parts of the brain and DNA normal humans don't. Since they are close enough species-wise, they can interbreed with and pass for regular-old humans."

"And vampires?"

Duncan stared at the empty pizza boxes for a long time. While my anxiety over my condition demanded answers, I had learned long ago silence brought out far more information than pestering my interviewees.

"Vampires are, or were, human."

"Oh geez, lighten up!" Tiffany's patience had left the building. She turned to me. "Like I said before, vampirism is caused by a virus. It's a disease, except you live pretty much forever, are allergic to UV radiation, and are on a liquid diet for the rest of your life."

"It is not that simple, Tiffany." A peeved expression filled Duncan's handsome features.

An expression I wanted to kiss away. I really needed to stop treating him like

Chippendales eye-candy. I was dead. Wasn't I? It's not like we could do the mattress mambo. Could dead chicks have sex?

Tiffany spread her fingers in a defensive gesture. "I'm not saying I want your germs."

I got the impression Duncan suppressed a groan when he turned back to me. "The V-virus was the AIDS of 10,000 years ago. It can only be passed through the exchange of bodily fluids. It also leaves you sterile," he said.

The bitterness in his voice made me want to wrap my arms around him and sooth his pain. Geez, dying must have permanently killed some brain cells for mushy sentimentality to cross my mind. And understanding the cost of such a disease crossed out any desire for hanky-panky. But if I was dead, could I still get sick?

Distraction. Yeah, distraction is good. "But if you're talking about immortality, I'd think everyone would want to be infected."

"Dammit, Samantha!" He smacked the granite countertop hard enough to make Tiffany and me jump. "You are not listening to me. We may not age but we can still die. If everyone has the disease, we are talking about the extinction of the human race."

I sat back. Part of my mind was screaming, *Too much information!* But I had to ask the questions. "Someone must have figured out what was going on back then. What did they do to contain the disease?"

"The old rulers segregated the populations. At first, anyway." He grimaced and tried to rub the tension from the back of his neck. Could vampires get headaches? "Then human nature took over."

His pronouncement was so matter of fact it took a second for the horror and tragedy of the situation to dawn on me. "They were ostracized and then treated as second class citizens," I whispered. Were we doomed to make the same stupid mistakes over and over again?

He nodded. "They eventually became a nation unto themselves. The dying would approach them for relief. Others would kill them for sport. Tensions hit a boiling point and war broke out."

A holocaust. And it's always the winners who paint the picture of the losers. "That's where the stories about drinking human blood came from, isn't it?" I would have done anything to wipe the sadness from his eyes.

"Yes," he whispered. "There were those who used it as an instrument of war."

"So you really drink human blood?"

His fingers stopped their play with the goblet stem as his eyes met mine. "No, I do not." He actually sounded offended.

I couldn't let the unspoken remainder rest. "But other vampires did or still do?"

"Once in a while, we'll have a problem with a rogue, but we deal with it immediately." And permanently from the tone of his voice.

"If you're a vampire, how'd you end up as Tiffany's guardian?" I turned to her. "You are human, aren't you?"

"How did you discover Tiffany is my ward?" Duncan's frigid voice drew my attention back to him.

I shrugged. "Court records."

"Those dealing with minors are sealed." He glared at me.

I glared back at him. "What matters is if I can find this out, so can Mallory. He had his people snatch me because he thought I was working for you." Another ugly thought popped into my head. "I need to call my brother and warn him. Mallory thinks the two of you are working together to investigate him."

"Your brother?"

"He's a reporter for the *Times*. Look, I'm not sure how this all fits together, but I'm not going to let Mallory's goon squad kill him." *Too.* We all ignored that unspoken word.

Duncan snatched the portable phone off the base tucked at the wall end of the bar and handed it to me. "Be careful what you tell him."

I shot him a dirty look. "Well, duh." I punched Max's home number. The phone rang six times before I clicked it off and tried his cell number. I didn't want to think about why Max's home phone didn't roll over to voice mail. His voice on his cell's outgoing message made me close my eyes in token relief.

"Max, I don't know what you're working on, but Tyrone Mallory knows about it. Duck and cover. I'll call you when I can." I sighed in disappointment as I hit the "Off" button. I would have felt better talking to him in person. Then again, maybe not. Mallory had probably already disposed of Max's beloved Camry. Now, if only my big brother would check his messages . . .

"Why is your brother investigating Mallory?" Duncan crossed to the refrigerator and pulled out a different bottle of red stuff. He unscrewed the top, and the coppery scent confirmed my suspicion this wasn't wine.

The pizza rumbled in my stomach at the thought of having to drink it. I would suck as a vampire. *Ha-ha.* Right now, I needed an ally, and I couldn't afford to insult the one person who seemed to be on my side. Something about Duncan made me want to trust him too. I prayed he wasn't using some vamp mojo to engender that trust.

I toyed with the condensation on my glass of cola and took the plunge of faith. "One of his street sources disappeared a few weeks ago. Also, one of my co-workers mentioned something about an increase in missing persons over the last few months. Both situations sound awfully similar to your friend Alex. I'm assuming he isn't the only one of your people missing." Maybe Agnes wasn't crazy after all. Maybe she'd been mind-fucked by vampires one too many times. Maybe I was drawing the line between two wrong dots. But I really didn't think so.

Duncan said nothing for a long time. He poured the blood into a mug he'd retrieved from the cupboard and set it into the microwave. Turning back to me as his dinner heated, he crossed his arms across that broad chest. "What kind of experiments were Mallory's people performing?"

His non-answer spoke volumes. I shook my head, the frustration welling through the contents of my stomach. "How the hell should I know? You can't even tell me what they did to me."

The microwave beeped and he pulled out the mug. "If I knew, I would tell you, Samantha."

So. I was no longer "Miss Ridgeway." Maybe there was a heart beating in his undead chest.

"I do not appreciate being referred to as dead." His face expressed his irritation more clearly than his snappish tone. Something must have shown on my face because the annoyed look immediately softened. "Yes, we can read minds, but if I may be frank, you just transmitted your thoughts."

"No, I didn't."

"Yeah, you did, Sam." Tiffany's face scrunched into a scowl. "I heard you too. Accidental broadcasting is pretty common in new vampires."

"But-but-but—" *Oh god! This is not happening to me.* "You said I wasn't a vampire!"

"No, you are not." Duncan took a sip from his mug before adding, "I do not know what Mallory is up to, but before this is over, I will find out what he did to you." His eyes gleamed brighter than the overheads. "And he will pay."

Chapter 11

A full-blown Tiffany-tantrum jerked me from another nightmare. This one had Zombie Charlie scooping brains from his cracked skull and forcing me to eat them. The bedroom was still dark, even though my funky awareness said the sun was up. I glanced at the LCD clock on the nightstand through grainy eyelashes as more high-pitched shouting filtered through the air. Dealing with the teen terror seemed a great deal more palatable at eight in the morning than more godawful dreams of the two people I had killed. Even better, the siren call of coffee floated in the air.

I straightened the replacement covers on Duncan's bed. The king-sized monstrosity turned out to be a heated, self-supporting waterbed, so the plastic mattress wasn't soaked with my blood. I had to grin. No crypt, no coffin, no sleeping in native dirt. He'd shot me a dirty look when I pointed out those myths last night. The man had no sense of humor at all. It was a wonder Goth Girl hadn't committed suicide in high school.

Ugly thoughts intruded as I tucked the corners. Maybe I should have taken the couch after all. Nightmares of Nurse Ratchett and Charlie, with their heads caved in and wanting my brains to replace theirs, had interrupted my sleep every hour or so. Those alternated with the emaciated Alex apologizing as he ripped open my throat and drank me dry. At one point, I woke to Duncan rocking me and stroking my hair. I wanted him to stay.

Instead, I had punched his chest and told him to get the hell out of the room. He grunted, rose, and warned me if I ripped open his bed with my thrashing, he would drown me in it. Maybe neither of us would have been so grouchy if we weren't exhausted and I wore jammies instead of my birthday suit.

I snagged the shirt and pants Duncan had given me the night before and pulled them on. In retrospect, I should've kept them on while I had slept.

Another whiff of fresh java enticed me out of the bedroom and down the hallway. I wiped gunk out of my eyes and sighed. Unfortunately, the coffee was in the same direction as the shrieking.

Something was wrong, and not just with Tiffany. Unlike the total darkness enveloping the bedroom, sunlight streamed into the downstairs rooms. And my insides twinged like they had in Mallory Labs after I'd thrown up and before I ended in a fetal position on the staff bathroom floor. Such intense pain wasn't something I wanted to experience again. I needed food and caffeine, not necessarily in that order, then I'd be coherent enough to piece everything together.

Tiffany didn't notice me entering the kitchen. Her flushed skin offset the usual stark black and white of her appearance. Duncan leaned against the sink and watched her scene with arms crossed over his fabulous chest until he saw me. Then he rolled his eyes as if to say, *Teenagers.*

Tiffany's voice had gone hypersonic, so only every other word was comprehensible. And most of those were obscenities. ". . . and I don't need a fucking babysitter. I can take care of myself against a Normal asshole."

When she paused for a breath, I said, "Duncan's right."

They both stared at me in shock. I shrugged. "Mallory's playing for keeps, and he admitted he knows Duncan's gunning for him." I crossed to the fridge, thirst and hunger twisting my insides to the point my caffeine addiction was an afterthought. I ignored the red bottles of what could only be blood and grabbed the milk. Thank God, this was a vampire who took care of his mortal guests.

I chugged the liquid heaven, the coolness taming the beast in my gut. It took a second or two to realize I'd demolished the entire gallon. Swiping my mouth with the back of my hand, I noticed their stares, Tiffany's of disbelief and Duncan's faintly of disgust. I glanced at the empty jug in my hand, then slammed the fridge shut. "I'll pay you back for the frickin' food," I muttered.

"You're probably still healing," Tiffany stated, crossing to join me. Tantrum totally forgotten, she yanked open the freezer door, pulled out two boxes of waffles, and shoved them into my arms. "There's butter if you want it. Syrup's in the pantry." She pointed to the tiny door in the wall next to the fridge.

She turned to pull a toaster and plates out of another set of cupboards. I dumped the boxes on the counter next to her and retrieved the rest of her list as well as a jug of orange juice.

For the next five minutes, we worked like a well-oiled assembly line. Tiffany would pop the waffles into the toaster and pour juice while I pulled them out and slathered them with butter, in between gulps of steaming coffee from the mug she'd shoved into my hand. When we sat down at the bar to eat, she had two waffles on her plate. I had the other eighteen plus my third cup of coffee.

As I dumped half a bottle of syrup on my pile, I noticed Duncan, still leaning against the sink, watching me with a bemused smile. Sunlight glinted off his dark hair, leaving reddish highlights in its wake.

Sunlight. God! I can be so stupid sometimes. All of his "woe is me, I'm a vampire" speech was bullshit.

New anger worked its way through my blood. Usually I can smell BS a mile away. Why was this time an exception? Because torture and death were such beautiful new experiences, that's why.

"Feeding me breakfast is the least you can do for lying to me," I snarled. I didn't bother with the knife and fork. Rolling up the first waffle, I shoved it whole into my mouth and chomped, taking my fury out on innocent breakfast food.

He frowned as he reached for his own cup still sitting on the counter next to him. The same heavenly aroma drifted from the ceramic in his hand as the mug by my side, which should have been clue number two.

"I find your thought processes very hard to track, Samantha." He eyed me while sipping his coffee.

"You lied to me about the whole damn vampire thing, you son of a bitch."

Tiffany blinked in surprise. "What are you talking about?"

This time I used the knife, jabbing it in his direction to emphasize my point. "You're standing in daylight."

That damn eyebrow of his cocked upwards in confusion. "I beg your pardon?"

Realizing he couldn't understand me with the second waffle in my mouth, I washed it down with a swig of juice before trying again. "You're standing there in freakin' daylight, drinking coffee."

He smirked, then turned and rapped on the window behind him. "It is called UV film, darling. Keeps the dangerous rays out. And I can drink other fluids. I simply cannot eat solid foods."

I shivered despite the sarcastic inflection he put on "darling." "Sorry," I muttered, though part of me didn't believe him.

He turned back to Tiffany. "Get your things."

She threw her fork down so hard the ceramic plate cracked. "I'm not going to hide like a baby! Besides—" She waved a hand at me. "You don't know if the zombie chick here can handle sunlight any better than you."

"Hey!" Only I could give people obnoxious nicknames.

"Sorry, Sam." She whipped back to Duncan. "You're going to need me—"

Her tirade stopped in midstream as Duncan strode over to me and yanked me to my feet. "Let us find out Samantha's limitations." He hustled me to the back door and shoved me through before slamming the door. The garage didn't even have an LCD clock to break the blackness. I swallowed hard to get the remains of the fourth waffle down my tightened esophagus.

Turning round, I shook the knob and banged on the door, but it didn't budge. "Dammit! Let me back in!" What the hell was he trying to do? I pounded on the door again. "I want the rest of my waffles!"

I frowned as my eyes adjusted to the dim light, so faint I shouldn't be able to see anything at all. Small dents from my brand-new, super-human strikes shadowed the door. Reinforced steel. I'd bet my next check the townhouse windows were bulletproof just like the SUV.

With a click and a hum, the garage door inched its way upward.

Oh God! He wasn't really going to do this, was he?

Why was everyone determined to turn me into his guinea pig? The bright sliver between concrete slab and garage door widened, and new fear jittered the waffles in my stomach. What if I really was a zombie now? What if I melted in sunlight just like the shambling undead on those late, late movies? Bright yellow crawled across the floor, seeking my bare toes. Total panic ensued. I turned and grabbed for the door handle to the SUV, but the damn thing was locked. In desperation, I shook the handle, which only rocked the SUV.

Then it was too late. Sunshine blinded me, and I screamed.

"Oh for cryin' out loud. I'm cleaning it up."

I blinked sun-induced tears from my eyes. An elderly woman glared at me from the sidewalk, pooper-scooper in one hand and the leash for her poodle in the other.

The dog could have been Mr. Cuddles' twin brother. He bared his teeth and growled despite his awkward crouch. Yep, complete with the same psycho attitude.

I gave the lady and the dog a half-hearted smile. "Sorry. I locked my keys in the car," I said, waving at the SUV. "Running a little late this morning."

There was a click and whoosh behind me. I turned to find Tiffany, all teen earnestness.

"Hey, Mom, you forgot your keys." She stomped over and held out the key ring. I was so stunned I was still alive and not melting goo, I let her drop them in my palm. Glancing down, she added, "You forgot your shoes again, too." Then she flounced back through the door.

Oooooo! Goth Girl was going to pay for the "Mom" crack. Right after I decapitated St. James for his little experiment.

With a jolt and a hum, the garage door began its downward track, shutting out Old Lady with Poodle. This time when I twisted the knob, the back door opened easily.

"You two are so dead meat!"

Tiffany sat at the kitchen table, laughing so hard tears streamed down her face. The serene look on Duncan's face was even more infuriating.

He looked at the girl. "I think my experiment answers your question."

—◦—

Tiffany still protested loudly from the back seat when I pulled into the garage where Duncan had directed me. He had given me the keys to his SUV before man-handling Goth Girl into the backseat and engaging the childproof locks. She finally gave up the physical fight when he threatened to chain her. The possibility of being clapped in irons hadn't stopped the steady stream of cursing from the backseat as I drove.

On the way, I had dodged a caravan of carnies beginning to unload their trucks. Street fairs were non-existent in Beverly Hills when I was growing up. Okay, they still were non-existent, and I envied Tiffany having the opportunity to hang out here today.

The attached garage and apartment sat behind an antiques store. The same antiques store I had followed them to last Monday. I'd googled the owner, Phillippa Mann, but I hadn't turned up a whole lot on her. At least, she had a California driver's license. After the shocks of the last couple of days, what else was I getting into? Who or what would a vampire trust with his living charge?

Okay, maybe not the best turn of phrase since it seemed I was already dead. With my luck and Mann's supermodel looks, she was probably a nymph or something.

"I still don't see why I can't stay at the townhouse," Tiffany whined while we waited for the garage door to close. Her pinched face pouted in the rearview mirror.

Duncan turned in the passenger seat to glare at her. Like it really made a difference with the kid's tantrum.

"As I said before, the same reason Samantha cannot."

I really wished he'd stop repeating that. It was bad enough I couldn't get any of my own clothes and I was wearing a pair of flip-flops one of Tiffany's ex-boyfriends had abandoned at Duncan's place. It was only a matter of time before Mallory and his goons put two and two together. Then Max and my parents were goners. With the parents God knew where in Europe, I had left two more messages to call me on Max's cell voice-mail and another three at the Times, all with St. James's cell number. I still hadn't heard from him, and I didn't want to admit how much his silence worried me. Especially since his home phone just rang and rang.

And I didn't dare call Ralph and let him know where I was. No doubt, Mallory's goons had bugged the *Scoop* offices when they searched them. The less I involved my editor, the safer he would be. So I tried to blame my roiling stomach on the eighteen waffles, half pound of butter, pint of syrup, quart of juice and gallon of milk.

God, Goth Girl was right. I was a pig.

The door between the apartment and garage swung open. The tall, elegantly coiffed brunette who appeared in the opening could have passed for Tiffany's older sister. You know, the one who does everything perfectly for Mom and Dad.

I just didn't remember her glowing when I took pictures of her last week. Now, a faint sheen covered her from head to toe. And it wasn't glitter lotion.

I climbed down from the SUV, and she stuck out a hand, gold bracelets chiming.

"I'm Phillippa, Samantha. Why don't you come in?"

I changed my mind. At least one member of this insane assembly had some class. My third impression vanished as I gripped her hand. She had the handshake of a Rams linebacker.

And yes, I still rooted for them even though the traitors moved to St. Louis.

A rueful smile curved her rose-painted lips when I tried to shake the feeling back into my fingers. "Sorry, I'm so used to dealing with supernaturals I forget my own strength."

Duncan joined us with Tiffany's elbow firmly in his grasp. "As I said when I rang you, I need you to look after Tiffany."

"I don't need a fucking babysitter!"

He shook his head and shared a look with Phillippa.

She laughed and linked her arm through mine, and we followed the Deranged Duo inside. I blinked in surprise at her kitchen. If Duncan's was understated, rich-jerk elegance, Phillippa's was . . . homey. A bowl of daisies anchored the blue gingham cloth covering the table. Matching curtains framed the windows, which must have had the requisite UV film. The butcher-block pine chairs gave off the same warm glow as the cabinets. Rag rugs protected the hardwood floor next to the stove and sink. And that smell! Could it be?

Saliva filled my mouth at the delicious aroma.

"You think you can bribe me with apple pie?" Tiffany snarled. Duncan had released her, but her boot tapped out a furious rhythm.

"Phil can bribe me with homemade pie anytime!" My stomach gurgled its agreement loud enough for everyone to hear.

—◦—

One homemade apple pie and a half-gallon of vanilla ice cream later, I sighed in contentment. The tantalizing scent of the second pie was tempting, but I had wolfed enough food for this hour. Teasing on the edge of the aroma of pie though was the sharp tang of ocean. I don't know why Phil bothered with the room deodorizer when her wonderful baking did the job.

Tiffany still toyed with the fruit and ice cream sludge on her plate. Phil eyed me, curiosity etched on her face.

"May I ask you a question?"

"Only if I can ask you some questions in return."

She smiled. "Fair enough. Did you eat like this before you died?"

My warm fuzzies evaporated at the reminder of my new status, but before I could answer, Tiffany chimed in.

"Oh God, Phil! You should see her car! She's got—"

"Thanks. Tiff." The look I shot her would have withered an ordinary person. Instead, she just shrugged and glared in return.

I turned back to Phil. "I admit my eating habits weren't the greatest, but I didn't eat as much as I have in the last twenty-four hours."

Tiffany opened her mouth.

"Bring up the brains, and you'll join me," I growled.

She shut her mouth and returned to poking at her pie.

The rest of what Phil said sank into my sugar-loaded brain, and I looked at her again. "What makes you think I'm dead?"

Her lips pressed into a thin line before she answered. "You don't look right." Her attention shifted to Duncan. "Have you called—"

He nodded. The way their faces twitched some kind of communication was going on.

It confirmed my suspicion that she wasn't human, so I interrupted what was obviously a rude conversation about me. I couldn't say it was behind my back. "My turn. What are you? You're not a vamp, so how'd you get hooked up with these two?"

Her eyebrow flicked upward and a faint smile tilted the corners of her mouth. "My. You're even more direct and to the point than Tiffany, aren't you?" She took a sip of her tea. "To answer your question, I would be considered a demigoddess."

Okay, that's not something I heard every day. My brain took a couple of seconds to process the new tidbit.

"But she was raised by Amazons," Tiffany piped in.

Ignoring Goth Girl, I tried to puzzle out Phil's real meaning. "So what you're saying is . . ."

She sighed, and said, "An Olympian was the sperm donor. Let's leave it at that."

"But—" I started.

Duncan's expression turned from irritated to downright pissy. "I did not bring you here to interrogate my friend."

"Really?" I shot him a nasty smile. "Friend? Or girlfriend?"

The comment was catty even for me. Vampires may not be able to turn red in the face, but his skin climbed towards a satisfying pink.

Phil, on the other hand, smirked behind her cup of black pekoe. "Amazing. Finally, someone has been born who can perturb the imperturbable Duncan St. James."

"So how long have you been seeing jerk-off here?" I aimed a thumb in his direction.

"You can relax, Sam. We're not dating, and I wouldn't dream of poaching on your territory."

"I knew you had better taste tha—" Her words smacked me in the head. "Hey, wait a minute!"

"Sam and Duncan sitting in the tree," Tiffany sang.

I raised my fork in a stabbing motion, and she stopped. I turned back to Phil. "Sorry, it's just when you were looking at him the other night . . ."

Amusement flashed in her eyes. "So you're the one," she said, then chuckled.

"What do you mean, I'm 'the one'?"

"The one who's been running background checks on us lately." A manicured finger stroked her cheek as she contemplated me.

"She was checking out Duncan because of the whole thing with Jessie's kidnapping," Tiffany chimed in.

A fine, perfectly sculpted eyebrow lifted on Phil's forehead. "You're a reporter?"

"Tabloid," Tiffany and Duncan said at the same time.

Their condescension irked me. "You say that like it's a bad thing. Do you know how many stories we beat the conventional press to?" I turned back to Phil and jerked a thumb in Duncan's general direction. "Seriously, how did you get mixed up with these two?"

Phil regarded me for a long time. So long I didn't think she'd offer anything else until she gave Tiffany a fond look. "After Tiffany's parents died, Duncan needed a daylight assistant so I volunteered to help raise her." She laughed again. "It was hard for him to attend parent-teacher conferences. And there were a lot."

I propped my elbows on the table, rested my chin in the palms, and regarded Duncan. "So she's not just your ward, is she?"

"Our relationship is none of your business," he bit out, fists clenched at his sides.

A horrible suspicion rolled out of my mouth before I could stop it. "Oh God, you didn't kill her parents and steal her, did you?"

Duncan's jaw dropped and his gorgeous eyes bulged. He looked on the verge of stroking out.

"Actually, she is his niece." Chestnut wisps artfully floated as Phil nodded her head. "She would be Duncan's—" Her eyes rolled toward the ceiling and her index finger tapped her cheek as she silently counted. "Is it fifteen or sixteen generations?"

"Sixteen," Tiffany mumbled around a mouthful of pie cream mush.

Green eyes flared with anger as Duncan fumed silently and jammed his fists into his coat pockets.

I, on the other hand, was impressed and gazed at Tiffany. "You can trace your ancestry back that far?"

Tiffany swallowed and shrugged. "Duncan's sister, Margaret, was my fourteenth great-grandmother on my mom's side."

His eyes went neon. "She doesn't need to know our family history."

"You didn't have a problem spilling history last night," Tiffany muttered.

He shot a furious look at her. She ignored him and shoveled more mush into her mouth.

Phil laid a hand on mine. "Never mind him. He's very touchy about family since Tiffany is the last survivor of Margaret's descendants."

Pain warred with irritation in Duncan's deep green eyes. I understood now why he was so protective of Goth Girl.

Before either Phil or Tiffany could say more, Duncan wrapped a huge palm around my wrist and yanked me from my chair. "I will ring you when I know more," he barked over his shoulder, and he shoved me into a garage for the second time that morning.

I yanked out of his grip. "What the hell is your problem!"

"I don't appreciate you invading my family's privacy," he shot back.

"You didn't have to bring me here!"

"No, I should have left you at the labs instead of saving your arse!"

Under the faint overhead garage light, I could see the muscle in his jaw tic.

He was right. As much as it galled me, I needed him more than he needed me right now. I swallowed the bile in my throat along with a huge helping of pride.

"You're right. I didn't say 'thank you' last night." I stuck out my hand. "So, thanks."

He stared at my outstretched hand like it was a rattler. After a couple of tense seconds, he reached for it. But instead of returning my shake, he drew my hand to his lips. The gesture was so old-fashioned and so . . . intimate I couldn't breathe. The brush of his lips across the back of my hand sent tingles through my body.

"My apologies as well, Samantha. I should not expect you to act contrary to your nature."

My system was so electrified it took a moment for his comment to register. "What do you mean by my 'nature'?"

He didn't answer. Instead he chuckled then crossed to the passenger side of the SUV and climbed in.

Irritated, I fished the keys out of my pocket and jerked open the driver's door. "By the way, St. James, join the twenty-first century! It's 'ass,' not 'arse'!"

Chapter 12

Duncan's directions fed us to the underground parking garage of Good Samaritan Hospital, his only words the entire trip. He wouldn't tell me why we drove here. I didn't think the argument in Phillippa Mann's garage was such a big deal despite his Neanderthal attitude. Maybe he liked being the strong, silent jerk. Maybe he was dragging this out to torture me. Maybe he was pissed about babysitting me.

He was out of the passenger seat before I shifted into "Park." I jumped out of the SUV and slammed the door shut. The eerie echo sent a shiver up my spine. I raced to keep up with him as he headed for the elevator. Other than his crack at my expense at Phil's, his foul mood permeated the ride over and spoiled my sugar-induced high.

"Wait a minute. Where are we going?" I wasn't puffing as I had when I chased after him a few nights ago. What the hell had Mallory's people done to me? Not that I was complaining.

"You have an appointment with Dr. Zachary this morning." Once inside, he jabbed the buttons for the private offices on the tenth floor. I resisted the urge to whistle. His Dr. Zachary must be damn successful to afford the rent here.

"What's a regular MD going to tell me?" I peered up at his face, but his stoic façade remained fixed on the elevator doors.

"Dr. Zachary specializes in treating supernaturals."

Interesting. His malpractice probably consisted of "don't screw up, and we won't eat you."

It didn't help I'd rather go another round with Mel Gibson's Dobermans than endure an exam. My gaze dropped back to my reflection in the hyper-polished stainless steel doors. I didn't look any different.

Well, maybe a little scared. Then I got pissed at the wussy woman looking back at me, someone who needed to hold her mommy's hand while getting a shot. The mom who worried I'd somehow damage her nail polish if she held me.

No, damn it! I've been taking care of myself for a long time. I could handle this too. The determined look of my reflection made me feel marginally better.

As we rose upward, Duncan's fists clenched and released in a rhythm, like he considered throttling someone. Probably me. He would have rescued his friend last night if the alarm hadn't been triggered over my escape. I couldn't stand the silent treatment any longer.

"Why don't you just get it over with?"

He started at the sound of my voice, as if he had forgotten I was there. "I beg your pardon?"

"Just kill me and get it over with."

"What the devil are you talking about?"

Fine. Pretend to be shocked, you pretentious SOB.

I turned to face him, itching for some throttle-action of my own. "That's why we're here isn't it? So you can figure out what they did to me? So why don't you just kill me and do the autopsy, and then neither of us will feel guilty about leaving Alex behind?" My voice ended with a quiver, but I didn't take my eyes from his face.

Neither of us breathed at the ugly truth shimmering in the air. His eyes turned to liquid emeralds, his pain a tangible thing sucking the oxygen out of the tiny space.

The elevator doors slid open, and I could breathe again.

"We're here," he mumbled, his eyes turning from mine. For once, he guided me with a gentle hand at the small of my back instead of yanking me by the arm. "Suite 1050."

Great. A man over four hundred who still couldn't deal with his feelings.

I blinked away furious tears as we went into the office, not sure why I expected him to be different. Maybe I harbored secret Cinderella fantasies since he did rescue me. Not that I would admit it to him. There's something inherently sexy in a man who can carry you. Especially if you're not Emmanuel Lewis or one of the Olsen twins.

Inside, I decided I'd have to reassess Dr. Zachary's net worth. Crappy, industrial mauve dominated the front office with a darker version of the color pretending to be the carpet. Holiday Inn starving-artist-sale landscapes decorated the walls.

One other person sat in the waiting room, an average-looking man who lounged on the couch. Lank brown hair fell across his face while he flipped through a magazine.

Average except the overabundance of musky aftershave smacking me from fifteen paces. I bit my tongue. One of my New Year's resolutions had been to refrain from commenting on other people's hygiene.

I'd already broken the other eleven resolutions.

I followed Duncan to the receptionist's window. As he spoke with the woman behind the counter, the hairs on the back of my neck rose. I eased a look over my shoulder. Mr. Average stared back with a confused look on his face. And then, I would have sworn, he sniffed me.

Right. Like he could talk. How could he possibly smell me over his aftershave? And I'd taken another shower this morning.

Duncan wrapped a large hand around my bicep and tugged me to where the receptionist held a different door open. A glimpse revealed a hallway, which probably led to exam rooms and offices. I glanced back. Mr. Average still stared at me with nostrils flared. As if I didn't have enough problems with creepazoids over the last few days. Though I had to admit, he seemed more curious, and slightly less threatening than Heckyll and Jeckyll.

The receptionist ushered us into an exam room. "Dr. Zachary will be with you in a moment, Mr. St. James." I knew the door only clicked shut, but to me, it sounded like a massive slam of doom.

Panic flared in the pit of my stomach as I took in the table and instruments. I backed into Duncan's chest. He murmured incomprehensible words in my ear. His voice disappeared along with all oxygen in the room. My heart thudded a terrible rhythm. Any second, the little pump would explode in my chest.

"I can't do this," I whispered. Images flew past my eyes, blood roared in my ears, and remembered pain bloomed in the rest of my body. Then mercifully, everything went black.

———•———

A god-awful smell interrupted my fluffy, warm grayness. I swiped at the offending aroma near my nose and connected with someone's skin. Regular human temperature skin, not Duncan's coolness.

"She's coming around."

I didn't recognize the voice, but once the ammonia odor disappeared, I inhaled the comforting scent of sandalwood and decided to risk a peek.

The woman kneeling next to me had an exotic look about her. Olive skin complemented her warm brown eyes and luxurious black hair swept into a loose bun on her head. She held my wrist in a loose grip.

I snatched my arm back at the sight of her white lab coat. Inching away from her failed because of Duncan's tight hold on me.

"Relax, darling. Let Bebe make sure you are all right."

Instead of reaching for me again, the woman held out her hand, a look of compassion and patience on her face. The kind of doctor who was great with screaming kids. "I just want to check your pulse. That's all, Samantha."

If Duncan trusted her, she couldn't be one of the bad guys. Since when had my opinion of him changed?

Since he dragged my bullet-riddled ass out of Mallory Labs. After a moment, I laid my hand in hers.

"Her pulse is fifty but strong." She graced me with a smile that, if I were a guy, would have made my toes curl. "Her aura is another matter."

"Huh?" I knew I was a little foggy, but did she actually say "aura"?

She shook her head in puzzlement. "I want to do a full work-up."

Duncan stood and, with no effort, lifted me to the exam table. I stiffened, every cell in my body screaming to fight.

The woman pulled a sachet out of her pocket and held it out to me. Another soft smile. "Inhale this."

Wariness prevented me from taking it. I'd had more than enough of doctors in the last few days, even if she was a friend of Duncan's. And why were all of his friends women? Gorgeous women. Didn't he have any guy friends? Oh god, was he gay? Had I been making a fool of myself over someone who would never take the slightest interest in my gender, much less me?

The doctor's voice dragged me back to my current dilemma. "It contains lavender and eucalyptus leaves, natural relaxants. Nothing more, Samantha." When I didn't take the cloth bag, she laid it next to me. "If you change your mind." Again, she graced me with a smile meant to calm children and crazy people.

"Samantha, this is Dr. Bebe Zachary." Mr. Impeccable Manners decided to speak up.

"You didn't bother to tell me she was a 'she.'" I couldn't stop my cattiness from spitting out a hairball.

"I thought you were a, what is the term?" His arrogant smirk covered his face again. "Ah, yes. 'Liberated woman.'"

"Oh, fuck off!"

Dr. Zachary tried to smother her own grin as she wrapped a blood pressure cuff around my arm. "Don't let Duncan egg you, Samantha."

"It's Sam." I couldn't stop the automatic correction, but somehow I felt a little more at ease with the good doctor. She relaxed noticeably as well.

"From what Duncan's told me, you're probably suffering from post-traumatic stress. I believe that's why you fainted."

"Oh, really. What else did he tell you?" Sarcasm laced my voice.

She laid a gentle hand on my arm. "Sam, I'm here to help you, but you're free to leave if you want."

Embarrassment hit me. I hated going to my own doctor. And I needed this lady's help. I couldn't exactly go to Dr. Brown and say, "Hey, I think I died last night. Can you explain why I'm still running around?" I nodded my consent.

Dr. Zachary bustled through the rest of her exam, checking temperature, heart, lungs, ears, eyes, nose, throat, and even reflexes. Like any other physician, she kept making "hmmmm" sounds until I was about to go batty.

"Well?" I jumped when Duncan said it at the same time as me.

"Sam, I'd like to take a blood sample." Her gaze flicked to Duncan before returning to mine.

Unease crawled up my spine. "Why?"

"You already suspect what I'm about to tell you." She took a deep breath and exhaled slowly before continuing. "By all rights, you should be dead. Your pulse is too slow, your blood pressure too low. And your aura—"

"Why the hell do you keep bringing up my aura? What the hell are you? A witchdoctor?"

She pursed her lips but amusement lit up her eyes. "Actually, I am a witch as well as a licensed physician."

"Oh." Why not? I've already run into mad scientists, vampires, and a goddess in the last three days. "I suppose the guy in your waiting room is a werewolf."

Surprise registered on her face. "Yes, he is." Her expression morphed into confusion. "How did you know?"

I had to give her credit for not lying to me. "His smell. At first I thought it was too much aftershave, but it reminded me of Mr. Cuddles before a trip to the groomers."

"Mr. Cuddles?" No mistaking the humor in Duncan's voice.

I glared at him. "My mom's toy poodle."

"And you normally sniff your mother's dog?"

I so wasn't going there. Ignoring him, I returned my attention to Dr. Zachary. "So what about my aura?"

For the first time, she truly looked uncomfortable. Her face held the expression all doctors get when they don't want to tell you the really bad news.

"It's black."

"And black means?" Was she fidgeting?

Her eyes couldn't meet mine any longer. "Ultimate evil."

"Or?" I prompted.

"Death."

It was relief to hear someone else say it out loud. Well, whisper it out loud any-way. "Okay, I think we can all agree I'm not Darth Vader."

She sagged as she realized I wasn't going to spaz out on her. "No, I don't think so either."

"I would have to disagree."

We both turned to glare at Duncan.

I returned my attention to the sane person in the room. "So we know I can't be cured," I said, deciding to ignore the vampire standing next to me again. I can deal with this. "What's the best course of action, Doc?"

"I'm still not sure what's going on. As I said, I'd like to take a blood sample, and—" She paused again, the supremely uncomfortable look plastered on her face.

She was getting on my last undead nerve. "Come on, Doc, spit it out."

"I'd also like to cast a spell to detect any magickal residue."

Maybe I'd been playing in "freaky" world a little too long. Dr. Zachary's words didn't even faze me. Instead, I nodded. "Sure. Whatever you need to do."

My courage didn't last though. I flinched at the sight of the needle she pulled out, anxiety setting my nerves on end. It was all I could do not to jump down from the table and run screaming for the Hollywood hills.

"Hold my hand, Samantha."

I screwed my eyes shut and clung to Duncan's words, and his hand, like a baby. If it had been anyone else, I would have crushed his bones to powder in the time it took her to extract five vials of blood.

Then I remembered whose hand held mine. More like what held my hand. I looked up at Duncan when she was done. "This isn't making you hungry, is it?"

"Unlike you, I had a sufficiently satisfying breakfast," he said, but he gave me a reassuring squeeze.

Dr. Zachary's spell was a lot easier to deal with than the blood samples she took. She prodded Duncan out the door. His protest at leaving sent a tremor of warmth through me. I just wished it had more to do with me than the fact I was his enemy's science project.

The doc flipped off the lights. Somehow, despite the darkness, I could still see the doctor. A faint yellow glow seemed to light her from within, not as bright as Phil's glitter, but obvious without the fluorescents.

A fruity smell tinged with flowers and spice filled the room and teased my memory. The doc's perfume or lotion was a hell of a lot more tolerable than the werewolf in the lobby. Maybe the heavy musk was a turn-on for lady werewolves.

She muttered a few words under her breath, and the glow flared. The thick, acrid smell of ozone filled the exam room. Tendrils of energy flowed from Bebe to wrap around and embrace my body. It tingled but didn't hurt.

The eerie part was I could see the doc's golden yellow light dance, meld, and then get swallowed by the nothingness surrounding me. The scene reminded me of a documentary I saw on the Discovery Channel, where the black hole ate a neighboring star.

Finally the remaining tendrils pulled back into her. She walked over to flick the lights back on. Her hand trembled as she held herself against the wall momentarily. Then she seemed to collect herself and called Duncan back in.

"Well?"

Geez, could this man do anything besides growl? When he wasn't making fun of me, that was.

"Let's go into my office." She gave us both a shaky smile. "I could use a drink."

Chapter 13

Dr. Zachary disappeared for a good fifteen minutes after she escorted us to her personal office. Duncan paced, but I sat hypnotized by the clown fish dancing inside the doc's aquarium. I didn't know why he was so worried. Okay, so he had an incurable disease. I was . . .

Oh hell. I didn't think the good doctor knew any more than I did.

She strode back into the office, closed and locked the door. A quick rummage through her desk produced shot glasses and a bottle of whiskey. After she handed Duncan and me a full glass each, she downed her own in one gulp, refilled it, then plunked the bottle of Jack Daniels on her desk within easy reach. Sensible shoes flew across the room before her stocking feet plopped on top of the desk beside Jack.

"It's nanites keeping you alive."

"Huh?" I blurted. It's a bad day when I can't even think of a follow-up question. I set my untouched glass on the desk before I dropped it in my addled state.

She sighed and sipped her drink. "If you can call it that. What I don't know is if the nanites are responsible for your death or are keeping your body functioning after you were shot." Duncan must have filled her in on the details of our little adventure last night.

"What the bloody hell is a 'nanite'?" At least Duncan looked as confused as I felt.

"It's a microscopic machine. In theory, they're meant for repair work on the cellular level."

The skin around my eyes tightened. "What do you mean, 'in theory'?"

She took another sip of whiskey before she answered. "Until today, I thought such a level of robotics and medicine were only that. A theory."

"You mean, there's little robots running around inside of me? That's why I'm alive?"

She winced and rubbed her temple like a bad migraine had started. "Something to that effect. I've sent your blood down for DNA sequencing."

"Huh?" God, I never liked science classes as it was, but she was talking way over my head.

"So you believe these machines are repairing Sam's body, not magick or the V-virus," Duncan said.

She nodded.

I was glad someone else was there to carry the conversation. The thought of things crawling around inside of me made my skin, well, crawl.

"But I'm dead, right?"

She leveled a no-nonsense look at me. And it wasn't as supportive as the pantyhose by the same name. "You saw what happened in the exam room when I cast the spell, Sam. If you were still Normal, you wouldn't have been able to see what I did."

I could hear the capital "N" in her words. Normal. As in an average, everyday normal human being. "How d-did you know I could—"

"The touching of our auras created a low level empathic bond. I felt what you knew, and you knew your aura was swallowing mine."

My throat convulsed in a painful motion. "I didn't mean to."

"I know." She smiled, the wry one of someone faced with an impossibility that had reared up and slapped her in the face. "But by magickal standards, you are dead."

"B-b-but I feel fine!"

"Except?" I didn't like the look on her face.

"Except what?" Then my stomach gurgled. Rather loudly.

"You told Phil you do not normally eat the amount you have in the last twelve hours," Duncan prompted.

Having a gorgeous guy notice my eating habits was not improving my day.

"Yeah, but I've been doing other things I don't normally do," I retorted. "Like, oh, I don't know, getting kidnapped, tortured, starved, experimented on, and shot!"

"Duncan told me about your gunshot wound. With your permission, I'd like to run some more tests, Sam. I'm not sure what the nanites are doing to you. Definitely accelerating your body's ability to heal, but I believe they may also be rewriting your genetic code."

"Huh?" I definitely needed better dialogue for this insane B-movie I was trapped in.

She set her glass down. Her elbows traded places with her toes as she leaned over the desk to regard me.

"You're not human any more, Sam. The problem is I don't know what you're becoming."

"Other than a zombie, you mean."

"You're not a zombie, Sam."

I waved my hand to shoo away her lame attempt to console me. "I know, I know." I rolled my eyes. "Duncan already told me they aren't real."

She shrugged. "According to my grandmothers, zombies were just stories used to scare children. It may be possible in theory, but a zombie would just be a magickally animated corpse. It wouldn't have a will of its own, much less a personality."

"Yeah, and you just told me nanites were only a 'theory.'" My fingers made quotation marks in the air. I clenched my eyes shut as a new *Fear Factor* stunt passed through my head—eat the zombie before it eats you.

"Oh, she has plenty of will and personality, all right," Duncan muttered next to me.

My eyes popped open, and I rammed a fist into his shoulder.

"Stop hitting me, woman."

"What? Your damn sixteenth century manners make you too good to hit a girl?" I really needed to hit something. Anything. I also knew I couldn't really hurt Duncan.

Unlike Nurse Ratchett and Charlie.

I shoved that thought back into its deep, dark hole.

I must have pushed Duncan too far. An evil grin spread across his face. "I would not strike a human girl."

He was teasing, but his comment was the camel's last straw. Next thing I knew, heavy sobs racked my chest. And like most guys, Super Vampire didn't know what to do with a crying chick. Even a dead one.

Dr. Zachary came around her desk with a box of tissues. She wrapped an arm around my shoulders and brushed damp hair out of my face as my sobs turned to hiccups. "It's a lot to deal with, I know, Sam. I'll do what I can to help."

She turned to Duncan while I awkwardly blew my nose one-handed. "I'll notify Caesar. The Council needs to know what Mallory's up to now that we have evidence. It would be best if you take Tiffany with you. Do you have a safehouse in mind?"

He nodded. I noticed why I had trouble holding the kleenex. His fingers were wrapped around the ones not clinging to the soggy tissue.

"Who's Caesar?" I asked.

"My, um, boyfriend." Dr. Zachary gave me a very big grin. "I guess it would be the best way to describe him."

"I will call him once we are settled," Duncan stated, as if his decision were the only one.

They both rose. Since he still had my hand, I had no choice but to follow.

Dr. Zachary hugged me, then gave Duncan a kiss on the cheek. "Be careful."

"Wait a sec." I yanked on Duncan's hand to stop him. Despite the madness, I had finally recognized the doc's perfume. "I've got to ask. Where did you get your secret stash of Peach Hyacinth?"

"I beg your pardon?"

"Victoria's Secret Peach Hyacinth. Where'd you find it? I love that lotion, and I was royally pissed when they discontinued it."

She shook her head. "I'm not wearing any lotion from Vicky's."

"Oh." I shrugged. "Sorry. My bad." Maybe the fruit, flower and spice scent she had was her normal odor, similar to the werewolf in her waiting room. Giving up on figuring out my over-sensitized nose, I let Duncan drag me out of her office.

We were in the elevator before I realized I had no more answers than before we came. If the doc was right and I was turning into something else, what the hell was I turning into? I shivered at the thought.

Duncan wrapped a large arm around me and pulled me close. I snuggled into his hard chest covered by a soft, gray sweater, hanging on to what comfort I had.

My stomach growled like crazy and my head ached by the time we reached his SUV. I pulled his keys out and handed them to him. "Would you mind driving? I just don't think I can deal right now."

As he stared at the keys, pink flared on his neck and ears. He handed them back. "I am sorry. I cannot."

"Cannot? Look I know you didn't bother to get a freakin' driver's license in the U.S. But c'mon! Stay within the speed limit and no one will be the wiser."

His face glowed neon bright compared to the dank concrete around us. "I mean, I do not know how."

"How can you be over four hundred and not know how to drive a freakin' car!"

His brow furrowed. "How do you know my age?"

"Quit changing the subject!"

"I am quite serious."

I took a very deep breath and ticked off one to ten, first in Latin, then in Japanese. "Because I can count, you moron. If Tiffany's the sixteenth generation from your sister, and there's roughly twenty-five years per generation, that's about four centuries. Let me guess. They didn't teach girls math in your day?"

That smile of his would be my undoing. It made me tingle all the way down to my toes.

"There were other things for women to learn in my day."

"Like cooking and cleaning?" I sneered.

He took a step closer, his thighs pressing against mine. He bent, his lips brushing my ear. "Serving their men," he whispered.

His voice felt like the best café mocha flowing across my body. Deep, dark, and oh, so rich. Maybe I wasn't quite so dead after all if I could feel this want. That was it. I wanted Duncan St. James. And I could never have him.

He stepped back, and regret dulled his eyes. He knew it too.

My stomach protested its emptiness. So loudly, the noise echoed off the low ceiling and support pillars.

Our shared laughter broke the tension. I gave him a playful shove.

"I need food. And clothes. If I'm driving, you're buying."

— • —

We headed for Arco Plaza. Well, City National Plaza, but I still had a hard time thinking of it by its new name. It wasn't the Beverly Center, but the underground shopping center in the middle of downtown was the safest place I could think of for both of us. I didn't relish a Mallory goon squad finding us in broad daylight, and I had to assume his people were looking for me. Billionaires don't become billionaires by letting their investments walk away. I hated to admit Duncan was right, but Mallory's goons probably watched or had wiretaps on all of our contacts. Odds were Mallory and his people thought I was stupid enough to be holed up somewhere, not cruising the Food Court with worker bees and the handful of kids skipping school.

After five Big Macs, two Mexican pizzas, and a 44-ounce root beer float, I felt satiated enough to shop. Late afternoon on a Monday meant we had most of the stores to ourselves. I figured I might be on the lam for a while so I kept to the practical—jeans, t-shirts, and pajamas. I did splurge on lingerie. Somehow, I resisted the urge to model those purchases for Duncan.

Once I had shoes and some cotton ankle-hi's, we headed back for the garage by unspoken agreement. Like last night, I knew it was close to sunset, and I had a feeling he knew too. But then, night came earlier in January. I sighed in comfort as I wriggled my toes in the clean socks and new Nikes. I slurped my extra-large chocolate shake while we walked back to the garage.

Duncan had paid for everything since my purse was long gone, and he had carried shopping bags without protest. When I asked him why, he shrugged. "You needed something to wear. Besides—" The evil grin was back. "I do not think I can resist last night's sleeping attire again."

Tingles skittered across my skin at his look. "You didn't have to come in and check on me." I had been naked and in his bed last night. It would have been so easy . . .

No, I needed distance from him before the naughty thought train continued. Except its absence left room for the uglier images I'd been trying to suppress all day. No, dammit! I was not letting Ratchett and Charlie back into my head.

I pressed the key fob and was awarded with an obnoxious beep that echoed between the forest of concrete pillars. Trying not to look at Duncan, I yanked the door open and pulled myself into the driver's seat.

His smile faded, replaced by a sober look. He tossed my bags in the back before rounding the SUV to climb into the seat next to me. He laid his hand on mine before I could turn the key.

"Sam—" He stared out the windshield, suddenly lost in another time and place, before he turned back to me. Bleakness seared its way into my soul at his gaze. "Killing someone is never an easy thing to live with, even if it was in self-defense."

I had managed not to think about last night for the last three seconds, but the bozo had to shatter my self-imposed blindness. Apparently, he wasn't as blind as I pretended to be. Tears welled in my eyes, visions of a sightless Nurse Ratchett swimming in the blurriness. "You didn't see them," I whispered, then shook my head in a vain attempt to erase the memory.

"They would have destroyed you." His thumb stroked my skin.

Anguish, guilt, desire, and regret mixed a strange concoction in me. I wanted to fall weeping into Duncan's arms. I wanted to erase the weekend from history. I wanted to kill the assholes who had turned my life, or death, upside down. I wanted a chance to be with a cute guy I had known less than twenty-four hours.

Except I wasn't getting any wishes fulfilled in this Rod Serling fairy tale.

"We need to get back to Tiffany and Phil." I pulled my hand from his, wiped away the couple of tears trickling down my cheek and started the SUV. Ignoring my feelings for the immediate danger of Mallory seemed the better option than pretending there could be something between Duncan and me.

Purple and pink clouds trailed between downtown high rises as I pulled out of the parking garage. We merged with rush hour traffic, folks on their way home to their regular lives. It was a beautiful sight, showing just how much my undead life sucked.

Chapter 14

Both night and the street fair were in full swing when we reached Phil's eclectic neighborhood. Between the street closures and the copious crowd, I had to park twelve blocks from her shop. Tiny white Christmas lights cocooned the trunks of palm trees while strands of larger, multi-colored bulbs swayed over the crowds. Hopped up on cotton candy and soda, kids ran screaming up and down the brightly lit streets, their parents trailing behind. Definitely not your typical LA scene-and-be-seen.

The delicious smell of popcorn wafted by on the chilly evening air. My stomach grumbled in answer.

Duncan chuckled and bought three corn dogs for me at the closest stand before we continued. We could have been like any other couple strolling up and down the carnival. I sighed as I sucked the last bit of bread off my last stick. This could have been a great first date.

Except for the zombie thing.

Teens across the way showed off for their girlfriends, trying to knock over milk bottles with softballs while the barker mocked them. Duncan grabbed my hand, tugging me through the crowd towards the game, one of many lining the street. Out of sheer curiosity, I let him. He shelled out the bucks for an entire bucket of balls and made a show of shoving up his sweater sleeves, playing to the crowd around us.

Maybe one of us was having a brain aneurysm. Yeah, he'd been affectionate with Tiffany, and to some extent Phillippa. Except for the flirtation in the shopping center parking garage, the rest of the time he'd been alternately angry or brooding. I stood watching him, trying desperately to figure out what was going on with the brand new show-off in Duncan's form-fitting sweater. Though I did notice his smile wasn't so wide as to give away his extra-sharp canines.

His first wild pitch almost took off the head of the barker. The kids broke out in hysterics while the barker glared at him.

"Turn around slowly and check out the crowd behind us."

Duncan's voice was pitched so low I knew I was the only person around us to hear him. Maybe there were advantages to these nanite things after all. I never would have been able to understand him in the controlled chaos of the midway otherwise.

His second pitch missed the milk bottles and bounced off the back canvas.

I did as he commanded, though it rankled me. I've never been good at the "obey" thing. I played the bored girlfriend and scanned the crowd. Maybe it was their designer clothing in the middle class neighborhood. Maybe it was their peculiar attention to our game from so far away. Or maybe it was strong thread of sandalwood not coming from Duncan's direction.

"The blonde and two brunettes at the sno-cone stand?" I whispered as I continued my pivot so our stalkers wouldn't notice. His vampire hearing would pick up my words despite the crowd.

He gave an imperceptible nod as he whipped a third pitch. I heard the distinctive crack of glass and bit my lip to keep from laughing. He must have taken out one of the colored light bulbs illuminating the booth. The barker swore as fragments tinkled to the concrete.

I had seen the women Duncan indicated on the sidewalk after we had parked. Damn! I had been expecting Mallory to send linebackers after us, not supermodels. I couldn't underestimate the bastard again. Assuming we got away from these gals. With my luck, they'd be some kind of super-ninja supermodels. The blonde looked familiar, but I couldn't catch the memory of where I might have seen her. Not someone I shot, but I'd seen her in someone else's work. I sauntered to Duncan's left so I could keep an eye on both him and our trio of possible assailants.

"Recognize them?"

He gave a slight shake of his head as his fourth pitch nailed the middle stack dead center and bottles crashed to the floor. The boys around us whistled and cheered. He shot me a cocky grin as he made short work of the other two stacks.

Grumbling, the barker handed Duncan the three-foot-high neon pink teddy bear my escort had chosen. Before I could make a sarcastic comment, he presented the prize to me with a flourish accompanied by catcalls from the teens.

I'd never had anyone win a prize for me, much less an obnoxiously bright stuffed animal. I was so surprised I didn't resist when he wrapped my free hand around his arm and guided me in the direction of the antique shop.

"If we've got a tail, how do you know Mallory doesn't have someone watching the shop?" I whispered.

"He probably does. Come on. We need to warn them."

He tugged my arm and picked up speed. I caught the reflection of Mallory's Angels in the shiny aluminum of a funnel cake stand. They were a block back and trying discreetly to catch up with us.

Duncan made a sharp left and yanked me into a picture booth just as another couple exited, folks dressed very similar to us. The bear disappeared from my arm and appeared in the other woman's as the flap closed behind me. I heard him tell the couple to keep it.

"Hey, I liked that bear." My harsh whisper didn't get his attention because he was already speed dialing his cell phone. He told Phil to get out of the place through the emergency exit—whatever the hell that was—and meet us where we had parked. She must not have questioned his orders because he snapped the phone shut and peered out.

"Let's go." He pulled me out and headed back the way we came.

After thirty yards, a familiar figure rose above the crowd. Heckyll might as well be wearing a sign saying, "Sadistic muscle for hire."

Panicking, I yanked Duncan between two tents, pulled his head down, and kissed him. His response was immediate. He pulled me closer and deepened the kiss, demanding and gentle at the same time.

The roar of the crowd disappeared under the thunder of blood in my head. Our tongues tangled and explored while his hands roamed my back and hips.

As much as I'd rather do some exploring of my own, I forced my hands between us and shoved. My breathing was as ragged as his as we stumbled apart. Something dangerous, alluring and very neon flared in his eyes, but I ignored the invitation and placed a finger against his lips even as I stepped closer to him.

"Behind me, next to the peanut stand. Jean jacket and black tee."

Duncan pulled his gaze from me, then nodded and frowned.

"Has he spotted us?" It felt like my heart would jump through my throat any minute.

He kept his eyes fixed on a spot behind me. "No. One of Mallory's?"

"Yeah."

We wouldn't make it back to the SUV. Jeckyll had to be nearby as well and God knew how many others were tracking us.

He grabbed my hand in a firm grip. "We will head for Phillippa's shop."

The sight of Heckyll shook me more than I wanted to admit. I didn't question Duncan's command. We rejoined the crowd meandering down the street and headed back towards the shop.

"Phil may be able to defend herself, but what about Tiffany? She's just a kid." For the first time in my life, er, death, I didn't have a problem talking and speed walking at the same time.

We dived around parents comforting a toddler screaming over a lost balloon. "They should be out of the shop by now." He smiled at me. "And Tiffany would surprise you."

"Knives tucked in her boots would not surprise me at all," I muttered.

He chuckled. "We will go out the basement same as them. Otherwise, we can make a stand there."

I glanced over my left shoulder. "Looks like we'll be making a stand. Mallory's Angels at seven o'clock. And the bitches have spotted us."

"Oh bloody hell!"

He picked up his pace, nearly bowling over the twenty-something quartet in front of us. The men shouted a few choice words in Spanish, but Duncan ignored them, intent on our destination. Sounds of the carnival faded as we turned the block. He had keys out and unlocked the door before I realized we were in front of the store.

I automatically reached for the wall, but he stopped my hand as I found the switch.

"They will see," he whispered. So I wasn't the brightest person while I was being followed. I was usually on the other end of the food chain.

Despite my enhanced vision, I stumbled over furniture as he pulled me through the dark store. We both turned as we heard the door rattle. Glass and splintered wood exploded inward. We dived for the floor.

Debris rained over me, pinging or clattering against the surrounding furniture. I didn't have time to check for injuries. Glowing yellow eyes hovered over my prone body. Brunette Number One flashed her fangs at me before seizing me by the throat and throwing me across the room. I crashed headfirst into some very heavy wood. Proverbial stars flared in my vision.

I blinked the stars away along with the birds chasing after them. A shadow stalked toward me, and I threw the first thing I grabbed. The ceramic shattered on the head of the shadow, which mumbled an unladylike curse. I just prayed I hadn't destroyed a Ming vase or something equally expensive.

I scrambled for the front of the store and yelled "Switch!" as I hit the lever. The sudden light startled the brunettes on top of Duncan. He tossed Brunette Number Two across the room before Number One hit him with a nasty uppercut.

I couldn't pay any more attention to his plight because Blondie was aiming a fist at my head. I dived and rolled as plaster crumbled above me. She pulled out her fist and a good chunk of drywall with it.

"Stake her!"

I could only spare Duncan a glance as I screamed back, "With what!"

"With wood! Oof! You bloody git!"

I wasn't sure if he meant I was the bloody git or the brunette he fought. Not that it really mattered at the moment. I avoided another punch, but Blondie's spinning kick caught me in the gut. Her second kick, aimed at my head, barely missed as I fell back. My nanite fortified lungs fought for a breath, any breath. A brass spittoon dived for my head. I rolled, and the spittoon cracked the one bit of concrete slab not covered by Persian rugs, the blow so close slivers of concrete and spittoon must have flown up my nose. The scent of metal was that strong.

My vision raked the room, but all the wood was connected to what I was sure were very valuable pieces of furniture. If it were Mom's expensive crap, I wouldn't have hesitated. Payback for all the lectures about dirt on her precious collector's items.

But Phil was a nice lady. For an Amazonian demigoddess.

I'd feel obligated to pay her back for the rest of my unnatural life, which was probably how long it would take. And I seriously doubted she'd make me any more of her wonderful pie if I trashed her store.

On the other hand, I had become attached to my own undead existence.

Scrambling to my feet, I snatched up a chair and brought it down on Blondie's head. It splintered on impact, and suddenly I had a usable stake-like leg in my hand. Without thinking twice, I jabbed the jagged end at Blondie's chest.

She knocked it out of my hand and threw another right cross at my head. This time the stars chased the little birdies when I landed on my ass with a distinct *thump*. Instinct made me roll, and a steamer trunk splintered as it crashed down where I had been.

Blondie snatched a fireplace poker, a determined look on her sculpted face. With some internal organ in my throat, I crab-crawled backwards. Her first blow missed me but shattered the glass case containing estate jewelry. Shards rained down on me, but a few cuts were the least of my problems. I scrambled to my feet and dived through the beaded curtain separating the store from the apartment.

The short hallway ended in a door. I grabbed the knob and twisted. In the bare instant my brain registered it was locked, I felt someone behind me. I jumped to the side to avoid the poker thrust at my chest. Her momentum drove the steel rod through the door. I turned to run, but the bitch grabbed me by my ponytail and yanked.

Not wanting to lose a hunk of hair, I threw myself backwards. We both crashed through the damaged door, landing in a heap of limbs and splinters on Phil's kitchen floor.

Knives! The cutlery next to the sink gave me some hope. I struggled upright, despite Blondie's kicking and scratching, and lunged for the counter.

Cold metal across my throat brought me up short. Blackness swam across my eyes and fingers clawed at the constricting steel. Blondie pressed the poker harder. My heart pounded and my lungs cried for oxygen. A miniscule crunch said my trachea wanted to give up the battle. Desperate, I racked my head back. From her muffled screech, I must have nailed her nose. Her grip loosened slightly, and I dived for the knives. She only hesitated for an instant before she tightened her hold.

My vision blurred as my air was cut off again. A wooden handle brushed my fingertips. I had no idea what I grabbed. Red and black dots flared, warning signs I was about to pass out.

I stamped down hard on Blondie's instep and was rewarded with a shriek of pain. The metal across my throat disappeared. I whirled and plunged the object I held into Blondie's chest.

Instead of a knife, the handle of a wooden spoon stuck out from between her ribs. Unlike the vamps on *Buffy*, she didn't explode into dust like I half-expected. She staggered back against the stove, her eyes wide and her mouth a perfect "O". In slow motion, the rag rug slid from beneath her and she landed in a sitting position, back propped up by the oven door.

I sighed with relief when her chest stilled and she didn't get up. Lids slid down over her glazed eyes. Thank God, I didn't have to deal a dead person looking at me. Okay, a dead vamp. The nightmares from the two humans were bad enough.

Except she didn't have the distinctive spicy wood scent I was coming to associate with vampires. She smelled more like . . . a steak knife. I took another deep whiff. The leftover apple pie made my stomach rumble.

A grunt followed by a triumphant shout from a female voice sounded from the store area. Worried, I raced back to the front.

Not that Duncan needed the help.

Unlike Blondie's quiet expiration, Brunette Number One screamed in fury as Duncan plunged half of a broken coat rack through her chest. At her partner's demise, Brunette Number Two ran for the gaping hole where the front door had been. Snatching up the other half of the coat rack, he threw it javelin-style. The force of the flying wood caught her in the back, shoved her through the doorway, and slammed her face-first into the sidewalk. Leaping over a dining table, Duncan grabbed her by the ankles and dragged her back into the store. Then he pushed an armoire, the same one I think dented my skull, across the entry.

With the shades down and the doorway blocked, no one could see the massacre from the street. I prayed the fight had been quick enough we hadn't attracted any other attention and the three dead vamps hadn't contacted any other members of the goon squad.

The godawful smell of rotten meat hit my nose. I gagged, searching for the source, and looked down next to me. Brunette Number One was melting. Literally.

Flesh and goo dripped from her bones, landing in a congealed mass on the Persian rug where she lay. I stepped away as dry heaves threatened.

"It's all right," Duncan murmured. He pulled me against him, and strong arms wrapped around me, holding me tight. I buried my head in his chest. Only to block the smell, I told myself, but I started shaking in earnest as the adrenaline from the fight phased out.

A second rush of rotten meat odor told me Brunette Number Two's body performed the same melting act. I stiffened as my stomach rebelled at the odor.

"Do you all turn to sludge when you die?" His sweater muffled my voice, but he must have heard from his rueful chuckle.

"I am afraid so. Let us go to the back," he said, steering me in the direction of the beaded curtain.

Then I remembered and muttered, "Shit."

"What's wrong?" Concern etched his face.

I gulped. "Blondie's still back there."

One of his eyebrow's rose. "You did kill her, did you not?"

I punched him in the arm. "Yes, damn it!"

He glared at me. "What have I said about hitting me, woman? Besides—" His scowl shifted to a reassuring smile that made my insides almost as gooey as the dead vamps. "If she is dead, you have nothing to concern yourself about."

"But she'll be all gross and yucky, too." I shuddered.

"Gross and yucky? This from the woman who drank an entire gallon of milk straight from the jug this morning." He rolled his eyes.

"It's not funny!" Tears threatened. I never thought myself capable of killing anyone, much less three people in twenty-four hours. Okay, two people and one vampire. Considering Blondie was just as strong as I was in my undead state, I had no doubt she was dissolving even as we spoke. My relief melted into more guilt, adding to the huge lake of it sitting in the pit of my stomach.

Duncan stroked my neck, and I had to admit it was comforting. "We must pass through the kitchen. Access to the exit is in there." His fingers drew my head up to meet his earnest gaze. "I will protect you, darling."

Ire pierced my self-disgust, and I knocked his hand away from me. "Why do you do that?"

Confusion replaced the concerned look on his face. "Do what?"

"Call me 'darling.'"

The amused glint in his eye did not amuse me one bit. "I did not realize I offended you, Samantha." I shivered at the way he drew out my name. God, I hated the way he made me feel. And I loved it too. I stomped towards the kitchen, wishing he couldn't read my mind.

He can still read your body, a little voice whispered inside me.

Not that we can do anything about that, I reminded my damned little voice.

Blondie was still intact and propped against the stove when I entered the kitchen. Something was definitely wrong.

"Why hasn't she—"

Blondie blinked. Blue eyes wide open, she looked down at the spoon sticking out of her chest. Then she and I both started screaming.

Chapter 15

"She's not dead! Why isn't she dead!" I couldn't stop shrieking the same phrases over and over. I'd practically shoved the entire long-handled utensil through her chest. Why the hell was she still moving!

Duncan tried to fend off my attempts to climb his back in my effort to get away from the not-quite-dead undead chick.

Blondie stopped screaming long enough to pull the spoon out of her. It came free with a stomach-turning *squish* and a gush of noxious-looking liquid down her silk blouse. Lucky for her, the shirt was also a noxious red. She sobbed as Duncan held the poker he had snatched off the floor in a threatening position. I stayed behind him, satisfied to peer over his shoulder as I clung to his back. He was better equipped to deal with her anyway.

"Who are you?"

She flinched at the menace in his voice.

He took a step forward. "I will not ask twice, and this—" He waved the poker at her. "—will hurt a hell of a lot more than a wooden spoon."

"S-s-sierra Mallory."

Holy shit! No wonder she seemed familiar. While researching Mallory, I had seen a picture of her with her father from six months ago at one of the many charity functions he sponsored. Even with the hole in her chest, she looked healthier now than she had in that picture. The gossip circuit held her disappearance from the blueblood social scene was due to a stint in rehab, but neither Agnes or I had found out which one.

I peered at her chest. The tiny hole from the spoon had already sealed itself. Just like the gaping wound in my chest had last night.

I gasped as the realization hit me. I had heard screaming in the lab last night. Hers.

With the chance to calm my own roiling panic, I analyzed Sierra's scent. Definitely not the sandalwood of a vamp. More like a frying pan. A just-washed, rinsed-clean Revereware frying pan. I poked Duncan's shoulder. "Does she smell like me?"

He didn't spare a glance over his shoulder, his attention on the weeping heiress. "What do you mean?"

"Metallic."

This time he looked at me. "Yes."

No wonder we couldn't confirm a rehab facility.

Sierra cried harder, spasms racking her body. Compassion waved through me along with a healthy amount of curiosity. What lunacy would possess Mallory to experiment on his own daughter? I eased around Duncan and knelt next to her.

"Samantha, are you insane?" he hissed. "She just tried to kill you."

Sympathy overrode my preservation instinct. I wrapped an arm around her, and she buried her head in my shoulder. I rocked her as Duncan stared at me in disbelief.

After a couple of minutes, Sierra's words became comprehensible. Her pleading mascara-streaked face looked up at me. "What did he do to me? Daddy said I'd be okay."

The childlike voice was not a good sign. Sierra was close to some kind of breakdown. After what the mad scientists had done to both of us, I couldn't blame her. I was pretty close myself after the last four days.

"The same thing he did to me." My whispered words didn't ease her distraught expression. I honestly didn't know what would.

She clutched my sleeves. "Help me, please," she begged. "He said I wouldn't be a monster."

"You're not," I murmured, stroking her hair. "It'll be okay." An eerie sense of deja vu hovered over me. I had mimicked exactly what Duncan had said and done after one of my many nightmares last night.

I looked up at Duncan. "We've got to help her."

Disbelief etched itself across his features. "She is the enemy."

"Not if her father did this to her," I mouthed back. Sierra's hearing would be just as good as mine, even in her state of shock. Her teeth rattled as she began shivering uncontrollably. "Duncan, would you please get us a blanket?" I said out loud.

He stalked out of the kitchen and down a side hall. I could hear muttering about New World women and lack of common sense, but he returned with a ratty patchwork quilt that saw its best days in the nineteenth century. I couldn't blame him considering the blood that stained Sierra's shirt even though the wound had healed.

I took the proffered quilt and wrapped up Sierra, then surprised myself by lifting her in my arms. Her shivering abated, but her eyes still held a glazed look as tears trickled down her cheeks.

"Where to?" I asked.

"You cannot be serious!" Duncan's eyes bulged, not to the extent of Jim Carrey's character in *The Mask*, but they bulged nonetheless.

"We can't leave her here." Some perverse need in me to help reared its head. The same one that drove me to ride in the ambulance and hold Fred's hand as he died.

"She just tried to shove a spittoon through your skull out there." He waved the poker towards the showroom before he shook it in my face.

"She goes with us, or we both stay." I prayed all my experience playing poker with Max and his buddies would pay off in this bluff. I didn't think Duncan's Elizabethan code of chivalry would allow him to abandon two helpless women, but he was pretty pissed. I wouldn't last two seconds against Mallory's people. I knew it and I knew he knew it too. Also, if I could get Sierra out of shock and away from her father, she may provide the answers I needed about our condition.

He tossed the poker across the kitchen in exasperation, smashing the bowl of daisies. Water ran off the table to splash on the floor. I clucked my tongue but refrained from saying anything further due to the murderous look in his eye. He opened the pantry and fiddled with the second shelf. The rear wall of the pantry swung backward on silent hinges. He gestured at the opening. I eased through with my load but looked back at Duncan.

"Would you grab the other pie for the ride?"

———•◦•———

My stomach gurgled loudly. Despite watching the street as I drove, I saw Duncan turn to glare at me out of the corner of my eye.

"I told you to bring the pie."

Tiffany snickered from the backseat where Sierra sat propped up between her and Phil. The heiress had passed out during our trek through the tunnel.

Phil and Tiffany had been waiting with the SUV at the tunnel's exit, which was fifteen blocks from the store in the opposite direction from where I originally parked. How they got to the vehicle and drove it back through the mob without getting caught freaked me out in itself, but given the proximity of Mallory's goons, I didn't ask any questions. Somehow, I got nominated to drive, and we rode in silence except for Duncan's terse directions.

The theme from *Buddies* jingled from behind me. In the rearview mirror's reflection Tiffany whipped out her phone. "What's up?"

Her eyes darted to Duncan, who glared over his shoulder at her.

"I dunno if I can go shopping tomorrow." A long pause while someone who sounded suspiciously like Jessie Alton prattled on about baby accessories. "Chill, cuz. Your hormones are out of control."

My attention alternated between the traffic and Tiffany's conversation. This super hearing could be invaluable to my job. I bit my bottom lip as Tiffany's caller burst into tears.

Tiffany sighed. "I know you're not supposed to go out without a special security escort, but I'm working on a case right now." Her gaze met Duncan's. "I've got to go." Another protest. "I'll tell him." A tiny click as she shut off the phone. "She wants to talk to you when you have the chance."

Duncan ignored his niece in favor of more orders. "Turn left up here."

Around the corner, I spotted a Mallory Mystery Machine facing the intersection with Jeckyll in the driver's seat, and I whipped from the turn lane back into main traffic. My brand-spanking-new zombie eyesight was barely keeping us one step ahead of the bad guys. Thankfully, I didn't cut off any vehicles by diving back into traffic, but Duncan's head hit the doorpost with a resounding *thunk* at my evasive maneuver.

"Bloody hell, woman!"

"Mallory's got your safehouse staked out, asshole."

His eyes widened, and all of us, except Sierra, looked back. No nondescript van followed, but we couldn't remain out in public much longer.

"How could they know?" Phil asked.

"The bitches read my mind," I muttered. How the hell was I ever going to hide from a bunch of freakin' vampires?

"No," Duncan drawled.

"Isn't that how Phil knew to meet us? Vampire telepathy?" I shot him a look before I flipped off the Mercedes who cut in front of us. Duncan proceeded to fill the girls in on Sierra's vampire friends who attacked us. I also noticed he didn't answer my question.

"Ahem."

He returned his attention back to me. "What?"

"Unless you want me to pull over and call Mallory myself, answer my freakin' question."

"The two we battled were dead before I told you of this condo," he said.

"What about others? What if Mallory had more than the Bitch Squad and Heckyll following us at the carnival?"

"I didn't sense anyone else, but . . ." Duncan shrugged. I wanted to smack him. How could he be that nonchalant about our continued survival?

From the reflection in the rearview mirror, Phil's brunette curls whipped as she shook her head. "Why would any rogue work for a Normal in the first place? It doesn't make sense."

"I thought a rogue was a vampire who drank human blood."

Tiffany took a little sympathy on my ignorance. "Technically, it's vamp not associated with a coven." She snorted. "And there's usually a good reason they were kicked out." There was a slight pause before she added, "A vamp might work for a Normal if he's offering a cure."

Duncan leaned over to look into the back seat. I gripped the steering wheel until my knuckles turned white when his hair brushed my cheek. "What are you talking about?" he asked.

"Think about it. From what I've seen, Sam's got all your abilities, but none of your weaknesses. What if he's offering the vamps who work for him a cure? You get to keep the cool stuff, but you can eat solids and walk in the sun again."

"Then why kidnap Alex or any of the other folks?" I piped in. I really didn't like the implications. I knew what happened to lab rats after experiments, and as far as Mallory was concerned Alex and I were his lab rats.

Duncan leaned back in his seat. "Unless the ones who are missing are folks who didn't accept his offer or are his research subjects." He reached into his pocket and muttered an oath. "My phone's missing."

"The shop during our fight?" I asked.

"Probably."

"Here's mine." Tiffany reached forward and dropped her silver box into his lap.

While he jabbed the number in, I glanced at the fuel gauge. An eighth of a tank. The way this behemoth drank gas, we would have to stop soon. And stopping meant we'd be sitting ducks.

He muttered another oath. "Caesar, call me on Tiffany's cell phone." He rattled off the number, then tried Dr. Zachary with the same result.

"Maybe they're busy getting busy." I peeked at Duncan. In the oncoming traffic's headlights, I could see face muscles twitch. "Come on, don't you have any other friends?"

"None that I would trust at this moment or would be close enough to aid us."

"You think someone on the inside of your organization is a snitch for Mallory?"

No one responded, which only confirmed my suspicions.

So Super Vamp was out of options. Now, I knew how Princess Leia felt after she made the crack about hoping to be around when Han Solo was wrong, and the Imperials were closing in on the *Falcon*. "Okay, then it's up to me to save our asses." I made a sharp right and headed west.

"Where the devil are you going?" he snapped.

I shot him a grin. "Apt description. We're heading for the Gates of Hell."

It was a serious gamble on my part, I admitted to myself as I headed towards Mom and Dad's place in Beverly Hills. Mallory knew I was with Duncan now. I hoped his obsession with capturing us blinded him from following up on Max.

Fifteen minutes later and with no tail following us, we rolled down Mom and Dad's deserted street and into the driveway. I thanked my guardian angel for the favor and punched in the six-digit code. The ornate steel gate swung open. White stone glowed in the wash of security lights as we cruised up the concrete. Much better was the fact the windows remained dark.

Thank God they stayed their extra week in Italy. I released air I didn't realize I had been holding. I wasn't sure how I'd explain things to them if they were home. I parked in the covered area behind the garage, so the SUV couldn't be seen from the gates.

We climbed out with Phil carrying the still unconscious Sierra. I was beginning to worry. Maybe the spoon to the chest did more damage to her than the bullet did to me. At least she hadn't turned into rotten meat goo in the backseat.

No one said anything as the group trailed me to the back door. A quick check of the ceramic frog in the neighboring flowerbed produced the key. I smiled at Dad's predictability. All this security and anybody could still get into the house.

A familiar beep sounded when I popped open the door. "Follow me. I'll get the alarm, and then we'll take her up to one of the guest bedrooms." The house was too quiet without Mr. Cuddles' hostile greeting. If Max really was in trouble, I hope he had sense to take the nasty little canine with him. I'd lay odds on the poodle over Mallory any day of the week.

I entered, crossed the kitchen and headed straight for the security pad in the front hallway, Phil hot on my heels with her load. I turned off the system, but something raised the hairs on the back of my neck.

Like I was being watched.

I whirled to see Max perched on the loveseat in the living room. My beloved older brother had Mom's .45 aimed at my head.

Chapter 16

This wasn't my big brother. Max would never aim a gun at someone. Anyone. But the ugly expression on his face scared the hell out of me. "Put that thing down before someone gets hurt."

Max gave a sharp shake of his head. "Sorry, Sam, I can't."

I planted my fists on my hips, trying not to show my fear. "I get kidnapped Friday night, I try to warn you Mallory knows about your investigation, and this is how you greet me." Pale yellow from the security lights outside reflected off the ugly metal in his hand. The barrel didn't waver from its focus on my forehead.

Static electricity pricked along my skin. Phil's harsh breathing contrasted with the slow, even intake by the still unconscious Sierra. *Oh god.* The last thing I needed was a demigoddess throwing lightning bolts at Max in the middle of Mom and Dad's living room.

He didn't answer for a long time, his attention flicking between me and the other two women. The switch in his attitude freaked me out. He's the one who tried to talk Mom out of buying the firearm years ago, citing endless statistics on how often handguns at home were used to kill occupants. And I was about to become one of his statistics, assuming I could be killed again. I really didn't want to test my survival capabilities from having my brains blown out.

"Well, I never thought you'd pull a Patty Hearst." His short bark of laughter sounded rough, so unlike the person I thought I knew. "You know, I was worried sick when you disappeared."

"Gee, thanks. I can tell. Now put the gun down." An ill feeling crawled through my gut. Any other time I'd have said Max was the analyzer, not a violent bone in his body. I half expected Rod Serling to step out of the shadows.

"Tell your other friend to get in here."

I didn't really want to get shot for the second time in twenty-four hours, but I wasn't about to put Tiffany in the line of fire. Maybe Goth Girl was beginning to grow on me.

Yeah, like a fungus.

"Now!" Max roared.

"I heard you the first time." The clipped British accent sounded right next to me, but I didn't dare look. "This woman needs medical attention."

Max's hand shifted so Mom's gun pointed at Duncan. "Like I'm going to believe one of Tyrone Mallory's lackeys." Max snorted to emphasize his point.

"Duncan's been investigating Mallory, too. He already thinks you two are working together." I raised both hands to where he could see them with his Normal vision. Damn. Less than a day and I was thinking like a supernatural. "You need to pool your information."

Max's attention never wavered from Duncan. "Let my sister go."

"Do you really believe your toy will work?" Duncan taunted.

"Long enough," Max countered.

Something clicked in my overstressed brain, but I was too concerned about Tiffany or Max getting hurt to analyze it.

Instead, I focused on the immediate problem. "Get. A. Clue. Snotface." I took a step forward with each word, and as I planned, the gun swung back towards me. Maybe not such a great plan after all. I clamped down on the fear spinning in my belly.

"Mallory kidnapped me because he thought I was spying on him for you." I took another step forward. "After he originally assumed I worked for Duncan." I jabbed a thumb in the general direction of the vampire behind me. "I'm not working for anybody but Ralph, so I'm getting really tired of people slamming me into walls and pointing guns at me for a story I'm not even writing."

The great thing about my new enhanced vision was I could see the doubt cross his face. Otherwise, the shadow from the partially opened drapes would have obscured my view of his ugly mug.

A familiar voice moaned behind me.

I kept my eye on the gun. "Now, Phil's going to take Sierra upstairs. She's had a very bad night." I really didn't want her to wake up with the .45 pointed at her. There was no telling what the nanite-enhanced heiress would do in her disorientation.

"Sierra?" The gun wavered. "Mallory? Here?" Nervous perspiration sparked along Max's forehead. He rose from the cushions. "What the hell did you do, Sam?"

"It's a long story. She tried to bean me with a fireplace poke—"

"Can I please put her down somewhere before you two continue your argument?" Phil asked. "She isn't exactly a featherweight."

Tiffany chose that moment to saunter through the entry to the dining room. "Hey, Sam, all I could find was cookies 'n' cream in your mom's freez—"

Startled by her appearance, Max spun to his left, his finger squeezing the trigger. Zombie speed saved Tiffany's brains from splattering across the imported hardwood floor. The shot went wild, shattering the Mikasa vase on the dining room table, as I slammed him back into the loveseat.

Awakened by the gunshot, Sierra started another round of her ear-splitting shrieks.

The living room lamps flared on, and I blinked at the sudden shock to my optic nerves. At least the same shock shut up Sierra. Thank God for Dad's kooky auto-timers.

"Give me that before someone does get shot!" I grabbed the gun away from Max and accidentally crushed the barrel in the process.

"Sam?" Raw fear shone in Max's watery gaze as his eyes flipped from me to the steel Silly Putty in my hand. "What the hell is going on?"

"Ouch! Get off of me!" Tiffany's muffled voice came from somewhere next to the china cabinet. Max and I peered over the arm of the loveseat to see Tiffany punch and kick her way free of Duncan's protective embrace from where they lay on the floor. Ice cream and chocolate cookie crumbles slid down the floral wallpaper behind them to puddle on the living room's very expensive Berber carpet.

"Mom is going to kill you," Max muttered in my ear.

———•———

After we calmed Sierra down, Tiffany and Phil cleaned up the ice cream mess the best they could, I stole a couple hundred from Mom's mad money stash to order pizza, and Max raided Dad's liquor cabinet.

I didn't question the cooler Duncan brought in from the SUV, and I sure didn't want to look in it either. He disappeared into the bathroom with it. I was thankful he didn't eat, or is that drink, in front of the rest of us. Okay, in front of me. This morning had left me a little sick as it was.

The cooler represented the one disgusting habit of your otherwise perfect boyfriend you ignore. Except I never could ignore the disgusting habits, which was probably why I didn't have a boyfriend.

And since when did Duncan graduate to possible boyfriend status? I decided to shove that thought into a deep dark hole and cover it with quick-drying cement. The whole subject of food was bad enough.

And I didn't have anything to brag about in the disgusting food habit department, considering the way I had been eating everything in sight for the last twenty-four hours. By the time the delivery girl rang the gate buzzer, Sierra's stomach had joined mine in a rousing chorus of rumbles.

After giving the delivery girl a hefty tip, I walked into the kitchen with two carriers full of pizza boxes. Taking a good look around me, I realized why I hated Duncan's kitchen. It must have been put together by the same designer Mom hired. The same stainless steel and black appliances with the same butt-ugly Italian tile on the floor. I really needed to re-evaluate my attraction to the man.

Max looked up from the virgin sex-on-the-beach he was mixing for Tiffany. "Geez, Sam! Who the hell is going to eat 20 pizzas?"

Duncan stuck his nose in his glass of wine—I was sure it wasn't blood since I had poured the damn bottle—to hide his chuckle. I shot him a dirty look.

Turning back to Max, I tried to change the subject. "You didn't leave Mr. Cuddles at your apartment, did you?"

He shook his head. "The break-in traumatized the poor guy. He's at the vet, enjoying some doggie tranquilizers."

Wonderful. Something else Mom will blame me for.

Max gave me a quizzical look. "You still haven't told me why we need twenty pizzas."

I swallowed hard, and my stomach warbled at the scent of pepperoni and cheese. "There's a few things I need to tell you."

The guys had grabbed the stools next to the kitchen island, so I joined the girls at the table in the breakfast nook. I'd much rather sit next to Duncan, but now was definitely not the time for lust.

Instead, I poured out the events of the last few days to Max between slices of nine pepperoni and mushroom pizzas. Well, I edited the story quite a bit. I wasn't going to spill Duncan's secrets without his permission, and I wasn't sure how Max would react to the whole vampire thing.

He did seem to take the whole nanite scenario rather well, though he'd probably hold it over my head later. While he chewed his slice of sausage and black olive, I could almost see the little wheels turning in his brain. "So which side is she on?" He nodded towards Sierra who was finishing her sixth veggie pizza.

She flushed a bright crimson against her dark roots. I frowned. Her hair didn't look that bad a couple of hours ago, but then I wasn't paying much attention to her 'do as she tried to bash in my skull and strangle me. Did the nanites consider hair color a problem to correct? If so, any highlights were in serious danger.

"I know you have no reason to trust me. Especially after . . ." She waved vaguely in my direction.

"You mean trying to brain me with a spittoon and skewer me with a poker?" I couldn't help the sarcasm dripping from my words.

"You're the one who wanted to bring her with us," Duncan said, an innocent look on his face.

I gave him another dirty look before turning back to Sierra.

She stared at her licked-clean plate. It took me a minute to realize she was crying again.

"Sierra, come on . . ."

"No." She sniffed and raised her head to meet my gaze. "You have every right to hate me. I listened to my father. I knew the things he was doing were wrong, and, and—" She gulped air to keep from totally breaking down. "I was sick, and I wanted to live so bad, I didn't care who he was hurting." She sniffed again. "Or who I was hurting. I'm so sorry, Sam."

She looked around the room, meeting each person's eyes squarely. "I'll help you stop him. He won't do this to anybody else." Maybe the spoon stabbing in Phil's kitchen had scared her straight.

Tiffany rose to grab another slice from the box she and Max were splitting. "So why were you checking out Mallory?" she said around a mouthful of pizza, using the rest of the slice to point at Max.

Max surprised me by turning beet red himself. The last time he looked that embarrassed, I had caught him in our bathroom fifteen years ago with one of Dad's *Playboys* and his pants down. The incident netted me an extra allowance for six months. It also taught my brother to lock the freakin' bathroom door.

"Come on, Max," I said. "Spill."

"I linked Anne's disappearance to Mallory."

"Who?" Tiffany mumbled around another full mouth.

"She's a runaway Max keeps an eye on," I answered. I turned back to Max. "That doesn't make sense. Why the hell would Mallory be interested in a street kid?"

He took a large gulp of his rum and coke. "This is difficult to explain."

"What? He's some kind of child perv?"

"Hey!" Sierra objected.

I glared at her. "Remind me to talk to you about your dad's basement." Sierra took a sudden interest in her seventh pizza.

Max plucked a sausage chunk off his slice. "I don't want to violate any confidences." The weird thing was the way he watched Duncan, trying so hard not to be obvious.

"Now you're the one stalling. Protecting your sources is one thing, but Anne's life and a lot of other people's are at stake!"

"You're not going to believe me." Max gaze shifted to an imaginary spot on the floor. "She's a vampire." He looked up. "Go ahead and laugh."

"Anne?" Phil held up her hand. "Anne Levy? About this high? Mousy brown hair down to here?" Phil gestured at the middle of her back.

"Uh-huh." Max looked thoroughly confused. "You know her?"

"Bloody hell!" Duncan swore.

My gaze flip-flopped between Duncan and Phil. "She's one of yours?"

Phil's hand clenched around the knife she was using on her pizza, and Mom's stainless bent like soft wax. Duncan nodded in confirmation. "She left to visit her living family in Ohio almost three weeks ago," he said.

"And no one called to check on her?" I shouted in disbelief. "With all the freakin' disappearances, you were too lazy to phone?"

"It is not that simple, Samantha," Duncan said.

"What do you mean 'it is not that simple?' You dial the freakin' number, you moron!"

"Her living family is Amish."

"Oh."

An Amish vampire. Who'd have thought? Not me, that's for sure.

"Sam knows what you are, right?" Max inclined his head in my direction.

Duncan gave one of his long-suffering sighs. He really needs to trademark those. "Unfortunately."

"Wait a minute." I glared at Max. "You knew what he was."

Max nodded. "The room temperature feel when I shook his hand. It's a dead giveaway." Then his expression shifted, and he launched a perplexed look at Tiffany and Phil.

"Hey, I'm just related to them," Tiffany said. She gave him a devilish grin. "And my sister's not a zombie."

Max's eyes shot to me. I shrugged.

"We're still waiting for her to eat her first brains," Tiffany volunteered.

"What?" Sierra shrieked.

"She's just teasing Sam." Phil laid a consoling hand on Sierra's arm.

"It's not funny," the heiress grumbled back.

"What does she mean you're a zombie?" Max looked thoroughly confused.

"I died last night. Got shot by one of Mallory's goons, but I'm still walking around. The nanites fixed me." I shrugged again when Max gave me a horrified look. "It's about the best explanation I can give you because I don't understand how it works myself."

Max's horrified expression melted into his super skeptical reporter face. "Zombies aren't real, Sam."

"So says the brother who's friends with a vampire," I retorted. "Do you have a better explanation of what I am with these damn robots inside of me?"

"Frankenstein?"

A wadded paper napkin launched itself from my hand and hit his forehead. "Snotface."

Max grabbed the napkin and tossed it into the waste can. "I had no clue what Mallory was really up to. I only figured out he was connected to Anne's disappearance because I got lucky. A couple of the homeless kids Anne watches over recognized the MLI insignia on the money clip of someone who was asking a lot of questions about her. They didn't believe his story he was her dad, so they didn't tell him anything."

Duncan set his goblet down. "But they told you."

Max shrugged. "I help Anne deliver food to them."

"Crap," Tiffany muttered. "All he needed was a vampire close enough to read their minds. When he questioned them, they couldn't help thinking about the truth."

Another puzzle piece fell into place in my shaken, not stirred, brain. "That's how you knew about Mallory?"

She nodded. "A few people recognized the pictures of some of the missing folks. Duncan could pull the memories. Employees of MLI or one of its subsidiaries were spotted by the witnesses shortly before or after about three-quarters of the disappearances. We just didn't have any solid evidence against Mallory until you."

Max's attention returned to Sierra. "You said you were sick. What was wrong with you?"

Sierra wouldn't meet anyone's eyes. Her voice barely rose above a whisper. "A rare form of leukemia. The doctors thought I was in remission, but it showed up again. They gave me six months, and that was six and a half months ago. When I woke up this morning, I felt normal for the first time in ages."

I whistled. "These things are a cure for cancer?" The implications hit harder than one of her punches.

Tiffany bit off the last of her slice that had sauce on it and handed me the crust. After nine pizzas, I was still a little peckish. Apparently, my appetite was not altered in the face of world-shattering events. Max stared at me, his look even more horrified than when Tiffany announced my zombie status. He hated people eating off his plate and refused to eat off other people's. But devouring something another had bitten into was the absolute worst.

Tiffany noticed him staring at the crust I bit into. "I'm sorry. Did you want my crust?"

"No, thanks," he mumbled.

The teen crossed the kitchen and tossed her paper plate in the trash before continuing. "If Mallory's looking for a cure for cancer and not for the V-virus, then how's he keeping his vamps in line?"

"He is looking for a cure for the vampires too." Sierra wiped her mouth. "According to Dr. Abel, the virus has similar properties to cancer cells."

"But why test it on me? I'm not a vamp and I don't have cancer!" The thought hit me like a freight train. "Do I?"

Sierra shook her head. "Not that I know of."

Okay, now I was starting to get pissed. If I had an incurable disease, then I'd probably be the first to volunteer as one of Abel's guinea pigs. But dammit! I'm a healthy twenty-six year old woman. Or at least, I was.

Sierra stared at the grease stain on her plate. "He wanted to make sure I would survive the nanites. They hadn't been tested on humans before."

Phil took a sip of her wine and frowned. "That makes sense. If the nanites are programmed to act similarly to the V-virus, he'd want test trials to confirm his data."

Max grabbed a clean napkin and a pen. "What do you mean?"

I really didn't want Phil to answer my brother's question. My stomach was threatening to heave nine pizzas as it was.

"Not everyone survives the initial infection of the virus," she said. "Otherwise, we'd be neck deep in vampires.

Everyone groaned at her atrocious joke.

"What doesn't make sense is the were and witch kidnappings," Tiffany said.

"It does if Mallory's not really looking for cures." Fury twisted Duncan's face. We all looked at him, waiting for him to finish.

"He's looking for immortality."

Chapter 17

With a sharp crack, the stem on Phil's wine glass split in two. The entire thing fell from her hand. Red liquid splashed across the table. "Gaia," she whispered.

Somehow, the rest of the goblet didn't shatter when it hit the wooden tabletop. Tiffany grabbed a handful of napkins to mop up the spilled liquid.

The implications of Duncan's words sank through my pizza-fogged brain. No, this was way too much for anyone to deal with, much less comprehend. I gulped a couple of times before I could jump on a decent train of thought. "Wait a sec here. You mean there's more than just vamps disappearing off the streets," I said. After everything we'd been through, I couldn't believe Duncan had been holding out on me. Maybe twenty-four hours didn't create a lifetime bond, but geez!

"I am aware of three that are missing. One werewolf and two witches."

"I know there're covenless witches, but don't the wolves keep close tabs on their packs?" Max said. The amount of his knowledge of the real occult world was beginning to scare me.

"Yes, they do." A wry smile crossed Duncan's lips. "Which is why we are looking at a potential invasion since the missing pup is the son of the San Antonio pack's alpha. Also, the two missing witches we know about belong to the Los Angeles coven."

No matter how I twisted the info, the pieces weren't fitting. I held up a hand. "Whoa. What does one set have to do with the other? Cancer and viruses are one thing. Why would Mallory kidnap the werewolves and witches? You guys told me they're just variations of humanity."

"Longevity is the commonality. Their lifespans are twice as long as normal humans. Not on par with vampires, but—" He shrugged, reached for his own wineglass, and took a sip. "They also have specialized abilities which we do not have."

The churning in my stomach grew worse. Dr. Zachary said the nanites were rewriting my DNA, but she wasn't sure exactly what they were doing to me. The bizarre appetite and uncontrollable telepathy were bad enough. Would I need a lawn mower to shave my legs once a month?

I turned back to Sierra, who stared at her plate again.

"How many people is your father holding in his rat hole?" My fingers flexed. I itched to wrap them around her scrawny little Paris Hilton wannabe neck since I couldn't get to her father and his mad scientists.

"Eight," she whispered. "Right now, anyway."

"How many more was he holding?" Duncan's voice held an edge of menace.

"Does it matter? They're dead . . ." She still wouldn't meet anyone's stare.

Phil not-so-subtly shifted her chair away from the heiress. Whether consciously or not, she cleared space for a potential fight.

"You stupid bitch." Tiffany was even less subtle than the demigoddess as she crossed to the island to throw away the broken goblet and soggy napkins. "People are dead because of you. Don't you care?"

"Yes." The word was almost lost in her sob. "Yes, I do."

"How many?" Phil rose from the table, her empty hand raised to strike. Instead of the calm, cool, collected Lauren Bacall look-alike I was used to, she resembled an avenging Fury.

Sierra flinched.

"Phil, no!" Tiffany leapt and grabbed her wrist. Not that she could stop an enraged demigoddess, but I had to give the kid credit for balls.

Tiffany's interference seemed to rattle some sense into Phil. She stalked across the kitchen to retrieve another goblet and poured more wine into the new one. She chugged it down before refilling the glass.

Sierra glanced up at Tiffany and whispered, "Thanks."

Tiffany glared at the huddled Sierra. "Don't go thanking me yet. Spill, rich bitch, or I let Sam and Phil rip you apart."

"I don't know exactly."

"Then give us an estimate." Duncan's voice could have dripped icicles. "I saw two dead weres in the facility last night."

"Maybe twenty, twenty-five." A sliver of defiance appeared on her face when she raised her head. "I was in a coma for the last week. My father was trying to save my life."

"And neither of you cared who you hurt in the process," Max said in disgust.

"I already said I was sorry. I can't change what happened," she said, pleading obvious in her voice.

I can't help rhetorical questions, and I knew we needed a quick change of subject before things got ugly. "So what do we do about Mallory?"

"We rest until we hear from Caesar," Duncan said.

"Who the hell made you boss?" I was so getting tired of him ordering me around.

He ignored my grumbling. "I'll take the first watch." His green eyes had the faintest of glows under the kitchen fluorescents. "The rest of you get some sleep."

Something pressed against my head, an unseen force. I shook my head, more in disagreement than discomfort, and the pressure disappeared. "When Mallory figures out Max and I are related, this house won't be safe."

"You said Mallory knew we were related," Max said.

I shot him a nasty look. "Get your ears cleaned, big bro. I said Mallory thought I was spying on him for you. He didn't know we're related, and I didn't tell during his little torture session. I pushed the Ralph connection, but it doesn't mean someone with his resources won't eventually check court records and find out we're brother and sister."

Max climbed to his feet and started clearing empty boxes. "Well, they haven't tossed Mom and Dad's place yet. Let's wait until Duncan hears from his boss."

I frowned. "But Mallory ordered his goons to search your place and your office."

"He did." Max smirked. "They didn't find my research. He even had them search the *Scoop* and Ralph's place too."

"Did they hurt anyone?"

Max shook his head. "Ralph was pissed as hell though and worried sick about you. We need to let him know you're okay."

"It's not safe—" I started.

"I know, I know. I wasn't going to call." He rubbed a hand across his face, the last few days obviously catching up with him. "I figure Mallory's got wiretaps on everyone, but it sounds like he's got his people working the Duncan angle to find you. We have a little time."

"Your files aren't here, are they?" I whispered. God, I hoped Max wasn't that stupid.

"Don't worry. There're in a safe place." He didn't clarify and the rest of us didn't ask.

———·•·———

Max and I went upstairs to scrounge blankets and pillows for everyone. I really hated staying here. It wasn't safe, but as my brother pointed out, our options were pretty limited at the moment. Especially if Mallory already knew about one of the vampire safe houses.

"I saw his picture in your bedroom," Max whispered in my ear as I pulled an extra comforter out of the linen closet.

I should have known Max's smirk earlier had nothing to do with his apartment getting searched and trashed. "You were in my place?" He was the only one with a key. Oh God, what if he'd been there when Mallory's goons had arrived?

"I was trying to figure out where the hell you had disappeared to. When my car vanished off the face of the earth, I got worried."

My evil glare didn't faze him. I shoved the comforter into his chest, knocking him back a step. "It's so nice you were more worried about your damn car than me." I turned back to the closet and yanked out a couple of pillows.

"Sam, from reading your notes—"

"How did you—"

He shot me a 'duh' look. "The plumbing access behind the tub? That is so amateurish, little girl."

My eyes narrowed. "Were you the one who messed with my computer? Mallory didn't find my notes, and he complained about a virus wiping out my hard drive."

Max shook his head, a confused look on his face. "You sure it wasn't something Fred planted? You said he'd been acting freaky before the accident. Maybe something he remotely activated?"

I shook my head. "Don't think so."

"Sure it wasn't your crush?" Of course. If my brother had been in the apartment, he'd seen the photo on my bedroom wall. Max's teasing look turned sober before I could whack him. "I was afraid St. James worked for Mallory, and you were in danger."

I held out the pillows, refusing to look at him. "He's not, okay." I wasn't sure why I was so pissed Max had seen the poster-sized photo of Duncan.

"I know that now. Sam . . ."

I looked at him, the concern on his face highly unusual for him.

"It won't work."

I frowned. "What won't work?"

"You and St. James."

"I don't know what the hell you're blathering about," I snapped, turning back to the closet.

He tugged on my shoulder with his free hand. "Sam, I'm not being a jerk. He's got what, a couple of centuries on you?"

"Four," I whispered.

"And Anne's got over a half century on me."

Confessions weren't an everyday occurrence between us. His crush on Anne must have been bad for him to spill.

"When did she tell you?"

A wistful smile crossed his face. "Fifteen years ago."

I gasped in shock. Max used to sneak out nearly every night during his junior year in high school. Anne explained a lot of his weird behavior during that time. "You've known vampires really existed all along and never told me?"

"Honestly, Sam, would you have believed me?" He shook his head. "I wasn't sure I believed myself, but as the years went by . . ." His self-deprecating laugh indicated his own amazement at the situation. His gaze met mine. "The point being, a relationship between a vampire and a human can't work. The age difference is bad enough. It's amazing the change in perspective a few years can make, much less a few centuries. Even so, would you be willing to give up sunlight, ice cream, your family, your life to be with him?"

I snorted. "In case you missed the memo, I don't have a life."

"You can still eat and go out in sunlight, right?" Max shook his head. "There's no guarantee the nanites can cure the V-virus or prevent you from being infected despite what Sierra says. Because that's what it comes down to. Most vampires won't have a human because of the guilt of cursing someone they love with an incurable disease. It's either that or watching the person you love wither and die from old age, never being able to touch them, to love them."

Fury raised its ugly head. Max spoke the thoughts racing silently in my mind since Duncan told me the truth. God, was that only twenty-four hours ago?

To hide my anger, I turned back toward the closet. "You don't have the right to lecture me just because things didn't work out between you and your high school crush," I hissed.

"I admit to my crush, but your copious files on this guy make you a psychotic stalker."

"Pictures of what guy?"

I jumped a foot at Duncan's soft baritone at the head of the stairs. "Geez! Can you just not sneak around for two seconds?"

"I'll take these downstairs." Max slid past Duncan and took the steps two at a time. I ignored both my brother and the hunky vamp standing next to me by grabbing a couple of light blankets.

"What guy?" Duncan repeated.

"It's a story I'm working on."

"Ahhh." He folded his strong arms over that fabulous chest and leaned against the wall beside me. "This wouldn't have anything to do with the black and white glossy of me on your bedroom wall, would it? Or the multitude of other photographs you've taken?"

I felt my face flush. Of course he heard every single word Max said. The only person in the house who didn't have super hearing besides Max was Tiffany.

Again, I turned back to the closet, praying there was another pillow I could smother myself with. "Max doesn't know what he's talking about." Then I realized Max hadn't mentioned any photos, and Mallory said Duncan had been seen at my place. Hell, *I'd* witnessed him and Tiffany leaving my apartment complex.

I whirled back to face him. "What the hell were you doing in my apartment?" I liked my privacy, and I really didn't appreciate everyone traipsing through my place like it was Walmart.

"Deducing why you were following me."

"I told you why Thursday night. I'm writing a follow-up on your rescue—"

"—of Ms. Alton from the Sunshine Believers." He pursed his lips. I couldn't take my eyes from them. Tingles ran up and down my spine at the memory of his kiss when I yanked him between the carnival tents earlier this evening. "At the time, I had no reason to believe you. And as I pointed out Thursday night by the river, you were stalking me."

I dragged my attention away from his lips. "Oh, really? And that gives you carte blanche to commit B&E?"

He shrugged. "While Tiffany believed you were harmless, I was not as confident you were not employed by Mallory."

"For crying out loud! Why does everyone think I'm working for someone else? Doesn't it occur to you people umf—" His mouth covered mine with a possessiveness that literally took my breath away. The blankets fell to the floor, and my fingers wound through his hair.

All of my indignation disappeared in the onslaught of his kiss. His hands wrapped around my waist to pull me even closer, his body against mine overloading my senses. Maybe it was the adrenaline rush from the last few days. Maybe it was something else. I wasn't sure what, but I didn't want the kiss to end.

Tongues and lips tangled and explored. Extra-sharp teeth nipped my lower lip, not hard enough to break the delicate skin, but a thrill of dangerous pleasure rippled through me at the risk. The rich scent of sandalwood rose, enveloping me in its embrace as Duncan's hands roamed over the sensitized skin under my t-shirt.

When he drew away, I almost keeled over. So this is the feeling all those sappy romances Mom read were talking about. He rested his forehead against mine, his breathing loud in the silence of the hallway. Dimly, I heard the other four downstairs, talking.

"I am sorry, Samantha. I should not have done that."

"Says who?" Why was he talking now? I pulled his head down for another taste.

Gently, he extricated my arms from around his neck. "Your brother is right." He brushed his fingertips lightly across my cheek, the sadness in his eyes overwhelming. "A relationship between us would never work."

"Like Max knows what he's talking about?" Anger replaced desire. I placed my hands on his chest and shoved. Hard. "So you were just leading me on? Is that it?" Silence reigned in the kitchen, which meant Phil and Sierra were listening to us. Fine. They wanted a show? I'd give them one.

"That is not true, Samantha, and you know it."

"You kissed me first, buster." I stepped forward and poked a finger at his chest. I was furious, at him for kissing me, at myself for wanting to believe I had a chance with him.

Irritation flared in his face. "No, you kissed me first. At the fair. After I told you what I was. So if anyone was acting dangerously, it was you."

"Excuse me? I figured out what you were at Mallory Labs. You did not tell me a damn thing! And that so-called kiss at the fair was to avoid the goon squad, not because I wanted to kiss you. You, you pervert!"

"So what is your excuse for kissing me back just now?"

God, I so wanted to smack the smirk off his arrogant mug. Mainly, because I knew he was right.

I whirled on the heel of my brand new tennis shoes, trying not to remember Duncan had bought them for me, and marched to my old bedroom. I slammed the pastel pink door behind me, but instead of the usual satisfying bang, there was a screech as the wood splintered down the middle. The side with the knob teetered for a second before it landed with a *whoomph* in the middle of the obnoxious pink shag covering the bedroom floor. The other section creaked on the bent and warped hinges.

This damn zombie strength would be my downfall.

Through the broken door, I saw Duncan still standing at the other end of the hall. He smiled, winked at me, picked up the blankets from the floor, and headed back downstairs.

I stared at the half door lying in the carpet. A broken hunk of it would make a very good stake.

Chapter 18

Tiffany's cell phone woke all the supernaturals but one at four a.m. I used to be able to sleep through mine when it sat on my nightstand six inches from my head, but with my new hearing, Tiffany's sounded like a grenade going off outside the house. It didn't wake Duncan because it sat in his pocket as he circled the grounds on lookout.

These new abilities were starting to be a bitch.

The good news in this insane situation? Duncan's friend, Caesar, had another safehouse for us. We had barely enough time to beat both the sunrise and L.A.'s morning rush hour.

The mysterious Caesar Augustine and Dr. Zachary met us at the canyon house he had directed us to. He seemed vaguely familiar, but I couldn't place him. Dark hair accented his olive skin. His deep brown eyes were warm and charming as was his old world personality, but for a split-second, they flashed gold when Duncan introduced me. Like I couldn't figure out what he was from his handshake. The unusually chill hands were a dead giveaway. Pun intended.

He also made it clear he wanted to speak with Duncan and Phil privately. Complaints, loud ones, from the rest of our little group convinced him otherwise.

Actually, Duncan's slight nod convinced him. Max, Tiffany, and Sierra didn't notice the byplay.

Dr. Zachary, on the other hand, did notice. I had the impression she didn't miss much. Still, she played the gracious hostess and escorted us to the family room.

A gray stone fireplace dominated one wall. Opposite of the fireplace, a wet bar with wooden shutters separated the family area from what was probably the kitchen. Heavy navy drapes covered the wall between the bar and the fireplace, giving the place a sepulcher feel. If this was the typical canyon home, behind the cloth were the sliding glass doors leading to the back deck and pool. Even though they probably were covered with UV film, and Caesar definitely seemed the careful type, I didn't try opening them. I didn't think the vampire contingent would appreciate being fried if the glass wasn't protected.

Seated in a wing-backed chair next to the fireplace, Caesar looked like a medieval king holding court, if medieval kings wore polos and chinos instead of silk and chain mail. The rest of us scattered on the couches and floor, except Duncan. He paced in front of the drapes, a feral jungle cat blending into his surroundings.

Caesar glared at Max, then Sierra, before turning his death ray eyes on me. "Anything said in this house will stay in this house. Am I understood?"

No threats, which meant something pretty bad would happen if we tattled. Caesar Augustine was one of those people my instincts knew wouldn't waste his time on threats. All three of us gave meek nods. Seeing Max intimidated would have thrilled me if our benefactor didn't cow me as well.

Before Duncan started into the events of the last thirty-six hours, Caesar held up his hand. "The Council has authorized us to rescue those we can and destroy Mallory's labs."

"Wait a minute! Who asked us to do what?" My little outburst escaped before I could stop it. Tiffany and Duncan shot me horrified looks. Dr. Zachary hid a smile behind her hand, but Phil openly smirked at my brashness.

Caesar's chin rested on steepled fingers as he regarded me. The look he gave me could have frozen Lake Tahoe solid for the entire year. "I tolerate your presence, Ms. Ridgeway, at my chief enforcer's request. Do not push my tolerance further."

Chief enforcer? Duncan? Was he a vampire police officer or more like head muscle? Instead of asking though, I murmured, "Sorry."

Part of me wanted to kick my own butt for such a rookie mistake. Getting info from someone like Caesar would take finesse and probably a butt-load of flattery, not me acting like the Grand Inquisitor. I chalked my slip up to dying a couple of days ago.

At least Caesar wasn't king of the vampires if he was taking orders from someone else. And I didn't want to meet the guy who was giving them because this vampire seriously gave me the willies.

"So they are finally taking our concerns seriously?" With his arms crossed and his stance wide, Duncan appeared likely to kick this unknown council's collective ass if Caesar said no.

"The Council needed proof, Duncan, not speculation." Caesar waved in my direction. "Ms. Ridgeway has provided that proof, albeit indirectly."

He turned his unblinking attention to Sierra, who paled noticeably. "You have a choice to make, Ms. Mallory."

Despite the tremor in her hands, she nodded firmly. "I'll do whatever you want, but—" She licked her lips and straightened. "I want your promise, no matter what happens, you won't hurt my father."

"She should not be involved in this," Duncan said. His defiant tone speared me. Was he still questioning my decision to bring her along?

I kept my tone logical. "Why not? She knows the compound better than anyone here."

Duncan's cool green stare turned from his boss to me. "You should not be involved either. You barely have any self-control at the moment. Or do I have to remind you of the basement?" he said. "Or that you cannot help broadcasting your thoughts?"

"Those were accidents." My protest sounded feeble, even to me. "And I only killed in self-defense."

Duncan arched a black eyebrow. "And you accidentally crushed your brother's gun."

"Technically, it's Mom's gun," Max offered.

I so didn't need his help right now.

Satisfaction flickered across Duncan's face, and he turned back to Caesar. "None of them should be involved in any rescue attempt. I'd prefer the Gryffudds or the Osakas—"

Caesar shook his head. "We don't have the time to fly in any other enforcers, and I want our daytime guard at the mansion."

Duncan opened his mouth, but a strange buzz cluttered my brain. Voices speaking so rapidly it sounded like multiple tracks of the guy from the old FedEx commercials playing at the same time. Except no one's mouth moved until Duncan's teeth clicked shut at the same instant the voices stopped.

Caesar turned to Max, Sierra and me, fixing us each with a pointed look. I felt more like a rat under a microscope than I did with Doctors Kane and Abel.

"You may be right," Caesar said, his comment aimed at Duncan even as his gaze drilled holes through my eye sockets.

Before I could throw a scathing retort, Sierra said, "After what my father did to your friends . . ." She gulped hard. Not that I blamed her. Her own guilt, the realization of what her father had turned her into, plus the whole Caesar intimidation factor must have weighed heavily on those debutante shoulders. "And Sam and me, my father needs to be stopped."

"How are we getting in?" Tiffany spoke up for the first time. "After Sam and Duncan's escape, they'll have doubled security."

Sierra seemed to gather her courage. "I can get you in."

Duncan took a menacing step toward her. "Why should we trust you?"

"You shouldn't." She met Duncan's measured stare, digging her fingers into her thighs probably to keep them from shaking. "You can't. But I'm the only hope the survivors have right now. She's right." She inclined her fake blondness toward Tiffany. "Daddy's already tightened security, but the guards will let me in."

I rose to my feet before I realized it and glared at the heiress. My support didn't lend itself to absolute trust. "Why should they? You're missing as far as they're concerned. Won't they be suspicious if you show up a day later with no communication?"

Sierra lifted one shoulder, her nonchalant manner at odds with the nails burrowing into her legs. "I tell them the truth, or as much as I can anyway. St. James killed my backup and captured me. I escaped but encountered difficulties with Augustine's people, which was why I couldn't take the chance of contacting them." She turned her puppy dog eyes toward Bebe. "Maybe jinx me so I can't use a phone?"

Voices buzzed around and through me again, even more this time. The sensation was akin to having my iPod playing every file at once, but I couldn't focus on any one voice. The weird thing was no one's lips were moving though eye contact between the supernaturals made it feel like a conversation was happening. Even worse, Tiffany had been included in the high-speed conversation from the way her eyes twitched. The entire incident happened within a second or two.

God, I really hated being left out of the loop and was about to make my displeasure known when Caesar nodded.

"Your assistance is accepted on the condition your father's life is forfeit for any betrayal on your part," he said.

Sierra gave a sharp nod in return. "Give me a pen and paper. I'll map out everything."

I've relied on insiders in the past for story tips. They want the money, the revenge, or the publicity. Generally though, the motive's revenge. The maid at the luxury hotel who saw the two married film stars (and not to each other) together and was stiffed on her tip. The bathroom attendant who saw and heard interesting things in the stalls—and was stiffed on his tip. I'd bet a year's salary Duncan and his friends were very good tippers.

While Sierra was adamant about her dad not being harmed, I'd bet another year's salary her motive was revenge. If anyone asked how I knew what she felt, I wouldn't be able to tell them. It was something in my gut, like the weird knowledge of sunrise and sunset without physically viewing the environment.

Just as I could tell by the look in Duncan and Caesar's eyes their guarantees concerning Mallory's safety were to placate Sierra in return for her information. If push came to shove, they'd take Mallory out in a heartbeat. I hoped the vampires could handle her when they did. Hell, I barely survived when she was stone cold lucid.

Since Sierra and Max had more knowledge concerning the compound than my scant memories of the basement, my contributions were largely ignored as were Tiffany's. The only redeeming point was Duncan's attitude was slightly less condescending to me than to his niece.

"Screw 'em," Tiffany whispered in my ear. She inclined her head towards the kitchen.

Best idea I'd heard since we got here. My stomach started the most tentative of rumbles as I sauntered after her.

I was surprised to find the good doctor already by the stove. She had slipped out of the great debate so quietly I never saw her leave. She stirred a large pot of—well, it sure wasn't spaghetti. The strange odor from the stove tickled my nostrils, sending me into sneezing spasms.

In countertime to my nose, my stomach started another round of gurgles, which sent Tiffany into gales of laughter. Even Dr. Zachary smiled as she stirred.

"Whatcha makin'?" the teen asked as she poked her own snout over the pot. The doctor rewarded her by smacking the tip with the handle of the wooden spoon she used.

"Sleeping potion for this little rescue mission." She reached into one of the bowls next to her and sprinkled a yellowish powder into the mix.

I glanced around. The kitchen had similar expensive stainless steel appliances as Duncan's. I don't know what was worse—vampires with gourmet accessories or that they all had the same decorating tastes as my mother.

The corners of my mouth quirk in amusement. Other than the fridge and maybe a microwave, what use would be the other stuff to them? I doubted too many of the vampires were in the position of serving homemade dinners. Well, except to their girlfriends and nieces.

I grabbed the fridge handle, praying to find a snack because the hunger pangs were becoming damn uncomfortable. What I saw would have made me barf if it wasn't for my zombie appetite. Blood bags packed two whole shelves of the side-by-side at eye level. I slammed the door shut.

"Don't you have anything not red to eat, Doc?" I wasn't normally a rude guest, but the gnawing hunger made me irritable.

Dr. Zachary smiled instead of firing back. Nothing rattled this woman. "There's a dozen chicken cordon bleu breasts in the freezer," she said.

"I can't wait for those to cook." My stomach seconded the motion.

She laughed outright. "Cherry tomatoes are in the veggie bin at the bottom, if you can tolerate the red. Carrots and celery if not. They should tide you over until the chicken bakes. That's all we have right now. I'll make a grocery run after I finish this potion."

Relief tinged with worry spread through my uncomfortable abdomen. What would happen to me if I stopped eating every five seconds? Even worse, what would happen to the people around me if I couldn't control my appetite? I didn't have the excuse of an Andes plane crash in the dead of winter.

My stomach grumbled again. Tiffany scrounged a box of crackers for us, forcing aside my worries about the future. While munching the stale saltines, I arranged the prepared poultry on a baking sheet, popped it in the oven and set the timer. She had to retrieve the salad dressing and vegetables. I couldn't handle seeing the vampires' dietary requirements again. Not when the crackers only blunted the slightly nauseous hunger feeling in my belly.

"Want a tomato?" Tiffany scooted the bowl of washed veggies toward me.

I grimaced. "No, thanks. The small ones remind me too much of eyeballs."

"Consider it practice for later." Tiffany popped one into her mouth and bit down. She rolled her eyes and made a spectacle of rubbing her stomach with accompanying yum-yum noises.

The urge to smack her arose, but after what I did to my old bedroom door, ignoring her seemed the safer option. But her jokes brought an ugly thought to the front of my consciousness. "Doctor?"

"You can call me Bebe," she said. "We don't stand on a lot of ceremony when it's just Family." She flashed a brief smile before returning her attention to her pot.

"Um, okay. Bebe." I tested the name on my tongue. It seemed weird not to address her formally, but she couldn't be more than five years older than me. Then I remembered what Duncan said last night about witches living longer than Normals. For all I knew she could be Grandma Neel's age.

"What's wrong, Sam?" Bebe's face carried a patience I didn't know if I'd ever master.

I swallowed the suddenly dry bits of cracker. "Did you check Sierra's aura?"

Again, discomfort flickered across her patrician features, and she took a sudden interest in her potion. "Yes."

"It was black, too." When she didn't answer, I added, "Wasn't it?"

"Yes."

Tiffany's attention whipped between Bebe and me. "Really?"

The doctor shrugged and sprinkled a greenish-gray herb into her pot. "I'm still trying to figure that out. Serious injuries were inflicted on both women before I could examine them. I don't know if the nanites killed them or—"

My hand automatically rubbed the spot between my breasts where the bullet had ripped through me. I might have killed Sierra. I might not have. Either way, my rising body count bothered what was left of my conscience. Almost as much as Bebe's inability to figure out what I was becoming.

I opted for a change in conversation. "So what all goes into this sleeping potion?"

"You are a curious one, aren't you?" Her brow furrowed in concentration as she tossed a handful of aromatic herbs from another bowl into the mixture. "A little bit of this and a little bit of that."

Vague answers irritated me. If someone doesn't want to answer my social chat question, they just need to say so. Those types of answers also increase my smart-ass quotient by tenfold. "Eye of newt and all that shit, huh?"

She looked up from the pan. "Well, if I'm out of newt eyes, I can always use cherry tomatoes."

Chewed orange bits exploded out of Tiffany's mouth as she choked on her laughter and a large piece of carrot. A few zombie pats on the back dislodged the hunk in her throat.

We munched on the carrot and celery sticks as the doctor stirred, bubbles in her brew popping in countertime to the conversation in the next room. The voices of the vampires and Phil sounded like Allied generals planning D-Day. I guess they were, in some supernatural equivalent.

At the ding of the oven timer, everyone from the living room swarmed in for food. Unabashed, Duncan poured a couple of mugs of blood and shoved them into the microwave. Tiffany and Bebe split a chicken cordon bleu while my brother and Phil scarfed a half-pound breast each.

I couldn't talk. Sierra and I wolfed down the other nine. The chicken, crackers and vegetables took the edge off, but I'd need to eat again—soon. Worry chewed on the back of my mind. What would happen if I didn't have access to food while we were on the run? Would my friends turn into dancing steaks to me, like in those old Warner Brothers cartoons? All zombie jokes aside, turning into a George Romero extra terrified me.

It dawned on me that Caesar hadn't come in with the rest of the troops. Duncan had slipped out while I ate. It's pretty bad when I pay more attention to a piece of chicken instead of the hot guy.

Okay, make that a couple of pounds of chicken.

I eased out of the kitchen, but the family room was empty. The boys had succeeded in having their little testosterone tête-à-tête while the rest of us were eating. Forget their little fight-against-world-domination plots. If they didn't want my help, then fine.

Except it was the Dr. Frankensteins who created me the vampires were going after, and I wanted in on the destruction of my mad scientists.

Crossing the room, I felt between the drapes until I found the lock to the glass doors. Flipping it, I slid the door open and walked into some glorious California sunshine. The cold front plaguing the area last week had moved west, letting warm air caress my face. Blue ripples reflected off the white-washed pool bottom. I really wished I had a suit. If it weren't for the house party inside, I'd consider skinny-dipping.

The few steps to the deck railing yielded a spectacular view of the canyon. In the distance, some bird of prey glided on the thermals. Even my enhanced vision couldn't see more than dark feathers. It was the kind of beautiful day made for playing hooky from work.

The soft murmur of voices rose from below the house. I strained to catch the words when Caesar's unmistakable tenor said, "You might as well come down instead of eavesdropping."

In the time it would take me to go back inside and climb the stairs down to the garage, they could find somewhere else to hide from me. I looked over the railing. Only a one story drop to the concrete parking pad below. If I had Jaime Sommers' strength and hearing thanks to the nanites, I probably had the rest of her skills. Hiking my legs over the redwood, I glanced down once more, uttered a quick prayer and jumped.

Heck, my landing was even semi-graceful. At least I didn't fall on my ass in front of Duncan.

Well under the shade created by the pool deck, the missing vampires reclined on lawn chaises, each with a can of beer in hand, looking for all the world like a couple of suburbanites discussing their lawns.

"So how is your grass doing this season, Duncan?" Caesar said.

That damn vampire mind-reading was really starting to piss me off.

Caesar grinned, gracing me with a full display of very sharp canines. Gone was the eerie mystique he'd affected earlier. He looked, well, normal. Apparently, he heard those thoughts also because he broke out into a hearty belly laugh.

"You know, eavesdropping on people's thoughts is rude." Heat seeped through the soles of my Nikes from the concrete. I strode into the shade to stand in front of the two vampires. I crossed my arms and glared at Caesar.

He tossed his beer can into the garbage bin in a behind-the-back shot that would have made any Sabretooth proud. *Eavesdropping in any form is rude, yet you have no problem indulging.*

I tried not to let the weirdness of his voice in my head get to me. If the jerk would tell me what was going on, I wouldn't have to eavesdrop. This craziness concerned me as much as it did his people.

True. But I won't risk my people's safety on guesswork where you're concerned.

What a load of sanctimonious bullshit. "I'm not the one who's a threat to you! And I don't get how you can be that concerned when you can read minds."

Confusion spread across Duncan's face. "What are you talking about?" He turned to Caesar. "You heard her?"

Caesar's eyebrow quirked up. "How can you not? She's transmitting louder than Tiffany's MP3 on full volume."

Maybe I was picking up on Duncan's confusion because Caesar's comment made no sense. "B-but I heard you in my head."

"You entered my mind, Sam. Not vice versa."

Interesting new trick, even if I hadn't meant to wing my thoughts in Caesar's direction or grab his. I stuck my tongue out at Duncan. In a way, it was a relief to know he hadn't read my thoughts. Especially the ones I'd been having about him.

He scowled. I couldn't blame him. I hate being the one person who's not in on the joke, too.

I scooted his feet over to sit next to him. "Told you Mallory's bitches read my mind."

His scowl deepened. "Or you told them."

I locked eyes with him. "I did not."

"Beer?" When I nodded at Caesar's obvious effort to change the subject, he dug into the cooler next to him and tossed me a can.

I popped open the top and, for a split-second, hesitated. I had no clue of what alcohol would do to me now so I hadn't indulged in Mom and Dad's stash last night. *Oh, screw it!* I gulped down half the can and waited for a few seconds. Nope, I didn't explode, melt, or keel over. The beer tasted the same as all the others I'd had before I died.

Unfortunately, Duncan wasn't about to let the telepathy thing go. "Maybe you accidentally told someone else. You did not know the whereabouts of the other safehouse when we encountered those women. It's likely there were other vampires scouting the area."

"And if Sam didn't accidently transmit the address, we have a different problem," Caesar said.

Duncan turned to Caesar, cocked an eyebrow and frowned. "A traitor."

Caesar shrugged at the statement. "Perhaps. Given what you've told me of your assailants, we may not have discovered all of the plants."

Reporter instincts took over. "Plants? As in vampire spies?"

Duncan ignored my questions in favor of his boss. "If you truly believe my security team is so incompetent—"

"This isn't only about you." Caesar's cool look would have had me shaking in my boots. Okay, my Nikes. "In case you haven't noticed, my own sister plotted against me for decades. I will not be that blind to any and all possibilities ever again."

I just love interesting dirt. There was history between Duncan and Caesar's sister from the dark look on Duncan's face.

Then an abashed expression spread over Duncan's planed features. "Yes, sir."

Caesar's posture eased a fraction. "It's equally probable Mallory could have recruited someone within the coven. There's been sufficient mutterings of dissent over the last two years between not executing Selene and my relationship with Bebe."

Interesting that the men's relationship was still intact. It made me wonder what this Selene had done to betray Duncan as well as her brother.

"To answer your question, Sam, yes, we do have internal problems from time to time." Caesar fixed me with his golden gaze, and I was very glad to feel the reassuring pressure of Duncan's legs against my lower back.

Not wanting to get deeper into vampire politics than I already was, I took a sip from the can to gather my courage, but I didn't have a chance to ask Caesar my question.

"Yes, you may," he said.

"No!" Duncan bellowed. If I hadn't transmitted to Duncan, then Caesar must have.

"She was well on her way to breaking out when you found her. Her assistance will be invaluable." The corners of Caesar's mouth crinkled in a wry smile.

"That does not mean we have a right to put her back in danger."

"Hey, I'm volunteering here!" I could yell right back. I turned to Caesar, lowering the volume first. "So, what am I volunteering for?"

"Sierra will escort you back to the complex as her prisoner in my vehicle," Caesar said. "Bebe's spells will cover the rest of us in the back."

"Oh." Helpless captive was not what I had in mind. I was thinking more of Linda Hamilton in *T2* or Sigourney Weaver in *Aliens*.

"Helpless, you are not," Caesar said.

"Wise vampire, you are," I said, mimicking his Yoda voice.

"Mallory's people will be prepared for us after my break-in from the other night." Leave it to Duncan to poop on the party. "And we now know we will not be dealing with only Normals."

"Yes, they will be ready for us," Caesar replied. "Which is why both Sierra and Sam will be the keys for our success. Once the captives are freed, we will have additional allies if it becomes necessary to fight our way out."

I lowered my voice to a whisper. "You're not using Sierra as a hostage, are you?" No point in taking chances that she'd over hear us, and I wasn't about to trust any telepathic talent I'd received from the nanites.

Caesar shook his head. "That's not our intention." A strange expression flitted across his face. "However, I don't believe Mallory will endanger his daughter, given the extremes he's gone through to save her life."

Duncan mumbled something under his breath I couldn't decipher. I didn't really try either since I was sure it wasn't complimentary. I ignored him and focused on Caesar's words while he relayed his plan. I just hoped our vampire Yoda's plan wasn't as disastrous as the little green Jedi master's in the last Star Wars movie.

Chapter 19

I rolled my wrists, trying to ease the bite of the manacles on my skin. While the quick-release catch was reassuring, Caesar insisted they appear as real as possible. I tried not to think about why he had them at the safehouse. There are things about other people's lives you just don't want to know.

The duck pond rolled past the passenger window of Caesar's Hummer, the last vestiges of sunlight bouncing off the surface. I couldn't repress the shudder at the memories of my last ride through this park.

"Cold?" Sierra asked from the driver's seat.

"No," I said, unsure whether she was deliberately mistaking my reaction. If she wanted to play the naïve heiress, that was fine with me. But I'd lay odds she knew exactly how I'd been caught by her dad's goons.

"I'm not either," Bebe hollered from the cargo area. "It's stifling back here. Wanna turn the A/C up?"

We had pulled out the back seats of Caesar's Hummer. Somehow Caesar, Duncan, Bebe and Phil managed to cram themselves on the floor. Gray tulle netting covered them, and with Bebe's illusion spell, it made the cargo bed appear empty. I knew the back wasn't empty, and I still had trouble seeing the folks, even with my super vision.

Max and Tiffany had stayed behind at the safehouse over the kid's very loud and very obscene protests. My brother, ever the voice of reason, talked her into common sense, not that she had a whole lot to begin with, but I wasn't sure about the speculative eye Goth Girl was giving him when we left. The thought of someone her age interested in my over-thirty brother was just—

Icky.

A hint of brakes forced my mind off that track. Thank God.

"This is it, folks," Sierra said. She turned down the back driveway towards the security gate for the delivery entrance. I slumped in the passenger seat, pretending unconsciousness but with my eyes open a slit. Just in case. I may have been the idiot to talk everyone else into trusting her, but part of me still had doubts.

Butterflies in the stomach were nothing compared to the roll of nausea filling my gut as we approached the guards. Semi-automatic weapons gleamed under exterior lighting that clicked on as the sun faded behind the horizon. One of the guards sauntered to the driver's side as we rolled to a stop. He ducked to take a good look at us as the driver's window slid down. His cocky smirk disappeared the instant he recognized Sierra.

"Ms. Mallory, what are you—"

"Doing your job." Gone was the sweet, shy girl who apologized for trying to kill me after I had skewered her with a spoon. The superbitch was back. Not a reassuring transformation.

As the guard stammered, she snapped, "Are you going to let me in or do I have to talk to my father, Irving?"

"N-n-no, ma'am." Irving stumbled back from the vehicle, signaling the guard inside the gatehouse to open the gates. Steel bars retracted smoothly along recessed tracks in the concrete.

Sierra floored the Hummer as soon as the opening widened enough for us to fit through. A relieved sigh emanated from her. She shot me a grin. "We're in."

"Not inside the building, we're not," I mumbled.

"Piece of cake," she said, as we approached a ramp that dipped into the complex. Two more guards flanked the closed rolled-steel door at the bottom. "Everyone in the back needs to keep quiet."

A whispered, "Well, duh," came from behind me, made funnier by the British clip. I stifled a smirk. Tiffany's lack of manners was wearing off on her uncle.

The new guard approached us as we coasted to a halt. He didn't look half as dumb as Irving did. I held my breath as he poked his head to get a good view of us and the interior. Bebe's cover spell better hold because this guy would shoot. My gut had no doubts on that score.

He nodded. "Ms. Mallory. You've been missing for a day."

Super cool, she inclined her head towards me. "She took a while to catch. Nailed Val and Chee. I lost contact with the rest of the retrieval team, but I knew how bad Daddy wanted her back."

Shit. She was changing the cover story. This whole scheme was going bad before we were inside the building.

The guard frowned. Damn, he wasn't buying it. My index finger poised a hair above the release catch. He took a long look at the interior again, stepped back, and motioned. His buddy didn't move, so someone had to be watching us on the monitors. Great, just great. Sierra had better be right about disabling the cameras inside the garage.

With a jerk, the door started its rise. She eased the Hummer forward. A small squad waited for us in the garage.

How many?

I nearly jumped out of my seat at Caesar's telepathic words. Even though I expected it, the feeling of someone else in my head was disconcerting despite the practice he and Bebe put me through before we left the safehouse. I bit my tongue to keep from answering aloud.

Six. Two more came through a side door to join their compadres. *No, eight.* Maybe I should be flattered that I required this many men to control little old me. I clenched my hand around the tiny PVC tube in my fist.

Sierra braked. The team swarmed to the passenger side to get me. I leaned against the door so when one of the goons yanked it open I fell partially out of the Hummer.

I looked up at six pairs of eyes and said, "Nighty-night, boys." Raising the tube in my hand to my mouth, I blew. Golden dust exploded across their faces, and one by one, they collapsed to the floor. Still holding my breath, I swung up and unlatched the manacles, then the seatbelt.

A few yards away, Sierra dusted the seventh guard. But one guard had stayed out of range of the sleep spell I'd blown. I panicked when Number Eight swung his gun towards her.

"Yo, bud!" Startled by my voice, he twisted in my direction but too late. I leapt. My right cross sent him reeling into the wall. It wasn't as satisfying as smacking the shit out of Alexander Radcliff when he put that rat down my shirt in fourth grade, but still . . .

I knelt and placed two fingers on his neck.

"Well." Duncan looked down at me. I smiled back.

"He'll have a nasty headache when he wakes up, but he's alive."

He gave a brusque nod. "I am relieved you did not kill this one."

I rose, brushed golden dust off my shirt, and sucked in a welcome breath. "Told you I'd get the hang of this super-strength stuff."

"You are not Lynda Carter," he replied.

"Oooo, two pop culture references in one shot. You sure American TV isn't turning your stuffy British brain to mush?"

"I don't think your brain is what he's interested in." Bebe popped up beside us, wicked grin on her face. "Speaking of which, here's a Snickers. I heard your stomach growling on the way in." She handed me the candy bar. Leave it to the doctor to monitor my less-than-desirable body functions in the middle of a rescue.

Duncan waved at her to hush while Sierra made some excuse that her nanites were interfering with the garage's video signal over the intercom. She told them the security team here would assist her in escorting me down to the lab. Either the folks Mallory hired were that stupid or she carried a lot of credibility as the boss's daughter. Either way, only Kane, Able and their fellow science geeks should be waiting for us downstairs.

Once she flipped the intercom off, Bebe threw a Snickers bar at her. She snagged it as neatly as an outfielder with a pop-up fly. While Sierra and I snacked on chocolate and peanuts, Phil and the boys stacked the unconscious security team in the back of another truck in the docking bay. If Bebe was right, her fairy dust would keep them out for eight hours.

We trooped through the inner dock doors and down the hall. Sierra waved towards the cargo elevator. She entered first and yanked out the wires on the security camera before waving us on. The butterflies circling in my stomach turned into Indy race cars. I prayed the Snickers wouldn't come back up. Going down into the rat hole where I was tortured? What the hell was I thinking?

Duncan and Caesar took stances next to the elevator doors, like SEALs with fangs, and motioned everyone behind them. I didn't argue. Getting shot once had been bad enough. I tucked Bebe behind me. She was the only person who came close to Normal in the group, and I wanted to keep her that way. I expected her to protest, but she kept silent.

Tiffany would have protested. Loudly.

The elevator took so long to move I figured I'd die of terminal boredom instead of anxiety before we hit the basement.

My stomach rumbled again. Duncan glared at me.

"I can't help it—"

Duncan laid a finger over my lips. I would have gotten the message if he had put his damn finger over his own damn lips. It was all I could do not to pull his finger into my mouth and start sucking. Which led to thinking about sucking on other parts. Which led to . . .

I clenched my fist against my thigh in an effort to clear the erotic thoughts from my brain. I should have asked Bebe if my super metabolism meant everything increased. Even worse, we were in a life-and-death situation. And from the grin on Duncan's face, he understood and enjoyed my internal struggle without the telepathic assist.

I reached behind and pinched him on the ass. His jump had everyone staring at us. Caesar appeared ready to reprimand both of us, but the elevator ground to a halt, and the doors slid open.

Tyrone Mallory stood in the hallway, behind a goon squad with very big guns pointed at us.

Chapter 20

There was a click to our left. "Elevator's locked, sir."

"Daddy!" Before anyone could stop Sierra, she plunged off the elevator and threw her arms around Mallory. "I knew you'd figure out my message."

Despite nearly getting knocked on his ass, Mallory hugged her back. "Are you all right, baby? They didn't do anything to you, did they?"

"I'm fine, Daddy." She waved at me and smiled. "I told you I'd get her back."

"When we found the bodies in the antique shop, I was so worried about you." He gave his daughter another fierce hug. "Let's have Kane double-check."

"Just a damn minute!" I stepped from behind Duncan, only to have all ten semi-automatics follow my movements. I should have been scared, but I was so pissed about Sierra's double-cross the possibility of turning into Swiss cheese only dimly registered. Duncan hissed at me to get back. I ignored him and marched out of the elevator.

"Mr. Mallory?" The lead goon stepped between us.

"Don't shoot, Bob," Mallory said.

"Yes, Bob," Sierra purred. "Sam has been sooo helpful. See, Daddy? Aren't you glad you didn't activate her self-destruct?"

Now, I really was going to puke up the Snickers bar. "What self-destruct?" I bit out.

"Ah, Miss Ridgeway, you didn't think I'd let my proto-type run all over Los Angeles without a fail-safe, did you?" Mallory actually had the nerve to smile. I wanted to grind the asshole to a pulp. My fists clenched while I fought the urge.

"Can we keep Sam? Please, Daddy?" Sierra stroked her father's cheek. The way she clung to her father triggered a different kind of nausea. I didn't want to think about the possibilities there.

"No, baby, it's not safe to keep her or the others. Now I know you're all right, we need to get rid of them."

From the look on Sierra's face, this was the first time she'd ever been told no. "Daddy, I know you love me." She played with his tie. "Please? I've never had a sister."

Despite Bob standing between us, I glared at Sierra. "After what your dad did to us, to you, you're just going to kiss and make up?"

"Well, you know, Sam . . ." One hand rested on Mallory's shoulder as Sierra slithered behind him. She peered past him as she placed her other hand on his opposing shoulder. "Sometimes a girl's gotta do what a girl's gotta do."

Her hands whipped up, and with a sickening crack, she snapped her father's neck. A surprised look was the only thing Mallory had time for in the split-second before he died. She dropped the body, which landed with a thud. My mouth fell open. Even Bob's face turned green.

"Well, Mr. Augustine, I guess you and your people no longer have to worry about my father." Sierra wiped her hands on her thighs.

I didn't dare look behind me. The vampires' one bargaining chip had just evaporated.

"Now, gentlemen," she purred as she stepped over the body. Bob backed away from her, only to run into my shoulder. "Unless you want the same thing to happen to you, you will follow my orders. Is that understood?" She smiled sweetly at each man in turn.

Then she looked at me. Her eyes carried her insanity. There was no other word for it. I didn't know if it happened when they injected the nanites in her, when I stabbed her with the spoon, or a long time before either, but Sierra Mallory was definitely psychotic.

"You'll always have a place here, Sam." She held her hand out to me. "We're two of a kind, you know. The only two in the universe."

I couldn't help looking down at her father's body behind her. I may have killed since becoming a zombie, but in self-defense. Not like this. Not in cold-blood. Suddenly, I couldn't breathe.

She clucked her tongue. "Really, it's for the best, Sam. You don't want him experimenting on more people anymore than I do."

My eyes rose back up to meet hers. She must have seen something in my face. She dropped her hand and shook her head. "Don't give me that look. I want you to stay here." She smiled again. "With me." She sighed, the kind you make when the kid you're baby-sitting gets on that last nerve. "To show you my good faith." She snapped her fingers, and the ten guards looked like they'd nearly pissed themselves.

"Bob, take your men and release the prisoners."

"Ma'am." Bob's gulp would have been audible from Nevada even without my super hearing. "Are you sure?"

Leave it to the goon squad to tick her off. The expression of distaste crossing her features left no doubt as to Bob's fate if he questioned her again.

"Ma'am, yes, ma'am!" he barked. He and his men trotted down the hallway and disappeared around the corner.

Keep her talking, Sam.

Gee, thanks. And how do I make conversation with Hannah Lechter here? I thought back at Caesar.

String her along. You need to buy enough time for her men to bring the prisoners back.

Do I look like Kevin Spacey in The Negotiator? *And what if she tells her bozos to open fire while we're trying to get the victims out of here? Not to mention the damn elevator's locked and she could blow me up at any time.*

I was starting to get really mad. Get in, get the goods, get out. That's my style. Not playing Jodi Foster to little Miss Patricide. I guess I should have been thankful she hadn't started eating him.

You can do this, Sam. You're the only one who can. Sierra Mallory's developed an attachment to you—

Oh, I so didn't need to hear that.

"What's your problem?" Sierra snapped.

I blinked in confusion. "What do you mean?"

"Your face keeps twitching." She stepped closer and stared me in the eyes.

Pretend she's Matt Damon. Pretend she's Matt Damon, I chanted to myself. Damon was a much harder target to nail than Affleck. But I got Damon's bare tush once before. I could do this.

Pretend she's who?

Shut up, Caesar! Yelling telepathically at the man, who in all probability was some kind of prince, even if he wasn't king of the vampires, wasn't my wisest move. But I needed to concentrate on my acting skills.

"I was just considering your offer, Sierra," I said. Waving nonchalantly, I added, "I tend to have conversations in my head when I'm trying to make a decision. Max would tell you."

A skeptical expression filled her face. "I'll be sure to ask him."

"You know, I don't know if I can get used to all the money," I said as airily as I could.

Sierra laughed without any humor. She made Margaret Hamilton sound positively benign. "I've seen your parents' place, silly."

Oh, crap. I should not have brought my family up. She knew where they lived. Panic formed a physical lump in my throat I could barely talk around.

"Well, you know teenagers. Gotta rebel. If the 'rents have the dough, I gotta be poor." I shrugged, praying I acted and sounded casual.

"Oh, Samantha." My full name never boded well for me. "This isn't about money." I tried really hard not to cringe when she grabbed my hand and began stroking it. "It's about power," she whispered. She leaned away from my ear, her voice rising. "Absolute power. We can control life and death."

Footsteps coming down the hall interrupted her evil-takes-over-the-world monologue. Slung between each pair of squad members were five supernaturals: three vamps, a werewolf, and a witch. I was starting to figure out the signature scent of each species. The fact humans and witches smelled delicious didn't help my worry over controlling my appetite.

I knew for sure they were alive. I could hear their hearts beating. But I've seen pictures of African famine victims looking healthier than these five. My heart rose as I recognized Alex as the second person. The guards carried Anne behind him.

"Where's the other three, Bob?" Sierra's tone promised pain to the poor security guard.

Bob paled underneath his eye protection. "They died while you were gone, ma'am."

She let out a dramatic sigh. "Oh well, I guess five is better than none."

Each pair of guards handed me a prisoner. I passed them to Duncan and Caesar behind me in the elevator. As I handed Alex back, he tried to wink at me. The garbled words from him sounded vaguely like, "Damn time the cavalry showed up." But I couldn't be sure.

Once the last person was on the elevator, I turned to board when Sierra grabbed my hand again. She squeezed and tugged, nodding towards the hallway. "Come on, Sam. I'll show you the rest of the compound."

"I haven't said yes yet, Sierra."

The National Weather Service should issue severe storm warnings about Sierra Mallory's moods.

Matt Damon. Matt Damon.

I smiled and said, "I haven't said no either. Why don't you give me a couple of days to think about it?"

The smile she gave me could have frozen liquid nitrogen. "All right then. You can have seventy-two hours." She leaned close to my ear and whispered, "Then Sammy goes boom." She stepped back, and in a normal tone, said, "Let them go, Bob."

Bob twisted the key, and the elevator doors slid closed. Ten people in the elevator, even if it was a cargo elevator, made for a tight squeeze, especially since five of them were prone on the floor. Everyone who was conscious held their breath as the car started to move. Bebe knelt next to the former prisoners, checking vitals.

The vamp I didn't know sniffed at her ankles. It was so starved and filthy I couldn't be sure of its gender. She rapped it on the nose. "Just wait a few more minutes. We have blood in our vehicle."

The vamp muttered something that sounded like, "Thirsty now," but it managed to stop treating her like a scrumptious doggy treat. If I were starved for three months, I don't think I would have any kind of self-control. Heck, I was already worried about my self-control after three hours with nothing but a candy bar.

The elevator finally jerked to a halt. For an agonizing minute, I didn't think it would open. Would Sierra order the cable cut? Or was this another sadistic game and she'd trigger the nanites' self-destruct anyway, taking care of me and everybody in the tiny space? Everyone outside of Mallory Labs who knew what she really was besides Max and Tiffany.

And blowing my nanites would turn the two Normals into sitting ducks.

Then Phil was through the sliding doors and pulling Alex upright before they fully parted. In a flurry of motion, the healthy folks carried, or in Bebe's case dragged, the injured and starved towards the Hummer. We all were waiting for Sierra to sic the security guards on us, but no one showed a hair in the docking bay.

We piled in, trying to make Alex and the rest of the former prisoners as comfortable as possible. It wasn't easy. Caesar jogged over to the garage door controls.

I climbed into the driver's seat, only to realize Sierra still had the keys. Duncan slid into the passenger seat, the witch cradled in his arms. I took a good look at her for the first time. Underneath the haggard appearance, she couldn't have been out of high school. Bile rose in my throat. Tiffany's age.

He held out his fist to me. "You did not think we would let her keep them, did you?" I raised my hand, and he dropped the keys into my palm.

Gotta love a sexy British pickpocket. I looked from the keys back to his grinning face. *Eat you heart out, Artful Dodger.*

"We're not out of the woods yet," I said, but my lips spread in a matching smile.

The engine roared to life, and I eased the massive vehicle into reverse. Once through the garage door, I slowed long enough for Caesar to jump in through the passenger door Phil held open. The two guards at the garage door stood by and watched as I executed a J-turn and sped down the driveway. I shared a glance with Duncan, then gunned the engine. With my questionable control, we may not be able to hear each other telepathically, but I was definitely learning his expressions. I had already figured out Caesar's Hummer wasn't the civilian issue version, despite the paint job. I just hoped the custom reinforcements would be able to knock down the security gate.

Sierra must have called ahead because the gates were wide open as we approached. Again, the guards just watched as we raced past them and into the night. A deep-felt sigh filtered past my lips at the temporary reprieve. Now, I could only pray we made it to safety before any more of the prisoners died.

Chapter 21

Selene eyed Sierra over the goblet she held and took a sip. "That wasn't necessary." Not that she hadn't planned to eliminate Tyrone anyway, but his premature death altered her timetable once again.

The petulant girl flung herself on the brown suede couch, a pout tugging her lips. "Father would have kept us apart. You know it."

Setting the glass of blood on the bar, Selene schooled her expression. This situation was no different than the maneuverings she'd done in Rome or with her own kin over the centuries. She only had to keep her focus on her goal.

She crossed what had been, until an hour ago, Tyrone's office and settled on the couch. Sierra automatically shifted until her head rested on Selene's lap.

"In my time, we believed the killing of a family member unleashed the Erinyes."

"Well, you're still here, aren't you? You haven't been dragged off by any Fury."

The whine in Sierra's voice joined with her words and sent a wave of cold through Selene's soul. Ptolemy's death had been an accident. It didn't negate her real intent, killing Caesar and his whore.

Sierra pulled her cell phone out of her pocket. "Maybe I should go ahead and kill her now."

Selene wrapped her hand around the hot pink device and tugged it from the girl's hand. "No."

"But—" Sierra rolled into a sitting position.

"Let Caesar and his boys play hero. They'll be too involved saving the reporter to give us any trouble over the next two days." She wanted to give Caesar and Duncan time to call in other Augustine enforcers. The more she could take out in one blast, the easier it would be to force the other vampires into compliance. She stroked Sierra's hair. "And we need to be ready for the shareholders meeting."

A sly smile filled Sierra's features. She trailed fingertips across Selene's silk clad arm. "I can think of other things to do in the mean time."

Selene wrapped her hand around the girl's and brought it to her lips for a kiss. "I have some last minute details to handle. Why don't you find one of the guards to play with?"

A loud, disappointed sigh filled the air. "You know what they say about all work and no play."

Letting a smile cross her lips, Selene leaned back. "You play enough for both of us. Record it and I'll watch with you later."

Sierra's delighted grin was her only answer before she flounced out of the office.

The fake flirtation faded as Selene's muscles relaxed. A slight headache twinged behind her eyes. The charade would have to hold until the end of the week. She didn't want to eliminate the girl until the board signed the paperwork giving her full control of the Mallory businesses in the event of Sierra's death. There would be fewer questions and fewer disappearances to deal with.

Rising from the couch and retrieving her dinner, Selene stood at the window and watched the evening traffic. It hurt that Sierra had become a liability. Mallory shouldn't have rushed into using the nanites. Now, the girl's mental instability could destroy everything she'd worked toward over the last two years.

She sighed. Maybe she truly was doomed to repeat Mother's mistakes and destroy everything she loved.

—————•—————

"We need to strike, and we need to strike now!" The sound of a body part hitting a solid object punctuated Duncan's statement. Despite the thick brick walls of Caesar Augustine's real house, everyone in the formal living room jumped, including the Normals. The argument in the study continued, but the voices dropped to the point I couldn't hear them anymore.

Apparently, you had to reach the century mark to earn Caesar Augustine's trust. Only Duncan, Alex, and Anne were allowed in on his little strategy session.

I stomped in a circle around the room, not knowing what else to do. The navy and gold upholstery and cherry paneling on the walls made the freakin' place feel like a funeral parlor. Not what I expected in the Mediterranean-style Brentwood mansion when we first pulled up to the steel gates.

The good news was Alex and Anne weren't rotten meat mush. A few gallons of blood, showers, and in Alex's case a shave, and the vamps were almost as good as new. Alex turned out to be better looking after he was fed and clean than I would have guessed.

Not that he had anything on Duncan.

I never did find out the name of the third guy. He took off while I whacked off the rats' nest Anne's hair had become after her weeks of imprisonment. I didn't have a choice. Now, her waist-length tresses gone, she sported a short, spiky 'do that rivaled Sharon Stone's. She didn't seem very pleased even though it set off her elfin features perfectly.

While I flaunted my ability with a pair of scissors, Bebe had called the teen witch's family. They collected little Sabrina, and the dad stated they were going into hiding. Alex's buddy, Logan, went with them as a bodyguard. When Duncan protested, the tall, hunky werewolf flashed a grin that raised the hairs on the back of my neck and said the assholes wouldn't catch him sleeping again. I pitied anyone who crossed this guy after everything Mallory's goons had done to him.

After contacting Los Angeles's head witch, Bebe had left for her medical lab. She had taken blood and tissue samples from all the former prisoners, including another round from me and the ones Tiffany had taken from Sierra while the heiress had been unconscious in the back seat of Duncan's SUV.

Phil had disappeared as well, muttering something about calling her insurance agent concerning the damage to her shop. I noticed she waited long enough to make sure Alex was all right, but as soon as he tried to talk to her, she got bitchy on him. There was a story behind the two of them, but my curiosity would have to wait.

Max and Tiffany had driven Bebe's car to the mansion, or vamp HQ as I called it. He phoned Mom and Dad and told them to stay in London for yet another week. When Dad questioned him, Max finally relented, keeping his story to the break-ins at his place and the Times. He added we were fine, but he was concerned about their safety if they returned to Los Angeles. Despite Max not spilling my new status, Mom still got on the phone and claimed his problems had to be my fault somehow.

Receiver still glued to his ear, Max had caught my grimace and rolled his eyes. I can't say I was fond of my new abilities at that moment. Suspecting Mom trashed me behind my back on a regular basis was one thing. Hearing confirmation of said suspicions was another.

"When are they coming out of there?" I muttered, more to myself than anyone else, and glared at the wall. Why couldn't the mad scientists have given me x-ray vision along with the super hearing?

"Whenever they're done, Sam."

I turned to find Max looking up from the couch, irritation on his face. I had tried to ignore him and Tiffany making googly eyes and whispering for the last hour. And here I was worried about Tiffany pulling a Lolita.

Duncan hadn't seemed to mind my thirty-one-year-old brother making the moves on his nineteen-year-old niece. Or maybe he had been ignoring them as well.

I don't know why it bothered me so much. Tiffany was an adult. Sort of. Or maybe I didn't like being reminded of the age difference between me and Duncan.

Another bang made the three of us jump, but this time the noise came from another area of the humungous house. I could hear Bebe shouting for everyone as she headed in the direction of the study.

"We're in here!" Tiffany yelled back.

Breathless, the good doctor paused in the doorway of the living room long enough to wave us to follow her before charging down the hall to where Anne and the boys held their strategy session. Despite her excitement, huge, dark circles had surrounded her eyeballs and taken them prisoner. She must have been up all night. Curiosity overwhelmed my wariness of Caesar, and I followed. Max and Tiffany trailed in our wake.

Bebe shoved the study door open without knocking.

Caesar's head jerked in our direction, annoyance plain on his face.

"You can have your snit fit later, sweetie. Everyone needs to hear this. Especially Sam."

Okay, she didn't say "Samantha". Full name equaled bad. The news couldn't be that terrible. Right? So why did my stomach fill with acid?

Duncan edged closer to me, his presence comforting in the insanity my world had become. He wrapped an arm around my shoulders and whispered, "It will be all right." I nodded at his words, but numbness spread throughout my body.

Bebe addressed her words to everyone. "All the prisoners' tests came back negative for alterations. The only problem is Sam." She kept eye contact with me as she continued. "As we suspected, your nanites are programmed to rewrite a person's DNA. Similar to the V-virus, but without most of the nastier side effects. Since cancer is your own cells gone wild, Sierra was cured by the nanites fixing them."

"What do you mean 'most of the nastier side effects'?" I already knew I wouldn't become meat mush under a small dose of UV. I steeled myself for the worst.

Bebe took a deep breath and launched into her lecture. "Ultraviolet radiation, silver and garlic are not detrimental to your cell structure. You have a lot of the positive attributes, such as increased strength and stamina, accelerated healing, and enhanced senses."

"What about my increased appetite?"

She shrugged. "You're consuming a Normal diet, which to me is a good sign. If you were a vampire or a were, the consumption would be expected with the changes in your body and your recent injuries. My guess is your appetite should taper off in a few days."

"And you're rehashing what I already know." My eyes narrowed as I regarded the doctor. "What bad stuff are you leaving out, Bebe?"

Her face blanked. "Maybe we should discuss the rest privately, Sam. There's—"

"No, dammit! We're talking about this here and now." My fists clenched at my sides, nails digging into my palms. Marginalization and patronizing attitudes didn't sit well with me.

Bebe paused for so long I didn't think she was going to speak, but she finally gave a slow nod. "You won't be able to have children, Sam." Tears pooled in her brown eyes, but she tried to blink them away. "It's the one component of the virus they couldn't eliminate. Other than that you're totally healthy."

I was fine. The relief sank as the import of the rest of her words registered.

No kids.

Nada.

Never going to happen.

I really hadn't thought about having babies. I just assumed when I met the right guy, it would happen. Like deciding to move to Beverly Hills or O.C. for the better school districts.

I never thought the choice would just be taken from me. Anger flared and died. I couldn't even smack around Tyrone Mallory now. He was as dead as me and my non-existent children.

Sympathy swam in Bebe's unshed tears. She understood part of how I felt. She loved a man who was in the same position I was. But dammit! She could still conceive and carry a baby.

If she walked away from the man she loved. Or if he consented to another man donating sperm.

Would someone be willing to make those kind of sacrifices for me?

I had to drag my attention from my pity party to concentrate on the conversation.

"What about the V-virus?" Max asked. "Could the nanites be a cure for the vampires?"

Bebe shook her head, disappointment etched in her face. Damn, no wonder she was so intent on discovering how the nanites worked. A possible cure for her sweetie would mean everything to her.

"The virus completely rewrites a vampire's genetic code, too," Bebe said. "The nanites aren't sophisticated enough to distinguish between what's original and what's been added. Maybe someday, but not yet." She turned back to me. "The irony is anyone with nanites can't become infected with the V-virus."

I didn't care for the knowing look she shot me. Infection of a potentially fatal disease was enough to keep my lust at bay when it came to Duncan. Was I that obvious to everyone around me?

Yes. Caesar's grin matched Bebe's.

I hate it when someone else figures out my feelings before I do. I didn't bother giving him the satisfaction of a reply.

"So basically Sam will have super strength, super speed, and live forever," Max said.

Bebe nodded. "There's no reason why she can't lead a normal life." She turned back to me. "You can't go to your regular doctor though. We can't let news of your real condition get out, to either the Normal or the supernatural communities."

"No, she can't pretend to be Normal."

I stared at Caesar. The look on his face was a mixture of pity and steel.

"I'm sorry, Sam, but if you don't age, someone will figure out there's something different about you," he said.

I shrugged out of Duncan's comforting hold. I couldn't accept Caesar's inevitable truth. "So I move every few years."

"What about your family?"

I waved in Max's direction. "My brother already knows about the supernatural community."

"And your parents?"

The desire rose to shove Caesar's relentless logic back down his immortal throat. I couldn't answer his question because frankly I wasn't sure they could accept the truth. But he wasn't the only one with logic as a weapon. "The point will be moot if Sierra activates the self-destruct."

Full-blown sympathy filled his eyes. "Which leads to our original problem with Mallory Labs." He drummed his fingers on his desk, the only outward indication of his worry. "We still need to destroy it."

"Why? If they are on the right track to finding a vampire cure—" Tiffany started.

"A cure potentially worse than the original disease," Duncan responded, more gentle with her than I would have been. "They obviously have not found a way to prevent the sterilization of the patient. And if they restore such functions, there is the possibility the robots might miss a snippet of RNA that will result in a future child becoming a vampire."

"It doesn't mean they won't find a way to solve those problems." Tiffany's eyes flitted from face to face, seeking an ally.

I hated to burst her bubble when her gaze met mine. "Tyrone's dead, and Sierra has no interest whatsoever in altruism."

"Think she'll sell to the highest bidder?" Alex said.

"Not necessarily," I ventured, a little surprised the vampires were now taking my opinions seriously. "She's more concerned with power. She'd exchange the nanites for personal favors, people she can control." I frowned and shivered. "She'd put a self-destruct in them in case someone gets out of line."

"Isn't that a little James Bond?" Max asked.

"You think it's fiction?" I raised an eyebrow and waved a hand at the assemblage in Caesar's office. "You're kidding, right?"

A scowl creased Duncan's face. "How can we be certain there truly is a self-destruct in your nanites? Sierra Mallory's claim could be a bluff."

"We aren't," I said. I could barely get my voice above a whisper. Tyrone Mallory was a lot of things, but stupid wasn't one of them. He'd have figured some way to keep tabs on me.

Everything dropped into place, and I smacked a palm on my forehead. "It wasn't telepathy. They've been tracking me through the nanites. But why'd it take them so long to catch up with me?"

"Magick."

Everyone looked at Bebe. She raised her hands and affected a Georgian accent. "I'm a doctor, not a computer geek."

"Seriously, though," she continued in her normal voice. "Between my spells for breaking into and out of the labs and my examination of you yesterday morning, there was probably enough magickal interference to disrupt the homing signal."

"Look," I croaked, throat dry at the thought of an impending, and very permanent, second death. "Sierra gave me seventy-two hours to take her up on her offer. Couldn't we create a computer virus or something to destroy the nanites?"

Caesar shook his head. "We're talking about very sophisticated code. My people could use one of your samples to reverse engineer, but they couldn't do it in less than two days. And we don't know what removing the nanites would do to you."

I felt the empathic wave of concern from him. From the little I'd learned about him, he had to be pretty upset to let that kind of emotion slip. Not that I was happy with his analysis either.

"Too bad we cannot drop a tactical nuclear device on the git's head," Duncan muttered. The flutter of air tattled his approach before both arms wrapped around me and pulled me snug against his chest. "We will figure something out, Sam," he whispered.

Damn, it was bad if he didn't use "Samantha". His hold felt comforting against the thought of dying twice within a week. Even in my limited knowledge, the nanites couldn't act as repair-bots when they were the explosive cause of damage. And there's no fucking way Sierra would let me live if I refused to join her little crusade.

"Too bad Mallory killed Fred. He's the only one I know who could backward engineer these damn robots," I muttered.

"Who's Fred?" Alex asked.

"A friend of mine who was a computer geek for the LAPD. Mallory's goon killed him because he . . ."

My voice trailed off as Max's eyes met mine. I could tell by the flash in his that he had the same thought.

"Oh shit," I whispered.

Max shook his head, his expression bleak. "Mallory's probably already searched his apartment, assuming Fred had anything with him."

"What the hell are you people talking about?" Tiffany's gaze flicked from person to person, totally lost. I could tell from the vamps' faces they had already read our minds. Duncan may not be able to read mine, but he sure as heck could read Max's.

I took sympathy on the kid. "We think my friend Fred may have been working for Mallory. It would explain why he warned me away and why Mallory's people killed him." I shook my head and stared at the floor. "I just wish I knew for sure."

Bebe cleared her throat, drawing everyone's attention. "There is a way we can find out."

"No!" Caesar roared, leaping to his feet. Red suffused his face, and the tidal wave of anger from his mind almost knocked me off my feet despite Duncan's hold.

"It's the only way, sweetie." Bebe's voice was velvet-coated steel. "You know Mallory wouldn't let anything regarding this project out of his control. But by murdering Sam's friend, he's done just that."

"And what if he refuses to leave your body when he's answered our questions," Caesar snapped.

"I'm willing to take that chance." Her chin raised in defiance, a slight tremble in her hands the only outward sign of nervousness.

"What are you talking about?" I asked.

"A séance to speak with Fred."

Damn. I was afraid Bebe was going to say that.

Chapter 22

Duncan and I closed heavy scarlet drapes against the late afternoon sun drifting through UV film into Caesar's conservatory. That's what he called the room. Sounded like a pretentious way of saying, "This is where Mariah Carey sings during her private performances."

I grabbed a couple of heavy upholstered chairs. "Don't we need to do a séance at midnight? Or at least wait until it's dark?"

Duncan shook his head and hoisted two chairs on each arm. Showoff. "Not with someone as powerful as Bebe."

He explained the danger to Bebe as we moved chairs into the hallway. If the ghost still hung around without crossing to the "other side", a witch could talk to him or her. No muss, no fuss.

But if the ghost had crossed the line, the witch would summon the spirit back to this plane of existence and allow it to possess her physical body for a short while. Most times the ghost would answer questions and then depart, leaving the witch none the worse for wear.

Sometimes though the guest phantom decides to take up permanent residence. If the witch's soul, spirit or whatever you wanted to call it isn't strong enough to fight back, then she is forced out of her physical body and dies. The ghost thinks it's home free in the land of the living, but it's not. The physical body reacts to the soul transplant just like an organ transplant, and there wasn't any way to stop the rejection.

Duncan said the one time he saw such an incident, the ghost lasted less than a week in its new body, and its second death still gave him nightmares. For Mr. Tough-Guy to admit any weakness, the reality had to be pretty bad, and it scared the hell out of me.

We carried the last of the furniture out of the room when Alex and Anne strolled in with armloads of white and black candles and set them in a corner. The four of us started rolling up the intricate red and gold Persian rug dominating the room, now that every other furnishing had been removed.

I wanted to reassure Duncan that Fred wouldn't do anything like trying to keep Bebe's body, but if he had worked for Mallory as Max and I suspected, then all bets were off. My heart felt like it would sink through Caesar's Italian marble floor. I didn't want to believe Fred had stooped so low as to whore his skills out to a sadistic asshole like Tyrone Mallory. If he had, I prayed Fred wasn't too busy burning in Hell to help me.

Underneath the remarkably dirt-free wool rug was an intricate pattern in the floor. We stood to lift the rug, and I looked back. A giant pentacle, done in various shades of white, black, and gray marble and outlined in silver, took up the entire room. I whistled, amazed at the workmanship and detail. The goods and labor had to have set Caesar back seven figures.

Maybe Bebe was a material girl after all.

The vamps and I lugged the rug out into the hallway. As we dropped our load against the far wall, the rest of the gang trooped towards us, Bebe, in the lead, dressed in a gauzy white robe, with Max and Tiffany right behind her. Caesar brought up the rear, a nasty scowl still plastered across his handsome face.

I caught a whiff of herbs emanating from the huge bag Bebe carried as she passed by. I couldn't say what they were, but ghosts probably loved them. They were a sweet counterpoint to the sandalwood pervading the house. We followed her back into the conservatory, and she began ordering everyone where to put equipment and which color of candles went where. Kind of like George C. Scott in *Patton* but without a cute little helmet and whip.

By the time she was satisfied, white candles followed the ring of silver, except each tip of the pentagram had a black one. Bebe sat in the center, surrounded by her bowls of water and herbs, incense burner, a goblet I was certain held wine with a little something extra from the musty odor, a laptop (of all things), and a couple of gross objects I didn't want to think too hard about. In the middle of her pile, Pooh's cracked crystal winked at everyone.

My eyes shot to Max's.

"She needed something personal of Fred's if we had it. I didn't think you would mind," he said with a shrug.

Bebe rose and shooed Tiffany and Max into a corner. "Go sit down. And no matter what you see—" She waggled her index finger. "Do. Not. Move. If you break the circle before I dismiss the ghost—" She lowered her voice. "The consequences would be dire."

Wide-eyed, Tiffany did what she was told for the first time since I'd met her. Max dropped to the floor next to her and wrapped an arm around her scrawny shoulders. I tried not to gag.

Bebe turned and gave me a secret wink. I didn't care if she was bullshitting the kid, but she wasn't reassuring my nerves one bit. I'd been holding Fred's hand when the doctors pronounced him upon our arrival at the ER. With everything I'd suspected and the wallowing guilt, I sure didn't want to face him, but the alternative was me splattered over Caesar's walls, ceiling and floor.

She flicked the light switch. With the drapes closed, total darkness enveloped the room except for the doorway's rectangle of dim ambient light that managed to penetrate this deep into Caesar's fortress. The illumination was sufficient for me, so I was sure the vamps could see as well. The mortals would be nearly blind.

The mortals. Shit, I was really beginning to accept this undead stuff.

Witches must have excellent vision, too, because Bebe moved unerringly and placed each of the vampires at a star point. She instructed them to sit inside the circle and hold one of the black candles. The vamps did as instructed, but they all were careful not to touch the silver embedded in the floor. Interesting. How many of the other Hollywood stories of vampire deterrents were true?

Before I could ask, Bebe tugged my arm and guided me toward the last one. My feet dragged in my brand-spanking new tennies.

"Uh-huh. I'm going over there," I insisted, pointing at Max and Tiffany's corner.

"Sam, I'll have a much easier time with this if I have five supernaturals."

"So get another vamp." I jerked my arm out of her grip.

"You're the only supernatural who also knew Fred. He'll respond to you much better than anyone else here."

I held up my hands. "Whoa, there. You didn't say a damn thing about me having to actually talk to a dead Fred."

Tiffany giggled behind me. I could feel everyone's eyes boring into me. Okay, everyone who could see me. I couldn't do this. I had watched the man die for Chrissakes!

Bebe's big brown eyes blinked. Twice. Three times. "It's your choice, Samantha. It's your life." Her soft voice wasn't threatening but pronounced my doom all the same.

"What life?" I muttered. I couldn't meet her earthy gaze any longer. I stared at the tips of my shoes and wrapped my arms tight around myself. Here was a woman willing to risk her real life for my undead one, and all I wanted was to run for the Sierras. And I didn't mean my psycho zombie twin either.

If nothing else, I would find out the truth about Fred. Maybe find a way to redeem him if he had been that deep in with Mallory. The scrawny-assed kid in me owed him. Raising my head, I took a deep breath, nodded, and headed for the last candle.

After I sat, Bebe picked up a butane lighter. As she approached me, I said, "Aren't you supposed to be able to light them with your fingertip?"

She rapped my head with the extra-long Bic before igniting the wick of the candle I held and proceeding around the room. Once all the candles glowed, she closed the door. The flickering flames resembled our church at Christmas, all lit up and pretty.

I hadn't thought of church in a long time, had stopped going years ago. Could I even go to a service now? Now that I was dead, did I even have a soul? I'd have to ask Duncan and Bebe when this was over.

Bebe curled up in the middle of the pentagram in some kind of yoga position.

The flexibility she displayed as she sat left no doubt in my mind as to the real reason Caesar was enamored with the beautiful witch.

That's none of your business, young lady.

I waggled the fingers on my free hand in apology at the still scowling Caesar across the room. Anne and Alex shared wicked grins. The fact Duncan, sitting to my right, rolled his eyes in confused disgust relieved me to no end. It was bad enough every other vampire in the room knew how sex-obsessed I had become. Maybe my attraction with Duncan did have more to do with my revved up metabolism than him.

Okay, my self-deception didn't extend that far. If I were that horny from the damn robots, I'd be after anything with a penis. My heavy sigh sent my candle's flame darting in every direction.

Ignoring the byplay of the vampires and me, Bebe lit her incense and rose. Starting once again at my point, she circled the outside of the silver ring, waving the burner as she went and muttering something under her breath. Even with my enhanced hearing, I couldn't quite make out her words, almost like the sounds were another language in another dimension. I shivered, as a chill seemed to seep from the floor. My candle flickered again and not from my breath. Drops of melted wax burned my skin, but it was uncomfortable, not painful. The nanites were already doing their job.

She reached me and began a second circle on the inside of the silver ring. Ozone mixed with the earthy incense. Her robes whispered as she strode past me. For the first time, I noticed her eyes were closed as she walked. Yet she avoided each candle.

If I were performing this little ceremony, my clothes and the house would be on fire by now.

The chill grew and was joined by an electric tingle in my fingers and toes. I glanced over at Max and Tiffany. The kid shook violently, and big brother now had both arms wrapped around her.

Part of me rejoiced the freezing temperature wasn't my imagination. Another part was concerned about the attention Max showered on her. Being a Normal surrounded by folks who weren't must be tough for Tiffany. Having Max around must be reassuring for her in some way, but the seeming attraction between them bothered me. Maybe because of my own reservations about the age difference between Duncan and me. I mean, how do you talk, really talk and not trade wisecracks, to someone who probably knew Queen Elizabeth I?

Bebe drifted by me again, but this time she returned to the center of the star and raised her arms. She shouted something in her unrecognizable language and golden light flared from the ring surrounding us, arcing upward until the six of us were surrounded in a half bubble of energy. Did the golden sphere extend through the floor to surround us?

With the completion of the half sphere, warmth spread through my body. I placed the flat of my free hand against the marble. Heat now seeped through the floor. Not uncomfortable. More like bed sheets fresh out of the dryer.

Damn, I could write an entire series for the *Scoop* on Bebe's tricks. Not that she'd let me though. What she was doing didn't come close to the crap my Blessed-wannabe roommate did in college.

Soft popping came from the little cast iron cauldron in front of Bebe, but no fire burned under it. She threw some of her herbs in the pot, and the contents hissed and bubbled. Muttering again, she held the silver goblet up in salute then drank deeply. She sat the cup down and picked up the remains of the Pooh watch.

Eyes closed, she rocked to the rhythm of her chanting. The only words I could make out were "Fred Nguyen."

I couldn't tell how long Bebe's ritual went on. My butt began to ache. The marble may have been warm, but the temperature didn't change the fact it was still rock.

The watch hit the floor with a clatter, and my attention jerked from the discomfort in my behind back to our resident witch. Her eyes were open, and a grin spread across her face as she eyed me.

"Hey, kid. Hear you're causing another ruckus."

Despite the warmth in our bubble, my veins turned to ice at the deep voice. Bebe had definitely left the building.

Chapter 23

I recognized the expectant look on Bebe's face from another person. Someone whose face I watched a nurse cover before the ER staff formed a morose line out the swinging doors.

I swallowed hard, but my voice still shook. "Hi yourself, Fred. How's it going?"

The witch's shoulders shrugged, the gesture unmistakably my dead friend's. "I'm okay. All things considered."

"Where were you?" I choked out.

She, or was that he, wagged a finger at me. "I can't answer questions about what happens after you die, Sam, so don't ask." The sound bursting from his lips could only be described as a cackle. "But then, you're as dead as I am."

"Yeah, but I look a hell of a lot better," I shot back.

He sobered and fixed me with a sad stare. "Didn't think I'd die this soon. Or that way. Thanks for staying with me until the end."

"You knew?"

He nodded, then grinned again. "Didn't think you'd join me so soon either." He picked up the cracked Pooh from the floor. "Or that you'd stoop to stealing my watch." He sighed and shook his head. "I really thought you'd be smart enough to drop the whole Alton story after I died."

Anger flared inside me, and I could barely hold my candle in my trembling fingers. "Your fault, asshole. You should have told me what was going on. And I didn't steal your damn watch."

He shrugged again. "Doesn't matter. Can't take it with me and all that jazz."

He noticed the fingers that held the watch for the first time. A look of shock crossed his delicate features and the watch crashed to the marble for a second time.

I wondered if the timepiece could ever be fixed with all the trauma it had suffered the last few days.

Fred yanked the gauzy robe away from his neck and looked down. "Hot damn! I've got boobs."

"Fred." I waved. He ignored me. Wonderful. His breast fetish had taken over.

Caesar growled and made to rise. I wasn't sure what would really happen if one of us broke the circle, but I figured it couldn't be good. I waved the vampire prince back down with my free hand.

"Fred! Fred!" I snapped my fingers to get his attention.

His eyes returned to me.

"Do you understand what's happening now?"

He licked his lips and nodded. "You need to talk to me about Tyrone Mallory." He grinned. "Heard the bastard got whacked by his own daughter. Serves him right."

I nodded, but he was already looking down into the robe again. I wasn't sure if Fred's boob obsession would override his common sense, but I didn't want to take chances with Bebe's life. I snapped my fingers, and his attention returned to me.

"Were you working on the side for Mallory?"

"Yes." His face turned almost mournful. "It was easy money at first, and when he approached me, what he was doing—" He shook his head. "It would have revolutionized medicine, Sam."

Concern tugged at me. "You didn't know what he was really up to?"

His head turned from me.

Realization washed through my conscience. "Oh my god. Fred!"

When he looked back at me, tears shimmered in his eyes. "It's not the first time, Sam. I—" Unreleased sobs choked his voice. "I didn't want you to know. I didn't want my sisters to know. What I am. What I was capable of." He swiped his hand across his face. "All of you thought I was some great hero. It felt good, and I wanted to be that hero, but—"

He turned away again. A cheek muscle clenched on Bebe's face as Fred fought his emotions. He swallowed, a rough grinding on the witch's delicate throat, and he met my gaze once more. "The only reason *they* let me come to you was to save your life. They said what I do now doesn't tip the scales enough to—" Another choking sound. "I-I couldn't let you get hurt."

Bitter laughter ripped from my throat. "You mean, any more than I am?" I didn't have time to worry about who Fred's mysterious *they* were.

"I'm so sorry, kid. Mallory kept tabs on me. I didn't put him and your mystery PI together until it was too late. I never meant for you—"

"I know." Tears gathered in my own eyes. "I know, Fred. But right now, I need answers. Is there a self-destruct in my nanites?"

He seemed to gather himself and blew out a deep breath. "Yes. I can tell you how to disable it."

"Can it be re-enabled?"

I jumped at the sound of someone else's words. The vampires had faded to my peripheral awareness as Fred and I talked, but Duncan's concern was evident despite the harshness of his voice.

Fred shook his head as he turned to face my guy. "It's all software, not hardwired. I'll show you how to remove the code and lock out access to Sam. Without me, Mallory's people won't have a chance breaking the encryption."

For the first time in a week, hope glimmered in me. I pointed to the computer sitting next to him. "Can you use that?"

He grinned as he flipped the laptop open and booted it up. "Piece of cake, kid."

"How do you introduce the disable code?" Anger still tinted Caesar's voice.

Fred shot a look over his shoulder. "Wi-fi, same way the destruct works. When the witch brings down her circle, log into your ISP. I'll set it to automatically download to Sam's friends."

"And how can we trust you?" Caesar snarled.

"Don't worry, big guy. I have no intention of staying in your girlfriend's body."

A shudder wracked Bebe's petite frame, and he turned back to the laptop. "I definitely don't swing that way."

For the next hour or so, Bebe's slim fingers flew over the keys as Fred typed. Candlelight flickered strange shadows through the magickal shield and across the walls.

The writer in me marveled at the juxtaposition of magick and technology. I had to bite my tongue to suppress a giggle. If someone had told me a week ago all this bullshit was real, I would have said he should be certified. I sighed, sending the candle flame dancing again. Max was right. I wouldn't have believed him.

Above the clicking on the keys, I heard the soft sounds of Tiffany snoring in the corner.

Finally, with a triumphant grunt, Fred set down the laptop and closed the lid. He eyed me with his shit-ass grin. "You'll be right as rain, kid." He patted the computer. "Just remember to download as soon as I'm gone."

"Wait. What about Sierra Mallory? Is there a self-destruct trigger in her nanites?" Duncan asked.

Fred shook his head, long brown curls flying. "No. Sierra was the one person Tyrone trusted. We told his partner there would be one." He shrugged again. "Tyrone was careful to keep her away from me after that."

Mallory's partner had to be a vampire. From the ugly looks on the other vampires' faces, they knew who she was.

Except Duncan. His mind continued barreling down the zombie heiress track. "Could we introduce a virus—"

Fred shook his head more vehemently. "No virus. Anything that would take down Sierra would also kill Sam."

"But—" I started.

A sad smile crossed his lips. "I'm out of time, kid. Just remember your key to Sierra's destruction is in you."

The weird surety the sun was setting filled me as Bebe's body collapsed on the floor. Fred was gone again. This time I knew it was for good.

Chapter 24

"How do you feel?" Duncan's tension sent his eyes into neon overload, a prelude to a full vamp-out I was beginning to discover. Somehow, I took comfort in the fact he was ready to take on the world for me. He scooted closer to me on the living room couch.

"Take a chill pill," I murmured and patted his cheek. Stubble grazed my palm, sending my thoughts to places I really shouldn't go. "I don't feel any different." My stomach gurgled loud enough everyone stared at me, including Caesar from where he sat in an overstuffed chair with Bebe in his lap.

Her energy bubble had dropped the second she passed out, but it took her a few minutes to come around after Fred had left her body. Apparently, sunset is as much a trigger for ghosts as sunrise.

Caesar hadn't let anyone else touch her in the meantime. He cradled the pale, drawn woman in his arms, trying to get her to take a sip of the protein drink he held. I didn't blame her for batting the glass away. I always thought they tasted like crap myself, but right now, I could probably drink Jonestown Kool-Aid with no problem as long it met my caloric requirements.

While his boss carried Bebe into the living room, Duncan had hustled me along behind them, Alex on his heels carrying the laptop. Maybe they were afraid the magick would interfere with the house's wi-fi if we stayed in the conservatory, but I didn't get the chance to ask. Fred's code had been uploaded to the Internet in less than a minute. Alex confirmed the self-destruct had been disabled.

Now, five minutes later, everyone still eyed me like I was the astronaut on *Alien* and they were waiting for my chest to explode. My stomach gurgled again. Louder. Maybe the gut explosion thing wasn't that farfetched.

"I really need to get some food, guys." I stood and stretched, the pain in my butt cheeks finally starting to recede. "What do you feel like, Doc? I make a mean omelet."

"Eggs sound a hell of a lot better than this crap. I can't believe people think this is good for them." Bebe dumped the remains of her glass into the fichus sitting next to the chair. I'd lay odds Caesar would need to replace the plant within the next couple of days.

I followed Bebe to the kitchen, biting my cheek hard to keep any Stevie Nicks wannabe comments from spewing forth. The woman had saved my life. If she wanted to wear floaty white dresses around her house, so be it. Now, if I could get "Rhiannon" to stop playing in my head . . .

Max, Tiffany, and the vamps trooped in behind us. Everyone pitched in on the prep work. Soon veggie and cheese omelets were frying and blood was poured.

I noticed the vamps weren't being as subtle about their eating habits around Max and me anymore, almost like we were now part of the gang. I'd still probably make Duncan brush his teeth after meals. Watching him drink the stuff was one thing. Kissing him afterward was another.

Oh god.

The omelet I flipped landed on the floor with a splat. Tiffany scooped up the mess, but I stared at the frying pan until it started to smoke from the burning butter. Anne gently tugged the handle out of my hand before she pushed me toward the table and into a chair.

What the hell was I doing, thinking about kissing him again?

The doc said it was okay. You won't get sick.

I told the taunting part of my psyche to shut the fuck up, and I dug into the stack of toast Anne plunked in front of me. But I wouldn't be able to avoid the subject forever the way Duncan watched me over the edge of his mug. I pushed any relationship thoughts into a black hole in the back of my brain and reached for a knife.

My second concern, a half hour and six dozen eggs later, was how I was going to afford groceries when I started back to work. Alone, I had eaten five of the six dozen with a pound of cheese and a couple pounds of veggies mixed in, not to mention an entire loaf of bread. Contrary to Tiffany and Bebe's estimates, today was day four of my zombiehood, and my appetite had not slacked off.

While it could be wonderful to eat a whole cheesecake in one sitting without packing it on my ass, what would happen if I didn't have food readily available? What if I go insane from starvation like a vampire? Would I eat people if nothing else was available?

Under the table, Duncan squeezed my thigh. "I will not let you go hungry."

Ire raised its ugly little head. I stared at those mesmerizing green eyes of his, not sure who had betrayed me or if he was lying about not being able to see into my thoughts. The anger lashed out at the most convenient target. "I thought you couldn't read my mind."

He smirked. "I did not have to with the way you were salivating over the remains on Tiffany's plate."

The teen shoved the last half of her one, and only, omelet towards me. "Go ahead and finish it if you're still hungry."

I should have hesitated. I wanted to hesitate. Instead I pulled the plate over and shoveled.

That is, I shoveled until I felt vampire eyes boring into my skull. I looked up to see Caesar contemplating me like, well, like Kane did before he and Able started experimenting on me.

I choked down the last bite I was chewing. The lump began an uncomfortable slide to my stomach. "What?"

He took a sip from his wine glass. "The phantom said the answer to defeating Mallory was inside you."

"And?" The way he eyed me frayed what was left of my nerves. "You think I have some secret knowledge?"

"It could be as simple as reverse engineering your nanites, Sam," Alex drawled. "You can't take ghosts too literally."

"And sometimes they deliberately mislead the living," Duncan snapped back.

"Fred wouldn't hurt me. He came back to help me." Annoyance crept into my voice. "He gave us the way to deactivate my little self-destruct problem, didn't he?"

"He did not have to. And he stated he had little to gain." Something flashed in Duncan's eyes, and not just anger. Shit, was that jealousy?

"He didn't have anything else to lose either," I said, my voice soft at the remembrance of the remorse and guilt Fred exhibited.

"He lied to you, Samantha," Duncan said, his voice low, concerned.

"Mallory probably threatened his family the minute he had an inkling Fred was backing out." I shrugged. "I just got in the way. Besides, Mallory's suspicion of me had as much to do with you and Max as it did Fred."

"I am trying to protect you." Anger colored his words.

I threw down my fork. It bounced and backflipped before landing with a clatter on the tiled floor. "Well, stop it! Your protectiveness got me in this mess to begin with!"

"What is that supposed to mean?" His voice dropped, the tone ice-cold.

"If you had just given me the goddamn interview, instead of playing Mr. Mystery Man, I wouldn't have followed you Friday night. And I wouldn't be dead!" I grabbed the napkin off my lap and threw it on the table before I rose and stomped out of the room. Blood roared in my ears as I headed for the garden. The audacity of that man!

Soft night noises greeted me as I stormed out the French doors. It took every ounce of self-control I had left not to slam them. I would have twisted the metal hinges and shattered the wood frame as well as the delicate glass panes. After everything Caesar and Bebe had done for me, they didn't deserve to have their home smashed up.

The backyard was classic Brentwood. Decorative lighting illuminated the pool, leaving sections of the flowerbeds in shadows. A romantic setting if I didn't want to deck the only person for whom I currently had lustful feelings.

I lay down on one of the decorative concrete benches scattered through the garden. A handful of the brightest stars glimmered through the hazy glow of the city lights. I stared at Orion drifting across the sky. How the hell had I gotten into this mess?

Deep down, a tiny part of me was thrilled by Duncan's attention. God only knew how I would have gotten away from Mallory without him. It wasn't just the knight in shining armor act though. He was a genuinely nice guy. Grandma Neel always said to trust how a man treats the females in his family.

Then again, maybe he needed to be a little harsher to Tiffany after all.

My issues with Goth Girl aside, he was sweet and a great kisser and cared about his friends to the point he risked his life to save them and . . .

He was a total chauvinistic jackass. This is the twenty-first century. I wasn't his freakin' lap dog.

"He knows you're not a dog, Sam."

I fell sideways off the bench at Alex's voice. Crawling back up, I glared at him while brushing off my clothes. "You could warn a girl, you know."

He chuckled and sat down on my bench. "You were too busy with your mad-on to hear me coming."

"So now he can't get the pole out of his English *arse* and sent you out here to suck up to me."

Alex ignored my rant. "Beautiful night, isn't?" He leaned back and gazed up at the few stars filtering through the Los Angeles light pollution.

I snorted. "No fair. I don't know how to read your mind, so just say what you're going to say."

He drew his attention away from the sky and regarded me. "I didn't tell you how I became a vampire when we were in the pit, did I?"

Now thoroughly confused, I shook my head and sat next to him.

"I dropped out of medical school to join the Texas Rangers. My father threw a fit of course. He always said being a Ranger would be the death of me." He laughed softly at the memory he was lost in before turning his attention to me. "I do understand loving what you do and the parents not comprehending." He stared back up at the sky.

Silence seeped into the garden as I waited for him to continue. I'd rather gotten the impression the vampires didn't cough up their personal information often. Alex wouldn't have brought up his transformation without it having something to do with Duncan. And I really wanted to know about my mystery man.

"We were escorting a group of cargo wagons headed west when we were attacked. Bandits." He shrugged and turned to look at me. "By the time they were done, everyone was dead. The drivers. The guards. And my fellow Rangers."

"Everyone but you?" I interjected.

He nodded and rubbed his jaw. "Not sure how many times I was shot. I passed out when they were ransacking the wagons. They must have thought I was dead." He chuckled again. "Which probably saved my life. Anyway, the vultures were circling when I came to. I figured I didn't have much time left. I managed to crawl under the shadow of one of the wagons and kept 'em away as best I could, but I passed out again. A noise woke me up about sundown."

I wished I had my recorder with me. This was a hell of a story.

He grinned at me. "Just can't let go of your journalistic streak, can you?"

"Quit reading my mind and tell me what happened next," I snapped.

"The bottom of the wagon fell out. Our Duncan had himself in a hidden compartment that could only be opened from the inside. Was on his way to California to meet up with Caesar."

His face sobered. "There wasn't anything he could do for me, Sam."

"Except Turn you," I whispered. Oh God. What a decision to make. Watch someone die, or condemn him to a horrible disease.

"He told me what he could do to save me and asked me if it's what I wanted. At that point, I would've said yes to Old Scratch himself. I didn't want to die."

"So Duncan . . ." I couldn't say the words.

"Yep."

My breath caught, waiting for him to finish.

Alex's gaze pierced me through. "You've got to understand, Sam. I'm the only one he's ever Turned. And he's been torturing himself with guilt ever since."

I blinked, all my assumptions flying out the window. "What about Anne?"

He shook his head. "Rogues. We think they may have been working for Selene."

"This Selene is Caesar's sister, right?"

Alex nodded. "And the vampire who Turned Duncan. Against his will, I might add. She thought Turning him would bind him to her, make him grateful for immortality. He was horrified by what she'd done, so she never forgave him for rejecting her."

A wave of jealousy poured through me at his words.

He chuckled. This whole telepathy thing was really beginning to piss me off.

The humor died as he continued. "Over the centuries, she's killed almost all of his living family. The rogues she sent would've slaughtered baby Tiffany too if Duncan hadn't stopped them in time."

"How old was Tiffany when it happened?"

"About six months if I recall."

For once, I had a little sympathy for Goth Girl. "So that's why Duncan raised her," I murmured.

"As best he could. We all chipped in to help." He grinned. "Phil and the day guards handled the sunlight duties, but a houseful of vampires makes the night-time tasks a little easier."

"I can just see him changing Tiffany's diapers." Humor laced my next comment. "So he was your Tonto, huh?"

Alex roared with laughter. It took him a couple of minutes to catch his breath before he commented, "Trust me, Duncan's not as stupid as the producers made Jay Silverheels act. More James Bond, I would think."

Oh yeah, he'd look great in a tux. I was sure he'd look great without a tux too. "So what happened after he Turned you?"

Alex's grin widened until his fangs glinted from the pool lights. "Three nights later, we went hunting."

I chewed on the information Alex gave me for a good long time after he went inside. It definitely put Duncan in a different light. To face someone who'd deliberately infected him with an incurable disease. To watch your family murdered one by one over the course of centuries. To raise a baby girl without the ability to do real dad things like picnics in the park and afternoon recitals.

This was Tiffany though, so maybe no recitals. I really couldn't see Goth Girl in a pink tutu.

Still, I'd give almost anything to have someone in my life who was that loyal, that concerned about my welfare, that loving. We may have a difference of opinion on what constituted manners and affectionate behavior, but I had to admit he meant well.

I stood up and brushed off my jeans. No more games. It was time to do a little hunting of my own.

When I stalked back inside the mansion, somehow I knew the location of each person in each room. All it took was a little concentration. Maybe I was getting the hang of my new abilities after all. Definitely would come in handy with my job. Since no one was nearby to hear anything, even with super auditory abilities, I removed my bra *Flashdance*-style on my way through the hall.

The sharp smell of whiskey greeted me when I walked into Caesar's library. Duncan sat in one of those large squishy chairs perfect for curling up with a good book. He wasn't curled up though. His boots were firmly planted on the plush carpet, all the better to support the laptop across his knees.

He watched me through hooded eyes but didn't say a word while I grabbed a glass from the wet bar tucked in an alcove next to the door and sauntered over to him. Maybe I didn't need the false courage, but it gave my hands something to do so they didn't shake. I made the most of my braless state as I bent over to grab the bottle sitting on the end table next to him. A whistle escaped my lips as I read the label. These boys didn't skimp on the good stuff. I poured a shot and tossed it back. The phrase "going down smooth" didn't do the whiskey justice.

I wasn't sure if the liquid fortification was to deal with my feelings for Duncan or the thought of him and Alex eating the bandits. Well, drinking their blood anyway. When I had decided the bandits sounded like they tasted better than lizards, which was probably the only other thing the two could find in the West Texas desert, I realized my real problem.

Duncan scared me and thrilled me at the same time. Nothing like the adrenaline rush I'd had with Jake. Deep down, I knew my ex couldn't hurt me. With Duncan . . .

I splashed another round in the glass. With Duncan, there was surety and not so sure at the same time. The physical aspect wasn't half as scary as the emotional. Could I bear to give this man my soul?

I was really glad he couldn't read my mind right now. I'd run. Or he'd run. Besides, some things are better when shown.

I poured the third shot before I could meet his eyes. He held his glass out for a refill, still not saying a word, watching me with those unnerving green eyes.

I sat down on the chair across from him and leaned forward, my tumbler cupped in my hands. "So what are we going to do?"

"Get back into Mallory Labs and destroy the nanite project before Sierra can distribute—"

"No," I interrupted. "I mean us."

"Us?" He raised an eyebrow.

"Yeah. You know, you and me." I waved my glass between us, sloshing whiskey over the side. Rather than waste anymore of the amber liquid, I drank the rest in one swallow.

"There is no 'us', Samantha." His attention shifted back to the laptop screen.

Ok-a-a-ay. I didn't expect him to throw me on the floor and start doing the nasty, but what happened to all the protection bullshit he spouted earlier? I wasn't going to let him yank my chain anymore.

"Look, I know you're in total denial, pulling the whole 'tortured vampire who can't love anyone because he's cursed' bullshit. But guess what? David Boreanez didn't get an Oscar for his role, and you aren't either."

"Emmy."

"Huh?" I blinked.

His eyes met mine again. "David Boreanez did not receive an Emmy for his role as Angel."

I grinned. "Ah, so you pay attention to the real world after all." And I would have sworn those green irises of his had the faintest of glows.

"No." A wry smile crossed his lips. "Tiffany made me watch the show."

"You poor baby."

"It was torture."

We both fell silent as his words hit way too close to home.

My gaze fell away from his. A change of subject was necessary. The glass clinked when I set it down on one of the stone coasters on the end table. A plan was forming, and I was really, really glad he couldn't read my mind. "So you're telling me you have absolutely no interest in kissing me again?"

"Samantha, we both know it is not a good idea to continue a relationship given the circumstances."

I rose from my chair and faced him. "So you're admitting a relationship exists?"

"I am admitting no such thing." His haughty expression transformed into one of puzzlement when I picked up his laptop and laid it on my chair.

"You didn't answer my first question, Duncan." I plucked the tumbler out of his hand and set it on another coaster. No one can say I'm a rude guest who gets water rings all over other people's furniture.

He blinked as I leaned over him and braced my hands on the armrests.

"Are you telling me you have no interest in kissing me again?" I repeated.

Our faces were inches apart. His breath brushed my cheeks as he fought to control himself. His oh-so-delectable lips firm, he shook his head. "We cannot."

I crawled into the chair and straddled his lap. An undeniable urge spread through me as I pressed against him. I couldn't resist a grin. His lips said no but the rest of him agreed with my point of view. Pun intended.

"Tell me why we can't," I whispered.

He groaned and closed his eyes. He was losing this battle and he knew it. Strong hands gripped my waist, but instead of pushing me away, he tugged me closer.

"You heard the doc. There's no reason we can't," I whispered. "Just no biting."

His eyes opened a fraction, neon giving the planes of his face an odd greenish cast. "You do not trust me."

"It's not about trust." Reaching up, I threaded my fingers through his dark, silky waves. "We don't know what my blood could do to you."

The briefest of smiles tilted his lips. "A sensible precaution."

Our lips brushed, melded, explored. He pulled me tight against his chest, the pressure delightful. The kiss deepened, electrified, sent waves of sensation slamming through my body. The rub of my nipples against thin cotton amplified my reaction.

He drew back slightly, and I nibbled my way across his jaw line to his ear. He moaned as I swirled my tongue around the curve.

"Even so, we should not do this." He made absolutely no effort to get up, so I pressed the advantage. So to speak.

"Why?" I asked once again. "We're two consenting adults in the twenty-first century." Leaning back, I tugged off my t-shirt, the movements rocking my hips against his erection. I threw my shirt on top of his computer and grinned at him. "Though I guess there is that pesky law concerning necrophilia."

"Samantha?"

"Hmmm?" That was all I could manage as he palmed my breasts. The pads of his thumbs stroked the tips. Shivers ran across my skin.

"You talk too much."

Then he seized a nipple in his mouth, and any thoughts flew out of my head, leaving pure want in their wake. His tongue traced circles around the tip, leaving me breathless. He turned his attention to the other, lavishing the same careful attention.

My breath hissed and tension thrummed when his teeth caught the areola. The extra-sharp canines brought both pain and pleasure, but he was oh-so-careful not to break the delicate skin. Muscles relaxed, wallowing in the desire. Another nip, not so threatening this time, the pleasure turning to raw agony.

He cupped my head, pulled me closer for another tangling of tongues and lips. A long, slow exploration that nearly made me come right there. God, the man could kiss. Broad hands caressed my back, moved down to my ass and scooted me closer. If that were possible.

When he ended the kiss, I mumbled a protest and opened my eyes. His eyes definitely glowed neon green. A knowing smirk played along his lips. Somehow the tables had turned.

I didn't really care at that point. Need had replaced want. Need for him, need to touch him.

I fumbled for the hem of his sweater, but he swept it off in one smooth motion.

And there on his totally masculine chest was a totally feminine gold locket.

My breath caught, and I brushed a finger across the shiny surface. Why would he be wearing something like that? "Is there something you're not telling me?"

Amusement sparked in his eyes. "Why? Jealous?" Underneath his playful tone swam a painful ache.

Without any stupid telepathy, I knew. "Margaret's."

His sad nod left a shadow over the original mood, one I needed to drive away.

My gentle kisses brushed his forehead, his eyelids, his lips. Soft nips reignited the fire. Hands splayed of their own accord across his chest. I ran my fingers through crisp, dark hair, following the trail to the button of his jeans.

Jeans?

Hormones, the séance and our argument had addled my head so bad I hadn't even noticed Mr.-I-don't-wear-anything-but-slacks wore denim tonight. Somehow the change made him even more enticing. I unsnapped and unzipped.

Oh yeah, I knew he had to be a boxers kind of guy.

His erection strained against the emerald silk. I ran my fingers along the covered shaft, eliciting another groan from his throat. My thumb stroked the tip before repeating the same action. His eyes watched me, the desire unmistakable.

I found my feet long enough to skim the remaining clothes off both of us before settling back in his lap. Amazingly, Mr. Alpha Male didn't argue about me undressing him. He pressed against my core, and slickness followed. My body seemed to have a mind of its own when it came to Duncan St. James.

I rose again, this time I slid over him, the fit perfect, full, wonderfully tight. A sigh of delight escaped as he yanked my hips hard against his. All control was lost. Our bodies ground, capturing every inch of delicious friction.

Internal muscles squeezed around him, pulled him deeper, wanted all of him inside. Lips swallowed his answering moan, so his hands answered instead. Grasping, massaging, parting cheeks in an effort to get even closer. One hand on his chest to maintain my balance, I reached behind, fingers stroking his velvety sac. His mouth followed similar motions along my breasts. The bolder my touch, the more I was rewarded, sharp nips mingling in a pleasure/pain, sending me into a frenzy.

I matched him thrust for thrust until the world exploded into a million stars. He buried his face in my neck as his body stiffened from his own release. I gasped when the exquisite spasms of his cock launched another round of answering convulsions. I'd never come that hard, that fast, that many times.

Ever.

God, he was better than a ride at Disneyland.

He leaned back and chuckled as he eyed me. "You are not comparing me to 'It's a Small World', are you?"

I blinked, trying to clear the mind-blowing orgasms. I didn't say the Disney ride thing aloud, did I?

One of his aristocratic eyebrows shot upward. *I delivered mind-blowing orgasms?* Male pride made his smirk even more irritating.

Then I realized his lips hadn't moved. *Can you hear me?*

He frowned. "You are very faint now."

Wonderful, just wonderful. Now he could read my mind.

I smacked his shoulder. "Think something to me."

I have half a mind to spank you for continually hitting me.

Really?

With a growl, he rose and threw me over his shoulder in one smooth motion. There's something to be said about men with superpowers.

I will give you a demonstration of superpowers, you little vixen.

He gave my ass a light slap, and I squealed. But I couldn't complain. My position gave me access to his backside as well. His gorgeous, taunt, muscular . . .

Then I realized instead of heading for the couch, he was marching through the door.

"Duncan?"

He ignored my protest and continued up the stairs. I am normally not a prude, but traipsing through someone else's house in my birthday suit stretched even my natural lack of manners.

"Duncan! Someone will see us," I hissed.

And?

He was right. No one was anywhere close to us as he made a beeline for his bedroom. Though I had a sneaking suspicion the other vamps knew what we were up to.

Do not worry, Samantha. He nudged the door shut with his free shoulder before tossing me on his bed. He stopped my slide across the slippery navy and gold bedspread by pouncing on top of me. Tickles led to a languid kiss that heated things up again.

Except I realized we hadn't used protection, which is so not like me. Granted,

Bebe had said I couldn't have kids, but what if she were wrong? What if Duncan and I couldn't make it as a couple? I'd certainly made a royal mess of things with Jake. And I didn't want to raise a kid alone. Hell, I had problems seeing me raise one at all.

A sudden desperation enveloped his touches and caresses, like he was afraid I would disappear. He stopped abruptly and gazed at me. A frown creased his forehead. "Do not do that."

"Do what?" A little confused and a lot frustrated, I wanted to yell at him to shut up and go back to what he was doing with that marvelous tongue of his. I wanted to tell my own insecurity to shut up as well.

"Do not shut me out," he whispered. He had this really weird look on his face, a mixture of sadness, anxiety, and something I couldn't quite put a finger on.

I blinked, now thoroughly confused. If I were a guy, I would have been deflating about now. I rose up on my elbows. "What the hell are you blathering about?"

"I could hear your thoughts, and then—" He shrugged and shook his head. "It was like you slammed a door in my face."

"I didn't mean to." I started to get a little peeved and a lot anxious. Why was I apologizing when he was the one who stopped the action? It wasn't lovemaking. I so wasn't going there. Just fun and games among the undead. Right? It was the only way I could deal with this.

I waggled my eyebrows. "Why don't you pick up where you left off and see if it clears up the reception?"

Rather than taking my suggestion, he took my face in his hands and started over from the beginning. He took his time, nothing like the frantic passion from downstairs.

But then I realized I couldn't hear him in my head either. Maybe that's what made sex in the library so exciting. I could feel his arousal in my mind as well as other places, and it turned me on even more.

Duncan seemed intent on driving me insane, bringing me to the edge, then backing off. Tears rimmed my eyes from frustration when his flesh teased the opening of mine. Teased, tantalized, tortured—

—you feel so wonderful, darling.

And suddenly I was in his head again, the sensations ping-ponging between us. There weren't enough adjectives in Webster's to describe . . . any of this. I wanted him deeper, and in response, he lifted my legs onto his shoulders, opening me even further. Slick, hot flesh plunging, caressing, contracting, releasing until I buried my head in his pillow to muffle my scream. With a groan and shudder, he collapsed on me, peppering my neck and shoulders with tiny kisses. His weight, a comforting blanket of solid muscle, felt oh-so-right.

How's that?

He rolled to his side and began kissing each of my fingers, sending aftershocks on top of the aftershocks. *Marvelous.*

I slapped his chest. *The reception, moron, not the sex.*

"What did I tell you about hitting me?" he growled. He flipped me on my tummy and pinned me down with one hand. I struggled, but it lasted only a few seconds. Talented fingers slid into me, hitting the spot of nerves that had my body shuddering under his ministrations. Apparently, there are some warnings that can't be delivered telepathically.

Chapter 25

I woke up with a start. Sunset. Damn. I had slept the day away.

It took another few seconds to realize I was alone in the huge bed. Then the shower spurted to life in the attached bath.

My lips curved as wicked thoughts raced. Sliding from the bed, I tiptoed into the bathroom. The intention was to watch him through the foggy glass.

I must not have been sneaky enough. Dark and wet, Duncan poked his head around the shower door and smiled. "Care to join me?"

I didn't dignify his stupid question with an answer. Steam billowed around me as I stepped into the double-sized shower.

———•———

An hour later, Duncan kissed the back of my neck because a towel covered the rest of my head while I rubbed the excess moisture out of the strands. "Meet you downstairs," he murmured before heading for the bathroom door. I flipped the ends of the towel out of my face to watch his backside as he left.

I hummed to myself and clicked on the hair dryer. A girl could get used to this kind of wake-up service. A few minutes later, I fished in one of the huge shopping bags sitting in the corner to retrieve my last pair of clean jeans. I wasn't sure when Duncan brought the bag to his room, but the thoughtful gesture wasn't lost on me.

Shifting through the bag didn't yield anything cleaner shirtwise, so I raided his drawer for a t-shirt. I winced before pulling one out. Black, of course. I needed to find out where Caesar and Bebe hid the washing machine in this place. I may not have the fresh-out-of-the-grave smell of George Romero's creatures, but I hadn't stopped sweating either. Creature of the night odor was not exactly the way to impress the new boyfriend.

I rolled the word around my head.

Yeah. "Boyfriend" sounded about right. It was a hell of a lot better than "chauvinistic asshole". And the benefits were way better.

It's not like we declared undying love last night. I winced again. I had discovered through trial and error, okay through sex and recovery, we could only "hear" each other while doing the nasty. I would need to seriously edit my thoughts while he was feeling frisky. And Lord knew men feel frisky ninety-nine percent of the time.

Stomach grumbling once again, I jogged down the stairs.

And stumbled into another argument. These folks really loved to fight in their kitchens. To be fair, only Caesar and Duncan were yelling. Alex's head swung back and forth like he was watching Venus and Serena during their last set at Wimbledon. I, on the other hand, couldn't understand a damn word the boys were saying.

It's Latin, Alex thought, and he winged an apple my way.

"*Veni, vidi, vici,*" I muttered before taking a nice big bite of my fruit.

You would have thought I dropped a dirty nuke in the middle of the Beverly Center the way the men stopped to stare at me.

I shrugged. "Sorry. It's all I remember from Latin 101."

"You're on your own in this one, kid," Alex whispered before slinking out the kitchen door.

"Do you have any idea of what you just said?" Duncan bit out. His eyes glowed neon. Definitely not a signal of impending nookie this time. Caesar's face was even scarier in its stillness, like a lion ready to pounce.

Sometimes the best defense is a good offense. Maybe I needed that phrase tattooed on my ass as a reminder not to put myself in defensive situations in the first place. No, the nanites would probably make a tattoo a total waste of money.

I took another bite and chewed before I answered. "'I came. I saw. I conquered.' It's the first line in Julius Caesar's account of his conquest of Gaul. Now known to the lowly Normals as France." I planted one fist on my hip and shook the apple in Duncan's direction. "I figured you'd like that part since you weren't exactly on friendly terms with them before your bloodsucking days."

"As for you—" I shot Caesar a dirty look. "I wouldn't be running around naming myself after his nephew if you have an objection to folks quoting him."

In the tense silence, I debated whether I could outrun two pissed-off vampires when Caesar dissolved into gales of laughter. Duncan didn't join in, but the unnatural glow in his eyes died out, though the outraged look remained plastered to his gorgeous jaw.

"Well said, well said," Caesar choked out as he wiped his eyes. "But I'd watch what I say around certain people without knowing them better, little zombie."

Curiosity welled, but a slight shake of Duncan's head deterred me from asking questions. It couldn't be what I suspected, could it? Was Augustine connected to the original Caesars somehow?

My stomach grumbled which sent Caesar into another laughing fit. "You cannot use your woman and not replenish her, my friend." He nudged Duncan in the ribs and gave me a knowing grin.

"Yeah," I said, putting the most pathetic look I could on my face. "At least Alex gave me an apple, and he didn't get any last night." I reached for the door. "I really should thank him properly."

Duncan yanked me into his arms and laid on a kiss so tender and so passionate it made me forget—well, everything. I don't normally go for PDAs, and I had forgotten Caesar was in the room until his not-so-discreet clearing of his throat caused Duncan to end the kiss.

"Now, where were you going?" he murmured.

"Don't remember." I grinned up at him. "But you still owe me breakfast for using me so thoroughly." I drifted from his arms and hopped up on one of the bar stools lining the island. "So whatcha going to cook for me?"

A slight look of discomfort crossed his features. "Cook for you?"

"Yeah. Cook for me." My stomach seconded the motion.

"Er," he fumbled and looked at Caesar, desperation in his eyes.

My suspected member of the ancient Roman Imperial family ignored Duncan's silent plea for help. Instead, Caesar poured himself a cup of coffee and propped himself on the stool next to me, looking at Duncan expectantly.

I'm not a morning person even when the morning starts at sunset, but realization smacked me between the eyes. "Holy boiled eggs! Batman can't cook!"

Caesar hid his smile behind his mug.

"I am able to cook," came the stiff British protest.

I looked at Caesar, and he leaned closer to my ear. "Grilled cheese."

Lucky for me I had finished my apple. Otherwise I would have choked on it from the laughter.

"It is all Tiffany would eat when she was five!" Dark pink flared along Duncan's cheekbones.

I slapped the counter, laughing so hard I couldn't breathe. Finally, I wiped my eyes and composed myself. "Is there anything else besides driving and cooking you can't do?"

He ignored me, stalked across the kitchen and pulled cheese and butter from the fridge.

Fine. Two can play that game.

"So can you drive or cook, Mr. Augustine?"

"Yes, to both."

Duncan slammed the skillet onto the stove with a bang that probably raised the rest of the household, undead or not.

"So, did you first learn to drive in your daddy's chariot?"

Caesar smirked as he played along with my game. Duncan must have really pissed him off for the vampire prince to take my side. "My older brother's actually."

"Did you have a problem switching from live mustangs to mechanical ones?"

"No."

Butter sizzled and a wisp of smoke rose from the skillet. Duncan flipped the first sandwich. Wonderful. He was going to make me eat charcoal.

I ignored his tantrum and favored Caesar with a bright grin. "Cool. Did you have any other siblings?"

Caesar was silent for a moment before he said, "A younger brother and a twin sister."

Ouch. I'd stepped in the dog pile even though I'd been warned more than once. Caesar's sister was the only sticking point in his and Duncan's friendship.

The first sandwich landed with a clink on the plate. I didn't think my zombie stomach could handle a whole plateful of burnt toast and extra-hard cheese. Even Caesar winced in distaste when Duncan slammed the plate down in front of me.

I reached for it. The sandwich was as hard as it sounded. I took a tentative nibble, chewed forever and flashed Duncan a grin after I finally managed to swallow the mouthful. "Thanks, sweetie." The bits of charred bread I was sure were embedded in my teeth convinced him to fry the rest of my sandwiches properly.

I heard a muffled "No, Tiffany, don't go in there," from Alex a millisecond before the door swung open. My brother followed close on her stilettos. The rich, lush scent of fresh apples and full-bloom roses followed in their wake. Frowning at the scent, I searched my memory. Apples I could understand, but I hadn't spotted any flowers in Caesar's place yesterday. Maybe Tiffany was wearing perfume.

The first real smile I saw from the teen wonder appeared on her face when she spotted my stack. She turned pleading, puppy dog eyes on Duncan. "Make some for me?"

He grunted in assent and slathered more butter on slices of whole wheat.

Tiffany smiled up at Max. "You want some? Uncle Duncan grills the best."

The smile Max gave her in return nauseated my cast-iron zombie stomach more than the burnt bread. He nodded and gave me an affectionate nudge before he propped his elbows on the counter next to me. "Morning, sleepyhead." The fresh rose odor was even stronger coming from him. He must have grabbed the wrong shower gel and shampoo this morning.

"Back at-cha." I had consumed half my current grilled cheese before warning bells rang in my head. He hadn't followed up with any lewd comments about last night's sleeping arrangements. I swallowed my last bite. Okay, maybe he had common sense not to say anything in front of the vampire doing his sister. Or maybe I was luckier, and he really didn't know in whose room I slept.

Duncan placed full plates in front of Tiffany and Max. Then he peered rather too closely at Max's neck.

"Hey, there's blood in the fridge," Tiffany protested.

Duncan ignored her, grabbed the collar of Max's shirt and yanked him halfway across the granite countertop. "What the hell have you been doing to my niece!" he roared.

Alex dove through the door and into the chaos. It took all of us to loosen Duncan's grip from Max's throat.

"Cut it out! I'm an adult!" Tiffany's shriek should have broken every glass in the cupboards. She and I formed a barrier between the straining madman and my wheezing brother. I wasn't sure Alex and Caesar were going to keep their hold on Duncan. The commotion was enough to draw Bebe and Anne to the kitchen.

When the women distracted me from the pissed-off vampire, I spotted the enormous hickey that set off Duncan. No wonder Max kept his left side away from me. I railed on him. "What the hell were you thinking? She's too young for you!"

Tiffany jumped between me and my idiot brother. "I am not!"

"Just please tell me you two used a condom." Everyone turned to Bebe with various expressions of fury and amusement. A bemused smile curved the edges of her mouth.

"Doc!" Tiffany wailed.

"Well?" Duncan's lips twisted into a feral snarl. The green glow of his rage sent eerie shadows in counterpoint to the overhead fluorescents. Hands clenched and unclenched as if he wanted to continue his throttling of my brother.

Tears streamed down Tiffany's face, leaving black trails of mascara behind. Despite my own anger at Max, I felt sorry for the kid.

"We—" Max started.

"He proposed!" The stunned silence lasted a full minute in the wake of Tiffany's announcement. Apparently, the vampires had ignored them as thoroughly as they had Duncan and me last night.

Then the full implication of Max's words registered in my altered brain. "What!" My turn to scream. I grabbed Max by the throat and took up where Duncan left off. I couldn't believe my brother would use such a cheesy line to get into her pants. "You low-life son-of-a-bitch! How could you even think—"

Anne and Alex struggled to pull me off my asshole of a blood relation.

"I-it's true," Max choked out once the vamps pried my fingers from his trachea. He turned to look at Duncan. "Look, I'm sorry, St. James. This isn't how we wanted to tell you."

"I am sure it was not," Duncan said, his voice icy.

"As if you and Sam have acted in an exemplary manner conducting your relationship," Bebe said.

Alex bent over nearly double, hiding his expression in what was left of Anne's hair. Even Miss Serious Amish Vamp had a smile on her face.

"But—" Duncan started.

"There's less of an age difference between them than you and Sam. And your sandwiches are burning," Bebe finished primly a split second before the smoke alarm sounded.

He cursed, skirted around Caesar to snatch the skillet off the burner, and dumped the now flaming contents into the sink. Steam billowed as he ran the faucet over the ruined cheese and bread.

I grabbed Max's arm and dragged him out of the kitchen. I didn't stop until we reached the pool. Drowning him seemed a legitimate option.

I yanked him around to face me. "What the hell is your damage? These people are trying to save our lives, and you go around boffing their kids?"

"Unlike you, I don't boff and run." He was calm as he rubbed his bicep. Way too calm. Then his words hit me.

"What is that supposed to mean?"

"As soon as you're done with the novelty of vampire sex, you'll dump St. James faster than your garbage diving clothes."

I opened my mouth, but nothing came out so I closed it. I tried again with no success. Finally, I muttered, "He's not fresh out of high school."

Max shook his head, a sad, pained expression on his face. "You just don't get it, Sam. Tiffany's seen and done things you can't even comprehend. Intellectually she's way beyond her years. I can have a conversation with her that doesn't involve the latest Hollywood boy toy."

"I don't talk about Hollywood boy toys all the time." The pout formed on my lips of its own accord. "Besides, it's business related."

He rolled his eyes. "Why am I even surprised by you working for a tabloid? Your master's thesis was based on the historical equivalent of a celebrity slut."

My eyes narrowed. "You worked for the *Scoop* long before I did, and Cleopatra VII of Egypt is a valid historical personage."

Rose flared under pale stubble. "Then why do you waste that poli-sci/history/journalism triple major for no other reason than to get your rocks off pissing off Mom? You let her tell you you're a screw-up, and then you go out of your way to prove her right. You chase off any guy who shows the slightest interest in you just because Mom wants you to get hitched. Isn't that the real reason you dumped Jake?"

Red swam in my vision at his change in tactics. How dare he! "That was low, Snotface. Even for you."

He looked away for a second. "You're right. I'm sorry." His gaze met mine again, his expression no longer furious. "In case you hadn't noticed, St. James is crazy about you. As crazy as Jake was once. But I know you. The first sign of things getting serious, and you'll break the poor guy's heart."

I snorted. "Duncan St. James isn't a poor anything. And quit changing the subject. What do you think he's going to do to you for messing with his niece?"

"I'm well aware he could do anything to me at any time," he replied, his voice cool. "All the vampires are telepathic, so he knows I'm serious about Tiffany. This isn't about me, Sam." He jabbed a finger into my chest. "This is about your issues. You're too damn scared to take any chances in your life."

"I take plenty of chances." I wanted to take a swing at Max so bad I thrust my clenched fists into my pockets. The denim ripping would give him a two-second headstart if I lost control. "I've had so many close scrapes—"

"With your heart, Sam?" He had that damn sad, pitying look on his face again.

The scent of roses was stronger than ever. I glanced around, more to avoid Max's puppy dog eyes than to really take in the garden. Caesar didn't even have rose bushes back here.

And then all the scents assaulting me the last couple of days clicked into meaning. Under the base scents for each species, scents also changed based on the person's emotions. Tiffany and Max smelled the way they did because they really were in love.

I hated Max then, more than I had ever hated him. My nails bit into my palms. This had nothing to do with any childhood rivalry, and everything to do with a basic fact. He was alive. I wasn't. He could love someone, marry, have children, be normal. I couldn't. Things had changed too much. For both of us, and in more ways than I could count. I wanted to bitch-slap him.

But if I hit him now, I'd probably kill him.

"Look, Sam, I'm sorry." He held out a hand, but a latent fear shone in his eyes. Fear based on the awareness of what I had done to Mom's gun, what I could do to him now.

I hated that fear as much as I hated him.

"Max, you really need to shut up." It was difficult to force the words past my gritted teeth, but obviously, he understood me because he adopted his oh-so-delightful sanctimonious attitude.

"Why? Because you're mad I've taken the plunge you're to chicken-shit to take?"

"Go fuck yourself." Not one of my wittier responses.

He fumed for a second before he stalked back into the house, leaving me to gasp for air like a beached shark. I couldn't follow and nail him with one of my fabulous sarcastic comebacks because . . .

Because deep down, I knew he was right. Maybe not about Duncan. I wasn't really sure where our whole situation stood. But as for the rest, he was right.

Damn him. Damn Mom too for that matter. I didn't need to damn myself. I was already there.

A tear trickled down my cheek. I didn't need him to point out I was dead and pretty much had nothing to show for it. Hell, I probably didn't even have my job since I hadn't called Ralph in almost a week. The old man will put up with a lot of shit, but he won't tolerate one of his people not calling in. My death was irrelevant.

"Sam."

I sniffed and wiped my eyes on my sleeves before turning to face Caesar. "Yeah."

"We have twenty-four hours before Sierra's deadline. We need to talk."

I sniffed again and nodded.

My petty issues would have to wait. Time for the dead to go save the world.

Chapter 26

Duncan's eyes burned as bright as kryptonite crystals in the Chris Reeve movies. "She cannot go!"

The realization Duncan roared a lot sank into my head. No wonder Tiffany adopted the goth persona. It was sheer self-preservation. At least, I now knew for sure Duncan's argument with Caesar in the kitchen had been about me.

"Sierra's offer was to me. Not anyone else." I waved across the assemblage in Caesar's office. "I'm the perfect decoy."

Instead of continuing his pacing, Duncan planted his gorgeous body in front of the office door. "She will be expecting just such a move," Duncan snapped back.

It took all my willpower not to roll my eyes. The big lug meant well, but he wasn't thinking straight. I rather got the impression he didn't anytime his maker was involved. Maybe I wouldn't be either if I were confronting Tyrone Mallory. But his death took a certain subjectivity out of my emotional equation.

Instead of pointing out the obvious, which he'd only deny, I nonchalantly perched on the corner of Caesar's desk and tried my most convincing voice. The one I used to reason with Ralph when he's on the fence about running one of my stories. "Most likely. Think about it. The only reason Sierra let me go was to plant a bomb, me, in Caesar's place." Again, I waved a hand to include the group in Caesar's office. "So far, we're her only opposition. She's probably already triggered the self-destruct in the hopes of taking out you guys. If I walk in on my own, she'll assume I didn't know she's already tried to kill me—"

"Again," Duncan muttered.

I threw up my hands. "Okay, you were right. I shouldn't have brought her with us. Happy?"

Caesar's quiet voice broke through our argument. "There's no way we'll be able to break into the complex a third time. If her father hired rogues, I have no doubt Sierra's retained their services as well." Nice to know I wasn't the only one avoiding the Selene equation around Duncan.

Duncan ignored his boss's logic. "We could still bring additional support to Los Angeles—"

Caesar's high-planed cheeks pinked. "Not before Sierra comes here. She undoubtedly knows exactly where Sam is, and she's not about to lose her father's prototype."

I was on his side, but I didn't like being referred to as Mallory's science experiment. Next thing you know, my hair'll turn black and white with electricity fizzing through it.

I apologize, Sam.

Apology accepted, oh great and wise Prince.

Caesar shot me an irritated look before continuing. "John and Ziva have already volunteered some of their people to assist us."

Duncan scowled. "I do not like relying on outsiders."

Bebe laughed, a soft musical tinkle in the emotions clouding the room, and shook her head. "Sweet Goddess, you sound almost as conceited as an uppity little witch did two years ago."

I swear I heard enamel and bone crack when Duncan clenched his jaw.

An amused smile flitted across Caesar's face. "Yes, I seem to recall a lecture around that same time on taking action based on a well-reasoned decision."

My attention flicked between Bebe, Caesar and Duncan. I may not have understood the reason for the intimate teasing, but I could still thoroughly enjoy Duncan's squirming.

Breath left Duncan's pursed lips with a whoosh. His facial muscles relaxed enough for him to say, "Very well. I am listening."

Caesar's fingers steepled below his lips. "I found out through some of my business associates Mallory Investments is holding a party tomorrow night at the lab facility before the private shareholder meeting on Saturday. An alternative to Sam's theory, Sierra may simply want Sam with her when she announces the cure."

"Yeah, except the only thing they cured me of was life," I muttered.

Caesar ignored my whining. "That will be the perfect, and the only, opportunity to get in."

"Squirt here and I can give them their obvious break-in," Alex said, gesturing at himself and Anne. "Two tortured vamps wanting revenge? It'll be perfect."

I noticed Duncan didn't protest Alex's plan. I was flattered he considered me more important than his best friend, but I resented he didn't believe I could take care of myself. Hell, even Tiffany was going on this little outing.

"No, she's not."

I jumped at Caesar's statement. Telepathy sucked the big one.

"Who's not what?" asked Tiffany.

"You're not going on this expedition," Duncan said.

"You left me out of the last one." Hands on hips, she glared at each of the vamps and Bebe in turn.

"And you'll be left out of this one as well. It's too dangerous," Duncan snapped.

I winced at the cliché. On the other hand, Tiffany hit her boiling point.

"I've held my own against Selene's best." Make that freezing point. She was eerily calm. Not the usual teen outburst I had come to expect. "As you've all pointed out, she's expecting us to try something. She won't be expecting me, and I won't be the helpless wimp left behind to be kidnapped for a trade by the bad guys."

"I think that's my job, honey," Max said.

From the look she gave him, he so wasn't getting any tonight.

"None of them should—" Duncan started.

"You're—" Caesar cut in.

"Enough!" I jumped to my feet at the same time I screamed. I couldn't handle the chest beating anymore. I just couldn't, not with my brother being a total wuss on top of everything. His girlfriend had more balls than he did.

"You—" I pointed to Max. "If you don't want to help, fine! Stay here and hide in the freakin' basement for all I care." Okay, so I was still pissed at him for the lecture by the pool.

"You!" I jabbed my index finger in Duncan's direction. "You were ready to slap the shit out of me for leaving Alex behind during my escape. Well, guess what? I'm not standing by while he risks his life to stop that psycho bitch. Caesar's come up with a viable plan. If you can't come up with something better, then shut the fuck up!"

"You are right."

I blinked in surprise. He couldn't have possibly just said what I thought I heard. "Excuse me?"

"You heard me the first time," he said, irritation plain in his tone. "I will not repeat myself." He crossed his arms over his chest.

Let it go, Sam. Just let it go.

Maybe I was too depressed from my argument with Max earlier, but I listened to Alex and returned to my perch on the desk.

Caesar summarized the whole plan. I was the first decoy. Basically I march up to the front door and ask my fellow zombie to come out and play. Alex and Anne play the second decoy at the back gate, and the rest would go through a different section of wall using one of Bebe's spells.

Was it only a week ago? God, I haven't been dead a week, and I'm out to save the world from the insane zombie queen. It was enough to make me crazy.

I tried to focus on what Caesar was saying, but all I could think about was how my stupidity put these people in danger. If I hadn't chased Duncan, would any of this be happening? Sierra would still be undergoing chemo, waiting for her daddy to save her. Duncan would have rescued his friends, and Caesar would have made some kind of ultra-rich gentleman's agreement with Tyrone Mallory to keep everything quiet. Life would have gone on for all of us.

When Caesar dismissed us, I wandered back out to the pool and sat on the edge, swirling my toes in the warm crystal water. I needed to do something to fix this mess. Normally, I do my best thinking at a coffee shop, but any private excursions were out of the question. And I was so tired of feeling like a prisoner.

Then there was the issue of Miss Zombie Queen. Not that I wanted to be the only one, but she presented a danger to the whole freakin' world. Everyone here had bent over backwards to save me—a total stranger. They didn't deserve to die because of me, trying to stop Sierra.

Fred had said I held the key to stopping little Miss Psycho Heiress. I just wish I knew what the hell he meant. Even if I couldn't figure out his cryptic statement, I had to face the bitch on my terms, not as a snatch-and-grab by her goon squad. Would Caesar's sister be with her? Doubtful, since she'd been doing her best to stay off the vampire prince's radar. The slender threads of an alternate plan started to weave together in my warped dead brain.

"May I join you?"

I jumped at Duncan's voice behind me. Plastering my fake smile on, the one I use for press agents I really hate, I twisted to look up at him. "Sure. What's up?"

Under the glow from the pool lights, a frown creased his forehead. "You have been unnaturally quiet since your outburst earlier."

I toed a floating leaf that had escaped the maniacal gardener who tended Caesar's place. He put the guys at Disneyland to shame.

"Sam?" Duncan knelt and took my hand in his, the pad of his thumb rubbing my palm. I tried to clamp down on the shivers of desire welling in my blood. That's the problem when someone can read your mind during sex. He knows what buttons to push.

"You did say I talked too much."

"Somehow, I do not think you were that offended by my teasing to take it to heart." Oh, he was so trying to play kiss and make up. And I wanted to play too, but I couldn't. Not tonight. He'd know what I was planning, and I would have a hard enough time hiding it from the other vamps.

"No." I choked on the next words but forced them out anyway. "I would have to care what you think to be offended."

He pulled back and his frown deepened. "Pardon me?"

God, this hurt. I knew then what I really felt for him. And I was about to crush any chance I had with him because if he knew what I planned to do in the morning, he'd find a way to stop me.

I inhaled deeply, trying to ease the ache in my chest. "Max is right." I turned to face him. "As much as I hate to admit it, he's right. I'm just using you. You're a novelty, something new and fun."

Pain clouded his eyes, and I couldn't look at him anymore. I gazed at the waves lapping the sides of the pool. "It's not fair to you. We need to end this now before someone really gets hurt."

"Do you love me?"

I froze at his question. My heart screamed to answer him. "What does that have to do with anything?"

"It is a simple question, Samantha. Yes or no?"

"No," I whispered.

I felt him rise and take a step away.

"You are lying," he said. "I do not know why when you were the one telling me to take a chance last night."

Ironic how I could dish out that little bit of advice. And now that I wanted to follow it myself, I couldn't. Not without getting the man I cared about permanently dead.

I dragged my eyes up to meet his. "I haven't lied to you since I met you, St. James. Last night was a mistake, and I'm sorry I hurt you." *Oh God, please make him leave before I start crying.*

"I see." His voice was as cold as his expression. "I am sorry too, Miss Ridgeway." I turned back to the pool and listened to the click of his boots as he strode back into the house.

The tears slid down my face as my heart shattered. My emotional bullshit would be enough to cover my thoughts from the other vamps, so for once in my life I let myself feel. Max was right. The few times my breakups weren't mutual, I initiated them to protect myself from falling for the guy.

Except Jake. He had been the one exception, and I deliberately fucked that one up too.

Yep, I deserved to be alone.

Surprisingly, no one came out to check on me. For once, the entire household left me alone. I wasn't sure if this was a good thing or not, but I didn't have to guard my thoughts for much longer. Close to dawn, the lights went out in the upstairs bedrooms one by one as everyone headed for bed. Except the kitchen light. They left it on, probably for me.

Voices speaking what sounded like Japanese filtered up from the guard house. The security detail's shift change. Good. The two Normal women who comprised the day guard wouldn't be a problem.

Fingers of pale blue light spread across the sky, followed by purple and pink. I couldn't remember the last time I had watched a sunrise. High school graduation maybe? The import struck me. If my plan didn't work, this could be my last.

I rose and went inside. The stillness was eerie in the early morning. Most people would be getting up and ready for work.

I crept up to Duncan's room and eased the door open. The sliver of light from the hall illuminated his broad chest and his right arm thrown over his eyes. The navy sheet covered him to the waist. Well, it did in theory. Certain parts were thrown into relief by the hall light. I sighed. His package was impressive at rest. And downright spectacular when he used it. Oh, he did know how to use it too.

His chest rose and fell in a steady rhythm from sleep. I eased the door closed and tiptoed to the bed. He deserved so much more than what I could give him, but I couldn't resist saying good-bye. I bent and placed a light kiss on his lips.

I never saw him move. I landed with a thump on the bed, pinned in place by his very powerful limbs. Okay, something new to add to my list of stupid things not to repeat—don't kiss a sleeping vampire.

Who was now a very wide-awake and irritated vampire. I squirmed, trying to get loose. Make that a wide-awake, irritated, and aroused vampire. And the pressure of his growing erection pushed my own thoughts south.

"What the bloody hell are you doing in my room?"

"Ummm . . ." I couldn't think with him touching me. All I wanted was to rip my own clothes off and join in the nakedness. And, lordy, the damn sheet wasn't covering anything anymore.

"Samantha." The evident warning in his tone didn't help.

"I don't know." I struggled some more, but with my hands trapped above my head, the only thing I did was rearrange my t-shirt. And not in a good way if I wanted to avoid sex.

He frowned at me, his eyes gleaming neon green in the darkness, also not a good sign. "What do you mean, you do not know?"

"I said I don't know," I snapped. "Now get off me!"

His frown switched to a sly grin. "In my day, there was only one purpose for a woman to be in a gentleman's bed chambers." One hand reached down to stroke the skin bared by my skewed shirt.

"So where's the chamber pot for me to empty?" I ripped back. My body betrayed my voice. His touch sent tremors through me, ignited my own desires. I was in serious danger, in more ways than one. I yanked my hands, but his one-handed hold was like steel cuffs.

Handcuffs are an excellent idea, darling.

His canines were white against his grinning lips. My breath harshened, and not from my fight to get free.

I licked my lips and tried to calm my racing heart. "Why are handcuffs an excellent idea?"

"All the better to keep you with," he murmured. His hand slid underneath my shirt, palmed my breast and thumbed my erect nipple through the lace bra.

I really should have bought the cotton granny underwear. The flimsy lace did nothing to restrict his access. If anything, the rasp of the material added its own sensual counterpoint to his strokes.

Keeping my mental shields intact under his sexual onslaught became impossible. A rush of desire flooded through me. I wasn't sure where his feelings ended and mine began.

His mouth found my other breast, his tongue keeping time with his thumb through the flimsy material until I squirmed and bucked. I wanted to touch him, but he kept me firmly pinned between his body and the bed.

He raised his head to blow lightly across the damp lace. The sensation sent ripples through my abdomen. Muscles clenched, demanding release and not from his imprisoning hold. A low moan started at the back of my throat.

No, I couldn't do this. I couldn't endure losing him. A strange pushing sensation rippled through my head, and Duncan jerked back as if I had slapped him.

"Do not shut me out." His voice half pleaded and half growled his words. "Samantha?"

"I can't do this, Duncan." I didn't realize I was crying until my voice sobbed out the words.

He released my hands and sat up. Pulling me into his lap, he cradled and rocked me against his chest. Incoherent murmurs whispered in my ear while I cried. The remaining tears I hadn't shed while sitting in the garden poured out.

After a while, the sobs petered out. I wanted to stay like this, just him and me. None of this other undead bullshit. Why couldn't I be a normal girl and he be a normal guy and we go on normal dates like the evening at the street carnival? I clutched my shoulders at the frustration.

He stroked damp strands of hair away from my face for a long time before he spoke, his touch comforting instead of arousing. "Are you going to tell me what tonight was about?"

I shook my head, not trusting myself to keep my plan secret.

His deep sigh ruffled the dry hairs on top of my head. "I am sorry if I frightened you."

I couldn't stop the smirk on my face. "Yeah, right. Like you ever scared me when I was alive."

He chuckled. "Forgive me for my assumptions."

I sat up to look him in the eye. "I'm sorry about earlier. I'm just not sure—" The unfamiliar emotions made me fumble for words. Until I discovered Duncan St. James, I had never had this problem in my life.

Desire rose, and I beat it back. Sex was too fucking risky no matter how much I wanted it. Hurting him again was not an option. I shouldn't have done it earlier.

A deep breath, and I tried again. "You're taking this way too fast. I died less than a week ago, and you're talking major commitment. The 'L' word." I grinned, hoping to ease the sting of my words. "Which in our case, literally means forever. I need some space and we'll see what happens."

His fingertips traced my temple and cheekbones as I held my breath. After a long, slow exhale, he nodded. "Would you stay?"

My eyes must have crossed in confusion because he added, "In my room." He smiled. "Just sleep."

"Put some pants on."

A bemused expression passed over his face, and he cocked an eyebrow. "Would that really stop us?"

"Please."

My tone convinced him to rise and scrounge a pair of silk pajama bottoms. Once we settled in his bed, he resumed stroking my hair.

Okay, stroking good, mind-reading not good. My muscles relaxed when I realized he was serious. He didn't push, didn't even try to cop an "accidental" feel. I don't think I ever had done the platonic in bed with a guy before.

It was . . . nice.

I snuggled closer and burrowed my head in the crook of his shoulder. The fresh scent of soap mingled with sandalwood and his own special maleness. My plan could wait a little while I indulged in some cuddle-time.

His caresses slowed then stopped as sleep claimed him. A half hour flew by as his soft snores filled the room. I didn't want to leave.

I couldn't see the man I loved get turned to meat slush either.

I eased from under the covers, but his eyes popped open the instant my feet hit the floor. "Where are you going?"

Thank God, my stomach decided to rumble before he finished his question. I flipped him a grin, and said, "You have to ask?" I bent to plant a quick smooch on his cheek, but he shifted his head at the last instant and grasped the back of my neck. His lips demanded mine open. His tongue lavished me in such a way I almost crawled back into bed.

Almost.

"Hold that thought until after I eat." I climbed back to my feet from my precarious perch on the side of the bed.

"I'll come with you." He flipped the covers back and started to swing his legs over. Oh mama, the p.j.'s were worse than just the sheets.

I waved him back. "No, get some sleep. Tonight's going to be insane enough." I leaned over and, this time, managed to peck him on the forehead. "I'll be back as soon as I clean out the fridge."

I'm such a liar.

The quizzical look he shot me made wonder if he actually heard my thought. Instead of confronting me, he nodded and lay back down.

Even with the UV film, the morning sun blinded me as I stumbled into the kitchen.

"Morning." Tiffany's cheery greeting made me jam my elbow into a cabinet. I really needed to remember to use my brand spankin' new zombie radar.

"Mornin'," I mumbled back. I snatched a mug out of the cupboard and poured the coffee Tiffany had already brewed.

"I didn't know if you wanted pancakes or waffles, so I made both."

Her appearance finally impacted the brain cells still obsessing over Duncan. Plain black tee, leggings, and sneakers. No fishnet, no hardware installed in or draped over various body parts, no make-up. The happy talk clinched my suspicions.

"You're pregnant, aren't you?"

Tiffany responded by flipping me off before flipping the over-easy eggs she had been frying onto a plate and shoving said plate into my free hand.

The jerk of the universe righting itself knocked me and my breakfast into a waiting chair.

"I figured we both needed a good meal before we head over to Mallory's." She plunked down in the chair across from me and proceeded to douse her own plate of eggs in a thick layer of ketchup.

"You know, Max hates ketchup on anything. And we have several hours before going to Mallory's." I frowned. "And you're not going, remember?"

She shoveled a forkful of the red and yellow mess into her mouth. "Max'll just have to deal. And I'm going with you."

"Your uncle said you weren't going. If my uncle was a vampire, I wouldn't be pissing him off." My eggs devoured, I forked a couple of waffles onto my plate.

"At least my uncle's not Satan spawn." She speared some sausages.

"Hey, that's your future mother-in-law you're talking about. And I'm the only one who's allowed to call her Satan spawn." I snagged a couple more waffles then slathered a quarter-pound of margarine over them. I frowned at her while I reached for the bottle of Aunt Jemima. "Where'd you hear her called Satan spawn anyway?"

"Max. And I didn't say I was going with the group. I'm going early with you when you drive over this morning."

Her statement startled me so much I didn't notice I was still pouring syrup until it ran over my plate and into my lap.

"Shit!" I slammed the bottle down, which sent a spray of sticky droplets over the rest of the table. "What the hell are you blathering about?"

She jumped up, snatched the roll of paper towels off the counter and tossed them to me. "You're going over early to confront the bitch queen." She shrugged, undaunted by my glare of death. "You'll need backup."

I dabbed up the syrup running off the table and onto my jeans. "It's too dangerous."

She ran a dish towel under the faucet. "I had five kills before I hit high school. You've only staked one person, and she wasn't even a vamp."

I knew Duncan would hate me for sure if I got his niece killed. "What makes you think I'll take you?"

"I'll wake up Duncan if you don't."

I sighed. Goth Girl had a point. I guess I was breaking in a partner.

Chapter 27

After an hour, I decided maybe the teen terror would be an asset after all. We had gone out to the guesthouse where Caesar had created an exercise room. It wasn't the typical Brentwood aerobics and weight room. Swords from various eras hung on one wall, their appearance hardly decorative. He collected everything from Roman pikes and Mongolian cavalry bows to the latest in Glocks.

Tiffany demonstrated a few moves and a few weapons. She outlined the best method to get past Caesar's day guards. It sounded like she had plenty of experience in that department.

I filled her in on my plans.

"Kill Sierra and blow up the lab?" Tiffany's incredulous look didn't reinforce my confidence. "That's it?"

I crossed my arms and gave her the evil eye. "You've got a better plan? Then let's hear it."

She sighed and shook her head. "We'll need some C-4." She pulled open another cabinet door, removed a lid from a plastic container and pulled out what looked like a handful of talcum powder. She started playing with it, and in seconds, she had a wad of what looked like white Play-Do in her palm.

"No." I held up a hand. From the little lesson Jake gave me when he was planning stunts for a Jackie Chan movie, C-4 was a very stable explosive. The knowledge didn't stop the nervous twitch in my gut when Tiffany started tossing the fist-sized mass into the air and catching it.

"No?"

I pointed at her R-rated toy. "Someone told me once the manufacturers put some kind of chemical marker in that stuff. Do you want to take the chance of it being traced back to Caesar?"

She looked at me, at the wad, and back at me. "Fine." She laid the C-4 in the canister and sealed it before closing the door. "What did you have in mind?"

Tiffany had the nonchalance I'd imagined in a Navy SEAL. Not that I was going to live long enough to meet a real live SEAL. Damn. And I'd always wanted to interview the ex-Governor of Minnesota.

"You have so gotta stop thinking terminally." Tiffany pulled her head out of the second storage closet. She rolled her eyes as she handed me a large messenger bag and a crossbow. "You're going to get us both killed."

"Would you stop reading my mind? It's creepy enough when the vamps do it."

A sour expression twisted her lipstick-free mouth. "I can't."

Not again. Anger at my own ineptitude with my new abilities flared.

"Would you freakin' stop screaming 'oh shit' in my head?" Tiffany slapped her hands over her ears.

Yeah, right. Like that would shield her from my mental shrieking. I had been so worried about keeping the vamps out I forgot my little nanite pals could transmit to everyone else as well.

"I remember what happened in the townhouse kitchen Sunday night." She reached up and smacked the side of my head. "Now, practice blocking or someone in the mansion is going to *hear* you."

I was getting very, very tired of everyone bitching at me about abilities I didn't want, much less could control. The same blackness welling deep inside I had felt earlier with Duncan snapped into place. Tiffany jerked and staggered back a couple of steps as if I had physically struck her.

Her eyes didn't just bulge. If she were a Looney Tunes character, they'd be out of their sockets and rolling on the floor now. "How the hell did you do that?" she whispered.

"I don't know." Guilt assailed me. I grabbed her arm to steady her. "Are you okay? I'm so sorry."

"Little bit of a headache." She studied me, more curious than fearful. "Your little talent may come in handy. Almost felt like a witch's psy-slap." She grinned. "The zombie equivalent of one anyway. Have you tried that stunt on anyone else?"

I grinned back, reassured I hadn't given her a brain aneurysm by accident. "Your uncle."

She laughed outright before she slid some silver knives into her bag. "He probably deserved it. So what did you have in mind for the lab?"

My grin widened. "Don't most laboratories have volatile chemicals?"

A matching smile spread across Tiffany's face and she nodded. "Make it look like an accident." She hefted the canvas strap over her arm. "Ready to go kick some zombie ass?"

I shouldered my weapons bag and gestured towards the garage. "Lead the way, Goth Girl."

She whipped around, fixing me with a stare more pointed than the dagger strapped to her ankle. "What did you call me?"

Oops.

——— •◦• ———

We were three miles away from Mallory Labs before Tiffany let my slip-up go. Sort of.

"So what the hell do you call my uncle behind his back?" she snarled. How she could sound so evil around the wad of bubblegum in her mouth was beyond me.

But I was so not going there. Besides Duncan would need a new category. Super Stud? Rod of Steel? Just thinking about him gave me warm, gushy feelings, totally inappropriate for the maiming, killing, and general destruction I planned to do in the next few hours.

"Well . . ." Tiffany's acid tongue brought my attention back to her. And the road. I stomped on the brakes to keep from mowing down the jogger who darted across the road. I returned his friendly middle-finger wave before answering her.

"Look, how many times do I have to say 'I'm sorry'?" I shot her a grin. "Besides, you're way cooler than Chris O'Donnell in *Batman Forever*."

She made a gagging noise. "The Olsen twins are way cooler than him. Unless you count *The Three Musketeers*. He was cute with long hair."

Whipping Caesar's Hummer around a corner, I snorted in amusement. "I can't see Duncan letting you watch any movie having to do with a French theme."

"It's the Disney version, so he cut me some slack." She laughed. "You're right though. In his book, the only thing worse than a French story is *Buffy* and *Angel*."

Our conversation halted at the same time I braked at the main gate. I couldn't see the point of driving into the employee spill-over lot Duncan and Tiffany had used for their surveillance missions. Besides it wasn't like we were bothering to sneak into the damn place.

The goon who checked our IDs wasn't one I had assaulted, mangled, or otherwise encountered in my two previous trips inside the labs. His intense scrutiny still made me nervous. Tiffany's gum made a loud *pop*, and I jumped.

I glared at her while the goon circled the Hummer. "Would you stop chewing that?"

"No." Snap, snap. "It keeps me focused."

The soft hissing of air followed her words. I swallowed the urge to prick the huge pink bubble.

"Ms. Mallory is expecting you, Ms. Ridgeway. Your escort will meet you in the visitor's parking lot."

I nodded as he handed back my ID and gave me directions before he waved us forward.

"See? No problem." *Pop, snap, snap.*

"Spit out the damn gum," I growled.

"It was your idea to waltz through the front door," Tiffany muttered, but she must have been afraid I'd brain-fry her for real. She fished out a scrap of paper and wadded up the mess.

Ignoring the butterflies chased by electric eels in my stomach, I guided the humongous vehicle into a spot and cut the engine. On the sidewalk, Kane rocked on his heels as he and a couple of more goons waited for us to join them. These two wore the standard rent-a-cop uniforms, but you could tell from their stance, they were anything but. And I could smell that they weren't vamps either, even if the early afternoon sun wasn't a dead giveaway.

Damn, this whole sixth sense thing came in handy.

"Weebles wobble but they don't fall down," Tiffany sang under her breath. She was right. Kane's pear-shape looked like it would pop right back up if knocked over, but I knew better.

"This one does if you hit him hard enough," I whispered back. We stepped onto the sidewalk, and both goons took a half step back. Then I caught the sharp, ashy scent emanating from them. Fear. I didn't understand why the odor would be a turn-on to vamps when the scent was more akin to a dirty grill. It made the eels and butterflies nauseous. Maybe my perception was due to my lack of bloodlust. But it was still good to know I made them half as nervous as they made me.

"I beg your pardon, Miss Ridgeway?" Kane smiled, but sweat beaded along the edge of his Adolph moustache.

Crossing my arms, I smiled back. "I was just telling the Girl Wonder here I'm surprised Tyrone didn't feed you to the werewolves for letting me escape."

If possible, Kane's skin transformed to a new, lighter shade of paste. His smile disappeared at the sniggers of the goons behind him. "Take their bags," he snapped before he spun on his heel and waddled for the door.

We handed over the totes to Goon No. 1 with the most token of protests. He unzipped and peered into each before giving a long low whistle. "Dr. Kane?"

Kane halted and peered over his shoulder. Goon No. 1 crossed the few yards and whispered to him, "These chicks are carrying some serious shit."

Have I said how much I love my new abilities?

Kane sneered. "Don't give it back to them, idiot." He continued his waddling.

Tiffany looked up at me and shrugged. Sierra's people would now relax, thinking they had disarmed us. We were fine as long as no one insisted on a strip search. And I seriously doubted Goon No. 2's interest in Tiffany's enhanced cleavage had anything to do with the weapons stuffed in her bra. The goons marched behind us while we followed Kane into the building.

As we crossed the lobby, I glanced up. Definitely a different view from the first floor, especially since I was conscious this time. I had to give a hand to their maintenance department. They'd patched up all the bullet holes from Sunday and repainted the walls.

Of course, Mallory's employee incentive program probably included the pit.

A nagging feeling of wrongness picked at me that had nothing to do with my own nerves. I peeked behind me as we followed Kane to a private elevator. More fear drifted from our escort. Heck, any werewolf or vamp would say I reeked of it too. But intermixed with the fear was something else, a tangy citrus coming from Tiffany.

I tried not to gulp when Kane pressed "1" after we boarded. I so didn't want to go back down there. I didn't have a choice now. The goons would shoot Tiffany and me in an instant. Tears threatened to spill from my anger at my own weakness. Fingernails dug into my palms as I fought for control. Lucky for me the nanites repaired my skin as fast as I shredded it.

To distract myself, I puzzled out the odd odor coming from Tiffany. Her lack of fear didn't make sense, but I was certain it wasn't exactly confidence either. Granted, she wasn't as fatalistic about our little expedition as I was. It was almost like . . . anticipation. But of what? She didn't have a personal grudge against Sierra. At least none I knew of.

I should be more concerned about why I know what a human emotion smells like.

For cryin' out loud! Quit wondering what I smell like. That is so sick, you perv!

Tiffany tried to glare at me without being obvious. I glanced at the men in the elevator. No one looked my way. Okay, good. I wasn't transmitting to everyone. A good thing Duncan wasn't with us. Then Kane and the guards would have a front seat to my X-rated fantasies.

Oh, gag me! I didn't need those thoughts in my head.

A loud groan filled the elevator at the same time as Tiffany's mental comment. The drama queen clutched her stomach and bent over. Everyone looked at her.

Kane eased away as far away as he could in the enclosed space. "What's wrong with her?"

"Motion sickness," I answered. I grabbed the kid to keep her upright. Instead of flinching, she quivered in my grasp. "And if she doesn't get a grip, I'm going to eat her." My stomach growled its agreement.

The goons plastered themselves in the back corners of the elevator, guns braced in front of them, but Tiffany stopped her silent giggles.

The elevator halted and Kane couldn't dive out fast enough. I released Tiffany, and she managed to keep her face straight when she rose. We followed Kane down the hallway with our guards several steps behind.

He escorted us into a large room, one that could have been something from an '80's video. Purple velvet hung from the walls, gold trimmed everything, and the furniture consisted of matching pillows surrounding low ebony tables.

Sierra reclined on one elbow in the middle of the room, giggling with a dark-haired woman. A woman who reeked of sandalwood. The frankly bullshit act on both their parts rubbed since I knew damn well they could smell us long before they saw us. Hell, Sierra's metallic odor nearly overpowered the vampire's signature sandalwood. When she glanced up us, she graced me with a seductive smile. That smile would have scared the bejeezus out of me even if I swung in the non-guy direction. The other woman sat up as well and slowly turned to face us.

I nearly had a heart attack when I got a good look at the second woman. The Elvira impersonator I thought had been a drug-induced nightmare smiled at me too, the tips of her fangs gleaming red in the subdued lighting.

She raised her goblet of blood towards us. "So glad you ladies could join us."

"Selene," Tiffany breathed.

I looked down at her in shock, but before I could ask anything, Goth Girl charged.

Chapter 28

Tiffany never stood a chance. The vampire was on her feet, holding the kid by the throat a foot off the ground before I could blink.

"Such a delightful gift, my dear. How did you know she was something I've always wanted?" The vampire's kohl-lined eyes narrowed, examining Tiffany with a mix of distaste and excitement.

"Let her go." My heart hammered triple time. I didn't know what to do. If I dared to touch her, she could break Tiffany's neck with a flick of her wrist. If the impression I'd received from Duncan and Alex was right, she wouldn't need much of an excuse.

The vampire looked at me, amusement flitting across her features. Tiffany's feet flailed, and her face shifted to an ugly bluish-purple color.

I'd gotten stories from sheer attitude and prayed my bluff would work this time. "Let. Her. Go." I stepped forward with each word. "If you want me on your side, Sierra, tell her to release the kid."

"Really, Selene. We don't want to upset poor Samantha by eating her little friend." Sierra had risen to stand beside her partner? Friend? She laid a hand on Selene's arm, the gesture weirdly intimate.

"She's a St. James. Worthless." Selene sneered, then she shrugged and tossed Tiffany to the side. Thank God, there were so many pillows. The kid bounced and rolled twice before coming to a stop against the wall. She lay there as she fought for oxygen, the continued racking sounds doing nothing to slow my heart.

"You okay?" I asked. I didn't dare move towards her and settled for keeping an eye on the bad girls. My gut clenched at the knowledge I wouldn't be able to stop both a zombie and a vamp from getting to the kid if they decided to kill her.

"Yeah." She coughed a few more times before sitting up.

Selene eyed me, curiosity evident. "She's not my offering?"

"Beg pardon?"

"My offering. To show your loyalty to me." She stepped towards me, giving me the rich bitch Rodeo Drive up-and-down.

Like I cared. Hell, I endured such torture every time I met a friend of Mom's. I checked her out in return. I had expected Duncan's maker to be some drop-dead platinum babe with a rack that wouldn't quit. She wasn't beautiful, not in any usual L.A. sense. More ethnic pretty like Nia Vardalos from *My Big Fat Greek Wedding*.

Then her words hit me, and I tried to paste an appropriately simpering smile on my mug. "Sorry, ma'am. I forgot the hostess gift. My mom'll tell you my manners are simply atrocious."

"What's she doing here?" Sierra nodded towards Tiffany.

I flicked my gaze between Sierra and Tiffany but addressed my remarks to the vamp. Even without Alex's warning about Duncan's maker, trust wasn't a word I'd associate with this woman. I'd have to play this very carefully. The struggle to act nonchalant frayed the few undead nerves I had left. I hadn't counted on dealing with a vampire queen in addition to Sierra.

"She got tired of her uncle bullying her around. When she figured out I was joining you, she asked if she could come."

Selene flicked an eyebrow upwards. "And you expect me to believe such an asinine story?"

A whisper touched the edge of my consciousness. Then a pressure, steadily increasing, a finger trying to drill through the middle of my forehead. I couldn't afford to give in to Selene's attempt to read my mind. They'd kill us both. Well, Tiffany would end up dead. Selene and Sierra would have to get extra creative for me.

Either way would be ugly.

"No, I don't," I replied, struggling not to show my effort. "But Augustine and his little group won't take the chance with an innocent kid's life and do something stupid, will they?" My lips curled into what I hoped was an appropriate evil grin. "I figured she'd be a useful hostage."

"You bitch." Tiffany's words devolved into another round of coughing. I couldn't warn her without tipping off the bad girls, so I crossed my toes she'd get a clue I was faking.

The mental pressure disappeared so suddenly I almost fell. Something very strange showed on the vampire's face at the mention of Caesar's name, a mixture of fury and regret. The Los Angeles vampires certainly had nothing on Peyton Place. If she was nuts enough to slaughter Duncan's family when he rejected her, I hated to think of what lay between Caesar and Selene.

"Then she's your responsibility." The vampire's soft voice raised gooseflesh on my arms. She edged closer until our noses were millimeters apart, Sierra sidling along beside her. "If she performs any inappropriate act, you both will pay."

I couldn't nod without head-butting her. I settled for muttering, "Fine," from between my clenched teeth.

"Sam will make sure the girl behaves," Sierra said, her tone a verbal stroke to match her free fingers running through my hair.

And I thought the vampire gave me the willies.

Sierra released Selene's arm and glided toward the door, executing little ballet twirls as she went. The switch between seductress and little girl so sudden I jerked when she paused at the doorway and spoke. "Cocktails begin at five. We need to find you both something suitable to wear, not to mention make-up and hair." She gave me a smile, one more predatory than seductive or innocent. "I can't wait to introduce you to everybody."

Selene followed the heiress, but shot me a look far colder and more calculating than Sierra's. She wouldn't hesitate to kill anyone who got in her way, including her so-called allies. I wondered if Sierra knew what she was getting into, not that it would matter to the psychotic bitch.

"Oh, Sam?" Sierra poked her head back in the room. "I'm glad you're here, but Kane told me something very disturbing." She clucked her tongue. "You really shouldn't have brought weapons, so I'll just have the boys put them in a safe place for you. Someone will collect you around four-forty-five. Can't have my new best friend late." She disappeared from sight, but I only heard the women's footsteps retreat down the hall.

Great. I rolled my neck, attempting to stretch the kinks out as Tiffany staggered to her feet. I had five hours to figure out how to kill Sierra, destroy the secret lab and get Tiffany out of here intact before the posse showed up and a lot of people died. My death was just getting better and better.

———•———

I can't believe neither of them even questioned why we had guns with us. It's not like regular bullets would stop either one of them, and we didn't have any vampire-specific ammo in those bags. Tiffany paused to examine her reflection in the full-length mirror before glaring at me over her shoulder. *Selene knows better.* Her nose wrinkled as she tugged at the gauzy neckline, her attitude more to do with the frilly LBD Sierra had selected for her.

Well, I did have that crossbow, and I don't think a vampire can recover from a full clip from a semi-automatic that fast.

She wrestled with where to hide the pencils she had been carrying, but the dress didn't leave a whole lot of options. *You'd be surprised, but still the whole thing was too easy.*

I'll remember that the next time a vamp plays softball with your skull. I'm amazed they didn't question my intentions further. I wasn't about to say anything aloud. Finally, I was starting to get the hang of this telepathy thing. The sending anyway. We hadn't found any cameras, but the bugs had been pretty obvious even to a neophyte like me, so we were trying to be careful. *Hearing* Tiffany had as much to do with her familiarity with the process than any talent on my part. It sure as hell wasn't as easy as Charlaine Harris made it out to be in her books. Though now, I began to wonder how much of her stories were true.

Tiffany raised her eyebrow as she watched me in the mirror. *Did Selene or Sierra try to read your mind?*

I hadn't figured out how to *read* other people on purpose who weren't intentionally sending their thoughts to me. But heck, it'd been less than a week since I died, and I had figured out the particular tickle signifying someone trying to poke her nose in my brain.

I nodded. *Selene tried. I don't think she got through. Otherwise, we wouldn't be having this discussion. Sierra couldn't find her own mind right now with both hands and a searchlight.*

Tiffany rolled her eyes in response before she continued her examination of potential hiding places in her dress.

After our little interview with the queens of the undead, the goon squad had escorted us to a good-sized bedroom with two double beds and a private bath. From the utilitarian look, it was probably a spare for when the staff spent the night.

Sierra had waltzed in a few minutes later with her personal dresser and a rack of frocks in tow. I never liked someone else picking out my clothes. The intense annoyance stemmed from Mom trying to dress me as her little princess. The stuff she had selected for me was worse than the number Tiffany currently wore. I started to rebel but then chewed a hole through my tongue to keep from making any flip comments to Psycho Zombie. Tiffany started to—once. A quick stomp on her instep changed her mind. It beat Sierra eating the kid's brains.

At least Sierra's armed escort hadn't followed Tiffany and me into the bathroom as we tried on each outfit. The fact Sierra picked out undies and a garter to match the royal blue sheath I wore was bad enough.

To top it off, Sierra had sent a make-up artist, manicurist and hair stylist in, so we never had a chance to ditch the guards, retrieve our bags, and blow up the joint.

Which meant we'd have to be creative with what little we had.

Tiffany settled on sticking the pencils in the built-in shelf bra of her dress. The goon squad missed them during the second pat down. *We'll have a better chance in the confusion of the party.* She gave a little wiggle to make sure nothing fell out.

I sighed and tugged at the too tight silk. *I don't want to be responsible for any more innocents dying.*

She pivoted to face me, her elfin face hard. *Buy a clue. Selene plays for keeps.* Eyelids pinched shut, but I already glimpsed the tears gathering. *She killed Ptolemy, her own brother.*

Bile gathered at the back of my throat. No wonder Caesar had thrown out his sister. Something else was in Tiffany's voice. Grief. She must have known this Ptolemy. If all of Duncan's friends had helped raise her . . .

Shit. I really didn't know how Tiffany kept it together. If I faced someone who'd taken everything important in my life from me, I'd be a basket-case right now.

Brown eyes snapped open, eyes that had seen too much ugliness in such a short lifetime. Tiffany sucked in a deep breath and focused with an obvious effort. *Anyone joining her won't hesitate to kill us either. Or have you forgotten what Sierra did to her own father?*

I shook my head. Only the crunch of Charlie and Nurse Ratchett's broken skulls beat the crack of Tyrone Mallory's neck in my memory. Psychiatrists would make a fortune off my nightmares for the next million years.

Tiffany examined the pointed heel of the stiletto Sierra chose for her. *Remember what I said about killing vamps?*

I nodded. Contrary to all the stories and movies from my childhood, Tiffany had explained there were only two sure ways to kill a vampire—anything through the heart or decapitation. Unless delivered in a concentrated, liquefied form into the blood stream, silver or garlic were unpredictable, just like some folks were highly allergic to bees while a sting was a mild irritant to others. Holy water and religious paraphernalia were all Hollywood inventions. She swore a No. 2 in the right spot worked a hell of a lot better than a stake. It didn't reassure me about our chances. Especially since neither of us had a clue whether the nanites conformed Sierra and me to the same headless limitations as the vampires. I'd already found out the hard way staking didn't work.

The thought of shoving something through someone's heart made me want to puke. More visions of Nurse Ratchett and Charlie swam in front of my eyes, taunting me. What was I thinking by coming here? I sank down on one of the beds and laid my head in my hands.

A scrawny arm wrapped around my shoulder. *You didn't have a choice. She would have chased you down once she realized the self-destruct failed if you hadn't come.*

I raised my head to look at her. A haunted kid returned my gaze. A groan issued from my mouth. She had seen everything I had just remembered. I really needed to watch my transmissions. "I'm sorry. You shouldn't have to deal with my shit. Not on top of yours anyway."

She tossed a quick one-shoulder shrug. "It's not easy killing anyone. I killed my first vamp when I was twelve."

It was hard to remember she was barely out of high school. And why was she talking out loud now?

So whoever's listening in on us knows we won't be easy snacks.

I grinned at her comment and played along. "What happened?"

A sad, ironic smile twisted her lips. "I skipped school and didn't make it home before dark. One of Selene's people caught me. And I staked him with the handiest available wood." She patted her chest where she had hidden her ammo. *Now, you know why I rely on these.*

A new sickness spread through my stomach. I saw all too often what happened to the regular kids on Hollywood Boulevard. Now that I knew what else could be preying on them, nausea wrapped a fist around my gut and squeezed.

"So how long were you grounded?"

She laughed at my obvious attempt to lighten the mood. "Two months of no phone or T.V. and another six months without my game system. Phillippa escorted me to and from school for the rest of the year. Do you have any idea how embarrassing that is?"

"I can imagine." Mom had done something similar when I was fourteen though it wasn't like I had Wonder Woman and the vamps looking over my shoulder like Tiffany did. I never figured out how I always got caught and Max never did. Maybe Anne put the whammy on Mom for him.

A sharp rap on the door jerked us both out of our nostalgic, morbid reverie. "Show time," I muttered.

The human goons escorted us back to the elevator and up to the main lobby. When we stepped out, polite chit-chat rumbled through my eardrums. A tsunami of scent assaulted my nose. Once the sensory overload washed past me, I took a good look around.

Strands of tiny white bulbs wound their way around indoor palms. A dais perched to the left of the main staircase, a huge LED screen showing the Mallory logo behind it. Men in penguin suits and glittering women milled around, performing the Los Angeles meet-n-greet, also known as bone crushing handshakes and air kisses. In other words, the reception area looked like any other ritzy corporate party.

A tentative sniff told me the mix of folks in the room was not the usual for corporate America. Over the last few days, I had started to distinguish which scents belonged to which species. The sheer quantity of sandalwood in the air indicated a large number were vamps despite the early evening sunlight streaming through the three-story high windows. I hated to think of how much the ton of bullet-proof, polarized glass cost. Apple indicated Normals. What I'd mistaken for a certain brand of lotion on Bebe had been a witch's ginger signature with her own unique smell. I glanced around but couldn't place who or what gave off a honey odor.

The intermingling of odors definitely made me wonder just who all really held stock in Mallory Labs. That and considering the sheer amount of muscle-for-hire decorating each possible entrance.

Buffet tables framed the room, piled high with shrimp, egg rolls and the typical hors d'oeuvres. We joined the line of people snaking around the food. Our tuxedo-clad escort hung back at the edge of the crowd, close enough to keep an eye on us, but not close enough for an accusation of eating on the boss's time.

Okay, maybe Sierra didn't serve typical hors d'oeuvres. The red stuff spilling out of the centerpiece fountain definitely wasn't cold champagne.

The coppery smell of blood overwhelmed me for an instant. I fought the urge to retch in front of the crowd. Even Tiffany wrinkled her nose in distaste at the bloody prime rib a caterer slapped on a plate of someone ahead of us.

Of course, my stomach chose that moment to growl so loudly the couple in front of us turned to stare. They both carried the musky scent I was learning to associate with weres. The man had a couple of inches on me, filled out his suit in the broad, muscular sense, and sported a ten o'clock shadow at five in the afternoon. I wanted to tell him his purple paisley tie had gone out with Prince, when he was the artist known as Prince the first time around.

The were gave me an appraising look before he smiled the predatory type of toothy grin men had been giving women for millennia. "I like a woman with a good appetite."

Before I could phrase a comeback, his face twisted in a spasm of pain. A quick check showed his companion's left hand gripping his package. She was barely taller than Tiffany, but she left no doubt of who was in charge.

"Apologize to the nice—" The brunette stopped to give me a delicate sniff. "I'm sorry, Miss, but what the hell are you?"

I wasn't sure how to answer her question. Not the weirdly rude politeness of the were, but I wasn't sure what to call myself.

Tiffany was. "She's a zombie, Pack Mistress."

I glanced at her. She had her neck at an odd angle, and she kept her eyes on the floor. All those articles I'd read about dealing with threatening dogs must apply to werewolves.

"Glad to see your pup has some manners unlike some people." She squeezed, and the male were whimpered softly. "What's your name, sweetie?"

"Sam. Sam Ridgeway." I started to hold out my hand and stopped. *What the hell is proper protocol when meeting a were, especially when she's holding her guy's balls in public?*

The lady were grinned at me. "Handshake's fine." She reached over to grab my hand with her free one, still not letting go of her mate.

My thought had been aimed at Tiffany. I prayed I hadn't just accidentally transmitted it to the weres.

"I'm Emily. This here son-of-a-bitch is my husband, George."

She finally released the male, and he edged back a hair. "I apologize, Miss." His voice carried the same Texas twang as his wife's.

My stomach took the awkward break in the conversation to growl even louder.

Emily slapped me on the back. "Let's get you some food, Sam."

Once our plates were loaded, the lady were led us to the tables surrounding the dais. Her husband kept his silence but regarded me with a speculative eye. He wasn't stupid enough for another obvious sexual leer. More like a puzzle piece he had been considering had fallen into place.

The human goons trailed behind us but didn't interfere.

"So, are you what Selene's big announcement is all about?" Emily asked once we sat and spread napkins.

My mouth was crammed full of crab cake so Tiffany responded. "I'm afraid we cannot answer your inquiry at this time, Pack Mistress." She kept her eyes fixed on her plate.

Wow, who'd've thought Goth Girl had a political bent.

"So how'd you become a zombie, Sam?" Emily wasn't about to let the subject go.

I swallowed and nearly choked on the cake. "That's a long story, Miss Emily." I frowned at my faux pas. "I'm sorry. Pack Mistress."

She laughed and laid a hand on my arm. The nails were manicured but short with no polish. I suppose hot pink lacquer wouldn't translate well on a wolf's claws. Probably why she had a short, stylish cut instead of the usual Lone Star bouffant.

"Emily, sweetie. Call me Emily. You'd be an Alpha if you were one of us. I can tell."

"Thank you." At least it seemed like a compliment. A strange gurgle came from Tiffany's bent head. I suppressed the urge to smack her.

A group of tall Scandinavian-looking folks started to sit at the table next to us. The men were as impossibly attractive as the women, and everyone's hair was an equally impossible shade of platinum blond. As one, they all turned to stare at me. Then they rose and glided to another table much further away.

"I thought zombies were a figment of Voudon imagination," George said. He didn't seem to notice the statuesque blond folks' strange behavior. His assessing look was starting to make me nervous.

"As far as I know, we're a pretty rare breed." I plastered a fake smile on my mug, but it didn't fool the weres.

"Rumor is Selene's latest girlfriend has come up with a vaccine to the V-Virus. Are you a byproduct?" George said.

This whole conversation verged on the edge of ugly. Not that I was offended, but I wasn't sure how much to tell the couple. They seemed nice enough, but who knew how much of their act was just an act. It had taken our little cadre a few days to put everything together. And if the weres were shareholders in the Mallory holding company, lord only knew how deep they were in this shit.

"I'm sorry, but I don't know anything about a vaccine."

George shrugged and dropped his question. "Doesn't matter. It's not like we can catch it. There's another rumor going around the younger witches can't catch it either."

The were's little tidbit was certainly food for thought. Is that how Bebe lived with Caesar without becoming infected? I didn't know for sure, but the witch doctor didn't appear to be much older than me.

And Duncan assumed Sierra was holding a potential cure over the vamps' heads, but Selene didn't strike me as so stupid that Sierra could pull that kind of blackmail on her. So what exactly were the two of them up to?

"My goodness, child! You sure can pack away the food." Emily held her hand to her chest. "You sure you aren't part were, Sam?"

I looked down. My plate was bare, and I couldn't remember eating a damn thing besides the crab cake. My stomach warbled its desire for more food.

"George, why don't you get Sam another plate?" It wasn't a request.

Once he was gone, Emily smiled at me but not the friendly Southern grin from earlier. "Now, dear, tell me how you came about?"

I felt her hand in my thigh and not in the friendly I'm-tired-of-pretending-I'm-straight touch. Several sharp somethings dug into my skin just above the edge of my stocking. I bit my lip to keep from yelping and glanced down to see a fur covered paw with very long claws piercing my skin.

"You can answer my questions, or I'll gut you and St. James' pup before you can scream." Golden wolf eyes replaced Emily's hazel human ones.

Tiffany jerked in response, but I didn't dare look at her.

"Yes, dear," Emily said. "I recognize you from the I.C. I don't forget a scent."

The I.C.? Was this Caesar's mysterious Council?

She returned her attention to me. "And I wouldn't count on your pathetic human escort to rescue you." My gaze flicked to our totally oblivious goons holding up the wall a short distance away.

A chilly, thin smile twisted Emily's face. "Considering the animosity between the Antonius twins for the last two years, I was suspicious the moment I saw your little friend. Now, Sam, who created you and why?"

Who the hell were these Antonius people she was talking about? Was a chasm I couldn't see opening under my feet, or could Emily and George possibly be potential allies? Time was running out on my options. Deciding Tiffany's intestines were worth saving, I gave the pack mistress an edited version of recent events.

After a minute, she released my leg. I blessed my speed healing and the blood fountain. Without both, I would have attracted every vamp in the place. As it was, the rents and tiny blood spots ruined the silk dress.

"That's why you and the Mallory girl smell like steel." She said it more to herself than to us. She smiled at me, the wide toothy grin far more feral than her eyes had been. "No wonder the sidhe have been giving you such a wide berth."

"The 'she'?" I had the distinct feeling of sinking even deeper into supernatural political quicksand.

She nodded towards the Swedish Bikini Team on the other side of the room, who had refused to sit next to us and kept giving me strange looks. I still must have had a stupid look on my face. Emily snorted in exasperation and rolled her eyes. "Fairies, dear."

Now, my attention was riveted on the group. They were all in the six-foot range, the women a couple inches shorter maybe. White-blond hair covered everyone's ears so I couldn't tell if they were pointed. "I thought they were smaller."

Emily shrugged. "That table's all Unseelie elves. They and the Seelie are the largest of the sidhe."

Fairies were nature spirits, and considering what bees did with nectar . . .

I shot Emily a curious look. "Is that why they smell like honey?"

She slapped her hand on the table and roared with laughter. "No doubt your nose works just fine, girl."

The organ in question twitched when George plunked a dish full of shrimp, apple wedges and brie in front of me. I crammed a piece of cheese-smeared fruit in my mouth, but not before I noticed a subtle look between the two weres and a slight shake of the head from Emily. At the same time, a couple of vamps across the room spotted us.

I swallowed hard. Time to take a chance. "What ever you want, ask fast. We're about to have company."

The words came out of Emily in a near-silent, breathless rush. "We're looking for our son, Logan, who disappeared four months ago. He's friends with an Augustine vampire named Stanton."

Holy crap! Somehow I could tell without telepathic contact she wasn't lying. Things were starting to look up in my little plan. "He was here. He's fine now, and he's escorting a witch family to safety." Apparently, the dumbass were hadn't called anyone before cutting out of Caesar's place. My words were so quiet I could barely hear them, but Emily's eyes closed in relief as the uglier of the two vamps clasped my shoulder.

"Her majesty wants to see you."

Wow, I didn't realize how full of herself Sierra had become. Or he could be referring to Selene. I nipped a shrimp to the tail, trying to ignore him and the smell of rotten lemons surrounding him. Someone was in a pissy mood.

"Now," he muttered and jerked me up. Last week, my shoulder would have been dislocated from the force.

Selene and Sierra must be done playing nice, or they decided they didn't want me talking to the Texas weres. It was beginning to look like the bad guys hadn't been snatching supernatural folks randomly after all.

"You forgot to say 'please', asshole." George's words came out in a growl, and he rose from the table. The air sizzled from Emily's tension beside me as she jumped to her feet as well.

"It's all right, Pack Master." I gave him a demure smile before I turned to the vampire. "I'm sure Selene's friend here didn't mean to be so rude." I leaned as forward as I could with the vise clamp on my upper arm and mock whispered, "I've noticed it's a failing common with male vampires."

Emily chuckled, and George's shoulders eased though the menacing scowl on his face didn't. Tall, Dark and Ugly didn't look one bit amused.

I nodded to the lady were. "It's been a pleasure, Pack Mistress. We must talk more later. Come along, Tiffany."

I spun on the ridiculously high heels so fast the vamp lost his grip on me. I amazed myself by not losing my balance and stalked off through the crowd. I felt Tiffany trotting behind me and the two vamps trailing her.

So intent on the fairies and weres, I didn't realize full dark had fallen until the lights dimmed as we approached the dais. The crowd quieted at the signal. When Selene stepped from a curtain draped across the entry to the private areas, the buzz of excited conversation echoed through the reception area.

The bodyguards flanking her sent cold slime down my spine. They looked like typical muscle, but a wrongness surrounded them. It wasn't just the scary predator stuff. I breathed deeply, trying to get a handle on our escort. It was more like . . .

Yes. I bit my tongue to keep from saying my thought out loud. A sharp, putrid lemony scent, mixed with ginger, ozone, and blood, began to fill the room. Selene's vamps had been amped somehow through magick, their anticipation and intentions somehow corrupting their normal odors. The bitches had one or more witches on the payroll as well as the rogue vamps.

Or the witches were more captives those two had threatened or out-and-out blackmailed. Either way, the end result didn't bode well for the folks in the room.

More vampires covered the exits, effectively imprisoning everyone in the reception area. Everyone was so intent on Selene approaching the microphone I don't think they noticed. I had little doubt to whom the guards owed their allegiance. Funny though, none of the human members of the Mallory goon squad were anywhere in the room now. Even our original Normal escort had disappeared. Did Sierra know her soiree had been co-opted?

"A bright new day dawns for all of us," Selene began. She really needed a new speech writer.

Tiffany slid her tiny hand into mine and squeezed. *Can you hear me?*

I nearly jumped out of my skin at her voice in my head. *Yeah.* I squeezed back in case I wasn't transmitting to her.

"You've all heard the rumors about a cure for the V-virus. Let me say they are partly true." A murmur ran through the assemblage. "What if you could retain all you've become and walk in the daylight?" Selene asked the crowd.

We're not going to make it out of here. Tiffany's voice in my head was firm and commanding, not the voice of a terrified teenager. Why wasn't she scared? I, on the other hand, was about to piss my designer panties.

"What if you could wear your silver jewelry again, ladies?" Her words brought a few sprinkles of feminine laughter from the crowd.

I tried not to be obvious as I scanned the room. *No shit. I need to get you out of here. Maybe I could leverage a favor out of George and Emily.*

"What if you could eat again? Even—" Selene paused for a breathless instant, "—chocolate?" Laughter rang through the room. I had to give the ancient vamp credit; she could work a room.

Tiffany ignored me. *You need to keep the bodyguards off me long enough for me to take out Selene.*

You're nuts! This isn't going to work. I don't know what I was thinking.

But I did know. I wasn't thinking. Just like I didn't think during the South Central riots. Just like I didn't when Ralph told me to lay off Duncan. Just like I didn't after Fred was killed. I was so damn intent on my goal I didn't stop and think of the consequences. Oh god, if anything happened to Tiffany, Duncan would never forgive me.

"I'd like you to meet the newest member of my family, Sierra Mallory." Polite applause accompanied Sierra to the podium. She could have been Selene's photo negative. Diamonds and black velvet covered her compared Selene's onyx jewelry and white satin gown. The dress cuts were exactly the same with the same upswept 'do.

Sierra didn't wince at Selene's claim on her either. Had the vamp mindfucked her? Was that the cause of the heiress's psychosis?

Sierra favored the crowd with a confident smile. "Ladies and gentlemen, thank you for coming tonight. For all of Her Majesty's theatrics, our product is simple."

"Her Majesty" was Selene. Fuck. Why didn't anyone tell me Duncan's maker was literally a vampire queen?

"My company has developed a solution to your problems." Sierra smiled at the crowd. On the LED screen, an image of a spidery-looking robot hovered over the heads of the two women. "This is a nanite." The spider began a slow rotation. "A microscopic machine that can rewrite any entity's genetic code. It can literally fix the defects in the V-virus, allowing a vampire to live in the daylight and eat without losing any of the benefits, such as superior strength and eternal youth."

Tiffany and I shared wide-eyed looks. I swallowed hard.

What'll happen when the vamps find out she's lying?

I don't want to be here when they do. Her grim look underscored her thought.

"I'm sure the rest of our guests are asking what's in it for you." Sierra's gaze swept the crowd before locking eyes with me. "Anything you want." Her attention returned to the crowd. "I was a Normal. Last Friday I was in the final stages of leukemia. The doctors said I wouldn't make it through this week."

She stepped back from the mike and twirled, the long velvet skirt of her dress flaring at the motion. "Thanks to nanites developed by Mallory Labs, I'm standing before you healthy." Her eyes glittered. "Strong. Alive."

There was a *whoosh* and a *thunk*. Scarlet feathers blossomed in the middle of Sierra's chest. Eyes wide in shock, she stared up at the balcony to her right.

"Sorry, Miss Mallory." Duncan's voice rang through the darkened reception hall. "I am fresh out of spoons."

Chapter 29

Chaos erupted. The bodyguards dived for the stage, their attempt to protect Selene thwarted when she shoved them aside. The guests charged the exits, some changing shape as they ran. Sierra still stood on the stage, staring at the crossbow bolt sticking out of her chest.

I whirled and smacked Ugly in the nose with the base of my palm. Dark blood spurted as Ugly howled in pain. Thank God, I remembered something from the Y's self-defense class Mom made me take in high school.

Tiffany had already pulled a pencil out of her dress and put it to good use. Meat mush that used to be Ugly's partner spread all over the marble tile. I grabbed her arm and headed for the nearest exit. With any luck, Duncan would meet us at the Hummer.

So much for my idiotic plan to deal with Sierra.

A hard jerk ripped Tiffany's hand out of my mine. I whipped around to see Selene in full vamp-out mode, Tiffany squirming in her arms. She opened her mouth wide to chomp on the kid when a gigantic ball of fur flew through the air and collided with the vampire's face.

She dropped Tiffany as she crashed down on the marble hard enough to crack the tile with her elbow. Both she and the furball came up clawing and biting. The furball resolved itself into a huge timber wolf. A timber wolf wearing a purple paisley tie. George hadn't bothered to fully undress before he shifted.

Another wolf clamped jaws on Tiffany's arm and started dragging her away. The kid must have landed on her head because she wasn't putting up any struggle.

"No!" I doubted anyone heard my scream in the surrounding bedlam. I dived for them only to slide into the pair. Blood and meat mush coated the floor and now the front of my dress.

The wolf let go of Tiffany and bared its teeth at me. It's pretty bad when Emily's wicked-ass grin looks the same whether she's wolf or human.

Her attention switched from me to the fight behind us. A whimper rose from her throat, and I turned in time to see Selene boot George ten feet into the air. He landed on the staircase and rolled down, his fuzzy form way too still.

With a growl, Emily launched herself at the vampire.

A whistle that would have been inaudible if I were still human was the only warning I had. I stumbled back, falling over Tiffany's prone form, as a silver sword whipped through the space where my neck had been.

A wild-eyed Sierra stood above me, feathered bolt still sticking out of her chest. Either Duncan had missed her heart or she was getting used to wooden shafts protruding from her body. Instead of passing out like she had in Phil's kitchen, she raised the sword over her head for another strike. I aimed a kick for her knee.

The bones shattered. Sierra screamed and collapsed to the marble. Rocking on the floor, she clutched the injured leg. I didn't have long to get lost before her nanites knitted her back together.

I gathered up the still unconscious Tiffany and stood. I tripped over a round thing, almost losing my bundle in the damned heels. Eyes from the disembodied head stared up at me. Now I knew elves did have pointed ears. I also had a pretty good idea of where Sierra liberated the sword. The poor elf's head had been ripped off.

A vicious battle raged around us. No rhyme or reason orchestrated the fight. Not all of the guest vamps were siding with Selene's contingent, which was good for the rest of us. Another set of wolves snarled and snapped from a defensive stand at the receptionist's desk. Emily and George had disappeared amidst the frenzy of bodies. My priority was to get the unconscious Tiffany to safety, but I doubted my ability to get us both out intact. Where the hell was Duncan?

I tried hard to ignore the bodily fluids and entrails littering the marble floor as I started for the main doors. Despite my sped-up metabolism, the shrimp I ate would be making an encore if I didn't get out of here soon. I swallowed the bile at the back of my throat and kicked off the heels for better footing. If I ever got the kid out of this damn war zone, I would have to bathe for a week to get the stench of death out of my toenails. Sliding and slipping my way across the tiles, I ducked and wove around combatants.

Something very large and doggy-smelling whammed into my back. Tiffany popped out of my arms, and I landed face-first in a melting vamp.

I didn't have a chance to throw-up before someone yanked me up by the back of my dress. Nails dug into my throat, pulling me to my feet. My hands reached for a solid purchase on something, anything.

"I'm going to rip out your guts, child. Did you think I couldn't smell *him* on you?" The jealousy in Selene's voice cut through me like the iceberg through the *Titanic* and just as frigid. No question the "him" she referred to was Duncan.

When she turned me to face her, I did puke. Thanks to George and Emily, her nose and lips had been chewed off and one eye was missing. And that was the least of the damage. The wolves had turned her into a living, bleeding exhibit from Body Worlds.

She squeezed harder. "How'd you disable the self-destruct? You and my brother should be dead."

Like I could answer while she choked me. Selene may have been shorter than me, but vampire strength hoisted me a couple of inches off the floor. Legs flailed, seeking a purchase on something, anything, to relieve the godawful pressure on my windpipe.

All seven of George Carlin's words ripped through my brain while I tried to wedge granite fingers from my throat. Selene's hands clenched tighter, and then I was drowning in my own vomit. Burning filled my lungs as stomach acid and lack of oxygen killed delicate tissues. Spots swam before me as I struggled to breathe. My fists beat at the talons crushing my airway. I could have been hitting Mount Rushmore for all the good it did.

Oh God, I'm going to die again. Why does dying have to hurt like this? The blows I landed barely registered in my oxygen-deprived brain. My toes were numb. The insanity of the battle blurred to dark gray, a prelude to the final black.

Something poked me in the ribs and then I fell, landing with a loud *splooch* on my ass. I bent over and coughed the rest of the crap out of my throat before I could suck in huge lungfuls of sweet, sweet oxygen. My throat hurt like hell, my chest worse, but cells and nanites alike rejoiced in the air. The scene snapped back into focus.

In slow motion, Selene collapsed to her knees beside me. Only when it was eye-level did I notice the tip of a crossbow bolt sticking out of her dress. Right where her heart should be. The golden glow faded from her remaining eye, and the bits of skin left began sliding off her skull. Her torso teetered for a moment before falling across my legs.

"Are you all right, darling?" Duncan knelt beside me, one arm wrapped around me, the other holding the crossbow. A crossbow I recognized. It had been the one I packed in my bag this morning. The one Kane and his boys had confiscated. I could only stare at him, totally dumbfounded.

"Samantha?"

I tried to talk, but nothing came out.

"Answer me, Samantha! Are you all right?" He shook me to emphasize the point.

So I smacked him in the chest and pointed to my neck.

"Oh." A delightfully sheepish smile spread across his face. "Sorry."

It was good to know the bastard had other expressions besides a scowl and a mocking grin. I tried to pull my feet out from under the melting and oozing vampire, but the gunk clung to my stockings. I really needed a shower.

"I guess that's what you'd call closure, huh?" Tiffany, bearing an awful resemblance to Sissy Spacek at the end of *Carrie*, stood on wobbly legs next to us. "Caesar isn't going to be happy you killed the bitch." An evil grin lit up her face. "But I'm pretty damned ecstatic right now."

Duncan looked up, a wry tilt to his eyebrow. "Are you all right?"

She started to nod but thought better of it. "Probably a concussion. Otherwise, I'm just fucking peachy."

"Watch your language," he said, but there was no bite in his tone.

I glanced away from their banter, and finally I noticed the fighting was pretty much over. Folks limped through the debris, searching for friends, relatives, and their own body parts.

"Where's Sierra? Better yet, where's George and Emily?" My words weren't much more than a croak. I didn't realize how much I missed the sound of my own voice.

"Who?"

"The Polks," Tiffany explained. At his confused expression, she added, "You know, the San Antonio Pack leaders?"

"Logan's parents are here?" Duncan rose. "Keep an eye on Sam. I'll find—" The rest of what he was about to say was swallowed by a hoarse cry as a silver swordpoint popped out of his shoulder. He crashed to the floor, his body racked by convulsions. Tiffany screamed.

Standing over Duncan, Sierra smiled at me. "You're next, bitch."

Chapter 30

I stared in disbelief. Why couldn't Psycho Zombie curl up in a corner and die like everyone else?

Time slowed to a crawl. Tiffany, crying, knelt next to Duncan and cradled his head in her lap. The survivors turned their heads in our direction. I stood up, each breath still torture from my partially crushed windpipe and vomit-filled lungs.

Duncan lay so still. His skin melded to the bones, anticipating the final disconnect before it began its slide to the floor. With every beat, I waited for my heart to explode out of my chest. *He can't be dead.* I gritted my teeth. *He just can't.*

Tears dripped down my face. The agony inside me, the inability to draw a breath without racking pain, had nothing to do with the damage Selene had inflicted.

My eyes met Sierra's mad ones.

Then everything whipped into fast forward. Sierra jerked the sword out of Duncan's body. She swung at Tiffany's bent head. I rammed her before the silver touched the kid. Sierra skidded through the debris.

"Don't you ever touch my boyfriend again!" I shouted. Or tried to. It came out more of a hoarse bark than a shout, but the nanites were doing their job.

The bitch scrambled to her feet and ran toward me, swinging wildly with the sword.

Well, she tried to run. The body parts and fluids made footing treacherous even without the heels she wore. I backpedaled. She slipped in what was at one time Selene's liver and went down hard on her backside. She was way too close to Duncan and Tiffany for my comfort.

"Aw, come on, Sierra" I taunted, sidling away from the vulnerable pair. "Is that the best you can do?"

Good plan, Sam. Piss off the maniacal, sword-wielding, bionic zombie. I told the logical portion of my brain to shut up and circled further away from Duncan and Tiffany.

My attitude had the desired effect. She ignored the people I cared about in order to behead me. Silver handle tight in her manicured hand, she kicked herself free of the remains of her former partner.

An even more disturbing thought occurred as Sierra stalked after me. What if I didn't die if she beheaded me?

She is going to behead you if you insist on such self-defeating thoughts. Duncan!

I risked a glance in his direction. He was barely conscious but alive. A human-shaped Emily, battered, bloody and naked, crouched next to him, helping Tiffany staunch his wound. Goth Girl stood, but Emily yanked her back. None of the other survivors ringing the room moved to interfere in this fight.

I ducked a wild swipe by Sierra and threw a chair at her head. She evaded my clumsy projectile. I dodged around a table, trying to keep out of reach of her sword. She leapt up on the plywood top.

I lashed out at the aluminum leg. It broke, but the jagged edge snagged my ultra run-resistant hose. She half fell, half jumped at me as the table collapsed. Sierra, the table, and I landed in a big tangled heap.

Except it wasn't the table that shot an elbow to my chin. My vision swam and the sharp, metallic taste of blood filled my mouth where I had bitten my tongue. A knee to my groin followed the elbow shot. For the record, it hurts pretty damn bad for girls, too.

I resisted the urge to cup myself. Instead, I shook my leg free of the table to gain some maneuverability, a nasty cut across my calf my reward for the effort. Before I could formulate a new plan, Sierra jumped behind me. With a yank on my hairspray-coated locks, she twisted my head back until it felt like a vertebra would snap.

An ugly smile filled my vision. "Let's find out just what you taste like." Beverly Hills-white teeth clamped onto my neck.

There's something intensely primal and terrifying when someone or something chomps a hunk of flesh out of you. I was sure Evander Holyfield would agree. My problem was I didn't have a referee and trainers to pull Psycho Bitch off me.

I thrashed and hit with everything left in me. A thick, dark heaviness gathered at the base of my skull. The pressure rose, gathering every thought, every breath. When it reached an unbearable level, I screamed.

Suddenly I was freefalling. The landing knocked the little air I had left right out of my lungs. Automatically, I slapped a hand to my neck for pressure and tried not think about the missing palm-sized section of muscle, ligaments and arteries.

Panicked, I felt around for a weapon, any weapon, with my free hand. My fingers closed around slick metal. I held the broken table leg between me and Sierra, who lay several feet away.

She sprawled across the disgusting marble, a sick grin spread across her face. My blood dripped from her chin and disappeared into the black material of her dress. She ran the back of her hand across her mouth. Red smeared across her cheek.

"I want some more," she whispered.

The aluminum makeshift stake wavered in front of me. I wasn't fooling myself about it killing her, but maybe if I stabbed her multiple times, she'd pass out long enough for us to chain her.

Yeah, right. And I'd suddenly develop J. Lo's figure.

Sierra rose to her hands and knees, the image unmistakably one of a jungle cat ready to pounce. Her muscles tensed, then confusion crossed her face. She rocked back, and her skin seemed to shimmer in the low light.

A raw scream of pain erupted from her throat. She rose to her knees, fingers scratching desperately at her face. Blood, a funky metallic scarlet color, dripped from the wounds. She started ripping at her clothing. No, not her clothing. Her abdomen. Skin hung in tattered shreds as she continued to tear at her own flesh. But when she clawed at her arms, instead of blood, metallic silver liquid oozed from her scratches.

What the hell? The table leg clattered to the floor. I dropped to my hands and crab-crawled away from her. Her agonized screaming rose in pitch. Sierra stood and continued to rip at her hair and skin. Skin which was no longer bleeding red or silver. Silver powder flaked from her body and drifted to the gore-coated marble.

With one last, horrific screech, Sierra Mallory exploded into a cloud of sparkling dust.

Chapter 31

Bebe tapped her pen against the clipboard she held. "Near as I can understand, your nanites thought they were still in your body."

"Thought? What do you mean 'thought'? They're robots. They can't think." I rubbed my damp hair with a towel.

She didn't answer and bent over the microscope once again.

Six hours ago, Caesar's search-and-destroy team had arrived at Mallory Labs and turned into a clean-up squad. Bob, the head of Mallory's security, hadn't argued over Augustine Research's "takeover" of the late Mallorys' assets. In fact, he seemed quite relieved. Additional "special" assistance arrived for the surviving guests. Tonight's chaos sure as hell wasn't going to be reported to the LAPD.

Bebe and a couple of paramedic weres had bundled me into an ambulance and drove me to Good Samaritan. I found out on the way that Caesar's generous donations paid for a special wing there. The board of directors believed Bebe headed up a cancer research program, but in reality, the folks working in the alleged program specialized in supernatural medicine.

While everyone else treated at the hospital had the luxury of a shower, or at least a sponge bath, the weres had wheeled me to Bebe's personal lab for an examination. A detailed examination. It royally sucked.

Didn't she have a clue of what decaying vampire smells like? After five hours of olfactory torture, she finally let me take a damn shower.

Bebe looked up from her microscope and rubbed her eyes. "Okay, bad choice of words. The nanites' program shuts them down when their sensors show they have left your body in minute quantities, such as in tears, saliva, or blood."

I tossed the towel on an empty stool and finger-combed my hair. I felt human again with the clean skin, clean hair and clean clothes.

My stomach grumbled.

No, I was never going to feel truly human again.

Bebe shrugged before she continued. "Before the shutdown engaged, Sierra's nanites attacked them as an outside threat or infection. That in turn triggered your nanites' self-defense and repair programs, which overrode the shutdown. It may also have to do with the size of the chunk she bit out of you."

I whistled. "Killed by a robot war inside her own body." Leaning against the lab table, I rubbed at the healed bite. No one could tell six hours ago I had a fist-sized hole in my neck. No redness, no scarring, nothing. Like the gunshot wound to my chest. The whole thing was so damn bizarre. "So Fred was right. My nanites were the answer to taking out Sierra."

Bebe nodded. Even without telepathy, I could tell from the twist of her lips that she was thinking the same thing I was. Why couldn't have Fred just told us that during the séance?

An open jar full of silvery flakes sat on the table next to Bebe's microscope, all that was left of the only other human zombie created by Tyrone Mallory. I reached over to poke at the "Sierra dust".

Bebe slapped my hand away. "Don't touch until I'm sure they're turned off for good."

I shook my head. "I had to have breathed in some of her nanites when she—" I stopped, not sure what to say. It's one thing to see someone go poof on TV, another in real life.

"That's why I want to see you in an hour for more tests."

I saluted her and barked, "Aye, Captain." As I closed the door behind me, the good doctor was shaking her head and muttering to herself about zombies and insanity.

Duncan waited for me in the hallway, his broad shoulders holding up the wall.

Like me, the holes in his luscious body had healed hours ago, but his skin was paler than normal, even for him. He favored me with a quick peck on the lips before his face turned grim. "Caesar wants to talk to us."

Right. My guess was the vampire prince would take another chunk of flesh from my ass for taking matters into my own hands and getting a lot of people killed. The very thing I'd been trying to avoid. But I nodded and fell in step with him as we headed down the hall toward Bebe's office.

I couldn't read Duncan's mind, but I also couldn't blame him for his dour mood. Ralph wouldn't be happy if I waltzed into his office, saying I had just shot and killed one of his siblings.

Ralph. Damn, I needed to call my own boss. My heart sank. The chance for the assistant editor position had poofed faster than Sierra Mallory. Hell, I probably didn't even have a job at the *Scoop* anymore, but I owed him the notice I was still alive and kicking. Sort of.

Duncan's knock on the office door was followed by a soft "Come in."

Caesar sat behind Bebe's desk, elbows propped on the surface and fingers steepled. After Duncan and I each detailed our versions of the night's events, ending with Selene and Sierra's deaths, the older vampire stood, turned and stared out the window for a long time. His fist raised and clenched against the glass. Duncan stood so still, as if waiting for recrimination. I held my breath, not sure if I could stop Caesar if he did try anything.

Hours seemed to pass before he whispered, "So I'm the last Ptolemy."

I couldn't have been more surprised if he had whipped around and kicked me in the gut. He couldn't be who I thought.

Could he?

Bits and pieces spun through my brain as everything slipped into place. His age. His mention of his siblings. Emily's comment about the Antonius twins.

Alexander Helios Antonius of Egypt, the oldest son of Cleopatra VII and Mark Antony.

All the sudden I couldn't breathe.

One thing didn't make sense.

He straightened and turned back to us. His hands slid into his pockets, and he regarded me with a sad half-smile. "You simply cannot stop asking questions, can you, Samantha?"

"With all due respect, Your Highness . . ." I stopped, not sure of the proper form of address for an Egyptian prince, but he nodded for me to continue.

"Why the hell would you use the name of the man responsible for the deaths of half your family?" I blurted.

Duncan jerked, probably pissed at my disrespect. I was too stunned to word my question more carefully. I had written my history masters' thesis on Cleopatra VII. If I'd had an inkling two of her kids were still alive . . .

Caesar seemed to find the question hysterical. He roared with laughter for a full minute before wiping the red-tinged tears from his face. "I get that question a lot." He exhaled and shook his head. "Selene and Ptolemy did not understand either." He grinned at me. "I think you, of all people, would."

I couldn't help smiling back. It was as much a screw-you to his parents' nemesis, the first emperor of Rome, as it was a tribute to his beloved older brother, who just happened to be Cleopatra's by Julius Caesar. Yeah. I could definitely understand.

"Master—" Duncan stepped forward but his words seemed to catch in his throat.

Caesar shook his head. "It's over. I would like to be alone now." He turned back to the window.

But Tiffany had mentioned Ptolemy as if she knew him. Had Caesar's youngest brother been Turned as well as his twin sister? It made sense considering the two boys had disappeared from the history books shortly after the Battle of Actium.

My millions of questions would have to wait until another time. Sympathy overrode my curiosity. As much as Max pissed me off at times, I didn't know what I would do without him. Duncan and I left Caesar to grieve.

George and Emily met us in the hospital lobby as we exited the elevator. George held out his hand to Duncan.

"Thanks for the use of the phone and the clothes, son," the were said. The men gave each other that emotional, masculine handshake they give when they really want to hug but are afraid it'll ruin their images.

Luckily, Emily's tight hug helped smother my grin at George calling Duncan "son". "Thanks for letting us know Logan's all right." She released me before my ribs actually broke from her strength. "You come and visit us sometime, girl."

Not ones for extended good-byes, the weres strode through the main doors and climbed into a waiting cab. Once they departed, I turned the evil eye on Duncan.

"I thought Logan was a lone werewolf."

"Technically, he is. The oldest sons are turned out by the pack once they reach adulthood to start their own pack. Logan came out to Los Angeles to find a mate."

"Here? In La-La land?"

"Yes."

"Oh." I was so tired I couldn't think of much else to say.

He smirked at me. "What? The great Samantha Ridgeway has finally run out of questions?"

I glared at him some more. "Have you checked on Tiffany? And where's Max? There. That's two questions."

Duncan shook his head, but the amused glint remained in his eyes. He took me by the hand and led me down a side hallway, which seemed to contain only private conference rooms. Angry words wafted down the corridor from the only one with a closed door. We looked at each other.

"—just one day. Quit making a BFD about it, Max." Tiffany's voice snapped with tension.

Uh-oh. Trouble in paradise, already?

Duncan rapped on the door. He was greeted by silence. He knocked again.

"Either come in or go away!"

He eased the door open at Tiffany's sharp voice. "I just wanted to see how you were feeling."

She stood at the edge of the table, not bothering to look at us. Instead, she glared at my brother, who leaned back on the couch and matched her expression with a determined one of his own. She was back in her Goth Girl gear, ripped black t-shirt and black leather mini-skirt.

"My brains are still intact," she snarled.

She was definitely back to her original attitude problem.

My stomach rumbled again, and she shot me a nasty look. "Unless your girl-friend plans on eating them."

Max rose from the couch. "Just because you're pissed at me doesn't mean you can take it out on Sam."

Tiffany turned her glare back to Max. "For the record, I am breaking up with you."

My heart leapt at the same time I felt a pulse of excitement from Duncan. Could it be?

"You can't. We're engaged." Max crossed his arms over his chest.

Guess not. I recognized his stance.

Tiffany stamped her foot. "You can't make me, asshole."

Max unfolded his arms and took a step toward her, more determined than threatening. "If you think I'm going to let my child be born a bastard, you've got another think coming," he said with surety.

I don't know what shocked me more—Max's news or his caveman attitude.

"You two have only known each other five fucking days! How the bloody hell did this happen?" Duncan roared.

Tiffany rolled her eyes at him. "It's called sex, Duncan."

"Then you are damn well going to marry the idiot!"

"Hey!" Max and I protested at the same time.

Pounding footsteps announced Alex and Anne's arrival.

"What's all the shouting about?"

I knew Alex's question was rhetorical. He and Anne would have had their heads encased in cement and buried two miles below ground not to have heard the commotion.

I answered anyway. "My genius brother knocked up the kid."

"We don't know for sure I'm pregnant." Her voice shook, the reality starting to sink in.

"Yes, you are," the vamps and I answered in unison.

Then I knew the source of Tiffany's citrus-y smell from earlier in the evening. Well, technically yesterday. The hormonal changes had already started, and deep down, she knew Selene had to die for her baby to be safe.

"We'll get out of here. You two need to talk," I said before walking over and giving each of them a hug. I shooed the vamps out and shut the door behind me.

Jealousy and excitement battled for supremacy. It stung I would never know the feeling of my tummy swelling or the kick of a tiny life inside of me.

Excitement won, with a smidgen of revenge assisting it. I would be able to spoil my niece or nephew rotten. The thought of hyping the tot on sugar and caffeine before sending him or her home to Max made me rub my hands in delight. My stomach chose that moment for a more insistent growl.

"I hope you're not planning on eating the baby." Duncan had a slightly horrified look on his handsome but still gaunt face.

"No," I said, smiling back at him. "But we'd better get down to the cafeteria before I change my mind."

Alex and Anne didn't follow us since they were still on security duty. The private cafeteria was an experience. Duncan snagged a bottle of blood from a cooler. While he set it in the microwave and punched the buttons to warm it, I pulled or requested one of everything from the counter.

Once we sat, Duncan kept his gaze fixed on the bottle. I tapped my foot, waiting for him to say something since I was busy inhaling a bowl of chicken noodle soup along with half of a basket of Zestas. After tonight, I had to wonder if the crackers really were made by elves.

Without a word, he drained and discarded the first bottle before he rose and retrieved another out of the cooler. While I was relieved to see color and tone liven his skin, the silent treatment sucked.

When he sat for the second time, I snatched the bottle out of his hand.

"Samantha." He swiped at the bottle I held out of reach.

"You'll get it back after we're done, buster." I glared at him.

"Sam—"

I reached across the table and touched his lips. "No, let me finish. I'm the last woman on earth who wants to have 'the talk'. I'm also not looking for a commitment."

"No, you should be committed," he mumbled against my fingers. His lips were sending signals to a part of my anatomy I sure as hell shouldn't be listening to. Duncan's eyes flared neon, and he nibbled on my fingers.

"Stop that!" I jerked my hand away. My fingers wanted his tongue back. Parts further south agreed. "And while you're at it, shut the fuck up and let me finish."

"We should get married."

Brain-freeze. So not what I was expecting.

Vampire speed caught the bottle plummeting towards the floor tile. He set it on the table before he scooted my chair closer to him and wrapped his arms around me. His chest rumbled with his chuckle as he hugged me.

"Had I but known what it would take to silence you, I would have proposed much earlier this week."

"No."

He cupped my chin and tilted my head to stare into my eyes. The cute little frown of his creased his forehead. "'No'? What do you mean 'no'?"

"First of all, that wasn't a proposal. It was a suggestion. Second, we haven't even been on a first date yet. And third—" Oh, God, I was channeling Max, but I couldn't stop myself. "You haven't even told me you love me."

"What are you saying? You want to court before we marry?"

I bit my bottom lip to keep from breaking into hysterics at his incredulous look. "Well. Duh." I rolled my eyes. If men didn't get a better clue with age, then the human race truly was doomed.

Hooking my upper arms, he set me back in my chair. He rose, grabbed his blood and sauntered toward the cafeteria door.

"Where the hell are you going?"

Duncan shot a wicked look over his shoulder. "Home."

"Without me?" I squeaked.

"Yes." The glowing eyes belied his stern look.

"But, but, but—"

"I do love you, heaven help me, but no more lovemaking until we are properly wed." His head disappeared. Sharp bootsteps retreated down the hallway.

That bastard!

I charged out of the cafeteria and caught up with him as he passed an empty patient room. A rough shove propelled him through the door. From the antiseptic odor, no one was currently staying in the room.

Once he caught his balance, Duncan cocked an eyebrow at me. "Excuse me?"

"What the fuck do you think you're playing at?" I growled.

The amused look was back in his eyes. "I am not playing at anything, darling. I simply refuse to go to bed with a woman who cannot do me the courtesy of replying when I tell her I love her."

"And what do I get if I tell you I love you?" I snapped.

He set his bottle on the patient tray before he lowered himself to the hospital bed and patted the blanket. "Come over here and I will show you."

Rational thought followed Elvis out of the building. Wary, I eased closer and sat next to him.

He reached for my hand and picked up nibbling where he left off in the cafeteria. I sighed and sank down into the nubby blanket, relishing the rough texture of his tongue snaking across my palm. Our clothes disappeared before I realized it.

Nerves ignited faster than a canyon wildfire. I bucked and moaned, but his fingers and mouth withdrew every time I closed in on an orgasm.

Within seconds, I begged him to enter me. He paused, his arms braced on each side of me. "Not until you say it."

"I already did."

"No, you asked what I would do if you said it. I've made a good faith demonstration. Now, I want to hear it."

"Duncan." It was a feeble protest even by my standards.

"Say it," he demanded.

"Duncan," I wailed. "You're not fighting fair!"

A wicked grin spread across his face. "I know." He teased his tip against my clit.

"Dammit, all right all ready. I love you."

I know. I love you too, darling.

He plunged into me, and my world shattered in an explosion rivaling Krakatoa.

Cool air replaced his warmth when he collapsed next to me. He snatched the extra blanket from the foot of the bed and spread it over my goose bumps before snugging me tight against his chest.

"See, was that so terrible?"

Ignoring his asinine question, I rolled to my side, an interesting maneuver considering the size of the standard hospital bed. Propping my head on my hand, I regarded him. "How did you hear me tonight at the lab? I thought the only time you could read my mind was …" I waved at the bed.

He stroked my waist and hip. I could almost see the little cogs whirring in his head. After I was sure he would ignore my question in favor of more sex, he answered. "Physical intimacy is not the trigger."

"Then what?"

"You have a very difficult time displaying your true feelings, especially where I am concerned. Tonight you were so afraid you would lose me you dropped your mental barriers."

"So you're the psychic equivalent of a Klingon battle cruiser? I get anywhere near you and I raise shields?"

His small smile indicated he was laughing with me for once.

"Something like that," he admitted.

"Okay," I drawled. "I'll buy your theory. Now, how the hell did you get to Mallory Labs by yourself in the daylight, Mr. I-Can't-Drive?"

"Caesar is correct. You simply cannot stop asking questions."

"Come on, give." I socked him in the shoulder, gently though since I didn't want to take the chance he wasn't completely healed.

"Obviously, you were not paying attention to Alex's story of how he and I first met." Now, he did smirk.

"Oh, shit!" I flopped over on my back at my own stupidity. Of course, the supply compartment under the back floor of the Hummer.

I peered at him with suspicion through slitted eyelids. "If you couldn't read my mind—"

He rose up on his elbow and cocked an eyebrow.

"I'm so going to kill Tiffany."

He chuckled. "As you would say, cut the kid a break. She did not leak her thoughts on purpose. You caught her by surprise with your psychic talent." He lifted my hand and nuzzled the palm. I floated on the erotic sensation when his next words registered. "However I suspected you would attempt some idiotic stunt."

I jerked out of his grasp, but he pinned me before I could slide off the bed.

"I was not about to let harm come to the woman I love."

Unfamiliar warmth curled inside of me, but I wasn't about to give in so easily. "Don't you ever fuck with me again, asshole."

"Are you sure?" He ducked to nibble my left breast. Soft laughter echoed through my head. That boy was going to find out just how nasty I could be. My toes curled as he paid extra attention to my other breast. Then he bent his head, his hair tickling my tummy as he laved my very sensitive flesh.

Paybacks could wait until tomorrow.

Chapter 32

Ralph was usually at the office on Saturday mornings, and he didn't disappoint me when I arrived the next day.

"Dammit, Ridgeway, you scared the shit out of me, disappearing like that. You're sure you're all right?" His gruff voice almost sounded emotional.

"I'm fine." I hesitated and glanced around the bullpen. Everyone's eyes immediately fell back to their tasks. Everyone except Bill Morton's. A salacious smile jeered back at me.

I couldn't blame Ralph for giving Bill the position since I was the one who fell off the face of the earth for the last week. I faced my waiting editor. "Can we talk privately?"

Ralph nodded. He hadn't missed the exchange. Once the door closed behind him, and he waved at the guest chair, he said, "I'm sorry, Sam."

I flopped in the seat. Emerson peered around the corner of the desk, and I held out my hand. He whined and ducked back behind the scarred furniture. It figured that the dog would freak over my new smell. Ralph eased into his chair, one arm moving rhythmically as he comforted the distressed bulldog.

Not sure how to start, I tapped the armrest. I mean, how exactly do you call in dead to your boss?

Ralph broke the silence first. "You should have listened when I told you to lay off St. James. And you got my offices trashed."

I couldn't help grinning at Ralph's pissed off tone. "You can blame the trashing on a story Max was working on. The bad guys thought you and I were hiding shit for my dumbass brother."

"Doesn't make you any less dead, does it?"

My jaw dropped. It took a couple of tries to close it. Finally, I stammered, "How do you know?"

"How do you think the covens and packs keep an eye on unusual happenings?"

This thing went far deeper than I realized. "The supernaturals own United Media?"

He nodded. "Augustine has controlling interest in our parent company." A sad smile followed. "You're not the first stray he's taken in, Sam."

I breathed deeply, trying to ground the raging turmoil in my head. Ralph knew he worked for a vampire. He fed unusual street information to Caesar.

And underneath the smell of paper and dog and cigarettes lay the faint musk of were.

"Where's your pack?"

He shrugged. "They tossed me and my brothers out years ago." A confirming bark echoed under the desk.

No fucking way. I shook my head, but before I could ask, Ralph handed me the answer.

"Emerson and I can't shift, Sam." He shrugged. "Waldo can, but he chose to stay with us, protect us." Ralph rarely mentioned his twin brother, a security consultant up in Seattle. Okay, litter mate.

Before I could formulate an answer to Ralph's bombshell, he leaned forward, resting beefy arms on top of someone's redlined story. Sharp, blue eyes bored into mine. "Are you going to accept Augustine's protection?"

Duncan had mentioned joining the vampire coven to me before I left for the *Scoop*. "I meet with Caesar in a couple of hours." I swallowed hard, slightly embarrassed. "He's still cleaning up some problems from last night."

"For what it's worth, Sam, I think you should take him up on it. The word about you is out thanks to last night's fiasco. You're going to need all the help you can get."

"About my job—"

"Talk to Augustine first."

I didn't like the finality in his voice, but for once, I listened. I'd screwed up enough to last a lifetime. Okay, a deathtime.

I rose and headed for the door.

"Sam?"

My hand on the knob, I looked at Ralph.

"Tell Max I passed his notes to the authorities like he asked."

"You had them all along?" I couldn't keep the disbelief from my voice. If the police had Max's notes, it could blow the lid off the whole supernatural world. How could Ralph do such a thing when he was one of them? Caesar was not going to be pleased. Nope, not at all.

"Yeah." Ralph smiled and reached for the pack of cigarettes lying on a pile of paperwork. "Now get the hell out of my office. I've got work to do." He made shoo-ing motions with the hand not busy pulling out a smoke.

The incidents of the last week chased each other around my head on the drive back to Brentwood. Some questions had been answered, but not all. Like what the hell the damn nanites were doing to me? I was still hungry all the time. All Bebe could say was they were still rewriting my DNA. But until they were done, we all agreed "zombie" was the best description for what I was.

The more I thought though, the angrier I became at Caesar for interfering with my employment. Unlike him, I wasn't independently wealthy. Dammit, I needed my job to pay for my ravenous appetite.

I wheeled my retrieved Honda into Caesar's drive and waved at Miko, one of the day guards. She waved back and the gates slid open. After I parked, I put my zombie radar to good use. Only three people in the house, two male vamps and one male human, all of them in Caesar's study. Good. I needed to bitch out my brother too.

I didn't bother knocking on the study door. In the split second I burst into the room, I realized the human sitting in the chair facing away from me had a full head of sun-bleached hair. He turned and shot out of his chair, piercing blue eyes wide with shock.

Then he lunged for me, and Duncan's firm grip on his arm prevented Brent Poole from tackling me.

"What the fuck is she doing here?" Poole tried to lunge again. "Let me go!" He struggled against Duncan's hold.

Damn. Attempted assault and me without my camera.

"Control yourself, Brent." Amusement and annoyance chased each other across Caesar's features. "I won't have you assaulting my guest."

"Guest?" Poole spat. "Uncle Caesar, you cannot be serious?"

Uncle? Caesar? Alton's soap star father was a distant cousin of the deposed Greek royal family. Was Poole and Alton's relationship a freakin' arranged royal marriage?

I clenched my fists. The story of a freakin' lifetime and I couldn't write it. Not without destroying people I'd begun to care about in the process. Death was so unfair.

At least Poole smelled like apples, which meant he was human. And I really wanted to put my new nose to work to find which stars were human and which weren't because I had some serious suspicions about Rebecca Romjin being elven.

"Duncan?" Poole looked at my man, trying to find an ally. "You know every-thing she's—" He pointed at me. "—done to me and Jess. Why would you let her in Uncle Caesar's house?"

"She's my fiancée," Duncan said.

"What?" Poole and I spluttered at the same time.

"I am not!" I yelled.

"She can't be!" Horror engulfed Poole's classic cinema features. He gazed at Duncan like a little boy who's realized his hero has feet of clay. He pointed at me again. "She's a tabloid reporter. She's using you to get to me."

Red hazed my vision. After the week I had, I didn't need his shit. "You have a really high opinion of yourself, don't you, jerkwad? Has it occurred to you the only reason I'm here in a vampire's house is because I died last weekend?"

"Oh my God." Poole rolled his eyes in disgust. He turned to Duncan. "You were my Qui-Gon, man." He whipped to face Caesar. "And you're family for chris-sakes! How the fuck could you two Turn someone like her?" He grabbed his de-signer jean jacket and gave me one last ugly glare before storming out of Caesar's study. A resounding boom of the front door slamming echoed through the house.

I looked up at Duncan. "Qui-Gon?"

He shrugged. "I gave Brent pointers when he was preparing for *Conversation with a Bloodsucker*."

As much as I wanted to snicker at the thought of Poole using Duncan St. James as a model, I couldn't forget the reason I came in and turned to Caesar. "I have a bone to pick with you, Your Highness."

"Yes?" Caesar knew, he was going to make me say it out loud, and he didn't even bother to look apologetic.

I crossed my arms and gave him my best Siamese cat stare-down. "Where do you get off telling my boss—"

"Technically, I am your employer."

"So what are you saying? I'm fired? Don't you think I can take care of myself?" I snapped. "I took care of Sierra, didn't I? I could have handled Ralph too."

"I have no doubt you could have, Samantha." Uh-oh. Warning bells began din-ging in my head at my full name. "But you are part of a whole other world now, the supernatural world."

"Gee, thanks, Caesar," I sneered. "Like I need the reminder."

"Maybe you do, Samantha. What are you going to do when someone notices you're not aging? What about when you move too fast or lift something a normal human woman shouldn't be able to lift?" Caesar steepled his index fingers and gazed at me, his expression reminiscent of the warning look he had given me once before in his safe house. God, that seemed a lifetime ago.

I took a deep breath to calm my nerves. "Look, Caesar, I have no intention of betraying any of you or your secrets, and I do appreciate all your help, but I need my own life. I need to feel as normal as possible."

My stomach decided to gurgle at that instant. Duncan chuckled, and I elbowed him in the ribs, none too gently. He rewarded me with a startled *oof.*

Amusement danced in Caesar's eyes even though his expression never wavered. "Samantha, you are newly made and still very vulnerable. If you were a recently Turned vampire, you'd have two options. You could tell your immediate family the truth."

I opened my mouth, but a cautionary look from Caesar made me hesitate.

"If you can't trust your parents with the truth, we will arrange for a new identity in a location far from Los Angeles with adequate resources to carve a new life."

"Like a Witness Protection Program?"

He gave me an approving smile. "Similar, yes. However, if you don't accept my protection, it not only will put you at risk for those seeking to capitalize on Mallory's research, your family could be in jeopardy as well."

Oh, fuck. I collapsed on the chair Poole had vacated. Black spots swam in my vision. This was not what I was expecting. Expecting . . .

A slim hope occurred. I glanced up at Caesar. "But wouldn't Max be part of your Family?" I swallowed hard. "Now he and Tiffany are engaged?"

The vampire nodded. "But not your parents. Protection only extends so far."

"Don't I have any time to decide?" I hated the whine in my voice.

"Ideally, a new vampire would have already finalized these affairs before being Turned, but vampire laws allow a coven master certain discretion in unusual situations." He looked up at Duncan. "Have Max and Tiffany set a date yet?"

My man's face carried a certain distaste though his posture remained at parade rest. "I believe they are looking at the first weekend in April."

Damn, that was fast. My attention swung back to Caesar, who gave a sharp nod.

"Seven weeks is well within the legal extension. You'll have until the day after the wedding to make your decision. Very well, then." His golden brown eyes swept over me. "I have a special project for you." He held up a hand to forestall my attempted protest. "You can work on this in your spare time when you're not on a *Scoop* assignment, and you will be paid accordingly."

I nearly choked on the figure he named.

"I believe that should be sufficient to cover the change in your grocery bill," he added.

I immediately became suspicious. "What do I have to do?"

"I want you to become our chronicler. With your history degree, your talent for the written word, and your—" He blinked as he chose his words. "—refreshing honesty, I believe you would do an excellent job."

Okaaaaaay. Not what I was expecting. "I figured you'd want me to inform you if anything suspicious came across at the *Scoop*."

Caesar smiled, a very dangerous smile. "I already have Ralph O'Malley covering that angle." He tossed a folder on his desk, clearly labeled Tyrone Mallory in Max's neat handwriting.

Holy crap! My mouth fell open. It took a couple of tries before I could speak. "Ralph said he gave it to the authorities."

"He did. At least, the proper authorities for him." A sly smile spread across Caesar's face. "Since you haven't answered, I will assume it is a 'yes'. Speaking of exposure, Duncan—" Caesar's smile disappeared. "Your work has been incredibly sloppy to allow a mortal to discover our world. As your punishment, you will be required to educate your fiancée—"

"I am not his fiancée!" I blurted.

Caesar ignored me. "—concerning our ways so we don't have any more accidental discoveries by the Normals."

"Yes, sir," Duncan muttered through gritted teeth.

"Dismissed." Caesar examined something on his desk, like we no longer existed.

"B-b-but—" My protest was cut short when Duncan dragged me out of the study and closed the door behind us.

"Wait a minute!" I yanked my arm out of his grip and jabbed a thumb at the door. "Where does he get off ordering us around?"

Green eyes bore into me. "He's my coven master and your employer."

Damn, I hated when he was right. And Caesar might be my coven master too, if I accepted his offer of protection.

I blew out an exasperated breath. Oh, who the hell was I kidding? I didn't really have a choice in the matter unless I wanted to become someone else's science experiment.

Duncan stepped forward, pressing me against the wall with his sheer presence. "Or do you really want to end up in a government lab?"

"No," I mumbled. "And stop reading my mind." It was really, really hard to think with one of his hands sliding underneath my t-shirt and the other stroking my cheek, the rough texture of his fingertips sending trills of sensation across my skin. "It still would have been polite to ask nicely."

"All right, would you care to accompany me to dinner this evening?" he whispered, his breath tickling my ear. The bastard was destroying all my attempts at pouting.

I know. Duncan's thoughts were as hot as the wayward hand fondling my bra.

Could you two please not have sex right outside my office?

Duncan and I jumped apart at Caesar's annoyed thought.

I eyed Duncan. "Your place or mine?"

He snorted. "Until we get your apartment modified for daylight use—"

"Your place it is." For once, I grabbed his hand and dragged him into the garage. "By the way, this does not qualify as an official date, nor does it mean we're engaged."

"Of course, darling," he said, his eyes gleaming neon green in the darkness.

We never made it out of Caesar's garage before sundown.

Zombie Wedding

Chapter 1

Tiffany Stephens leaned close and whispered, "Sam, get your mother out of my face, or I'm going to stake her."

My sympathy for my future sister-in-law didn't last long while we waited for Mom and Antoine to come back with a load of designer bridal gowns. I should have known the lunch invitation was a con job. And I knew Mom would start on my bridesmaid dress once Tiffany's wedding wear satisfied her Beverly Hills sensibility. Mom had already complained all the way to the boutique about buying off the rack with the wedding a week from Saturday.

I cast a surreptitious look at my brother's homicidal fiancée. With all the mascara and eyeliner, her squinted eyes were little more than black slashes on her nearly white face. A quick glance around the Rodeo Drive boutique reassured me that everyone else was out of hearing range. Normal hearing range anyway.

I leaned closer to her and whispered back, "Killing her would be the perfect Christmas gift for me."

She snorted at my teasing and pursed her purple-black lips. Her size two combat boot tapped an irritated rhythm. As one of the few human enforcers of the Augustine Vampire Coven, she could hold her own against any supernatural menace.

Standing up to my mother was another story. Not that Tiffany didn't do a superb job, but resistance didn't register in Mom's self-centered, materialistic universe. The bridal gown issue was a prime example.

The subject of our discussion charged back toward the dressing area where she had planted the two of us. Antoine, Mom's personal image consultant, floated in her wake, loaded to the gills with fluffy white material.

I wasn't precognitive—at least not yet—but I could see what was about to happen. Hell, the blind guy who panhandled outside of my apartment complex could have seen what was about to happen.

Mom shoved her purse in my arms. Mr. Cuddles, her toy poodle, poked his head out and growled. I wished the dog's hostility were because he detected my "change" two months ago. Unfortunately, his attitude toward me had more to do with his owner's and had existed from the moment Mom brought him home from the breeder. I set the purse on the floor, and Mr. Cuddles hopped out and trotted over to sit primly at Mom's feet.

She held up the first filmy concoction.

"No fuckin' way." Tiffany glared at her.

"Now, Tiffany, darling, since you don't have any family to assist you with planning your wedding, you really need me."

Smooth move, Mom. Remind the psychotic future daughter-in-law that her parents are pushing up daisies. I bit my tongue to keep from saying those thoughts aloud.

"I have my uncle, and I already told you I have a dress."

Even I could barely understand Tiffany through her gritted teeth.

Mom sniffed. "Really, dear, fishnet is inappropriate in a society wedding." Tossing the first gown aside, she snatched the next one in the pile.

Picking up the hanger, I straightened to find a perfectly coifed woman with a fake smile surgically grafted to her skin. The owner took the dress from my outstretched hand.

"Sorry," I mouthed.

Her eyes flicked from me to Mom and back, the pleading evident. Like I could stop Mom's rampage.

"No, no, this one won't do, either." The bundle of satin flew in my general direction.

Tiffany planted her fists on her non-existent hips, silver bangles on her wrists jingling. "I don't need—"

Mom just tutted and reached for the next dress in Antoine's arms. She held the blinding whiteness in front of the seething enforcer. "What do you think, Antoine?"

He shook his head. "I really would suggest off-white or pale rose with Ms. Stephens's coloring," Antoine simpered. "Nothing fitted considering her—" His cough barely registered as semi-discreet. "—delicate condition," he finished sotto voce.

Mom shot him a nasty look. I switched to gnawing on my lower lip and stared at the ceiling to keep from laughing. Tiffany's pre-marital pregnancy was a touchy subject—for everyone except Max since it proved my brother's manhood. But she was only a little over seven weeks along, so it wasn't like the baby would be showing on her petite frame at the wedding.

"I'll give him delicate," Tiffany muttered. I held my breath, but she didn't reach for the silver dagger tucked in her right boot.

A gusty sigh blew from Antoine's artificially puffed lips. "Not much we can do about the hair."

Red flared across Tiffany's pale cheeks. I released the pent-up breath when she didn't reach for the dart gun in her messenger bag either. A dose of the concentrated garlic and silver iodide solution may not be lethal to a human, but it stung like hell.

Antoine shook his head. "And that atrocious make-up she has on simply won't do—"

Tiffany leapt, black-nailed hands reaching for Antoine's throat.

Okay, I didn't foresee that one. Mr. Cuddles yipped and dove back into Mom's purse.

Honestly, I could have stopped Tiffany, but it was more fun to watch the nineteen-year-old goth try to strangle Mom's snobby image consultant. That is, if she could find his pencil neck amid all the taffeta.

"Samantha! Do something!" Mom's shriek had more to do with her mortification at the scene Tiffany was making than concern over harm to Antoine. Especially now that everyone in the boutique, not just the owner, watched Tiffany pound Antoine's head against the floor. Lucky for him, it was plush carpet instead of something harder.

I sighed and rolled my eyes. "Tiff?"

She was too far gone, screaming insults that definitely wouldn't win her brownie points with the Gay and Lesbian Alliance. I scooped her up under my left arm, but she still had a firm grasp on Antoine's emerald collarless silk shirt. I shook her, as if she were Mr. Cuddles and I'd caught him humping one of my stuffed animals. Unlike Mr. Cuddles, Tiffany ignored me and continued her assault.

I shook Tiffany again. Antoine's head bobbed, but she still wouldn't let go. On the third shake, it registered in her pea-brain that I had her hoisted on my hip. She dropped Antoine, whose skull hit the carpet with a dense thud.

"Put me the fuck down, bitch!" She began fighting me in earnest. Not that it had much effect in her awkward position or with my new gifts.

"Let me go, you freak! So help me, I'm going to whip your zo—"

I slapped my free hand over her mouth. Tiffany bit me. Hard. I discovered how difficult it was to keep a smile planted on my face while Goth Girl gnawed on my palm, but I managed.

"We're just going to step outside and have a little girl-to-girl chat. Be right back, Mom." I hauled the still struggling Tiffany out the boutique door and into the hot afternoon California sun. Mom said nothing behind me. I guess she wasn't too worried about Tiffany's "delicate condition."

Once outside of the boutique, I set Tiffany upright. She stomped back a couple of paces, her breathing heavy. She glared at me, fingers flexing, but she didn't reach for the silver dagger, the gun or the pencils in the pockets of her camouflage pants. She was the only enforcer I had met whose favorite weapon against rogue vampires was a yellow No. 2.

Eyeing her just as warily, I shook my right hand to get some feeling back into it. A quick glance showed that she had nearly severed off a large chunk of flesh. I may heal fast, but a wound like that still hurts like a sonuvabitch. After a few seconds, not even a bruise showed, but I had to fish in my shoulder bag for a tissue to wipe off the excess blood.

"You still haven't told your folks, have you?" Tiffany's expression wasn't friendly, but it no longer had that endearing maniacal quality.

"No, I haven't." I shoved the nasty-looking tissue back in a Ziploc I kept in my bag for these types of occasions, crossed my arms and glared back at her. I didn't like the reminder of the ticking clock over my head. "But you have no excuse for screaming the z-word in public. You know better."

She had the grace to look abashed and muttered, "Sorry." With a gusty exhalation, all the fight rushed out of her. She slumped against the boutique's brick wall. "You're right. I've never slipped up in front of Normals like that."

I believed her. Ignorance was bliss when it came to John and Jane Public. The less they knew about the supernatural world, the better off everyone was. And Tiffany had been living in the dual cultures far longer than my measly two months.

The tears welling up in her big, brown eyes disturbed me on more levels than I cared to admit. Weepy was not a word anyone would use to describe Tiffany. I stepped forward and laid a hand on her shoulder. "It's probably the hormones talking, but—"

"I know, I know." She wiped the tears away on the hem of her black t-shirt, leaving streaks of blue-black mascara across her pale cheeks. "I'll be more careful."

I let my hand fall from her shoulder, reassured that Tiffany had regained control of her temper. As I turned back for the door, her touch on my sleeve stopped me. My initial tension released at her uneasy expression.

"Sam, it's not my business, but—" She paused as if searching for the right words. This had to be a first. I mean, Tiffany? Using tact?

She glanced around to make sure no one was near, but she still lowered her voice. "Maybe you should tell your parents." Her hand dropped. "Before they find out accidentally."

"Ri-i-ight." I glanced around myself, but few shoppers were on the sidewalk this time of day with the unusual spring heat. "The only thing Mom and Dad are going to love more than Max knocking you up is finding out I'm a zombie."

Chapter 2

Later that night, my erstwhile boyfriend, Duncan St. James, took a sip of his wine and leaned back against the red vinyl seat. "Tiffany is correct. You should inform your parents before they discover the information on their own. Assuming you plan to tell them and not obtain a new identity and relocate."

"You're just taking her side because she's your niece." I glared at him while I shoveled the last forkful of lasagna into my mouth. I was hungrier than normal after Mom's failed wedding dress expedition. The rich flavor of oregano and tomato swirled over my taste buds, and I sighed with delight.

One of the few joys of my new undead existence was that I could still eat normal food. So what if it was an obscene amount? Unfortunately, it meant watching the restaurant budget unless someone else was paying. Like tonight.

"Tiffany is a niece sixteen generations removed, and I was not taking her side because of our blood relationship. I am merely stating the obvious facts, which you have chosen to ignore." Like the centuries made a difference when he had raised Goth Girl since she was a baby.

"I'm already joining the damn coven." I reached for the bread basket. *Yes.* One slice of garlic bread was left. "Why is everyone pressuring me now?"

Duncan set his glass down. "Because it would make planning security more efficient."

I glared at him. "So I'm just a check mark on your to-do list? The fairies know I'm part of Augustine Coven. They haven't done anything."

Except it didn't mean they wouldn't either. As the only remaining sentient zombie, I was a pretty unique individual. So damn unique that the fairies wanted to drop me in the middle of Three Mile Island when they found out about me. Of course, their attitude might have more to do with the teeny-tiny robots that kept me functional. They viewed my body full of nanites as the equivalent of a dirty nuke in their backyard. And according to the supernatural rumor mill, the fairy queens had put a price on my head.

Which meant I needed supernatural help. Which meant joining the Western U.S. Vampire Coven. Which meant I had to follow their sucky rules.

Ha! Sometimes I crack myself up.

"You are assuming a direct attack, Samantha. The sidhe rarely work that way."

I mopped the last of the sauce with a hunk of crusty Italian bread. "Caesar gave me until the day after Max and Tiffany's wedding. I still have a week."

Duncan's eyes narrowed. "If you do not believe your parents can be trusted, then the matter is moot."

"Dammit, I hate when you get all logical." Max wasn't an issue since he'd known about the supernatural community for years and had kept his mouth shut, but the risk of exposure was too great for the supernaturals to take the chance of Mom gossiping at the country club without "assurances." My other choice was ending up in the vampires' equivalent of the Witness Protection Program.

Duncan gestured for our waiter. "I am assuming you want dessert."

"That's a stupid question." I jabbed the sauce-soaked bread in his direction before stuffing it into my mouth. "And you're changing the subject," I mumbled around the soggy crust.

"It was more a statement of fact than a question." He signaled our waiter, Jimmy. "And yes, I am. I do not wish to argue tonight."

Two minutes later, Jimmy plunked two plates of the house specialty, chocolate mousse pie, in front of us while giving Duncan a come-hither look. The Little Sicily staff had fought over who would serve us since I started bringing Duncan here. I wanted to chalk it up to Duncan's generous tipping, but it really had more to do with his vampire charisma.

Though truth be told, Jimmy would have flirted with anything with a penis. And Duncan was definitely all male.

Duncan's mojo kept the staff and other patrons from noticing I ate both my dinner and the one he ordered while he drank a bottle and a half of wine by his lonesome. What else were we supposed to do when he's on a liquid diet and I ate more in one meal than the Rams' entire offensive line?

Jimmy filled our coffee cups and gave Duncan a seductive smile before returning to the kitchen. I ate half my pie and washed it down with the rest of my wine before I continued.

"This isn't an argument. And it's not that I don't think Goth Girl has a point—" Duncan grimaced at my nickname for Tiffany, but I ignored him. "—but do you really think my parents could handle the fact that I'm the z-word?"

"Your father loves you, Samantha." He practically purred my name, which sent warm wet fuzzies through my pelvic region until I realized he said it in conjunction with Dad.

Ewwwwww.

"Stop it, Duncan. I'm serious. Mom's having enough trouble with the whole pregnant teen thing."

He smiled as wide as he dared in public with his extra-sharp canines. "I take it neither you nor Tiffany have bothered to enlighten your mother that Tiffany's twentieth birthday is next Friday."

I grinned back. "What? And spoil all the fun? Besides, Max could have told her and didn't bother." I sighed and took a sip of coffee while I contemplated my dilemma. "Finding out her daughter and half the wedding guests are the living dead would give her a heart attack. No problem then, right?"

Duncan's eyes narrowed. "I am not dead."

I sighed again. Technically, he was right. Vampirism was caused by a virus and considered a chronic human illness with no cure by the rest of the supernatural community. I, on the other hand, was very much dead according to my local witch doctor. Well, she's really a witch who happens to be a licensed M.D., but it was so much fun to piss Bebe off by calling her my witch doctor.

"I'm sorry I called you dead, but you know what I mean," I said.

Duncan raised one of those damn aristocratic eyebrows of his. "I believe the current term is 'win-win situation'. You would fulfill your obligation to the coven and eliminate your mother in one stroke."

I rolled my eyes. That British accent of his could convince me of almost anything. "Don't tempt me. Anyway, if Mom knew Tiffany could run rings around most SEALs, she'd blow an aneurysm, but I'm saving that little tidbit for a special occasion. Maybe Mother's Day." I took another sip of coffee and decided to ignore my situation for now. "So what's the plan for tonight?"

"*Dawn of the Dead* is playing at the revival theater." He reached across the table and began stroking my wrist. Tremors spiraled through my body.

I smiled sweetly. Two could play that game. "How about the new *Underworld* movie instead?"

Duncan's eyes turned neon green, which would be a good sign if we were about to have sex. "That is not amusing. Those films are an insult." Displeasure tinged his voice. He bent his head, shoulder-length raven hair falling over his face to hide his internal struggle. Glowing eyeballs don't exactly reassure the rest of the restaurant's clientele no matter how much mojo a vampire has.

Jerking my hand out of his now uncomfortable grip, I leaned across my booth seat to check under the table. Damn. From the appearance of his jeans, maybe it *was* the sex thing and not the pissed-off thing. I popped back up. "If I'd known you had a thing for Kate Beckinsale, I would have put on my black wig and skintight leather ages ago."

He didn't look up. "You do not have a leather catsuit."

"But I do have the black wig." My breath matched his short, rapid pants. I shouldn't be teasing him, especially since I was the one who instigated the latest break-from-sex rule.

Air blew from his flared nostrils and ruffled the dark strands spilling across his face. "This would be so much easier if we were wed."

He might as well have thrown a freezing bucket of ice water in my face. I tossed my napkin on the table. "Now why'd you go and ruin the evening by bringing up *that* subject?"

Our age difference emphasized the gap in our views of relationships between men and women. Duncan had insisted that we get married to protect my honor just because we did the mattress mambo. More than once. In several different places. In several different positions.

It wasn't like I could get knocked up since I was already dead.

Chalking up his antiquated POV to his sixteenth century upbringing, I also hated to point out to the big lug that I had lost my "honor" at senior prom. I had insisted that we date for a while to make sure we had something in common besides mind-blowing orgasms. Right now, I really wondered what we did have in common.

Duncan's head rose. His eyes were their normal, everyday green, but his brows twisted in an angry frown. "Why do *you* treat matrimony as if it is one of George Carlin's seven words?"

"Because it should have been the eighth."

"It was your idea to—" His face scrunched in pompous distaste. "—date."

I leaned closer to him. "FYI, buster, this is our fourth date."

He crossed his arms again. "And?"

"Normally, I put out on the fourth date, but you blew it."

"I put out on the first."

Duncan and I both looked up. Jimmy stood next to the table, check in hand. He shot me a skanky look before giving Duncan a not-so-demure smile.

"Thank you, Jimmy. That will be all for this evening." Duncan reached for his wallet and handed a couple of Ben Franklins to Jimmy, who stalked off in a snit. You'd think the kid would be ecstatic over that kind of tip. Little Sicily was one of those places that had only one dollar sign next to it in restaurant guides.

Then I saw the phone number Jimmy had scribbled on the receipt.

I glared at Duncan. "Did you have to put the whammy on Jimmy just to make me jealous?"

I did not *put a whammy on Jimmy!*

I crossed my arms. I *so* wasn't stooping to his telepathic level. "Uh-huh. If it weren't coming from a guy who's worn hose longer than I have, I'd take it a little more seriously."

Duncan was out of the booth faster than even my undead vision could follow. He grabbed my hand and practically dragged me out of my seat.

"Slow down," I whispered. "Someone's going to notice us."

His pace eased a fraction.

"We haven't decided which movie to see."

He ignored my token protest and continued his beeline for the exit, hauling me in his wake.

"Where are we going?" I ignored the jealous looks from Jimmy and the rest of the waitstaff.

"Home." Duncan didn't bother looking at me.

"Why?"

This time he stopped and turned toward me. His eyes glowed neon. The sexy neon. He leaned close and whispered, "To show you my codpiece."

His warm breath tickled my ear, sending another kind of warmth surging through my nerves.

Without another word, we headed straight for his SUV. I fumbled the keys out of my pocket and climbed in. "You know, you're not helping your manly cause when you can't drive your own freakin' vehicle." In the two months I'd known Duncan, I still hadn't found out why he couldn't or wouldn't drive anything with a combustion engine.

He didn't have a problem riding in them since he was already in the passenger seat. The shoulder strap across his black long-sleeved tee only emphasized his broad chest. His long fingers stroked my thigh, reaching higher and higher as I flipped the ignition. And that was the only answer I got out of him until we reached his townhouse.

Chapter 3

"Cleopatra Selene Antonius is dead."

The basketball sailed through David Head's outstretched hands, his first rebound miss in three years. He turned and stared at Francois "Frankie" LeBeau. The werewolf snagged the orange ball and loped down the custom-built court in Head's New Orleans mansion. The rhythmic thump of leather matched the slap of rubber soles on the wood, the only sounds in the wake of Frankie's announcement. The were's dunk belied his five foot two frame. Human frame, that is.

The harsh sound of the buzzer filled the practice room, triggering a grin from the smaller man. David wasn't sure what surprised him most, the bomb Frankie had dropped or the fact the little bastard used it to win their scrimmage. No, the latter shouldn't have surprised him at all. Then the realization of what Antonius' death meant exploded in his overloaded skull.

Frankie retrieved the ball and dribbled back to where David stood. The pounding echoed through the cavernous room. "Man, you're drooling all over the floor."

David clamped his jaw shut before he seized the were's arms and shook him. The orphaned ball bounced three times before rolling toward the free throw line. "You're sure about this? How reliable is your source?"

Frankie's eyes narrowed, and he shrugged off the grip. David sucked in a deep breath, a desperate attempt to get hold of his excitement. Even though he towered over the were by nearly two feet, there was no doubt who was the stronger, and meaner, of the two men.

"My cousin works security for the San Antonio Packmaster. He saw the whole damn thing when he escorted his boss to some big-ass meeting Selene held in Los Angeles a couple of months ago." Frankie grinned, a ruthless look that would have sent anyone with common sense running. David was the first to admit he didn't have much common sense. Otherwise, he wouldn't be lusting after the hottest vampire he'd ever met.

His heart pounded as Frankie continued. "Duncan St. James shot his maker right through her fucking heart with a crossbow in front of everyone. She melted faster than Margaret Hamilton."

"Ding, dong, the bitch is dead," David whispered. He slumped to the floor, disbelief coursing through him. He never thought he'd live to see this day. Cleopatra Selene Antonius, the Augustine Coven's queen, no longer stood between him and the one person he desired most in the world.

Frankie's words sunk through his dazed brain and he glared up at the were. "Two months ago? Why are you just telling me now?"

Frankie shrugged. "Just found out last night." Another grin. "And you now owe me five big ones."

David shook his head at his friend's tactics. "Asshole." Frankie's maneuver to win the bet didn't matter though. Nothing mattered except getting to Los Angeles as fast as possible.

"Thought you might say that." The were grinned even wider at David's unconsciously spoken words. He thumbed toward the doorway. "Already got reservations on the eight o'clock direct flight to LAX. Miz Claire's packin' our bags as we speak."

"Davy, what the hell are you planning?"

He turned. Yvonne stood in the doorway to the court. From his sister's glare and fists on her hips, she'd heard his exchange with Frankie.

"Nothing that concerns you. Stay out of it."

She stalked across the hand-sanded planks. He didn't know what pissed him off more—that she deliberately stomped her stilettos into his pride and joy or her I-have-my-powers-and-you-don't attitude. Her client must have left. He didn't get why she bothered with the additional income. Even if Jean-Pierre Rousseau didn't pay her an exorbitant amount, he could more than take care of his own sister.

Fear etched lines around her eyes. "Don't you even be thinkin' about courting no vampire, boy." She wagged a manicured fingernail at him. "Even if you're smart enough to use protection, he could still get carried away and bite you. Then where'd you be?" she said, tossing her cornrows so the clacking beads emphasized her point. "No juju can save you once you're infected."

"Maybe the risk is worth it." He gave her a devilish grin. "Besides, you're the one who introduced us."

Anger lit her hazel eyes. "Don't you even go there, David Jebediah Head. I had to call in favors to make sure you were protected when you were playing in Los Angeles." Other than Frankie, she was the only person who could get away with talking back to him.

"Yeah, playing for both teams." The were's low voice was followed by a snicker.

David ignored him. Maybe the L.A. coach and owner hadn't been ecstatic when one of the tabloids outed him, but they loved the ticket sales and his ability to fill the arena with fans. His breath seized at the memory. First, Brandon had walked out after the harassment by the paparazzi. Then, the nutcase Bible-thumping stalker had picked up where the media left off. St. James gave him something to focus on, someone to hope for . . .

But L.A. had been two years, several million dollars, a free agency, and one broken heart ago.

He glared at Yvonne. "And what kind of favors do you trade with Jean-Pierre? You telling me you don't want to get down and dirty with a certain vampire master?"

Instead of laying into him as he half-expected, she merely shook her head, a sad look on her face. "Davy, honey, it isn't good to want something you can't have."

"Who says I can't have St. James when I haven't said shit to him about how I feel?" The ache inside could only be relieved by pursuing the cause. He didn't need any of Yvonne's lame-ass love potions either. Not when he laid his case before St. James. Now, if the man didn't respond to the direct approach, *then* he wasn't above a little hoo-doo to help pave the way.

Frankie crouched next to him. "So what do you want to do, boss-man?"

"L.A.," David whispered. He climbed to his feet, barely conscious of his movements. Desire, thick and hot, rose in his mouth. "I need to get to L.A."

Yvonne stepped in his path. "Wait until next week, Davy. Then you can accompany me with Jean-Pierre—"

"I'm not waiting for some lame ass political bullshit junket. Why don't you come out with us since you have to be there anyway? Have some fun for once."

Yvonne shook her head again, staring at the polished floor. "This isn't a good idea, Davy."

David ignored her as a glimmer of suspicion flared through him. Was her reluctance because she was jealous? No, asking the same damn question wasn't worth dealing with her shit. Instead, he eyed the were. "You got first class?"

Frankie raised a hand to the sweat-soaked t-shirt covering his chest in mock horror. "Is there any other way to fly?"

———•—•———

The shrill electronic version of Elton John's "The Bitch is Back" jerked me awake. In the darkness, it took a minute to remember I was at Duncan's townhouse.

Duncan groaned next to me. "You cannot find another song for your ringtone?"

I elbowed him in the ribs. "That's no way to talk about your fellow countryman." Besides, that particular ringtone applied to only one individual. A person I had no interest in talking to this freakin' early in the morning, but I knew if I didn't answer, Mom would just turn around and call my home number, which I had forwarded to Duncan's place.

He rolled over and buried his head under his pillow. The comforter quickly followed over top the goose down cushion.

Resigning myself to the inevitable, I grabbed my cell off the nightstand and punched the "Talk" button. "Good morning, Mom."

"Good morning? Samantha! It's two in the afternoon!"

"Thanks for the time check, Mom. To what do I owe the pleasure of your melodious voice this afternoon?" I flopped back against my own pillow in anticipation of her latest tirade.

"That girl insists the reception *must* be catered by someone named Epstein."

Mom sniffed, her distaste with Tiffany's selection obvious. "I've never heard of these people and none of my friends have either."

"Mom, Jacob Epstein is a family friend of the Stephens. I hardly think he'll deliberately ruin Max and Tiffany's reception. And it's great that he can do it on such short notice." I resisted the urge to add the Epsteins were witches and could quietly keep the supernatural guests in blood and whatever the hell else they might consume.

"Well, I'm not paying for it. It's bad enough I have to take care of the entire wedding." My mother, the drama queen, sighed. A long suffering sound that only a Beverly Hills snoberati could produce.

"Mom, Max and Tiffany did not ask you to plan the wedding." I tried to keep my voice calm and even, but her repeated tirades about the ceremony were wearing thin. And I wasn't even the bride.

"No," she snapped. "*She* wanted to have the ceremony in City Hall. Downtown Los Angeles is no place to have a wedding." Another long-suffering sigh. "But what can you expect from a girl who has no money and has to trick a man into marrying her?"

Duncan shot up from under the covers, eyes glowing neon and fangs bared. With his super vampire ears, he'd heard every nasty word out of Mom's mouth. This was a guy who'd staked other vampires through the heart and beheaded werewolves to protect his niece. If I wasn't careful, he'd do something equally ugly to my mother.

Then again, maybe that wasn't such a bad idea.

Against my better judgment, I waved him down. "Mom, Max is a big boy. He knows how to use a condom."

"Samantha, don't be so vulgar!" Another gusty exhalation sounded through the receiver. "Besides, that girl probably poked a hole in it."

Of course. My dear older brother could do no wrong in her eyes. I snorted. "They probably used the one Max has been carrying around in his wallet since he was fifteen. They have an expiration date, you know."

Laughter erupted next to me.

"Who's with you, Samantha?"

I sat up, grabbed my pillow and shoved it over Duncan's face to smother the loud guffaws issuing from his mouth. "No one, Mom. Just watching Comedy Central." Our supernatural strength was pretty evenly matched. When Duncan couldn't pry the pillow off his face, he resorted to tickling me. I dissolved into a shrieking giggle fit.

"This isn't funny! Samantha? Samantha! Are you listening to me?"

Stop it, Duncan! When he didn't, I resorted to the next weapon in my new arsenal. I dipped into my welling irritation and let loose a psy-bolt. Duncan tumbled backwards off his king-size waterbed, dragging the covers with him, and landed with a loud thump on the hardwood floor.

Bebe was still trying to figure out where that little half-telepathic, half-telekinetic talent came from. Supposedly, only witches had a similar skill. And if I wasn't careful, I ended up with one hellacious headache. My nanites were supposedly patterned after the vampire virus, but without the nasty side effects like an aversion to UV rays. Obviously, something had gone awry in the lab.

"Sorry, Mom. I was watching an old Tim Allen routine." I wiped the tears from my eyes. Duncan's head popped over the edge, and we matched glares. "Was there anything else you needed?" I said into the cell.

With one last dirty look, a very naked and very gorgeous Duncan stood up and stalked into the bathroom. Naked except for the gold locket that had been his sister Margaret's. I'd never seen him without it around his neck. I had thought that maybe after the death of Margaret's murderer, the same bitch who'd Turned Duncan, he'd let go of the past, but no such luck.

After the door slammed shut, the hum of the double shower caught my attention. I loved Duncan's shower with its wide marble ledges and flexible show massager. Moisture flooded between my thighs. Maybe it was time to test the shower in a new capacity.

"You're still coming over tonight, aren't you, Samantha?" Mom's voice jarred me out of my fantasy. Crap, I'd forgotten about that damn family dinner. Mom continued without waiting for my reply. "That girl is bringing her uncle, so you need to be here on time."

Why the hell was everyone expecting *me* to be the buffer between the families? I had gotten the same plea from Max, Tiffany and even Duncan. How could I possibly keep the peace when I was the last person any of them listened to?

Against my better judgment, I said, "I'll be there at seven sharp. See you tonight, Mom." I clicked off before she could launch another round of Tiffany bashing. Plumping my pillow behind me, I leaned back against the headboard. If I went into the bathroom right now, Duncan and I would never make it to Mom and Dad's Beverly Hills McMansion. Sitting up and looking around the bedroom, I tried to remember where I left my jeans when my cell beside me started singing again, this time to Huey Lewis's "Workin' for a Livin'."

Dammit. I was supposed to have the weekend off from *The National Scoop* for once.

I punched the "Talk" button once again. "What's up, Ralph?" A series of hacks and wheezes greeted me. I rolled my eyes and waited for my boss's coughing fit to finish. "You know, Ralph, that carton a day habit of yours is going to kill you."

Ralph snorted. "Right. Like I need health advice from the dead chick."

Ouch. Well, at least I could trust no one else was in his office since Ralph O'Malley, editor-in-chief extraordinaire, was on the Augustine Coven payroll and had his own little secret.

He didn't wait for my fabulous comeback. "We got a tip there's a semi-private party that purple freak's throwing tonight." He had a low opinion of Duke Miller, the grand master of danceable funk. "Your boy, Head, is supposed to be there." As a die-hard L.A. Sabretooths fan, his opinion of David Head was slightly higher. Two years ago, Ralph hadn't been happy when I showed him the photos I took of Head playing tonsil-hockey, among other things, with a member of a certain boy band. But bless his heart, Ralph did his job and ran the story. It'd been my first cover.

"Ralph," I whined. "You promised."

"The only other person I got is Agnes. Do you really want me to send her to scoop you on a David Head story?"

He was right on two counts. There was no way Agnes Durley could con her way into an exclusive party. The woman wore a tin foil hat to protect herself from the FBI reading her thoughts for chrissakes. Not that the aluminum could really stop the rest of us who had a little telepathic talent. Also, Ralph knew my weakness too well. The chance to nail a photo of Head's latest paramour wasn't an assignment I could pass up.

"Ralph, you know I've got a dinner at Mom and Dad's tonight. And His Freakiness's parties don't start until two in the morning at the earliest." I kept the protest in my voice as reedy as possible.

"You're a freakin' creature of the night," he shot back.

"You can't hold next week's edition of the *Scoop* past four a.m." I had to keep my warning delicately balanced.

"Fine, fine," he muttered. "One thousand bonus on top of the usual rate if you can get the pics here by three-thirty."

"Five thousand."

"Twenty-five hundred, and that's it, Sam." He gave me the address for the after-hours shindig.

"Deal. I'll see you in thirteen hours, Boss."

Ralph responded with a grunt and a slam of the phone.

I smiled and said, "I love you, too, Ralph." I couldn't take it personally. Ralph was crotchety with everyone. The job also meant I needed my higher-res minicam as well as a change of clothes for tonight.

Duncan? I need to run home before we head over to my parents. I've got an assignment for tonight.

For a minute, I didn't think he was going to answer me. Then wet feet slapped against the marble and the bathroom door opened. I swallowed hard at the vision of six feet, four inches of dripping male nakedness.

God, save me from temptation.

His eyebrow swept upward as he gave me a suspicious once over. "And you could not plan how to use tonight's torture of some unsuspecting celebrity to extract yourself from your mother's dinner party?" He shook his head and tsked. "Samantha, I am highly disappointed."

"It's a secret concert that doesn't start until after the bars close." I crossed my arms, suddenly realizing I was still naked as well. The best defense was a good offense, otherwise we seriously would not leave his bedroom. Maybe last night wasn't such a good time to break the sexual fast. "And I'm highly offended you would even suggest I would renege on my promise to go with you," I said, matching his tone.

He crossed the floor in two quick strides, his grace reminding me of a leopard. "I am sorry, darling." He bent and I let him pry one of my hands loose to kiss the palm.

Shivers ricocheted down my spine. I couldn't stop the breathy gasp that escaped from my lips. Duncan's mouth slid to my wrist, the light press of his fangs sending an electric wave in counterpoint to his wet locks tickling my hyper-sensitive skin. He didn't dare actually bite me though. The last person who tried that stunt had exploded in a cloud of metallic dust.

Reluctantly, I disengaged his attention with a quick peck on his mouth and a hand on his chest to prevent any follow-through. Hunger flared in his eyes, but he managed to pull himself upright.

Along with a very large portion of his anatomy.

"Let me get dressed and I will come with you," he murmured.

I shook my head, knowing all too well what would happen if I did. "No garage and no UV film at my place makes my sweetie a crispy critter."

"Move in with me."

My just-found pink satin panties dropped from my suddenly nerveless fingers. He didn't just say what I thought he just said. I looked up at his very serious green eyes. "Why the hell are you bringing this up now?"

"I had planned to bring it up when you woke, but your mother interrupted." He rocked on his heels, his expression a mix of hope and impatience.

I blinked and swallowed hard. Was that what last night's seduction had been all about? It was difficult to think clearly with Duncan's erection bobbing a few inches from my face. Sucking in a deep breath, I pretended to ignore the tantalizing body part and retrieved my panties from the floor.

"You are not even going to do me the courtesy of a reply?" It sounded like the impatience was winning.

I snagged my panties over my feet, pulling them up as I rose. We both knew I was stalling, but God, I so didn't want to get into this discussion right now. I couldn't deal with Max's impending wedding and deciding whether to come clean with Mom and Dad. Duncan's repeated attempts at commitment only added to the suffocating weight on my head.

Grabbing his hands in mine, I gazed up into his eyes. Honesty was my best bet to get out of this. "You threw me for a loop, you big lug. We don't have the time for a real discussion, and I sure as hell don't want to go to Mom's fighting with you."

He jerked his hands out of mine, anger cooling his expression. "I see. I am trying to compromise here, Samantha, and you throw my offer into my face."

I sucked in another deep breath. The effort to check my own temper burned an acid hole in my cast-iron zombie stomach. "All I'm saying is that I can't deal with your offer and the fiasco of tonight's family dinner at the same time."

My vision started swimming from the tears collecting in my eyes. Why was he dumping the commitment thing on my head now? I died a little over two months ago, and I was still adjusting to that little bon mot. Not to mention my new role as Jimmy Carter at Camp David. Actually, the former president had an easier time brokering peace between the Egyptians and Israelis. I was stuck between—

God, I couldn't even come up with a comparison remotely as bad. Top that off with possibly having to walk away from what little I could call a life in my undead existence.

The wave of anxiety shocked me as the floodgates opened, and I collapsed in a heap back on the rumpled bed. Strong arms wrapped around me and rocked my body in time to my sobs. The words "just can't" slipped out into between each gulp of air. Dammit, James Bond didn't cry while the clock was ticking, so why couldn't I hold it together?

For a few minutes, we sat on the edge of the bed, waiting for my pathetic weeping to stop.

Duncan brushed damp strands away from my cheek. "I am sorry, darling," he whispered in my ear. "I truly did not realize you were under this much pressure."

"No," I said, swiping away the wetness with the backs of my hands. "I've got a couple of major decisions to make in nine days, my brother's getting married in eight, and everyone expects me to play fucking mediator tonight." I sucked in a deep breath to steady my voice before I eyed him. "Cut me a little slack here."

Suspicion flared in his eyes. They closed and a deep, heartfelt exhalation escaped from him. I couldn't bear the pained expression on his face and turned to stare at my newly-painted green toenails.

When I polished them yesterday, a zombie with green toenails had sounded hysterical. Now, the grass-toned toes seemed oddly prophetic. I may be dead for real before this month was over. Could a zombie die a second time from a stress-induced heart attack?

"Not only have you not told your parents about your new status, you have not told them about our relationship, have you?" he said, giving voice to his realization.

I shook my head. Misery seeped through every pore in my body. I wasn't sure if he felt my movement or had opened his eyes, but he kept talking anyway.

"Samantha," he said, keeping his voice gentle. "Have your parents met any of your courters?"

I shook my head again. They had met Jake, but I sure as hell wasn't bringing up my ex-fiancé right now.

"Oh." When I was sure he wasn't going to say anything else, he added, "There is no reason they need to find out tonight."

I flung my arms around him and kissed him soundly on the lips. "Oh, thank you, thank you, thank you for understanding, Duncan." I squeezed him hard in my joy. Thank God, he could handle my rib-crushing hug.

When I broke the embrace, he leaned back, concern in his gaze as he stroked my cheek. Tendrils of love and caring wove through my brain, the sensation of being cocooned a little overwhelming. *You are going to have to tell them the truth soon, Samantha, or you will be required to cut ties with them. You agreed to our laws in return for Caesar's influence.*

I snuggled against his shoulder, taking what little comfort I could before facing the Gates of Hell. *I know, honey. I know.*

Chapter 4

Contrary to my four-hundred-year-old boyfriend's opinion of my flakiness, I thought long and hard about the pros and cons of dealing with the parental units on the drive back to my place.

I parked at my apartment complex, switched off the ignition and let my head hit the steering wheel. That's what it came down to, wasn't it? Either I trust my parents with my little undead secret, or I give up my career. My family. My life.

Okay, maybe not my life. That was already gone.

Fuck it all to hell! I kicked the car door. If not for the reinforced steel of my brand-new, customized Accord, I would have ripped the door off its hinges in my pique. As it was, I cracked the interior panel. I sighed and made a mental note to call the "special" body shop tomorrow. The nice thing about being part of the supernatural world was the access to an array of after-hours services.

In less than half an hour, I had showered, swiped on a little mascara and blush, slicked my hair back in a ponytail, and slid on an LBD that would work for both my parents' dinner and an after-hours party. I also took ten minutes to ingest a loaf of wheat bread and a pound of colby longhorn. It wouldn't do to have my stomach growling before Mom's dinner. Duncan and I would still have to stop somewhere for my third evening meal on the way to Duke's party. I thanked God on a regular basis that Taco Bell's drive-thru was open until three a.m.

I wove through the beginnings of Los Angeles's rush hour traffic on the drive back to the townhouse. By the time I arrived, Max's brand-new Volvo sat in Duncan's driveway.

My big brother still hadn't forgiven me for the loss of his Camry a couple of months ago. It wasn't my fault my creator's thugs had totaled Max's baby in their attempt to kill me. Which goes to show how much the bad guys sucked at their job because I was still human when they rolled the car with me in it. I'd survived though the Camry hadn't.

When I walked into the kitchen, Max and Tiffany sat at the kitchen table, looking anywhere but at each other. Duncan, on the other hand, stood at the counter and sucked blood straight from the bottle.

O-k-a-a-y. Not a good sign. Duncan always nuked his meals in mugs. This was the first time I'd ever felt waves of nervousness roll off my guy.

I crossed my arms. "This ain't a funeral, folks."

"Could be," Tiffany muttered.

"Don't worry, kid. If anything goes wrong tonight, Mom will be sure to blame it on me."

"Sam—" Max started.

Tiffany stood, the unconscious brush of her hand across her thigh a weapons check. "She's right, honey. Let's get this over with." Wow. Goth Girl on my side?

Either that, or she planned to finish off Mom if the subject of the wedding dress came up.

I strolled over to Duncan while he sucked down his last drop of blood and gave him a quick peck on the cheek.

"Let me brush my teeth and I'll be ready," he said. The brushing was for my benefit. I was still a little queasy when it came to his dietary needs, so I distracted myself by admiring the view of his butt in his tailored trousers as he strode from the kitchen.

"Ewwwww! I'm scarred for life." Tiffany covered her eyes with both hands.

I must have shot her a confused look because Max said, "You were transmitting again, Sam."

"Oops," I murmured. "Sorry about that." Getting a handle on my brand-new telepathy had been a major struggle over the last two months. I slipped every once in a while, but it was worth it last week when I accidentally made half the male staff at the *Scoop* question their sexual orientation.

I checked the waste can as I strolled over to the fridge. The unusual number of empty bottles tinted with red residue sent a shiver of unease through my nerves. Was there something wrong with Duncan? Every time I turned around I learned something new about vampire physiology, but the only time I had seen Duncan drink this much was after Sierra Mallory stabbed him through the chest with a silver elf-forged sword. He was damn lucky the heiress couldn't aim worth shit and missed his heart. I grabbed a soda, but before I could ask Tiffany about Duncan's consumption, he stalked back into the kitchen.

Tossing me his keys, he muttered, "I am ready." No one said anything as we trooped through the back door into the garage. Once Duncan and I were safely in the SUV, I flipped the control for the garage door, and the last evening sunlight spilled in.

I eyed Duncan. I couldn't help it. Every time we left his place before sundown I was a nervous wreck, scared shitless that I'd screwed up and left a window in his Suburban cracked open or a door ajar. Anything that let in that tiny sliver of fatal sunlight.

Thank God for UV film.

Duncan shot me a reassuring smile, and I backed out of the garage once Max and Tiffany were clear of the driveway. The endless drive to Beverly Hills was even more unendurable thanks to full-blown rush hour. The only terrific thing about the whole ordeal? Pulling through Mom and Dad's front gate fifteen after seven, a full four minutes after sundown and fashionably late.

I parked behind Max, but Duncan made no move to get out. His face twisted like he'd been sucking lemons instead of blood as he stared at the white monstrosity my parents called home.

I grinned at him. "Don't worry. They don't know you had anything to do with trashing the place."

He snorted, not taking his eyes from the house. "I was not the one who shot your mother's favorite Mikasa vase. Nor was I the one who shattered the bedroom door."

"Yeah, well, I'm not the one who smeared cookies 'n' cream ice cream down Mom's very expensive wallpaper. Do you have any freakin' clue how hard it was to get a match to repair that?"

He turned to me, an evil look in his eyes. "We could ditch. As you have repeatedly pointed out, your parents would expect such an action from you." For Duncan to suggest such an action, as well as use American slang, showed how nervous he was.

I patted his knee, one of the few spots I could touch that wouldn't result in immediate hanky-panky. "Do you really want Tiffany to have her baby in prison? Because you know Dad and Max won't be fast enough to stop her when she goes for Mom's jugular."

He exhaled, a drawn out, tortured sound if I'd ever heard one, before he said, "I would rather experience the Spanish Inquisition." He opened the door but stopped and shot me a very pointed look. "Again."

"Hey, you two! Get your asses moving!" Tiffany stood at the bottom step to the front door, hands on hips and looking perturbed.

"Show time," I muttered under my breath. I prayed the house and everyone in it would be intact at the end of the Dinner From Hell.

—•—

Yvonne shifted her awareness, using Sight to examine Davy's aura as he tipped the bellboy. The excitement over his hair-brained scheme rippled bloody crimson over the normally cheerful salmon pink. Underneath that, a silvery gray crisscross pattern overlaid the shards of black diamond, just as it had for the last sixteen years.

Davy shut the door and turned. His flashy smile faded to a scowl when he noticed her watching him. "You got a problem?"

She shook her head. "Tired." A weak smile followed to enforce her excuse. "It's my bedtime in our zone. You know I've never been good with jetlag." An involuntary yawn slurred the last word.

Brotherly concern replaced the scowl. "You want some supper first?"

Another shake of her head sent beads clicking. "I'm going to get some sleep." She headed for her room in the hotel's presidential suit before he could convince her to go out with him. Shutting the door behind her, she released the pent-up breath she'd been holding. Was it her imagination or was the binding on Davy duller than she remembered?

Wrapping her arms to ward off the chill of the A/C, she sat on the edge of the king-sized bed. It had to have been her imagination. The New Orleans coven had said the bindings would last his lifetime. Her eyes squeezed shut, a desperate attempt to block the ugly memory of what Davy had done all those years ago. It wasn't how she wanted to remember their mother.

She swiped the couple of tears that had escaped and reached for the phone. Her hand shook as she punched Jean-Pierre's number. Talking to him always reassured her.

It took only one ring. "*Chére?*"

"Hi." She cleared her throat. "You said you wanted me to call when we got to Los Angeles."

A throaty chuckle sent a shiver of unrequited desire through her. How pathetic was she to have a crush on her boss. Her drunken confession to him years ago should have squelched the feelings. Except he'd shared his own feelings that night.

Not that either of them could ever act on those desires.

"I wish you'd waited and flown with me."

"I—" Sweet Goddess, how did she explain this? "Someone needed to keep an eye on Davy and Frankie."

The silence lasted so long, she began to believe the connection had dropped. Then Jean-Pierre's soft French accent said, "What's wrong, Yvonne?"

The giggle caught her unaware, the situation so ludicrous. "Remember the security Augustine Coven provided for Davy a couple of years ago? He has a crush on their chief enforcer."

Hearty guffaws filled the earpiece. "St. James?"

"Ridiculous, I know." She joined in Jean-Pierre's laughter. Davy's childish infatuation warranted the humor, though she would never hurt her baby brother by throwing it in his face. "That's the reason he wanted to come out a few days early."

"I doubt if the boy's impatience will be rewarded." Jean-Pierre made a rueful noise. "Can you keep him from causing a major diplomatic incident, or shall I fly out early?"

Relief spread through her. Leave it to the coven master to show how ridiculous her fears were. "No, I can handle him."

"Save a dance for me, *chére*. I haven't been to a good wedding in decades."

"Of course. And thank you."

As she replaced the handset to its base, a tremor of unease rippled up her spine, replacing Jean-Pierre's suave confidence in her. After gathering her magick supplies, she sat cross-legged on the plush carpet. She needed advice, advice Jean-Pierre for all his charm and age couldn't provide. So why did she worry that for once she might not be able to save her baby brother from his own stupidity?

— • —

Mr. Cuddles' greeting barks turned into a high-pitched whine the moment Duncan stepped into the foyer. The toy poodle launched himself out of Mom's arms and scurried out of sight. I prayed it would be the only weird incident of the night.

We made it past introductions and were seated in the living room with pre-dinner drinks before Mom made her first snide comment.

"You're awfully young to be raising a teenager, aren't you, Mr. St. James?" Mom gave him a withering smile before sipping her martini. She shifted in her chair and crossed her ankles, attempting to look every inch the society matron, an act she'd been practicing long before she'd left Wheeling, West Virginia. Well, technically, she ran away since she was a minor when she boarded that bus for California.

I caught Max's attention from where he sat next to Tiffany on the couch. *Less than ten minutes. You owe me fifty bucks.*

He grimaced and rolled his eyes. The doofus had really thought Mom would go easy on Duncan and Tiffany if he and I were sitting there to run interference. Like my interference ever made a difference to her.

"Please call me Duncan." He flashed Mom a charming smile, one I had to admit worked pretty damn well on me. He shrugged. "A man does what he must to help family."

Mom wasn't about to be deterred in her digging. "To give up your life in England like that and come all the way to America to raise your niece? And you couldn't have been more than a child yourself."

Oh crap. She'd noticed how young he looked. I opened my mouth, but a reassuring mental touch nudged the new subject from my head.

Duncan chuckled. "I was already living in the United States, and I assure you I was of legal age when I was made Tiffany's guardian. Ellie and Rick would not have left their precious daughter to anyone in whom they did not have full confidence."

Taking a gulp of my gin and tonic to cover, I had to give Duncan credit. He didn't fidget next to me on the loveseat while under Mom's barrage. Old-world charm exuded from him.

Mom sipped her martini, taking a moment to calculate the next shot before continuing her interrogation. "Yes, but the work and the cost to raise a child these days? It had to have been overwhelming for you."

Her coyness didn't fool anyone. Tiffany's jaw dropped, but Max reached for her hand and squeezed it. Hard, I suspected, from the way her fingertips turned white. She closed her mouth and gave him a glare that promised he would pay for his actions later. Dad stared at his scotch on the rocks, but the tips of his ears turned red. I knew from bitter experience he wouldn't interfere when Mom pulled this kind of shit.

Duncan eased forward on the loveseat and set his own scotch on the coffee table. He stared at my mother with such an intense look, I thought for a second he was trying to put the vampire whammy on her.

"You have made it very clear to Tiffany you believe she got pregnant on purpose in an effort to have your son support her," he said. "Not that it is any of your business, but Rick and Ellie left a substantial trust fund for their daughter. *My* first assumption was that Max was trying to take advantage of Tiffany." He glanced at Max before returning his gaze to Mom. "But I believe your son when he says he loves Tiffany. I am not enthusiastic about the situation anymore than you are, but I will accept it because I care about my niece's happiness. As I know you will accept it because you love your son."

Mom's mouth fell open, then it shut with an audible click of her teeth. Even Dad looked up from the depths of his tumbler in surprise. Few people had the guts to stand up to her, and Duncan did it with a finesse I sorely lacked.

"I see." Mom's frosty voice held a wary edge. Maybe she'd finally met her match.

Thank God the maid interrupted the silent, shocked tableau by announcing dinner.

— • —

David paced the length of the presidential suite's sitting room while Frankie yakked with an old buddy. With legs as long as his, it amounted to a whole five steps. "Well?" he asked when Frankie hung up the phone.

"If you don't chill, I'm gonna break your kneecaps, man." The were's voice was icy calm.

And deceptive. David had heard Frankie threaten to shatter the fingers of someone who'd cheated him at pool once with the same tone. And the were had proceeded to do exactly that when the man refused to return Frankie's money.

David dropped to the couch and held his hands up. "I'm cool. I just want to know what you found."

Frankie tossed him the pad with Duncan's number and address scribbled on the top sheet. "I got his business info, but the place is closed for the night. No go on the home."

David shrugged, not surprised. Few vampires advertised where they lived, even to the supernatural community. God, he hated the delay in his search.

Frankie leaned back in his chair and raked his fingers through his greasy locks. A gigantic yawn racked him. "Let's take a tip from Yvonne and get some shut eye. Then we'll hit Duke's party and throw back a few before heading over to Reno's."

David shot to his feet. "I want to go to Reno's now." The bar catered to L.A.'s supernaturals, the best place to start tracking down Duncan. His mouth watered at the thought of the tall, dark-haired vampire.

Frankie shook his head. "My friend won't be there until close to dawn. Besides, if you want to keep your image as basketball's bad boy, you need to make an appearance at Duke's. We'll sling back a few drinks, get you to relax, then hit Reno's."

Fuck. Frankie knew his buttons too damn well. Staring at his reflection in the wall mirror hanging above the were, David ran a hand over his close-cropped lime curls. He had tried to explain the color of Duncan's eyes to his stylist, and this was the best the bitch could do. Nerves itched to be out on the street. He'd gotten tired of playing by everybody's rules a long time ago, but Frankie wasn't making rules, just common sense. He needed to take his approach with Duncan slow, or he'd blow any chance he had with the vampire. Maybe Duke's party would take the edge off his jitters.

He nodded his acquiescence to Frankie, headed to the suite's bar and grabbed a bottle. He didn't bother looking at the label. He needed something, anything, to calm his nerves.

"Wake me when it's time," he said as he headed for his bedroom, not bothering to look over his shoulder. Frankie grunted an acknowledgment behind him.

David kicked the door shut and took a long swallow of alcohol, letting the fiery liquid burn away his impatience. He set the bottle on the nightstand before stripping off his sweats and t-shirt. Throwing himself on the bed, he reached for his dick and imagined Duncan St. James stroking the shaft.

Chapter 5

Through salad and the main entrée, everyone managed to keep the topic on wedding preparations. Mom drilled Duncan about the Epsteins. He assured her Jacob and his family had catered the wedding for Tiffany's parents and had done a wonderful job.

I nibbled on my asparagus stalk, not liking the speculative gleam in Mom's eye. Since Duncan's revelation concerning Tiffany's financial status, her expression left no doubt that she was calculating Duncan's net worth as well.

"What do you do for a living, Duncan? Tiffany wasn't exactly clear." Mom probably thought her smile charmed everyone, but it gave me the willies. That smile also meant she would make sure Duncan would know the appropriate pecking order in the family. Now I understood Caesar's explanation of the attraction of gladiatorial games in his day.

"I am a private security consultant." He didn't elaborate, but Mom wouldn't leave well enough alone.

Damn. If she'd stop staring at him for two seconds, he could slide the huge slab of prime beef from his plate onto mine.

She leaned her chin on her hand. "I'm sure that must pay well."

"As you remarked earlier, well enough I could raise a child." His cool, polite voice held a hint of steel.

I wanted to cheer my man on to victory. No one stood up to her except me. And she always made sure I was punished for my transgressions. Someway, somehow.

"So who do you provide security for?" The smile she gave him would have scared the shit out of a great white shark.

"I am not at liberty to discuss my clients, Elizabeth." The tight smile Duncan gave her in return was the only visible indication that irritation with Mom crawled under his skin. Unfortunately, his nerves started inching along my spine, despite my attempts at shutting out his emotions using all the little witch tricks Bebe had shown me. Nothing worked, which didn't help my peace of mind.

Max wiped his mouth and said, "So, Dad, how do you like your new car?"

Mom batted aside big brother's attempt at redirection. "Some celebrities? Maybe one of your clients has thrown Samantha out—"

"Hey, why don't I show Duncan the new landscaping you put in the back, Dad?" I jumped out of my chair like someone had jammed a cattle prod to the cushion.

Dad nodded, for once playing along with my attempts to minimize the destruction in Mom's wake. "Elizabeth, why don't you check on dessert while I show Max and Tiffany our latest addition?" He rose, waving the other two to follow him. "Safety ratings are important, but you kids need to think about room. I remember everything we had to haul around when Max and Samantha were little . . ."

Dad's voice faded as he disappeared around the corner, Max and Tiffany scrambling after him. I made a beeline for the back door, Duncan tight on my heels. I dared a peek over my shoulder. Mom sat with her mouth hanging open at everyone's abrupt departure.

Once we were outside, Duncan twined his fingers through mine. Neither of us said anything as we wandered past the pool and wove around the heavy foliage. Apparently, Southeast Asian jungle was the new in-thing thanks to Angelina Jolie's latest series of adoptions. Duncan's touch comforted me now I was outside of Mom's sphere of evil. I sighed. *If we could make a break for his vehicle . . .*

He chuckled. *She is not that terrible.*

I glanced up at his pale face shining in the moonlight. *Do you realize she was calculating your net worth and gender preference in order to decide if it was financially feasible to ditch my father?*

He winced before he brushed my cheek with his fingertips. *I am sorry, darling. I had hoped you had not* heard *that thought from her.*

My heart sank into the prime rib and asparagus fermenting in my stomach. I had been making my usual wisecrack. I hadn't caught Mom's gold digging scheme in my efforts to keep Duncan's irritation and my nervousness from blowing my shields wide open. Still, it cut to hear Mom's true nature laid out before me.

His soft, soothing strokes shifted from my face to the nape of my neck in his attempt to distract me. I felt rather than heard his rumble of amusement. *Fear not, Samantha. I evaded the plots and wiles of many women interested only in my fortune for years in Queen Bess's court. Trust me to handle your mother as well.* He tugged me closer until I was nestled against his chest.

A disturbing thought crossed my mind, and I raised my head to meet his eyes. *Then why do you insist on marrying me?*

He grinned, a full one that displayed his extra-sharp canines under the silvery light. *Because I know you only want me for my body.*

"Hey!" I shoved against his chest hard enough to break his embrace. "Just for that you conceited assumph—"

Too busy being pissed off, I missed his step. Vampire speed and strength had me wrapped in his arms. He kissed away my protests with a slow languid exploration that left me breathless. Wanting. So aroused, I considered ripping my panties off and jumping him.

When we came up for air, I licked my lips trying to remember why I was angry with him.

Are you reinstating your no-sex rule?

Oh yeah, that's why.

"I'll give you a no-sex rule, you jerk." I leapt on him, landing us both in the middle of some weird fern thing. Grabbing his head in both hands, I gave him a wet, tonsil-exploring kiss. His hands roamed in their own exploration, sending my nerves dancing. Teeth nipped my neck, not enough to break the skin but enough to drive me crazy. His very erect cock pushed and throbbed against my thigh, trying to find its way past all the material we were wearing.

Okay, material he wore. My dress was hiked up to my waist, and talented fingers worked their way past my thong.

"SAMANTHA!"

Mom's shriek brought us both sitting upright in a flash, trying to tug everything back in its place. Dad, Max and Tiffany stood behind her, their smirks a counterpoint to Mom's expression of absolute disgust and horror.

"Five minutes, you two." Tiffany rolled her eyes. "We cannot leave you alone for five minutes."

Chapter 6

"I want an explanation, Samantha Marie Howell! And I want it right now!" If anything, Mom's shriek was higher-pitched and more appalled than in the garden. She slapped her palm on the bar counter to emphasize her point.

"It's Ridgeway now, Mom." I was surprised at how calmly my voice came out. Duncan, sitting next to me on the loveseat, squeezed my hand.

"I don't give a shit if you call yourself Sunbeam Moondoodle. Your birth name is Howell and I will damn well use it!" Nice to know she still hadn't forgiven me for legally changing my name once I graduated from high school. But what reporter wants to be accused of riding on the coattails of her Pulitzer Prize-winning older brother?

"Now, Elizabeth, give the girl a chance to tell her side." Dad gave me a reassuring look from his seat on the opposite couch. Max had already handed him another scotch. "Samantha obviously felt the need to hide an important relationship from us, and we should give her a safe place to talk."

Max and I shared a quick look as he mixed Mom another martini. Mom must still be dragging Dad to her shrink, not because she wanted to improve their marriage, but because it was the "in" thing to do.

"Relationship! Is that what you call her humping *our* guest like she was—"

"Mr. Cuddles?" I offered.

An answering bark echoed from somewhere in the house.

For the second time tonight, Mom's mouth gaped open, but nothing came out. She was, however, turning an interesting shade of purple. Max handed her the martini, and she downed it in one gulp.

Dad jumped into the silence. "So how long have you known my daughter, Duncan?"

"Two months, Ted."

"I see." Dad took a sip of his scotch before he continued his Ward Cleaver act. "And how long have you been dating?"

I bit my lip to keep from laughing since Duncan had nearly four centuries on Dad.

Serves you right for not introducing your father to any of your gentleman callers. While silently chiding me, Duncan answered Dad without missing a beat. "We have only been courting for four weeks."

I pinched Duncan's thigh. *Hey, it's been almost seven weeks.*

He refused to look at me as he answered. *Intercourse and courting are* not *the same thing.*

Mom thrust her glass in Max's face for a refill. "You should have gone with your first instinct if it took you a month to decide to ask Samantha out."

A soft, cottony warmth swallowed the anger and pain threatening to explode my skull into a million shards. I wanted to scream at Mom for all the snide comments. I wanted to get mad at Duncan for using his mojo on me.

She is not worth it, darling.

In his mental voice was all the affection I'd ever desired. I didn't have to beg for it or debase myself to earn it. And the realization hit me that he wasn't using his mind control at all. Sitting on the couch surrounded by Duncan's love, my vision blurred.

I swallowed the tears and their accompanying lump for the ultimate surprise of the evening.

Dad rose from his chair, setting down his tumbler with a sharp click of ice. Dark pink suffused his face, but his blue eyes were glacial. "That will be more than enough, Elizabeth. If you can't be civil to your own daughter, there's no reason for you to be in this room."

"You're taking her side?" If possible, Mom's voice rose even higher. She stalked over to Dad and jabbed a manicured nail in his chest. "She rejects us, rejects our name. Embarrassing us at every opportunity—"

My tongue went dry, then I realized my mouth was hanging open. This was an event for the Guinness Book, the first occurrence of Dad openly defying Mom.

Dad covered her hand with his and pushed it down. "The only person embarrassing herself right now is you, Elizabeth. And I'm not losing the chance to know my grandchildren because you drove the kids away!"

Grandchildren? Holy crap, did Dad think I was pregnant too? Mom and Max's face wore shocked expressions that probably matched the one that stretched mine. Tiffany snickered.

Dad turned to Duncan and me, his hands spread. "Not that I'm putting any pressure on you two."

"Thanks, Dad." For once, sarcasm didn't fill my voice. Did this mean he approved of Duncan? My throat grew tight with the wishful thought.

Dad cleared his throat. "Are you pregnant?"

"Dad!" I didn't know whether to be shocked or amused.

"You do not have to worry about such a thing," Duncan said as Dad retrieved his scotch and resumed his seat. Pink flushed Duncan's pale neck and face.

I opted for amused.

"Really?" Dad's voice was nearly as dry as Mom's martinis as he rattled the ice in his tumbler. "Because I rather got the impression in the backyard that you two were already having sex."

I swallowed my laughter at Duncan's embarrassed expression. He actually hemmed a little before answering, "Things weren't as they appeared."

His irritation crackled through my brain. *This is not funny, Samantha, and you are not helping.*

I can't promise anything if Dad asks what your intentions are.

"Then what exactly are your intentions toward my daughter, Duncan?"

I slid off the loveseat and hit the expensive Berber amid loud guffaws.

"Samantha, get off the floor!" Mom found her voice as she marched to the bar, glass out for another refill.

"I had wanted to ask your permission to wed her shortly after I met Samantha, but she refuses to allow me to do so."

Dad nodded, a sage expression on his face. "She can be rather stubborn."

"You've known Samantha for only a month, and you want to marry her! Are you fucking insane?" Mom shrieked, stomping back over to the couch.

"Mom!" Max yelled.

"Elizabeth!" Dad hollered at the same time.

I stopped laughing. Dad and Max presenting a united front between me and Mom's anger? Tonight's wonders were never ending.

I glanced at Duncan as I resumed my perch on the loveseat. His eyes narrowed, and he slowly rose to his full height until he towered over Mom. "Elizabeth, with all due respect, you will not insult Samantha." He folded his arms over that fabulous chest of his, all raw intimidation. And he didn't bother with any vampire whammy either.

Mom melted under his withering glare. Her eyes widened until white surrounded her icy blue irises, and weird, little burble sounds issued from her mouth. Finally, her gaze dropped to the floor. "Well, of course, um, I suppose we need to talk about the rehearsal dinner."

Mom's classic way of dealing with a losing argument—change the subject.

Which, frankly, was fine by me.

— ·◦· —

Two uncomfortable hours later, I sat in the nearest McDonald's, scarfing down my second Big Mac. Duncan came back from the counter with three more plus a large carton of fries, two chocolate shakes, and a large Coke. He swapped trays before sliding into the seat next to me.

Sitting across from us in the booth, Max rolled his eyes. "I don't know what's worse, you inhaling everything in sight or Tiffany puking everything she eats."

Duncan glanced over his shoulder toward the short hallway leading to the restrooms. "Should one of us check on her? She has been in the ladies' room an abnormally long time."

"No!" Max and I said simultaneously.

"Trust me, honey," I said, patting Duncan's thigh. "Interrupting Tiffany in the throws of morning sickness will just leave you with something sharp shoved through your eyeball." In my case, it had been a metal nail file at Max's house last week.

Duncan took our warning in stride. He busied himself with clearing the trash from my first round of food while I started on the second.

Max leaned an elbow on the table and rested his chin on his hand. "I just wish she'd get morning sickness in the morning instead of ten at night. You're not supposed to have sleepless nights until *after* the baby is born."

Tiffany stumbled back to the booth, drawn and even paler than normal. She sank down next to Max. "I wish I hadn't just wasted a perfectly good prime rib dinner."

"So do I," I mumbled around a mouthful of hamburg and pickles. "Consuela gave me an odd look when I asked for seconds. If I knew you were going to puke it all up, I'd have stolen yours."

Tiffany must have felt super crappy because she didn't even flip me the bird.

Max wrapped an arm around her hunched shoulders. "Why don't I get you home, sweetheart? A little Seven-Up and some saltines will settle your stomach."

"Sounds good *urp*—" Tiffany slapped a hand over her mouth and raced for the restroom.

There was a loud *plunk* as Max's head hit the table.

"Do you need assistance taking her home?" For a sixteenth century guy who supposedly hadn't been educated in the finer points of women, Duncan could be awfully supportive. It kind of made me wish we could have babies.

Max rolled his head to peer up at him with bleary eyes. "No, but thanks for the offer. I covered the back seat in plastic garbage bags and keep extra bags and clothes in the trunk. Normally, we're not out after nine, but Mom kept rambling on and on about the damned rehearsal—"

He shot up at the pissed look Duncan gave him and waved his hands frantically. "Not that I don't want to marry Tiffany! I love her, and I want our baby." He blew out a breath. "I just wish we could do it without Mom involved."

Duncan relaxed and gave Max a curt nod. "Apology accepted. After dinner with your mother, I now understand Samantha's severe aversion to marriage."

Tiffany plopped back down next to Max and leaned her head on his shoulder. She looked terrible except there was no color beyond white to describe her face. "I think we're safe to make a dash for home, sweetie. I've lost every meal I've had since I started eating solids."

I slurped the last drops of milkshake, tossing the cup in the trashcan while I followed everyone out to the parking lot. A minute later, Duncan and I exchanged looks. I could hear Tiffany dry heaving as the Volvo raced by us, Max waving a half-hearted good-bye. Which meant Duncan could hear the poor kid too. For once, I felt sorry for both Max and Tiffany. It was going to be a long night for the two of them.

I climbed into the SUV, a difficult procedure in the sheath I wore. "You sure you want to go to Duke Miller's party?" I peeked at Duncan as he buckled his seatbelt. Someone could have dropped a unicorn in the middle of the Beverly Center, and I would have been less surprised than when he volunteered to go on this assignment with me.

"Will it not be less suspicious if you arrive with an escort?" An adorable frown creased his features.

I grinned. "You obviously haven't heard about any of Duke's parties."

"Yes, I have, which is why I am accompanying you." His seductive smile made me wet my panties. "I will be the only man you couple with today."

Starting up the SUV, I pulled into traffic, narrowly missing a Lexis when Duncan slid a finger up my inner thigh and nestled it underneath my thong. Three orgasms and two near-misses later, I still hadn't told him to remove his hand.

Chapter 7

David glanced at his watch again. Two-thirty. Frustration pounded in time with the music blasting through the sound system. Bodies pumped and thrust to the tempo, except for one couple tucked in the alcove formed by some amps and a potted palm. Yep, those two were having their own personal party by the way the girl's dress failed to cover her naked ass. Watching them didn't ignite the usual itch.

For the first time, he understood why Yvonne looked so fucking bored at these parties. She'd been awake when he checked on her, but she refused to leave the hotel room, stating with her annoying surety that the loa weren't inclined in his favor tonight.

The loa didn't fucking understand a man's needs.

"Someplace you have to be, sugar?" The redhead clinging to his arm pursed her lips into what he was sure was supposed to be a sexy pout. "And here I thought we were having a good time." She sidled around him and rubbed her barely covered breasts against his stomach. "It could be even better," she practically purred, reaching for his dick.

He grabbed her hand before it made contact. Any other time, he'd have taken both her and her blond girlfriend upstairs in a heartbeat. Maybe his reputation as a party animal would go to shit, but he just wasn't in the mood for pussy tonight.

"Sorry—" He tried to drag her name out of his memory but couldn't care enough to give it much effort. "—Red, I've got places to be." He raised the scarlet-clawed hand to his lips. "Give me your number, and I'll look you up the next time the Blues are in town."

She smiled and pulled a lipstick out of her purse. Bending in front of him so he could get a thorough look at her D cups, she lifted his shirt and wrote a number in a bold scrawl across his abs. Red also swirled her tongue around his bellybutton while she was at it. Probably would have moved further south too, if he hadn't pulled her upright and given her his promise in the form of a kiss that went way past French. He sent her on her way with a solid smack on her behind.

The antsy feeling demanded his full attention as he wove a path through the writhing dancers. He didn't have all of Yvonne's talents, but he'd learned long ago to trust the anticipation racing along his nerves. He owed the national rebound record to it. And he needed to get out of here.

Now.

Frankie leaned against the wall, whispering in some starlet's ear, his paws staking possessive claim on the girl's hips when David clapped his shoulder.

The irritated expression on the were's face turned to disappointment. "Aw, come on, man! Give me a break. Just a few more minutes."

Little Miss Starlet flung a hank of dyed blonde hair over her shoulder and glared at Frankie. "Excuse me? A few minutes?"

"Now." Damn. It wasn't like Frankie didn't get enough on every other road trip.

"Sorry, babe. Boss calls the shots." Frankie pinched her tit hard enough to elicit a squeal. He fell in step as David pushed his way through the crowd.

"What's the hurry?" Frankie asked.

"Feeling." A sliver of relief shot through him that Frankie didn't question his motive this time, but for the were to say absolutely nothing . . .

He looked back only to find Frankie frozen in place two paces behind him. Turning to follow Frankie's stare, he found the emerald eyes that had haunted him the last two years.

———•———

I'd gotten used to vampire reticence when entering crowds. For them, it was probably like a starving human walking into a bakery, surrounded by mouth-watering aromas. Or I thought I had until we got past the foyer to Duke Miller's club-in-a-mansion and Duncan jerked to a stop.

What I didn't expect was David Head, standing a yard away and looking like his mama had just bitch-slapped him.

"Hello, David." Duncan held out a hand, but his move was almost . . . hesitant.

The normally egomaniac basketball player trembled, actually trembled, as he reached for Duncan's outstretched palm. "How ya doin', man?" His voice was a little more stable. Not by much though. The strong scent of roses filled my nose.

Head was in love, but who . . .

My eyes traveled from the b-ball player to Duncan. No way.

Somehow I'd gone from the Dinner From Hell to the Twilight Zone. What was I missing here? No hint came from Duncan, his shields tighter than I'd ever felt.

A sharp musk hit my nostrils, and I followed it to the were standing at Head's right arm. His nose wrinkled as he evaluated my scent in turn, the normal reaction I get from a were because I smell like a steak knife rather than steak. Then his eyes narrowed, his look downright ugly.

From his and Head's body language, they weren't bedmates. So why was Head at a party with a were? Was he Head's bodyguard?

"I am well, thank you. And your sister?" Duncan tried to extract his hand from Head's grip, but the Blues' new star player clung to him like a life preserver.

"Yvonne's fine. She's here in town too." Head now carried that dewy wide-eyed look. You know the one. The kind his ex-boyfriend's preteen fans used to carry before I outed the two of them.

Duncan finally managed to pull free, in a semi-non-insulting way. A pleasant, and way-too-fake, smile spread across his features. "Please give our coven's regards to her and to Jean-Pierre." He turned to tug me further into Duke's mansion, but Head laid a platter-sized hand on his shoulder.

I felt like I was watching one of those PSAs of a slow-motion auto accident. Except I was the crash test dummy in the passenger seat. My assignment was exploding into as many shards as the proverbial windshield when my face smashed through it.

"Maybe you'd like to meet up with us for dinner tomorrow night?"

Head's puppy dog expression looked so pathetic and hopeful I almost felt sorry for him. The broccoli scent of his desperation joined the heady roses and hung in the air around us.

Duncan shook his head. "My apologies, but my fiancée and I have a family obligation."

I nearly choked on my spit, but before I could clear my throat, Head registered my presence. His eyes widened slightly, but not just in recognition. More like someone sizing up the competition.

A smile to match Duncan's filled Head's prominent features. "I didn't know you were engaged. Congratulations."

A vinegary aroma filled my nostrils, and behind it was the spicy tang of ginger. The double revelation sent my reporter's instincts racing, but I'm not sure which surprised me more, that Head was jealous of me or that he had witch blood in his background.

"We'll be in town for a while. Maybe some other night?" A pleading tone filled his voice.

I wasn't about to spend the evening playing nice to someone who had a crush on my guy. Even if my guy was a lying fink. Why hadn't Duncan said something about knowing David Head when I mentioned my assignment?

Screw the bonus. I had bigger vampires to fry. "I'm sorry, Mr. Head." I gave him a smile that I was sure was far more sincere than the ones he and Duncan wore. "But my brother's getting married a week from Saturday, and with both of us in the wedding, we just don't have the time, but thank you so much for the offer."

This time, I pulled Duncan away from the two men. When I glanced over my shoulder, both of them were staring at me. But their expressions carried two different forms of intense scrutiny.

Why didn't you tell me you knew David Head? I didn't bother quashing my irritation.

If I had known he would be here, I would not have come. Orange and red colored Duncan's mental voice.

While I was relieved he was talking to me, I still couldn't get past his surface thoughts. I twisted to face him. *He was my assignment tonight!*

Duncan twitched under my arm. *I am sorry, Samantha. I assumed your target was Duke Miller. You did not mention David.*

I did too!

No, you did not. Before I could protest, he flashed me his recollection of our conversation. Damn, I hated it when he was right, but I couldn't see past the immediate memory to find out his connection with Head.

Which meant Duncan was definitely hiding something.

I made a face at him. *Yeah, well. You know what they say about people who assume.*

Humor returned to his eyes. *You were the paparazzo that exposed David's occasional predilection for young men.*

I couldn't meet his eyes anymore. For some strange reason, equal parts of worry and embarrassment raced through my nerves that he'd put two and two together regarding my past experience with Head. Without having a clue, I'd crossed a witch two years ago. Did things I'd done as a human count against me now? I sucked in a deep breath and released it. *After seeing some of Bebe's spell-slinging, I should be thankful that I hadn't had an "accident" before now in retaliation for outing Head.*

I looked back up at Duncan. Needing an anchor in reality, I dropped the telepathic connection. "How did you two meet?"

A wry smile twisted Duncan's lips. "A gentleman objecting to David's personal preferences threatened him. Since David's sister works for Jean-Pierre, he asked Caesar to resolve the situation."

Oh, crap. Puzzle pieces lined up in my brain and dropped into place. The rumors about Head's stalker were true. When I'd pitched the follow-up on Head to Ralph, he'd nixed the idea.

No, he hadn't just nixed the idea. He'd drop-kicked it into lunar orbit. At the time, I'd thought he'd been furious the Sabretooths were considering a trade of their top rebounder thanks to my story.

In reality, Ralph had accidentally brought unwanted attention to a supernatural.

I had outed a bisexual pro ball player who happened to be a supe.

And the stalking may have been about more than just Head's switch-hitting.

Oh God, Caesar must have been pissed.

Which meant I'd gotten someone killed.

Nausea overwhelmed the Big Macs I'd eaten earlier.

"It was not your fault, Samantha." Duncan's whispered words did little to comfort my churning stomach.

I blinked back tears. "Yes, it was. If I hadn't done the story, you wouldn't have had to protect Head. Y-y-you wouldn't have had to-to . . ."

He shook his head, and a wave of yellowish exasperation washed against my shields. "Now you are the one making assumptions. We did not kill David's assailant."

My veins froze. There were worse things than death. Right now, I wished I didn't know that, and I really wished I could have stopped my next words. "W-what did you—"

A disappointed look filled his face. *He was a mentally ill young man. I erased his knowledge of David Head, and Bebe had him admitted in a facility where he could get the care he needed.*

My gaze dropped from his again as heat flooded my cheeks. Of course, they had. Guilt joined the swirling emotional mud. No wonder he'd shut me out. I'd hurt Duncan's feelings by even suggesting he hadn't done the honorable thing.

My shields quivered under the dual pressure of my own feelings and the charged atmosphere of Duke's guests. Unable to handle the overload, I pivoted on my heel and made a beeline for the front door. A whisper of movement and a hint of sandalwood told me Duncan followed me.

A beefy arm stopped me at the door. "The boss wants to talk to you."

My blurry vision followed the black-clad arm to its owner. Stern brown eyes met mine.

"If you'll just wait here for a moment ma'am," he added.

"What's the problem? I'm leaving."

"That is the problem, Ms. Ridgeway." The internationally recognizable voice came from behind me. A voice so rich and smooth it could make a woman shed her clothes just to hear more of it.

Gathering the shreds of my dignity, I turned to find Duke Miller standing in the foyer. Tonight, instead of his signature purple, the diminutive entertainer dressed in pale gray slacks with a matching fedora. A bright yellow silk shirt fell unbuttoned to his waist. To accessorize his appearance, his background singers, Ruby and Sapphire, clung to each arm. Since I couldn't tell the twins apart, I didn't know which one wore the black mini-dress and which one wore the white.

An impish grin filled his delicate features. "First, you chase one of my guests away, and then you don't even bother taking any pictures. Your readers, and my fans, will be sorely disappointed."

That's when the tantalizing scent of rich honey reached me. I cursed my abilities and fate in general.

Miller and his girls were fairy.

And I didn't mean that in the politically incorrect sense that some of our rival magazines had suggested. It definitely explained his musical genius. But it was one revelation too many tonight. Add into the mix the rumors the fairy queens had put a contract on my head, and the urge to flee sucked my breath away.

"I'm sorry for crashing your party. We were just leaving." I took a step back toward the door.

Ringed fingers flicked a dismissal of my apology. "I wouldn't have had Ruby leak the information if I didn't know it would attract your attention."

I stiffened at Duke's admission. And I'd lay good money the real reason Duncan insisted on coming with me was he knew Duke's status. Oh, someone was *so* going to pay!

My arms crossed over my chest. "What do you want?"

Duke's gaze moved in a slow up, down, up examination, not really sexual though the man exuded sensuality. "I was merely curious." His lips formed a pout. "I must say that I don't share the Courts concerns."

I glared at him. "Concerns about what? I'm not violating IC law by coming here, and you just admitted to luring me on false pretenses."

The International Council was the Supernaturals' equivalent of the U.N. Duncan and Caesar had made me memorize the IC code. All 28,440 pages. Thank God, I had retained my terrific memory after my death, the earlier lapse with Duncan notwithstanding.

Duke's eyes widened slightly. "No, you certainly didn't." He sidestepped his own complicity. Another amused grin appeared. "And the Queens' concern ever an army of tabloid journalists invading sidhe territory is ludicrous." He nodded at Duncan. "Good night, Chief Enforcer."

"Good night, Your Grace." Duncan returned the polite nod before grabbing my elbow and steering me out the door.

We were in his Suburban and half-way back to his place before either of us spoke. Of course, I was the one who finally broke the silence.

"What is Duke Miller?"

"He is Sidhe."

I smacked a palm against the steering wheel. "Tell me something I don't fucking know! Like what is he to the fairies that he'd host a party for the sole purpose of attracting my attention?" I stole a glance at Duncan. Headlights played across his pale face, but he didn't turn in my direction.

"He is Millanthropas de Dannan. A duke of the Seelie Court."

A whistle escaped through my front teeth. "A real duke, huh? But why lure me? Aren't the Seelie supposed to be the good fairies?"

"Good and evil are nebulous terms, Samantha. Vampires are the spawn of Satan, according to certain authorities." No mistaking the mild sarcasm in his voice.

"You seem pretty damn evil to me right now. Next time you and Caesar want to use me as bait, ask first." The snarl in my voice sounded like a were's to my own ears. L.A.'s alpha were would rip apart anyone who'd pull this kind of shit on him. I was sorely tempted to follow his example.

Silence. Duncan didn't even bother to deny the accusation. My chest ached. He and his boss, my boss too since I had accepted vampire influence, had deliberately dangled me in front of a fairy noble, knowing damn well how most of the fairies felt about my existence. The pain fed the fury itching to cut loose.

"Was Ralph in on setting me up?"

"No."

Good. That was one less person on my shit list.

Why? Nothing. Nada. His shields were tighter than Fort Knox. I knew he could hear me knocking, but he refused to open the mental door, not even a crack.

I clutched the steering wheel to keep my fingers from trembling and cleared my throat. "Why, then?"

He shrugged, but at least he answered. "Given the Sidhe Courts concern that Caesar will create more . . ."

I shot him a glance before returning my attention to traffic. "Go ahead. You can say it. Zombies."

"Samantha, you are no more a—"

"I'm technically dead, and I'm walking, aren't I?" I snapped.

"Technically, you are driving." He laid a cool hand on my thigh.

I wanted to slap his touch away. I wanted to break every bone in his fingers. I wanted him to say, "I'm sorry. I didn't mean to betray you."

Instead, he said, "And as Tiffany has repeatedly pointed out, you have not started eating brains yet."

My stomach chose that moment to gurgle. Loudly.

Duncan's amusement tickled my psyche, but that just pissed me off more. It had been almost five hours since the McDonald's stop. As Bebe had predicted, my appetite had tapered off where I wasn't eating five-course meals every two hours, but I still ate an obscene amount. It wasn't like the extra calories showed up on my thighs, but I still hated it. All of my so-called disposable income fed my undead appetite, and that was by working two jobs.

If I quit working for Caesar, I'd have more problems than paying my grocery bill. I wouldn't stand a chance on my own against the entire might of the fairy world.

I didn't know what to do with all that anger, so I did what any semi-prudent hungry zombie would do. I pulled into the closest Taco Bell drive-thru.

———•———

"How could he!" David pitched another bottle at the suite's wall. The shattered glass and spray of alcohol did nothing to alleviate his fury, any more than the other twenty bottles. He was running out of ammo. "It's only been two fucking months!" He snatched a vase and hurled it at the ruined wallpaper.

With a wave of her fingers, Yvonne threw up a shield to protect her and Frankie from the crystal shards as the vase exploded. "Davy, calm down." Even muffled by the condensed air, her voice rose.

Her tone penetrated the fire filling his vision. The last time he'd heard her sound that scared, they'd been kids. The same night he'd brought their mother home. He turned to find Frankie standing between him and Yvonne, like David had stood between Yvonne and their stepfather years ago. He had never wanted to be the cause of that same expression on her face.

Hot wetness replaced the flames. He swiped a hand across his face and through his lime curls, trying to hide the tears that escaped. "Damn, I'm sorry. Yvonne—"

She took a hesitant step past Frankie, but the were grabbed her arm. The fact that Frankie thought he needed to protect her from her own brother lashed across David's soul, the pain worse than the ache that racked him when Duncan introduced that bitch as his fiancée.

No. David shoved the pain aside before he sucked in a deep breath and released it. "It's okay, man. I'm not going to do anything stupid." If anything, he needed to be smart about getting what he wanted.

Yvonne rushed into his arms, her hug hard against his ribs. "Don't you ever scare me like that again."

"I'm sorry," he whispered into her hair. "I didn't mean to scare you."

"It's okay, Davy." She patted him on the back. The same comfort she had given on those dark nights when their mother and stepfather's drunken shouting matches got physical. "It's okay. Let's go home and forget about all this."

He pulled back so he could look her in the eye. "Come on. We came all the way out here. Let's stay a few days. Have some fun."

She shook her head, a bemused smile on her face. "Our ideas of fun are two different things."

"Let me make this up to you. We'll do Disney or Universal. Maybe hop the shuttle up to Napa." He shot her an impish grin, the one he used to con his way into and out of a whole lot of messes.

Sure enough, it still worked on his big sister because after two seconds, she laughed and shook her head again. "I swear, David Jebediah, the things I let you talk me into."

He pushed her gently toward the door to her bedroom. "Go get some sleep. We'll plan out the rest of our vacation tomorrow."

Yvonne raised a suspicious eyebrow. "You promise you're staying in for the rest of the night?"

Crossing his heart, he nodded solemnly. "Hope to die."

She stared at him for a long time before smothering a yawn. "Good night then." She crossed the suite and the door *snicked* shut behind her.

The prickly feeling on the back of his neck made him turn and face Frankie. An ugly frown pinched the were's sharp features.

"What are you planning?" Frankie asked.

"Nothing." David stalked over to the phone.

Before he could punch the numbers, Frankie's hand covered his wrist. "I think you've had enough tonight, boss."

"I haven't had a goddamn thing to eat since we got to L.A. Now get your paw off me." Not that his words carried any real threat to the were, but Frankie let go of him anyway. "You want anything?"

Frankie nodded and folded his arms across his chest.

Once David placed both of their orders, he plopped down on the couch and propped up his feet before he snatched the remote on the side table and started flipping channels. The weight of Frankie's stare finally snapped his last nerve. He twisted around to face the other man. "What?"

Frankie shook his head, his expression definitely not mirroring Yvonne's earlier amusement. "I know you, man, and you're not my baby brother. What are you really planning?"

Irritation washed over David. He knew he wasn't that fucking easy to read. Otherwise, he wouldn't have so many national title trophies on his shelves back home. "How can I be planning something?"

"I recognized the woman with St. James, too. Samantha Ridgeway, right?"

David turned back to the T.V. and thumbed the button. The tall, hot chick from the Weather Channel, the one who needed to ditch that damn orange lipstick, popped up on the screen. "So?"

"There's some things you may not know about her." From the soft *whoomp*, Frankie had dropped into the overstuffed chair next to him.

"I know enough." Brandon hadn't been the same when his bandmates kicked him out rather than lose their record deal shortly after the piece appeared. David had offered to help him put together his own label, but the stress of the ugly press had been too much on his boyfriend's fragile ego. Thanks to the bitch, he'd lost the best relationship he'd ever had.

The relationship that kept him from doing something stupid like getting his throat ripped out by pursuing the wrong supernatural.

"According to the rumor mill, she's the reason St. James killed Selene Antonius."

David shot upright on the couch. "What? Why didn't you tell me that earlier?"

Concern brightened Frankie's eyes. "I didn't take it or the other thing I heard seriously. Until I got a good whiff of her tonight, that is."

The urge to wring the information out of the were seeped into his brain. "What'd you smell besides garbage?" he sneered.

Frankie leaned closer. "That's just it. She smelled like stainless steel. According to my cousin, the story is Antonius turned her into a zombie using some kind of mini robots."

David stared at Frankie for a full ten seconds before he slapped the couch cushions. Laughter rumbled from his belly. "Good one. Good one, man. You had me going."

"I'm not joking."

The snarl in Frankie's voice quelled some of David's humor. He shook his head and propped his elbows on his knees. "I'm not making fun of you, but there's no way Ridgeway could be a zombie."

"Oh, yeah. Since when are you an expert?"

The memory of his one experience with the undead sobered him completely. "I may not be in Yvonne's league when it comes to magick, but I can tell you this." He held up his index finger. "A little too well preserved for one thing." He thought about his conversation with Duncan and Ridgeway and held up his middle finger. "And a little too bossy for the other."

Frankie dropped the subject when a sharp knock brought him to his feet.

As the were dealt with the room service, David considered this new information. If Frankie's cousin was right about Ridgeway, this might work out even better than his original plan for St. James. He was no longer a kid messing with resurrection spells out of grief. This time he'd do it right.

Nothing would be more delicious than fucking over the New Orleans coven. Except stealing a man from the woman who'd ruined his ex-boyfriend's life.

Yep, the old folks were right about how to serve revenge, and he would remain frosty until he eliminated the competition and got Duncan St. James in his bed.

Chapter 8

I would have preferred cutting off my toes, just to see if they grew back like the cheerleader on *Heroes*, rather than deal with Ralph in the wee hours of Saturday morning. But I couldn't sleep without fessing up to the man to whom I owed my career. I had *never* missed a fucking deadline until now. And I was too angry at Duncan to even want to join him in bed. After leaving him at his place, I drove to the *Scoop* offices and strode into the bullpen at three-forty-five.

"Where the hell have you been, Ridgeway? I've held the line for your damn pictures." Ralph's bark resembled that of the English bulldog at his heels. Emerson gave a low growl to back up his brother. The O'Malleys gave true credence to Caesar Augustine's penchant for taking in strays.

"Don't have 'em. We need to talk." I could be just as blunt.

"Goddammit, I need pictures, not—"

"Family business, Ralph. Now."

Ralph's tirade turned to stone-cold sobriety at my mention of Family. Yeah, he recognized the capital "F". "Family" as in supernatural business. "My office." He turned to Bill Morton, the newly appointed assistant editor. The job that should have been mine if I hadn't died. "Use the second cover lead and have printing start the run."

Amid Bill's ass-kissing reassurances, I followed Ralph and Emerson through the frosted glass and wood door. He had the only private office at *The National Scoop*, other than the publisher's executive suites upstairs.

Despite the no-smoking ordinance, Ralph lit up before his ass hit the cracked chair leather. He sucked in a lungful of smoke before he said, "What happened, Sam?"

I dropped into one of the visitor's chairs and swallowed my fury as I met Ralph's concerned gaze. He so rarely used my first name, but I needed to know the truth. Duncan hadn't let me read him after the showdown at Duke's place, which bothered me. A lot. Probably more than his initial betrayal.

But even James Bond would try to get the truth before he whacked the bad guy. I'd follow his example though I wouldn't have to rely on threats. "Ralph, I want permission to read your mind."

His mouth dropped open, and the cigarette hit a pile of papers amid a shower of sparks. After tossing the butt in the overflowing ashtray, he swatted the embers smudging someone's story.

Emerson whined before trotting over to rest his huge head on my knee. I scratched his ears, the same as I'd always done before I found out he was a werebulldog. Just as Ralph was trapped in human form due to a genetic quirk, Emerson would forever be a man imprisoned in the shape of an ugly, slobbering dog. I wasn't sure which of us had it worse at the moment.

When Ralph's eyes finally met mine again, I said, "Just surface thoughts, Ralph, so I will know if you're lying."

"Sam." For the first time I ever witnessed, fear tighten his craggy features. The thick smell of ashes filled the air, an odor that had nothing to do with Ralph's two-pack-a-day habit.

"You know I wouldn't ask unless something was seriously wrong." My vision swam slightly, as much from my own emotions threatening to break through as Ralph's scent. "I respect you too much, you old fart."

Ralph's ashy fear melted into the acid sharpness of worry. I hated being able to smell/taste other people's emotions, a by-product of Mallory's little science experiment, but never more so than now.

He gave a curt nod before he said, "Ask."

I dropped my outer psychic shields, and the mustard wave of Ralph's thoughts rushed into the space. "Did you know Duke Miller was a fairy?"

He shook his head, but frustration replaced the worry. "Damn, girl, you know that rumor's been floating around—"

Despite the bizarre chaos of my night, a laugh worked its way out of my throat as I held up a hand. "No, I mean a, um, sidhe."

Ralph grinned as the clean cotton of truth swept through him. "No shit. Really? Explains a lot." He reached for another cigarette.

"So you didn't know the fairy courts have been gunning for me?"

Emerson raised his head and barked. I couldn't read his thoughts and emotions the way I could Ralph's, but he was obvious in his own way.

Ralph clicked his lighter and took a puff before answering. "All the Families know. That's why I'm so freakin' happy you're dating St. James." His eyes narrowed as my unspoken suspicion hit him. "I didn't set you up, Sam."

Blessedly, his thoughts remained Downy fresh, but with the tinge of laundry left out on the line during a lightning storm.

"But you knew David Head was a witch."

Mildew replaced clean cotton. Another whine reverberated from Emerson's throat and he ducked under the desk.

"Dammit, Ralph, why didn't you tell me?"

In all the time I'd known him, I'd never seen regret in his eyes. Until now. It took a couple of seconds, but Ralph changed his mind about lying to me because the mildew cleared from my perception. The sad part, he was probably scared I'd force my way into his brain, which contrary to the stories Normal folks believed was a gross, painful process, for us as well as them.

"I couldn't Sam, you know the rules. You were human then." He sucked in a lungful of smoke before he blew it toward the ceiling. "You weren't Family either."

Family again. A supernatural or a normal human who was related to a supernatural either through blood or marriage and could be trusted with that knowledge. Occasionally, the term was used for a Normal who worked for a supernatural.

The thought only dredged up the morass of my own problems, and I could no longer meet Ralph's eyes. Could I trust my parents with my new status?

Max? Yeah, him I could trust, though he did try to shoot me the day after I died. He knew about supernaturals long before he knocked up a certain vampire's niece. Anne Levy, the homeless girl I thought was one of his street sources, had turned out to be one of Duncan's enforcers.

My head swung up so I could glare at Ralph. "Wait a minute! Max knew Anne was a vampire long before he ever met Tiffany. How come he got a free pass, and I didn't?"

Ralph's gaze pinned me through the smoky haze hanging over his desk. "Sam, do you really think Augustine would've cut me slack for breaking the rules just because he did for her?"

Damn, I hated admitting Ralph was right. Caesar took Anne into his coven after a rogue had bitten her. The vampire master practically regarded her as his daughter. It still didn't answer my original question.

"So why'd you send me after Head tonight if I'd gotten you into trouble the last time?"

Ralph sighed, a loud gusty exhalation that stirred the microscopic layer of ash that lay over everything on his desk, and crushed the butt. "The supernatural celebrities understand the business the same as Norms, Sam. As long as I don't publish anything that'll reveal their supernatural status, they're fair game. And frankly, they like the publicity as much as anyone else." His fingers twitched in the desire for another smoke. Instead, he ran a hand over the scraggly remains of his hair. "The problem wasn't the original story. The guy stalking Head after you, uh we, outed him as bi may have been nuttier than a Baby Ruth, but he knew way too much about supernaturals. Augustine and Rousseau couldn't take any chances."

I could understand the need for secrecy from Joe Average, but something wasn't quite right here. Just as Caesar was the master of the Western U.S. Vampire Coven, Jean-Pierre Rousseau controlled the vamps in the southeastern states.

"Why would Caesar and Jean-Pierre care when Head's a witch?" I frowned, twisting the complicated jurisdictions and political connections around in my brain. "A witch living in Los Angeles would come under Silver Bear's purview." For a tiny little Jewish woman, the Silver Bear Coven's high priestess was just as formidable as the vampires.

"Not when his sister is Rousseau's eclectic."

Ouch. This situation was getting more screwed up by the minute. I should've just walked out of Ralph's office, but now all of my reporter's instincts had kicked into high gear.

He chuckled before he broke down and reached for another cigarette. "I recognize that look. Go ahead and ask. I'll tell you what I can."

My right eyebrow rose of its own accord. "What you can or what you know?"

Another chuckle before he took a drag of the fresh smoke. "Okay, okay. What I know."

"Is Head eclectic too?"

Ralph nodded and leaned back, his chair creaking ominously. "Some incident when they were teens got 'em kicked out of the New Orleans witches' coven. Don't know the details but I heard it had something to do with their mom and stepdad's deaths. The Laveaus hushed everything up." He shrugged. "Most of the witch covens don't want the embarrassment splashed around, and perpetrators are usually ecstatic to get exiled from witch society rather than the death sentence."

Interesting. I would have pegged Head as the chooser, not the choosee, of exile. I'd have to ask Bebe for dirt when I got the chance, but she'd already given me the scoop on the reasons why a witch would voluntarily become an eclectic. The rest of the witches didn't like one of their own working for the competition instead of pretending to be a Normal, so if a witch wanted to work for one of the other supernatural groups, he or she cut ties with their coven.

Except something didn't make sense. I eyed Ralph. "Why pro basketball instead of working for Jean-Pierre too? He'd make a hell of a lot more money."

Shifting forward, he tapped the cigarette against the ashtray and took another puff as he leaned back in his chair. The clean cotton of his thoughts didn't override the stench of smoke filling his office. "From what I've heard, Head doesn't have a whole lot of talent in the magick department. There's always been some question of who was the real culprit in the incident that got the kids exiled. Head claimed responsibility so his powers were bound by the coven."

My grin matched Ralph's. "Really? I can't imagine why." Head's penchant for boasting had been cause for jubilation in the Sabretooth locker room when he'd used his free agency to join the New Orleans Blues.

Ralph blew a smoke ring toward the overhead fluorescents, and his mood turned serious. "Ridgeway, I expect something a little more substantial for next week's edition."

So much for our little heart-to-heart. My editor was back.

"And I want to get this puppy put to bed before Saturday morning," he added with a smile. "I've got a wedding to go to Saturday night, and I'd like to get *some* sleep." Max had worked for Ralph under a pseudonym in high school and college, so of course the old fart had been invited.

I rose from the guest chair and reached for the doorknob. "You and me both, Boss."

Emerson crawled out from under the desk and gave my hand a good-bye lick, but Ralph's not-so-discreet cough made me pause at the door. I looked over my shoulder.

"If this is going to be your last issue, I'd like it to be pretty damn spectacular."

Damn, him. He wouldn't ask me straight out, and I hated that he knew me so well he'd already assumed which decision I'd make. I nodded and stalked out of his office before the welling tears could fall.

Chapter 9

I avoided Duncan over the next four nights. The bastard had stabbed me in the back. It would have been less painful if he'd actually used a knife. A dull, rusty butter knife. How could anyone say he wanted to marry me, then turn around and use me as fairy bait? Why didn't he tell me Duke Miller was literally a duke of the Seelie Court. I ignored his repeated voice-mails. The bastard couldn't even say he was sorry in his messages.

Wedding preparations and hours spent staking out local celebrities helped keep me out of my apartment. At least until Brittany and K-Fed provided me with the perfect cover story late Wednesday morning. Ralph was on cloud nine, and as I unlocked my front door, I thought I had plenty of time to finish planning tomorrow night's bachelorette party.

"Samantha."

I jumped back, swinging my camera bag. Duncan caught it before it connected with his head. If I'd known it was him, I would have swung harder. No, I would have weights in the bottom, or used some fancy martial arts move like Jet Li.

The bastard had stayed upwind, so I missed my opportunity.

We stood there for several seconds, staring at each other under the security light.

He blew out a breath. "I understand you are still angry with me—"

"Get off my front step." I jerked my bag out of his grip.

"I would like to talk—"

"I don't want to hear it." I really wished I could walk through my front door, and he wouldn't be able to follow me. But the story of vampires unable to cross a threshold without an invitation was bullshit.

Just like Duncan saying he loved me.

I looked at him, really looked. There was no hint of remorse, only that stony visage of Mr. Chief Enforcer. "If you'd—" I clenched my jaw shut. There was no use rehashing the same old issue, and I wasn't going to beg him to apologize.

"If I would what?" He reached for my face, and I slapped his hand away.

"If you won't leave, I will." I stomped out to my car. When the Honda's door slammed shut, the broken panel rattled. Between deadlines and the wedding, I hadn't had a chance to take it to the shop.

I glanced back at my apartment in the rearview mirror as I pulled away. He stood there, not chasing after me with vampire speed. Not doing…anything. The bastard just stood there and watched me drive into the night.

The problem was I had nowhere to go. I didn't want to deal with Tiffany's morning sickness at Max's. Mom and Dad's was a joke. Ralph would tell me to suck it up and get over myself. As far as I was concerned, Caesar was as much to blame as Duncan, so his and Bebe's place was out of the question. Anyone else I knew in the supernatural community would call Duncan the minute I showed up on their doorstep. So I drove in an aimless pattern through the dark streets.

Maybe my driving wasn't as aimless as I thought when I recognized which neighborhood I cruised a couple of hours later. My driving must have been on autopilot because the car pulled into the driveway of an all-too-familiar little bungalow.

Jake Wong pulled open the front door, even though I didn't remember knocking. Water dripped from his short blue-black hair, and his dark brown eyes widened in surprise. He tightened his grip on the towel wrapped around his waist. Every muscle on his delectable body was as honed as it had been when we'd been a couple. For a minute, it was like two years had disappeared.

"Sam? You okay?"

I burst into tears.

———•———

Jake's bungalow was as warm and cozy as I remembered, the décor an odd mix of Eastern and Western styles, but it worked. He handed me a steaming cup of oolong tea. I had never been able to convert him to coffee. What was it about me and tea-drinking guys?

He sat down across the kitchen table with his own cup. He'd taken a minute to throw on jeans and a t-shirt before making the tea. Part of me regretted the change in his attire.

"Why do I get the feeling this isn't a booty call?" he said, sliding a fresh box of tissues to me.

Dammit, James Bond did booty calls, but he didn't bawl his eyes out on an ex's front door step. I wiped my nose and gave Jake a weak smile. "I'm sorry. I-I just didn't know where else to go."

He laid his hand over mine. "You know I'll always be here for you." His expression turned serious. "Is this about Max's wedding?"

My mouth dropped open. It took a couple of attempts to make it work. "God, no! How'd you even—"

"I saw the notice in the paper a couple of weeks ago." He let the silence grow for a minute before he said quietly, "What's his name?"

"Who?"

"The guy who broke your heart."

My anger resurfaced, and I could no longer meet his steady gaze. Instead, I stared at steam rising off my tea. "Who says it's about a guy?" When he didn't answer, I stole a peek.

A sly smile had spread across his lips. He let go of my hand, and leaned back in his chair. "So . . . you want me to beat him up for you?"

Despite all his training as a martial artist and a stunt man, Jake was severely outmatched, but the idea that he'd defend my honor eased my tension.

"No." I shook my head. "If anyone's going to smack the shit out of him, it'll be me."

"So what's his name?"

Part of me wasn't sure how much I should reveal without crossing the supernatural line. The other part was uncomfortable talking about the current boyfriend with the ex. So, did I still consider Duncan my current?

"I'm sorry. I shouldn't have come here." I started to rise, but Jake laid his hand on mine again, his touch comforting, and far warmer than a certain British jerk's.

"He asked you to marry him, didn't he?"

I didn't answer him. I couldn't. Not when I'd turned down Jake's proposal two years ago.

"Sam," he said softly. "It took me a while, but I finally figured out you ran because what we had scared you."

Frozen in place, I stared at him. I couldn't move as he tossed the harsh truth at my feet. "I'm so sorry. I—" Swallowing the renewal of tears, I looked away. "I never wanted to hurt you."

"I know that now, Sam," he whispered. "But don't throw this thing with . . ." He waited, letting the silence stretch and crack.

"Duncan," I finally said.

"Duncan," he repeated. "Don't throw things away with Duncan because you're scared."

"I'm not scared," I muttered.

"So why are you at your *ex*-fiancé's house right after another man proposed to you?"

"You're right. I shouldn't have come because you're an asshole, Jake Wong." I swiped at the tears that had managed to escape and stood.

"Uh-huh." He grinned, the brightness reminding me of things best left forgotten. There was just too damn much water under our bridge.

He rose from the chair and pulled me in a tight hug. "Go home, Sam. Give this Duncan a chance to make up for whatever he did to piss you off." His fingers tilted my chin up, forcing my eyes to meet his warm gaze. "Before we both do something we'll regret."

I couldn't deny the temptation. Jake was familiar. Comfortable. Safe. And I'd screwed him over completely. I knew if I told Jake things were over with Duncan and asked him for a second chance, he'd give it to me in an instant. But it wasn't fair to him. I'd ripped holes in both of our souls because of my fear two years ago.

And how would he handle the whole zombie thing?

No, I couldn't do that to Jake. But I wasn't sure if I could trust Duncan to replace the emptiness in my heart.

Chapter 10

Duncan was gone when I got home. The only trace of him was the faint scent of sandalwood on my front step. I needed to think, but instead I threw myself into the last minute preparations for Tiffany's party. I was probably avoiding again, but I found inspiration always came when I focused on something else.

So, shortly after sunset on Thursday night, a limo full of rowdy women headed into the desert night with me, bound for Las Vegas.

Okay, rowdy except for Mai, who made a point of locking the partition in the "up" position while she drove. I wished Miko had come, but Mai's baby sister had bowed out, claiming one of the senior daytime security needed to be in Los Angeles in case supernatural wedding guests arrived early. Tiffany had been bummed

Miko was the only bridesmaid not coming, but when I said I'd talk to her, Goth Girl threatened to shove her nail file somewhere even more uncomfortable than my eyeball.

Personally, I suspected Caesar or Duncan ordered Mai to come in Miko's place. She was the only Augustine enforcer more dour than Duncan.

And he must not have mentioned our fight to anyone because no one even broached the subject of why we weren't talking. Instead, a current of excitement enveloped the bridesmaids, and Mai had raised the partition out of annoyance. Or maybe it was the champagne corks ricocheting through the limo.

Even the bride-to-be exhibited good spirits, probably because Mom declined to come when I told her our destination. And here, I thought it'd be Anne, the Amish vampire bridesmaid, who'd protest the mostly naked entertainment. God, for once, I loved being the maid of honor.

"I'm telling you," Tiffany said as she sloshed more sparkling grape juice in her flute, "the last two nights of sleep have been pure bliss!"

"I told you the morning sickness wouldn't last forever." Dr. Bebe Zachary, our resident witch, took a sip of her champagne.

"Really?" Tiffany flashed her a smile that promised trouble. "When was the last time you puked every night for a month straight?"

"Tiffany." Passing headlights shifted along Phillippa Mann's face, making her skin glow more than usual. Not that Normals could see it. "No picking fights tonight."

I wasn't sure if Tiffany accepted Phil's chiding because she helped Duncan raise my future sister-in-law or because she was a freaking demigoddess. Either way, Tiffany leaned back against the plush leather bench.

Ever the peacemaker of the group, Anne Levy held up her goblet of blood. "Here's to Tiffany and Max. May their union be blessed."

"Well, it's already fruitful," I said, tinking my own champagne glass against the others, and everyone, including Tiffany, burst out laughing.

"So? Where're we going?" Tiffany bounced up and down in her seat.

I grinned. I hadn't been able to keep it a secret from the other gals, thanks to my ineptitude with my mental shields. But I was rather proud that I'd managed to keep it from Tiffany.

The bride's smile fell. "Tell me or I use my nail file on the other eyeball."

"Geez, is this how you treat Santa Claus too?"

Anne snickered. "You don't want to know what she did to him."

I could feel the blood drain from my face. "Please tell me we're talking about a department store variety and it didn't involve a felony."

Phil laughed. "We wish."

Bebe shot confused looks between Phil and Anne. "What'd she do? Run over one of the reindeer with the SUV?" Like me, she was a relative newcomer to the Augustine Coven, even though she and Caesar had been an item for a little over two years.

Anne tucked a lock of hair behind her ear and sighed. "That would've been so much easier to deal with."

We all were laughing hysterically for the rest of the trip as Phil and Anne told stories of all things Tiffany.

—•—

Frankie shifted on the balls of his feet. "Are you sure you want to do this?"

David ignored the nervous were and concentrated on the lock. A muttered spell, a soft click, a push. He smiled to himself. Good to know he hadn't lost his touch.

"Why couldn't you pick a funeral home?" Frankie's voice hissed in David's ear.

"Because fresher is better. Now shut up. I need to focus." He'd never had the chance to master blurring or invisibility spells, which left a good, old-fashioned power surge. The security camera promptly spat a flurry of sparks. He slipped through the door stenciled with "Clark County Morgue," Frankie so tight on his heels the were practically climbed up his ass.

"Damn, I hate the smell of these places."

For the first time, David felt sorry for Frankie. No matter how much anti-septic and disinfectant cleaner they used, decay permeated the air of a morgue. While the stench bothered him, he could only imagine what his friend's hyper-sensitive nose picked up.

"Ridgeway's still going to have a witch and a vamp with her," Frankie continued. "Not to mention at least two human enforcers, and no one knows what the hell Mann is!"

The continued stream of complaints grated on David's nerves. "Why do you think I'm getting back-up?"

Between the two of them, it hadn't been hard to track Ridgeway in the course of preparing for her brother's wedding. It was the social event of the season for the L.A. supernatural community. And there had only been two logical places for the ladies to go once he found out Ridgeway planned the bachelorette party for tonight in Vegas. A couple of franklins confirmed which show time she had bought tickets for.

"We could have hired someone to take care of her *after* we left Los Angeles." Frankie stood next to the door, peering out through the glass and mesh window. "That way St. James won't think it's you."

David settled cross-legged on the scrubbed linoleum before he flicked a scarf from his backpack and spread it before him. He eyed the were. "Why would he anyway? He doesn't know how I—" He swallowed the rest of the statement. Taking out the other necessary items, he arranged them carefully on the scarf. "Besides you're the one who's always saying it's best to take care of these things yourself."

"*Now* you decide to take my advice?"

"Keep your voice down before someone hears us." He poured the tiny bottle of Baccardi in the shot glass. Nerves jangled so he inhaled a deep breath and shook his arms to drive out the memories of the last time he'd performed this ritual. It sucked that this was his only magickal talent besides picking locks and blowing up electronics.

The Laveaus thought they were so fucking clever. *Lifetime my ass.* The binding spell was slipping, but he'd been careful to keep the illusion going, even around Yvonne. No sense courting trouble with the coven before he was ready.

Knowing he was running out of time, he clipped the cigar. A flick of a match and a couple of short puffs ensured the end glowed. A welcoming curl of smoke floated toward the stark ceiling.

David began the summoning spell. He only hoped Papa Ghede was in the mood to listen.

— •◦• —

"C'mon, Mai! You've got to come with us. I got you a ticket too." I reached over the front seat and waved said ticket under her nose. Okay, technically it was Miko's, but her big sister didn't need to know that.

Mai's expression was tighter than her glossy black French braid. "I'm on duty." She had dropped us off at the Karnak long enough to stow our luggage at Caesar's penthouse and say a quick hello to her grandfather, the vampire who ran Las Vegas in Caesar's name. Damn, it's hard not to love a billionaire boss. Now, she wove through Strip traffic toward the Rio.

Tiffany's head poked over the front seat to join mine. "No one said you had to drink. C'mon, it'll be fun!" At Mai's silence, she switched to a baby voice. "You know someone will be vewy, vewy angry wif you if someting happens to his pwecious baby awound all those big, bad, *naked* mortals."

Mai snorted and reached up with one hand to shove the ticket out of her face.

Tiffany looked at me and return to her normal voice. "You know the only reason she's not cursing us out right now is because you're screwing her boss."

"And your uncle."

"Eeewww." Tiffany ducked back into the rear compartment.

"Mai, you can honestly say you were doing your duty by keeping your boss's niece from sticking her hands down strange men's pants." I grinned. "And you know I'll tell him."

Almond-shaped eyes flicked up to stare at me in the rearview mirror. "Your attempts at blackmail are pathetic, Samantha." Her attention returned to the surrounding pedestrians, who were starting to spill from the sidewalk into the street.

"So's your reason for not coming with us." I stuck out my tongue.

"It is not."

"Is so."

She sighed. "You're all drunk."

"Are not!" Tiffany's voice rang from the back.

"Neither am I," Anne added.

Mai shook her head. "Someone should keep an eye on the lot of you."

A cheer went up from the back compartment.

I clapped Mai on the shoulder. "You're not going to regret it."

She sighed again. "I always regret coming to this damn city."

— • —

A deep chuckle echoed inside and around the stainless steel refrigeration units. Frankie LeBeau had seen and done enough freaky shit in his life that the invisible entity drinking the rum and puffing on the illegal Cuban didn't bother him.

But the muffled sounds of someone, of several someones, moving around inside the units made him want to wet his jeans. As much as he loved David like a littermate, what that boy could do wasn't fucking natural.

Unseen hands released all the latches at once. David's sing-song bass voice died until there was total silence. The stench of grave dirt and rot rose, threatening to overwhelm his canine senses. Then the sounds of scrabbling, fingernails on steel, cloth and skin sliding along the trays rippled through the air. Limbs covered in mottled flesh emerged from the units, followed by heads. Finally, the corpses crawled out of their little cubby holes.

Frankie tried not to look at the blue-gray skin and vacant stares on their faces. Most of the dead were in decent shape. Except for the three obvious victims of this afternoon's pile-up on I-15. Even his mind had trouble wrapping itself around the fact meat shouldn't be moving once it'd gone cold.

Someone screamed behind him. He whirled to find a petite blonde in navy scrubs. Her clipboard clattered on the floor, and shrieks of panic continued from her wide-open mouth. Cursing his inattention, he reached for her, only to see his partially shifted hand rake the pale flesh of her arm.

The pain seemed to knock away her fear. She pivoted out of the cold storage room and raced for the alarm. In two bounds, he'd caught her. He had to give the bitch credit; her thumbs thrust straight for his eyes. But her attempted blinding wasn't enough to stop the snap of elongated jaws that tore out her throat.

Shit! Damn! Mother-fu-

The remaining air in her lungs bubbled out through the blood filling the cavity once containing muscle and cartilage. With a sick, wet thump, the body crashed to the floor. Red pooled around the head, soaking the blond hair before spreading across the linoleum.

He reached up for his snout, only to feel skin on skin, his form already shifting back to human. He'd been so careful not to lose control over the past ten years. Jean-Pierre would not be pleased, but the vampire master's anger would be inconsequential if John Lannigan's wolves caught up with him. The Los Angeles Packmaster would order him shredded in a heartbeat for killing a Normal.

Frankie paused in wiping the blood from his jaw. The woman's body continued to twitch and jerk. This wasn't right. The death spasms should have stopped by now. He took a step back, then another.

And bumped into something clammy and unyielding. He jumped to the side. The corpse had been a fifty-something male. Dead hands reached for him.

"No!" David's command echoed in the empty hallway. Shuffling behind him came the other six zombies. The corpse let its arms fall to its side.

Frankie's relaxation lasted less than a second. A warm hand grabbed his. A shout rammed out of vocal cords as he leapt away from the woman he'd just killed.

"Ah shit, man! Did you have to kill her?" Disgust filled David's voice.

Frankie couldn't look away from her blank eyes, the film already creeping across the big, blue irises, to answer David. She reached for him again.

"Stop." David's order halted her movement, but it seemed like her attention was fully on Frankie.

"Frankie?"

He licked his parched lips, nerves on a hair-trigger, wanting to shift so he could run far, far away from this place. Swallowing hard, he struggled to remain on two feet and not sprout fur.

"Frankie?" David said again, this time laying a platter-sized hand on his shoulder. A warm, blood-pumping, living hand.

"I-I'm sorry. It was an accident. She attacked me and-and—" He gulped. She stared at him with those unseeing eyes, instead of lying on the floor like a proper dead person. "I'm sorry. Instinct kicked in—"

"'Sokay, man. We need to get them loaded into the van and head out. Are you going to keep it together?" David shook him slightly.

Frankie nodded before inclining his head toward the assistant coroner, according to her red-stained security badge. "Do we have to bring her?" Dammit! It was an accident. He didn't mean—

"Yeah," came David's soft reply. "We can't let her run loose. She was too close—" He took a deep breath. Even without him saying it, Frankie heard the unspoken accusation. "She'll be looking for revenge without me to control her," David continued. "The spell will be over at dawn, and she'll just be dead again."

Frankie nodded then fell in step behind David and his little troop of zombies. He wasn't going to hell like his mama had said.

He was already in it.

Chapter 11

Tiffany's shriek nearly pierced my undead eardrum. The cowboy thrust his package in her face, and she shoved the five-dollar bill into his fake suede G-string. Bebe waved a fistful of cash at the dancer, and he gyrated over to her.

Stone-faced Mai actually cracked a smile as a "police officer" showered her with attention. Then again, maybe it was the handcuffs dangling from his hip. Or it could have been the gold embroidered badge that barely covered his assets.

Even Anne had loosened up. Instead of peeking through fingers as she had during the first half of the show, she bounced her black flats in time to the music. But every time one of the performers approached her, she edged back in her seat, shaking her head.

The only one looking absolutely bored was Phil. I didn't know what James Bond would do in this situation. For one thing, he wouldn't be caught dead at a male strip show.

I dropped cash on the waiter's tray and plucked up the two strawberry daiquiris. Nudging one in front of her, I caught her eye. *You okay?* There was no other way she could've heard me with all the women screaming around us.

I'm sorry. She gave me a wistful smile. *You worked so hard putting this evening together. It's just—* Sadness filled her blue eyes. *When you get to my age, you've seen it all. Literally.*

Somehow I didn't think she was only referring to male genitalia. *Max isn't taking her away from you, you know.*

Phil shook her head, the gray rain taste of her thoughts threatening to drown my own alcoholic-assisted good mood.

And it took a *lot* of freaking alcohol these days to even get a slight buzz.

I . . . She sucked down half the pink drink. *I know it's stupid, but she's the closest thing I've ever had to a daughter.*

Who'd have thought Phillippa Mann had pre-wedding mommy blues? I laid a hand over hers and squeezed in sympathy while the last notes of the current number died amid thunderous applause. Dancers strutted across the stage and behind the curtains. Tiffany and Bebe's cowboy blew them kisses before jogging after his fellow performers.

Anticipation lay thick in the air though the pause between numbers couldn't have been more than a couple of seconds. The stage lights dimmed to an eerie blue, and the opening beats of "Thriller" filled the air. Women screamed in excitement as the dancers shambled on stage. Each one's monster make-up and costume were a weird blend of sexy and bizarre.

"Oh, gross!"

I followed Tiffany's line of sight to the last man on the left. Instead of the ripped and buff men entertaining us all night, this guy had a spare tire Homer Simpson would envy. Compared to everyone else on stage, his expression was slack, not flirtatious.

"I thought Vegas didn't allow . . ."

My gaze dropped, and my realization met Phil's at the door. The man hadn't bothered with his G-string. I cocked my head as I examined the goods. Why on earth had he used body make-up on his privates instead of wearing the G-string? In a stiff lockstep out of time with the music and the rest of the dancers, he aimed for our table.

Goddess! That man's really dead!

The same time Bebe sent her warning, Mr. Naked plowed through the table closest to the left side of the stage. The ladies he knocked over shouted insults. One took a swing at him.

I didn't see if she connected. Something frigid grabbed my neck and jerked me backward. I landed hard on my ass and looked up. Decay and rot filled my sinuses as I stared into unseeing, filmy eyes. I didn't have any room to duck the fist headed straight for my nose. Flinching to one side, bone cracked when the blow landed on my left cheek. It felt like my eyeball exploded along with the nerves. Sucking on the pain, I aimed a vicious kick at the asshole's groin.

Only to have my red stiletto stuck in the way-too-giving flesh.

Before I could pull free, my shoe disappeared along with my opponent. Something crashed into the bar from the loud shattering of glass. Another hand, this one warm and definitely alive, yanked me upright and tottering on one heel.

Phil peered into my good eye. "You okay?"

"Yeah. Nothing thirty minutes won't fix," I muttered.

The music died as the DJ realized there was something wrong. Two of the dancers closest to Mr. Naked grabbed his arms. With a shake, he sent them flying into other customers. Angry shouts around us turned into screams of raw panic. The crowd around Mr. Naked had parted at the sight of Mai's semi-automatic and were stampeding toward the main doors. She squeezed off a couple of shots.

Mr. Naked didn't even grunt. Sheer physics made him pause, but he resumed lumbering toward us when he regained his balance.

"Sam!"

Tiffany's warning didn't come fast enough. I caught a hint of musk and death before I was jerked off my feet again, much easier this time thanks to the missing four-inch heel. Hovering over me was a blonde in navy scrubs. At least, I thought she was blonde. It was hard to tell with the semi-dried blood matting her hair. Semi-dried blood that probably came from the huge gap where her throat used to be. What concerned me more than the horrendous wound was the scalpel she held in her right fist.

Fear and anger built. Deep down, I knew I wouldn't get a second shot and cut loose with a hard-core psy-bolt, one that'd leave me with a migraine for the next three days. Light bulbs popped behind my eyeballs and something stabbed the center of my brain.

Flashing spots cleared in time for the results. The woman flew backward and landed in the middle of a group of vacated chairs. Plastic crunched under her dead weight. One down.

Except the shattered chairs kept crunching. Acid gathered at the back of my throat. Like something out of a slasher movie, she rose, kicking aside crumpled bits of furniture. My telekinetic blow didn't faze her.

A flash of lightning blinded my good eye, almost as instantaneous as the crack of thunder that destroyed what was left of my poor eardrums. The smell of barbequed meat hit me. When I could see again, Psycho Doc was nothing more than a crispy critter. A grim smile lit Phil's face. So glad to know she'd found some enjoyment in the evening.

Mai had given up on the gun and had pulled out a couple of Japanese-style short swords. If we survived tonight, I'd have to ask her how she hid all that hardware underneath her black business suit. Whirling around Mr. Naked in a complicated dance, she chopped bits and pieces off him, but he still kept coming.

A quick glance at the rest of the group showed we were all in various degrees of trouble. Tiffany had smashed the kneecaps of one of the creeps and proceeded to beat him over the head with a chair. Using her vampire talons and fangs, Anne tore her opponent limb from limb. So much for her Amish pacifism. Meanwhile, Bebe took her cue from Phil and threw fireball after fireball at another zombie.

My heart stopped. That's what they were. *Real* zombies.

Phil jumped between me and another lumbering corpse. "These things are fixated on Sam!"

"No shit-ugh!" Tiffany's final blow crushed the man's skull. He twitched, but there were enough broken body parts he couldn't get up.

The corpse Phil faced off looked like it might have been a man in his late twenties when he was alive, but way skinny, even without part of its cheekbone and jaw missing. My own broken cheekbone throbbed in sympathetic pain. We were too close to Tiffany for Phil to risk another lightning bolt. Instead, she threw a punch at the zombie's stomach. Her fist went clear through his mid-section, spraying bits of vertebrae across the floor and splashing assorted goo all over her gold lamé dress.

Paralysis from lack of a spinal cord obviously wasn't a problem for him. Dead fingers wrapped themselves around Phil's throat.

I couldn't help her. Another nightmare smashed a fist into my already broken cheekbone, sending a tsunami of pain through my skull before I landed on a table ten feet away. Attempting to roll with the hit saved what was left of my face. The zombie Phil had thrown into the bar cracked the table in two with a double-fisted blow.

The daiquiris threatened to erupt from my stomach. What I'd missed earlier was the fact that the woman's entire ribcage had caved in. No blood oozed from the millions of shards of glass embedded in her naked body.

Or from the entrails dragging along the floor.

And my shoe's heel was still embedded in her crotch.

I backed away, only to have her buddy join her in stalking me toward the stage.

"Get behind us, lady!"

Two hard bodies pulled me up onto the platform and inserted themselves between me and the zombies, so I wasn't sure which man had spoken. I did have a very nice view of the backsides of Mr. Cowboy and Mr. Policeman, but they were about to die for their chivalry.

There was a loud crack as Phil broke one of the zombie's arms. "Tiff-*cough*-Tiffany! Quit-*choke*-messing with that-*cough, cough*-corpse and call for backup!"

Phil's order seemed to get the attention of the remaining zombies. Their undead stares turned toward Tiffany, who dived under our old table to retrieve her purse. Once she was clear, Phil electrocuted the dead boy still trying to throttle her.

While my dancers and I backed away from the shambling zombies, Bebe took a running jump onto the other side of the stage. How she did it in the red leather mini-skirt and heels, I'll never know. Behind her, smoke trailed from the corpse she had charcoaled. "Sam! Get their attention back on you!" She skidded to a stop next to me and swiped my damaged cheek with both hands, sending fire across my overloaded nerves. "And get the Norms off the stage!"

My rough shove sent the boys sliding across the polished wood on their perfect pecs. I'd apologize for the friction burns if I survived tonight. Clapping my hands, I yelled, "Tiffany! Phone!"

Her throw from a kneeling position under a table would have done any professional quarterback proud. The little cell arched over the heads of the zombies. However, my attempted catch would have ended my career as a wide receiver. The bit of plastic and metal slipped through my nerveless fingers to shatter on the stage.

It did get the three remaining zombies' attention. Mr. Naked joined my two assailants. Apparently, he had too much fat for Mai to cut off because, other than his now missing hands, the rest of his limbs were working.

Bebe appeared at my elbow. "Back up two steps."

Fear made me a bitch. "You'd better have a fucking good plan."

"I do." Under her breath, she added, "If it works."

I did as the doctor ordered and glanced down. Under the blue stage lights, the stuff smeared in a circle around us looked black. A hard gulp rattled my throat when I realized I saw my own blood. It was a heck of a lot of blood too.

The zombies crawled on stage, their movements stiff and awkward but still menacing.

"When I tell you, jump left out of the circle," Bebe whispered.

Perspiration soaked my little black silk number as the zombies lumbered closer and closer. Since I'd died, I'd ruined more clothes with more bodily fluids than humanly imaginable. Focusing on my wardrobe kept me from pissing my panties when Mr. Naked reached for my neck.

"Now!"

At Bebe's shout, I launched my body to the side. Raw agony blacked out my vision for an instant. I blinked tears out of my eyes. Or maybe it was blood. The zombies had lumbered into the circle Bebe had drawn. As one, they turned their blank faces toward me.

With both of us clear, the doctor slapped a hand on the blood circle, muttering alien words under her breath. At least, they seemed alien to my pain-filled head. A hemisphere of golden light sprang into existence.

And the zombies collapsed in a heap. No movement. Not even a twitch.

The same couldn't be said for the other five zombies. Even the three fried corpses were trying to crawl, except ash and chunks of meat fell at a rate that almost made them comical instead of threatening. Mai gave Anne one of her swords, and the two of them proceeded to hack the remaining bodies to bits.

Tiffany crawled out from under her table just as the smoke wafting from the crispies triggered the sprinklers. "Anybody else got their cell phone?"

Chapter 12

The back of the limo lightened despite the UV film as dawn poked her head over the mountains behind us. I'd never been so glad to see the "Welcome to California" sign in my life.

I leaned my head against the cool glass of the limo's window. The smashed cheekbones had healed over the last few hours, but I still had a ringing migraine thanks to the telekinetic stunt I'd pulled at the Rio.

Mai's umpteenth-great-grandfather Kensai Osaka and his boyfriend Jamal had originally planned on hitching a ride back to Los Angeles with us for the wedding. What the boys hadn't planned to do was clean up mutilated corpses at a strip club.

It may have been business as usual for the rest of the supernaturals, but I was at a total loss. No one I knew ever had zombies show up at her future sister-in-law's bachelorette party.

I eyed the physician seated across from me. "Are you sure, Bebe?" I couldn't stop asking for the umpteenth time.

"Yes, I'm sure!" Her ever-calm demeanor cracked, but it felt so good to share the headache. "I've always been taught that real zombies are impossible."

Next to the doctor, Kensai stroked his chin. "Something animated those corpses, Bebe. Perhaps the victims gave permission to sacrifice their lives to be reanimated. If so, it wouldn't be true black magick."

Bebe closed her eyes and let her head drop back against the leather seat, but her clenched fists revealed her exasperation. "Goddess, how many times do I have to tell you people magick is neither black or white."

I wanted to say Caesar's Vegas lieutenant had a point, but I also didn't want a fireball shoved up my ass.

Jamal reached through the partition and patted her shoulder. "Take it easy, girl. No one's questioning your expertise. We just need answers."

"Perhaps, Grandfather, we're looking at this problem from the wrong angle." Mai met my eyes for an instant in the rearview mirror before returning her attention to the freeway.

Something about her look sent a shiver up my spine, which ended with a spike of pain in my frontal lobe. Unfortunately, there wasn't anything in Bebe's bag that would work on me. Damn nanites.

"What do you mean?" Kensai twisted on the side seat to look at her, almond eyes wide. The entire fourteen generations removed thing still unnerved me, especially when he looked more like her baby brother home fresh from college.

"We're agreed that the . . ." She paused, searching for a politically correct term.

I sighed. "You can say it, Mai. Zombies."

She nodded. "Very well. The zombies were fixated on Sam. Perhaps if we can discover the reason for their attraction to her, we can backtrack the magick to their animator." She cleared her throat. "There is another possibility though."

I swallowed the desire to smack our driver's head. "Spit it out, Mai. No one back here is in the mood for twenty questions."

She flicked another glance in the rearview mirror before she said, "Perhaps you're responsible for their animation."

"Hey! They were trying to kill me!" Pain spiked again when anger-based adrenaline flooded my bloodstream. Or maybe it was the fact Mai had voiced the same ugly thought that popped into my brain while I shoveled body parts into buckets.

"You've already exhibited talents other than vampiric ones," Bebe pointed out.

"Yeah, and it was no secret Selene and Mallory experimented on weres and witches as well as vamps when they were designing the nanites." Heat edged my voice.

"Perhaps you are evolving beyond your original programming," Mai said.

I waited for Tiffany to make some snarky Trekkie comment while everyone digested Mai's suggestion. And waited. And waited.

Tiffany sat next to Phil, tucked in the corner of the rear bench seat, arms wrapped around her knees, nearly motionless except for the slight expansion of her chest muscles when she drew a breath. From the look in her eyes as she stared out the window, she wasn't anywhere in the state of California.

Before we left Vegas, Bebe had "borrowed" a sonogram machine to check both Tiffany and the fetus. I knew she wouldn't have risked either patient by clearing our return drive, but Tiffany's withdrawn behavior was freaking me out.

"Tiffany?" I whispered.

Gray, gooey fear washed through my migraine-shredded shields when she met my gaze. "All I could think last night was they were going to kill my baby, Sam."

"But that's just it." We all turn to look at Anne. "Those things didn't hurt any-one unless the person was between them and Sam."

"But—" Bebe started.

"No." Anne edged forward on the leather. "Think about it. The first one? Who came out with the dancers? He knocked those ladies over because they were be-tween him and Sam, but he didn't deliberately hurt them. Yes—" she held up a finger when Phil opened her mouth "—he backhanded the lady with the beehive. But she jumped in front of him and hit him first. Same with those two, um—" Pink tinted her cheeks as she obviously remembered the half-naked dancers.

For the first time in hours, animation returned to Tiffany's face. "She's right. The rest of the zombies came through the audience. I don't remember any com-motion behind us before that one with the crushed ribs decked Sam."

"Maybe because you were too busy playing with the scenery," Phil teased.

"No," Bebe said, waving an index finger at Phil. "They're onto something. They ignored Tiffany too until you told her to call for help."

I could almost see the hamsters spinning the wheels of her mind into overdrive.

"There's a common thread here. All of the corpses were fresh too. Less than twenty-four hours dead. And they all came from the county morgue."

Kensai grunted. "Don't remind me. You will all be getting Clark County morgue scrubs for your next one hundred birthdays to pay them back for the dam-age we did." He had a team take the chopped and fried bits, along with the three more intact corpses, back to the morgue once his people had figured out who was missing some bodies. The Vegas vampires then used their whammy to fudge mem-ories and clear the building. As far as L.V.F.D. was concerned, a chemical flash fire had damaged the cold storage room. The only fatality was the assistant coroner, who'd been on duty at the time.

Something about the whole situation still smelled rotten, and it wasn't the zombie stench all six of us ladies had scrubbed off before we climbed back in the limo. Okay, a couple of somethings.

"Giving Mai the benefit of the doubt here," I began, "if I *accidentally* animated those bodies, why would I send them after myself?"

"Suicide?" Tiffany offered.

I stuck out my tongue at her.

"You have been under a great deal of stress lately," Phil said. Soft, blue eyes watched me. "Maybe their animation was accidental. Maybe it was an unconscious attempt to avoid the wedding and the decision of whether to leave Los Angeles."

Jamal grinned, fangs too white against his dark skin. "I've got my fingers crossed you'll leave."

Kensai took pity on what I was sure was a very puzzled look on my face. "The contingency plan is already in place."

"What contingency plan?" I didn't want to know the answer.

"You and Duncan moving here." Jamal's expression turned serious. "Is there anything I can do to sweeten the pot? I miss Los Angeles, and I hear you've got a thing for dark chocolate." He waggled his eyebrows.

"Jamal."

The Moor shut up at Kensai's admonition, but the urge to scream filled my aching head. Was this the real reason Duncan asked me to move in with him? Just another manipulation in his bag of tricks?

I couldn't deal. Not now. Instead I focused on my other concern about the attack. "What about the coroner? Bebe, you've said blood magick is one of the strongest forms."

She nodded. Her fine black eyebrows knitted in worry.

"Would it make a difference what species' blood is used?"

She shook her head. "No, and I used yours to set the circle. It worked just fine. I don't get where you're going with this, Sam."

I waved a hand. "Nowhere, I guess. I thought maybe supernatural blood might be more powerful than Normal blood. I could have sworn I smelled were on the assistant coroner back at the club."

Again, Bebe shook her head. "If the coroner was a werewolf, which she wasn't, it wouldn't make any difference as far as blood magick is performed."

This would be so much easier if I could think through this damn headache. I leaned forward, rubbing my temples. "We still don't know how she died."

"You mean, other than the gaping hole where her trachea used to be?" Phil's wry smile did nothing to alleviate the anxiety aggravating the ache in my brain.

I blew out a deep breath, trying to shove the awful vision of the poor woman out of my mind's eye. "What I mean is, did she get in the way of the zombies like Anne pointed out? Or was she sacrificed to animate the other corpses?"

"I didn't detect any blood magick—" Bebe muttered through gritted teeth. She squeezed her eyes shut and pressed the heels of her hands against the lids. "Okay," she said before dropping her hands to her lap and fixing me with a pointed stare. "Assuming your theory has merit, yes, it is possible that she was a sacrifice. But—" She held up an index finger when I opened my mouth. "A blood spell practitioner would need all of her blood for something of that magnitude. That usually means a draining cut to the throat, not to mention how it taints the magickal energy . . ." She frowned as she worked through the idea. "I didn't see her before Phil had to fry her. Tell me more about her injury."

Phil and I repeated all the gory details we could remember from the insanity.

"That sounds more like werewolf or vamp damage," Jamal offered when we were finished. "Sam, you said you thought you detected were musk. Did anybody else? Because all I smelled at the club was dead human and fear."

Phil, Anne and Kensai shook their heads.

We all fell silent as the limo rolled another couple of miles from the site of Tiffany's disastrous bachelorette party.

"It could be a vampire," Anne said. "Maybe some of Selene's people who escaped. She'd been trying to wipe out Duncan's family for centuries, and it's no secret Duncan killed Selene to save Sam. In that kind of, um, crowd it would be hard to distinguish individual vampire scents."

Gotta love a mass of horny women. I kept the thought to myself though because the limo grew even quieter at the implication that Caesar's twin sister was still wreaking havoc even after her death.

"No," I finally said. "This was aimed at me personally."

"Uh, Sam?" Tiffany raised an eyebrow. "Selene's attack on you a couple of months ago was pretty fucking personal."

I shook my head. "Not the same. I was her experiment that escaped as far as she was concerned. Okay, I happened to be sleeping with her ex-boyfriend too." I didn't like thinking about the bitch, or her Normal partner, Tyrone Mallory. Maybe no dead person ever likes thinking about the assholes who killed her. Especially if they brought her back from the dead to be their immortal prototype to display to potential human customers. All the glam of vampires with none of the nastier side effects, like a severe aversion to ultra-violet and a liquid diet.

Except the pain of the transformation made my current migraine feel like a Hawaiian vacation. I still woke up from nightmares of what they did to me, cold sweat drenching my nightshirt. One of the reasons I started the break from sex with Duncan was to work on sleeping alone again. I couldn't depend on him forever to deal with the post-nightmare shakes.

"Besides—" I shrugged, trying to regain my emotional equilibrium. "—she's dead. If anyone would hate me now, it'd be the fairies." I jerked upright. "Wait a minute! What about fairy creatures? Are there any that could tear out a person's throat like that?"

Phil grinned. "Maybe a ticked-off reindeer?"

Tiffany flipped the bird at her former guardian.

———•———

David tapped the steering wheel in time to Kanye West on the digital player as they wove through the Los Angeles rush hour traffic back to their hotel. Frankie still wasn't talking to him, but the rising sun promised a brand new chance in his quest. He'd approached the situation with Ridgeway from the wrong angle. Frankie had been right. Brute force in a public arena hadn't worked. All right, it failed dismally. If she was really a zombie, he needed an alternate idea.

Grabbing the spiral notebook off the dash, he glanced at her schedule. Wedding rehearsal at her parents' place tonight, followed immediately by the rehearsal dinner at Anthony's. He grinned. Getting into Anthony's wouldn't be a problem. Getting back into the kitchen would take some serious sweet talk and greasing of palms.

Yeah, on any court, a player needed a Plan B.

"We should go to your old place," Frankie muttered.

David turned to stare at the were. A horn blasted next to his ear, and he jerked the steering wheel, whipping the rental back into the correct lane. "Damn, man! You don't talk for hours, and *that's* the first thing you say!"

"I shouldn't be around Normals." Something shook in the unflappable were's voice.

"That woman was an accident, Frankie. No one's going to find out about her. They've already burned all the evidence." The Las Vegas radio stations had talked of nothing but the early morning fire at the morgue, which was why he'd switched to the digital player long before they'd hit the state line. Supernatural standard procedure demanded the destruction of evidence, but he had to admire the Augustine Coven's efficiency in cleaning up the fiasco at the Rio.

"You don't know that!"

"Well, I sure as hell don't want to go back to—" He swallowed hard. It'd been almost two years since Brandon walked out his front door. He shouldn't care—

"Then why don't you just sell the fucking place and be done with it?" Frankie bit back.

David tightened his grip on the wheel. He'd been asking himself the same question for a very long time, but something in him couldn't quite let go of hope. Maybe part of him saw himself moving back to L.A. once he retired.

Maybe because he saw himself living there with someone else. He'd already had the light blocking drapes installed to cover the massive windows overlooking the pool months ago, along with UV film on all glass.

"You're right," he said quietly. "No sense staying at the hotel when I've got a perfectly good house in Los Angeles."

For the first time since the accident at the morgue, Frankie's tight frame relaxed. "Only thing you've said that's made sense all week."

Neither man said another word the rest of the drive into the city.

Chapter 13

Yvonne scanned the hotel lobby crowd with her Sight. No supernaturals. Good. Slipping down a quiet corridor, she spotted the old-fashioned pay phones. Any calls from their suite would show up on the bill, and she couldn't risk Davy or Frankie borrowing her cell phone and checking the call log.

She hated going behind her brother's back, but his obsession with the vampire was getting out of hand. He refused to say where he and Frankie had gone last night. And the mix of ginger and mold surrounding him when they'd come back this morning had been too thick to ignore. He was practicing again. The coven's binding hadn't held.

Her hand shook when she lifted the receiver. It took three tries to insert the coins, but she punched in the old number without hesitation. If Davy wouldn't listen to her, only one other person could talk him out of this madness.

"Hello?"

Her breath caught in her throat. She forced it out. Davy's sanity, maybe even his life rode on this slim chance. "Brandon?"

"Yvonne?"

"Yes." She gulped. "I need your help." Tears threatened. Davy would be so furious if he knew, but he'd listen to Brandon.

"Anything for you."

"We're in Los Angeles."

For the few seconds of silence, she wondered if Brandon would hang up on her. "He never stays here. Did he decide to sell?"

"No, *chére*." Nails dug into her palm. "He wants to stay at the house. I—"

"I'll get my things packed."

"Brandon, no. I want you to be there when we arrive."

"I—I can't, Yvonne. I love him, but—" The silence weighed between them. Finally, Brandon sighed. "Thanks for letting me stay here. I close on my new place next week. A hotel will do until then."

"Brandon—"

"I'm sorry, Yvonne." A click, then static filled her ear.

She leaned her head against the cool stainless steel of the divider. Now what was she going to do?

———•———

"A bad dress rehearsal is always a good sign." That statement earned me glares from the entire bridal party, not just Mom. I shrugged. "That's what Matthew Broderick told me."

Tiffany slapped a makeshift bouquet of soggy toilet paper flowers in my gut. "Ferris Bueller is not running my wedding," she bit out through clenched teeth. She stomped out of the banquet room at Anthony's to begin the run-through for the fifth time.

Unfortunately, the toilet paper wasn't the only thing soggy. The entire wedding party was a little damp. A freak thunderstorm had started as Tiffany walked down the staked-out aisle in Mom and Dad's backyard. A power surge from the storm blew the backyard lighting system, a necessary item for nighttime nuptials. And they weren't the first problems we had today.

Neither the tent, the runner or any of the chairs and tables had arrived at Mom and Dad's at noon as promised. The rental company claimed they had no record of the reservation. Then the florist called to say a malfunction with their refrigeration units had destroyed their entire flower supply, including the arrangements she'd already put together for the wedding. She promised she'd have something for us by tomorrow, but the substitute flowers weren't acceptable to Mom. Dad pulled the phone out of her hand when she threatened to shove a cactus up the florist's ass.

Mai and Miko had whipped together beautiful origami bouquets made from toilet paper of all things, just so the bridesmaids had something to practice with.

But Mom's tension hadn't started with the florist. Phil had intervened on Tiffany's behalf in the wedding dress search earlier in the week, pissing Mom off to no end. None of us knew what the two of them had picked out, but Tiffany was happy, which satisfied Max. While Mom bitched about Wal-Mart specials, I prayed the unseen matching bridesmaid dresses weren't totally hideous.

When Caesar suggested we adjourn to Anthony's a little early to practice there, we all sighed in relief. Except no one kept track of Reverend Mitchell, a buddy of Dad's from the country club, who'd agreed to perform the ceremony. He'd taken a wrong turn and arrived a half hour behind the rest of us.

The situation hadn't improved after he finally showed up. Anne, of all people, had tripped walking down our practice aisle and fallen flat on her face. Greg Evans, Max's best friend and best man, forgot Tiffany's ring. And Phil had rammed a door into Alex Stanton's nose, breaking it. We played it off as just a nose bleed so the Normals wouldn't suspect anything when the usher/vampire healed within minutes.

Given Phil and the sexy blond enforcer's history, I don't think that "accident" had anything to do with our stream of bad luck. Luckily, everyone kept their mouths shut until Mom stomped back into the banquet room to restart the canned music.

"This is too much for coincidence," Bebe said as we followed Tiffany out of the banquet room. She looked over her shoulder. "Anne?"

"With the storm, there's ozone everywhere," the vampire grumbled. "How would I know if there's a spell? You'd see it before I'd smell it."

"Sam's right. A bad rehearsal is a sign of good luck," Miko said.

"Only in the theater," Bebe muttered.

"All of you need to shut the fuck up," Tiffany growled.

"Tiffany." Duncan's eyes glowed neon green in the dark hallway. Lucky for us, it was just us girls and he wasn't in full vamp-out mode.

His gaze shifted from the pissy bride to me. The two of us hadn't been alone since I had arrived at Mom and Dad's, deliberately late, I admit.

I wasn't sure how much of his irritation was the same as everyone's general bad mood or because I walked away from him Wednesday night and continued avoiding him. Despite Jake's advice, I was scared to find out Duncan's real feelings. Maybe I'd pushed him too far by refusing to talk to him for the last week. Maybe

I'd screwed up by not giving him the chance to explain. Maybe I'd lost the man I loved.

Maybe I was still furious because he'd already made plans to move us to Las Vegas if I didn't tell Mom and Dad the truth.

More than anything, I hated other people telling me how to live my life. I'd hated Mom trying to shove me into her Beverly Hills princess mold. I'd hated Dad's not-so-subtle pressure to go to law school. I'd hated being compared to my Pulitzer-winning brother while I was on the freaking high school paper.

Honestly, if I never saw my parents again, it wouldn't cause a sleepless night. As opposed to the severe insomnia I'd suffered the last week because I couldn't snuggle up to Duncan and talk out my worries. He would have stroked my hair, whispered reassurances in my ear, made me feel normal again.

Ah, damn. Jake was right. I did love Duncan, and my chicken-shit commitment issues had reared their ugly heads.

And honestly, I'd miss Dad. Maybe Mom, too.

The music started again, and first Bebe, then Anne, and finally Miko glided through the door. I counted off the beats and had taken my first step when Duncan seized my arm, whirled me around and planted a kiss on my mouth.

A very thorough and passionate kiss.

I had the vague sensation of something cold and wet pressing against my stomach in contrast to the liquid heat deep inside me.

He broke our contact. Green eyes gleamed in the dim light. "We *will* talk after the rehearsal."

"Sam."

Mom's hissing and waving at the doorway barely penetrated the fog in my head. Luckily, she was too intent on me to notice Duncan's eyes. I floated down the aisle, smashed toilet paper flowers glued to the front of my dress, and took my place by Reverend Mitchell. Turning, I watched Duncan escort Tiffany into the room. The look he gave me could have melted steel. I loved him. I wanted to trust him.

I didn't know if I could.

The entire wedding party got through one whole run-through without any more screw-ups, and Reverend Mitchell declared it a raving success. Everyone either headed for the bathrooms or the bar while Anthony's staff started wheeling in the buffet. Except for me. I snatched a handful of hors d'oeuvres from a passing tray and crammed them into my mouth. The taste of the stuffed mushrooms was a little off, almost like taking a drink of Coke after eating an Andes mint. I tried to figure out the unusual flavor when Duncan appeared at my elbow, millimeters away but not touching.

"May I speak with you outside, Samantha?" The heated look in his eyes belied the formal tone of his voice.

I nodded, not daring to answer with my packed mouth. Grabbing a handful of pigs-in-blankets, I followed Duncan through the main dining room of the restaurant and out the front doors.

The parking lot pavement shone under the security halogens, and everything had that fresh rain smell. Everything, except Duncan. Sandalwood rolled off him, giving the night an exotic scent. Once we were well away from the valets, he turned and asked, "Are you all right?"

I blinked. Out of everything I expected him to say when I had rehearsed tonight's encounter over and over in my head, a stiff inquiry to my wellbeing was not it. Swallowing the last of the funky tasting mushrooms, I said, "I'm fine." At a total loss as to where this conversation was going after that fabulous kiss he'd laid on me, I added, "How are you?" before popping the a couple of the mini hot dogs in my mouth.

He shoved a hand through his dark locks, a sure sign he was already exasperated with me. "Bebe and Tiffany said you were injured last night. Bebe suspected a fractured skull on top of everything else, but she said you refused to let her check."

Tattletales.

I finished chewing, the dogs a hard ball as they went down, and crossed my arms, only to be reminded of the soaked paper flowers pasted to my mid-section. Peeling toilet paper off my cotton floral print dress kept my eyes and hands occupied while I answered. "Tiffany should have been her priority. Beating a zombie's skull in was a little too much exertion for a pregnant chick."

The thick foliage surrounding the restaurant muffled the street traffic. Otherwise, we were both silent for a long time, except for the faint squish and plop of the toilet paper hitting the concrete.

"I understand you are upset with me—" He held up a hand when I looked up and opened my mouth. "Let me finish."

Crossing my arms over my chest again, I closed my mouth. I'd give him his chance. He'd better make it pretty damn good, though that kiss had gone miles in muting my anger.

"Caesar is concerned about last night's attack. We agree with the ladies' assessment that it was aimed specifically at you."

My heart dropped at his words. "Caesar is," not "I am." Hugging my arms tighter, I closed my eyes, so he wouldn't see how his words cut my soul.

Duncan continued his relentless dissection of my heart. "Caesar recommended, and I concur, that for your safety, you move in with him and Bebe for the time being. With the estate's twenty-four-hour guard, it is unlikely another attack will occur. If it does, you will have a more than adequate defense."

This wasn't my boyfriend concerned about my safety. This was the chief enforcer of the Augustine Coven analyzing a potential threat to a member. The difference sliced the still beating organ out of my chest and served it up, hot and steaming. And with all this zombie crap, he didn't even want me staying with him. I swallowed the huge lump of tears forming in my chest. Or maybe it was the dogs coming back up.

After clearing my throat a couple of times, I managed to croak out a "No."

"This is not a game, Samantha." His eyes brightened under the halogens. "Someone tried to kill you."

"And who waved me in front of the fucking fairies like a red flag." My voice was flat, my angry tears solidifying into a ball of ice in my gut.

"Bebe does not believe either of the Sidhe Courts committed last night's attack."

"Oh, really? Dr. There's-No-Such-Thing-As-Real-Zombies is absolutely su-u-ure the fairies aren't involved? That makes me feel so much better." I wasn't about to point out Duke Miller had set a trap for me and didn't bother to trip it because he deemed me inconsequential. Truth was, by focusing on the fairies, I ignored the real fear. That somehow those shuffling nightmares had been attracted to me because I was one of them.

Dammit, James Bond did *not* have these kinds of problems. Why couldn't I have a nuclear bomb to diffuse?

Duncan rolled his eyes in a passable imitation of Tiffany. "Bloody hell, woman! For once in your life, listen to reason—"

"I am being totally reasonable." Numbness seeped in, not replacing my anger but surrounding, enveloping it. "I'm not taking the chance of someone getting hurt or killed at the mansion because they *accidentally* got in the way of a bunch of walking corpses."

The stone mask dropped, along with his canines. Anger flamed his eyes into raw neon. "You were fortunate last night."

"I know." And I couldn't help but wonder at the weirdness of the role reversal, my voice remaining calm, his rising. "I had three enforcers, a witch and a demigoddess with me, and we could barely handle eight of them. If there are more the next time, we'd be fucked. I'd be fucked. And I don't want my future niece or nephew, much less anyone else I care about, to be following me down that long, dark tunnel." I sucked a huge breath of rare damp air to stave off the tears hovering behind my lids. "With my luck, the light on the other side would be a Red Roof Inn."

No hint of a smile appeared on his face. Maybe it was another twenty-first century colloquialism that sailed over his head.

He threw his hands up. "I cannot—"

"Hey, if y'all are finish necking—"

At the Texas drawl behind us, we both turned to glare at Alex.

"Or not. Dinner's started." The poor vampire pivoted on his boot heels and raced back to the front door at more or less human speed after the matching death glares we shot at him.

"You will obey a direct order, Samantha," Duncan said. I turned to face him again. The stone mask was back in place.

His words should have royally pissed me off. The best I could muster was a half-hearted bird. "You're not my boss."

"Caesar is. Or are you forfeiting his protection?"

The numbness settled deep in my bones. Caesar's protection. With it, Duncan would guard me, not because he wanted to, but because Caesar ordered it. Without that kind of security, I was on my own. I searched his face, looking for a hint of love, compassion. Hell, at this point even a little of the lust from earlier. Didn't he care? Or had our whole relationship just been an act, a way for the Augustine Coven to control a rare resource?

Disappointed at his lack of emotion, I shrugged. "Whatever." The threatened tears disappeared under the weight of losing everything. My job. My so-called life. Duncan. Everything real sunk into a deep morass of non-feeling nothingness.

He muttered something under his breath I didn't catch. Maybe I didn't want to catch it. I couldn't summon the desire to care either. He spun on his heel at my non-response and stomped back into the restaurant.

Standing there in the parking lot, I wasn't sure what to do next. I hardly felt like partying, but the maid of honor should probably have her ass at the rehearsal dinner. A soft breeze ruffled my hair as I tried to decide what to do next. It was difficult to think though, and I couldn't blame that on the lingering headache. Styrofoam worms had invaded my skull, making everything distant, vague.

The faint thump of drums traveled on the wind. Or maybe it was a stereo bass. Tha-thump. Tha-thump. Like a heartbeat. I felt the pounding through the pavement more than heard it. Some idiot with more money than sense who'd turned the entire rear of his over-sized vehicle into one gigantic sub-woofer. The sound/feel seemed the only thing connected to reality.

I took a step backward. I should go inside to the party. Then someone called my name.

Pivoting slowly, I scanned the parking lot. Nothing there, except one of the valets taking a smoke break. And he was too busy puffing away to have spoken.

Another difficult step backward, but I could have been wading through cotton. The pounding became more insistent. Not a request, a demand. It must be followed.

I shook my head. *My imagination. I'm letting last night's creepies get to me.*

But I couldn't move. The numbness I felt while talking to Duncan turned into a deep lethargy. I tried to will my feet to move, but it was almost like my brain had short-circuited. Were the nanites malfunctioning? Was I finally dying?

No curiosity, much less fear.

I felt nothing. Nothing, except . . .

Need arose. A desire to follow that strange beat swallowed whatever thought I might have had. I started across the concrete, passing the valets and their little traffic cones. Something summoned and all I knew was that I must answer it.

Chapter 14

The screeching brakes and annoying honk should have made me jump. In the back of my fuzzy awareness, the noises meant danger, but I couldn't gather the strength to heed the signs. Headlights flashed in weird colors, chocolate pie and lemon meringue. The flavors in my eyes were much more interesting.

A head popped out of the driver's window of the Mercedes. I waited for the pie dough skull to fall on the pavement from the weight of obsidian-framed diamonds covering its eyes. A single finger rose, bisecting the length of black and white.

The universal gesture registered.

A director. One I should know, but I couldn't think past the pounding beat in my gut, in my blood, in my head. All I knew was the little man in his car and all his desserts were in my way. Another high-pitched beeping. My ears hurt. Centipedes in the shape of music notes crawled out of the metal box, and hands slapped over my ears in a vain attempt to keep them from flying into my brain. I struck the metal box making the irritating cheeps. Steam rose and I kicked the red metal box aside.

I continued on, leaving the raspberry sorbet lights behind. I didn't belong with the sweet lights anyway. I belonged in the dark, the rich earth swallowing me. A satisfying meal of succulent meat and steaming blood as I returned to my real mother's welcoming arms. Wet greenery and decay filled my nostrils, the scent of home.

Dark figures rose around me, surrounding me, welcoming me as one of their own. I could sleep now, safe and warm.

A lightning flash of pain. I screamed.

And woke up from the dream in the middle of a nightmare, surrounded by zombies trying to rip me apart.

I lashed out with my left fist, my right arm useless. I didn't want to think about the white gleaming in the middle of the shredded bicep. Dust exploded along with a skull. Unlike the party at the Rio, these things were so dead they weren't juicy anymore.

Sickly black diamond and red haze played along the edges of the zombies. I elbowed another corpse. Amid the mold and powdered flesh I inhaled was the acrid smell of ozone. *Damn it, Bebe!* It *was* magick that animated these freakin' things!

I kicked, jabbed and clawed, but it was useless. They tore into me, ripping my dress, leaving bloody furrows in my skin. A couple of them even left their brittle fingernails embedded in my body.

Don't panic! A scared giggle burbled in my throat while I popped another skull off a crumbling neck. Ford and Arthur never encountered zombies in their hitch-hiking adventures.

An eerie silence enveloped the whole bizarre scene, punctuated by my grunts as I fought them. I tried to yell for help, only to have some elderly woman shove her entire desiccated fist into my mouth the second it opened. I gagged, trying to spit out the bones and dried flesh even as the hand, severed when I jerked my head away, struggled to yank out my tongue.

I couldn't even call out telepathically, my head still aching from the incident at the Rio. Where was the fucking prince who was supposed to rescue me? I'd settle for a duke. Duncan had been a duke once upon a time. Why wasn't he here?

Because I told him to go away, that's why.

I swung and flailed, blocking the attempted gouging of my eyeballs. Desperate to stay upright, because if I went down now, I was a goner.

The nanites couldn't keep up with the injuries the corpses were inflicting, though the tiny robots kept me on my feet in the chaos. It turned to my advantage because the zombies started having trouble grasping my blood-slicked skin. I kicked one guy's knees out. He landed with a crunch, breaking into several pieces on the damp concrete.

My few seconds of luck didn't last. One of them landed a nasty blow on my back, and I crashed to the cold, hard pavement. Another stomped on my calf when I tried to roll clear. The bones broke with an audible snap.

Pain twisted into fury. I snatched a thigh bone of the zombie I'd knocked over and started swinging with everything I had left. My offensive cleared enough space for me to climb awkwardly upright on my one good leg.

"C'mon, you motherfuckers!" My voice croaked with the dust I hadn't been able to cough out. "You want another piece of me? Come and get it!"

With each swing of my makeshift weapon, I'd scream, "Die!" Okay, it was more of a hoarse whisper, but the words added to my temper as I whaled and smashed the zombies. Bits and pieces flew around me. They didn't belong here. It was a freaking time of celebration, of life. Tiffany's face, stark with terror, flashed in my mind's eye, begging me not to let them kill her baby. I didn't stop pounding them. Not until—

"Sam?"

I whirled. Mai stood there, her eyes wide with fear, her semi-automatic in both hands. Pointed at me.

I looked around me. The zombies weren't moving. Not even a twitch. Just body parts scattered over this little corner of concrete behind the restaurant's dumpsters.

Then I looked down at my body. Blood mixed with grave grime to coat what was left of my skin. My dress hung in tatters off my shaking shoulders. I had no clue where my sandals were. The adrenaline started fading, leaving pain in its wake. I knew it was about to get worse. A hell of a lot worse. Not like the time I'd been shot point-blank in the chest two months ago. The nerve receptors in my brain weren't a repair priority with a fist-sized hole between my breasts. My pain perception had changed since then. The crushed lower leg bones and black spots in front of my eyes announced how much.

Maybe I'd get lucky tonight and pass out first.

Facing Mai again, I croaked, "Get the Normals out of the banquet room. M-my parents can't see me like this."

Rubber on wet asphalt squealed behind me. Mai rushed past me and dived through the shrubbery. I hopped on the one intact leg behind her, the small branches digging into my raw flesh. The boutique next door was dark, except for taillights as a sedan peeled onto the street. Mai leveled her gun at the escaping car, but I pushed it down with my good hand.

"Never mind. I saw the license plate." And the two assholes in the car and I were going to have a very serious talk about the misuse of magick when I got a hold of them.

Mai holstered her gun and reached out to sling my left arm over her shoulder. With her help, I limped to the kitchen door.

And this time I knew it wasn't my imagination. Mixed with the odor of grilled steak, tilapia and grave dust was the distinctive musk of werewolf.

Chapter 15

I flashed Anthony Monroe a weak but sincere smile when the restaurant owner set another bottle of Jose Cuervo Gold on the floor next to where I sat. Thank God, the zombie attack had happened at a Family-owned establishment. Tables were shoved aside in the private room where the aborted rehearsal dinner had started to make room for me and my impromptu trauma team.

I shoved my sixth bottle into Anthony's waiting hand before I put the seventh to my lips and chugged. With a sigh of resignation, I set the empty down on the floor and wiped my mouth with the back of my hand. The room gave a lazy merry-go-round spin. I was pretty close to human drunk with my nanites overloaded from the zombie-inflicted injuries.

Trying not to look at my bizarrely angled left leg, I reclined on the plush carpet. "Do it." I really could have skipped the torture, but if James Bond could survive it, I could too.

Bebe shoved a thick silicone cooking spatula between my teeth. Biting down, I closed my eyes against what was coming. Hands braced my shoulders and the less damaged leg. One of the vamps, from the room temperature touch on my injured leg, twisted the half-healed bones.

I jerked as they broke again, my scream turned into a muffled groan as I bit through Anthony's expensive utensil. I could feel Bebe working quickly to realign the leg so it would heal straight this time. As fast as the nanites could regrow bones, she wouldn't bother with a healing spell. It didn't exactly make my next five minutes Disneyland though.

Cool hands held me still as the pain raged through my body. Cool, except for the warm touch on my right shoulder, which had to be Phil. She whispered in my ear, but the agony turned her words into gibberish.

When the pain faded to a bearable ache, I blinked the tears out of my eyes and spit the rest of the spatula out of my mouth. At Bebe's nod, Caesar, Anne, Alex and Phil released me. My stomach chose that moment to rumble. Loud and strong and continuous.

Phil and Alex help me into a chair, and I started shoveling food into my mouth before Alex had scooted the chair to the table.

It felt like something inside me would gnaw its way out. I couldn't eat fast enough. The second I cleared one plate, someone thrust another in front of me. I didn't know what I was eating, only swallowed and took the next bite. Anthony's voice called back to the kitchen, but the words were vague in the all-consuming hunger. There was no taste to anything I half-chewed before swallowing. I didn't bother with forks or knives, ripping, tearing and stuffing with my bare hands. Anything to quell the monster growling its displeasure in my gut.

"Damn. I thought my pups could eat."

I looked up, realized I had half a quail hanging out of my mouth, and pulled it out before I reached for a napkin.

John Lannigan, Packmaster of the Los Angeles werewolves, stood there, grinning at me. If Caesar reminded me of a young Marlon Brando, then John was Harvey Kietel. Average height, with thick graying hair and naked power in his frame. So secure in that power, he didn't bother with an escort. One of those men who could be your best friend as easily as your worst enemy. His piercing brown eyes examined me.

I swallowed the last bite of quail before turning my gaze to Caesar. "What's he doing here?"

John's eyes narrowed. "If there's a rogue wolf in my territory, it's my business, little girl."

I reached for another dinner roll, but kept an eye on the werewolf. "How do I know he's a rogue?"

John stepped forward at my insult, threat obvious in the subvocal growl. All he needed was his hair standing straight up.

I'd had enough though. Enough beatings in twenty-four hours. Enough grave crap in my mouth and under my skin. Enough pain.

Simply *enough*.

I shoved back my chair and stood, meeting his glare. The effect was probably diminished by the roll stuffed in my mouth and the fact I tottered on one leg.

Caesar stepped between us. "Sam. John." His head swiveled back and forth, catching our eyes. "Until we know what exactly is going on, no one is going to do anything stupid." His smile wasn't meant to be reassuring with the bared fangs.

I chewed the roll slowly. John, I could take out before he shifted, even with the half-knitted leg bones and most of the meat on my right arm missing. Caesar was another story. He was the oldest and most powerful vampire on the North American continent. Even the other two U.S. vampire masters would think twice before going mano a mano with him.

I sank back into the chair and reached for the bowl of steamed broccoli Anne handed to me. But I didn't take my eyes off John for a second as I alternated bites of quail with the vegetables.

Bebe sighed and wiped her hands on another napkin. "If you two can remain calm, I'm going outside to have a look at those remains." Caesar gave her a quick peck on the forehead as she passed him. And the look he gave her reminded me too much of the one Duncan gave me earlier.

Duncan. He'd charged out into the night when Mai half-dragged my butt into Anthony's kitchen. Not a word of comfort. Not even asking if I was okay.

All right. I had to admit that was a stupid question given my mangled state at the time. But dammit, after that kiss he'd given me during the rehearsal, he could've at least pretended to care.

An uncomfortable silence filled the room while I finished the bird and nibbled on the broccoli. At least I was eating at a semi-reasonable rate now. When those disappeared, Anne passed a plate of cream puffs to me. The pastry I bit into was delectable, the first thing I really tasted all night. The monster had quieted. I looked over at the two tables next to me. Dishes were piled two feet high on both. Two months ago, the sheer idea of eating that much in one sitting would have made me puke. The last time I'd eaten like this was after Mallory's guards had shot me during my escape.

The night I died.

Apparently deciding I was no longer a threat, John glanced at Caesar. "Where's Ziva? I thought she was coming too."

"Here, darling!" Ziva Epstein swept into the room, her husband, Ben, a cheerful shadow to her flamboyance. His dark trousers and white dress shirt contrasted sharply with her neon pink running suit. "Where's my baby?"

Of course. In any kind of incident, the Silver Bear High Priestess's first priority would be her granddaughter, Bebe.

"Out back." Anthony inclined his head toward the rear of the restaurant. "I'll show you."

"And check those mushrooms too," Caesar added as Anthony led Ziva out of the banquet room. She acknowledged him with a backward wave and disappeared around the corner.

The mushrooms. "Oh God," I groaned. "Did anyone else eat them?"

Alex grinned. "Just your mother. And only because Tiffany said they smelled funny."

It finally registered that Max and Tiffany weren't in the room. Good. My brother had the common sense to remove his pregnant fiancée from the line of fire, though the vamps probably had to hogtie her and toss her in the back of the car for him.

"But your mother didn't suffer the same effects you did," Anne said. She took the plate I had unconsciously cleaned of puffs and set a huge helping of tiramisu in its place. "And Bebe stopped anyone else from eating them after Duncan's concern over your behavior in the parking lot."

Their reassurance produced a small wave of relief, but it lasted less than a second. Whatever had drugged me hadn't affected anyone else, and there weren't many pharmaceuticals that affected me. This was so not good. I picked up a fork and dug into the cake and cream.

A thoughtful expression passed across Alex's face. "Though your father may have appreciated a mindless, unspeaking zombie for one night."

Phil gave a wry smile. "We all would have appreciated Elizabeth in such a state for the next twenty-four hours."

The instant Phil realized she was sharing a joke with Alex, her face fell. I didn't know what had gone on between the two of them before, but I was making it my mission to find out and fix it, assuming I survived whatever the hell was going on now. For folks as old as they were, they were being utterly ridiculous.

Of course, everyone else in the room probably thought the same concerning Duncan and me after Alex had narc'd about our fight in the parking lot. I didn't lower my shields to find out for certain everyone deemed me an idiot. Our fight was part of the excuse the supernaturals used for my absence, adding for good measure that I'd taken off in my car after the fight. Mai got the valets to move my Accord behind the building before Mom and Dad walked out the front door.

Ben sat on the chair to my immediate right. White fringe danced a semi-circle around his bald head. Sparkling brown eyes peeked out of crow's feet. In contrast to Caesar and John, he came across as the sweet grandfather next door. The type who kept a lookout for the little kids in the neighborhood and passed out the good candy at Halloween.

But it didn't mean the old witch exuded any less power than the vampire or the were.

He peered into my eyes. "You okay, kiddo?"

I had the sneaking suspicion he was trying to read my aura, get a handle on my physical state. But every witch who'd tried eventually gave up. According to Bebe, my aura was pure black. Black as death itself.

Or ultimate evil.

The fairies voted for door number two.

At my nod, he examined the mess that was my right arm. As the Water Elder of Silver Bear, his forte was healing. I dropped my good hand on his as he reached for the terrible wound.

"It's okay, Ben. The nanites are doing their job." I gave him what I hoped was a reassuring smile. And sure enough, now that I'd eaten and they'd finish repairing my bones for the second time that night, the tiny robots set to work on the flesh of my mangled arm.

Under our watchful gazes, skin and muscle rebuilt and stitched itself back together. By the time the enforcers and the witches returned from their examination of the scene of the attack, not even a scar remained from my formerly mangled arm or the zillions of scratches and cuts I'd received in the fight. Absolutely nothing to show for the night's activities, except for the blood, sweat and zombie dust coating my skin.

Oh, and the fact that my secrets were more exposed than Victoria's.

Anthony interrupted that realization when he followed the supernatural CSIs into the room. In one hand, he carried a bottle of Jack Daniels, which he set in front of Bebe who had plopped in the chair across from me. Walking around the table, he handed me the cloth bundle, which turned out to be a pair of navy sweats and a matching t-shirt.

"Thanks, Anthony." I flashed him a grateful smile.

"*De nada*. I learned a long time ago to keep extra clothes here." He shot Bebe a glare before he thumbed over his shoulder. "You can use the bathroom in my office."

I raced out of the room and around the corner. Bless him, he had real towels and washcloths on a little shelf over the toilet as well as a corner shower stall. The hot water felt so good, but I couldn't enjoy it like I wanted. I needed to hear what Bebe and the enforcers discovered. After rinsing off the worst of the corpse grime and dried blood, I jumped out and pulled the soft cotton over damp skin. The remains of my poor dress and underwear I wadded up and stuffed in the trash.

I jogged back to the banquet room in time to catch Bebe saying, "—not sure what this residue is."

"What residue?" I asked.

Everyone, even John jumped at my voice and turned to stare at me.

"What residue?" I repeated. I didn't want to think about the fact that I'd snuck up on the major leaders of the Los Angeles supernatural community and the equivalent of their police. If I could do that, it might alienate the few people left on my side.

Bebe cleared her throat, a soft delicate sound. "There's a type of energy residue on the remains of the corpses you destroyed."

"Magick residue? From the spell that animated these fuckers? And you can trace it, right?" At her fidgeting, my anger reared its ugly head again. "Don't you dare tell me it wasn't magick! I could smell the freaking ozone! And the funky light show surrounding them—"

"I'm not saying it wasn't, Sam." Bebe's voice held that same patronizing tone all doctors had when confronted by an irate patient. She sucked in a deep breath.

God help me, this was going to be bad. Really, really bad.

"The residue may have come from you," she said.

"What!"

Familiar masculine sandalwood washed over me before the British accent murmured in my ear. "Sam, let her finish." Duncan wrapped his arms around my waist and pulled me against his hard, strong chest.

I should have been pissed at him, but I wanted his touch so bad I didn't object. Hell, after the last two nights of mayhem, you couldn't pay me enough to object.

Underneath the sandalwood though was a slight tinge of ash. In the two months I'd known him, I'd never smelled fear emanating from him. I twisted to look up at him. "The license plates—"

"I ran them," he said, his eyes filled with worry. "The automobile was reported stolen earlier this evening by the owner. A Normal with no Family connections."

Shit! I closed my eyes. I'd depended too much on that little tidbit of info.

Opening my eyes again, I turned back to Bebe. "How could magickal residue have come from me? According to you, the nanites rewrote my DNA to match vampires."

Bebe downed a shot of whiskey, so Ziva answered instead. "We're eliminating the obvious. It's not witch magick, sweetie." She held up a hand to forestall my protest. "It's not elf magick either. We're not sure what this energy is. Mai . . ."

The old witch hesitated, and I looked at the enforcer.

Ramrod straight as always, Mai met my look squarely, but there was unease in her sharp features. "You were saying something with each strike against your opponents. I couldn't hear the actual words, but with each blow, there was a, a—" She blinked rapidly as she grasped for the words. "A flash of nothingness."

"Huh?" I stared at her. "Are you sure you didn't eat one of those funky mushrooms?"

"That's the other problem, sweetie." Ziva was young by witch standards, only seventy-five, but right now, she looked every inch a Normal of the same age. "Someone laced the stuffed mushrooms with devil's horn."

"Huh?" My conversational skills were rapidly declining.

"Datura," Bebe said. "It's a hallucinogenic plant."

I blinked and tilted my head. "But drugs don't work on me. The nanites negate the effects too fast."

All three witches shifted uncomfortably in their chairs.

"Out with it," I commanded.

"According to the old stories, devil's horn is used by Voudon sorcerers to raise the dead," Ziva said.

I looked at Bebe, who was suddenly fascinated by the shot glass she rolled between her palms. Returning my attention to Ziva, I said, reasonably politely, "I've been told zombies are impossible to conjure."

"There's always been rumors about the New Orleans and Haiti covens," Ben said quietly. "But no real proof. They've flaunted their abilities in public over the last couple centuries, but nothing serious. The rest of the covens chalked it up to boasting for profit. Enhancing their status among the Normals in order to separate the public from their money." Ben shrugged. "Of course, the New Orleans folks have been quiet lately, their hands full with other problems since Katrina."

Something wiggled in my overloaded brain, a connection I wasn't making. Or maybe the nanites were still dealing with the devil's horn in my system. "So why'd this drug work on me?"

"It was spell-enhanced," Bebe said, her voice so soft I could barely hear her. "It was targeted to affect you specifically because—" She took a deep breath and released it. "Because you're dead." She finally met my gaze. "It made you highly susceptible to such magickal influence and clouded your rational mind."

"So my mom's going to be okay?"

She nodded. "Elizabeth may have some weird dreams tonight due to the hallucinogenic properties inherent in the drug, but no, it won't do to her what it did to you."

Relief swept through me. Despite our differences, I didn't want my mom ripped apart by the undead.

Looking back at Mai, I said, "Thanks for your help. How'd you know I was back by the dumpsters?"

Mai shrugged. "I didn't. When Bebe discovered the doctored mushrooms, Duncan said you had eaten some and you hadn't returned, so we spread out to search the facility."

Duncan hugged me tighter. "Kensai and Jamal have taken the corpses to the crematorium for disposal. Though you seem to have eliminated any animation by your destruction."

"I did save some of the remains, boxed and sealed," Bebe added. "Stan and Harry are already on their way down, so they can check them before daybreak."

My stomach clenched at the thought of the San Francisco enforcers. "Are you sure you want them to check this out? They're half-fairy—"

"Samantha," Duncan said, his breath tickling my ear, "the Gryffudds' allegiance is to Caesar for that very reason. They are persona non grata as far as the Courts are concerned, and they will not lie about their examination."

I still didn't like trusting any fairy, half or not, even if they were enforcers and reported to Duncan. But I wasn't getting anywhere by throwing a—

The memory of what I'd done shot home, even if it was a little fuzzy. "Oh crap! There was a car in the parking lot. Scorse—"

"Marty and his wife are fine," Caesar said. "We had to alter their memories, but as far as they're concerned you and they had a fender bender in the parking lot, which resulted in damage to two additional vehicles. Restitution has been made to all parties, and your car is on its way to our mechanic's—"

"You didn't." That little vampire shit was leaving me stranded!

"It was my idea."

I jerked free of Duncan's arms, whirled, and smacked him in the chest. "You didn't even ask!" *Smack.* "You never ask what I want!" *Smack.* "You didn't even ask if *I* wanted to move to Las Vegas." *Smack.* "You just make the decision—" I overbalanced on the last swing and would have landed on my ass if he hadn't caught me.

"If you are finished with your temper tantrum?" Amusement glinted in his eyes.

"I haven't even begun, buster!"

Chapter 16

In the end, my temper tantrum made no difference. In a way, I was a little embarrassed. James Bond wouldn't have thrown a tantrum. He would have just shot the person holding him back.

But what could I really use to threaten a vampire? Not proud of myself, I switched to begging. Not even my pleas concerning the need of a car for wedding preparations swayed Duncan. He gave me a choice of following Caesar's orders to stay at the Brentwood mansion or he'd have the witches trap me in a protective circle. My so-called friends and John volunteered to hold me down while Bebe and her grandparents cast the spell.

I had pouted and snapped while Alex and Mai escorted me in his truck to my place to collect some things. Ziva and Ben followed us in their car to the apartment complex and then back to Caesar's mansion as an additional precaution.

Alex pulled into the gated drive, and Ziva leaned out the car window, yelling "See you at the wedding!" as they drove past. The taillights of their Caddy disappeared into the night.

I *heard* Alex's exchange with the guard on duty, a vampire I didn't recognize. The gates slid open with the barest whisper of metal on metal. When the pickup pulled to a smooth stop behind the house, I grabbed my overnight case and jumped out before Alex or Mai could say a word.

When I stomped into the kitchen, Bebe sat at the island sipping from a cup, one of her herbal concoctions from the flowery odor. "Which room?"

She eyed me, waiting a couple of heartbeats before she answered. "The usual."

"No." I shook my free index finger at her. "No fucking way. I want the guesthouse."

"Jean-Pierre and his escort are using the guesthouse." She peered at her watch. "They should be arriving any minute." Vamps.

"Then I'll use the east wing."

"Virginia and her party are already here." More vamps.

"The downstairs mother-in-law suite."

"The Polks and their entourage." Werewolves.

My bag dropped to the floor. "This is just fucking peachy." I so didn't want to spend the night in Duncan's room. "Can't I bunk with you or Anne?"

"I like you, Sam, but you're not my type." She took another sip of tea. "And my cousin, Alice, is rooming with Anne along with Mai and Miko. If it makes you feel better, he probably won't spend the day here."

My eyes narrowed, and I considered trying to throw a psy-bolt at her out of spite. That's when I realized my head didn't hurt anymore. No pulsing behind my eyeballs. No nagging ache in my frontal lobe. Nothing.

Bebe must have misinterpreted my expression because she hopped off her stool. "What's wrong, Sam?" Golden light danced along her fingertips.

I frowned. "My headache's gone."

"You're sure?" Bebe's magick played along the edges of my body. After a few experimental tries over the last few weeks, she'd figured out how to check my vitals without her aura getting sucked into mine.

"I still had it during the rehearsal . . ."

Our eyes met, and Bebe's forehead creased even more. "Before you consumed the laced mushrooms."

I nodded. "Could the devil's horn—"

"Datura," she corrected. "And I doubt it. You said you started hallucinating shortly after—"

"I know, I know." My hands waved aside her objections. "But what if it's the plant itself that's the painkiller? My funky mind trip could have been the spell."

Brunette curls flew when Bebe shook her head. "I'm not experimenting. Your health and safety is my first priority as your physician."

"I've heard that before." My pout was back. All those claims that my safety was Duncan's first priority? *Ha!* Instead he left me in the tender care of his boss's girlfriend and his minions. "Where is the rat bastard?"

"Following up some leads." Alex strode into the kitchen and headed straight for the fridge. A bag of blood was quickly emptied into a large mug and placed in the microwave.

"He said the getaway car was stolen." I glared at the back of Alex's blond head.

He punched in the time and pressed the start button, before turning to face me. "Yup."

"So what leads are you talking about?"

He shrugged and leaned back against the counter. "Dunno."

It'd be so easy to fall for the easy-going Texan if I weren't already obsessed with Mr. Tall, Dark, and Asshole. I opened my shields, trying to get a hint from Alex's surface thoughts.

Alex grinned at my amateur probing. "And that's exactly why he didn't tell me and Mai what he was up to."

I needed a new plan. *Anne might know and she might even tell me.*

"No, she doesn't," Bebe said. "She and Jamal are heading up tonight's security detail."

Damn, I hated it when I accidentally transmitted my thoughts.

Bebe smiled. "Only when you're this tired. It's not unusual in young witches and new vampires. Go get some rest. You've had a rough night."

I opened my mouth to protest.

"Don't make me lock you in the conservatory for the night." A titanium will lay behind her words. And spending the night on the marble floor of the room she used for spell casting was about as appealing as spending it in Duncan's room.

At least, Duncan had a mattress.

I grumbled under my breath all the way upstairs. Alex and Bebe were laughing in the kitchen, which meant Alex, with his super-vamp hearing, repeated every insult I uttered.

———•———

I woke to a familiar hardness snuggled against my back. The arm hugging my waist wore the same jacket sleeve it'd been wearing at the restaurant. The clock on the nightstand silently blinked from "10:00 AM" to "10:01 AM." Last night's anger sat in my stomach, a lead weight on top of a dull ache.

"Phillippa and Tiffany have arrived. Bebe and Anne are trying on their bridesmaid dresses first. It should give you a chance for breakfast." Duncan's warm breath hit the sweet spot behind my ear.

Warm tingles in my pelvis decided to argue with the lead weight. "So they sent you up as their errand boy?"

He ignored my insult. "I volunteered." A slight hesitation marred his voice. "But essentially you are correct."

"Well, that just makes a girl feel special."

A soft sigh ruffled my hair at my sarcasm. "I wanted to make sure you were all right. And . . . I did not want you to think I was lying, even by omission."

"What a token apology." The lead weight crushed the tingles. I flung the covers and Duncan's arm aside and sat up to shoot the evil eye at him. "That's all I get this morning? A half-assed apology for waking me up?"

He sat up as well, the stone face in place. "What do you want from me, Samantha?"

"I want you to quit telling me what to do."

His voice rose to match mine. "I would not have to if you would use the sense God gave to a horse."

I jumped out of the bed. His bed. And planted my fists on my hips. Otherwise, they'd be planted on his handsome mug. "Are you calling me a horse?"

Vampire speed had him towering over me in less than a blink. "A mule is more like it. You are the most stubborn, infuriating—" His long fingers raked through his hair and yanked. Surprisingly, no clumps came out. His voice lowered with his next words. "Someone is trying to kill you, Samantha. Permanently, this time."

"No shit! I don't need some half-assed vampire detective telling me that!"

The door slammed open to reveal a scowling Alex in his tighty-whities. "Would you two mind keeping it down? Some of us are trying to sleep."

"Fine." I shot Duncan a dirty look. "We're finished anyway." I stalked past Alex and headed for the stairs.

———•———

Hellfire! She was not avoiding this discussion by running away again. Duncan started to follow, only to have Alex hold up a hand. The younger vampire leaned back to check the hall before facing him.

She's right. You're being a prick.

Duncan's lower jaw dropped. *She is totally disregarding her safety, and you're taking* her *side!*

Alex shook his head. *You just don't get it, do you? She wouldn't be this difficult if* you *hadn't been making plans behind her back.*

I did not do anything behind her back!

Alex crossed his arms and cocked his head to the side. *Vegas doesn't ring a bell?*

Mouth snapping shut, Duncan glared at his second. *I was waiting for her decision concerning her parents, and there is a difference between having a contingency plan and outright lying.*

Then why'd she have to find out your little contingency plan from Jamal instead of you? At Duncan's silence, Alex wiped a hand over his pale face before shaking his head again. "I can't help you if you're this clueless. I need some sleep." He turned and ambled in the direction of his room.

Duncan clenched his fists. He wanted a life with Samantha. She refused his proposal. So he had swallowed his pride and common sense. She refused his offer to live together. He tried to protect her, and now she refused to even have a civilized conversation with him.

All he wanted was to make sure she had a place to go to if she chose the Supernatural Protection Program. Las Vegas was a perfect choice. She could still work for O'Malley under an alias and have a multitude of celebrities to harass. It was fairly close so they could visit Tiffany, Max, and the baby. And . . . and . . .

Anger drained from his blood as Duncan contemplated Alex's pointed observation. Samantha knew none of this because he hadn't said a word to her. And now, she wouldn't listen to anything out of hurt feelings. In Tiffany's words, he'd royally fucked this one up. He wished desperately he had an earthly clue on how to make amends with Samantha.

Chapter 17

Still fuming, I stalked into the kitchen and into organized chaos. Emily Polk, the San Antonio pack's alpha female, had commandeered Caesar's kitchen for those guests looking for a non-liquid breakfast. She shoved a plate full of egg and cheese sandwiches into one of my hands and a glass of orange juice in the other.

"Go," she said with a shooing motion. "The girls are trying on the dresses in the conservatory. I'll have lunch ready for y'all between fittings and make-up."

Bless her heart. And I really meant it. Emily had witnessed my gargantuan appetite after my transformation two months back, and not only had taken it in stride, but had provided for me. I shoved half a sandwich in my mouth and chewed as I made my way down the hall to the back of the house.

And nearly dropped everything in my hands when I reached the doorway.

Three impossibly beautiful women fluttered around Tiffany, who stood on a stool and looked impossibly beautiful herself in an impossibly white outfit reminiscent of something a Greek goddess would wear. Gold trim sparkled in the late morning sun. A crown of white flowers nestled in her black hair and anchored a veil of the same whisper-thin fabric. Contrary to Antoine's opinion during the disastrous shopping expedition last week, the robes brought out the lovely, translucent pink shade of her skin.

She smiled at me, a radiant expression that would have dazzled me even if it wasn't such a contrast with her usual Goth accoutrements. "How do I look?"

My mouth opened and closed several times before my brain caught up. "Stunning." I took a deep breath. "Max is going to fall ass over heels when he sees you come down the aisle."

She blushed. She actually blushed. Smoothing down fabric across her still flat abdomen, she turned to look in the full-length mirror. "Do you really think so?"

Sucking in another deep breath, I noticed the strange odors from the three women arranging the folds of fabric draped across Tiffany's petite form. It took another whiff to identify oak, pine and what I thought might be sassafras.

Something wasn't right. They wore the same casual clothes any California twenty-something would wear. Then it hit me. Little motions of the three ladies were disjointed, out of place. One cocked her head in a birdlike manner while she examined the hem. Another fussed with nonexistent lint in quick, squirrelly motions. The third fluffed the veil streaming down Tiffany's back in the slow dreamy gestures of a butterfly spreading her wings.

A sharp clap spoiled my concentration. I turned to find Phillippa standing near me, a look of motherly pride on her patrician features.

"All right, ladies. Let's get started on Sam since she finally crawled out of bed."

Within seconds, the women, or whatever they were, had Tiffany off the stool and undressed. As Butterfly Woman hung the bridal dress, Phillippa divested me of my breakfast and the other two divested me of my jammies and underwear.

Before I could protest, they covered my nakedness in an outfit made of the same gauzy material as Tiffany's. With deft, sure motions, the women wrapped silver cords across my breasts and around my waist, eliminating the need for a bra.

Not that I needed one anyway with my pitiful B-cups.

Then I caught sight of my image in the mirror. Pale pink set off huge sapphire eyes in a startled face. My face.

Tiffany whistled and flashed a thumbs-up gesture. I turned to Phil to find a frown marring her face. Glancing down, I checked the material. Nope, no crumbs or juice stains.

I looked back up at Phil. "What's wrong?"

She opened her mouth, then shut it before giving a sharp shake of her head. "Nothing."

I would have let it go if her three buddies didn't share the same expression of discomfiture. Planting hands on hips, I swiveled to face them. "What's going on?"

All three of Phil's helpers ducked behind her before peering over her shoulders. Yeah, right. Like I was the one who could throw lightning bolts.

Phil muttered to them in a language I didn't recognize, and the women darted out the door. Tiffany's head swiveled, confusion smeared over her face, but Phil didn't bother to elaborate.

And I wanted some elaboration. "Phil—"

She held up a hand. "Don't start with me. I'm not sure . . ."

The anger simmering since I woke up hit a full roiling boil. "Then don't take that holier-than-thou tone with me, Little Miss Demigoddess. What the hell is going on?" When she remained silent, I added, "Your friends saw the same thing you did. Who are they? Forest creatures you made human to help you with your goddaughter's wedding?"

"Don't take your anger at Duncan out on me." Lightning flashed in her eyes, a not-so-subtle warning.

I waved my hands, the only way to express the exasperation that threatened to turn my anger into a steam explosion. "I'm sick to death of everyone keeping secrets from me."

Tiffany snorted in a vain attempt to swallow her laughter.

"What's so fucking funny?"

My snapping didn't deter her. "You're sick to death." She collapsed to the floor, rolling in hysterics.

I rolled my eyes, but her humor served to dispel the literal storm clouds swirling around Phil and me.

Phil smiled before she said, "I'm sorry, Sam. I don't—" Her attention flicked to the sunshine streaming through the window again before returning to me. "I called in some favors from the local nymphs to help with the dresses. As for what we saw—" Her expression grew pensive. "We're not sure."

Concern drank the steam of my exasperation and anger. No, not drank, sucked it down like an alcoholic on a binge. Mai had the same worried look last night Phillippa had now. "You mean, the nothingness Mai reported, or the strange magick the witches detected?"

Phil shook her head, curls from her loose bun bobbing in an erratic motion. "That's just it. It was neither of those things. It was more like—"

"Pure beauty."

We both faced Tiffany at her oddball words. She shrugged. "I don't know what else to call it. Do you?" She shot accusing glares at us.

A thoughtful expression crossed over Phil as she tapped an index finger on her cheek. She slowly nodded. "Yes, you're right. Sam's whatever-it-was reminded me of Aunt Aphrodite's glamour—"

I held up my hands. "Whoa, whoa, and whoa. Mai described the end of existence, and now you two are talking about me throwing off sex goddess vibes?"

Tiffany shrugged again. "Makes sense. This could be how the nanites manifest their version of vampire mojo."

"But—" I spluttered. "You're girls!"

"Geez, Sam." Tiffany matched my fists-on-hips pose. "It's not like we jumped you or anything."

Phil smirked. "Besides, you've seen the effect Duncan has on other men."

I snorted. Unfortunately, they were right to a point. "Jimmy the waiter is gay, and David Head's bi, so it's not like he converted . . ." My brain went into overdrive. The were musk I picked up both in Vegas and at Anthony's restaurant in Beverly Hills. I *had* smelled it before. Head's buddy at the party last week. "Shit!"

I jumped off the pedestal and raced through the door, gauze trailing behind me. The tree nymphs darted out of the way from their eavesdropping positions as I plowed past them. *Duncan!*

He was in front of me, pulling me into his arms before I cleared the hallway. "What is it? Samantha?" His gaze darted around, looking for a foe.

His worried tone cleared my shakes. Except I wasn't sure if it was anger or fear causing them. "The scent I told you about last night? I knew I smelled it before. It's the werewolf who was with David Head last Friday. That doesn't make sense though. Why would he be after me?"

Warm sandalwood covered my body, my thoughts. *Breathe, Sam.* Strong arms guided me to the kitchen and a chair. "Emily, would you please make a cup of tea for Samantha?"

I shot him an irritated look. "Coffee." I swear. How on earth do I keep picking tea-totalers?

The alpha bitch's husky laugh filled the kitchen. "No sissy drinks for my girl." Two seconds later, a mug radiated its reassuring aroma in front of my nose. I scalded my throat gulping it, but I didn't care. I needed some semblance of normalcy.

I stared at my liquid love, hoping to find answers in its velvety sienna depths. "It doesn't make sense. What the heck did I do to have a were send real zombies after me?"

"Were? What the fuck is she blathering about?"

I glanced up at Emily. Her brows pinched into an ugly scowl. I shuddered. I'd been on the receiving end of her claws once, and she'd only been mildly irritated that time.

Duncan's eyes glowed, another not so good sign. "What do you know about a were that accompanies David Head?"

"The New Orleans basketball player with the crazy hair?" Emily's eyes unfocused while she thought. "One of the Cajun pack's pups works for Jean-Pierre. He might know." She whistled, a sharp, piercing noise that had both Duncan and me wincing.

A tall, rangy man with reddish brown hair appeared in the doorway leading to the dining room. "Yes'm?"

"Marvin, who's the cousin on your mamma's side working for Jean-Pierre Rousseau?"

"Frankie?" The big were's attention flicked from the pack mistress to me. I didn't like the guilt flashing in his eyes.

Emily snapped her fingers. "Yeah, would he know what pup's hanging with—"

"That'd be him." Damn werewolf had been eavesdropping. "Frankie's just a runt. How could he be any threat to—" He waved a hand in my general direction.

I stood. How, I didn't know because the shakes were back in full force. "What. Did. You. Tell. Him. About. Me?" My voice had dropped a full octave.

"I—" Hair sprouted across his skin in response. "Pack Mistress." His head canted to reveal his throat. "Everyone's been talking about what happened at the Mallory Labs' shareholders meeting. I didn't mean nuthin' by it."

A pissed expression filled Emily's tight features. "Answer the girl's question." If my voice had deepened, hers was an outright growl. I glanced down past her waist. Crap. Claws extended from her furry hands.

A canine whine spilled from the were's throat before he answered. "We were just havin' a couple of beers over cards." Whites shone around his irises. "I told him how the Augustine queen had died, who did it, and why. And I told him about the metal zombie girls Mallory created, what they smell like and how she—" he jerked his head in my direction "—took out the other one."

This was probably the most stupid thing I've done in my death, but I stepped between Marvin and Emily. I laid a hand on his shoulder, and he flinched at my touch. "It's okay. Nothing's going to happen to you."

Emily wasn't quite as forgiving. "Get out of here!"

Marvin slunk out of the kitchen. Lucky for him, he hadn't morphed all the way. It'd take a month to get his tail out of his ass.

"Of all the stupid—"

"Let it go, Emily." Focusing on the empty doorway, I tried to process the why of everything. "Marvin's right. Everyone's talking about me these days." I sure didn't like being on the other side of the gossip column, but there wasn't a damn thing I could do about it.

I looked at Duncan. "Think Jean-Pierre knows one of his boys is hooking on the side?"

For once, his stony enforcer face had been replaced by an analytical expression. He blinked. "'Hooking on the side?'"

I crossed my arms in a vain effort to quell the shakes. "What are the odds Frankie's trying to collect on the fairies' bounty?"

Duncan nodded. "The thought had crossed my mind, but it does not explain the presence of zombies, much less how they came to be."

Tiffany appeared in the doorway. "Dammit, Sam! You are so not spilling coffee on that bridesmaid dress." I let her drag me back to the conservatory. I had to focus on one major crisis at a time.

———•———

Yvonne's hands shook as she sorted through her luggage, trying to decide what to wear to the Normal wedding. The last time had been Mother's second wedding, and the daisy print she'd worn as a ten-year-old would hardly be appropriate at an elite Los Angeles function. Being back in this house where that lunatic stalker had tried to kill her baby brother did not help her nerves either.

She laid the clothing out on the bed. A fingernail tapped her chin as she examined the five outfits she'd brought with her.

She tried to talk Davy into coming with her, but he pointed out the wedding was a business function and Jean-Pierre needed her. Then he stormed down the hall and disappeared into his bedroom. It did no good to speak with him when he was in one of his funks, but she'd hoped to distract him from whatever trouble he and Frankie were involved in.

"How long has the ex been living here?"

Nylons and panties flew from her hands in every direction. She turned and glared at Frankie. "Can't you knock?"

He rapped on the open door, a wry look on his face. "How long has David's ex been living here?"

She should have known the were would pick up the fresh scent, but there hadn't been time to come out and cast a spell to cover it. Not without both Davy and Frankie knowing. She still wasn't sure what prompted Davy to leave the hotel. He hadn't been inside this house in nearly two years, not since the night he and Brandon broke up. The same night the stalker broke in.

His flippant answer about not wasting money on the hotel contrasted sharply with his normal spendthrift ways. But then he'd never bothered to sell the house either. Like he hoped Brandon would come back to him someday.

Plucking undergarments off the floor, she stacked them in the open drawer. "Brandon needed a place to stay while he looked for a house here. It's only been a couple of weeks."

Frankie shook his head. "You shouldn't be keeping secrets from your brother, *chére.*"

She slammed the drawer and whirled to face him, beads clacking her anger. "I shouldn't be keeping secrets? What about you and Davy sneaking out at all hours and not one word about where you were? I know damn well it hasn't been your usual partying." When the were didn't say anything, she flung a hand upward. "What? No answer? How surprising."

Frankie crossed the bedroom, weariness hanging from his frame, and sat on the bottom edge of her bed. His gaze never left the open doorway, his body poised to bolt. "He's practicing again." The admission hung in the silence.

She edged around the bed and sat next to him, rolling and unrolling the stockings she had rescued from the floor. A deep sigh spilled from her. "And you've killed again."

The chartreuse shame rushed from his aura, nearly pulling her under in his despair. "Yes." The acknowledgement didn't even qualify as a whisper.

What a trio they made. None of them could outrun the mistakes they made as children. Maybe they were fated to repeat them over and over again. Linking his cold fingers in hers, she squeezed in gentle reassurance. "Jean-Pierre's here for the Augustine wedding. He'll know what to do."

Frankie leapt away. The sudden motion shook her. His face elongated into a snout. Hair sprang from every pore. "No! You can't!" The garbled words were more barks than English. "He said if it happened again, he'd turn me over to the pack."

She hated giving voice to her own disturbing suspicions. "Not if Davy forced you. How long has Davy known the binding is no longer holding his powers?"

Desperation and hope warred in Frankie's golden eyes. Then his snout sank to his chest. "He didn't make me do anything, Yvonne. I'm not hanging him out to save myself." Sorrow laced the gruff words.

Yvonne kept her voice gentle. "I won't say anything about you. But I need to know, Frankie. How long has Davy known that his *full* powers were back?"

Fur receded back into his skin. His despairing gaze flicked to the window before returning to her. Good. He'd stay, and Goddess knew she needed all the help she could get.

"I don't think he knew for sure until two days ago." He shrugged. "That's the first time I've seen him try to cast a complex spell."

She snorted. "Except for shorting out security systems."

Frankie nodded. The boys' penchant for sneaking out hadn't changed in all this time.

Her finger resumed tapping her chin. The binding spell was supposed to last Davy's lifetime. But from the ancient scrolls and books Jean-Pierre had acquired for her, it was nearly impossible for a binding on a true necromancer to last. Something about them being a fundamental force of nature. And that force of nature was now loose in Los Angeles.

She sucked in a deep breath. "Last night the first time he's raised the dead?"

Frankie shook his head. "Night before too."

That explained the absences. Damn it all, why couldn't the two men simply have gone to a brothel? *Aizan, what should I do?* But the loa was silent.

Yvonne rubbed her sweaty palms on her slacks. "I'm meeting Jean-Pierre in a couple of hours. Maybe he'll have an idea of how to contain Davy." The loa knew she had none. She didn't have the raw power alone to bind her brother, and the Lord knew he wouldn't quietly submit. Not this time.

She would need assistance. Maybe Jean-Pierre could petition the Silver Bear coven on her behalf. Frankie stiffened at her words, but she held up her hand. "Don't worry, I'll keep quiet about your situation, but we can't have Davy running around, animating every dead body in Los Angeles."

The were's head bobbed in silent agreement.

———•———

Fuck 'em both! David gunned the engine as the rental tore down the street. Good thing a house intercom was right outside Yvonne's room. His suspicion than Frankie would narc on him had been right. Dammit! He would have covered the were's ass for the murder of that girl. Frankie was practically blood. Knuckles tightened on the steering wheel at the blatant betrayal.

Maybe after he took care of that zombie chick, he'd deal with those backstabbers. Yeah, once she was in tiny pieces, then he'd clean house. And he knew just what would convince her to come to him. Alone. This time she wouldn't have her friends to protect her.

The car shot through a yellow light before whipping into the Hollywood Cemetery driveway.

Chapter 18

Once again, I piled into the limousine behind the girls, Mai at the wheel. This time though we resembled a series of pale moths, not jeweled beetles. The mood was quiet compared to two nights ago. Tiffany's hands trembled when she smoothed her veil back.

"You can still call it off. Max'll understand," I whispered.

If possible, her eyes would have shot daggers. Or No. 2 pencils.

"My baby is *not* going to be illegitimate. And quit foisting your commitment phobias on me."

The rest of the gals carried various expressions of annoyance. Time to back off. Besides, I hated to admit the kid was right. I prayed my own nerves were due to my own relationship issues and not my worries over another zombie attack. All we needed to do was get Max and Goth Girl hitched and on the plane for the honeymoon.

Except I couldn't call her Goth Girl anymore. She'd let the nymphs apply a delicate, natural-looking make-up, not the stark black and white stuff she normally favored. The kid looked absolutely freaking unbelievable. The maiden bride. A mother-to-be.

"Would you quit staring at me? I swear, Sam—" Tiffany jabbed a finger over the bouquet of white lilies and blue-green carnations she held.

I grinned like an idiot. "Max is a lucky man."

"Damn straight he is." Then her own idiotic grin lit up her face. "He's going to shit when he sees me, isn't he?"

"Yup." She joined me in a round of giggles.

When we finally stopped laughing for lack of air, she pinned me with a shrewd look. "You're breaking his heart, you know."

"Max?"

"Duncan, you moron."

"We're different than you and Max."

Her eyeroll wasn't as dramatic without the black eyeliner and mascara. "Yeah, you're both stubborn. And self-pitying. Oh, boo-hoo, I'm not Normal so I can't have a *real* relationship."

Now, Phil, Bebe and Anne were staring at us while Miko covered her mouth to hide her grin. Tiffany shot each of the supernatural women a disgusted look. "Oh, *puh-lease*. You all do it, and you know it."

She turned back to me, her fixed look sealing me to the limo seat. "Every relationship has problems. Pregnant at twenty wasn't *my* first choice, but condoms break." She shrugged. "I love Max and we'll figure out how to make it work. *You're* not even trying."

I couldn't answer her, couldn't even look at her. Damn, I hated when the kid was right. I stared out the window at passing headlights. Duncan and I, in a brief moment amidst the flurry of preparations, had agreed to talk after Max and Tiffany were on their plane tonight. How'd things get so complicated? I wanted him, but I was afraid of losing myself in his expectations. Just like I almost had with my parents. I locked my fingers so I wouldn't twist the stems of my own bouquet.

It wasn't just his expectations; it was my irrational need to rebel against any expectations. And Duncan hadn't said one word about me having to leave my job or my family. He left the decision up to me, despite making his contingency plans behind my back.

Was that what I was really angry about? That he didn't dictate terms, so I had nothing to protest? That he was trying to give me alternatives? That he actually cared enough to give me a choice?

I swallowed the lump gathering at the top of my throat. And I was pissed at him for what? Having an undead life I hadn't chosen? It wasn't his fault. Just my own pig-headed nature for not letting go of a story that had been bigger than I could handle.

A deep breath calmed the growing butterflies. One thing at a time. Get Max and Tiffany hitched. Catch the were rat-bastard trying to kill me. Then maybe Duncan and I could find a tolerable compromise.

———◆·———

Yvonne twisted the beaded evening purse as she paced in front of the gated estate. Augustine security had refused to admit her into the Brentwood mansion without an invitation. Not that she blamed the two blond half-fae watching the dark street. The beads slickened under her sweaty hands. Where was Jean-Pierre?

When Yvonne hadn't been able to reach him on his cell phone, she'd ordered the driver he'd sent for her to come to the Augustine estate instead of the wedding location in Beverly Hills. Had she already missed him?

A familiar essence, sandalwood and sea salt, filled her mind the same moment headlights appeared in the driveway. The iron gate began to slide open. She dodged through the narrow gap and ran to meet the SUV—as best as she could in heels.

The vehicle screeched to halt in order not to hit her, and the two front doors sprang open. Arms cabled with muscle caught her, and she writhed in a vain attempt to escape the half-fae's grasp. "Jean-Pierre!"

A familiar figure slid from the vehicle's passenger side. "Let her go, *mon ami.*"

The comforting face loosed the tears she'd been trying to contain the last two days. The second the imprisoning grip disappeared, she leapt into Jean-Pierre's arms.

"What's wrong?" No vampire suggestion in his smoky voice, just raw concern.

"It-it's Davy. He came out here b-because he thinks he's in love." Tears soaked the front of his dark purple suit jacket. The skull and crossbones tie clip dug into her cheek, but she didn't dare let go. To do so meant facing the ugly reality.

Warm comfort slipped into her mind, *seeing* the reason why she came with

David to Los Angeles. A soft chuckle rumbled beneath her ear. "*Chére*, there's nothing wrong with love."

"The b-b-binding's dissolved."

The vampires, the half-fae, even the night around them, stilled. A world holding its breath at the news a necromancer had been loosed upon it.

"Where is he?" He resumed stroking her braids.

"I-I don't know. He may have overheard Frankie and me talking about him. We heard tires squealing in the drive and the rental's gone."

"And where's Frankie?" The deep, dark bass fed reassurance into her soul.

"Out looking for him."

"Shifted?"

She nodded. "He said he'd have better luck as a wolf."

Patoi swear words rang in her ears. A soft buzz filled her mind as Jean-Pierre fed the information to someone approaching them.

"Yvonne?" There was no mistaking the authority in the Greek accent behind her.

Hating to leave the haven of Jean-Pierre's embrace, she broke away to face Caesar Augustine. Golden eyes glowed as he regarded her, followed by the brush of a master vampire's mind against hers.

"Why is your brother trying to kill Samantha Ridgeway?"

A deep breath didn't banish the tears, but it did ease some of her shaking. "The person he's in love with is Duncan St. James, and St. James told Davy he's engaged to Miss Ridgeway."

———•———

Mold and rot filled David's sinuses, perfume accenting the heady power. Firelight danced shadows across decaying skin. His neck and shoulder muscles ached with the strain of holding so many zombies in his thrall. He needed more, but his efforts pulled at the fraying threads of his aura.

More power, heh? I'll take something else in trade. Low-pitched laughter followed the words in David's head.

Dammit. He didn't have anything else. Fingering the bloody blade, he racked his mind for something he could use to bargain with.

What's that slinking behind you?

At Papa Ghede's question, he twisted to find canine eyes reflecting the firelight. Most of the shape was hidden behind a pedestal. The angel on top of the grave raised its hands in supplication. Relief and wariness swam through his blood at the familiar head. "Frankie?"

The dark figure whined, a plaintive sound in counterpoint to the sharp crackle of flames. He crept forward on his belly, inching across the disturbed earth. The acrid stink of fear rolled off the wolf. He reached Davy, shoving a cold nose in the crook of his elbow.

Don't do this, man.

Davy shoved the wolf's head away. "You've got no right telling me shit."

Frankie's sharp yellow eyes flicked from the blood dripping from Davy's arms, then back to his face. *Yvonne's gone to the wedding. She'll tell Jean-Pierre what you're up to. They'll be ready for you tonight. You won't get near that stupid reporter. Let it go.*

Davy stood and glared down at Frankie, anger reigniting. "Sis wouldn't have jack to tell him if you hadn't blabbed." The zombies shuffled restlessly in response to his emotions.

Ears flat, Frankie cringed at the nearest corpse stepping closer to him, but he didn't run. *She already knew you were practicing magick.*

Bitterness flooded David's mouth. "Bullshit! You were ready to run to the vamp too. I heard you."

Frankie rose to his paws, teeth bared. *I fucked up, too. You think I want both of us executed? I'm trying to help you.*

A glacier spread over David's fury. "Thanks. I appreciate that." The wolf got the hint, but too late. Claws and teeth were no match for the avalanche of corpses falling on him.

Frankie thrashed and bucked, but with legs and head pinned, he wasn't going anywhere. One golden eye rolled to meet David's. *Maybe I deserve this, but don't seal your fate with my death.* Weariness laced his mental tone, not the pleading David half-expected.

"I want you to know I always admired you." He plunged the knife into Frankie's chest. The wolf jerked once, twice.

Harsh laughter filled the bright, noisy Los Angeles night. *Done.*

— • —

The bee buzzing of rapid telepathic communication hummed outside and around my old bedroom at Mom and Dad's. Phil and Bebe primped the bride, but they couldn't disguise the split-second worried look they shared. I glanced at Anne, who resembled a Sixties flower child in her lilac dress and straight brown tresses. Complete with the acid trip look on her face.

Anne? What the heck's going on?

The faraway look disappeared, and she met my gaze. *There was a problem at Master Augustine's estate with one of Jean-Pierre's party.*

With her Amish upbringing, the vampire couldn't lie worth shit. Even telepathically. *Don't mess with me, girl.* In bare feet, I towered over the diminutive woman. *If you don't tell me—*

She checked Tiffany, but the kid was totally oblivious. Anne flashed fangs at me in warning. *Duncan doesn't want Tiffany to know. We are* not *ruining her wedding.*

Before I could add my opinion of Duncan's orders, a sharp rap brought everyone to their feet. My heart skipped a beat as the man in question entered the room. The sandalwood and spice that was uniquely Duncan filled the room. For once, he wasn't dressed in his ever-present black and gray. The pale azure suit matched Phil's dress, but where her outfit flowed, his hugged all the right places. The tie, a darker hue than the suit, knotted at his throat while the platinum tie pin winked at me. But his loving smile was solely for the bride standing before him.

Damn, would he look that good if this was our wedding?

"I believe you need something old." He fished in his pants pocket.

Tiffany shook her wrist so the gold and lapis lazuli beads on her bracelet tinkled. "Phil's bracelet stands for both borrowed and old."

He pulled out a gold locket from his pocket. "You should have this."

"But—" Tiffany's eyes were wide with shock. Actually, we all mirrored her expression. Duncan *never* took off his sister's locket.

"Your great-grandmother Margaret would want you to have it."

Tiffany bent her head and pulled the veil out of the way. "Just add fifteen more 'great's there, Uncle Duncan." Her smartass comment didn't hide the emotion in her voice as he fastened the locket around her neck. She fingered it before whispering, "Thanks."

Duncan smiled at her while she fluffed the veil back in place with Phil's help. "Everything is in place. Are you ready?"

Tiffany's big brown eyes grew even bigger, but she nodded.

An instant of the insect sound filled my head as he relayed the news downstairs, then he held the door while we traipsed through. Just when I didn't think he'd acknowledge my presence, his long fingers encircled my arm. Cool lips brushed mine.

It isn't Head's were behind the attacks. I'll tell you the rest after the ceremony. And then we'll discuss our future.

I must have been struck dumb. By the kiss, the news or the offer to *talk*, I wasn't sure. All I could do was nod. It didn't make sense. Why was there were musk all over the zombies that had attacked me the last two nights if Head's buddy wasn't involved? And why is Duncan acting Mr. Attentive all the sudden?

Trying not to read too much into the kiss or the promise of disclosure, I carefully maneuvered down the stairs in the freaking long dress and joined the girls behind the drapes leading to the patio.

Instead of last night's rehearsal fiasco, every step of Anne, Miko and Bebe was precise as they each strode down our makeshift aisle. Shoving my problems aside, I bent and gave Tiffany a quick peck on the cheek. "Break a leg, kid."

She squeezed my arm, and then I joined the parade. The patio concrete still held a hint of afternoon sun beneath my soles, but all too quickly gave way to cool grass. Guests sat on mismatched folding chairs. I tried to ignore the curious gazes and whispers coating my skin. And the sniffs as vamps and weres who hadn't met me marked my unusual scent. Nerves tingled and my face warmed at being on the receiving end of the gossip mill.

Mom and Dad sat to my left. Dad's face glowed with pleasure while Mom examined me with a critical eye. I gave them a smile as I approached.

Ahead of me stood Max, a ridiculous grin plastered to his face. His white suit glowed under the jury-rigged outdoor lighting. Thank God, Tiffany hadn't asked him to wear a toga. Those scrawny pale legs of his would have blinded the guests. I flashed him a thumbs-up as I joined the girls in front of Reverend Mitchell.

The trio of vampire musicians broke into the Bridal March, and the crowd rose. Flanked by Duncan and Phil, Tiffany strode down the aisle, head high and expression radiant. My eyes stung at the picture they presented, family no matter the circumstances. A small green monster snorted its displeasure. I couldn't see myself doing the same with my parents. Mom would claim it wasn't traditional for the mother to walk down the aisle with her daughter.

From the corner of my eye, I could see Max. His mouth hung open. It took him a couple of tries before he could close it. I knew the moment his and Tiffany's gazes met. His face held such an expression of utter happiness I wanted to hate him.

Tiffany and her guardians reached the altar. Duncan and Phil presented Tiffany to Max, and to my embarrassed pleasure, Duncan winked at me before they took their seats. Everything else receded into a wash of white noise as the minister droned on about the responsibilities of spouses to each other. Despite the boredom, I had enough presence of mind to exchange Max's ring with Tiffany's bouquet at the appropriate point.

I breathed a sigh of relief when Reverend Mitchell finally reached, "I now pronounce—"

I should have known better.

All the electric lights exploded.

Chapter 19

The screams of the Normal women swallowed the crack and sizzle of the shorted halogens. Somehow, Mom hit the daughter disappointment note by being one of them. The woman could bitch out the CEO of a Fortune 100 company for taking her parking spot at the country club, but a few blown bulbs sent her in a tizzy. Okay, not a few bulbs. Every light inside the house had failed too.

The entire assemblage on Tiffany's side rose as one, spreading out in a defensive stance. As if they had expected something like this. Maybe they did on a regular basis considering how many supernatural leaders stood on Mom and Dad's lawn.

Goosebumps rippled over my skin at the other possibility. But dang it, the lights hadn't gone out at the Rio or the restaurant.

The electrical failure didn't leave us totally in the dark. A nearly full moon floated on ambient city glow. Multitudes of candles bobbed in the pool. Tiny blue flames wavered under the buffet's warming pans. Animal eyes reflected the light balls and fireballs glowing in many witches' hands as the weres started stripping off clothing to Change. Neon colors sparked where vampires interspersed themselves between the shifting weres. Ozone from the electrical surge mixed with that from the witches' spells.

The fact that the power outage was serious enough to disregard supernatural rules about exposing their abilities in front of so many Normals sent my heartbeat into overdrive.

Duncan stepped between me and Tiffany. Reverend Mitchell thrust his crucifix at him. Not that I blamed the shaking minister. With fangs fully extended and eyes glowing neon green, my guy was an awesome sight.

"Be gone demon of Satan—"

Tiffany reached out and slapped the minister. "With all due respect, Reverend, shut the fuck up."

Duncan pressed his keys into my hand. "Get to my vehicle. Stan made sure it is at the end of the drive."

"But—" I glanced wildly around. Dad pushed his way over to Max, who now clutched Tiffany to him. Not that she looked real happy about him doing the he-man protection thing.

Duncan shook his head. "Do not argue with me this time, Sam. They will follow you. Mai!"

The enforcer jumped to my side, weapon drawn.

"LAX. You should be able to outrun the zombies to the airport. Get Sam in the air."

Anxiety nibbled the edges of my sanity. This was different from the last two attacks. I dug fingers into Duncan's arm. "What if they don't follow us?"

A flash of green light and a sonic crack swallowed Duncan's reply. The harsh grumbling of stone warned we were too late.

The fae shield's fallen! Bebe's warning echoed in my head.

Fallen, my ass. Those two bastards probably let the zombies in the front door with a bow and a smile.

In the wake of the good doctor's telepathic shout, the witches, both guests and catering staff alike, raced and darted, trying to encircle the crowd. An all-too-familiar moaning filled the air, but instead of the earth shaking beneath our feet, the masonry of the estate walls rippled and cracked. With a roar, a large section behind Mom's new foliage collapsed inward. Rock shrapnel flew at us and carved through the outer ring of witches before they had a chance to get their protective circle up. Cries of pain ripped the air, followed by the metallic scent of blood. Bebe's grandmother shouted orders, attempting to stitch the magickal ring back together, but too many of her people lay on the ground.

A flicker of movement caught my eye. Silent as ever, the corpses crawled and clambered over the rubble of the estate wall. Silent except for the rub and scrape of decaying flesh and bones against stone and trees.

"RUN!"

Duncan's combined vocal and telepathic yell almost knocked me over. Mai clutched my arm, dragging my stunned body toward the house. Bile ran thick in my throat at leaving Duncan and my family behind. But I couldn't fault his logic. Those things had been fixated on me both times before, and that many corpses would crush anyone in the way. The only chance the guests had was for me to draw them away.

Stan, one of the half-fae enforcers, met us in the kitchen. He supported his partner, Harry, with an arm under the smaller man's shoulders. Both men were covered with gouges and cuts under equally shredded clothing. I hurt just looking at the thigh-length slice on Harry's leg. Moldering flesh clung to the silver short swords they both carried. Any question I had about their loyalty to Caesar and Duncan dripped away with their blood onto Mom's immaculate white tile.

Stan shook his head, red droplets flipping from the ends of his blond buzz cut. "Bastards are in the front yard too."

"Duncan's vehicle?" Her gun was steady, but Mai's arm shook as it held mine.

"Can't get to it." Harry gasped out the words. "Too many of them."

"What if I clear a path?" All three enforcers stared at me like I'd lost my last marble. Maybe I had.

"Those things are obsessed with me. They'll follow me. If they don't, I can use a psy-bolt to knock them out of the way. Once you get to the SUV, I can outrun them and meet you on the street."

"Using one at the Rio—" Mai started. Like she had to remind me of the blinding migraines.

"No time to argue. Go." Stan waved his sword in the direction of the front door.

Now, I was the one pulling Mai through the house, leading the guys back to the front door. She was right though. I wasn't sure I could pull off another telekinetic stunt. My head no longer ached like a sonuvabitch, but it didn't mean I'd regained the mental strength.

Odd thumps from outside rattled Mom's knick-knacks on the wall shelves, and scratching assaulted our ears. Knowing what made the noises didn't help my nerves, but I charged forward anyway. It helped that three enforcers were covering my butt. I stopped in the entrance hall long enough to hand the keys to Mai. "Don't stop for me no matter what. Just get to the wheels."

Whites shown around her irises, but she gave me a curt nod. Drawing on her professionalism shoved my own gnawing fear out of the way. No more people were getting hurt on my account. I sucked a deep breath and launched myself forward.

Kicking open the front door knocked over two zombies. The third one lost his skull with a well-placed right hook. I jumped over the stairs, bowling over a few more in the move. Black terror rose when I got a good look at the front yard under the moonlight.

Zombies packed the lawn. The section of stone wall to the right of the gates had been destroyed on this side of the house too. More of them stumbled over the blasted rocks and clambered over the vehicles lining the drive. A rancid, coppery odor mingled with the ozone, and a thick, ugly black diamond and red haze surrounded the corpses.

This definitely wasn't like before.

Gibbering panic tried to drive me back to my childhood bedroom. *Hide under the covers where the monsters can't get you.* Except I knew such an act wouldn't save me. No, the zombies'd just pull the house down around my ears before stomping my liver to shreds and eating my brain.

"Move, woman!"

I jumped at Stan's shout. Snatching up one of the stupid concrete garden gnomes Antoine insisted Mom needed as a yard accent, I flailed at the closest zombies. Dust and gooshy body parts flew around me as I whacked the undead out of my way, making progress across the grass. A bullet whistled past my ear and blasted the face off a corpse I'd missed. I twisted and flashed Mai a grateful look.

"Pay attention." Coinciding with her reprimand, she aimed the semi-automatic at my head and fired. No, not my head. The upraised arm of the zombie about to bean me. The bone snapped with a dry crack, but the fallen hand grasped the blades of grass to crawl toward me. The gnome smashed through the torso of the still-standing corpse, and my heel crushed the inching finger bones.

We were half-way to the gates. But it was getting harder to swing the gnome without hitting one of the enforcers. The boys were having the same problem with their weapons. Mai had given up on her gun as well. Two slim swords gripped in each hand hacked in a vain attempt to clear us some space, but corpses pressed us together.

"Sam?"

The tremor in Mai's voice kicked my fear up a notch, and I pulled all that yellow emotional sludge into a massive ball. Facing the gates, I yelled, "Fire in the hole."

The psy-bolt slammed through the zombies in front of me, shattering many and knocking apart the rest. Despite the amount of power I expended, I didn't collapse under a wave of agony. A ghost of the leftover headache from Thursday nagged my head instead of the full-blown migraine I'd normally get using that much telekinetic force. I wasn't about to stop and analyze the situation. The four of us raced the remaining yards for the SUV. I threw the poor garden gnome at the zombies ambling toward us before I grabbed Harry from Stan and tossed him in the backseat. I scrambled in after him.

Mai shifted into gear before the vehicle doors slammed shut. The Suburban jerked when Mai mowed over the first couple of zombies who reached us. It rocked again as tires rolled over the fallen front gates. Then we were clear of the estate and racing down the street.

I peered over the backseat. No. That could *not* be right. I blinked and focused again, a new iciness filling my veins. More zombies shambled over the rubble and into the grounds. Not one of them looked in my direction.

"Mai, stop!"

She slammed on the brakes, and the SUV squealed to a halt.

"Are you fucking insane?" Harry's eyes widened beneath his crimson-soaked bangs.

"They're not following us!" If I hadn't been afraid before, gut-churning horror filled me now. As one, the others looked out the rear window, and their eyes reflected my fear. Dammit, I couldn't leave innocents behind to be slaughtered by the undead.

There was no question or vote. Harry slid into me as we tilted on two wheels when Mai whipped the Suburban in a U-turn. The engine revved as she punched the accelerator, and we raced back to the house.

Chapter 20

Mai plowed over more upright zombies, gunning the Suburban up the driveway. The boys and I hung on as best we could with all the bumps and jerks. Swerving past guest cars, she cut across the lawn. In her wild careening over the grass, she hit as many walking corpses as possible while still making progress toward the back of the estate. The SUV tires churned soil and body parts when Mai whipped it around the garage in a slick ninety-degree turn and slammed on the brakes.

Splashes of lightning and fireballs illuminated the scene. Wolves raced, leaped and dived, using guerilla tactics to pull down and shred zombies. The three vampire masters and their people formed a protective ring between the Normal guests and the zombies not engaged by the werewolves. But in their panic, the Normals were more of a threat to the vamps than the zombies. Screams and the smell of burnt sandalwood filled the air. Dammit. The Normals had figured out the effect of silver on the vamps. Another group of zombies surrounded a clump of people by the temporary pulpit.

There wasn't enough room to get past the pool without dunking the Suburban. We piled out and charged toward the carnage. Okay, three of us charged. Harry limped to the driver's seat, revved the engine and mowed down the corpses shuffling around the garage to keep them from joining the backyard fray.

Mai tossed me one of her swords, and I waded into the mess, swinging and hacking. We couldn't reach one of the vamps in time. Two zombies played taffy pull with him. His head popped off, followed by the stench of rotten meat when the vamp's body dissolved into goo.

Sorrow and anger raged at the waste. With a single chop, I sliced the zombie on the right in half. Mai did the same on the left. Stan hacked his way through the clump at the altar, shouting Bebe's name.

I couldn't take the time to figure out the half-fae's plan. A sharp shove sent me crashing backward over one of the buffet tables. Three zombies stomped through steaming broccoli and green beans, reaching for me. In the seconds it took me to untangle the sword from the tablecloth, bony fingers arched and slashed across my neck.

Bright red arterial blood spurted up and over me and the zombies before I could slap a hand over the deep cut. Rotten tongues snaked out to taste the splashes. One of the zombies removed the aviator glasses dangling from his intact ear and slurped red liquid off the rims. My stomach heaved at the sight, but the three were no longer interested in me, instead licking as much of my blood off their arms and hands as they could. I waited for them to explode into silver dust like Sierra Mallory had when she tried to drink from me.

Nope, I wasn't going to get that lucky. They were real zombies, not cybernetic wannabes like Sierra and me. The three licked each other's body parts out of reach of their own tongues. In a gross and unsettling way, the picture reminded me of the time Max sprayed catnip all over me, much to our cat, DC's delight.

The blood seeping beneath my fingers slowed as nanites worked to repair my sliced carotid. I rolled to my feet to face more immediate concerns, only to catch sight of a zombie punching Tiffany in the stomach.

She fell backward, her head smashing into the coffee urn at the end of the line of tables. *No!* All her fears spoken in the limo ride home from Vegas were coming true. I ran, but somehow, Max beat me to her. He swung a music stand at the corpse coming after Tiffany. The zombie caught Max's wrist and squeezed. Max's howl didn't block the crack of bones breaking. The zombie raised its other fist.

No, no, no! "No! Go back to hell, you fuckers!"

I yanked the zombie off Max. Just like last night behind Anthony's, I punched and kicked with every scream and swear word emphasizing my emotions. The zombie disintegrated under my blows, and I stamped its entrails into Dad's formerly pristine lawn.

I bent and wheezed, trying to catch my breath. Exhaustion blackened the edges of my vision. It didn't make sense. Beating one freaking zombie shouldn't have sapped my strength, unless it was a delayed reaction from the telekinetic stunt I'd pulled in the front yard. My skin prickled and I looked around.

Everyone in the yard who was still conscious stared at me. No sound whatsoever except my harsh gasps for oxygen. And the zombies . . .

They lay scattered around the people and wolves, all of them in the same state as the one I had just pummeled. My heart lodged in my throat. They weren't the only ones not moving. Quiet sobs rippled the air. Mobile guests knelt next to prone figures, helping where they could, covering the bodies where they couldn't. What had been a joyous occasion had been turned into a carnage scene out of a horror movie.

A tap on the shoulder made me jump. I whirled to find one of the zombies who'd attacked me at the veggie table. Except his flesh was no longer hanging off his bones. Pink skin surged with blood. Vitality. Life.

"Ya wouldn't happen to have a stogie, would ya, toots?"

Chapter 21

I blinked blood and sweat out of my eyes. Nope, he was still there. In fact, his two buddies joined him. I blinked again. I wasn't seeing things. No aggressive moves, just looking at me as their desiccated skin knitted back together and filled out while I watched.

"By the way," Zombie Number One waved at the chaotic scene, "where are we?"

Eyeballs plumped and cartilage elongated the nose once again. *No, it couldn't be.* He shoved the huge aviator glasses back on his restored nose. *Dammit, I covered his funeral last fall.* I blinked for the third time, and any air I'd reclaimed left in a whoosh.

Mortimer Stern stood before me. Uncle Morty. Mr. Comedian, himself. The man. The myth. The rejuvenated corpse.

Like my death could get any stranger.

Uncle Morty waved a hand in front of my face. "You okay, toots? You're kind of pale." His eyes traveled down my body, taking in my blood-drenched gown and gore-encrusted feet, before working their way back to my boobs. Figured. The man had been a notorious lech in life. "What kind of production are you working on, toots?"

"Who's the kid?" Familiar red hair haloed around the face of comedienne Lily Bell. And behind her stood the Nose himself, Bill Faith. Three major stars from my grandparents' generation in front of me. Three major stars looking like they did in their prime instead of wrinkly old people. Okay, three dead major stars dressed in their moldy burial clothes, and I couldn't think of one coherent thing to say.

Bill Faith leaned over to whisper in Uncle Morty's ear. "She mute?"

"Don't know. Hey, toots? Can you talk?" He lifted a hand and pantomimed a moving mouth. "You know, talk?"

I relaxed my jaw muscles and muttered, "Stop calling me 'toots.'"

"Sam!"

"Stay here." I jabbed a finger at the ground and took a step away. They didn't so much as twitch, the curious expressions remaining on their restored faces. After shooting another glare at the trio, I stumbled the couple of steps back to where Max huddled with an unconscious Tiffany in his good arm. The right one bent at an unnatural angle that churned my stomach.

"Where's Bebe?" Tears coursed down his face. Ashy fear leaked out of every pore. "She's—"

I bent and checked Tiffany's pulse. It was there, and she stirred under my touch. But . . .

"This is all your fault!" Mom's screech rent the air. She stomped over to where I crouched next to Max. "You just couldn't let Max have his day, could you?"

Caesar grabbed her shoulder. "Stop." She sucked in a breath to yell. "Now, Mrs. Howell," he finished. No *suggestion* at all, but from the look in his neon yellow eyes, his bloodlust was barely in check.

I prayed Mom would get a clue, but she was just getting her groove started. She shook an index finger less than an inch in front of his fangs. "Don't you think you can scare me with your vampire act, you undead freak."

I rose and joined Caesar. "Mom, shut up. We've got to get the injured to the hospital."

She opened her mouth.

"I said stop, Mom." Everyone around us froze. Ri-i-ight. Like I was scarier than the Prince of Vampires.

The ugly stench of fear rolled off Mom, but she disguised it well. Her familiar haughtiness filled her eyes. "Or what? You'll smash me like you did all the zombies?"

God help me, I had done it. Just like last night. I couldn't worry about this new ability right now. Instead, I matched Mom's nasty look. "Don't tempt me."

"Duncan? Max, where's Uncle Duncan?" In the silence, Tiffany's hoarse voice carried across the crowd. No one answered her plaintive plea.

I took in the various piles of sludge that formed vampire remains. I reached out with my thoughts, but met with empty blackness instead of the familiar warmth. No. No, this couldn't be happening.

My heart stopped before it broke in two.

———•———

The vinyl waiting room couches in the Maura Lannigan wing of Good Samaritan Hospital were Federal blue instead of the avocado of Los Angeles Memorial. It didn't make them any more comfortable. For the second time in two months, I slouched in crappy cushions, mourning the death of someone close to me.

At least Fred Nguyen's assassination back in January had been a normal death. Not that a van smooshing my LAPD source into road pizza was a good thing for him or me. His death had been the red pill for my trip to the supernatural wonderland.

A trip made more surreal by the events of the wedding. The Los Angeles leaders pulled strings to get their people, both supernaturals and Family, transported here while the non-Family Normals were sent to Cedars-Sinai. Probably with a little memory-erasure during the ambulance ride.

As far as the outside world knew, this wing specialized in treating rare forms of cancer. The cover of John Lannigan's late alpha female allowed money to be donated by the supernatural community. The hospital board never questioned the only stipulation for the donations, that Bebe supervised, and had sole discretion, over the wing.

The fingers of Max's good hand twined around mine as we sat. I'd offered to sign his cast, but he murmured, "Later."

There was nothing worse than waiting in a hospital. Dad shoved a cup of coffee in my free hand and dropped a few packages of cheese crackers he'd scrounged for my growling stomach in my lap. Mom took up the role of pacer when he took the chair next to Max and me. My trio of restored zombie comedians perched on the couch across from us, and for the most part kept their mouths shut. No one knew what to do with them, so Caesar ordered them to stay with me until Bebe could examine them. Right now, our witch doctor needed to care for the living.

A few yards away, Caesar stood in a whispered conference with the other two vampire masters. Jean-Pierre wouldn't meet my gaze. Virginia shot me withering looks from time to time. She was the only vampire master with a bodyguard, a tasty hunk with straight blue-black hair and cinnamon-flavored coloring. A witch I didn't know stood with the vampires, an eclectic from her simple ball studs and hoop earrings. A multitude of braids were gathered at the top of her head, each ending in a bead of a different kind of stone. From the way she inched closer to Jean-Pierre under my watch, she probably worked for him.

Closing my eyes, I leaned back against the couch. I'd been so excited to talk to Virginia. When Caesar had arranged for me to interview her after the wedding for the vampire histories he wanted me to write, I'd been ecstatic about talking to one of the first Europeans born on American soil. When I told Duncan, he said to tread lightly with her . . .

Tears streamed from beneath my lids. Damn, I'd gone almost five minutes without thinking about him. I wanted to believe he wasn't one of the piles of vampire sludge scattered around Mom and Dad's back lawn. God, how I wanted to believe!

The naked, raw silence reigned in my psyche.

Max's hand slipped from mine, and he tugged my head to the crook of his shoulder. "They'll find him."

I sniffed, shooting for a subject change to keep the floodgates in check. "You need to worry about your wife and your baby."

A dry chuckle thrummed through his chest. "You mean fiancée. The ceremony wasn't completed." His voice dropped to a whisper so Dad wouldn't hear. "And I think the vampires have already erased Reverend Mitchell's memory."

I would have laughed if I didn't have a lead weight sitting on my chest. Swiping my nose, I said, "It's probably for the best."

Max stiffened underneath my cheek. "Me and Tiffany not getting married?"

Blinking gummy, swollen eyes, I looked up at him. "No, I mean Reverend Mitchell. He almost stroked out when Duncan—" The words jammed in my throat.

Max sighed. "Maybe Tiffany was right. The civil ceremony at the court house would have been less—" He stared at the operating room doors for a long time before he finished. "Just less."

I squeezed his knee. "Tiffany'll be fine. They'll both be fine." Now, if Bebe would come out and verify my wishful thinking . . .

With a pneumatic hiss, the doors at the other end of the corridor opened to reveal Alex. Compared to my gore-crusted gauze, his jeans were pristine. It made me wish I'd had a chance to clean up. Gross was becoming my natural state. And my tears would be a little less obvious in the shower.

Cowboy boots tapped a somber rhythm as he strode down the hall to report to Caesar. A status report Duncan should be giving to the coven master. Alex glanced our way, but wouldn't meet my eyes either.

He kept his voice low, but damn it all if he didn't switch to French for his update. I should have paid more attention to the private tutor Mom insisted on in high school. If I had the energy to care, I would have given Alex hell for hiding stuff from me. All I could do was stare at the floor.

At Alex's mention of Jamal, my head jerked up to see Caesar's still expression.

Eerily still expression. The last time he had that look had been two months ago. The night Duncan had killed Caesar's twin sister to save my ass.

Oh God! Even my exhausted brain could put two and two together. Jamal was dead. His laughter flickered through my memory. He and Kensai had been together nearly four centuries. How the hell was Kensai dealing?

This was all my fault.

I couldn't breathe when Alex flicked a look in my direction then whispered something else.

"What do you mean he's missing?" Mom's voice jerked me out of my wallowing. She strode over to the vamps, arms crossed.

From the looks she got from the vamps, I would have thought she'd grown another head.

"*Oui, je parle francais*," she snapped. "Now, what do you mean Duncan's missing?"

My heart jerked. Missing? The vinyl crackled when I rose. Or it may have been the dress. Caesar and Alex shot worried looks my way before Caesar's expression turned imperious.

"This is a private conversation, Mrs. Howell."

Mom's arms loosened and a manicured index finger waved underneath his nose. "Don't you dare take that tone with me, you undead freak." Weird. The sounds she made weren't her normal high-pitched screech. More like Mr. Cuddles growling a warning.

I couldn't bear to let go of the tiny sliver of hope. "Mom." I crossed to them and laid a grimy hand on her arm. She didn't so much as flinch at the possible stain on her designer suit.

Instead, she met Caesar's mojo head on. "And don't you dare try that mind control shit with me." Her body shook, but her voice remained steady. "My grandbaby may be dying in there. The last thing poor Tiffany needs is for you to lose her uncle's body too."

"Mom."

She turned to me. Unshed tears shimmered under the ugly fluorescent lighting. "Don't defend them, Samantha. You and Max should have told me."

What? She never blamed both of us for anything.

Caesar's sharp voice sliced through the frigid hospital air. "This isn't your business."

"Listen up, you undead son-of-a—"

"Mom!"

"Stay out of it. Samantha."

"Mom, they're not undead. I am."

Mom's head turned toward me in slow motion. Total blankness that had nothing to do with her Botox injections filled her face.

I sucked in a harsh breath, trying to get air past the lump of grief in my throat. "I am, Mom. I-I died two months ago. Duncan tried to save me, but—" There. I finally said it. After agonizing over my decision for two freaking months, I blurted the truth out in the middle of a hospital waiting room after zombies crashed my brother's wedding.

Horror dawned on her face, and a fist rose to her mouth. "Oh, my God. He turned you into one of them?"

"No, Mom."

The fact that Dad stood behind her, hands gripping her shoulders, finally registered. "What happened, honey?"

Within two minutes, the Reader's Digest condensed version spilled from my lips, including my kidnapping, death and transformation at the hands of billionaire Tyrone Mallory and Caesar's twin sister, Selene, as well as Duncan's rescue of me.

"Wait a minute." Dad held up an index finger, a puzzled look on his face. "Did you die from the nanites or the gunshot wound while you were escaping?"

"Well . . ." My dirty toes brushed against the formerly sterile linoleum. "We're not sure."

"But surely the Mallory girl—"

"Um—" The wheels in my brain turned furiously, but there's no easy way to admit you've committed homicide to your parents. "I kind of stabbed her through the heart after the nanites had been injected into her."

"You what?" Mom's mouth dropped open.

"With a wooden spoon. I couldn't reach the butcher knife." If Mom's eyes could have jumped out of her skull, they would have. "It was self-defense. She was choking me with a fireplace poker," I finished lamely.

"Dr. Zachary didn't have a chance to examine either Sam or Sierra Mallory between the introduction of the nanites and their mortal wounds." I didn't notice Max had joined us until he spoke.

Mom's shrewd gaze shifted from Max to me. "So what really happened to Sierra Mallory? The rumor around the club was she had cancer. Or is that a cover story for you killing the poor girl?"

Nice to know things were back to normal between us. "She did have cancer," I said with gritted teeth. "I was the guinea pig for the cure. The nanites eliminated the leukemia, but somewhere along the way, Sierra turned psychotic. When she sucked my blood, both of our nanites hit a programming glitch, and she exploded."

"She exploded?" Not even the Botox treatments could keep Mom's eyebrows from climbing halfway up her forehead.

"But you're saying you're a zombie, right?" Poor Dad. From the furrows in his forehead, he was trying to accept this. Maybe it hadn't been such a good idea to tell them.

"Damn. After that load of bullshit, I need something stronger than a cigar," Uncle Morty muttered.

In unison for once, the entire family turned to Morty and said, "Shut up."

"No." Mom shook her head. "No, I don't accept that. You're nothing like those things." She jabbed a finger in the vampires' direction.

I rolled my eyes. "Of course not, Mom. Vampires aren't dead. They just have a chronic disease. I'm a zombie, and yes, I am dead."

"But you're not like the ones that-that—" Dad cleared his throat.

I shook my head. "Because of the nanites, Dad. Those were real, summoned-by-magick zombies."

A snicker sprouted from the other couch. "With that story, it sounds more like she's the bride of Frankenstein."

I turned to Bill Faith. "Opinions of the 'normal'—" My fingers made air quotes. "—zombies are not welcome. So keep your mouth shut unless you want to end up as Dad's new lawn fertilizer."

Bill's jaw snapped shut, and he went back to flipping through a *Better Homes and Gardens.*

I couldn't deal with everything at once. Wrapping my arms around my body, I took stock. Jamal was dead. Tiffany was still in surgery. It wasn't like I could help either of them, so the next priority was Duncan. My attention focused back on Alex. "Spit it out. What's going on?"

The tall Texan twitched. It sucked being the bearer of bad news, but I wasn't about to let him off the hook. I had to know, so I gave him the Siamese stare-down I'd practice for years on our cat, DC. And it wasn't like Mr. Psychoanalysis-for-everyone-but-him to avoid the truth.

At a slight nod from Caesar, he met my eyes and took a deep breath. "We've been able to identify all the remains through personal effects." *Jewelry and watches mired in goo,* my mind filled in. "We haven't found anything that we know is Duncan's. Not even his sister's locket." His eyes closed in resignation, then opened with a pleading look.

Like he needed my forgiveness. Hell, I was the one who needed everyone's forgiveness. If I'm the one animating the dead as Mai suggested . . .

Then his statement of evidence registered. "He wasn't wearing Margaret's locket." Caesar and Alex jerked at my revelation. "He gave it to Tiffany as her 'something old' right before the ceremony." A small blister of hope developed on my heart. God, it was going to hurt when it popped.

"This one?" Max dug awkwardly with his left hand in his suit trousers. Blood had dried in reddish-brown spatters across the white legs. He pulled out the handful of jewelry Tiffany had worn during the ceremony. "Bebe took these off her in the ambulance." In his open hand lay the simple gold wedding band, Phil's bracelet, and the locket.

I reached for it, only to have Jean-Pierre's eclectic slap my hand away. "No. Don't contaminate it any more than it is. I may be able to trace where my brother's taken St. James."

My overloaded gray matter finally regurgitated Ralph's story. David Head's sister was Jean-Pierre's eclectic. And before the wedding ceremony, Duncan said it wasn't Head's were buddy behind the attacks . . .

"You bitch!" I reached for her throat. She scrambled away, running for the doors.

Except I never touched her. Caesar and Jean-Pierre grabbed my arms when I was millimeters from her neck. Writhing and yanking, I tried to reach her, but the master vampires' grip might have been concrete for all the good it did.

"Stop it. Samantha, stop. Killing her won't help Duncan." Caesar's words penetrated the red haze covering my vision.

I gasped and stopped fighting the men. "Okay, fine. I won't kill her." Caesar and Jean-Pierre's hold relaxed. Shooting her a murderous look, I added, "Yet."

"Tracking spell?" Alex's words floated somewhere behind me, and the bitch nodded. She didn't take her eyes off me, or release her death-grip on the door handle.

I shook my head, vigorously enough Jean-Pierre's hand tightened on my upper arm. "No, Bebe'll do it. Not her."

"I'll do what?"

With our little homicidal tableau, I don't think anyone in the waiting room heard Bebe and Ben Epstein come out of the operating room. She turned and gave her step-grandfather a one-armed hug. "Go get some rest. And thank you."

He patted her on the back. "You too, little girl." Dark circles ringed his eyes, and their normal twinkle had been ground under the foot of exhaustion. Giving everyone a curious look, he shuffled past Head's sister and out the doors.

Ignoring the eclectic's advice, Max pressed the jewelry in my hand and approached Bebe with an anxious expression. "How's Tiffany?"

"She'll be fine." Bebe pulled off her operating room cap, and wild curls sprang everywhere. "We got the internal bleeding stopped and healed. Same with the concussion." She gave Max a tired smile. "A few days of bed rest and she'll be back to her charming self in no time."

"The baby?" Fear tinged Max's voice. Mom stepped closer to him and wrapped an arm around his uninjured side.

Bleakness filled Bebe's face. "It's too early to tell."

"What kind of doctor are you?" I could hear the sneer in Mom's voice.

Bebe's posture stiffened. "I'm sorry, Mrs. Howell. They don't cover zombie assaults in med school." She turned to Max, her body language freezing Mom out. "The first twenty-four hours are critical after this kind of physical trauma to the mother. Ben and I healed the damage, but the body still registers it." She sucked in a deep breath. "If Tiffany's body doesn't spontaneously abort, she should be able to carry to term just fine."

Max shrugged off Mom's embrace. He reached out and pulled Bebe to him in an awkward one-armed hug. "Thanks," he whispered. Lilac gratefulness mushroomed in a cloud around him.

She nodded. "You can go on back and sit with her in recovery." When Max disappeared behind the doors to the operating section, she strode to where the guys still stood between me and the eclectic and eyed me. "Now, what do you want me to do?"

Rapid-fire buzzing brushed my mind as Caesar filled her in.

She sighed, her relief palpable. "And here, I thought you people wanted something difficult." She held out her hand, and I untangled the chain from the bracelet before dropping the gold in her upraised palm.

"You need to set a circle—"

Bebe eyed Head's sister. "I don't need jack, little girl." She paused and grinned. "I take that back. A fat bottle of Mr. Daniels would be highly welcome after the night we've had." Her mood sobered. Eyelids dipped and ozone spiced the air. After a couple of seconds, her eyes blinked open, and she dangled the locket in the air. "Here you go, Sam. Just hold it in front of you, and it'll point the way." The locket swung on its chain for a second before hovering to the right. "It'd be best if you—"

A scream choked off her words. Her body convulsed and shook, collapsing to the floor. I reached out to help, but the moment I touched her, black diamond fire seared my skin and incinerated my mind.

Chapter 22

Agony racked Duncan St. James's skull, driving him away from comforting unconsciousness. Tiffany's wedding. Samantha in danger. The desire, the need to chase those thoughts drove him. Unfortunately, full coherence lay in the same direction of his pounding head. Resigning himself to the inevitable, he opened his eyes. The darkened bedroom seemed vaguely familiar, but recognition escaped him, and not because of his blurred vision.

Instinct said it was after sunrise, but the heavy drapes blocked the fatal rays. He blinked, tried to lift his head to check his surroundings. Cheeky idea. A spike of pain drove the wave of dizziness, and sweat trickled into his eyes. Maybe Tiffany would have suggestions on combating the swirling nausea.

Another tactic then, but trying to raise his right arm seared his flesh. An ugly odor confirmed the burning long before he could gather the strength to look. Silver encircled his wrists. A painful glance down showed similar shackles on his ankles. Not to mention he was stark naked.

How humiliating.

Last night. He closed his eyes, trying to concentrate on the previous evening's memories. The attack on the wedding. He'd sent Sam out of the Howells' estate with an enforcer escort. He turned to Tiffany and then . . .

And then . . .

One of the zombies must have bashed in his brains, considering the level of discomfort and lack of memory. Bloody hell. Where had he been taken? He took a deep breath to calm the nausea. Sharp, acrid ozone coated with ginger and an earthy masculine scent wafted through aching sinuses.

David Head. His home in Los Angeles? A possibility since the hotel said Head and his party checked out Friday morning. Yvonne was right. The boy had gone off the deep end if he was kidnapping vampires in addition to trying to kill Samantha.

Duncan jerked the manacles again, only to have the silver fry more skin. God only knew where Head was. The throbbing made detection of anyone else in the building difficult. He had to escape, find Samantha before Head—

No, the idea didn't bear any more scrutiny. She was a resourceful and clever woman. If she could escape Selene, she could escape Head. Those thoughts didn't make his current predicament any more palatable.

Metallic noises reached his ears. It took precious time to recognize a key in a lock. Head was returning. He renewed the painful efforts to extract himself from the manacles.

———— •◦• ————

Brandon shoved the key in the lock. His therapist was right. Running away from admitting his identity hadn't solved his problems. Neither was using Yvonne to touch and not touch the man he still loved. He needed closure with David, even if it meant David kicking his ass. He turned the key and entered.

The odor of something burning smacked him in the face.

He raced for the kitchen. No, stove and oven both were off. He ran down the hallway, the acrid odor worse with every step.

Oh shit! Had David left incense or candles burning? His carelessness with both had been an ongoing source of irritation when they were together.

He hit the master bedroom door at full speed, and it slammed open. His mouth opened in shock. In the near darkness, a naked man lay in the middle of David's custom-made bed, spread-eagle and chained. Brandon flicked the light switch. The stranger blinked rapidly, but it was Brandon's stomach that did a queasy somersault. Around the cuffs on the man's wrists and ankles, ugly burns oozed blood and mucus.

"Who the bloody hell are you?"

Brandon absorbed the sight. Longish, black hair, one heck of a body, and a British accent. Yeah, he could understand why David might want to chain the stranger to his bed. But the David he knew wouldn't hurt someone. Not like this.

"I said—"

"I'm Brandon." He almost added "David's boyfriend," but that wasn't true anymore, hadn't been true for a long time, and he didn't think the stranger would appreciate the comment. Not the way those intense green eyes practically glowed. "Brandon Tyler."

"Find the bloody keys!" Somehow this guy was freaking intimidating while chained to the bed and stark naked.

Brandon crossed to the bureau, set down his keys and the plant he'd brought for David, and yanked open the top drawer. Yep, David still kept his toys in the same place. He rummaged through various lotions and plugs until his found a key on a slender silver chain.

"Here we go." Reaching the top post, he unlocked the first cuff. The stranger hissed when the metal brushed the top of his right hand. Ugly redness spread across the skin, and small blisters popped to the surface.

"What the—" Brandon checked the manacle, then his own hands. Cool metal and unmarred pale skin. "Are you allergic to this?"

"Yes, you imbecile!"

Brandon glanced down. If he didn't know better, the stranger's canines were longer, too long for a normal mouth. He took a step back.

Air whistled as the stranger sucked down a lungful of air and released it. "I apologize for calling you names. My head aches, and—" He glanced down his body before giving Brandon a rueful smile. "This is not normally how I meet a young gentleman. I am Duncan."

"Um, sure." *Figures.* This Duncan was just someone David picked up at a bar or something. "Where is David, by the way?"

Duncan's eyebrows rose. "You do not know?"

He shook his head and released Duncan's ankle, holding the appendage away from the silver as best he could. "I came over, hoping to talk to him." Dang, the man had cold feet. What the hell was the attraction when frozen toes were one of David's pet peeves? He walked around the bed.

"Hey, Duncan, I've got tea, scones and—"

Brandon whirled to find David standing in the doorway, holding two bags and a drink tray. Chocolate eyes widened as David took in what he was doing. He took a tentative step toward his ex. "David?"

Steaming tea spattered over the hardwood floor and bags flew. David dropped to his knees, his hand slamming down on the silver piping near the doorway. Blood orange light sizzled across Brandon's eyes. When he blinked the spots out, David was gone.

Brandon strode to the open doorway and literally hit an invisible wall. Banging on the nothingness in the doorway produced no sound, no knock, nothing. It was like the air itself was solid. His heart skipped a beat. No. All David's stories, all those insane tales told in dark nights as they held each other couldn't possibly be true.

Turning back, he tripped over one of the paper sacks. A plastic bag full of scarlet liquid poked out of the top. He knelt and reached for it. And nearly threw up.

He looked back at the bed. The stranger had unlocked the last two manacles and now stood beside him. Neon green eyes met his. Fangs extended in a snarl. And his stomach convulsed at the knowledge of just what his ex-boyfriend had locked in the bedroom with him.

Chapter 23

The beast inside me roared, howling its hunger for all to hear. Meat, bloody and raw. The smell, the desire, It wanted the rich flesh, to savor the juices.

"Sam?"

"Goddess dammit, Jake! Stay back!"

The voices meant nothing. Not when the hunger was all that mattered. Then a wedge entered my mouth, not the delicious odor that teased, but something else. The beast didn't like it. Not this wimpy, pale imitation.

Cold, dead fingers stroked our throat. "C'mon, toots, swallow."

We shook our head, but the fingers and the voice persisted. Our throat convulsed and the mouthful slid south.

"C'mon, toots, another bite." Meat, hot, but not the right hot.

The beast grumbled its displeasure. A heartbeat. Two. It gave in and grudgingly accepted the offering. Then we devoured everything shoved at us.

I hiccupped and looked down. A zillion Big Mac wrappers lay on top of hospital blankets on my lap. Twinkie boxes stood open with only scraps of cellophane in them. And they weren't just the regular supermarket variety boxes, but the mega boxes you get at the wholesale cost clubs.

I lifted my head. My three zombie comedians were closest to the bed, obviously the ones who'd fed the beast within me. Mai stood between the bed and the door, Stan behind her. She holstered her gun as I took in their presence. The defense to my possible zombie rampage. Tiffany sat in the opposite corner next to the window, her semi-automatic pistol in her lap. Max stood next to her.

Just like last night at the restaurant, everyone in the hospital room, except Bebe and Mai, alternated between staring at me and the food debris left in my wake. My brain kicked into gear and sped past the satiated beast. Stan hadn't witnessed one of my gorge-outs, and this time wasn't like the ones Tiffany and Max had seen in the past. I blinked. And what the hell was Goth Girl doing in a wheel chair so soon after surgery?

And Jake . . .

I pointed at my ex who peered over Uncle Morty's shoulder. "Holy crap! What's he doing here?"

A lazy, sardonic smile spread across his face. "Thanks a lot. Maybe I was worried about you."

Bebe elbowed Bill Faith out of the way and lowered the safety railing. "She's coherent. Let me check her vitals." When I shot her an inquiring look, she snorted. "Two of John's boys were on duty downstairs." She glanced at Jake and turned back with a disgusted look. "Your *boyfriend* here said he was Family."

Uh-oh. I wasn't sure if she was angry at the security weres for screwing up. It's not their fault they didn't have telepathic abilities in their human forms. Or if she was furious at Jake for figuring out how to finagle his way past the guards. Or pissed at me for, well, involving a civilian in this mess. An ex-boyfriend at that.

"Actually it's the asshole who tried to fry my brain who's ticking me off," she muttered.

Oops. My head ached a little, but nothing like the previous migraines. Still, with Jake here, I needed to be extra careful with stray thoughts.

Instead of using magick, Bebe wrapped a blood pressure cuff around my bicep. I winced when she jerked the pressure cuff a little tighter than necessary. "If it wasn't for you and your minions, I don't know what would have happened." Her wave indicated the zombies hovering beside the bed.

I twisted to find Lily Bell sitting behind me stroking my hair. Uncle Morty clutched the raised railing in one hand, a bag of Mickey Dee's fries in the other. And I don't mean one of those itty, bitty paper envelopes, but the small bags used for Happy Meals. Full to the top. An unlit cigar dangled from his mouth.

I turned back to examine the doctor. The circles under Bebe's eyes were bigger and darker than Ben's had been. With a jolt that had nothing to do with the air-filled plastic pinching my skin, the memory of the waiting room slid into view.

I grabbed her arm. "Are you okay?" No wonder she wasn't using magick to examine me. The doctor was lucky her brain wasn't barbequed.

She nodded and slid the flat end of the stethoscope through the neck of my hospital gown before she shushed me and said, "Breathe in."

I inhaled. Mother of pearl, it hurt. My entire ribcage seemed constricted to the point my lungs had no room to expand.

"Again."

"You're a fucking sadist, Zachary," I muttered, but I sucked in another pain-filled lungful anyway.

She snorted. "Yeah, I'd say you're fine." A sober expression drove away her amusement. "Thanks for saving my ass last night."

"Last night?" I croaked. No, I wasn't out that long, was I?

I must have accidentally transmitted again because Bebe nodded. "Yeah, you've been out a little over fourteen hours."

"What happened?" I glanced at Jake before I waved a hand. "You did the . . ."

She grimaced. "Someone anticipated the tracking spell."

"Huh?" A quick check showed my ex with a nonchalant expression, considering Bebe had just admitted she's a witch.

Tiffany rolled up to the bed, and over Bill's toes from his curse as he jumped back. "Like a computer hacker spiking a trace. Whoever took Duncan put a spell on him, so when Bebe tried to find him with Grandma Margaret's locket, boom!" She smacked a tiny fist into the opposing palm, her endearing homicidal look fixed on her sharp features. "A magickal back surge to liquefy her brain."

Joy flooded through me. He was alive. Duncan was alive.

A wild grin replaced the nasty look on Tiffany. "Yeah, he's alive." A shadow fell. "For now."

"When you touched Doctor Zachary, you went into convulsions too," came Lily's smoky husk from behind me. Her tender strokes through my hair were far more comforting than I wanted to admit. It was something a real mother would do for a troubled daughter. I hadn't missed the fact Mom was nowhere to be seen. Neither was Dad.

"We could *see* you pulling the spell out of her." Lily's voice held a touch of wonder.

Bill gave a quick nod. "Yeah, it was like we knew you were trying to ground out the power, but you were having trouble. We jumped in to help." His wave indicated the other two dead comedians.

Uncle Morty plucked the cigar out of his mouth and tucked it in his jacket pocket. A pocket connected to a brand new suit jacket. Nice to know my little zombies weren't wearing their moldy grave clothes anymore. "Doc, here, was a little shaken but fine. You took the brunt of the surge. We couldn't wake you up for anything though." A handful of fries replaced the cigar, and he chomped away.

"But the spell still worked, right? We know where Duncan is?" I glanced from Tiffany to the rest of the group gathered around me.

"That's the problem, Sam." A scowl twisted Stan's features. "We know where he is—"

"But Caesar nixed any rescue missions," Tiffany finished with a snarl.

Chapter 24

Duncan brushed past the trembling Brandon and tried not to think about a certain infuriating blonde. She damn well better have survived the zombie attack. He couldn't bear contemplating the alternative. The dryness of his throat prevented him from swallowing his guilt. Why didn't he deduce David was behind the zombies? He knew the boy's history, and he'd put Samantha, everyone, in danger with his ineptitude.

The smooth nothingness of a witch's circle met his touch. He knelt at the doorway, but the ring of silver burned with just a fleeting brush of his fingertips. There was no getting a telepathic message through the shield. David had planned well. Too well.

With a grunt, Duncan rose. He needed to prioritize the actions he might accomplish, to prepare for his next encounter with David and find an escape. A quick examination of the room resulted in an empty phone jack. Not that the line would have worked with an activated circle intersecting it, but it had been worth the try.

Returning to the center of the room, he considered the next step. The tea was a total loss, so he snatched up the plastic, red-filled bag and tore it open with his teeth before upending the contents. The taste nearly gagged him.

Human.

Well, that was just bloody perfect. What the hell was Head thinking? He considered flushing the contents down the toilet.

A slight movement caught his eye. The Normal boy had wedged himself between the dresser and the table holding stereo equipment, crouching there with his back plastered against the wall. His fear flooded the room, setting Duncan's fangs on edge.

No, he'd have to drink what David had brought. He couldn't risk losing control of his thirst with an innocent trapped in the bedroom with him.

Steeling himself, he swallowed the contents of two of the three bags. He knelt and stashed the third bag in the mini-fridge tucked under the nightstand. No sense in being a pig. Only the Lord on High knew when David might return.

He stood and flexed his wrists. The blood was already doing its work. The pain of his burnt skin eased. He turned to the boy shivering in the corner. "Brandon?"

The ammonia-stench of urine filled the air.

Duncan sighed and raked a hand through his hair, the strands stiff under his fingers. Probing further, he found the tender spot on the back of his skull, all that remained from his zombie-inflicted injuries. "I believe I will shower first. After you have a chance to clean yourself, we will talk."

The only answer was a squeak of fear.

He scowled. "I am not the one who sealed you in his bedroom."

A step toward the young man produced another squeak. Duncan held up his hands. "I will not harm you."

"Y-y-you—" Brandon pointed at the trashcan where the blood bags had been disposed.

Duncan shrugged. "Beggars can't be choosers." The lightest of mental touches eased the boy's tangled emotions. Truly, his actions were for his own relief. Canines retracted at the lessening of the boy's fear scent. "Are you hungry?"

Brandon's eyes widened and his ashy scent sharpened.

Duncan swallowed another sigh. The boy was totally useless. He retrieved the soggy pastry bag from the puddle of tea and glanced inside. The heady smell of cinnamon and sugar wafted into the room. The waxed paper had saved the contents from a thorough dousing. Pulling open a dresser drawer, he yanked out a white t-shirt and used it to mop off the dark brown liquid that trickled down the sides of the little sack. After being kidnapped, he couldn't feel guilt over permanently staining his abductor's clothing.

"If you change your mind," he said, placing the bag on top of the stereo. On reconsideration, he should have let the tea drip all over David's expensive components.

The boy didn't budge unless one counted the quaking fear.

Duncan gave up and strode into the bathroom.

— · —

"What do you mean he won't let us rescue Duncan?" My words came out in a throaty growl, more animal than human. Dammit, I couldn't even picture Caesar leaving any of his people, much less Duncan, to the mercy of another supernatural. "Where is he?"

Tiffany glared back, the anger in her eyes matching mine though not aimed at me. "Duncan's at David Head's mansion in Malibu."

I glanced between the furious Bebe and the equally seething enforcers by the door. "What are you talking about? He's an eclectic. He's got no fucking standing in Los Angeles. There's no reason we can't bash down his door." My hands wrapped around the guardrails. Metal squeals filled the air as my fingers twisted the metal into new shapes in my efforts to escape Lily's arms.

Stan's glower promised someone would be hurting once the half-fae got his hands on the culprit. "Head made a deal with Duke Millanthropas."

With his words, I froze. This was so not good. "Why would a Seelie duke deal with an eclectic witch?" My tone matched Stan's frigid voice. "Especially one under a vampire coven's jurisdiction?"

Bebe covered my right hand. "Jean-Pierre repudiated Head after Lannigan's pack found a dead were in the Hollywood Cemetery. His heart had been cut out. A couple hundred graves disturbed."

A blood sacrifice to raise the dead. The zombies that had crashed Max and Tiffany's wedding. All one hundred Twinkies surged in my stomach. "Not one of his?" *Please, God, not one of John's people.* Maybe I didn't totally trust the Los Angeles packmaster, but I wouldn't wish that kind of death on anyone.

The doctor shook her head. "The runt from the Cajun pack who works—" Her eyes closed as she corrected her words. "Worked for Jean-Pierre."

The image of the short were from Duke's party flashed through my mind. A formerly living, breathing were. The one whose scent I'd detected on the other zombies. I swallowed hard, trying to keep the Twinkies contained. "Head killed his own bodyguard? To raise those zombies?"

Another nod. Teary eyes opened to meet mine. "He knew Jean-Pierre would call a death hunt on him for the murder. So he went to Millanthropas."

A death hunt. Acid coated the back of my mouth. The supernaturals were great believers of capital punishment, even here in California. If Jean-Pierre Rousseau leveled an execution order on one of his people, Caesar had every right to carry it out if Head was still in his territory. In fact, he'd be required to if he didn't want to start a war with the southeastern vampires.

The nanites put the food I'd gorged on to good use because neurons began firing, trying to make two and two equal four. "If Rousseau's called a death hunt, why would the fairies get in the middle of an internal vampire matter . . ."

Everyone in the room, except Jake, gave me the "duh" look.

Jake raised his hand. "Hey, someone want to explain it to the dumb mortal here?"

Max took pity on my ex. "To the fairies, Sam's the equivalent of Saddam Hussein."

I rolled my eyes. "No, Caesar's Hussein. I'm more like the alleged WMDs hidden in the desert, except I'm real."

Jake's eyes still had an incredulous look.

"The steel in the nanites," I pointed out.

Understanding registered on his face. "So they'd want a necromancer in their back pocket as their assurance the vampires won't launch a first strike."

Mai's quiet voice filled the hospital room. "Except Head doesn't have the control over Sam he would over other zombies."

The scene behind the restaurant surged to the forefront of my thoughts. "He had enough control over me a couple of nights ago."

"Only because he was able to slip a drug into your food. He won't catch you that way again." Mai's pain and rage simmered behind her eyes. Jamal was her family. For someone with no extra gifts, she could be freakin' deadly in her own right.

Just one problem with the enforcer's theory. I looked up at Bebe. "What about Head's sister?"

The doctor snorted. "She claims she doesn't have the necromancy talent like David. You can't just bind one aspect of a witch's power. According to Jean-Pierre, David confessed to raising the dead so the New Orleans coven bound only his powers."

I eyed Bebe. While I believed her, Rosseau's story was suspect just from his and his eclectic's body language. There was definitely an emotional attachment between them, even if she wasn't one of the new witches who were immune to the vampire virus. "Then why was she kicked out of the coven?"

"Because she knew what her brother was doing and didn't try to stop him or report him to the coven." A sad sigh followed Bebe's statement. "Sam, Yvonne's waiting outside to talk to you." She held up a hand when I opened my mouth to argue. "I think you should hear what she has to say."

A new beast growled inside me. Bebe was making a mistake trusting this woman. How could we be sure Head's sister wasn't involved in Duncan's kidnapping? She had already been found guilty of complicity in Head's actions by her own coven.

There was only one way to find out, and if she refused me, I'd have my answer.

I nodded my acquiescence. Bebe's shoulders eased, but just a hair. Good to know I wasn't the only one who didn't trust the New Orleans witch.

Stan poked his head out the door. A soft voice with a Caribbean lilt answered, one I recognized. I wound my fingers in the standard hospital blanket, not trusting myself to keep my hands from her throat.

She slipped into the room, the clicking of her braid beads the only sound. Stan held out his hand. She hesitated a moment before handing the designer bag slung over her shoulder to the enforcer.

"Jewelry too." Mai's hand on the butt of the gun on her hip indicated her seriousness.

Fear flashed in the woman's eyes, but she complied without a word, handing necklaces, rings and a billion bracelets to Stan. Mai still didn't remove her palm from her weapon.

Through it all, the witch never took her attention from me.

Bebe cleared her throat. "Sam, this is Yvonne Head."

Head took a step closer to the bed. Uncle Morty dropped the half-empty bag of fries into my lap. The former comedian moved to block her before I laid a hand on his arm. He glanced at me. I shook my head slightly. His body language remained tight as his attention returned to the woman, but he didn't take any further steps. I'd have to sort out the whys of the dead comedians' protective streak later.

Once I had Duncan back.

There was something incongruous about the whole situation. Here I was in a hospital bed, surrounded by a pile of fast food wrappers and with my ass hanging out of one of those standard issue hospital gowns. Meanwhile a beautiful, and no doubt powerful, witch stood in front of me, dressed in the latest designer-wear, twisting her fingers like a kindergartener caught picking a booger in class.

I took a really good look at her. Her expertly applied make-up didn't cover the dark smudges under her eyes, much less the bloodshot whites or puffy skin. Manicured nails ended in jagged tips. Ashy splotches showed on the skin of her neck and arms. The signs of someone under a hell of a lot of stress. I almost felt sorry for her.

It was an emotion I couldn't afford right now. Not with Duncan's life at stake. "Why are you here, Ms. Head?"

She jerked at my lowered voice. Her attention fell to her twined fingers. "I-I want to help you, and I need your help in return."

The space between my eyebrows tightened. "You want me to help you how?"

Her head rose, naked pleading in the tears trickling down her cheeks. "I need help saving my brother."

Tiffany snorted. "A little late for that." Max shushed her.

Head's attention flicked from my almost sister-in-law in the corner and back to me. "I don't have anyone else to ask." She sniffed and swiped at the wetness on her face. "The fairies don't care about him, and he's—" Her gulp was audible before she met my eyes. "He's sick. The binding the coven elders placed on him has failed. I can't bind him alone. He's too powerful."

Granted, her brother had rattled my clock with the magickal feedback, but she probably wouldn't make sense anyway. Was she really trying to plead the insanity defense for Head? I stared at the nervous witch. "What do you expect me to do?"

She flicked a look at Bebe and sucked in a deep breath. "He's as much a danger to himself as to everyone else. I spoke with Dr. Zachary—"

That earned Bebe an ugly look before I focused back on Yvonne. "And?" I prompted after too many seconds of silence.

"Instead of relying on a binding, you could take away his powers."

My mouth dropped open. Lily tensed behind me, her hands gripping my shoulders. I floundered a few times before I found my tongue. "How the hell do you expect me to pull that rabbit out of my ass?" My attention turned to Bebe.

Her arms were crossed, a thoughtful expression on her round face. "The same way you destroyed the spell animating the zombies."

A quick peek at Yvonne standing there with a hopeful expression on her face didn't help my nerves. I glared at Bebe. *Are you fucking insane? Did you see what happened to the zombies when I broke the spell? I don't have that kind of finesse!* As much as I despised Head's guts at that moment, I couldn't conceive of smashing him to bits. I barely handled the nightmares from the three times I'd killed in self-defense.

She winced at the mental shout. "Stan and I can tutor you. David's not going to hurt Duncan. Not if we keep our distance before we're ready to strike."

"You've got no guarantee—"

"David's in love with St. James."

My head whipped around at the surety in Yvonne's voice.

What game was she playing at? My eyes narrowed. "Tell me something I don't know. But if he's as nuts as you say, there's no reason to believe he wouldn't hurt Duncan."

In return, her eyes widened and blinked several times. "How-how did you know about his feelings?"

"David smelled like roses when we ran into him at Duke Miller's party." I took a deep breath and released it. "I want to read your mind."

Horror spread across Yvonne Head's angular features. There was no other word for the expression. "W-why?"

Muscles tightened as I hardened my expression. "That's the price for my help. For all I know, you're setting me up so he can knock me down. We both know there's no love lost between your brother and me since I'm the one who outed him. So let's cut the bullshit."

All my cards lay on the table. Getting into Head's estate would be easier with her help, but not impossible. I was gambling Duncan's life that her concern for her brother's would outweigh anything else. Then I'd know for sure what the stakes were.

Or she could fry my brain if I screwed up.

I tried very hard not to think of that possibility as we locked eyes for a very long minute.

Finally, she nodded. "I will submit, but—" A diamond glint flared in her light hazel eyes. "I want your promise you will not kill Davy."

I nodded as well, but I had the terrible feeling I'd just told the biggest lie of my life.

Chapter 25

Humid air followed Duncan out of the bathroom. His eyes fell to where his fellow prisoner sat in the same spot. The boy still had his arms wrapped around his knees, his chin tucked. But instead of shaking in fear, he rocked, trying to comfort himself no doubt.

Duncan gestured to the open door. "I am finished if you would care to use the facilities."

The boy's head rose. Bloodshot, puffy eyes stared from between the dark locks hanging in his face, a suspicious cast in them. He said nothing.

"Has David come back?" It was a moot question since he would have heard, but it was the most neutral subject he could conceive at the moment.

The boy shook his head.

Gripping the towel wrapped around his waist, Duncan knelt next to the boy, who tried to become one with the wall again. At least this time he didn't squeak in fear.

"Brandon, right?" Duncan tried to inject as much calm and patience he could muster into his words and mind-touch.

The boy nodded.

"Those damp clothes cannot be comfortable. Please, clean up."

Brandon's posture tightened further. He remained silent.

"I promise not to harm you."

"You're a vampire."

The boy's choked words were spat at Duncan's feet. It reminded him too much of his earliest years. Of Margaret's fear upon her discovery of his transformation.

"Yes."

"You want me alone and naked so you can do perverted things to me." Anger replaced the fear in Brandon's eyes. All in all, a good sign if his words didn't cast aspirations at Duncan's manhood.

Amusement twisted his lips. "As my fiancée would say, I do not swing that way." Duncan rose to his feet. Was David's abduction of him due to the young athlete's infatuation with him? Or was he bait to lure Samantha to her permanent death? Experience already answered that question. *Hellfire!* With Selene's demise, he'd simply traded one obsessed, not-exactly-sane suitor for another.

He tamped the growing concern and kept his tone light. "Frankly, you would be far worse off if you were trapped in here with her." Pulling open a drawer, he rooted for something to wear. Nearly everything David owned was far too colorful for his taste.

"You mean, girl vamps are worse than guy vamps?" Brandon's posture eased. A dread curiosity filled his youthful features.

"She is a zombie, not a vampire." Duncan held up a pair of black athletic shorts. As much as he detested the feel of synthetics, they would suffice.

"Z-z-zombie?"

Duncan glanced at the boy while he worked the shorts over his feet and up under the towel. "I would not be too concerned." He grimaced. "She prefers Taco Bell over human brains." A shrug as he tossed the damp towel on the bed. "There is no accounting for taste." He resumed rummaging for an acceptable shirt.

"Is there anything worse than a zombie?"

"Oh, yes." Duncan tugged a gray t-shirt over his head. "My niece is mortal, but she would have shot you out of spite by now." He eyed Brandon as he smoothed the Sabretooths logo over his chest. "And that is without suffering the effects of her current morning sickness."

———— •—•—— ————

I twined my vanilla hand around Yvonne's chocolate one. Damn, less than ten minutes and I was already thinking about food again. Sucking in a deep breath, I closed my eyes and lowered my shields. The rich scent of loam and mulch filled my head. Sparkling green swirled behind my eyelids.

My eyes popped open. I wasn't in the hospital room. Instead, I stood on a chair, my hand on a spoon stirring a bubbling liquid. Warm colors filled the kitchen. The stove before me looked older. Maybe a '50's model like the one in Grandma Neel's house.

My hand, but not my hand. A melodic voice behind me said, "Now baby, what's next?"

"A teaspoon of dragon's blood to amplify the power?" I glanced up at the woman. The exotic cheekbones were familiar. I knew her and didn't at the same time. Warmth and affection suffused her smile, a pride and acceptance I'd never received from my own mother.

She gave me a teasing look. "Be sure, Yvonne. A spell works as much from your will as it does the ingredients."

"Man, the kitchen smells like girl farts." A boy stood in the doorway. He appeared to be around seven. His short hair was its normal dark brown, not the day-glo colors he would affect years later.

"Davy." My voice wailed in protest.

Mama turned, a stern look on her face. "David Jebediah Head, that is no way to speak in my house."

He waved a tiny hand in front of his nose. "When's supper?"

"When Daddy gets home." I stuck out my tongue.

"Yvonne."

At Mama's admonition, I turned back to the boiling pot. After carefully measuring out the dark red powder from the jar on the counter, I dumped the spoonful in the mixture. Pink steam puffed from the addition, and I resumed stirring.

"I'm hungry."

Davy's plaintive whine struck my last nerve. "You're always hungry."

"Can I have a cookie, Mama?"

"One." She held up her index finger for emphasis. "And I'd better not hear you complaining you can't finish your dinner."

He fished a molasses cookie from the jar before disappearing back into the living room.

A sharp knock on the front door, and Mama reached for the towel to wipe her hands. Confusion bent her brow.

"Mama!" Davy raced back into the room, his eyes wide, the half-eaten cookie in his hand forgotten. "There's a policeman at the door."

And I knew. Daddy wasn't coming home tonight. He wasn't ever coming home again.

———•———

Green tilted, and David's voice was older but still hadn't cracked with adolescence. "I'm tellin' ya, he's evil."

"David." Mama's admonishment didn't hold the strength it used to. "He's your father."

I blinked my eyes to clear the green spots. We were in a different house, smaller. Mama's bedroom. She sat in front of her dressing mirror, stroking make-up over the new bruises. Pain wrenched my heart. Mama wouldn't let me heal her split lip. It would only make Mr. Jenkins more furious.

And I wouldn't call him "Father" no matter how many times Mama lectured me or he beat me.

"He's not my father!" Davy swiped furiously at his tears, embarrassed he'd let them slip.

I shared his anguish. Reaching for her hand, I whispered, "Please, we need to leave before he hurts you bad."

Mama closed her eyes and said nothing.

——— • ———

Another green shift. My stomach wrenched. Mama lay at the bottom of the stairs, eyes staring at nothing. I flung my body next to hers. Her aura faded from green to dark gray. Reaching for her wrist, then her neck. No thrum. No beat. Nothing.

"Davy, call 9-1-1!"

No hint of movement. I looked up at my baby brother.

Murderous fury darkened his eyes, his face, his aura. He stared up at the top of the stairs.

Jenkins stood there. No remorse, no concern on his blank face.

"Davy." No one moved at my whisper, not even me. Mama's aura turned black, then disappeared completely.

——— • ———

A green flash.

"You murdered her!" My throat burned from my screams. Arms and hands ached from hitting and slapping him. I didn't care anymore. No one believed me and Davy. Not the police. Not Bishop Samuel. Not even Grandmama.

"Shut your mouth, bitch!" Another blow to the face. My head slammed into the doorframe and rebounded into Jenkins's fist. I couldn't focus, couldn't think of a spell, couldn't find the strength to pick myself up before he grabbed the front of my nightgown. The fragile cotton ripped under the weight of my limp body.

An ugly gleam appeared in his eyes, one he showed before he and Mama disappeared into their bedroom. His attention flicked over my naked bosom, making me feel awful and dirty. He reached for me. "Guess you do have some magic after all."

"Leave her alone." Davy's voice cracked and broke.

Jenkins and I both turned. Davy stood in the hallway, his aluminum baseball bat in both hands. He gave an experimental swing. "Wanna play ball, *Dad*?" A dangerous anger filled his face.

Jenkins rose to his full height. He still towered over Davy, but not by much. "This is my house."

Davy took a threatening step forward. "Not tonight."

Eyes darting between the two of us, Jenkins muttered, "You'll get yours, boy." He spit on me before he wheeled and marched down the stairs. The front door opened, then slammed shut.

I clutched the torn nightgown over my nakedness. "He'll be back."

Arms reached around me, helped me to my feet. When had my baby brother grown so strong?

"We'll be ready for him," David said as he guided me in the direction of the bathroom.

———•———

I blinked to clear the green spots. We sat in the stifling attic. I eyed Davy's set-up. "I don't think this is a good idea. We don't even know if it'll work."

"It will." His voiced broke again as he poured a measure of whiskey.

"How do you know?"

He wouldn't meet my eyes. "I brought Mr. Whiskers back."

Hot air caught in my throat. Jenkins had strangled our pet bunny two months ago after Mr. Whiskers had chewed up one of his slippers. "Y-you did?" I was afraid and impressed. Davy sucked at most spells.

"Yup."

For the first time, I really looked at his aura, to *see* the black sparkles underneath Davy's pretty salmon. Not the sad black of Mama's death or the tainted black of Jenkins's fury, but a beautiful diamond pattern.

My breath left in a whoosh. Baby brother was a real live necromancer.

He gave a sharp nod. "You ready?"

Anxiety welled again.

"Yvonne?" He looked at me. "I can't do this without your help. You in?"

I matched his nod. "What do you need?"

"Just a little blood." He pulled out the hunting knife Jenkins had used on a couple of the neighborhood dogs stupid enough to do their business on our lawn.

I swallowed the hard lump in my throat and held out my hand. He pricked the tip of my index finger and squeezed a few drops into the glass of whiskey. After performing the same operation on his own finger, he set down the knife and chanted. A cold wind swept through the small space, cold enough to set my teeth chattering, even though it was deep summer in New Orleans. Something whispered at the edges of my awareness. I watched Davy's eyes close. A smile lit his face.

"Now, we just have to wait," he said in his cracked voice.

———•———

A crash downstairs jolted me awake. Shouting filtered up through two floors, but the words were so slurred, I couldn't understand them.

"Davy?" I sat upright, pushing braids out of my face.

"It's okay." He patted my knee.

I may not have been able to understand the words, but I recognized the voice all too well. Fear solidified into a lump in my gut.

A gunshot cracked so close my heart paused. More shouting, nearer this time. Another shot. A hole appeared in the attic floor less than a foot from Davy's make-shift altar.

"I can smell your shit up there, you bastards! Get down here!" The third shot ripped through Mama's Book of Shadows, sending shreds of paper into the air.

Davy climbed to his feet and headed for the fold-up ladder.

I grabbed his ankle. Clammy flesh and damp socks met my touch. "Davy, don't." I barely breathed the words. "He'll kill us."

"Maybe." An oddly confident boy grinned down at me. "I doubt it." He eased the trapdoor open and shouted, "We're coming down."

Jenkins met us at the bottom of the steps. The reek of alcohol, smoke and old sweat wafted through the hallway. He waved the gun in the direction of his and Mama's bedroom. "In there."

I shot a glance at Davy. Didn't he realize what terrible things Jenkins would do in there before he killed us?

When neither of us obeyed, Jenkins aimed the gun between Davy's eyes. "I said move!"

Pink floral print flashed at the other end of the hallway. Chemicals and mold rolled through the hot air in a noxious wave. My eyes widened. "Mama?"

Jenkins turned and his mouth fell open. Mama stood at the top of the staircase. Her burial dress was stained and filthy, her shoes missing. Gray tinged her skin. Purple filled her bloated lips, black stitches tugging the swollen flesh.

Oh, sweet Oshun! What had we done?

Mama, or rather the thing that had been her, shambled forward.

An explosion rattled my ears, and I collapsed to the floor.

A wisp of smoke drifted from the barrel of the shotgun Jenkins now aimed at Mama. A clear liquid oozed from the neat round hold in her forehead, but no blood. She took another step forward.

Whites appeared in a solid ring around his midnight eyes. He pulled the trig-ger again and again. Some of the bullets hit Mama. Others left scars on the walls. She didn't stop. Jenkins made an odd sound, almost a pig squeal, before he bolted for the big bedroom. The door slammed, then I heard the harsh scrape of furniture on hardwood.

"Mama?" I reached for her, but cold skin brushed past my outstretched hands. A whimper escaped my throat.

Hands stroked my hair, my hot, wet face. "It's okay, Yvonne. It'll be over soon."

I looked up at Davy. Puce lay underneath his mahogany skin. My own stomach heaved.

The bedroom door shattered under the first blow of Mama's fists. A shove sent the antique dresser sliding across the floor. Jenkins's terrified face disappeared as Mama stalked him out of our view.

Then the screaming started.

I buried my face in Davy's t-shirt and clamped hands over my ears. His arms wrapped around me, but nothing shut out the awful squishy ripping and the pain-filled howls. When quiet reigned again, I dared to look.

Mama stood in the smashed doorway. Bits of unnamed things added their own stains to her once beautiful dress. Crimson slicked her cold, dead skin and dripped from her fingertips. She stumbled toward us.

Davy released me and rose.

Terror filled my mouth. I clutched his leg. "No!"

"It's okay." He shook free, but not before I saw the queasiness in his face. Striding forward, he said, "That'll do, Mama. That'll do."

She halted. My own nails dug into my thighs. This wasn't my mama. It was something unnatural. A scream rose in my throat as I waited for my mother's corpse to tear Davy and me apart as well.

"Sleep in peace, Mama." He reached out and closed the filmy, unseeing eyes. The body collapsed to the hardwood, a meat puppet with its magickal strings cut. Then Davy fell to his knees and puked all over the dirty, bloodstained floor.

Chapter 26

Sitting before the silver ring embedded in the floor, Duncan pulled apart the remote and flipped the batteries onto his palm.

A freshly showered Brandon watched him from the edge of the bed where he rolled up the legs of the overlong sweatpants he'd found in David's bureau. "Whatcha doing?"

Duncan set one battery aside. "Attempting to escape." Using the tiny file on a pair of nail clippers he found in a drawer, he pried the casing off the remaining cylinder. His breath hissed and fire flared in his nerves when a white flake landed on the base of his thumb. Not as damaging as a silver burn, but he needed to be more careful with the scarce resources on hand.

Concentrating, he scraped the potassium hydroxide out of the battery. If he could break the circle before David returned, they'd have a chance to summon help. He pushed the white powder into a line across the silver using the clippers.

Feet thumped to the floor behind him. "How's the insides of a battery going to help?"

Duncan held up a hand and Brandon halted. "The chemical is highly caustic." He stood and eyed the boy. "I am retrieving water. Do not touch anything."

Brandon took his bared fangs seriously. The boy retreated back to the bed and held up his hands. "No problem, man."

As he filled the glass from the tap, Duncan tried not to think about why David hadn't come back to the house yet. Too many possibilities, most of which ended with Samantha never smiling again.

Damn it all to hell! He resisted the urge to throw the glass against the mirror. This whole scenario was something Selene would have concocted. He really had traded one sadistic bitch in his life for another.

Taking a steadying breath, he returned to the bedroom doorway with the crystal tumbler filled with water and a toothbrush. *St. Simeon, protect your fools.* Dipping the toothbrush in the liquid, he dribbled a tiny amount on the line of white powder. Heat slapped his face as the potassium hydroxide dissolved.

Movement whispered behind him again.

He didn't bother looking. "Brandon, if you do not wish to have lye burns, I suggest you retreat to the bathroom." Soft pattering told him the boy obeyed.

Noxious fumes burned his eyes and nostrils. Retreating to the bathroom as well, he prayed the alkaline solution would work.

Brandon gasped at the fumes working their way into the bathroom when the hissing metal dissolved with a soft *pop*. Duncan crossed the tiled floor and released the catch on the frosted glass window. Wrapping his arm and hand in a clean towel, he pulled it open. Fresh air flooded the area, brushing away the ozone from the spell along with the alkaline fumes. He took a grateful breath and reached through the opening with the encased arm. No circle.

And despite the high, bright sun, his reach didn't extend past the shadow of the house.

Summoning all his will, he targeted a mental shout. Nothing but a tinny echo came back. Bloody hell! Head must have another circle around the estate. But how could a witch with his minimal talent cast that size of a spell? Odds were a larger circle shield would be far weaker than the one that had imprisoned him and Brandon in the bedroom. If so, it could be broken with enough force. He shook his head. Best to deal with one problem at a time.

The problem was the noonday sun. He turned and examined Brandon. The boy was his best hope, but he would be vulnerable to whatever traps David may have set on the grounds.

A shudder rippled through Duncan at the memory of zombies climbing the walls and shambling across Ted Howell's precious lawn. Whatever David Head may have been two years ago, he'd grown in his abilities. Dangerously so.

"Did you come in your vehicle?"

Brandon nodded. "If we can get past David, we can make a run—" Crimson spread up his neck and lit up his ears. "You can't go outside, can you?"

"Not right now anyway. Not unless you have UV film lining all the windows of your automobile."

The crimson migrated from ears to cheeks. He shook his head.

A bitter smile twisted Duncan's lips. Daylight was more of a cage than anything David could devise. "Do you know where Anthony's Restaurant is?"

Brandon's snort resembled one of Tiffany's so much Duncan had difficulty restraining a laugh. "Only one of the hottest places in the city? I think I can find it."

"When you reach the restaurant, tell the staff it's an emergency Family matter and you must speak with Anthony's Uncle Caesar. Tell Caesar everything that's happened here." He paused. The last thing he wanted was to frighten the boy more than necessary, but he grabbed Brandon's shoulders and looked him squarely in the eye. "You may be pursued. Do not stop for anyone. Do you understand?"

Despite the ashy fear scent rolling off the boy, he gave a sharp nod. "No stopping. Get help at Anthony's." He hesitated. "Caesar's l-like you, isn't he?"

"Yes." Duncan smiled as wide as he dared to reassure Brandon. "He will not harm you. And this may be your only chance to escape."

"David wouldn't—" Brandon sucked in his cheeks and looked away. "Never mind."

Sympathy for the boy filled Duncan. He'd learned the hard way as well that someone he thought he cared for could have a horrible, vindictive, selfish side.

Still no sounds of any living thing inside the house except for those made by the two of them. He released the boy. "David's not inside the house. You need to go." He clapped Brandon's shoulder. "Now."

The boy trotted from the bathroom, stopping long enough to shove his feet in the leather loafers he'd originally been wearing and to snag his keys and wallet.

After stepping carefully over the still smoking gap in the silver ring, he glanced back. "Will you be okay?"

"I will if you hurry."

Guilt passed across Brandon's face before he turned and ran down the hallway.

Duncan followed at a more sedate pace until he reached the living room. Sunlight flooded the huge room. The rapid slap of the loafers ended with the creak of a door opening. He blinked watery eyes and stayed in the edge of the shadowed hallway. Then with a prayer, he indulged in one of Tiffany's childhood quirks and crossed his fingers.

Outside, an engine purred to life then dipped in tone. When the vehicle was about a hundred yards away, shouting began. The engine whined as if a foot pressed the accelerator to its limit. A clang. A thud of metal on flesh. Screams of pain but none he recognized as Brandon's voice. The roar of the engine as it moved further away.

A smile tugged his lips. The boy did better than he expected.

A door slammed. Heavier footfalls, rubber on hardwood. David Head appeared in the opposite entrance to the living room, panting. His wrist flicked with a mumbled word.

The floor heaved under Duncan, tossing him into the air. He rolled with the landing in the sun-bright room. Gaining his feet, he expected the bite of UV charring skin. Only seconds to take down Head before he was incapacitated by the radiation.

Nothing.

No pain. No burning. Not even an itch.

Fangs extended, he launched himself at the witch. Despite the extra inches Head had, he didn't stand a chance. In less than a second, Duncan pinned him to the floor, both arms wrenched behind his back. "Why are you trying to kill Samantha Ridgeway?"

David wiggled, trying to find an opening. If the situation weren't so dire, Duncan could almost admire the man's tenacity.

He pressed a knee against the witch's neck. "Answer me."

"He's not your real problem, vampire."

Ozone filled the air. Green and yellow lights exploded in Duncan's vision. He couldn't move, couldn't breathe, couldn't do anything except fall headlong into a black tunnel.

Chapter 27

Green spots cleared from my vision. Worms twisted my intestines in intricate knots. I bent over, trying to deal with the shit in my head. Oh God! Yvonne . . .

I straightened at the tight clasp on my hand. The witch still held my palm in hers. Tears ran down her face, washing away the make-up she so carefully applied before coming to see me.

"I'm so, so sorry." I squeezed her fingers lightly because my lame words were so fucking inadequate.

She said nothing, merely squeezed back and swiped at the wetness on her cheeks with the back of her free hand.

I cleared the hard lump out of my throat and eyed the rest of the assemblage. "You guys need to get out of here."

A resounding chorus of "No" slammed into my eardrums, along with a "Fuck you, bitch" from Tiffany.

"Look, guys," I said, trying to meet everyone's eyes. It was a little hard with Lily still sitting directly behind me. "Head wants me dead." After everything, Yvonne showed me, I couldn't blame him. The shit he'd dealt with before he'd ever left middle school explained a lot of his screw-the-world attitude. And the failure of his last relationship rested squarely on my shoulders. I'd never faced the fallout of one of my stories. Never really saw the aftereffects.

I swallowed hard and focused on Duncan's face in my mind. Because if I didn't remind myself of the consequences to the man I loved if I didn't face Head, I'd chicken out.

There. I admitted it. I loved Duncan.

Another swallow. "Head'll do a trade if I show up, but not if the cavalry follows me." My hand shot up to forestall the beginning protests. I eyed the doctor. "Bebe, so far this mess is between the vamps and fairies. You can't drag your family into it." She gave me a reluctant nod. If nothing else, she had a practical mind.

Not so for others in the group. When I turned to Tiffany, her mouth was already moving. "Don't you even think of cutting me out. He's my uncle. My family!" A French-manicured nail shot in Yvonne's direction. The incongruity of the missing black lacquer nearly derailed my thought train. "If she's going, I'm going."

"What about my niece or nephew?"

At my quiet point, her mouth snapped shut. A single drop trailed from the corner of her eye down her murderous visage.

My attention switched to Max behind her. He held up his uninjured hand. "I know, I know. I'm worthless in a fight. I'll keep an eye on them." He laid the hand on Tiffany's shoulder. She buried her face against him so the rest of us wouldn't see the tears.

I looked at Jake.

A shit-assed grin filled his mug. "You're not cutting me out of this one. I want to meet my replacement." He shrugged. "Besides, if Head's expecting a lot of woo-woo stuff, I'll be your ace in the hole."

He made sense as much as I hated to admit it. Jake could give Mai a run for her money in fighting and weaponry. I turned to the female enforcer. She stared back.

I started to say something and found I couldn't. That stare of hers made me uncomfortable, so uncomfortable I couldn't meet it any longer. I shifted and plucked at the blanket. "Mai . . ."

"My sister is still in ICU and Jamal is dead." No inflection on those words. No emotion. No argument.

"Ok-a-a-y then." I turned to Stan.

A pale blond eyebrow rose, almost meeting the edge of his buzz cut. "Do you really want to walk into Head's without a sidhe ally yourself?"

"You're half-fairy," I spat back.

"And my cousin Harry's still in the hospital too, thanks to Head." He shrugged boulder-sized shoulders. "Bebe and I have been working on some magick combinations." He inclined his head toward Yvonne. "Give me a couple of hours with her."

Yvonne returned his acceptance with a gracious nod of her own.

I was now officially worried. From the little Bebe explained to me, witch and fairy magick could be a lethal mix, usually to the casters. We had no clue what my peculiar black light crap would do to such a mix. And speaking of my unknown abilities . . .

I pivoted on my butt to face the three zombie comedians. "You three need to stay with Bebe."

Uncle Morty gave a sharp shake of negation. "We're with you, toots." Bill and Lilly nodded in support.

I sighed, more from sympathy than exasperation. I hated to be left out of the loop, too. "Look, guys, I appreciate the thought. I really do. But—" My voice hardened at the memory of the rehearsal dinner fiasco. "Head controlled me once before, and I almost didn't break the spell in time." Hell, I still wasn't sure how I'd broken it, or if I really had. Maybe Head let it slip so he could enjoy my pain and fear while his zombies were skinning me alive. "The bastard pulled you out of your graves. I'm not putting you at his mercy. Not again."

Bill shuffled, the eyes behind the famous nose shifting with uncertainty. This was a man who'd done USO shows in combat zones, and he obviously didn't like the fear he was feeling. Lily's expression was solemn, contemplative. I couldn't read the inscrutable emotion in her eyes. However, Morty's eyes glared with ferocity. "Just a damn minute, toots—"

I reached for his hand, grabbing warm, living flesh. "Please, Morty. I've attended your funeral once. Don't make me do it again. Not yet."

Morty plucked the unlit cigar from his pocket. Fingers searched for a light. He finally gave up and returned to glaring at me. "Don't get yourself killed, toots."

I smiled up at him. "Don't plan too. Didn't like it the first time." I let go of his warm grip and handed the greasy bag of fries to him. "Besides, these things will kill me faster."

— • —

Brandon shivered in the dimly lit back room of Anthony's restaurant. Not sure if it was the temperature or the company, he stammered through his story. The man, no, the vampire seated across from him listened as he told the tale of David imprisoning him in the bedroom with Duncan, the British vampire's ingenuity and his subsequent flight from the estate. Occasionally, the vampire Duncan had referred to as Uncle Caesar asked for more specifics. Otherwise, the vampire stared over his steepled fingertips at Brandon with those oddly yellowish eyes.

Two other people sat across the table with the vampire. The graying, middle-aged man with a predatory air kept looking at him like he was something to be dissected. The older woman kept giving him reassuring nods as he related the story. He had the impression neither of them were vampires but just as dangerous.

"And then these creatures, uh, people," Brandon amended with a nervous glance at Uncle Caesar. "They seemed to melt out of the shrubbery and jumped at my car. I-I think I ran one of them over, but Duncan said not to stop for anything." He should feel guilty over that, he knew he should, but he was just too damn grateful to be alive. The arrow sticking out of the ruined stereo reminded him of that on the reckless drive to the restaurant.

The vampire sat, looking at him. Another shiver stole over the raised goose pimples covering his arms. The guy appeared close to Brandon's age, but the vibe he gave was older. Much, much older.

Finally, Uncle Caesar lowered his steepled fingers. "Thank you for your assistance, Brandon." He sighed. "For your own safety, I think it's best that you don't remember any of this."

Cold sweat broke out on his forehead. "Wait a minute. You don't have to kill me. I won't tell anybody. I swear!" He couldn't stop the rising pitch from scraping his vocal cords raw.

"Don't be silly." The woman waved a manicured hand. "We're not going to kill you."

A cold, iron vise clamped onto his arm. Brandon looked up.

An Asian guy dressed in black jerked him up from the chair. "I shall deal with him, Master." At Caesar's nod, the other vampire dragged Brandon from the room.

"Please, man, don't do this!" He yanked and pried, but the Asian guy's fingers might as well have been iron chains for all the good his struggles accomplished.

"Hush," Asian Guy hissed. He dragged Brandon to a covered unloading dock and shoved him into a black Ferrari waiting in the shade.

Brandon threw his weight at the door and yanked on the latch. No luck. A flick of the switch showed the window was secured as well. Before the thought of climbing over the console and out the driver's door fully formed in his brain, the vampire climbed in and turned the ignition key.

Asian Guy eyed him. "Put on your seatbelt."

Brandon hesitated a moment before reaching for the strap. It didn't make sense. Why would the vampire be concerned about his safety if he had been ordered to kill Brandon?

"I'm not going to kill you." The vampire's growl acted as a counterpoint to the purring Ferrari. He accelerated around the building and whipped the car into traffic.

"Wh-what are you going to do to me?" Brandon swallowed a screech at a near-miss with a produce truck when the vampire changed lanes. Fingertips dug into the soft leather armrest. Then again, he may die as a normal Los Angeles traffic fatality before the vampire could drain his blood.

"I'm taking you to Yvonne."

Fury surged. How could this vampire ninja wannabe know about Yvonne? "Don't fuck with me, man."

Darkness filled the vampire's profile. "David Head is responsible for my life-mate's death." Glowing yellow eyes glared at him before returning their attention to traffic. "While I would take great delight in exacting my revenge on you, Yvonne has convinced Samantha of your usefulness."

Bile surged in Brandon's throat. David, or at least the David he thought he knew, wouldn't have harmed a soul. Maybe a little jostling on the court in a heated game, but not deliberate murder. And from the furious look on the vampire's face, anything he wanted to exact on Brandon was bound to be painful. *Focus, man. Focus.* "W-who's Samantha?"

"Samantha Ridgeway." An evil smile curved the vamp's lips, exposing elongated fangs. "Our resident zombie."

Oh God! Not her! Acid billowed and the vampire grimaced as Brandon bent over and heaved chunks on the floor of the Ferrari.

He sat up and wiped his mouth on the shoulder of the oversized t-shirt he wore. David's t-shirt. As if the fear and weirdness of the last few hours weren't bad enough, now he had to face his worst nightmare. The woman who destroyed his career. Destroyed the one real relationship he'd ever had. Destroyed his entire fucking life.

And he couldn't even kill the bitch because she was already dead.

Chapter 28

Another round of pain greeted Duncan as he swam toward consciousness. He lay still, praying for the ache behind his eyes to subside before he tried to open them. The constant assaults were becoming bloody inconvenient. If this is what his wedding to Sam would be like, maybe she had a point in refusing such a ceremony. He reached for his skull, only for a dollop of searing agony to halt his wrist. Forcing his eyes open, he raised his head.

Damn it all to Hell!

Once again he was chained spread-eagle in David Head's bed. His only consolation was this time he was still clothed.

At the rustling of the bedcovers, the villain himself looked up from where he knelt next to the doorway. "This is just cold, man." David gave a sad little shake of his head when he bent to continue examining the damage to the silver circle. "Do you know how hard it is to cast a ring of silver this big? Do you have any idea how much something like this costs?"

"I can imagine," came Duncan's dry reply. Bracing himself against the pain, he tugged experimentally at the right manacle. No give. He relaxed the muscles, trying to wrap his mind around anything else besides the burning skin on his wrists and ankles.

Patience. He needed patience, but the gut knowledge that he had hours to go before sunset screamed in outrage. "If you release me, I can go to the bank before it closes. Reimburse you for the damage."

David chuckled and climbed to his feet. Tension in Duncan's body ratcheted as the witch crossed the room and sat on the edge of the bed. "Maybe tomorrow. When the bank's actually open." His focus shifted to the floor. His hands clenched and released but he made no move to touch his prisoner. "This isn't how I meant everything to go down, you know."

It took Duncan a few seconds to realize David was weeping. With an effort, he kept his voice low, soothing. "You can still fix it. Release me. I will speak with Caesar and Jean-Pierre. We can work out some sort of arrangement."

David gave another shake of his head and swiped away the wetness on his face. "Too late for that."

Queasiness filled Duncan's abdomen. Too late? What had happened while he was unconscious? *Please, Lord, let no harm have come to Samantha.* He chose his next words carefully. "Both masters are fair. Recent events—"

David faced him squarely, and the words jammed in Duncan's throat. The odd light in the witch's eyes sent an uneasy frisson through his body.

"I love you. This all started because I love you."

An odd combination of horror and sympathy swept through Duncan at the boy's whispered declaration. He sorted through everything he could possibly say, and there was nothing, absolutely nothing, that wouldn't shatter David's fragile ego. "I appreciate the sentiment, but I—"

"You love that bitch. Why else would I want her dead?" The statement held so much bitter resentment it was difficult for Duncan not to flinch.

"I was under the assumption you were still angry over the pictures she took months ago."

A dark expression shadowed the witch's face. "Hell, yeah!" He rose and began pacing along the foot of the bed. "How'd you like pictures of you and a lover in a private moment plastered all over the fucking country?"

Everything fell into place. David blamed Samantha for two losses. Not sure how to counter the angry glare, Duncan sighed. "You are correct. I would not."

"Damn straight." The witch gave a sharp nod. "This whole situation is so totally fucked up. Brandon shouldn't have run off either. I wasn't going to hurt him. You'd think he'd want to be in on this. She hurt him more than she did me. Totally fucked up his music career."

During David's rant, Duncan took a good look at him. Dark circles marred the skin under his eyes. Had the boy slept in the last three days? He gambled on information Yvonne had given Caesar shortly before the aborted wedding ceremony and the thick rose scent in the house. A scent that didn't come from David alone. A scent even Brandon's fear could not totally override. "He still loves you."

David jerked to stop, bloodshot eyes wide. "What'd you say?"

It wasn't the reaction Duncan expected, but nevertheless David deserved honesty. "Brandon still loves you."

The witch strode to the head of the bed, fist raised to strike. "Shut the fuck up!"

Duncan didn't miss the flare of hope under David's furious visage. "I am conveying the truth. Do not toss this chance away. Release me. Let me help you."

"He's lying, David."

The familiar mellow voice from the bedroom doorway smashed the glimmer of belief in the witch's eyes. Duncan turned his head to find Duke Millanthropas. The fae no longer dressed as the effete persona he affected on stage. This time he was decked in the leather and silver mail of a sidhe warrior. As Samantha would have said, this so was not good.

Focusing on the truth was the best option, and Duncan aimed his next words at David. "Brandon's scent coats this room. Read my mind if you do not believe me." Inviting a possibly insane basketball player inside his head wouldn't have been his first choice, but it was his only chance to break whatever hold the sidhe had on the young witch.

Millanthropas crossed his arms. A raised eyebrow on his sharp features conveyed his disbelief. "Then why did Ruby track your Brandon to Anthony's where he met with Augustine, Lannigan and Epstein?"

"I sent him to the restaurant for his own safety." Duncan shifted to glare at David on the other side of the bed. The witch was smart enough to lower his upraised fist. "I was not the idiot who sealed the boy in a confined space with a severely injured vampire and scared the piss out of him."

"I panicked when I saw him unlocking the cuffs!" David's protest held a slight whine. "I haven't seen him since he-he—" He could no longer meet Duncan's stare and started shifting his weight from foot to foot, a schoolboy caught in a foolish escapade.

"It doesn't explain why Kensai Osaka disappeared with Brandon shortly after the boy's interview with Augustine." Millanthropas's honeyed voice carried an annoyed hint, his focus solely on Duncan. "And it doesn't explain why two other members of Augustine's inner circle along with your fiancée and David's sister have vanished and we can't track them."

Duncan couldn't stop his smile at the fae's peeved tone. The duke's bodyguards were two of the best trackers of the Seelie Court, which meant Bebe and Stan's experiments to combine witch and fae magicks succeeded. "Given David has made three attempts to take the life of someone under Master Augustine's protection, I am shocked at your question."

Millanthropas smiled in return, but the expression cast an ugly shadow across the fae's flawless features. "And how does one kill something that's already dead?" He stepped closer, his posture far more menacing than the witch's, who was nearly twice his size. "Now where would your master hide his precious little zombie?"

The kitchen in Duncan's townhouse stank to high heaven from the concoction Yvonne stirred on the stove. I considered opening a window when the double beep of a car horn sounded outside the garage. Even with feeling Kensai's presence outside, I waited for Mai's shouted confirmation from the living room. With fairies involved in this mess on top of a necromancer who hated my guts, it paid to be careful. Really, really careful. I'd already parked Duncan's Suburban in the alley behind the townhouse, so I hit the switch on the wall.

Another honk, closer this time, and I hit the switch again. When the rumbling of the garage door stopped, I poked my head in to confirm it had closed properly. What can I say? After the last three days, I was turning into a safety girl.

Kensai had already exited the Ferrari, giving me fewer seconds to drool over Caesar's beautiful machine than usual. He eyed me as he crossed over to the passenger side. "You're cleaning the vomit out of the carpet."

I blinked. Vomit? Please let it be Normal puke. I'd have to replace the carpet otherwise. The last two months had taught me nothing's worse than trying to get bloodstains out of upholstery. Not to mention, I could barely afford my grocery bill on two salaries, much less new Ferrari carpet.

Brandon Tyler's face was as pale as the Caucasian vamps when Kensai helped him climb out of the car. He took one look at me, and he somehow managed a new shade of green.

I raised my fingers in a half-hearted wave. If Head really wanted me dead, he should've sicced his ex-boyfriend on me. The laser-like intensity of his gaze conveyed his hatred almost as effectively as the gagging stench of brimstone filling the garage from the open door to the kitchen.

Kensai tugged the singer forward, and Brandon's hatred switched rapidly to green-gray nausea. Funny how the mental flavor of that feeling matched the physical one. Kensai got the garbage can in front of the guy, but all he produced was dry heaves. My cast-iron zombie stomach twitched in sympathy.

I reached out to steady Brandon when it seemed he was finished. "Let's get you upstairs."

He jerked back. "Don't touch me, bitch."

The miasma of grief at touching Kensai's mind lurched in my gut. *There's crackers and soda in the kitchen.* I wished I had said the words aloud instead.

The Japanese enforcer showed no sign of his inner turmoil, merely nodded in acknowledgment as he escorted the stressed-out singer into the townhouse.

I headed to the wooden shelving Duncan had installed and pulled off carpet cleaner and a package of sponges. With a quick trip into the stinky kitchen, I filled a bucket with water and retrieved some rubber gloves. Kneeling next to the sports car, I started cleaning up another one of my messes.

It was hardly the worst I was responsible for, but it was a start.

Duncan had just better keep his ass alive long enough to appreciate my efforts.

—— · ◆ · ——

David paced the length of the living room, listening to Millanthropas on his cell phone. At least it looked like a cell phone, but considering the amount of residual fae magick the device exuded, it was something else glamoured to look like a cell. The duke's voice still held a hint of irritation.

The fae hadn't been happy when David had stopped him from plunging his silver knife into the helpless vampire. When the hell had he lost his stomach? Frankie's canine features floated in his mind. He quickly shoved the thought back in the deep dark hole along with memories of his stepfather. Or what had been left of him.

"I understand, my queen." An odd look glimmered in the fae's mahogany brown eyes. "I will look into the matter." Millanthropas snapped the phone shut, his uncanny eyes unblinking. He tapped an index finger on the black casing. "Is there something you wish to tell me, David Jebediah Head?"

He halted, hands flexing. "What're you talking about, man? Are you going back on your bargain?"

Millanthropas stood there, looking at him, his stillness as unnatural as the vampires. Or a raised corpse. The only thing moving was the slow climb of crimson under his dark-fuzzed cheeks.

David stomped across the floor. "She's not alive! I have the right to destroy the bitch for what she did to me!" Hysteria filled his voice. He tried to clamp down on the panic. What the hell was the fae hinting at?

"I am not referring to Samantha Ridgeway. She's as much a danger to us as she is to you." Millanthropas took a menacing step closer. "I am referring to a dead were the Los Angeles pack found in the Hollywood Cemetery."

David spread his hands wide. The duke was no fool, but he'd have to spin this carefully. "I told you Yvonne planned to turn me over to the vamps even though I was in my rights. She sent Frankie to stop me." The remembered smell of bowels and entrails clogged his throat. "I had raised too many, and-and—" He swallowed the hard lump of memory. "I couldn't stop them in time." His gaze dropped to the floor. "It was an accident."

A soft snort from Millanthropas made him raise his head. "I swear. It *was* an accident."

The fae's unnerving eyes bore into him. "Rousseau has called a death hunt on you for Francois Charles LeBeau's death. He's *requested* my queen turn you over to him." A cool smile spread his lips. "Or present your body."

Ice filled David's veins. "He wouldn't. Yvonne wouldn't let him."

Mild surprise raised the duke's fine eyebrows. "You just said your sister planned to turn you over to the vampires anyway."

David collapsed in the couch, fear chewing on his belly. Where the hell had this thing gone wrong? "Turning me in, yeah, but-but—"

The fae stood over him, rebuke in his voice. "I couldn't care less about the Normal you killed in Las Vegas—"

David's head jerked up at those words, hot anger replacing the fear. "I told you. I didn't kill the bitch." He licked his lips. His best friend was gone, had stabbed him in the back, so protecting him no longer mattered. "Frankie did when she surprised us in the morgue."

Amusement twisted Millanthropas's mouth, and his warm hand clasped David's shoulder. "As I said, we will keep our promise in return for your aid." He squeezed to the point of pain. "As long as you are useful to us, David Jebediah Head."

With those words, he pivoted and stalked out of the room, his footsteps making no sound.

David lowered his head into his hands. Any other time in his life, he'd talk over a problem with Yvonne. She always had an idea, a plan, hell even a clue. Why had she betrayed him? And how in Papa Ghede's name was he going to get out of this mess without her?

Chapter 29

The smell of Yvonne's spell cooking in Duncan's kitchen was marginally better than my gloves and sponges, but not by much. I tossed the reeking cleaning materials into the trash. I peeled the gloves off my sweating hands and quickly tossed them in with their compatriots. Two seconds later, the trash bag was safely deposited in the wheeled garbage bin in the garage.

When I came back in, Yvonne glanced in my direction before turning her attention back to the brew she stirred. "You should talk to him."

I didn't have to ask who she was referring to. Brandon Taylor's rancid anger filtered through the stench of puke and the witch's spell. "What makes you think he wants to talk to me?"

She laid the wooden spoon in the ceramic holder next to the stove and faced me. It was the most action Duncan's stove had seen since Tiffany moved in with Max last month. I bit my lip to keep my wisecracks to myself. This was not the time. I just prayed Head wasn't hurting Duncan because he couldn't reach me.

Yvonne's light hazel eyes tracked my path to the refrigerator as I retrieved a gallon of o.j. and started chugging the contents. I could have read her mind, but we'd both kept our psychic distance since the hospital. I suspected she'd seen my past as easily as I had seen hers. When I didn't think she'd add anything, she said, "You have the rare chance of making amends after your death, Samantha. I suggest you take it." She turned her back to me, picked up the spoon and resumed stirring.

I drank the rest of the jug before tossing the empty plastic into the recycling crate. The witch was right. I'd started this fiasco two years ago by pursuing a story. A legitimate story. Dammit, I hadn't been the one in the wrong.

I hung my head. No, I took away what little privacy David and Brandon had in their fledgling relationship. And now, those closest to me were paying for my story-at-all-cost work ethic.

Stalking through the living room, I gave Mai and Jake a curt nod of acknowledgement. My steps slowed the closer I got to the top of the stairs. What the hell was I supposed to say to fix this?

The muffled voice that answered my knock on the guest bedroom door held a hint of tears. Sucking in a deep breath, I twisted the knob.

Brandon must have been expecting Yvonne because he sat abruptly at my entrance. "What do you want?"

I released the air in my lungs and closed the door. "We need to talk."

The petulant glare he gave me through red and puffy lids would have been funny if it weren't for the circumstances. "I told Kensai everything I could remember about our—" He swallowed and his attention dropped to his clenched hands. "Everything about David's place."

"That's not—" Despite the gallon of juice, my throat dried out faster than a raisin in Death Valley. "I mean, I—" I shoved my hands in my jeans' pockets. "Dammit, why are you making this so hard?"

"Me?" He held a hand to his chest in mock horror. "And how, pray tell, did I wreck your recording career?" He climbed to his feet and padded over to me. "Ruin your love life?" He jabbed a finger at my chest. "Destroy your existence?"

Brandon had maybe an inch on me. So between his bare feet and my Nikes, his bloodshot eyes stared directly into mine. Brimstone filled the air once again. I had to give him credit for not having a mental breakdown after everything he'd been through since this morning.

"Well, I'm dead. If you want a pity party, I've got you beat on that one."

His face stilled. The quick switch between brimstone and cotton candy was the only warning I had before he exploded into gales of laughter. He turned and collapsed face first on the bed, the comforter muffling the noise.

"It's not that funny," I muttered.

Brandon rolled over and sat. "Yeah, it is." Swiping at his eyes, he tried to get his humor under control. "Yvonne gave you the same lecture she gave me, didn't she?"

Face muscles twisted my expression into a frown. "What are you talking about?"

"She gave you the 'kiss and make up before it's too late 'cause life's too short', blah, blah blah." Both of his hands flapped in time to his words.

My eyebrows lifted. "Wow. Braid your hair and you could pass for her."

He rubbed his cheek. "Don't think I can shave that close."

I eased down next to him on the bed, not meeting his eyes and a little surprised he didn't scoot away from me. After sucking in another deep breath and releasing it, I whispered, "I am sorry."

Brandon snorted.

Heat flared under my skin and I glared at him. "Look, I'm trying to give you an apology."

"Only because my ex had your boyfriend chained to his bed."

My mouth fell open, and I tasted his thoughts. Clean cotton. Shit. Kensai had kept that little tidbit from me.

From Brandon's wide eyes, he'd come to the same realization. "Oh fuck. I thought you knew."

Sandpaper filled the back of my throat. "Silver?"

He nodded.

I stood. The thought of going without Kensai crossed my mind, but I'd made enough mistakes lately. And I needed all the help I could get to rescue Duncan. My fists clenched. Sundown couldn't come fast enough.

Heading for the door, I was stopped by Brandon clearing his throat. I looked at him.

Pink flared under the faint peach fuzz on his cheeks. "I accept your apology and—" He found a sudden interest in the area rug under his feet. It took my enhanced hearing to catch his "I'm sorry too."

I crossed back to him and laid a hand on his shoulder. "Brandon, do you think you can talk David out of doing something stupid?"

His head lifted, and his dark brown eyes met mine. "I think so. Maybe." He shook his head. "I'm not sure anymore." He took a deep breath. "I wanna try."

"Stay by Kensai. David'll be gunning for me, so I don't want you in the line of fire."

He licked his lips. "Yvonne—"

"Will be backing me up." I tried to give him a reassuring smile. "Kensai won't hurt you."

"He's a—" Brandon glanced at the door.

I laughed and gave him a reassuring squeeze. "Trust me. It's the witches and fairies you want to stay away from."

He shook his head. "Not all of them." He closed his eyes a moment before eyeing me again. Tears filmed the orbs. "Try not to kill him."

Sobriety filled my head. "I'll do my best."

I was so going to hell for making promises I might not be able to keep.

⸻ ·•· ⸻

Millanthropas admired Sapphire's lithe form as she paced a healthy distance from the steel gates but close enough to watch for her sister's return. She must have sensed his presence because she whirled in his direction and crouched, her hand dropping to the hilt of her sword.

Straightening in recognition, she sketched a bow, but her eyes flashed with her emotions. She didn't bother to hide her contempt at the queen's previous command. "Instructions, Your Grace?"

"We wait." He fingered the curl on her cheek that had escaped her warrior's knot. How he missed its leaf green color.

Dark flooded her skin. "The vampires—"

"Are seeking a political solution rather than put their precious weapon at risk." He smiled, and his fingers moved to stroke the tight lines of her neck muscles.

Her slim eyebrow rose. "The queen doubts your assessment of the zombie?"

He shrugged. "It matters not. Samantha Ridgeway is more of a danger to herself than to us. But Head lied to gain our protection."

Humor lit her golden eyes at her understanding. "We are no longer needed here."

Tugging her closer, he pressed his lips to hers. A sigh escaped as her body pressed to his. Her yielding drove his body rock hard with desire. She reached for him, slim fingers cupping, caressing, demanding.

He forced a hand between them, as much to tantalize a soft, full breast as to halt the proceedings. "Have the warriors return to our mound except for a dozen."

Confusion drove away her dreamy expression. "But you're not leaving?"

Another smile tugged his lips. "Not yet. I want to observe how events unfold tonight."

Sapphire blinked. "The vampires will attack—"

He shook his head. "No. They won't. She will come, though. She's marked young Duncan as her own, and she will come for him tonight." Fierce emotion heated his blood at the thought of watching the necromancer and the nestling battle. "Our queen simply doesn't realize she has wagered her throne on the outcome."

Chapter 30

I fingered the paintball gun on my lap, the one now loaded with pellets of anti-zombie potion. It felt weird not sitting in the driver's chair of Duncan's SUV. I glanced at Mai as she focused on traffic. The collective mood molded a grimmer than usual look on her face.

I twisted around and peered at the rest of the group. Brandon and Yvonne huddled in the second seat. Concern over tonight's outcome gave them sour looks that matched Mai's expression. I couldn't blame them. They cared about David, didn't want to see him hurt, but we didn't have a clue what kind of a fight the fairies would put up defending him.

With his pink-tinged cheeks and nasty scowl, Stan resembled a Rams linebacker prepping to throw the first punch after an illegal hit. He did have a clue, and even though he didn't sugarcoat his assessment, listening to someone's war stories was very different than living through a battle. I found that out the proverbial hard way when I was twelve and had the terrific idea of snapping pictures of a riot in South Central.

Kensai and Jake crowded in the back seat next to Stan with nearly identical stoic looks. Except the muscles in my ex's jaw twitched occasionally. The vampire's face could have been carved from tan marble with neon lights inserted for eyes.

And don't get me started on the flood of scents in such a tiny compartment. I didn't blame them for being wound up, but it was all I could do not to gag as I addressed the troops. "Let's go over this one more time."

Brandon groaned. "Jesus, Ridgeway. You're not fucking Eisenhower, and this isn't D-Day."

Stan snickered, easing the stress lines on his face. His humor was probably due to the fact he'd worked with Ike during WWII.

"And I've had enough people die over this bullshit, so we are going to review the plan." I glared at the pop singer. "One. More. Time."

He fingered a matching paintball gun slung over his shoulder, but the fairies must have scared him enough this afternoon. He dropped the attitude and said, "I stay with Kensai and shoot any zombie that comes our way."

I eyed him.

He gave a dramatic sigh. "And talk David down if he tries to stop us."

The vampire picked up the recitation. "We enter the house, find and release Duncan, and take him back to the SUV."

""Meanwhile, I keep Millanthropas and his troops busy." Stan's bass held a nasty delight, which would have scared the piss out of me in any other circumstances.

Jake shot me a reassuring smile. "Mai and I guard the SUV until Kensai and Brandon return."

"We head directly for Caesar's Brentwood estate." Mai still wasn't pleased about that part of the plan. It wasn't in her nature to run from a fight.

"And if David doesn't interfere with Kensai and Brandon, he's our responsibility," I said, gesturing between me and Yvonne. The odds were our renegade would stick with his murderous obsession to eliminate me from the planet.

Damn it. James Bond went into situations with a better plan even if he was the bait. No, Bond was luckier than me. If he shot a bad guy in the head, the bad guy stayed dead.

Well, at least I had a plan for once. I just didn't have a fucking clue of how to stop one pissed-off, nothing-left-to-lose necromancer.

Morty Stern pressed the non-existent gas pedal on the passenger side floor. "Damn it, Lil! Speed up or we'll lose her!"

Lily said nothing underneath the surgeon's cap still holding in her hair, but the speedometer crept higher as they followed the black SUV.

"We shouldn't have stolen the doc's keys," Bill muttered from the back seat of the BMW.

Morty snorted while he fiddled with the unlit cigar in his fingers. Considering they were all wearing scrubs emblazoned with the Good Samaritan logo and had knocked out the werewolf assigned to guard them, grand theft auto was the least of their problems. "I don't think Doc Z. would've ordered me not to smoke in her car, then left the keys on her desk if she didn't know what we were planning."

"What *you* were planning, moron."

Leave it to Bill not to call him a liar directly. Morty twisted to look over his shoulder. Not too long ago, such a move would have left him wracked in pain from the damn arthritis. Now, he felt forty years younger, and he wasn't about to let go of the second chance providence had granted him.

He glared at Bill. "This jerk is the reason we're not camping out in our graves. Toots is the reason we don't look like George Romero extras. We owe her."

Guilt tugged Bill's face under the passing headlights, and he nodded.

"What do we do after that, Morty?" Lily's voice carried a serious tone under her smoky husk. She glanced at him before returning her attention to the vehicle—and the woman—they chased. "We can't go back to our families."

Leave it to the broads to try to be practical when he was trying to save the damsel. He hadn't thought about what they'd do after they saved the kid's ass. Hell, the doc still had no clue why they were running around, and younger than when they died, in the first place. What would Molly do if he showed up on her doorstep?

He played with the stogie as he contemplated that thought. Interesting that Ex-wife Number Two popped in his head instead of Wife Number Three, who stood by his bedside when he took that last breath.

An audible gulp sounded in Lily's throat. "I don't want to die again. Call me a chicken, but the cancer hurt too damn much the first time."

Bill leaned forward and patted her shoulder. "That won't happen, Lily. Samantha's not that type of girl."

A bitter laugh erupted from Lily. "She doesn't even know how she restored us."

Morty shoved the end of the cigar between his teeth and bit down. Hard. Lucky for them, Lily and Bill had only the haziest of recollections of last night's events. He remembered though. It was all he could do not to puke at the pictures flashing in his brain. How he slashed her throat open. How the crimson liquid sprayed all over the place. How sweet it tasted.

The stogie seemed to suck the spit from his mouth. If Toots's blood was the only way to stay alive, then by God, he'd drink it. But he needed her intact, and that meant facing the bastard who'd dragged him out of his grave.

——— ·•· ———

David's eyes snapped open, and he glanced around the living room. Shadows filled the space, daylight long gone from their depth. Surprised at having fallen asleep, he sat up and rubbed his eyes. The only sound was the twin hums of the A/C and the refrigerator, but something had awakened him.

No, not the presence of something. The absence. The fae shield surrounding his place was gone.

"Millanthropas!"

One shadow next to the widescreen parted from the rest. "Do you require something, David Jebediah Head?"

One of Duke's bodyguards. He couldn't tell which girl in the darkness. "Where's the shield you promised me?"

Her laughter prickled his skin. "*I* promised *you* nothing."

Panic skittered underneath his puckered flesh. "Your queen did through Duke Millanthropas."

Again, the cold laughter filled the room. "Based on your assertion of inno-cence." The midnight outline of face, hair and pert breasts moved closer to the couch. "We both know you're hardly innocent, David."

From the purr in her voice, he was dealing with Ruby. And humans were noth-ing more than toys to her. Fuck. Sapphire at least had some affection for him.

Yeah, Davy, the same affection some rich bitch has for her lap dog.

Funny how Yvonne's remembered words made him feel a little better. Didn't make Ruby any less of a threat. "I want to talk to Millanthropas." He licked his lips. "Now."

Ebony heat slid across his body as she straddled him. "I'll get him." Steel velvet fingers tugged his dick, and honey filled his head. "When I'm done with you."

Fear overrode lust. He shoved at her, but deceptively thin ankles locked under his thighs. Diamonds sparked in his vision. "Get off me, bitch!"

The diamonds exploded, sending the fae ass-first into the TV. Ruby dropped to the floor in a crouch, her normally soundless heels crunching the plastic shards of the widescreen.

"That's no way to treat your only allies, David." Fire laced her voice. Only the static electricity skating across his nerves warned him.

Reaching down with magic, he pulled at the house's slab. Hardwood groaned, cracked and shattered as the concrete underneath the floorboards shifted and molded over his body. It blocked the spell she threw at him.

He counted to two, and Armageddon shook the walls and frame of the house as the two magicks reacted violently against each other. The boom of plate glass imploding rang his ears. His skin baked in his self-made oven. Wild energy cracked the concrete encasing his form.

He waited, but the need to breathe overwhelmed him. A mental shove sent the concrete crashing to the floor. The resulting dust launched a coughing fit.

Once he caught his breath, he noticed the still form by the remnants of the widescreen. Staggering past the smoking couch, he knelt beside Ruby. Her leather and matte black armor had protected everything below the neck. Only a couple of small nicks from flying debris marked the flawless skin of her face.

Then his mind registered the thick wood shard protruding from her left eye. The wide-open right eye stared unseeingly at the ceiling.

He staggered back to his feet. Pissed would be an understatement the minute Millanthropas knew about this. He pivoted, looking for help that wasn't there.

Clenching his fists, he glared at the stupid bitch. What the hell had she been thinking? Anyone with common sense knew not to pit fae magick against a witch. Hot white anger chilled as the missing shield registered. Duke had pulled his warriors and had probably sent Ruby to . . .

Shit.

His sister, his best friend, and now the fucking fairies.

No doubt the vamps were on their way. Well, they would find out he wasn't an easy target. He knelt next to Ruby's dead body once again. A man had resources, and he'd use whatever he had at his disposal. Pulling a silver dagger from the fae's boot sheath, he started chanting.

Glass crackled underneath footsteps on the patio. Wild magick tickled his mental shields. Millanthropas hadn't sent the other fae away after all.

Chapter 31

I staggered and blinked tears from my eyes while white spots continued flashing on my retinas. Ozone filled my nostrils. "What the hell was that?" I had barely climbed out of the SUV at the gate to Head's mansion when my vision and nose had been assaulted by the explosion of energy. The scary thing was the total lack of noise from the blast.

Something grasped my shoulders. No, not something. Someone. Jake, by the Granny Smith odor trickling past the acrid stench. "Sam?"

"I'm okay." I lied. My head felt like it would blow up any minute. The experience wasn't as bad as Head's backfire spell last night, but it came in a close second.

"It was fae and witch magick interacting." Pain laced Stan's rumbling bass.

The damn spots did not help the confusion in my brain. "I thought you guys could work together."

"He means someone's throwing attack and defensive spells up at the house," Yvonne choked out. In addition to the migraine-type pain in my head I was sure she and Stan were also feeling, terror edged her words. The only witch tossing magick up there would be her baby brother. "If the energy's not tuned, it's like throwing a piece of magnesium in a toilet."

Oh, jeez. "Except a lot worse."

"Yes."

Something slithered to my right, and I jerked out of Jake's grasp. Soft honey wafted past the ozone. I raised the paint gun in that direction, even though I couldn't have hit Mom and Dad's garage at point blank range with my blurred eyesight. "Freeze, asshole."

A familiar chuckle rippled across my ears. Duke Miller. "Do you really think you could hit me right now, Samantha Marie Ridgeway?"

I still found it hard to think of him as anything but an R&B star, and that was a good way to get my friends killed. The fact he hadn't ordered his people to attack meant they were as incapacitated as Stan, Yvonne and me. I smiled in the direction of his voice. "I've got a load of witch potion in my gun. Wanna take a chance?"

Icy grief tainted his next words. "David Jebediah Head killed one of my bodyguards. I will not stand between you and your goal."

The spots eased enough I could see two purplish forms a few yards away. From the white lines running across them, they stood on the other side of the gate.

I frowned. Something wasn't right. I'd never seen Duke without both girls in arm's reach. Why would he leave one of the twins alone with Head? Brain cells tried to fire despite the ache. Head hadn't killed anyone without a reason. Granted, his reasoning was totally warped.

A whisper of movement next to me preceded the hint of sandalwood. Not Duncan's rich, woodsy smell, but spice overlaid with the rotten egg smell of grief. Anxiety sent another wash of acid through my stomach.

The *click-hiss* of Kensai drawing his sword came before his words. "Head discovered your betrayal."

Thank god, vampires could only smell magick. Otherwise, he would be blind too. Bracing myself against the emotional anguish, I reached out mentally for the vampire.

What betrayal?

Ruby has always performed Millanthropas's dirty work, at least for the four centuries I've known her.

Gerbils began swimming in my stomach acid pool. *Who's with Duke besides Sapphire?*

I do not detect any other fae in the vicinity. And the fae shield is down.

That explained some of the weird silence. *Duncan!*

No answer.

"He was alive before we left the house a few minutes ago."

My sight had cleared enough to detect the movement of Duke's mouth at the top of the deep purple pillar of his body. I aimed the paintball gun at the tiny black opening. "Doesn't mean you didn't have Ruby kill him first before she went after Head."

Decaying flowers drifted past my over-sensitive nose. "She didn't touch your mate." The deadness in Sapphire's voice matched her scent. "We have no wish for your attention on us."

"Huh?" The bitch was lying. She had to be. It was no secret the fairy queens wanted me gone. Why would Duke and his minions care about attracting my notice?

The laugh from Duke blew more fear across raw nerves. "What is the human proverb?" The second dragged forever before another laugh. "A bull in a china shop." Sharp white teeth appeared in the black hole of his mouth. "It would be rather idiotic of me to wave a red flag in front of a bull like you, wouldn't it, Samantha?"

Any time someone used my full name it never boded well for me. "Then open the freakin' gate and get out of the way, or I pull the trigger."

Apparently, Duke decided not to call my bluff. The two now-black forms shifted to the left. A quick series of electronic beeps, then the gates swung inward.

My aim shifted to cover Duke and Sapphire as they gave the steel latticework a wide berth. "Where're the rest of your fairies?"

A soft intake of breath came from Duke, then his scent rippled. Putrid lemon and dead roses overlaid his honey. "They are no longer here."

Fuck. There had to be more fae than just Ruby throwing magick at the top of the cliff. "Stan?"

"There's just the three of us anywhere near Head's house. Don't worry." A hint of satisfaction lay beneath the bass rumble. "These two aren't going anywhere."

"Sam." Jake's hand grabbed my elbow again. "You can't go in there." His voice lowered. "You can't see a damn thing."

I swallowed the laugh at his attempted discretion. Reaching for the warmth on my arm, I patted his hand. "You worry too much."

"How many fingers am I holding up?"

I batted at the black thing waving in front of my face. "We stick to the plan."

— • —

The scrape of boots drew Duncan's attention away from the shackles and back to the doorway. Silence and darkness had reigned for the last few minutes since the explosion of ozone. Who'd been foolish enough to throw the first spell? Even worse, who had survived the battle?

A lithe form appeared in the bedroom doorway. He peered at Ruby through the one eye not swollen shut by her previous exercises. She stood perfectly still for an instant, then the fae woman shambled toward him.

Bloody wonderful. His good eye closed. No doubt the fairies would try to use him to bargain for Samantha.

The wash of blood and decay swept past the ozone that clogged his sinuses. His good eye popped open. The silver and black mail covering her upper body was gone. Her leather jerkin gaped open, revealing pristine fae flesh smeared with crimson and a fist-sized hole over her heart.

Or where a heart should have been.

Film covered the malicious glitter that normally shone in her eyes. The awkward gait no longer resembled a fae's light step. In four hundred years, few things grabbed his intestines and twisted them like the sight of the zombie fae bending over him. He sent a quick prayer to the Virgin Mary that the zombie wouldn't literally twist his guts before he had a chance to run.

She reached for the silver chains holding his arms. A solid yank snapped the links. She shifted and bent over his legs. At the groan and crack of overstressed silver, Duncan whipped the arm chains forward. The links caught the zombie across the cheek, ripping blotchy skin. She, no, it, Duncan corrected himself. The woman who'd tortured him less than an hour ago no longer inhabited the body that tumbled onto the bed. Using his legs as leverage, he tossed the dead woman across the room.

He rolled off the bed, but muscle weakness from the fae's ministrations and the lack of blood sent him reeling to the floor. Using the dresser, he dragged himself to his knees. Shuffling sounds behind the bed warned him of his fate if he didn't get out of this house. He forced aching bones upright and stumbled through the bedroom door.

The scent of fresh blood triggered the extension of his fangs as he entered the living room. Splatter patterns decorated the floor around the smashed widescreen. The hardwood and concrete had buckled as if an earthquake had centered in the room.

A shadow fell over him. David stood near the shattered floor-to-ceiling windows overlooking the patio and pool. Wetness shone silvery red under the moonlight streaming through the opening and across his naked body.

"Sorry, man. Can't let you leave yet."

Nutrient-starved muscles refused to move at Duncan's command as the fist flew at his face. Beneath the crack of his skull ricocheting from David's blow and crashing into something hard and sharp behind him, Duncan could have sworn he heard Samantha screaming his name. Before he could answer her, the scarlet stars darkening his eyes turned black.

Chapter 32

The four of us started up the drive, Kensai leading me and Brandon doing the same for Yvonne behind us. White spots had stopped exploding in my vision, but the magickal A-bomb still compromised my eyesight. Without streetlights, I'd been reduced to Normal vision.

I'd forgotten how much being mortal sucked. But then from the tension in the hand that guided me, Kensai wasn't happy about moving at regular human speed either.

We'd trudged halfway to the house when something bit me. Before I could slap at the offending insect on my arm, it exploded in a silvery white puff.

"What the hell was that?" Brandon's voice hit the falsetto pitch that had grated my nerves when he was still with his boy band. It didn't sound any better with super hearing.

"A mosquito. Or it was." Kensai shot me a puzzled expression. Or at least it appeared to be. The moon wasn't as full as it had been a couple of nights ago, and its glow along with his gold eyes gave the vampire's face some pretty odd shadows. "What happened?"

The last thing that bit me and blew up had been Sierra Mallory, the only other cybernetic zombie. I shrugged. "The nanites don't like it when something does an unauthorized blood withdrawal."

But the exploding mosquito set off alarms in my head. Bebe had theorized my nanites were incompatible with Sierra's, so when the former heiress started gnawing on me, the robotic smackdown literally consumed her from the inside out.

Except the damn mosquito didn't have any nanites.

A stillness settled on the estate in the few seconds I tried to figure out the exploding bug problem. I blinked, peering through fuzzy eyeballs, but nothing came into focus. Even the mosquitoes stopped buzzing under the building silence. Then the fresh wave of ozone followed by musty decay proved my olfactory nerves were back to normal.

"Run!" Yvonne's scream ripped a ragged gash through the air.

I sensed more than saw the things flying, running or hopping toward us. I twisted out of Kensai's grip to catch the ginger-smelling figure of the witch. Tossing her over my shoulder, I sent, *Grab Brandon. I'll follow you.*

The vampire didn't argue. Brandon was too scared to protest from his silence and the waves of ash rolling off him.

I did my best to keep up with Kensai, but the pavement rolled under my toes, making balance even more difficult. Behind my shoulder, Yvonne whispered foreign words. The ground swelled and receded on both sides of us in time to her rhythm. It finally sunk into my brain she could see the animal zombies on the manicured yard through her abilities and used the sod to crush them.

A zombie rabbit slipped by and latched on my ankle. I stumbled and nearly dropped Yvonne. *Can't go down. I can't go down.* A shake of my leg and the decomposing bunny flew into the air. A wet thump hit the grass. It hadn't exploded into sparkly dust.

The vision of the zombies licking my blood at the wedding flashed through my head. I clamped down on the nausea. We didn't have time to deal with resurrected rabbits. Lungs sucked air as I raced after Kensai.

Unfortunately, Yvonne couldn't do a darn thing about the chitonous bugs dive-bombing us. Brandon shrieked as the things landed on him and proceeded to snack on his exposed skin. I chewed and spit out the few that flew into my mouth. But it was difficult to focus on running, keeping my trap shut, and breathing through my nose as black specks filled the night.

And I really wished my eyesight would go away again when I spotted the resurrected feral cats covering the ground in huge leaps.

Then we were inside the main door. Kensai threw the lock. Brandon crumpled to the floor. Yvonne and I smashed the remaining zombie bugs. Both the vampire and I breathed hard, though the entire episode had lasted less than a minute.

Kensai was still bent over, and I reached for him. He slapped my hand away and growled, "Don't touch me."

He straightened. Neon yellow filled his eyes, and his fangs were fully extended. Brandon squeaked and scrambled across the tile, away from Kensai. Even I took a step away from the vampire.

Then the metallic odor filled my nostrils, followed by the nasty tang of recent death.

No. Please don't let us be too late.

I crossed the foyer, following the scent that had set off Kensai. When I entered the living room, gorge rose in my throat. Blood was splattered over the floor near the remains of a big screen television. The hardwood in the center of the floor had been splintered. Smashed concrete showed through missing or damaged planks. Acrid smoke wisped from the remains of leather couches. A couple of strides brought me to the shattered TV. Sweet honey and sweeter decay coated the scarlet splashes.

This was where Ruby died, but where the hell was her body?

"This is Duncan's." Kensai's words drew me to where he stood next to the smaller stains on a hallway wall leading further into the house. A whiff of distinctive sandalwood confirmed his assessment.

My stomach lurched. Were we too late? I didn't think I could take facing a zombie Duncan. What we'd have to do if Head had already killed my man.

Glass crackled behind me. I whirled in time to catch a glimpse of blank, filmy eyes before Ruby launched herself at me. My back took the brunt of the impact against the wall. Plasterboard cracked and shuddered. Wood framing groaned. White powder filled the air.

Before I could clear gypsum dust from my throat, a slim fist wrapped itself in the folds of my shirt, using it to jerk the rest of my body clear of the dent. My knees smacked hardwood, shooting pain up my thighs. Silver flashed above my head.

The clang of metal interrupted the whole life flashing before my eyes thing. With a shove and some fancy sword work, Kensai drove the dead fairy away from me. He parried her next blow and countered with a thrust to the heart.

Okay, where her heart should have been. A short syllable of Japanese exploded from his lips as he realized the same thing I did.

Zombie Ruby's backhand sent him reeling into the innards of the widescreen.

I struggled to my feet when the first pop sounded. Noxious liquid exploded from the blue balloon and across the gory mess of Ruby's chest.

The zombie hesitated for an instant before raising her sword, blank attention fixed on me. Four more balloons impacted. The former fairy seemed to collapse in on her body. She, no, it slumped to the floor. Yellowish fumes wafted from the corpse.

I glanced at Brandon as he lowered the paintball gun. "Thanks."

"*De nada.*" The singer stared at the immobile body, looking a little green. He swallowed hard.

I couldn't blame him. My stomach was trying its best to rebel, too.

"He's outside." Yvonne's harsh whisper froze Kensai as he tried to extract himself from the wires and circuit boards of the ruined television.

"Where?" My voice sounded down right gravely compared to hers.

Her forehead wrinkled in concentration. "The other side of the pool. Near the guest house."

I took a step toward the ruined sliding glass doors when a cold hand on my shoulder halted me. Twisting to glare at Kensai, I mouthed, "Let go."

With a sharp shake of his head, he slipped between me and the doors. *Duncan would flay me if anything happened to you.* Glass crunched under his boots as he eased his way closer.

"Do you have a freakin' death wish?" I hissed. "There's a necromancer out there who doesn't give a shit who's in the way when he tries to kill me."

He ignored me and used his retrieved sword to peer around the tattered curtains. The crackle of more bits made me look. Yvonne stationed herself by the curtains at the other side. Brandon stood behind her, knuckles tight around the paintball gun.

It reminded me of my own gun slung over my shoulder. I pulled it forward, only to have wetness meet my fingers. The plastic barrel was bent, a neat crease in the center I'd bet matched my backbone. The cracked casing had sent a shard through one of the balloons. I shook liquid from my hand. The last thing I needed was for the anti-zombie spell to work on me.

"Are you okay?" Concern laced Yvonne's voice.

I concentrated for a moment. Nope, no dizziness, no tingling in the extremities. The nausea I could attribute to other causes. I nodded.

Unsnapping my hopper, I tossed it to Brandon. He promptly scooped out a handful of balls to replace the ammo he'd used, and dumped the rest in the messenger bag slung across his chest.

Peering over Kensai's shoulder, I shuddered at the scene. Red tinged the pool water. Crimson puddled on the concrete patio.

"Come on out, Ridgeway! I know you're in there!" No mistaking Head's voice, but it had an odd timbre to it, like two soundtracks a split-second out of synch.

Yvonne caught my eye and shook her head.

I stepped around Kensai's outstretched arm. "Stick with the plan. I'll distract him."

Glass snapped and popped underneath the rubber tread of my Nikes. The magick clash had blown out the pool and patio lights, but the moon overhead set everything in sharp relief. A dark figure stood at the edge of the deep end, a pale bundle at his feet.

A deep breath sent reassurance through my soul. Decay didn't mar the familiar sandalwood, but from the sharp metallic aftertaste, Duncan was hurt. Bad. That was why he hadn't answered my call.

"If he dies, you'll have nothing to bargain with, David." My voice should have echoed against the bare walls of the main house. Shadows swallowed the sound. Hell, there wasn't even the faint hum of traffic that normally echoed off the bluffs and canyon walls of Malibu.

"I don't have *anything* because of you, bitch!"

Anger rolled across any guilt lingering over the damage from a two-year-old story. "I'm not the one throwing away a multi-million dollar contract to settle a score."

Harsh laughter filled the air. "Like I give a shit about the money."

"You're right." Déjà vu settled over the bizarre tableau. Why did I attract the supernatural crazies? "From what you did to your supposed best friend, it's obvious you don't give a shit about people either."

"I'm going to take the same pound of flesh you took from me."

I didn't even get the whiff of ozone before the concrete bucked under me. My body shot through the air. Chlorinated water sprayed as I hit the surface with the nastiest belly flop on the face of the planet. Sinking down, my legs contracted in anticipation of pushing off the bottom.

Cold, clammy hands wrapped around my ankles. In the murky water, pale figures surrounded me. I struggled and thrashed, but I couldn't break free. More fingers clutched at my wrists, my clothes. Not the dried up bodies or the squishy, freshly dead of before. These were the bloated corpses of drowning victims.

A silent scream blew the little air left out of my lungs. I'd found the rest of Duke's people.

Chapter 33

Chlorine burned tender nose membranes. My lungs wanted to suck anything to replace the expelled air. Burning need warred with dizziness. Being dead didn't mean I wouldn't pass out from lack of oxygen. Once I was totally helpless, the fairy zombies would rip me apart.

And Head wouldn't have any reason to keep Duncan alive.

A desperate kick freed one leg. The water hampered the zombies as much as it did me. A wild grab missed when I coiled and scissored off the concrete. A couple of them were jerked along for the ride to the surface.

Blessed air met my gaping mouth. The threatening numbness in my limbs faded, and I struck out for the side, my two passengers still trying to claw my left leg apart. Damn, why were all of Head's zombies obsessed with that particular appendage?

I wasn't the world's greatest swimmer, but the nanites made up for my lack of style with raw strength. I grasped the side and heaved my torso out of the water. The fairy zombies clinging to my leg tried to drag me back under, but a hard swing against the edge of the pool knocked them off. Another heave and I rolled onto my back. Wet coughs brought up the water that had managed to seep down my throat.

Slow, mocking claps reached my ears. I leveraged an elbow under me. Head's teeth gleamed under silvery light.

He shook his head. "Stupid bitch."

I swiveled my head. The rest of the fairy zombies waded out of the shallow end, their aim obvious.

My attention jerked back to Head. "You'd kill your own sister?"

Head's eyes widened. I didn't take the bait. He knew Yvonne was in the house, the same way she knew he was out here.

"Stop this now, David," a masculine voice rang out.

Surprise brought me to my knees. Brandon, not Kensai.

The pop singer stood in the ruined doorway, a Rambo-wannabe from his stance and the aim of the paintball gun. Only the death grip on the trigger gave away his anxiety.

"I said, stop it, David." He squeezed off a couple of shots at the nearest zombie. Yellowish fumes encircled the dead fairy before it collapsed to the patio. The rest paused, robots waiting for their next orders.

Except the zombie master was having difficulty processing his ex playing pissed off 'Nam vet. "How c-c—" An audible gulp broke the tension. My attention swung back and forth between the two men. Finally, Head choked out, "What the fuck are you doing with her?" He jabbed a finger in my direction.

"Trying to keep you from doing anything stupider than you've already done." Anger snapped in Brandon's voice.

I didn't dare move. No sense distracting the witch if Brandon could talk him down.

"After what she did—"

"She didn't lock me in her bedroom with a pissed off vampire!" A rush of air, as the singer took a diaphragm-level breath. Roses mixed with the ash and brimstone rolling off him. "Let these folks go. I'll do what I can to help you, David. These people are fair. There's extenuating circumstances—"

"You left me, you bastard!"

If the tears and pain in Head's voice hadn't warned me, the ozone and a deep rumble under the concrete would have. I was on my feet racing for Brandon. *Too late. I'm too late.*

Kensai shot through the door. He shoved the kid into the grass, hard enough Brandon's chin and chest dug a furrow in the pristine yard. With a horrendous crack, concrete yawed open underneath the vampire's feet.

A split-second turned into an eternity. Kensai hovered over the chasm, Wile E. Coyote still running before he realizes nothing's underneath him. A soft, sad smile filled his features. Then he was falling. Earth and stone roared.

I stumbled as the ground flowed under my feet. My knees and hands cracked the concrete when I landed. I looked up. A jagged scar marred the patio where the enforcer had stood.

"Kensai!" No answer. I scrambled for the crack, the opening blurred by tears. I dug and pried the broken chunks, tossing them aside. I reached out, trying to sense where he was, the best place to dig. This couldn't happen. I wouldn't let it.

Something pulled me away from the collapsed hole, something cold and clammy and unyielding. Dead flesh and razor-sharp nails tore at my skin and clothes. Pain stabbed through my abdomen. Screams of rage and pain filled the air, too high-pitched to be Head's.

Obnoxious liquid exploded around me, yellowish fumes filling the air. The ground bucked and twisted under me. I screamed and tore and thrashed at my attackers.

Then warmth gripped my chin, forcing my attention to brilliant blue eyes and flaming red hair. A husky voice murmured, "We've got you, kid. Quit fighting us. You're safe."

No, I wasn't. None of us were with David Head running around and no checks on his power.

Lily pulled the silver fae knife out of my gut. I couldn't stop my scream. After a round of intense pain and a lot of panting, I realized my trio of zombie comedians crouched around me. The fire in my belly subsided enough for me to notice it wasn't lightning illuminating the back yard. I glanced around.

Under the flashing lightshow, Mai crouched next to Brandon who sat a few feet away. Blood poured down the singer's face from an ugly cut across his hairline. Jake stood over them, his paintball gun sweeping the scene.

Fairy zombies sprawled across the ruined patio. Some obviously shot by Brandon, Jake and the enforcers from the smell, the really gross ones just as obviously dismembered by me.

Near the pool house, energy flared and sizzled between the siblings in a deadly game of magickal dodgeball. Even though she was outmatched in raw power, Yvonne made up for it in accuracy. If David hadn't been holding an unconscious Duncan as a shield, she would have gotten him.

Stan prowled around the other side of the pool toward the dueling pair. My heart lurched into my mouth. He wouldn't do something stupid like start throwing fairy spells in the mix, would he?

But any wishful thinking on my part was quickly nipped. A wild shot by the necromancer didn't hit Yvonne, but the chunk of wood sheared off a nearby tree smacked her in the temple. She collapsed sideways into some charred foliage.

Mai jumped to her feet. "Stan!"

Then I realized the giant tree hadn't lost a chunk, but half the trunk. Three loud pops and the tree was falling. Falling on the half-fae enforcer in its path.

When a tree falls on a half-fairy in a bisexual basketball-playing necromancer's yard, it's pretty fucking loud.

Quiet reigned for a moment before Bill muttered, "Oh, shit." Head turned in my direction. "I hope you got a plan, kid."

Morty and Lily's hands wrapped around mine and pulled me to my feet.

Anger burned cold in my gut now that the knife wounds were healing. "Yeah," I said. "I do." With me being the only supernatural standing between the Normals and a necromancer, I took a page from James Bond. I leapt straight for the bad guy.

Chapter 34

Head's eyes widened and his mouth dropped. I surprised myself too. My diving launch arced over the pool, and I caught him around the waist in mid-turn as he tried to shift my unconscious boyfriend between us.

The three of us tumbled to the concrete, Head and I wrestling for purchase. Duncan, on the other hand, flopped around like a dead fish.

I winced at that mental image. My distraction let Head plow one of his huge elbows into my cheek. Stars exploded behind my eyeball. Damn, no wonder the other basketball players avoided going mano a mano on rebounds with this guy.

I rolled, not waiting for his follow-up. A wet-sounding crunch came a second later, and Head bellowed.

Crab-crawling, I scooted away from Duncan and Yvonne. Would Mai take the hint and get them out of the line of fire? Oh, hell, was Stan even still alive?

I didn't dare send anything to them telepathically with my lack of control. I needed Head's attention solely on me.

Except I lied to Bill. I didn't really have a plan. I just had to stall long enough for the surviving enforcers and Jake to come up with one.

A wrought-iron patio chair skidded in my direction. Okay, keeping David's focus on me wasn't going to be as much of a problem as I thought with his telekinetic stunts. I flung myself out of the way and onto the cool grass. A chunk of concrete exploded inches away, shrapnel slicing across my face. I rolled to a crouch and grinned at the enraged basketball pro.

"C'mon, Davy. Is that the best you can do? Throw rocks at the zombie?"

"You can't call me that, bitch!" I swear specks of foam flew from his mouth as he stalked toward me.

"Awww, is poor wittle Davy mad?" A flower pot whistled past my head, and I side-stepped further down the sloping yard. "Is poor wittle Davy taking his toys home?" Another chunk of broken concrete flew toward me, and I dodged to the right. Good. My taunts had ignited his rage to such a pitch he wasn't bothering with spells, just telekinetics.

Right now, it was the only point in my favor. My physical strength topped his, but could I take him without killing him? My promises to Yvonne and Brandon clanged in the back of my head.

"Whatsa matter, Davy? Don't like it when someone can fight back?"

He grunted as he launched a folded table umbrella javelin-style. I hopped backwards, and the tip buried into the soft soil a foot from my toes.

"Forgot to bring your mama's corpse to sic on me, Head?"

"Don't you dare talk about her. Don't you fucking dare!" Head stalked after me, fingers flexing like he wanted to squeeze the life, or death, out of me. The whites shown around his dark eyes.

I deliberately lowered my voice. "Y'know, Head, maybe Al Jenkins really is your father. He liked to hurt women too."

A roar filled with pain and rage and grief echoed through the night. He charged, but I side-stepped, leg outstretched to sweep his out from under him. Not taking any chances, I jumped on his back. He bucked and I went tumbling across the grass.

Three dark shapes raced out of the night, grabbing Head and wrestling him back to the turf. He was no match for the three zombies.

Morty pinned a flailing arm with his knee. "We got him, toots! Do your thing."

I crawled over to David's head and laid a hand on his cheek. The bastard actually tried to bite me. Dammit, it was Sierra Mallory all over again. I closed my eyes, wanting words to convince him to stop this insanity. Words had always been my weapon of choice . . .

. . . and I blinked green spots away from my vision. I sat on a bedspread decorated in stitched basketballs, my hand resting on the cheek of a familiar little boy.

"You're not Yvonne," he accused, scooting away from me. Cobwebs covered him, twining through his dark curls and glowing against his coffee skin. Odd-looking, glowing cobwebs.

"No, I'm not." I glanced around. We were in David's bedroom in the old Nebraska farmhouse. What the hell was going on? How'd I get here? Yvonne was out cold in the yard of his Malibu house. Wasn't she?

Except I knew this wasn't a memory.

I turned my attention back to the six-year-old staring at me through slitted eyes. "She asked me to watch you." It was the best explanation I could come up with.

He eased closer. "What are you?"

"Umm . . ." How the hell was I supposed to answer that?

He peered at my face, an analytical expression on his. "Ya ain't got no wings, so you can't be the tooth fairy." I noticed his missing front teeth. "And your eyes are glowing like a vamp's."

"Look, David, I'm supposed to tuck you in." I reached for the bedspread and stared at my outstretched hand. My skin had a silver sheen under the starlight twinkling through the open window.

"And you don't look like no white woman I've ever seen."

Kids could see through any line of bullshit, so I opted for the truth. "I'm not sure what I am. Someone made me, but I don't think he even knew what he was making." Not for the first time I wondered how much Fred was following Selene and Mallory's orders and how much he experimented on his own when he programmed the nanites that now inhabited my body.

I took a closer look at David. "What do you have all over you?"

He stared at the funky cobwebs a moment before he looked up at me and shrugged. "Dunno."

Then I realized they weren't exactly cobwebs. More like writing. Almost.

The top layer of red looked odd, jerky, reptilian. Like the language a lizard would use, if lizards could use a pen, that is. The middle layer was a deep brilliant green. Not modern writing, but Afro-centric symbols. The bottom layer consisted of a sparkling black pattern. Something so alien that if I studied hard enough, I'd know the secrets of the universe.

I brushed at the fine threads. They dissolved under my touch, turning from their original color to silver before disappearing totally.

"There. Now that you're cleaned up, why don't you lay down? Growing boys need their sleep."

He squirmed under the covers, and I pulled the bedspread to his chin. Earnest eyes stared up at me as I stood. I bit my lip. For a moment, I would have sworn it was the adult David looking at me, no longer filled with hate and bile.

The need for forgiveness tore at my soul. "I'm sorry for hurting you. I was wrong and I shouldn't have taken those pictures of you without your say-so."

A sage nod preceded his words. "S'okay. I'm sorry I got mad at you. Mama says I got a temper and I let it make my decisions."

I bent and kissed his forehead. "Goodnight, David." I rose and turned to leave.

"Am I ever gonna wake up, Miss Sam?"

I looked back at the little boy ensconced in basketballs made of thread. How could I answer when I didn't understand myself? "I hope so, David. I hope so."

Chapter 35

I blinked. The vanilla taste of Twinkies filled my mouth, and the antiseptic smell of a hospital filled my nose.

"Aw, shit. Not again." My head fell forward and landed in a crinkling mass of cellophane.

"Out of my way, boys."

I raised my head to find Bebe elbowing Bill and Morty away from my bedside. A loud belch exploded from my lips.

"Samantha!"

I blinked once more. Mom and Dad hovered at the foot of the bed. I looked around. Mai stood by the door, but her hand wasn't on the butt of her semi-automatic this time.

"What day is it? How's Duncan?"

Bebe shoved the frigid stethoscope down my hospital gown. "Monday morning. Now, shut up."

The damn thing was marginally warmer when she moved it to my back. It didn't stop me from noticing she hadn't answered my question. A ball of ice, far colder than any stethoscope, rolled through the Twinkie mash in my stomach.

"Bebe—" I couldn't say anything more without the ball of ice turning to tears.

She reached for my hand and squeezed. "He's stable. That's the good thing."

Stable? The V-virus healed anything short of beheading or a stake through the heart. What the hell had Head done to Duncan?

I flipped the covers and swung my legs around. "I want to see him."

"Samantha!" Mom screeched.

"Nice to know the color's natural, toots." Morty grinned around the unlit cigar in his mouth.

I flipped the blanket, sheet and my gown back over my lower half. "Anyone who's not a doctor needs to clear the room." I turned to look at Mai when no one moved. "Can I borrow your gun?"

Even Mom barreled through the door. Mai flashed a grin before following my parents and the zombie trio. It was the first time I'd ever seen the woman smile a genuine smile.

The Twinkies curdled in my stomach. Mai had smiled at me even though I'd gotten her grandfather killed last night. If I were Mai, I would have unloaded the full clip into my skull.

— • —

Fresh jeans and a clean t-shirt against showered skin improved my mood before I traipsed up to the ICU. I made a quick side trip before heading down to Duncan's room.

Yvonne sat quietly by David's bedside when I entered. Monitors beat a steady rhythm. All of them except for one vital indicator.

I tensed as she rose and rushed toward me. But instead of the attack I half-expected, she embraced me in a hard hug.

She stepped back, holding me at arm's length, and nodded. "Good to see you up. I feared Master Augustine had lied about your true condition to spare my feelings."

The soft beeping filled the silence before I found my voice. "I'm so sorry, Yvonne."

She shrugged. "He's alive." Looking back at the unmoving form in the bed, she still talked even though she kept both hands on me. "Medically, the Normals would write him off as brain dead, but he's not. Deep down, I can still feel him."

When she turned back to me, unshed tears glimmered. "I don't know how you bound him, but it's tight."

Too tight. So fucking tight, the man was essentially in a coma. And I didn't have the slightest clue of exactly what I did or how. "Yvonne—"

She placed warm fingers to my lips. "He's a necromancer. It will fade with time."

Damn it. She wasn't sure any more than Bebe or me. For all intents and purposes, I might as well have killed him.

A soft *whoosh* behind me made me turn. Brandon stood there, a little surprised to see me from his wide eyes. "Hey." His fingers fluttered, then he couldn't seem to meet my gaze. He focused on Yvonne. "The jet's ready. Nurse said they'd be up in a few minutes to take him down to the ambulance."

"Jet?" My attention flicked between the two. "Where're you taking him?"

Yvonne raised her chin. "To a private facility in Miami. Jean-Pierre has made arrangements for his care."

Made sense. Miami was the vampire master's capital. Yvonne could visit her brother as often as she wanted. "Have you come up with a cover story?"

A wry smile tilted the witch's lips. "He was drunk and fell into the pool."

I sighed. It'd be hard to dispute, and knowing the vamps, a second set of medical records supporting the story had been "accidentally" leaked to the tabloids thanks to my former boss.

Former boss. I guess I'd made my decision after all.

I turned to Brandon. "I'm really sorry about—" About what? Ruining his love affair? Destroying his singing career? Sinking him deep in an alien world he wasn't prepared for? I settled with saying, "For everything."

He shuffled his feet. "My bags are already in the car, Yvonne. You want me to take yours down?"

Okay, I didn't expect him to hug me, but I wanted some acknowledgement. "You're leaving Los Angeles? What about your new recording contract?"

Finally, his eyes met mine. "I can fulfill it in Florida." His eyes slitted. "Plan on fucking that up too?"

"Brandon!"

I held up my hand. "It's okay, Yvonne. He's got every right."

He held up his hands. "What am I supposed to say? Thanks for only putting my boyfriend in a coma instead of killing him?"

Guilt sucked on my conscience. I pivoted to leave, but Yvonne didn't release her hold on my arm. The last thing I wanted was to hurt her any more than I had. I stopped.

"For what it's worth, *merci beaucoup, chére.*"

I nodded. "You're welcome. *Bon voyage.*" Her throaty laughter followed me through the door. I could almost have laughed too at my piss-poor French. Almost.

At the end of the hallway, I peeked through the thin window set in the door to the windowless room. Tiffany sat curled in the recliner next to the bed. Black eyeliner and dark purple lipstick decorated her face, a good sign. Her fingers tapped against the pad cradled in her lap to the beat of the EKG. She obviously wasn't concentrating on whatever she had pulled up online.

I followed her gaze to the man lying in the bed next to her. Duncan's skin nearly blended into the sheets. Dark bruises and various cuts marred his chiseled features. My stomach flipped. If his skin still held evidence of his imprisonment, it meant the virus worked on repairing more serious injuries. Blood IV's ran into each arm. I swallowed hard to contain the tears. Bebe had warned me.

Pulling open the door, I edged in as quietly as I could. "How's he doing?" I whispered.

"I have felt better."

The kid and I jumped at the wheezy voice coming from the bed. My stomach righted itself at the dry clipped humor contained in Duncan's croak.

"Hey." I crossed over to his side. There was a spot of skin relatively intact on his forehead, and I planted a kiss there.

A chuckle rippled into a cough. Tiffany jumped up and her pad crashed to the floor. I gripped the bed rails, unsure of how to help him. He waved Tiffany back before he resumed laughing.

"This isn't funny, Duncan." She glared at him, tiny fists propped on her hips. "You've gone through sixteen pints of blood since they brought you in last night."

The familiar affectionate smile filled his face. "Where's your husband?"

Tiffany's scowl deepened. "They really knocked you on the head. Reverend Mitchell didn't have the chance to finish the ceremony, remember?"

He frowned, and I laid a hand over his fingers. "It's okay. As far as the Normal guests are concerned, the ceremony went off without a hitch, but a freak windstorm blew over a tent and hurt a bunch of people."

Tiffany crossed her arms. "Only because Satan Spawn threatened to stake Caesar with her Manolo Blahniks if the vamps laid any other memory."

I fixed Tiffany with a dirty look. "How many times do I have to tell you? Only I get to call my mom Satan Spawn."

She stuck her tongue out at me.

"Then we call Reverend Mitchell and arrange—"

I squeezed his fingers gently. "Reverend Mitchell got his memories altered too, which is probably a good thing after the way he reacted when you vamped out in front of him."

Another chuckle. "Oh, yes."

I didn't know how much he really remembered and how much he was humoring us. I caught Tiffany's attention and inclined my head toward the door. "Why don't you go get something to eat? I'll stay with him."

Her lips puckered, but before the protest could spew, she gave a sharp nod. "I'll be back."

I toed the standard visitor's chair closer and sat, not daring to let go of his chill fingers. "How are you really feeling?"

"Like I have been run over by a tractor-trailer, then the operator reversed to run me over again." He closed his eyes. When they opened, glowing green eyes pierced me. "If I try to have a real conversation with you, will you flee?"

A lump filled my throat. He was lying in a hospital bed after zombies beat the crap out of him and fairies tortured him, and he still wanted to have *the* talk. I crossed my heart with my free hand. "I promise not to leave until you're finished." I certainly didn't want the lughead to climb out of bed to chase me.

His eyes closed again, making the bruises around them even more pronounced. He said nothing for a very long time.

The pause nagged at me. "Are you okay? Do I need to get Bebe?"

An answering squeeze caressed my fingertips, and his eyes flew open. "No."

An undercurrent of fierceness filled his scratchy voice. "I had time to think while Head kept me prisoner. I understand your feelings, however—"

"Yes."

A sigh passed his cracked lips. "Please let me finish—" He blinked as my answer registered, then his eyes narrowed. "What are you affirming?"

I sucked in a deep breath and released it slowly. Yep, the feeling deep in my gut was still there. "Yes, I will move in with you." I held up my hand to forestall him. "But we're not announcing any engagement." I counted to three in English before I added, "Yet."

He nodded, a crazy, happy light in his eyes, even though his face remained its usual stolid countenance. "Agreed."

I couldn't help my own crazy, happy grin in return.

Chapter 36

A glance at my watch confirmed I was very, very late. Jitters ran along my nerves as I stood across the street from the courthouse, waiting for the light to change. Mom was going to raise holy hell, and it was the last thing Max and Tiffany needed today. Okay, it wasn't just the civil ceremony. I'd been pacing at my apartment all morning in anticipation of a call.

A call I was now receiving from the vibration from my suit pocket. I pulled out the cell phone and punched the button. "Yes?"

"It's a go," Marshall Wagoner's voice warbled over the cell phone. If it wasn't for my super hearing, I wouldn't have been able to hear him over the sax player wailing away behind me. "Loved the video. Absolutely loved it! How soon can they start?"

My face tightened into a wide grin. As the producer of the Vegas Parade of Stars showcase, I knew he'd be interested in my three zombie comedians. A little pride filled me. For the first time in two months, I'd done something without relying on supernatural contacts.

It didn't mean I was stupid though. "Send me the contracts, Marshall. Then we'll talk."

"Gotta ask, honey. Why are you leaving the *Scoop*? Managing comedy acts is a whole different enchilada."

"I needed the change, Marshall. When can I expect the contracts?" I wanted to get my people settled before I dealt with the insanity of packing up my miniscule belongings. Las Vegas was going to be . . . fun. Warmth filled me. A whole new start with Duncan. A whole new career. Maybe it's what I really needed in life. Or death.

"I'm e-mailing them now, sweetheart."

As I flicked the lid shut on the conversation, the white walk figure appeared. Dodging the mass of people parading in the crosswalk, I took two steps outside of the appropriate lines.

The street tilted. My vision blurred. My stomach threatened to heave its contents. *What the fuck?*

Then everything righted again, except . . .

I whirled around, a full three-sixty. The intersection was deserted. No people. No cars. Nothing. The building, the pavement, even the sky had a sepia tone. It felt like I was looking at an old photo of downtown in the library archives.

"What the fuck?" My voice echoed against the concrete. There was no other sound. I looked behind me. The sax player on the corner was gone, too. An empty case lay on the sidewalk. Wind picked up the bills that had been deposited, pushing the greenbacks along the way with an invisible hand. Rod Serling was going to step out of one of those doors any minute. I turned to face the courthouse again.

A man stood in the middle of the intersection. His dark skin contrasted sharply with the white tails he wore. His matching top hat sat at a rakish angle, not even quivering under the onslaught of the hot, dry wind. Dark glasses covered his eyes. Both glove-encased hands gripped the white cane he leaned on.

"I would have a word with you, Samantha Marie Ridgeway." The nasally voice scrapped against my spine.

"I'm sorry. Do I know you?" I took a step forward, trying for the life of me to place him. The man looked like he had tissue shoved up his nose. It would explain his voice.

He tapped his cane on the pavement. "You took something of my father's that was not pledged to you. Return it. Now."

The wind plastered the linen skirt to my legs. "What are you talking about? Who are you?"

Teeth whiter than his suit flashed. "You may call me Baron." The wide smile disappeared. "My father wishes his property back."

Definitely Twilight Zone material. The weird wind pulled strands of my hair out of the neat French braid I'd managed to tame it into this morning. "I've got no idea what you're talking about. I don't know your father."

"Don't play, girl. Return David Jebediah Head to me. Now."

My thoughts tangled as fast as my hair. Was this some fairy trick? "I don't have David. His sister took him to Miami."

The strange man tapped his cane again. "His soul was not yours to take. You have no right to it." Anger laced his words.

What the hell was going on here? My eyes blinked as the wind picked up speed. "Look, I don't have David or his soul. I can't give you what I don't have."

"Fine. If that's the way you want to play, I'll take something of yours in payment." A third tap and he disappeared.

The world tilted again. A car horn blasted in my ear. I jumped. More horns joined in a symphony of noise along with shouting and a few not-so-friendly waves. I raced to the other side of the street. Cars peeled through the intersection, the one with the now-red light. I took a deep breath and looked around me.

Normal. Everything looked totally normal again. People marching on the sidewalks to their various destinations. Cars weaving to avoid buses, pedestrians and other cars. Even Mr. Sax Guy wailed an off-key version of "Moon River."

A fairy illusion. It had to be. They were messing with me because they lost their little gambit. Another glance at the watch said I didn't have time to wonder about my bizarro visitor. But I glanced back at the now busy intersection. A shiver rippled up my spine.

———•———

Music blasted through the speakers of the back room at Anthony's. I set the tray on the table, passing out blood, champagne, and in Tiffany's case, sparkling grape juice. Glasses clinked in various salutes. I took a sip of my own flute of bubbly and watched the partiers on the makeshift dance floor. Mom actually looked like she was having fun with John Lannigan boogeying to some retro number until the judge cut in.

I nudged Bebe in the seat next to me. "Think Her Honor is aiming for alpha female."

She grinned back. "Probably. His official mourning period's been over for a year. I think he's enjoying the freedom, but the pressure to mate or abdicate . . ." She shrugged.

Mourning period. The champagne fizz burned its way down. For two minutes, I'd forgotten we'd attended funerals for the last three days. Kensai and Jamal's joint ceremony had been especially tough.

"Master Augustine?" Mai stood next to Caesar. Her staccato delivery drew everyone's attention. Her words rushed out as if she was afraid to stop. "I'd like to volunteer as Duncan's personal daytime guard in Las Vegas."

Caesar was silent for a moment. "May I ask why?"

Mai shot me a look before she answered. "He needs someone experienced with zombies."

Bebe, Max and Tiffany snickered. Duncan tensed next to me, but I had to give Caesar credit for keeping a straight face.

The vampire master turned to my guy. "And your opinion?"

Duncan inclined his head. "The transfer is acceptable."

I had a sneaking suspicion Mai had already approached him.

"We knew we'd have to do some personnel shuffling." Caesar turned to me. "And from what I hear, Sam will need assistance with packing. I've heard horror stories concerning her apartment." He shuddered.

"Hey!" I protested.

Before the pick-on-Sam fun escalated, Alex appeared at Tiffany's elbow. He set a package wrapped in gold with a silver bow in front of her with a flourish. "For you, Mrs. Howell."

Tiffany eyed it suspiciously before looking up at the blond enforcer. "You open it."

He spread his hands in a defensive gesture. "I promise. No tricks. When I cleaned out the photographer's place and erased her memory, I took the rolls she shot before everything went to hell. Got 'em developed for you. Congratulations, sweetheart." As Tiffany's posture eased, he bent and pecked her on the now flaming red cheek.

"Thanks." She ducked her head, trying to rein in the flowing embarrassment. Max reached for the package, only for Tiffany to slap his hand away. "Mine."

She tore open the wrappings and passed around the mini-albums, retaining one for her and Max to view.

Duncan flipped open the one handed to him, and I leaned closer for a look. His arm wrapped around me, cocooning my body against his broad chest.

Tiffany's voice brought me out of my feelings of snuggly contentment. She held up her album to Max, a finger pointing to a specific photo. "This one of your college friends?"

Max shook his head. "I don't even remember this picture getting taken." He shrugged with his good shoulder. "I don't recognize him, but then most of that day is one big blur. I take it he's not one of your friends?"

Duncan reached for the album, and Max pushed it into his waiting grip. Caesar rose to peer over his shoulder, and Bebe pushed closer to me.

My heart froze in my chest. In the glossy four-by-six, a grinning Max stood next to a familiar man in white tails. White teeth gleamed against coffee bean skin. Baron's arm snaked possessively around my brother's shoulders.

Oh, shit.

Turn the page for a special preview of the next Bloodlines novel, *Amish, Vamps & Thieves!*

Amish, Vamps, and Thieves

Nerves tingled along the back of Anne Levy's neck as she strode across her brother's hay field under the ripe moon. A deep breath tested the scent in the humid Ohio night air. The spicy apple of a Normal human mixed with the sweet clover and summer maple, confirming the watcher's presence. She glanced to her right. A shadow shifted within the woods bordering the east side of the field.

Her watcher was unimaginative at best, using the same cover as last night. Enforcer training jumped into play despite Anne being home for the first time in decades. A telepathic check found her partner. *Sam? My friend's back.*

The black diamond tickle of Samantha Ridgeway's humor rippled through Anne's mind. *You're sure he's not one of us?*

Yes. Anne let the crimson wash of her irritation filter through the link. Like she couldn't tell the difference between a supernatural and a Normal after sixty years.

Amish or English?

The tips of Anne's fangs pricked her bottom lip as she smiled at Sam's use of the Amish term for an outsider, but her humor was short-lived. She'd already lost everything she cared about in her life. Her home. Her chance for children. Jacob. And Thomas had sacrificed everything he desired to keep the old ways for the sake of their parents. She wouldn't, she couldn't let his sacrifice be in vain.

But if the church elders learned Thomas had contacted her for help, her brother would be shunned. He was in enough trouble for pushing the leadership of the Amish community into hiring an attorney to fight the developers and the state. If the elders found out exactly what she and Sam were . . .

Yo, Anne? You still there?

She shoved away the disconcerting thoughts and drew another deep breath. The various scents were too mixed in the still, thick air to tell if the whiff of plastic came from something the man carried or trash floating down the Killbuck River. *I can't tell from this distance, but he's definitely the same man who observed me from the woods last night while I patrolled.*

The other woman's annoyance swept back in salmon orange wave. *Then maybe you should have questioned him* last *night.*

Based on what? Anne flung the thought back. *He's made no action against me or the livestock.* And there hadn't been an animal attack since she and Sam had arrived in Millersburg. That fact lent credence to Thomas's theory that the culprit behind the livestock mutilations was indeed a supernatural. It also bolstered Sam's opinion they were dealing with a rogue. Anne had learned decades ago not to make assumptions despite the evidence. She needed proof the killings weren't linked to Birkenwald's attempts to force her brother and the other farmers out of their homes.

Sam's mental sigh whispered through her mind. *Doesn't mean he's not a look-out. It's time we had a talk with your* friend. *I'm at the north fence line of Jacob Miller's property. I'll swing around.*

Anne swallowed her discomfort at the mention of Jacob. No sense giving Sam's tongue any more ammunition. *Are you sure trapping him is a wise course of action? He may be a distraction from the real culprits.*

Oh puh-leease! If a vamp and a zombie can't handle one measly human . . . Sam's mental voice dissolved into peals of laughter. *Besides, the boys would never forgive me if I let you get slimed because the asshole's carrying one of those reaper thingies.*

It's called a scythe. Anne didn't bother to correct her on the other point. Technically, Sam wasn't a zombie, but no one knew what else to call a walking, talking dead person. At least, she hadn't stooped to eating human brains.

Yet.

Anne shoved a lock of hair behind her ear. The short strands irritated her as well, but not nearly as much as Sam's laughter, her poor estimate of Anne's abilities, or the offer of hair accessories earlier. Not that she didn't appreciate Sam's kindness, but the clips weren't—they just weren't . . .

Plain.

The prohibition against adornment stuck to her soul even after all these decades away from Holmes County. Assuming vampires still had souls. She hoped the fact that she still cared about her brother meant she did.

Anne shook her head as she walked, dislodging the hair again. She shouldn't have come home. Crickets chirped in counterpoint to the frogs along the banks, their summer song a reminder she'd never belong here again. Maybe the "boys," as Sam referred to the older vampires of the Augustine Coven, were right. Maybe she *should* join the twenty-first century. But in the sixty-plus years since rogue vampires had forced her into this existence, her faith had brought her comfort—still brought her comfort, even in her darkest times. Wearing her hair and clothes in the old style was part of that comfort as well.

And Jacob had always told her how much he loved her hair. But he wouldn't have loved it quite so much if he knew the monster she'd become.

She suppressed a shudder at the mix of old and new anxieties, and she continued stalking through the clover. She couldn't blame Sam for cutting off her waist-length locks. The zombie had done what was necessary to the ruined tresses. Her hair had become tangled beyond any hope of redemption during her month of captivity at the hands of Sam's creators.

No, she was angry with Master Augustine. She couldn't fault his generosity by giving Sam a place in the coven considering some of the other supernaturals' attitude toward the zombie. But when he charged Sam with the responsibility of being Anne's daytime guard for this trip, neither woman had been fooled about who was supposed to watch whom. Maybe the confrontation with the Normal would cleanse her of the aggravation of having to babysit.

Anne let the mix of irritation and humor slide from her consciousness. From the corner of her eye, she gauged the man's progress as he drifted from tree to tree, matching her pace. He had to be one of the local English boys, his shirt too bright of a blue to be an Amish. Maybe a youth hoping to claim glory or notoriety by discovering what the Millersburg Monster really was. It wouldn't go well if a Normal discovered the perpetrator first and Thomas's suspicion of a supernatural culprit was correct.

No, it would not go well at all.

She sampled the night air again. Her watcher's scent was too rich, too spicy, too heady, for a child. A trickle of warmth seeped through her belly. He was definitely an adult male. Vampire instincts rose, only to be quelled by her will. Her blood need had been well satiated before she and Sam set out tonight, but the desire to hunt her hunter filled her being. Angling her course toward the trees, she closed the distance between them.

— • —

Colin Fitzgerald let the night goggles he'd bought at the army surplus store drop from his eyes. The silhouette of the girl headed for the edge of the woods lining the river. For a split second, he would have sworn her eyes glowed, but it had to be a trick of light from the goggles. He shook his head and rolled his shoulders to ease the chaffing of the backpack straps. Keeping to the shelter of the trees, he paralleled her course. A stroll through the woods in the middle of the night was never a bright idea under the best of circumstances. He crossed his fingers he wouldn't break an ankle in a groundhog hole. The damn pests were more of a threat than the wisp of a girl traipsing through Thomas's hay field.

This whole situation was growing weirder by the minute. She couldn't possibly be the person killing and mutilating his clients' livestock. He couldn't believe someone that slight could have the strength to drag a full-grown bull around a pasture.

Not by herself anyway. Even after removing the internal organs.

But she'd been by herself the last couple of nights, just as she was tonight.

Hitching his thumbs under the backpack straps, he dodged around a tree dressed in ivy. Under the full moon, the shadow in the hay field continued toward the fence line separating Thomas Levy's property from the Millers'. Dark clothes cloaked her. A long-sleeved, oversized shirt and a calf-length skirt. He didn't have a good look at her lower legs in the foot-high clover, but he'd lay odds she wore plain black stockings and shoes. If it weren't for her uncovered, chin-length locks, she could be any other Amish or Mennonite girl in the area. But something wasn't quite right in her posture as she stalked through the clover. Definitely not one of the demure, humble women he'd come to know since leaving the Philadelphia D.A.'s office and moving to remote, out-of-the-way Millersburg, Ohio.

A quick peek through the goggles showed her continuing on the same course. She might know who was behind the livestock loss. Why else would she be sneaking around his clients' farms this time of night?

Except he couldn't quite call her confident stride sneaking.

He almost wished the girl was a party to one of Matt Jessup's practical jokes. No, not even Matt would sink to that level. He may have a quirky sense of humor—Colin had been the butt of several of the other attorney's stunts—but Matt wasn't vicious. Not like the bastard who was destroying people's livelihoods.

His fingers tightened around the goggles. He knew what it'd cost the Amish farmers to come to him for help. To them, approaching an outsider for aid was unheard of. But an attorney?

The church elders had pitched a fit when they found out Thomas Levy and Jacob Miller had visited Colin's office. An ironic smile twisted his mouth. Well, as much of a fit as an Amish would allow himself. Simon Yoder's face had been beet red, though he never raised his voice, when Colin met with the men of the Millersburg Amish community at Thomas's house. In the end, Simon had been outvoted, the majority agreeing that Colin was best suited to fight Birkenwald Group's attempt to buy out their farms.

At least until Birkenwald decided to play dirty.

Their attempts to pressure state officials into seizing the land through eminent domain was bad enough. Colin swallowed the bile collected at the back of his throat. Torturing the farmers' livestock to death to drive the Amish out constituted raw evil in his book.

He swung the backpack off one shoulder to trade the goggles for a bottle of water.

"What are you doing here?"

He jerked to a halt. A darker shadow separated itself from a maple trunk and glided into a patch of silvery moonlight in front of him. The girl from the hayfield. A sharp gasp escaped his throat. Even though she wore the dark, simple clothing of an Amish, plain was hardly the word he'd use to describe her. Silvery light worshipped her pale face. Dark eyes peered at him through equally dark locks. Elfin features twisted into a frown as she regarded him.

And how had she managed to overtake him? Two seconds ago, she'd been a hundred yards away in the middle of the freakin' clover.

"You're on private property." A challenging step forward, such an assertive move for the slight wisp of a girl. "Who are you and what are you doing here?"

His dry tongue rasped the roof of his mouth. A fairy queen. That's what she reminded him of, the poster of an Unseelie temptress tacked on his nephew Evan's bedroom wall. And that brief memory cracked the wall he'd carefully built over the last year. Maybe he was going insane from guilt if he was imagining fairy queens.

An amused snort silenced the soft rustling of birds and other animals settling in the trees for the night. "If you think I'm a fairy, you really need to get out more."

Oh, shit. I said that aloud? Colin winced. He hadn't made such a fool of himself with a girl since Missy Johnson in sixth grade. Old habits reasserted themselves, and he matched her aggressive body language. "I could ask you the same thing. This is my client's land, and I know for a fact you're not one of his granddaughters."

She blinked, eyes luminous in the moonlight. "You're Thomas's attorney?"

"Yeah. And you haven't answered my question."

Her confused expression melted into one of acid fury. "What are you doing out here? Are you trying to get yourself killed?"

It was his turn to snort in humor. "Last time I checked, I don't moo and I don't chew cud."

"That's no guarantee . . ." Her head tilted, and she—

He shook his own in disbelief. No, she really was sniffing the air like one of Matt's coonhounds.

Her pale face turned back to him. "You need to leave here. Now."

He took a step back, not that he took her warning seriously, but something sent a cold shiver across his skin and raised gooseflesh. It was more than her voice. Her eyes glowed, a warm gold that had nothing to do with moonlight or fairy queens. Human eyes didn't reflect light like that, and there was little light besides the moon. No, not a reflection. Her eyes emitted the glow, a glow growing stronger and brighter.

Colin took another cautious step back. "What are you?"

Hot breath on his neck was the only warning he had before something shoved him face first into dirt and dead leaves. Something heavy landed hard on his back, slamming his temple back into the musty soil. Something that stank the putrid, coppery stink of old blood as well as its own godawful body odor.

Then the smothering weight was gone. High-pitched yips and a higher-pitched battle cry brought his head out of the loam. And into a nightmare.

Air petrified in Colin's lungs. His mind refused to wrap itself around the furry *thing* that clawed and bit at the girl. The beast hunched on its rear limbs, neither totally upright nor on all fours. Colin's eyes refused to focus, as if the shape of the thing declined to stabilize into one form or another.

And the girl wasn't a *girl*. She was the angel of death. Or a demon. This was the dark queen incarnate, dancing and dodging the monster's blows. Her eyes glowed neon yellow under the shade of a massive maple. Fangs extended past lips twisted in a feral snarl. This time Beauty was a beast too, and she charged the furry version.

The two figures tumbled across the branches and decay littering the floor of the woods. Their thrashing threw detritus in the air as each struggled to subdue the other. The thing tossed the girl away. She rolled, coming up in a crouch. When she leapt, the thing landed a solid kick in her gut. The girl slammed headfirst into a trunk, the crack still echoing through the trees when she crumpled into a heap at the roots.

The furry thing limped into the small pool of moonlight. Dark liquid oozed from its left shoulder. It gave Colin a dismissive glance and turned its attention back to the girl, a jagged piece of deadwood clutched in its upraised right claw. There was no mistaking its intention in its awkward steps as it staggered toward the unconscious girl.

Colin fumbled with the backpack lying next to him before he yanked out the flare gun. With a quick prayer, he aimed at the thing and pulled the trigger. A nova burst to life in the clearing, followed by a scream of pain. The nasty odor of burnt fur confirmed he hit his target. From the scuffling against the brush, the thing beat a fast retreat toward the river.

Blinking white spots out of his vision, Colin crawled in the direction of the fallen girl. Guilt dug its way out of the hole where he'd buried it. Once again, his decision made him responsible. *Please let her be okay. Please.* He dropped the flare gun and reached for the dark form. Fingers automatically went to her neck. No pulse. New fear joined old guilt in his intestines. *Dammit! Calm down so you can help her. This is not like Patrick and Evan.*

There! He breathed a sigh at the faint thrum under his touch. The beat was way too slow but steady. He checked for other injuries, trying not to jostle her too much. And trying not to think about the fact they were in the middle of the woods and over two miles from the nearest telephone. He pulled out his cell phone from his jeans pocket, but as expected, the words "No Service" flashed on the screen. Heat surged through his face and hands. He shoved the useless piece of crap back in his pocket.

With tender strokes, he brushed her hair out of the way. Shaking fingers probed her skull, and his heart convulsed at the mushy feeling in the base. Sticky wetness coated his hands. The guilt and fear curdled into a fetid mass.

Something grabbed his shirt collar and yanked him backward, adrenaline overloading his nerves. He twisted to punch at the monster when a feminine voice said, "Just what the fuck are you doing to her?"

Amish, Vamps, and Thieves is available at your favorite e-book and paperback retailer!

About the Author

Suzan Harden transitioned from writing information technology manuals for companies and legal articles for a law enforcement magazine to her first love, fantasy and science fiction in all their forms. She's the author of the Millersburg Magick Mysteries, the Soccer Moms of the Apocalypse series, and the Books of Apep series.

Contact Suzan Harden

Facebook: Suzan Harden
Email: suzan@suzanharden.com
Website: www.suzanharden.com

Sign up for Suzan's Mailing List